THE ORLOJ OF BOSTON

Erasmus Cromwell-Smith II

The Orloj of Boston
© Erasmus Cromwell-Smith II

© Erasmus Press

ISBN: 979-8-9996225-6-3

Publisher: Erasmus Press

Proofreading: D. Suster, Tracy-Ann Wynter, Janet Bartos

Cover Design and Interior Design: Elisa Arraiz Lucca

www.erasmuscromwellsmith.com

First edition

Printed in USA, 2025.

Books written by the author

In English,

As Erasmus Cromwell-Smith II:

- The Equilibrist series,
 (Inspirational/Philosophical)
- The Happiness Triangle (Vol. 1)
- Geniality (Vol. 2)
- The Magic in Life (Vol. 3)
- Poetry in Equilibrium
- The Equilibrist (Trilogy)

(Young Adults)

-The Orloj of Prague (Vol. 1)
-The Orloj of Venice (Vol. 2)
-The Orloj of Paris (Vol. 3)
-The Orloj of London (Vol. 4)
-The Orloj of Boston (Vol. 5)
-Poetry in Balance

As Erasmus Cromwell-Smith II
The South Beach Conversational Method

(Educational)
 -Spanish
 -German
 -French
 -Italian
 -Portuguese

The Nicolas Tosh Series,
 (Sci-fi)

- Algorithm-323
- Algorithm-325
- Algorithm-326

As Nelson Hamel (*)
The Paradise Island Series,
 (Action Thriller)
-Miami Beach, Dangerous Liaisons
The Rebel Hackers Series,
 (Sci-fi)
-The Rebel Hackers of Point Breeze
-The Rebel Hackers of the Glacial Dawn
-Threshold of Embodiment

En Español,

Como Erasmus Cromwell-Smith II:

 -La serie del Equilibrista,
 (Inspiracional/Filosófico)
- El triángulo de la felicidad (Vol. 1)
- Genialidad (Vol. 2)
- La magia de la vida (Vol. 3)
- Poesía en equilibrio
- El Equilibrista (La serie completa)

(Jóvenes Adultos)

-El Orloj de Praga (Vol. 1)
-El Orloj de Venecia (Vol. 2)
-El Orloj de Paris (Vol. 3)
-El Orloj de Londres (Vol. 4)
-El Orloj de Boston (Vol. 5).
-Poesía en Balance

Como Erasmus Cromwell-Smith II
El Método Conversacional South Beach

(Educacional)
 -Inglés
 -Alemán
 -Francés
 -Italiano
 -Portugués

La serie de Nicolás Tosh,
 (Ciencia ficción)

- Algoritmo -323
- Algoritmo-325
- Algoritmo-326

Como Nelsón Hamel (*)
La serie de la isla paraíso
 (Acción Suspenso)
-Miami Beach, Relaciones peligrosas
La Serie de los Hackers Rebeldes,
 (Ciencia Ficción)
-Los Hackers Rebeldes de Point Breeze
-Los Hackers rebeldes del amanecer glacial
- Umbral de la encarnación

(*) in collaboration with Charles Sibley.
All titles are or will be available in audio book

Table of Contents

Poems and Fables

Previously in the Orloj Saga

The Orloj Saga follows six young wizards on a quest to restore magical astronomical clocks (**"Orlojs"**) around the world. At each stop they face deceptive illusions—vices and fears—and must summon true virtues to dispel them.

Over four consecutive summers, six friends discovered that the world's great cities hide living astronomical clocks—**Orlojs**—that set a 24-hour countdown and test them with illusions born of human vices. Guided by eccentric "antiquarians," harried by a **Sly Dark Goblin**, and strengthened by fables that teach right action, the group advances in rank each year from **Apprentices** to Young Wizards, then **Master Wizards**, and finally **Orloj Wizards**—by practicing virtues that dissolve the illusions.

Their journey so far has spanned four legendary cities:

Prague (age 12) — The Orloj awakens. Beneath the Vltava and up to Hradčany, the six learn humility, generosity, and compassion to master pride, envy, and greed, earning their first badges as Apprentices.

Venice (age 13) — Under the clock of San Marco, they face betrayal and resentment with honesty, loyalty, and forgiveness, crossing an "endless bridge" to San Giorgio Maggiore and rising as Young Wizards.

Paris (age 14) — A hidden Orloj at Notre Dame and a surreal double Eiffel Tower force them to choose respect, tolerance, and selflessness over arrogance, indifference, and willful deafness, graduating as Master Wizards.

London (age 15) — An invisible Orloj behind Big Ben culminates in six trials at the Tower of London. By embodying kindness, perseverance, loyalty, tenacity, and the renewed importance of humility, and generosity they defeat despairing illusions and become Orloj Wizards.

Each city's trial built upon the previous one: mentors reappear in new guises, the antagonist grows craftier, and every virtue learned becomes the key to the next door. This volume—**The Orloj of Boston**—stands on its own for new readers, while returning readers will hear the echo of those earlier clocks in every choice the characters now make.

Author's Note:
Embracing the Journey

An Orchard's Lesson

Long before I became an author, at fifteen, I wandered an old orchard at dusk, the air heavy with the scent of ripe apples and sunlight filtering through rustling leaves. My heart was shadowed by doubts about my path. A family friend, sensing my turmoil, shared a gentle truth: humility and courage can root any dream in fertile soil. That moment—bathed in warm light and whispered breezes—years later sparked The Orloj Series, a tale of young wizards who confront illusions to discover wisdom, unity, and their truest selves.

"Humility and courage—soil where dreams take root."

That simple orchard lesson became the series' blueprint. Each new city tested the young wizards with illusions of vice, dispelled only by discovering the corresponding virtues.

The Orloj of Boston challenges the young wizards' mastery in a new land. One where deceptive glamours threaten to unravel reality itself. Boston's hidden Orloj, etched into cobblestone streets and historic corners, demands that their newfound powers be wielded with integrity. Guided by mentors echoing the orchard's wisdom, these friends face cosmic battles beneath Boston's Custom House Tower. Their journey will prove that unity and empathy triumph over division. Dear reader, as you wander Boston's enchanted paths, may this orchard lesson linger: illusions may obscure the way, but courage and connection illuminate the heart. Let the Orloj's chime spark wonder and guide your own journey through these pages.

Prologue I —
Sedona Sparks, Boston Echoes

Sedona — Summer 2059:
Ember Before the Tale

The red sandstone cliffs of Sedona blazed under the Arizona sun, their vibrant hues shifting with every subtle play of light. The desert air held a quiet mysticism, its silence punctuated only by the occasional whispering breeze and the distant trill of a canyon wren. Amidst this quiet grandeur, Professor **Erasmus Cromwell-Smith II** and his steadfast companion, **Lynn Tabernaki,** wandered along an ancient trail, absorbing the profound peace emanating from the sacred land.

The previous summer's introspection in Scotland had gently guided Erasmus back into a rhythm of reflection. Memories swirled in his mind: Prague's lessons on seeing through illusions, Venice's clarity amid fantasy, Paris's call to unity, and London's trial that lifted them beyond Master Wizards. He understood that the tale of Boston could stand on its own—an adventure anyone could begin anew—even as it rewarded those who had journeyed with him through Prague, Venice, Paris, and London. Yet this year, surrounded by Sedona's towering spires and sweeping vistas, the professor felt a particular pull to revisit older, deeper memories—a journey to the city of his birth, Boston, where a rumored Dark Goblin threat once simmered beneath colonial streets.

That evening, nestled on the terrace of their adobe retreat overlooking Oak Creek Canyon, Erasmus watched embers rise from a crackling fire pit. Lynn sat nearby, her reading glasses perched on her nose as she observed him thoughtfully, recognizing that familiar contemplative quiet settling over him once more.

"Another voyage into memory?" she prompted softly, setting aside her tea.

Erasmus smiled gently, eyes reflecting distant flames. "Indeed." The word lingered between them, filled with unspoken weight.

Lynn tilted her head. "You've shared so much already—Prague, Venice, Paris, London. But Boston… you've never truly explored that one with me."

Erasmus paused, letting the silence stretch before responding. "Boston was unique," he began carefully. "It was… more personal. The city of my birth, of childhood innocence—and it harbored illusions that cut deeper than any we had encountered before. Rumors of a malevolent presence—what we came to call the Dark Goblin—shadowed everything there."

Her curiosity piqued, Lynn leaned forward, eyes shimmering with interest. "Hidden clocks again? An Orloj obscured from mortal eyes?"

"Not just hidden," Erasmus replied softly, gaze distant. "Boston's Orloj was buried beneath history itself, interwoven with myth and truth that blurred together in Boston's past." In turn, we were guarded by mentors who knew our vulnerabilities intimately. A profound magic, both beautiful and perilous. It awakened new abilities within us, powers that tested not only our skill but also our integrity, each gift as challenging as it was extraordinary."

"And these powers," Lynn asked gently, sensing a deeper complexity, "they carried risks?"

"Significant ones," Erasmus confirmed soberly. His voice grew steady, professor-like. "Misuse of Invisibility, for instance, threatened to turn one of us permanently translucent, while Mind-Reading risked violating the trust between us."

Lynn regarded him thoughtfully, understanding deepening in her gaze. "How did you manage such potent abilities without losing yourselves?"

Erasmus looked into the flames, reflecting quietly. "We relied on **Antiquarians** who became our mentors—wise guardians who guided us through structured moral lessons. They taught us virtues like humility, integrity, and unity, each lesson carefully woven into challenges tied to historical clocks like Bern's Zytglogge or the Stará Bystrica astronomical clock. These encounters were more than magical training; they tested our souls and strengthened our character."

Lynn leaned closer, captivated. "I still find it fascinating how your outfits changed with your conscience… did that truly help you?"

"Reliably, yet mysteriously," he smiled, eyes flickering with the memory. "Our clothes would subtly shift to warn us whenever we strayed from our quest or whenever danger lurked near. It was an ever-present reminder of whether we remained aligned with the deeper truths we sought."

Silence fell gently between them again, the desert night wrapping them in its warm embrace. When Erasmus spoke next, his voice was low and thoughtful. "Our greatest tests came when our powers failed us—inside sacred spaces like the hidden Orloj itself, or in tunnels connected to it. There, stripped of magic, we had to depend solely on the wisdom imparted by our mentors. We faced illusions crafted not by spells, but by our own fears and vulnerabilities."

Lynn reached for Erasmus's hand and gave it a reassuring squeeze. "That must have required immense courage."

"It required more than courage," Erasmus admitted quietly, eyes glistening. "It demanded trust—trust in each other, in our mentors, and ultimately in ourselves."

Stars sparkled overhead as the night deepened, and the fire pit settled into glowing embers. Erasmus inhaled deeply, the cool desert air steadying him. "Mentor spirits also appeared to us from time to time, providing emotional and moral guidance. They echoed lessons once taught to my father, Erasmus Senior. One such guide—Mr. M.—had mentored my father decades ago, and his spirit watched over us in Boston when we needed him most. Each spirit was a voice from the past guiding us forward, reminding us of the wisdom my father valued deeply. He often told me how humility and courage, planted like seeds in the heart, can grow into greatness"—Erasmus smiled at the recollection—"a timeless lesson that kept us grounded in moments of doubt."

Lynn smiled warmly, her voice filled with gentle admiration. "You faced incredible challenges, Erasmus."

He nodded slowly, eyes reflective yet resolute. "And each challenge deepened our understanding of who we were—and who we needed to become."

They sat quietly after that, the desert's tranquility settling comfortably around them, each lost in thoughts of past and present. Finally, Erasmus stood and offered Lynn his hand to help her up.

"It's time I share this tale fully," he said softly, a note of determination in his voice. "Boston's story has waited patiently, but now it must be told."

Lynn rose beside him, gazing confidently into his eyes. "Then let's tell it together."

The desert night deepened around them, Sedona's ancient silence carrying the unspoken promise of stories yet to be shared.

By the time autumn's first chill touched Sedona's red cliffs, Erasmus felt the familiar pull of nostalgia—and a readiness to return to the Institute.

A few days later, as the desert's hush gave way to the Hyperloop's soft whir, Erasmus boarded a transit pod in San Francisco. On the journey, he found himself reflecting on the whispered legends of Boston—the hidden Orloj, the mysterious Dark Goblin stirring in the city's oldest chambers. His lips curved into a faint, knowing smile as he sent a quick message to Lynn: "On my way."

Her teasing reply made him chuckle aloud: "Of course. Don't be late this time. He was, predictably, seven minutes behind schedule.

The Hyperloop thrummed quietly beneath Professor Erasmus Cromwell-Smith II as it whisked him toward his annual academic pilgrimage. Dressed in deep emerald tweed, he felt his anticipation build when the familiar silhouette of the Central Institute came into view.

With Sedona's tranquility still echoing in his heart, Erasmus stepped onto the bustling campus. Hundreds of students and dozens of virtual participants were already gathered eagerly in the grand auditorium.

"Welcome back!" he greeted them warmly, eyes twinkling as the audience burst into enthusiastic applause.

"Great to see you again, Professor!" came a familiar chorus from the front rows.

Erasmus held their gaze, a warmth in his voice. "Today, dear friends, we turn to another page in the book of my wizarding past—one very close to my heart, one deeply personal. Let me take you back to the summer of 2034." He smiled as a hush fell over the room. "I was sixteen, and my friends and I journeyed to Boston—a city with no famous astronomical clock, yet one that held secrets which challenged us more profoundly than we ever anticipated. Whispers of an elusive Dark Goblin lingered there as well. In that hidden magic, we found great triumphs… and faced our greatest flaws."

He paused deliberately, ensuring he had every eye and ear.

"Once again, poetry and ancient wisdom were our guides. Illusions awaited us, virtues beckoned us, and hidden truths revealed themselves at every turn. Together, we would unveil Boston's unseen Orloj."

Lowering his voice, Erasmus leaned toward the rows of students and added in a conspiratorial whisper, "So join me, my dear friends, as we step into the streets of Boston and uncover its long-kept secrets."

As the auditorium gradually fell silent, the last murmurs fading into an expectant hush, Erasmus drew a slow breath beneath the lights and began his tale – at last, Boston's story would be told aloud.

Prologue II —

Boston Common, Dawn (2034)

Boston concealed an ancient Orloj unlike any the young wizards had encountered before. It was intricately tied to the city's deepest past, guarded by subtle, sinister illusions woven by the Dark Goblin. The trials awaiting them here would test not just their magic but their character. They would demand wisdom, humility, and trust far more than any arcane skill.

Just before dawn, Boston lay wrapped in a silence charged with expectation. It was as though the city itself braced for a hidden unveiling. Thin wisps of mist drifted off the Charles River, weaving pale patterns around the venerable stone bridges and the timeworn walls of Harvard Yard. Beneath this hush, an undercurrent of magic hummed. An unseen stirring hinted at deeper secrets poised to break the surface.

High on Beacon Hill, where dignified brick brownstones caught the first glow of morning, Mr. M. materialized like a figure from a half-forgotten dream. His spectral half-cape fluttered in an invisible breeze, eyes quietly luminous with calm awareness. A guardian of ancient Orlojs and one of Erasmus Senior's own mentors, Mr. M. now watched over them with timeless vigilance. Raising a gloved hand toward the dark spires etched against the brightening sky, he spoke in a voice that merged seamlessly with the rustling leaves:

"They're coming," he murmured, as if to the city itself.

"Balance will lead them through old perils and new. Courage, my dear ones—courage above all."

A subtle shift rippled through the predawn air. Mr. M's figure shimmered like an image reflected in turbulent water.

In that fleeting moment, threads of prismatic light revealed the intangible bond he shared with an older lineage of mentors—the very guides who had once entrusted wisdom to Erasmus Senior and who now, through him, safeguarded them. Then, as softly as the coming dawn, Mr. M. dissolved into twisting streaks of light, leaving only a whisper of magic on the breeze.

From somewhere deep in the city's still-slumbering streets came a distant echo—a hollow, fading laugh reverberating from the darkness of alleyways and old burial grounds. It stirred the low mist, faint but unmistakable—a reminder of the rumored Dark Goblin said to roam Boston's hidden corners. As the shimmering remnants of Mr. M.'s presence melted away, that echo drifted across Boston Common, where it brushed against lamplit paths and beckoned six figures to emerge into the gray early light of morning.

One year had passed since these six young wizards—Blunt (the leader, Erasmus's nickname), Reddish (quick to act), Firee (fiery in more than name), Checkered (analytical), Breezie (ever optimistic), and Greenie (empathetic and wise beyond her years)—transcended Master Wizardry in the secret chambers of London's Orloj. Their bond, forged by trials and illusions across Prague, Venice, Paris, and London, had not waned. If anything, each new journey had deepened their trust and sharpened their respect for the ethical weight behind their powers.

Vow on the Common

Now those faint rumors of a Dark Goblin—whose presence they had only ever sensed in restless dreams—had drawn them here, to a city renowned for its Revolutionary history but reputed to host no famed astronomical clock. Under the dim glow of Boston Common, an enchanted gaslight flickered. Though none had burned in these gardens for a century, the six friends converged beneath the bronze gaze of a venerable statue. The early-morning hush was broken only by the soft rustle of nearby trees. Dew clung to the grass under their boots, and the damp dawn air carried a faint briny whiff of sea breeze, reminding them of Boston's harbor and its centuries of maritime lore.

Firee tightened his grip on a small runic pendant he'd kept since London—a talisman recalling a moment of bravery when illusions had nearly consumed him. He glanced around at his friends, his resolve solidifying. Greenie inhaled deeply, remembering the humility she'd learned in Prague, where power alone had proved meaningless without honesty and restraint. "It's like Prague all over again," she said softly, eyes on the drifting mist.

A stray ripple of magic buzzed between them, causing Reddish's attempt at an Invisibility spell to flicker inadvertently—just enough to remind them all how quickly even a well-meaning spell could backfire. For a heartbeat, Reddish's forearm vanished into translucence before snapping back into view. She winced, more at the memory of the potential consequence than the misfire itself.

Their gazes shifted as Blunt—Erasmus Cromwell-Smith II himself, though his friends always used his wizarding nickname—gently withdrew a familiar leather-bound tome from his satchel. Its ancient cover glowed with a faint inner warmth. Across the title page, an inscription shimmered into view with measured clarity:

"You stand once more at the threshold. Boston holds truths masked by history. Virtues and flaws await—a tapestry of trials to overcome. Ascend beyond Orloj Wizards…or fall prey to shadows unseen.”

A hush fell around them as Blunt read the words. It was as if the bronze statue above—its metal eyes catching the first glint of dawn—were also awaiting their response. Breezie cast a thoughtful glance at the brightening horizon, a determined smile on his lips. “We’ve braved illusions before,” he said, his voice gentle but sure, “and we’ll do it again.”

Blunt looked to each of his friends in turn. In this quiet moment, beneath the dawn sky, they all understood what was unspoken: the trials ahead would demand everything they had learned. With solemn precision, each of the six placed a hand over the bronze plaque at the statue’s base, an unspoken pact passing between them.

“We face this together,” Blunt said, his water-blue eyes reflecting the first rays of morning. “No matter what comes.”

Around the circle, six voices murmured in agreement. In that instant, a silent vow was sealed on Boston Common—a promise of unity against whatever darkness lay ahead.

Introduction

Boston, Mid-Morning — Ghost Lights Stir

Boston greeted the six young wizards with a bright mid-morning sky and streets alive with summer bustle. Erasmus Cromwell-Smith II—known to his fellow wizards as Blunt—led the group onward, his hometown pride evident yet tinged with a ripple of unease. For months, cryptic messages had hinted that astronomical clocks were awakening unseen magical forces across the United States. Some of these clocks were newly built, others ancient but newly unearthed—yet all of them were stirring long-dormant powers. Now a secret library here in Boston promised crucial clues, if they could interpret its contents in time.

Outside a stately brownstone near the old North End, the young adventurers spotted two familiar figures—their chaperones from previous adventures. Blunt's uncle, Bart Sutton-Leigh, and his aunt, Antonella Cromwell-Smith, stood by the front steps and waved them over. The warm air smelled faintly of fresh bread and salty harbor water—a blend that spoke of Boston's storied past. Tucked beneath light jackets, the six wizards kept their Harlequin garb discreet; they were well aware that the city's mounting magical disturbances were already stirring curiosity—and fear—among everyday people.

Suddenly, a shriek cut through the busy sidewalk. From inside a nearby café, a terrified woman staggered backward, eyes locked on twisting coils of pale light dancing near the ceiling. Startled patrons rushed to her side, some muttering about "ghost lights" that had drifted past the windows before disappearing like morning fog in sunlight.

"It's already happening," Reddish whispered, her fingers hovering near the pocket where her wand was concealed. Normally she was the quickest to act, but now she cast a wary glance toward Blunt. "We should check this out…."
Before they could rush toward the commotion, Bart ushered the group firmly toward the brownstone's vine-covered doorway. "Inside," he urged in a low voice. "We can't help anyone if we don't first understand what's happening."

Antonella gave the shaken woman in the café one more concerned look, then offered the young wizards a reassuring smile as she held open the door. "The reading room is ready for you," she said. "We've gathered some old diaries— including some of Erasmus Senior's own journals—that might connect these new American clocks to the Orlojs in Europe."

Exchanging a knowing look with Reddish, Blunt recalled how the Antiquarians—those wise mentors of theirs—had a habit of hiding vital lessons in unexpected places, whether in ephemeral shops or puzzling riddles. If dark forces had indeed infiltrated the new clocks cropping up across the country, those diaries might contain the only roadmap to stop the chaos from spreading.

"Let's move quickly," Breezie murmured as they filed into a narrow foyer paneled with oak. He closed the heavy door behind them. Outside, a faint, unsettling laughter echoed down the street—unclear, but undoubtedly otherworldly—as if carried on a breeze from the harbor. The six friends exchanged uneasy glances, hearts pounding with the realization that these illusions threatened not just Boston, but possibly the entire country.

The Brownstone Briefing

Within the cozy reading room's dimly lit walls, timeworn volumes lay open on a broad oak table, waiting. Motes of dust swirled in a slant of sunlight coming through a high window, giving the air a sense of quiet gravity. Blunt and his companions gathered around the table, while Bart carefully spread out the crackling diaries, some bound in cracked leather and filled with spidery handwriting from decades past.

"These diaries mention a hidden Orloj here in Boston," Bart said, tapping one dog-eared page with a thoughtful frown. He paused as the six young wizards leaned in, exchanging looks of surprise. "Your father, Erasmus Sr., believed this city's Orloj served as a sort of central hub. He suspected it linked the astronomical clocks being activated here in the States to the older ones in Europe. That would mean Boston was more than just the starting point of your journey—it was the keystone, awakening forces long dormant on both sides of the ocean."

Blunt muttered a determined oath under his breath after hearing his father's theory confirmed.

Antonella nodded, gently smoothing another diary's yellowed pages. "We've also discovered notes about something strange—ephemeral shops called 'The Six Statues' that vanish as soon as they appear, much like the hidden markets you encountered with the Antiquarians abroad." The six friends exchanged uneasy glances; they had encountered such vanishing shops during their travels abroad, and the thought of them appearing here in America now was unsettling. "We don't know yet how they fit into this, but if such shops are popping up here too, it can't be a coincidence."

Reddish lifted her gaze toward a nearby window, recalling the pale ghost lights that had flickered moments before. They were gone now, but the anxiety they left in their wake was not. "If illusions are intensifying this quickly," she said, "we can't wait for them to spread further. We need to contain this before it gets out of hand."

"Cedar Rapids is the first site that's raised a major alarm," Bart continued, flipping to a page marked with a ribbon. "We've had scattered reports of strange happenings in places like Monticello, Grafton, Columbia, and others. But Cedar Rapids—where they just built a new clock tower—seems to be the epicenter right now."

Antonella picked up a typed report lying beside the diaries and read out a highlighted snippet: "Time skipping randomly around the new Orloj tower… illusions of entire streets vanishing." She looked up, her expression grave. "Locals are terrified. If these illusions keep getting worse, the panic alone could cause real harm even before the magic does."

Greenie's normally calm composure cracked; her eyes widened in alarm at the description of a town's streets disappearing into thin air.

Blunt exhaled slowly, a memory surfacing of the illusions they had faced once in Venice. "We overcame illusions there by seeing through elaborate fantasies," he reflected, "but what's happening here… these new illusions feel stronger. More hostile."

Greenie gently touched one of the open diaries, her fingers tracing a line of her father's neat script. She shot a meaningful look at Firee. "Remember how in Prague we learned the power of humility?" she said softly. "We might need that lesson again now. If we charge in overconfident—assuming we can control everything—these illusions could trap us the way our own pride nearly did back then."

Firee nodded, posture tense as he leaned over the table. "I have the same feeling," he muttered. "Like there's a catch. The illusions here might be disguising something bigger. If I sense any kind of trap when we get near Cedar Rapids, I'll alert everyone immediately." His innate Danger Sense had saved them before, and they all took comfort that it hadn't failed him yet.

Bart glanced around at the six young faces, his voice steady but edged with concern. "Erasmus Senior always believed the six of you could restore balance wherever illusions take root. That's why he sent these diaries to me, and why I'm counting on you now." The weight of responsibility in his tone was unmistakable.

For a moment, Bart's words hung in the air, and the six friends felt the weight of responsibility settling on them. Then, a soft knock at the front door interrupted the moment. Everyone froze. A courier peeked into the reading room—a young man in a rumpled uniform with his cap askew and eyes wide with fright. "Uh, sir?" he addressed Bart in a shaky voice. "Urgent rune-telegram for you… and this was stuck to your mailbox." He held out a sealed cream-colored envelope and a small parchment slip marked with strange glowing runes. His hands trembled slightly as Bart took them.

"Thank you," Bart said quietly. The courier bobbed a quick nod and backed out, casting one more worried glance over his shoulder. Through the doorway, ghostly greenish lights could be seen flitting above the street outside. "Strangest morning of my life," the courier mumbled to himself as he pulled the door shut.

Antonella swiftly broke the wax seal on the envelope and unfolded the telegram within, her eyes darting across the hastily written lines. As she read, her face fell. "It's from Iowa," she said, voice hushed. "They say the illusions around Cedar Rapids' newly built Orloj tower are growing worse by the hour. Strange apparitions, flickering time shifts… rumors of entire buildings dissolving into thin air."

Reddish watched one of those ghost lights outside streak by the window and vanish. She swallowed hard. "So that's our focus then. Cedar Rapids," she declared, trying to keep her voice steady. There was a tremor of excitement—and worry—in it.

Blunt tapped one of Erasmus Sr.'s diary pages, jaw set with determination. "We can't ignore the other sites entirely, but we should start where the threat is strongest. If these illusions feed on public fear, Cedar Rapids could spiral out of control fast."

Bart held the little rune-marked slip up to the light. The runes pulsed faintly as he handed it to Antonella. She squinted, translating the archaic symbols aloud:

"Shadows stir at your threshold. Cedar Rapids wavers next. Seek the truth beneath illusions—your father's diaries hold the key. Remember humility, or illusions consume you."

Firee's brow furrowed. "It's like a direct warning," he observed. "Could be from the Antiquarians… or from an enemy trying to rattle us. Either way, someone knows what's happening."

"Whoever sent it, the message is clear," Blunt said, exchanging a resolute look with Greenie. "Cedar Rapids is in immediate danger—and we're meant to stop it."

Suddenly, a spiral of pale green light snaked across the outside of the window frame, outlining for just an instant what looked like the sneering visage of a phantom face. It hovered there, smirking at them, then vanished in a blink. Firee edged closer to the glass, flames already curling faintly around his fingertips in reflex. Breezie joined him, a breeze swirling about his coat sleeves, ready to dispel whatever might come next. But the apparition was gone as quickly as it appeared.

"That settles it," Checkered said, snapping shut one of the diaries with resolve. Her analytical mind was already in strategy mode. "Whatever these illusions are, they're aware of us now—and taunting us. We need to move."

Bart carefully gathered up the diaries and handed them to Blunt and Checkered for safekeeping. "Take these with you. They contain everything we know that might help," he instructed. "Antonella and I will stay here in Boston to keep digging for more information and to handle anything else that arises."

Antonella placed a gentle hand on Blunt's shoulder. "Be careful," she urged. "And remember what Erasmus Senior always emphasized in his notes: every illusion, no matter how powerful, has a weakness. Often it's a virtue or simple truth that will reveal it for what it is."

Blunt nodded solemnly. "We'll remember. And we'll be back with good news," he promised.

With that, the six young wizards steeled themselves for the journey ahead. As they stepped back out onto the sunlit street, the everyday bustle of 2034 Boston continued around them— vendors calling out and the distant hum of a Hyperloop beneath the city—yet hints of an older era bled through the veneer of normalcy. A pair of translucent carriage wheels clattered for a moment over phantom cobblestones, and a faint steamship horn echoed from the harbor, as if sounds of the past were seeping into the present.

The uncanny mix made the young wizards feel as if they were teetering at the edges of reality. Already, a few civilians were cautiously peering skyward for more ghost lights.

Blunt took the lead, the old diaries clutched under one arm and his wand hand resting at his side. Reddish and Firee flanked him, alert for any sudden disturbances. Checkered, Breezie, and Greenie followed close behind, each quietly summoning the lessons and courage they'd need for what lay ahead.

Above them, the clear mid-morning sky gave no hint of the illusions lurking just beyond sight. But they all knew better now—shadows were stirring. Together, they would shine a light on those shadows before the darkness could spread any further. Their path now pointed westward toward Cedar Rapids, where they would have to contain the spreading disturbance at its source.

Chapter 1

From Cedar Rapids' Silent Watcher to Bern's Zytglogge Astronomical Wonder

The Silent Watcher's Warning

Morning sunlight bathed Cedar Rapids' Czech Village, illuminating red-tiled roofs and cobblestone lanes. Curious locals drifted past the newly unveiled Orloj with a moving zodiac — a one-of-a-kind astronomical clock in North America — yet kept a cautious distance, as though sensing an ancient heartbeat thrumming beneath its gilded dial.

Blunt shouldered his satchel, the edge of his harlequin-blue cloak concealed under a weathered jacket. Reddish, Firee, Checkered, Breezie, and Greenie trailed behind, their footsteps slowing as they neared the imposing timepiece.

"Strange," Firee murmured, squinting upward. "The air feels charged." Indeed, the very atmosphere hummed with the Orloj's pulse, a quiet call to action.

Breezie ran a hand along the clock's stone base, eyes drifting to small carvings of farmers and blacksmiths representing the town's heritage. "It's more than a mere replica. Feels like it's watching us."

Blunt nodded, his gaze catching on something embedded in the clock's face. A faint sigil — almost like a Swiss rune — glinted on the edge of the Orloj's dial, hinting at a connection far beyond Iowa. Under his jacket, his harlequin cloak shifted to a wary silver sheen, signaling potential danger.

A gentle gust stirred the plaza, rustling a cluster of pamphlets advertising the new clock. From a narrow alley, tendrils of silvery mist curled forward, brushing against the wizards' senses. Firee felt the hair on his arms stand on end.

"Glamour," Blunt explained softly, noticing confusion on a bystander's face. "A spell that cloaks a clock's truth behind illusions."

Greenie let her fingertips graze one of the Orloj's carved figures, empathy sparking. "I feel it stirring — something old awakening." *Unity strengthens our resolve, shielding us from illusions' deceit,* she reminded herself silently.

Reddish inhaled, bracing for action. "We'd better prepare."

Suddenly, an eerie half-laugh echoed from the misty alley, so faint that passersby merely shivered and walked faster. But the six young wizards felt a prickle of warning. A fleeting shape — almost Goblin-like — slipped through the fog, then vanished. Whether Dark Goblin or rogue Harlequin, its shadowy malice was fueling the illusions, a threat they knew all too well.

Breezie exchanged an uneasy look with Checkered. "We can't ignore that."

Reddish's eyes narrowed toward the swirling mist. Part of her wanted to slip into invisibility and scout ahead, but the charged air made her hesitate — she still remembered how a stray distortion that morning had caused her cloaking spell to flicker. These illusions could destabilize even their best magic if fueled by overconfidence. Instead, she gripped her wand tighter.

Blunt quietly gathered the group closer. "Let's proceed carefully. Our powers have purpose, but we must use them wisely. No recklessness."

They drew nearer to the clock, hearts thudding in sync. The Orloj's gilded astrolabe flickered, as if urging them on. Warm sunlight caught the Swiss rune again — a silent invitation, or perhaps a warning.

Whisper on the Cobblestones

"Stick together," Reddish whispered, scanning the empty alley flanking the clock tower.

Firee nodded, trying to quell an undercurrent of fear — the fear that he might miss a vital sign and let illusions slip past unnoticed. His heart raced, senses sharp against the unseen threat.

Above them, the Orloj's hands swept forward, softly announcing the next hour. In the distance, that ghostly laugh echoed once more, sending a chill down Greenie's spine.

The Pulse Behind the Dial

The Orloj let out a low hum, its golden sun hand shimmering like a ripple on water. Locals paused, unsettled by the subtle tremor in the air. Blunt's eyes sharpened as he harnessed his enhanced perception. He saw the zodiac ring on the clock quiver at the edges, hazed by layers of illusion.

Reddish bristled with restless energy, her fists clenching. "Feels like the clock is calling to us."

Checkered pressed a hand to the Orloj's cool stone. "If illusions are weaving around this dial, we need to see what's underneath."

As if on cue, the silvery mist from the alley curled across the plaza. Firee tensed, scanning for that shadowy shape that hinted at a lurking goblin presence. When nothing emerged, he exhaled slowly, though his heartbeat refused to settle.

A moment later, a swirling current of light fanned out from the Orloj's center, bending reality like a lens. Breezie, watching from the rear, placed a steadying hand on Reddish's shoulder. He masked his own private fear — a fear of isolation, of being left to face these horrors alone.

Blunt took the lead. "Form a circle around the clock's base. If illusions are intensifying, we might access whatever lies beyond with a unified approach."

They joined hands around the Orloj, recalling a technique from their earliest training. The cobblestones felt warm beneath their feet as a sudden wind gusted, rattling nearby shop signs. On the clock's dial, the faint Swiss rune blazed brightly, as if acknowledging their unity.

The Rune Gate

Their circle tightened. The six cloaks pulsed beneath their jackets, each adopting a subdued glow. Blunt focused on the swirling energy gathering at their center, letting his portal-crafting spell spark to life. The Swiss rune pulsed in response — a beacon linking Cedar Rapids to its European counterpart. The air rippled with prismatic hues, coalescing into a translucent doorway: a swirling vortex laced with faint Alpine etchings.

Checkered inhaled deeply. "Ready?"

Without hesitation, the six stepped forward into the portal. In an instant of weightlessness, the world flipped; vibrant colors streaked past their vision, and clockwork echoes ticked at the edges of hearing, as though time itself held its breath.

Then their feet found solid ground again. A crisp chill caressed their faces, and the distant toll of a bell announced their arrival in another land entirely.

The Zytglogge's Call

When the ancient mechanism stirred, carved bears began to circle, and a bronze bell tolled a measured pattern — resonant and old as the stones beneath them. The six friends stood on a cobbled street bathed in dawn's pale light, gazing up at a medieval stone tower crowned by an imposing astronomical dial. It was the Zytglogge of Bern. Ornate hands swept across a midnight-blue clock face etched with zodiac symbols and a rotating moon disc. An early morning hush enveloped the Swiss capital, accentuating the tower's quiet authority.

Behind them, the portal's glow faded. They had arrived at the source of the disturbance, Bern's medieval heart, where the Zytglogge's ancient wisdom — and its hidden perils — awaited.

Breezie turned in a slow circle, awe momentarily overcoming apprehension. "Bern, Switzerland," he breathed. He recognized the tower from illustrations in Erasmus's diaries — chronicles from the original Orloj scholar. "This place is nearly eight centuries old. Legend says it was built to remind people that time humbles all."

Checkered brushed a windblown curl of hair from her face. "Then we're here to see if that legend holds true. The clock's energy feels… off."

Indeed, as they listened, the Zytglogge's massive gears emitted a strained, subdued grinding, as though the machinery were laboring under an unseen weight. A brisk breeze carried the scent of fresh bread from a nearby bakery, mingling with the crisp Alpine air.

Firee rubbed his arms and scanned the shadows near the tower. "No illusions swirling out here yet, but my gut says we're not alone." His senses prickled with the same vigilance honed in Paris's catacombs.

The Six Statues Roll In

Reddish caught a glimpse of movement in a narrow side street. She tensed, expecting to see that same shadowy figure from Cedar Rapids. Instead, a small traveling shop rolled silently into view on bronze wheels engraved with pulsing runes. As the wooden panels unfolded elegantly, a sign at the top glowed softly with the shop's name:

The Six Statues

Greenie's eyes widened. "The diaries mentioned a store by that name. It appears wherever illusions gather."

Before they could say more, the shop's interior revealed itself. Shelves of antique books, arcane instruments, and glimmering trinkets lined the walls. At the center stood a marble statue of a robed figure with downturned eyes and open palms — a posture of absolute humility.

Cornelius and the Humility Key

From behind the statue emerged a tall man with long white hair pulled back into a neat ponytail. He wore a flowing robe of muted silver, and faint runic scars were etched across the back of his left hand.

His voice was low and measured. "Welcome, travelers. I am Cornelius Tetragor."

A gentle surge of calm emanated from him, as though the man carried humility in every breath. Blunt felt tension ease from his shoulders. "We sensed corruption in the Orloj back home," he explained, "and it led us here through a portal."

Cornelius gave a respectful bow, echoing the statue's humble posture. "Indeed. Corruption seeps into these ancient gears as well. But humility can restore what arrogance seeks to break."

Trials of Humility

The shop's wooden panels gleamed in the weak sunrise, the runes on its wheels pulsing in time with the rhythmic ticking of the Zytglogge. Cornelius guided the six wizards closer, his demeanor calm and purposeful.

"I know of the illusions plaguing your Orloj," he said softly. "This clock, too, is under threat. Bern's tower has stood since the 13th century — built to remind citizens that no one stands above time. But something is seeking to distort that lesson." The air around them thrummed with the Zytglogge's pulse, a warning of the corruption's grip.

He reached out and brushed a hand across the marble statue's folded robes. In response, the statue glowed faintly, as if acknowledging his devotion. "Humility is more than a word. It's the key that allows us to see beyond illusions — and beyond our own pride."

Checkered took in Cornelius's silver robe and the deliberate, gentle way he carried himself. "How do we help?" she asked.

A hint of weariness touched Cornelius's gaze. "Inside this tower lies a corridor of illusions — a trial that will test your willingness to bow to truth over ego. Succeed, and the clock's corrupted gears can be cleansed. Fail… and the illusions will only strengthen."

Blunt exchanged looks with Reddish and Firee, recalling the quivering clock dial they had left behind in Cedar Rapids. "Lead the way," he said, resolve solidifying in his voice.

Cornelius nodded and stepped toward a small wooden door at the tower's base. He placed his palm on its ancient latch; the runic scars on his knuckles glowed, and a hushed click echoed as the door unlocked, as if the tower itself recognized him.

Breezie inhaled deeply, nerves fluttering. He could already imagine the lines along which these illusions might try to break them — his loneliness, his doubts, the fear of being separated from his friends. But he squared his shoulders, determined not to be consumed by such worries. He had overcome fears in London's trials, and he would do so again here.

The Corridor of Illusions

Sensing Breezie's trepidation, Greenie gently touched his arm. "We'll face it together," she promised, offering a comforting smile.

Cornelius pushed the door open and gestured for them to follow. "Remember: illusions prey on your desire to be more than you are," he warned quietly. "Embrace humility, and the illusions will lose their grip."

They stepped inside the base of the clock tower. Dim torchlight revealed a narrow stone staircase spiraling upward. Ancient walls pressed close on either side, whispering with memories of centuries past. As the group ascended, the rhythmic clang of clock gears grew louder above them. Now and then a distortion warped the air — wavering shapes flickering at the edges of their vision.

Reddish's harlequin cloak shimmered from silver to a faint amber hue, mirroring her heightened vigilance. Firee closed his eyes as he climbed, focusing on the tiniest magical tremors around them. Each step felt heavier than the last, as if this tower were a place where time itself tested hearts as much as it did resolve.

At the top of the stairs, they entered a long corridor suffused with unsettling energy. Faint pulses of light skittered across the stone walls, and distant ticking reverberated like a giant heartbeat. Along the corridor, stone arches shimmered with illusion, their surfaces rippling to reveal fleeting images before turning solid again.

Breezie paused as he caught a glimpse of a reflection in one archway. Instead of his real, anxious face, he saw himself utterly alone, wandering a silent, empty city. A cold ache knotted in his stomach — the illusion was laying his fear of isolation bare. He tore his eyes away and steadied himself, remembering Greenie's reassuring words: they were in this together. *We're not alone here*, he told himself firmly.

Firee steeled himself as well, scanning the dim corridor for any sign of the Goblin's silhouette. A quiet voice of doubt nagged at him: *If you fail, the illusions will overwhelm your friends.* He shook off the thought, repeating a silent mantra of vigilance and trust.

Cornelius moved with quiet purpose at the corridor's center, his robe brushing over stones worn smooth by ages. "Glamours twist reality here," he explained gently. "Stay focused. Pride or panic will only feed the illusions."

The very corridor seemed to pulse quicker at his words, as if challenging their unity.

Confronting the Mirrors

Greenie stepped forward and pressed her palm firmly against the cold surface of her mirror. She refused to flinch as she met the eyes of her grandiose doppelgänger. "I don't want to overshadow anyone," she said, loud enough for all to hear. "Humility means we serve, not dominate."

Her words sent a visible ripple across the mirror. The dazzling images within it began to dim. A sibilant, frustrated hiss echoed through the corridor as if the illusion itself recoiled. Drawing strength from Greenie's resolve, Reddish lowered the flame flickering in her hand. "Power without humility leads to ruin," she added, her tone sharp with conviction.

One by one, the illusions of grandeur began to crack. Breezie exhaled in relief as the reflection of his lonely ascendancy flickered and vanished. Firee watched his own image — once an unstoppable firelord — recede back into the glass and disappear.

At last, each mirror's hold shattered completely, the glassy surfaces dissolving into swirling motes of light that scattered down the corridor. The path ahead cleared, revealing a wide stone chamber beyond, where deeper, more resonant clockwork noises boomed and echoed with an unhealthy lurch.

The False Heart of the Clock

Without further warning, the smoky figure launched itself at them. Tendrils of black mist lashed out across the floor, each tip sharpening into a claw that hissed temptations of power as it came. Reddish reacted instantly, flinging a wave of flame across the nearest tendril. The fire burned through one coil — but the smoke simply re-formed, unharmed, a moment later. Checkered's eyes narrowed; through the swirling dark she caught a glint of something metallic.

"There's a hidden gear at its core!" she shouted. "That's the real target!"

Blunt swept his wand in a wide arc, calling up a stream of cleansing water. The purifying wave hissed against the smoky creature, and the entity swirled away to avoid the full torrent. Firee darted aside and summoned a pinpoint lance of flame aimed straight for the exposed inner gear. But the figure's billowing cloak of shadow closed protectively around its core again, thwarting the direct attack.

At the same moment, Breezie felt that old flicker of isolation — an urge to prove himself by tackling the threat alone: *The others might only slow you down,* a deceitful thought whispered. He clenched his jaw and forced himself to breathe steadily, recalling Greenie's voice and the lesson they had just learned. They would not win alone. *We stand together,* he reminded himself, pushing the isolating illusion aside.

Greenie raised her hands and sent forth slender vines of shimmering green magic. They twined gently around the smoky silhouette. The figure's voice hissed, "Weakness... you'll never quell me," as if mocking her supportive spell.

Greenie only narrowed her eyes, pouring more of her steady power outward. "Humility is not weakness," she answered calmly. "It's the bond we share."

Her enchanted vines tightened, holding the shadow-creature just enough to slow its writhing. Blunt seized the opening, directing a blast of icy water that washed over the entity, freezing portions of its smoky shroud in place. Reddish followed with a focused burst of flame, the controlled fire scorching away the last wisps protecting the exposed gear. In the same breath, Firee's earlier spark finally struck true, landing on the revealed gear teeth with a crackle of energy.

Seizing the moment, Checkered darted forward. With a cry, she channeled a beam of shimmering light from her outstretched hands. The magic speared into the corrupted gear and dissolved the dark residue in a final burst of brilliance.

The shadowy figure let out a furious wail. Its smoky form shuddered and then disintegrated, leaving only a rain of fading embers drifting to the floor. They had done it — the pride-fueled phantom was gone. Their vigilance and teamwork, anchored in humility, had guided each strike and led them to victory.

Return to Cedar Rapids

With that final warning, Cornelius raised a hand in farewell. The air shimmered at the chamber's edge as the magical shop reappeared by a side arch. Its runes pulsed calmly on its bronze wheels, and a gentle rush of light unfurled into an open doorway leading back the way they came.

One by one, the six stepped through the portal for their return journey. Crossing the threshold felt gentler this time — as though the Zytglogge's restored harmony now guided them safely home. In mere moments, they found themselves standing again in Cedar Rapids' bustling Czech Village square.

Sunlight gleamed on the Orloj's dial overhead. Below, a few locals fanned themselves with pamphlets and wiped sweat from their brows, feeling nothing beyond the ordinary warmth of a summer morning. Townsfolk bustled nearby, blissfully oblivious to the momentous clash that had just transpired an ocean away. Blunt carefully withdrew the brass astrolabe from his satchel and pressed it against the Iowa Orloj's face. The engraved instrument sparkled and clicked softly into place on the clock's dial.

Greenie placed a hand on the Orloj's stone base and closed her eyes. She could feel a new, reassuring hum in the mechanism — as if the American clock recognized the piece of its Swiss counterpart now protecting it. "The illusions... they're fading," she said softly. "Everything feels quieter."

Then Blunt lifted his hand toward the clock's gilded dial, tracing a slow arc through the sunlit air. Threads of amber light spiraled outward, weaving a gentle ward around the Orloj. The shimmer settled like morning dew, binding the last echoes of distortion beneath a calm, enduring glow.

Reddish let out a long breath, a cautious smile tugging at her lips. "We overcame the Zytglogge's test. Cedar Rapids seems safe for now."

Firee traded a glance with Breezie, and the two shared a silent understanding. Confronting those illusions had required each of them to face down inner doubts — and they had done it by trusting in each other. Breezie gave a small nod, relieved that his fear of being isolated had not pulled him away from the team when it mattered most.

Checkered turned to Blunt, her eyes bright with determination. "Cornelius did warn us — the illusions are spreading like a web. This was only the beginning."

Blunt's cloak settled back into a calm, steady hue now that the immediate danger had passed. He looked around at his five friends, pride and gratitude shining in equal measure. "Then we stand ready," he said firmly. "We won't face them alone."

Their shared resolve — forged in Bern's trials — anchored them for the challenges ahead. For a moment, a hush fell over the square, as though the city itself acknowledged their vow. High above, the Orloj's hands moved with peaceful precision, each tick resonating with renewed clarity. And somewhere in the distance — faint yet unmistakable — that eerie ripple of laughter sounded once more, a reminder that not all shadows had been banished.

Yet as the six young wizards departed Cedar Rapids' Orloj, they carried the lesson of humility with them. United in purpose and braced by vigilance, they felt ready to face whatever new illusion or darkness lay ahead. Their journey was only beginning, but they knew one truth for certain: as long as they remained humble and stood together, no cunning illusion could ever prevail for long.

As they turned away from the Orloj's gleaming face, a faint shimmer rippled across the cobblestones — the lingering trace of Cornelius's portal. Its hum deepened, resonating like a whisper carried across worlds. Cornelius Tetragor's portal left them not in their next trial, but back home in Boston — on Beacon Hill, at dusk.

The air folded once more, revealing a swirling threshold lined with flickering runes.

Blunt paused, sensing its pull. "Another summons," he murmured.

The others gathered close, the glow of the portal reflecting in their eyes. From its depths came a faint aroma of sea mist and iron—Boston's scent, unmistakable.

Without hesitation, the six stepped through, their silhouettes swallowed by light.

Chapter 2

Chasing Tetragor's Traveling Bookstore

Ghost-Lights Over Beacon Hill

Moments ago, the six young wizards had stood within Bern's ancient clock tower; now Cornelius Tetragor's portal deposited them back home in Boston – on a Beacon Hill sidewalk at dusk – rather than into another far-flung trial.

The hum of magic faded as they stepped onto familiar cobblestones. Streetlamps flickered awake against towering brownstones and ivy-wrapped railings, their warm glow mingling with the last purple streaks of daylight. Though the street lay quiet, each of the six carried subtle echoes of the clockwork trials they had recently overcome. Something about the evening felt expectant, as if Boston itself were holding its breath. For an instant, a whiff of warm parchment and smoke wafted up from a nearby cellar grating – then vanished as quickly as it came. A passing gentleman paused and frowned at an empty patch of wall. "Odd," he murmured, shaking his head as though he'd imagined a bookseller's door where none stood. In another moment he continued on, and Beacon Hill's hush settled once more.

Blunt brushed a hand over his harlequin-patterned cloak, recalling how its unruly colors had been calmed by humility rather than force. At his belt hung the brass gear they'd retrieved in Europe, the old motto Innovare Contra Stagnatio glinting in the lamplight. Inhaling the familiar city air, he felt the night's stillness grounding him. All around, narrow alleys and curtained windows glowed with everyday life, yet an unspoken question seemed to drift through the atmosphere.

Checkered's keen gaze swept the brick facades. Out of the corner of her eye, she caught a faint greenish flame flicker behind a distant chimney – a ghost-light ordinary eyes would have missed. "Something feels different tonight," she murmured, alert to every shifting shadow.

Greenie pulled her emerald cloak tighter around her shoulders. "The city's heart is steady," she observed in her soft, lilting voice, "but a chord of anticipation hums beneath the usual bustle." Indeed, even passing pedestrians slowed and grew quiet, as if sensing some unseen drama on the verge of unfolding.

Firee stood a half step apart from the group, scanning the street with guarded intensity. A ripple of crimson magic flared at the edge of his cloak – an instinctive warning signal. "We learned important lessons in Bern," he said under his breath, resisting the urge to speak too openly of illusions in public.

"Whatever awaits us here, we must not lose our humility." His sharp intuition, honed by their recent trials, kept him vigilant.

Breezie exhaled slowly, letting a calm optimism wash over him. "Master Tetragor did hint that Boston would bring deeper challenges," he noted, his tone hopeful. Closing his eyes for a moment, he attuned himself to the city's magical undercurrent. "It almost feels like the city is waiting for us to notice something," he added gently, as if the secret were a shy creature he didn't want to startle.

Reddish's eyes darted over wrought-iron fences and dancing gaslight shadows with restless energy. A subtle tension in the mild night air set her nerves on edge, as if an invisible stage had been set and the first cue could come any second. "Then let's not just stand here," she burst out, a spark of impatience in her voice. She took an eager step forward. "We should head back to Bart and Antonella – they might have news by now."

The six young wizards exchanged resolute nods and set off through Beacon Hill's lamp-lit lanes, each of them sensing that the night's tranquility was only the prologue to something significant.

The Second Brownstone Briefing

Before long, the narrow street widened to reveal a familiar ivy-covered brownstone. A single lantern glowed by the front door – Bart and Antonella's subtle signal welcoming their apprentices home. Inside, the foyer was warm and still, redolent of old books and lemon polish. From the oak-paneled study came the low murmur of the two mentors' voices.

Reddish shrugged off her light jacket, revealing the embroidered hem of her wizard's cloak beneath. "It's good to be back," she admitted, tension unwinding from her shoulders in the cozy entryway. The quiet crackle of a hearth and the sight of overstuffed bookshelves eased a worry she hadn't realized she'd been carrying.

In the lamp-lit library, Bart and Antonella rose from a table strewn with ancient diaries and notebooks. These two seasoned wizards – steadfast guides through trials in Venice, Paris, and London – greeted the returning six with relief. "You're back," Antonella said, smiling as her eyes flickered over them to check for any harm. "Did everything go well in Bern?"

Before anyone could answer, the lantern by the door hissed sharply. A thin ribbon of green flame licked the inside of the glass, then vanished. Antonella's and Bart's eyes met in alarm. "It's near," Antonella breathed, her voice suddenly tense. The young wizards traded alert looks; something magical was stirring in the Boston night.

Blunt stepped forward and inclined his head respectfully. "We succeeded in Bern," he reported briskly. "We recovered what we needed from the clock tower. But it's clear our journey isn't over – we've uncovered a new clue about humility, and perhaps deeper illusions here in Boston." His tone was calm but carried an undercurrent of urgency. If the green glow at the door was any indication, time was of the essence.

Antonella and Bart exchanged knowing looks. While the six had been abroad, the mentors clearly had not been idle. Bart gently closed the cracked leather diary he'd been poring over and tapped a page marked with a ribbon. "While you were away, we continued our research in the diaries," he said, motioning the group closer. "One phrase kept appearing: Veritas in Humilitate."

At the Latin words, the young wizards pressed in around the table. "Truth in humility," Checkered translated softly, tasting the phrase. Her analytical eyes narrowed. "Is that a warning… or a location?"

Before Bart could answer, a shrill ring cut through the hush from the hall telephone – one abrupt chime that stopped almost as soon as it started. Everyone froze for half a heartbeat, listening. The old phone fell silent again, as if it, too, were playing at cryptic clues. Bart allowed himself a faint, wry smile. "Perhaps both," he murmured, the interruption oddly affirming his suspicion. He rotated the aged diary so the others could see a spidery Latin entry on the yellowed page.

Greenie leaned in, tracing the faded ink with a gentle fingertip. "The handwriting looks the same as the entry about Bern's Orloj," she noted, recognizing the flourish of letters. Her heart skipped a beat. "So the next clue really is here in Boston?"

"We believe so," Antonella replied. She drew a folded newspaper clipping from between the diary pages and slid it across to them. The headline read: Ghostly Green Lights Mystify Beacon Hill Residents. Beneath it, a grainy black-and-white photo showed faint emerald flares curling above Boston's rooftops. The mentors had clearly been connecting dots while the team was away.

No sooner had they absorbed that than the telephone rang again – a single jarring peel that this time did not stop. Bart crossed the hall in two strides and lifted the receiver. The others watched, tension mounting, as he listened to the tinny voice on the line. Bart's eyes widened and he went very still. Gently, he set the handset down. "The night porter at the Athenaeum just called," he reported, turning back to the group. "He says the Long Room suddenly smells of smoke… and the lamps there just guttered green."

Reddish straightened up fast, her pulse quickening. "The Long Room? That's at the Athenaeum," she exclaimed, shooting a glance at her friends. The Beacon Hill ghost-lights, the green lantern flame, and now this – the pattern was clear.

"Exactly," Antonella said, her tone turning grave. "The Athenaeum has long been a place of scholarship and modest pursuit of truth. If illusions are seeping into Boston again, they may have chosen ground rich with that very energy."

The thought sent a quiet ripple of unease through the room. The idea of new illusions taking root in their own city made each of the young wizards unconsciously edge closer together.

Breezie frowned thoughtfully and piped up, "And the traveling bookstore – does it connect to these lights somehow?" He had a hunch the phenomenon wasn't just random magic in the air. The diaries had mentioned something about a mystical shop…

Bart shuffled through a few more loose pages on the table until he found a scribbled note. "We're not certain," he admitted, "but the name The Six Statues appears in several firsthand accounts." He placed a finger on one such entry and read aloud, "'…a peculiar shop that appears and then vanishes, leaving only the scent of parchment and smoke.'" He looked up meaningfully. A mystical traveling bookstore that came and went like a ghost? It was exactly the sort of thing Cornelius Tetragor might be involved with.

Greenie's eyes widened in disbelief. "That shop is real?" she whispered. Tales of magical bookstores had always seemed like storybook lore – yet here it was in Bart's research.

Antonella nodded gravely. "Cornelius mentioned it to us once," she said. "A gateway disguised as a bookstore, surfacing wherever illusion and truth converge." Her voice held both respect and caution, as if speaking of a capricious old friend.

Blunt's expression hardened with purpose. The clues all pointed to one course of action. "Then that's where we start," he declared. "The Athenaeum first – if a phantom shop is hiding nearby, we'll find it." There was no hesitation in his voice. The last trial in Bern had taught them that facing illusions required swift, decisive action.

"Carefully," Antonella added, resting a gentle hand on Blunt's arm. Her mentor's instinct flared with concern.

"Illusions born of pride are often the hardest to see. If this trial is anything like the last, it may run even deeper. Stay on your guard, all of you." She swept her gaze over the group, a motherly worry in her eyes.

Blunt met her look and gave a confident half-smile. "We will," he promised. He glanced around at his teammates, who all wore expressions of calm readiness. They had confronted illusionary pride once before and come out stronger for it.

"We have each other," he said firmly, "and we remember what we've learned." Six heads nodded in quiet agreement.

Their eyes shone with unified resolve.

Without another word, the young wizards gathered their cloaks and gear. Bart and Antonella followed them to the front door, then held back, allowing their protégés to take the lead. This was a challenge the six needed to face on their own. With determination pulsing in their veins, the students stepped out into the night once more, venturing toward the Boston Athenaeum to unravel the mystery awaiting them.

Seeking the Athenaeum

Leaving the brownstone behind, the six young wizards moved quickly through the lamplit streets of Beacon Hill. Nightfall had deepened the sky to a velvety violet. The air itself felt charged with potential, as though the city were holding its breath. They headed east toward the Boston Athenaeum, following the tug of the clue and the faint trace of green-tinged magic that still hung in the air.

As they turned a corner onto a broader avenue, an older gentleman on a bicycle pedaled by and slowed to tip his hat in courteous greeting. Blunt returned the nod reflexively, but something about the man's watchful smile gave him pause. It stirred a memory of illusions they had dispelled far away. Before the group could decide if the cyclist was merely polite or if the city itself was sending them a subtle signal, the man had vanished around the bend, swallowed up in the deepening dusk.

Gas lamps cast golden halos on brick sidewalks and wrought-iron fences as the six crested Beacon Hill. Marble statues on corner pedestals stood silent sentinel, their stony faces flickering in the gaslight as the group hurried past. Within minutes, the white dome and elegant façade of the Boston Athenaeum came into view. Soft uplighting illuminated its grand windows and marble pillars. The sight sent a small thrill through each of them – this venerable library, devoted to truth and knowledge, might well be the stage for tonight's challenge.

Reddish slowed as they neared the Athenaeum's imposing entrance. The great double doors were closed at this late hour, and the surrounding street lay nearly deserted. She peered intently into the nooks and alcoves around the building's perimeter. Nothing obvious… "If something's here, it's keeping itself well-hidden," she whispered, frustration edging into her voice. Reddish was not fond of waiting games; the quiet and darkness made her skin prickle.

Firee stepped up to the heavy wooden doors and laid his palm flat against one. He half-expected resistance, but to his surprise the door yielded under his gentle push. "It's unlocked," he reported in a low voice, exchanging a wary look with Blunt. It was well past public hours – perhaps Cornelius had arranged after-hours access for them, or perhaps the Athenaeum's own wards recognized the urgency of their quest.

One by one, they slipped inside, disappearing into the shadowy library.

The Athenaeum's Hush

The Boston Athenaeum welcomed them with a cathedral hush. Pale moonbeams spilled through tall arched windows, illuminating motes of dust above rows of mahogany bookshelves. Marble busts of philosophers and scholars glimmered in alcoves, casting long silhouettes across polished wood floors. Every footstep the wizards took produced a soft echo that was immediately swallowed by the venerable silence, as if the library itself were enforcing quiet.

"Spread out – but carefully," Blunt whispered. They fanned out into the main reading hall, each on high alert for any glimmer of magic or illusion. A few of them had pulled up their hoods; a group of robed figures wandering the

Athenaeum wouldn't raise eyebrows (the old library had seen its share of eccentric scholars), but stealth was still wise.

Reddish drifted along one wall of bookshelves, her fingertips lightly trailing the spines of weathered tomes. She strained to listen for anything out of the ordinary. But no phantom whispers reached her ears; no inexplicable green lights danced in the rafters. The only movement came from the gentle sway of the gaslight sconces on the walls. Reddish pursed her lips in disappointment – she had hoped for a quick, dramatic reveal.

Greenie closed her eyes in the stillness and sent out a subtle wave of empathic magic. The building was suffused with the benign emotions of learning – curiosity, concentration, the calm of accumulated knowledge. Yet beneath that, she sensed… anticipation. Greenie's brow creased. "The library itself feels like it's waiting for something," she murmured, keeping her voice barely audible. "But I don't sense anything wrong in here." No fear, no deceit – just that strange expectancy.

Checkered moved methodically between reading tables and glass display cases, a silver detection charm dangling from her hand. Its gentle glow lit oil paintings of Boston's founders and illuminated the marble floor that had felt the tread of generations of truth-seekers. She knelt to inspect the edges of an Oriental rug, then straightened and shook her head. "No traces of glamour or hidden doorways," she whispered. "It's as if the building is hiding something – but holding its secrets close." There was no obvious illusion in play, which in itself was telling. An illusion born of pride wouldn't reveal itself so easily in a place devoted to honest inquiry.

After a thorough quarter-hour of searching the Athenaeum's halls, balconies, and shadowy alcoves, the six regrouped by the grand circulation desk. One by one, they shook their heads. Nothing overtly magical had been discovered inside.

"It might not be inside at all," Checkered said, her voice hushed but determined. She recalled Bart's notes about ephemeral shops that appear and disappear. If she were a tricky illusion trying to avoid notice in a sanctuary of truth, she wouldn't hide in the well-lit reading room. "If I were an illusion here," she continued, "I'd lurk just outside, somewhere in the Athenaeum's shadow – rather than within these walls where truth holds sway."

Blunt considered this and nodded. The Latin clue "Truth in Humility" had led them here, but perhaps the actual trial lay just beyond the library's honorable walls. "Let's take a look around outside," he decided softly. "Courtyards, alleys – anywhere nearby that we might have missed."

With quiet efficiency, they made sure everything was as they'd found it and slipped back out the Athenaeum's front door, pulling it closed behind them. The Boston night greeted them with the chirr of late-summer crickets and the distant whoosh of a lone car on Beacon Street. Steeling themselves to find whatever elusive magic was lurking, the young wizards set off to circle the Athenaeum's perimeter.

They walked along the library's side, entering a narrow alley that ran between the Athenaeum and an old adjoining residence. The granite blocks of the Athenaeum's rear façade loomed above them, bathed in the flickering glow of a lone gas lamp at the alley's mouth. In the deepening darkness, they moved slowly, scanning every brick and shadow for something out of place.

Checkered raised her lantern, casting long shifting shadows over the cobblestones. Firee's crimson cloak suddenly rippled and darkened to a wary maroon – his magical senses picking up a faint disturbance just out of view. He halted and held up one hand. "I sense movement… there, in that corner," he whispered, pointing toward a cluster of ivy-draped stone near a wrought-iron gate at the alley's end.

They converged on the spot: a small, ivy-choked courtyard tucked behind the Athenaeum. A rusted gate hung ajar, supporting a single dim lantern that barely illuminated the space. Breezie knelt and pressed his palm to the ground. In a thin layer of dust on the cobbles, he could just make out footprints that didn't match their own. "Someone – or something– passed through here recently," he noted, keeping his voice low and steady so as not to betray the excitement fluttering in his chest. A thrill of mingled fear and hope coursed through him; at last, a sign they were on the right track.

The Six Statues Unveiled

Without warning, a fleeting silver shimmer rippled across the old brick wall at the back of the courtyard – like a splash of moonlight where moonlight had no business being. Everyone tensed.

Checkered narrowed her eyes, focusing her innate truth-sense on the wall. To her magic-tuned vision, the shimmer sharpened into distinct threads of energy. "It's an illusion," she breathed. "There's a distortion right in front of us." Something was camouflaged here.

Blunt lifted an arm in a silent signal for the group to stick together. "Easy now," he cautioned, voice a calm murmur. "We approach as one." Wands in hand but pointed downwards, they stepped forward in unison. Hearts pounded beneath their ribs, but their resolve was firm.

Whatever lay hidden would be faced together.

Greenie closed her eyes briefly as they advanced and sent out a gentle pulse of empathy. At once she felt them – traces of emotion clinging to the air like ghostly fingerprints: uncertainty… curiosity… and a spark of awe. Whoever (or whatever) had been here before had experienced those feelings. It was as if the place itself remembered a recent visitor standing right where they stood now.

Another soft shimmer rippled across the bricks. The silvery distortion coalesced slowly into the hazy outline of a wooden signboard. As the shape grew clearer, ghostly letters on its surface glinted with faint gold light.

"The Six Statues," Reddish read aloud, her earlier tension blooming into bright excitement. Her heart leapt – that name! It was the very one they'd seen scribbled in Bart's accounts. They had found the fabled shop from the diaries.

As if summoned by the sound of its name, the illusion finished unfurling. Before their astonished eyes, a small traveling shop materialized in the courtyard, nestled snugly between the stone walls as though it had been there forever.

Oil lanterns under the eaves flickered to life, casting a gentle glow over wooden panels carved with arcane symbols. The entire shop rested on six stout bronze wheels, and the hanging sign above the door proudly depicted six little statues arranged in a circle. The front door itself stood slightly ajar, releasing a sliver of warm, golden light – and an inviting hush – into the night.

They had done it: they'd found Cornelius Tetragor's mystical traveling bookstore, The Six Statues. For a moment, the six young wizards simply stood and grinned at one another in disbelief and delight. In the stillness, they could smell the faint aroma of old parchment and candle wax drifting from inside, exactly as the legends described. This was no mere illusion – it was real, and it was waiting for them.

Cornelius's Welcome

Blunt took point, gently pushing the shop's door fully open with the tip of his wand. A brass bell mounted above the frame gave a soft chime as they crossed the threshold. The interior was cozy and dim, lit by a few hanging lanterns that swayed as if in greeting. It smelled heavenly – like aged paper and leather bindings with an undercurrent of wax polish, and just the faintest tang of something metallic, like a distant blacksmith's forge.

They stepped in cautiously. Shelves packed with leather-bound tomes lined the walls from floor to ceiling. Between books lay curious mechanical gadgets and stoppered jars filled with glittering ingredients. In the center of the shop stood a circular wooden table draped in burgundy velvet, and beside it, a familiar figure in flowing white robes.

Cornelius Tetragor turned toward them with a serene smile. His long silver hair cascaded over his shoulders and his kindly eyes shone with recognition – and pride. He inclined his head in a slight bow of greeting, every movement humble and composed. "Welcome, friends," he said softly. His voice carried the same calm warmth it had in far-off Prague and Bern, as though he had expected them all along. "Boston's quiet pursuit of knowledge has been awaiting you… and so have I."

At the sight of their mentor – the very one who had guided them through trials in Prague's halls and Bern's clockworks – now here in Boston, the six young wizards couldn't help but break into relieved grins. Cornelius's mere presence was a balm, soothing the last remnants of anxiety from their search. They bowed respectfully in return.

"We followed the clue here," Checkered explained eagerly. The usually stoic girl's relief was evident in her voice. "The phrase Veritas in Humilitate led us to the Athenaeum, but we found no illusions inside. We realized something might be hidden nearby… and then we discovered your shop." She gestured back towards the door, marveling still that the tiny courtyard had concealed an entire bookstore.

Cornelius inclined his head, pleased by their deduction. "Boston's Athenaeum provided the stage," he said, "but as you saw, illusions rarely reveal themselves openly in a place devoted to truth. Thus, my traveling bookstore lingers at the threshold – just outside the obvious – where curiosity leads the humble a step beyond." He swept his arm in a gentle invitation for them to gather around the central table.

Greenie let out a small sigh of pure relief and stepped further in, feeling Cornelius's calm confidence wash over her like a reassuring tide. "We're so glad to see you again, sir," she said earnestly. There was genuine affection in her eyes for this mentor who always seemed to appear when they needed him most. "What lesson must we learn tonight?"

Cornelius's eyes twinkled at her eager question. He rested a slender hand atop a neat stack of scrolls that lay on the round table. "Tonight, humility must face a subtler foe," he replied. "You've seen how humility guards against the grand illusions of vanity. Now you will learn how corruption can masquerade as virtuous ambition."

Blunt folded his arms, brow furrowing thoughtfully. "Corruption in the guise of ambition…," he echoed. "Like someone pursuing a lofty goal, but being secretly led astray by pride or deceit?" It was an unsettling notion – a good intention twisted into something harmful.

"Precisely." Cornelius nodded. The golden embroidery on his robe caught the lantern-light as he began to circle the table, meeting each of their gazes in turn. "Temptation often arrives shrouded in noble intent. A shortcut offered "for the greater good," a flattery disguised as an opportunity – these can poison even the purest heart if not recognized for what they are." He glanced around at the ring of young faces watching him, his demeanor kind but serious. "Humility and honesty will be your lanterns in the dark when such temptations arise." The six apprentices exchanged sober looks. Cornelius's words settled over them like a light mantle; each understood that a new test was on the horizon and that their understanding of humility would be the key to overcoming it. They straightened their postures almost in unison, silently taking the lesson to heart. They had learned to conquer pride by being humble – now, they would have to spot corruption hiding behind promises of greatness.

Readings by Lamplight

Cornelius's enchanted bookshop radiated a timeless aura around them. The shelves overflowed with delicate tomes and crackling scrolls. Brass instruments and astrolabes ticked softly on high shelves, the rhythmic sounds blending with the gentle creak of the swaying lanterns. In the very center of the room, a life-sized wooden statue of a cloaked figure knelt in a humble pose, its head bowed. The statue's presence suffused the air with a quiet reassurance – a silent reminder of the virtue they would need tonight.

Around this central figure, the young wizards arranged themselves in a loose circle. A thrumming undercurrent of energy hummed in the shop's wooden walls, as if the very space anticipated the lesson about to unfold. Breezie felt a slight prickling at the nape of his neck – not of fear, but of expectation. They all knew by now that Cornelius's lessons were never idle: whatever wisdom they gained here would soon be tested in the trial to come.

Cornelius ran a finger along one of the rolled parchments on the table. "Here are the voices of those who faced similar tests ages ago," he said. A fond smile crossed his lips as he regarded the scrolls. "Tonight, by lamplight, you will read two fables. Each will shed light on how humility stands steadfast against the alluring whisper of corrupted ambition."

At a nod from Cornelius, Blunt struck a match and lit an extra oil lantern, placing it at the center of the table. A warm glow spread out, illuminating the parchment rolls and inviting them to begin. The six young wizards drew closer, their shadows mingling with the statue's in the gentle light.

"Our first tale," Cornelius said, selecting the top scroll from the stack. He offered it to Breezie with a respectful incline of the head, "is called 'The Scholar Who Refused the Crown.'"

Breezie accepted the scroll with reverence, handling it as gently as an infant. The parchment crackled faintly as he unrolled it, revealing lines of graceful script in an old, flowing hand. He met the eyes of his friends for a moment – they all gave him encouraging smiles – then he cleared his throat. In a soft, measured voice, Breezie began to read aloud. The only other sound in The Six Statues was the quiet pop of the lantern's flame as it cast dancing light across the faces of those listening intently.

"The Scholar Who Refused the Crown."

They say he lived in the quiet bend of the river,
beneath the flowering plum trees
that leaned gently over his roof like old friends.

His name was not known in cities.
No statues bore his likeness,
no ink sang his praise in ledgers of kings.

But scrolls he wrote were copied in secret
by those who knew where truth slept.
His students came in sandals and silence,
and left with eyes more open than before.

The Court heard whispers.
"A sage," they said,
"with clarity rare as spring water in drought."
And so they sent messengers—
with cloaks of silk and promises dressed in gold.

The first arrived with a jeweled ring.
"The Chancellor's seat is yours," he said,
"if you will only lend your wisdom to the Crown."
The scholar bowed low and replied,
"A mind in chains cannot think freely.
Let me serve truth, not thrones."

The second came in the rainy season,
offering scrolls inked with titles and honors.
"The world should know your name," she smiled.
"You could guide generations."
He looked at her gently.
"A tree does not ask the wind to carve its name into the
mountain.
Its fruit is proof enough," he answered.

The third came cloaked in shadow,
whispers trailing behind like rustling leaves.
He made no promises of glory or fame.

He spoke instead of what could be lost:

your home, your scrolls, your students…

"Every great oak must bow in a storm," he warned.

The scholar lit a lantern

and held it up between them.

He answered softly:

"Then I will be the seed that grows again after fire."

Years passed. The empire changed its shape.

Chancellors fell. Gold grew tarnished.

And the scholar's house remained — a little more

weathered,

but warm in the glow of morning light.

One day, a young girl knocked at his door.

She carried no titles.

Only questions.

He welcomed her in with a smile

that had never once sought to conquer a crown.

As Breezie finished the final lines, his voice trailed into the respectful silence that had settled over the shop. A profound hush followed the fable's end, as if the very walls of The Six Statues were absorbing the gentle wisdom of the tale. The young wizards let the story's quiet power wash over them. In their minds, they could see the humble sage bowing under his plum trees, steadfast in his integrity; they could imagine the bright-eyed girl arriving years later to learn from him in that modest riverside home. It was a victory without fanfare – quiet and hard-won – and it resonated deeply with them all.

For a long moment, no one spoke. They simply exchanged thoughtful glances. Reddish's eyes shone with admiration for the scholar's unwavering courage. Firee's expression was distant and pensive, as if he were replaying each of the scholar's replies to the tempters in his mind. Checkered gently ran a finger along the scroll's edge, marveling at how a simple story could carry such weight. Greenie had placed a hand over her heart; her cheeks were damp with quiet tears, the tale's truth having moved her greatly. Breezie himself sat still, the empty scroll trembling slightly in his hands as he let out a breath he hadn't realized he was holding.

Cornelius observed their faces, a gentle smile on his lips. Satisfied that the first lesson had taken root, he reached for the second scroll. In the flickering lamplight, he held it out to Greenie. "This one is yours to share," he said softly.

Greenie accepted the parchment, carefully untying the silver ribbon that bound it. "It's titled 'The Mountain, the Mirror, and the Seed,'" she announced. She took a steady breath and began reading, her voice as tender and clear as a stream at dusk. Each word was enunciated with the care of a storyteller weaving a spell:

"The Mountain, the Mirror, and the Seed"

In an ancient land where the sky brushed the peaks of towering mountains, there lived a young scholar named Lior. He had mastered the scrolls of every kingdom, debated philosophers into silence, and received honors from kings. And yet, a quiet unease bloomed in his chest that he could not explain.

One day, hearing of a legendary teacher who dwelt atop the highest mountain, Lior set out to climb it. Villagers warned him, "Many seek answers up there; few return the same." But Lior, confident in his intellect, only smiled. "I seek truth, not comfort," he said.

After many days of ascent, he reached a weathered temple perched near the mountain's icy summit. Inside, an old woman sat beside a small fire. Her robe was plain, her eyes ancient and kind.

"I've come," Lior declared, bowing stiffly, "to learn what remains when all knowledge is known."

The old woman nodded. Without a word, she placed before him three objects: a mirror, a seed, and a feathered scale.

"Return to me when you understand the weight of these three," she whispered.

Perplexed but determined, Lior left the mountaintop carrying the mirror, the seed, and the scale.

First, he studied the mirror. At first it showed only his own confident face. But as days passed, the reflection began to shift. He saw the faces of peers he had dismissed, ideas he had scorned, the pride coiled behind his wisdom. This mirror revealed not just his image, but his impact on others.

Then came the seed. Lior planted it in rich soil and watered it diligently, day after day. But no sprout ever emerged. Baffled and frustrated, he finally cracked the seed open — only to find it was hollow. Lior wept as understanding dawned: only honesty bears fruit. A seed that lacks a living core will never grow. Knowledge, without humility, is empty.

Last, the feathered scale. Lior placed all his accolades on one side — his scrolls, his medals, his trophies — and then he stepped onto the other side. The scale did not tip. Only when he set the mirror and the hollow seed beside him did the balance shift, slowly bowing in his favor. In that moment, Lior realized: one's true worth isn't measured by what we achieve, but by what we willingly set aside. Only by letting go of vanity could he find equilibrium.

Years passed. When Lior at last returned to the mountaintop temple, he was no longer draped in silk or certainty. The old woman welcomed him with a quiet smile and poured him a cup of tea.

Greenie paused at this juncture, lowering the scroll slightly. She let her gaze drift over her friends, gauging their reactions. The shop had fallen even quieter, as if the very air itself was listening. In the dim lantern glow, each of the wizards found themselves reflecting on their own lives – on moments they might have let pride dictate their actions, times they might have brushed off others' ideas too quickly or too sharply. More than one of them swallowed hard, feeling the fable's truth resonate uncomfortably in their chest.

Cornelius remained silent and still, allowing the lesson to sink in. The statue of the humble figure cast a long shadow across the floorboards. Breezie unconsciously stepped a half pace closer to Reddish, as if taking quiet comfort in their unity. Firee's green eyes glistened; perhaps he was recalling how easily knowledge and pride can become entangled. Checkered's analytical face softened into remorse as she considered whether she'd ever valued being right over being kind.

Seeing that the tale had pricked each of their hearts, Greenie gently cleared her throat and continued, her voice as gentle as falling twilight:

Then came the seed. Lior planted it in rich soil and watered it diligently, day after day. But no sprout ever emerged. Baffled and frustrated, he finally cracked the seed open — only to find it was hollow. Lior wept as understanding dawned: only honesty bears fruit. A seed that lacks a living core will never grow. Knowledge, without humility, is empty.

Last, the feathered scale. Lior placed all his accolades on one side — his scrolls, his medals, his trophies — and then he stepped onto the other side. The scale did not tip. Only when he set the mirror and the hollow seed beside him did the balance shift, slowly bowing in his favor. In that moment, Lior realized: one's true worth isn't measured by what we achieve, but by what we willingly set aside. Only by letting go of vanity could he find equilibrium.

Years passed. When Lior at last returned to the mountaintop temple, he was no longer draped in silk or certainty. The old woman welcomed him with a quiet smile and poured him a cup of tea.

"What have you learned?" she asked.

Lior replied, "That wisdom isn't in knowing more, but in needing less. That humility isn't silence but refusing to place oneself above truth. A seed, though silent, can split stone — and a mirror, though still, can shatter arrogance."

The old woman nodded. "Then you may stay… or return, as you wish. Your choice is no longer driven by the need to be right," she said, pouring tea into his cup, "but by the grace to be whole."

As Greenie spoke Lior's final revelation, her voice nearly broke with emotion. She gently set down the scroll, her hands trembling ever so slightly. The closing words of the second fable hung in the air, and a deep sense of peace stole over the bookshop's interior. The six young wizards sat or stood in thoughtful silence, absorbing the rich tapestry of images: a mirror reflecting hidden pride, a hollow seed that would never sprout, a scale that weighed intangibles like humility and sacrifice.

Firee released a breath he hadn't realized he was holding. He felt both humbled and inspired. Without any need for discussion, each of them understood that these two fables were like mirror images of each other – one showing a humble life that refused corruption, the other a proud life transformed by humility. Both converged on the same truth: ambition means nothing if it forsakes honesty and humility.

Cornelius allowed them several heartbeats of quiet reflection. Then, in a voice barely above a whisper, he said, "Understanding is but one step." The gentle words drew all eyes to him. Cornelius's expression was calm and resolute. "Now," he continued, "show me how you stand in truth when illusions come bearing promises you'd rather not refuse."

At that soft challenge, the oil lanterns in the shop flickered. The very air around them began to shift and quiver. Greenie hastily rolled up the delicate scroll she had just read as the rows of wooden shelves wavered like a heat mirage. The lantern flames elongated into glowing greenish streaks. Along the edges of the room, a pearlescent mist gathered, coiling around the legs of the table and creeping toward their feet.

Before the six could utter a word, the mist thickened and the cozy shop around them began to dissolve. The walls of books and curios faded, replaced by distant gleams of gold. The familiar floorboards under their boots smoothed into cold, polished marble. They realized, collectively and with a thrill of adrenaline, that Cornelius's challenge was triggering an illusion — the next trial was beginning.

None of them resisted the change. It was gentle—almost like slipping into a dream. Their vision blurred, then refocused. In moments, the cozy lamplit shop had melted away entirely.

The Gilded Temptation

They found themselves standing in a grand hall that might have been lifted straight from a royal palace. Every surface glimmered with opulence. Marble floors gleamed underfoot, mirroring the towering gilded pillars that supported a domed ceiling painted with triumphant scenes. Golden light poured in through high arched windows, though beyond the glass lay only a bright, indistinct haze. Ornately dressed courtiers drifted through the hall, offering gracious smiles that felt subtly unsettling—each polite grin seemed to conceal an ulterior motive.

At the center, atop a pedestal of white marble, rested a crystal sphere as large as a pumpkin, glowing from within with a mesmerizing ethereal light. As the six wizards cautiously approached, disembodied whispers swirled around them like perfumed smoke. The voices murmured of alliances, of patronage, of destinies shaped and futures secured—all in hushed, enticing tones. The crystal sphere pulsed softly with each seductive suggestion, a subtle tug in the air as if attempting to draw the young companions closer.

Reddish felt her gaze drawn irresistibly to the sphere. The longer she stared, the more it seemed to reflect her own aspirations. In its shimmering depths, she thought she saw a flicker of herself standing triumphant on a grand stage, her fiery passion celebrated by thousands. A voice—perhaps from the sphere, perhaps from within her own mind—whispered, "Imagine how much more you could do, if you just reached out and took it… just a little compromise…" Reddish's fists tightened at her sides. The temptation to channel her bold spirit into something bigger and widely recognized tugged at her heart. It sounded so reasonable—just a small concession in exchange for the power to accomplish so much good. The realization sent a chill through her; it wasn't like her to even consider cutting corners. She gritted her teeth, struggling to keep her mind clear.

Nearby, Breezie's attention was caught by a polished patch of floor that gleamed like a mirror. For an instant, he saw not his real self but a vision: himself draped in fine robes, celebrated and important. In that phantom reflection, he stood alone on a high balcony, waving to an adoring crowd far below. The sight tugged at Breezie's deepest insecurity. A honeyed voice breathed in his mind: "If you had more influence, you'd never be left behind. You could ensure no one ever abandons you. You could keep everyone safe and together." Breezie's heart thudded. The idea of having the power to guarantee unity—to never feel isolated again—was dangerously tempting, making his palms damp with sweat. He swallowed hard and tore his gaze away from the illusion on the floor, shuffling closer to Reddish and Blunt for reassurance.

Blunt surveyed the hall with a wary, level stare. He recognized the trappings of an illusion designed to seduce. The reverent hush in the air, the too-bright gleam of gold, the deferential courtiers drifting at the edges of his vision—everything felt carefully orchestrated to lull them into lowering their guard. *This was just like the fable's lesson, he thought: false grandeur hiding an empty promise.* He recalled the humble scholar who would not trade truth for a throne. Blunt's jaw tightened with resolve. "We must stand firm," he whispered to the others, his voice barely audible over the soft, flattering murmurs that filled the hall. He caught Firee's eye and received a quick, affirming nod.

Firee had been scanning the periphery of the hall. His sharp instincts noted that while everything appeared sumptuous, a hollowness lay beneath the shine. The courtiers' laughter was a shade too distant, their features slightly blurred at the edges. When Blunt spoke, Firee quietly drew his wand, his fingers tightening around the handle. "Corruption here wears a welcoming face," he murmured. He could practically smell the deceit—like sweet incense masking the scent of rot.

Checkered closed her eyes and reached out with her innate truth-sense. When she opened them again, the hall's splendor dimmed in her sight. The fine details of tapestries and costumes had blurred, and threads of half-truths coiled through the air around them. "I sense no outright lies," Checkered whispered, "but twisted sincerity is everywhere—a noble cause slowly sliding into vanity." It was as if the illusion itself spoke in half-truths: Yes, do good, it implied, but do it my way. Give up a sliver of your virtue, and I'll reward you.

Even as Checkered finished, one of the illusory courtiers drifted toward them. He was a tall figure draped in opulent fabrics, his face obscured by the golden glow. In his arms he carried a polished tray holding six scrolls, each sealed with glimmering wax. "No harm in a minor compromise, dear ones," he cooed, extending the tray invitingly. His voice was soothing and persuasive. "Sign these, and you can do greater good—only a small piece of your integrity is all it costs. Think of the lives you could change with the influence you'll gain." The six wizards pressed together shoulder-to-shoulder, eyeing the offered contracts. Golden script shimmered on each scroll, but not one of them moved to take a scroll.

Reddish's eyes flashed, the hall's light catching the fiery red in her irises. "That 'little piece' of our integrity is everything," she shot back, her tone hard with resolve. "We won't trade who we are for all the power in this hall." Her passionate words echoed off the marble columns.

At Reddish's defiance, a tremor rippled through the illusion. The crystal sphere on the pedestal flared abruptly brighter, as if feeding on any flicker of doubt lurking in their hearts. The honeyed whispers grew more insistent, probing each wizard for weakness. Greenie felt a tug at her empathy—a subtle promise that with just a small concession she could heal every hurt—but she recognized the trap for what it was and stood firm.

Sensing the illusion tightening its grip, Blunt drew a deep breath and summoned the calm unity that had carried them this far. He reached out and clasped Breezie's hand on one side and Checkered's on the other. In an instant, all six joined hands in a small ring—a united front. "We reject any promise that asks us to abandon our honesty," Blunt said, his voice clear and unwavering. His words rang out like a bell, slicing through the chorus of whispers.

The robed figure's ingratiating smile faltered and then twisted into something cold and brittle. All around, the drifting courtiers froze in place. Their gracious smiles vanished as dozens of eyes fixed unblinkingly on the young wizards. The gentle background music that had been playing in the hall turned discordant. The trial was clearly escalating. The golden light sharpened into a harsh glare, and shadows began pooling in the corners, as if the illusion were preparing to pounce now that subtlety had failed.

In that charged moment, the very opulence of the hall began to warp. Marble columns stretched taller, twisting unnaturally as if they were made of melting wax. In the dark corners, the coalescing shadows swelled into vague shapes with glinting eyes—watching, waiting for any of them to falter. Echoes of both promises and threats now reverberated off the high ceiling, blending into an overwhelming, wordless hum.

A sudden pang of loneliness gripped Breezie as the shifting light and shadow toyed with his senses. One moment, he felt his friends beside him; the next, it was as if he stood isolated on that high balcony from his vision, the others nothing more than distant specks below. An old fear churned in his chest: the fear of being truly alone. Breezie squeezed Blunt's hand tightly, anchoring himself in reality. "I won't be fooled into thinking I need any power that separates me from my friends!" he cried out, his voice trembling with emotion but strong enough to carry. "No promise of glory is worth losing our unity!"

Greenie placed her free hand over Breezie's, lending him strength with a warm pulse of empathy. Gentle by nature, she had never spoken with such conviction before. "Our real strength comes from being true—true to each other and to what's right," she said firmly. "No shortcut, no prize is worth sacrificing our integrity."

A rush of wind whipped through the hall, as if the illusion itself hissed in frustration. Firee's scarlet cloak snapped and billowed behind him in the sudden gale. Illusory voices swarmed around him, offering visions of him commanding torrents of unstoppable magic—if only he would accept the gilded contract. Firee gritted his teeth and squeezed his eyes shut. In the darkness behind his eyelids, he summoned the image of that hollow seed from Greenie's tale—shiny on the outside, empty within. "No matter how grand it looks," Firee shouted over the roaring wind, "a hollow seed bears nothing!" His eyes snapped open, burning with determination. The tempting vision around him wavered, recoiling from his fierce declaration of truth.

Checkered released her friends' hands and lifted her wand—aiming not to strike, but to shine light. Channeling her magic, she sent a beam of silver-white light toward the largest shadow lurking near the pedestal. "Let's see these illusions for what they really are!" she declared. The brilliant ray sliced through layers of shimmering glamour. Beneath the veneer of opulence it revealed something mechanical and corroded: grinding, rusted gears of a clockwork device concealed at the base of the crystal sphere. It was as if the illusion's heart was nothing but a broken machine feeding on their doubts. "False grandeur, fueled by lies," Checkered announced, as cracks began to spiderweb through the gilded floor underfoot. The illusion was being laid bare.

Nearby, Reddish conjured a small flame in her palm. Its genuine warmth pushed back the cold, false light of the hall. She held it high, and the little fire's glow painted their faces in honest gold. "We've seen illusions take many forms," Reddish called out, turning in a slow circle to confront the phantoms closing in. "They always crumble when met with humility and truth. This one is no different!"

Bolstered by each other's resolve, the six moved in unison, a coordinated force. Blunt stepped up to the marble pedestal where the crystal sphere vibrated violently, struggling to prop up the collapsing illusion. He thought of the mirror Lior had carried—the mirror that reflected the impact of one's choices. In the sphere's glassy surface, Blunt saw not a promise of power at all, but the reflections of his friends standing beside him. With steady determination, he pressed his palm flat against the sphere. It was cool and slick under his hand, pulsing like a panicked heartbeat beneath his fingers. Blunt met his own eyes in the crystal and spoke calmly, "I do not desire to rule or to control. I choose to serve the truth."

A soft blue glow blossomed from Blunt's hand—the gentle tide of water-based ward magic he had learned in earlier trials. It flowed into the crystal sphere like cleansing water washing over a stained shore. Everywhere the soothing light touched, the sphere's hypnotic shimmer dimmed. A spiderweb of cracks suddenly raced across the crystal, and the entire hall shuddered around them.

A chorus of dissonant voices erupted from all directions in one last desperate barrage. "Fools! You would turn down the chance to shape destiny? Think what you could have done!" the voices shrieked in a cacophony, equal parts anger and fear. But it was too late. The integrity of the illusion had been irreparably shattered. The crystal sphere gave a final shudder on its pedestal and then CRACK!—it split apart, a thunderous sound pealing through the hall as a burst of blinding white light seared out from its core. In that instant, the grand hall itself quaked. Gilded columns fissured, and the painted ceiling began to crumble. Shards of illusory gold and glass rained down, dissolving into streams of harmless light before they could ever reach the floor.

Currents of gold and shadow whirled chaotically around the young wizards, searching in vain for any heart that would give them purchase. But they found no anchor—not a single shred of vanity or deceit remained in the six united hearts. Having nothing left to cling to, the illusions let out a last wail and began to dissipate like smoke torn apart by a gale.

Reddish threw up an arm to shield her eyes from the hall's dazzling unmaking, while Firee planted his feet, cloak whipping around him as he braced against the final magical gusts. Greenie closed her eyes and breathed steadily, silently trusting in the virtue that had carried them through. Breezie gripped Blunt's shoulder to steady himself, and Checkered stood at Blunt's other side, her wand-light unwavering as the false paradise was swept away.

Humility's Triumph

At last the storm of illusions subsided into a gentle swirl of colored lights... and then was gone. A deep hush fell. The oppressive gilded glow had vanished, replaced by the warm, steady lamplight of Cornelius's shop. The six young wizards found themselves once more standing on the wooden floorboards between shelves crowded with books and curiosities. Their circle remained unbroken, hands still linked from when Blunt had first reached out.

The carved statue of Humility in the room's center glowed with a soft, approving luminescence, as if acknowledging that the trial had been overcome. A short distance away stood Cornelius. His white robes were unruffled and calm, his hands clasped serenely before him. Quiet pride shone on his face. He stepped toward them, the floorboards creaking gently under his footfall.

"You have done well," Cornelius said, his tone warm and serene. In those simple words lay a wealth of praise. The six had not only understood the lessons of the fables—they had lived them, even when temptation beckoned with sweet promises.

Blunt let out a long breath and released Breezie's and Checkered's hands. The tension slowly drained from his shoulders. "That illusion tried to seduce us in such a subtle way," he said, his voice still a little awed by how close it had come. "It didn't attack our pride head-on this time. It offered us ways to do better—if we'd just give up a bit of truth." He shook his head, marveling softly. "A very clever trap."

Checkered brushed back a stray lock of hair that had come loose; her brow was damp with perspiration. "Good intentions can twist into something else so easily, without humility to keep ambition in check," she observed quietly. Even as she spoke, Checkered realized she didn't need to over-explain the lesson this time—they had all seen it with their own eyes.

Around them, the bookshop itself felt lighter, as though a heavy weight had been lifted from the air. Firee pressed a hand over his heart, feeling it still hammering from the adrenaline. "Those fables..." he said softly, "they echoed in our minds at just the right moments. I nearly listened to those whispers at first," he admitted with a half-smile of relief. He understood now that the humble scholar and Lior had been with them in spirit, guiding them. "I'm glad we remembered what emptiness lies down that path. Ambition without integrity truly is hollow."

Breezie nodded, remembering the fleeting image of himself alone on that balcony. "It's tempting to believe in a quick path to greatness, especially when it sounds like you could help others by taking it," he said. He cast a grateful glance at his friends. "But if that path means losing who we are—losing the trust and honesty that bind us—then it leads nowhere but loneliness."

The six shared a moment of quiet understanding. They had been tested in a realm of illusion and emerged victorious not by brute force or arcane might, but by staying true to the humble principles they'd pledged to uphold. No one needed to say aloud that they'd learned something profound; it was evident in their faces, in the ease of their breathing, in the renewed light shining in their eyes.

Cornelius watched them with a benevolent gaze, the faint smile on his lips full of satisfaction and hope. Gently, he broke the silence. "Remember this lesson well," he said softly. "Humility is not a treasure you win once and lock away; it is a light you must carry and tend every day. Each time you uphold it, you strengthen it for the trials to come."

They turned to him and listened as they would to a beloved teacher. Cornelius's tone remained gentle, not admonishing—simply guiding them onward. A nearby stack of old maps fluttered in a slight draft, highlighting that outside the shop, the night was quiet and still. The trial was over, but that didn't mean every mystery in Boston had been resolved in one stroke.

Reddish glanced toward the door, where through the open doorway she could see a sliver of the alley and the Boston street beyond, still cloaked in midnight calm. "Do you think the illusions haunting this part of Boston are gone now?" she asked Cornelius. "Did we free the city tonight, or will those temptations just creep into some other corner?"

Cornelius inclined his head thoughtfully. "Illusions seldom vanish forever," he replied. "They tend to adapt and change form. However"—he lifted one long finger in gentle emphasis—"your victory here means those particular whispers cannot easily take root in your hearts again. You've denied them purchase, and so they'll wither without the nourishment of your doubt." He turned his gaze toward the door, as if peering beyond it into the soul of the city. "As for the city… there may yet be other shadows or tricksters to face.

But you have become more aware now—better prepared to see through them. Boston is safer tonight because of what you have accomplished."

Blunt stepped forward and bowed his head respectfully. "Thank you, Cornelius. You set the challenge, but you allowed us to find our own way through it," he said sincerely. His voice carried gratitude toward the mentor who never forced answers upon them. "Just like the scholars in the fables, we had to choose truth for ourselves."

Cornelius's eyes crinkled with a deeper smile. "It has been my honor to watch you grow." With that, he turned and walked to a small cedarwood cabinet at the back of the shop. "And now," he continued, "you have earned one more reward for your efforts—one more clue on your journey."

The cabinet was carved with intricate runic patterns. When Cornelius pressed his palm to its door, the etchings glowed faintly blue and the latch clicked open. From inside, he drew out a rolled parchment tied with a deep green ribbon, along with a small faceted crystal that shimmered with inner light.

The young wizards stepped closer, curiosity piqued. Cornelius unfurled the parchment on the table, revealing a detailed, old-fashioned map of the northeastern United States. Tiny inked sketches marked various locations—forests, hills, towns. He set the crystal gently on the map, and it immediately glowed brighter over one spot: a town labeled Hazleton, Pennsylvania. There, beside the name, was a tiny illustration of an ornate clock tower. Next to it, written in looping script, were the words Engle Monumental Clock.

Breezie's breath caught. "The Engle Monumental Clock..." he breathed in awe. "Pennsylvania… that must be our next site," he said, excitement and wonder brightening his tone.

They all leaned in over the map. Indeed, around the tiny drawn clock were several little figures, almost like mechanical statues, and above it Cornelius had sketched a faint ring of gears. But something was odd—across the drawing of the clock's face were a few small scorch marks, as if someone had singed the parchment with the tip of a flame.

Greenie gently touched one of the singed spots, feeling the faint char at the edge. "Do the diaries mention this clock?" she asked, her mind rifling through the records they'd studied. "I recall something about Hazleton… The Engle Monumental Clock was a 19th-century clock famous for its moving statues and music."

"Yes," Cornelius affirmed, tapping the map where Hazleton was circled. "The diaries and notes gathered by your mentors suggest that your next challenge will take place there. And I suspect the virtue at play will not be humility this time." He gave them a knowing look. "Each clock, each trial, tests a different facet of wisdom."

Checkered peered at a fine Latin inscription penned below the clock drawing. Her Latin was rusty, but she could pick out a couple of words. "Innovatio... in spiritu..." she murmured.

Cornelius nodded. "Innovatio in Spiritu—innovation in spirit," he translated. "I will hint only this much: the next illusion you confront will deal with the danger of stagnation versus the power of innovation and progress. Just as corruption here disguised itself as ambition, complacency can disguise itself as safety and tradition. Remain open-minded and forward-looking, as well as humble."

The six companions absorbed this, trading intrigued glances. Innovation versus stagnation—it sounded like an entirely new kind of challenge. Reddish already looked eager at the prospect of something different, while Firee grew thoughtful, no doubt pondering how a clock might test one's drive to innovate.

Blunt accepted the glowing crystal from Cornelius's hand. It was warm in his palm, pulsing with gentle energy that felt familiar—like an echo of the water magic he had just used. "This will guide our next portal, I presume?" he asked.

"Indeed," Cornelius said. "This travel crystal resonates with the humility you all just demonstrated." He closed the cabinet and stepped back toward them. "Use it at a place of magical convergence—I suspect you know how to find one after so many journeys—and it will open the path to Hazleton's Engle Monumental Clock."

Firee turned the crystal over in his hands, watching its light refract in rainbow hues. He could sense faint strands of magic within, perfectly aligned with the virtue they had strengthened. "We'll apply everything we've learned here," he promised, tucking the crystal safely into a padded pouch on his belt. His green eyes flashed with determination. "Humility will remain our anchor as we step forward. And if stagnation or complacency awaits us, we'll break those illusions by seeking truth and progress, just as we did tonight."

Cornelius's expression grew distant for a moment, reflective. Perhaps he was recalling trials from his own youth, or imagining the challenges these six would soon face. He rested a hand lightly on Firee's shoulder and gave a confident nod. "Stay true to that anchor," he advised. "Every clock you encounter, every new illusion, is another thread in the tapestry of your journey. Virtues you've already mastered will support you, and new virtues will be tested. Trust in each other and in what you know is right."

Reddish took a final, sweeping glance around Cornelius's magical bookshop. The lamplight danced off the spines of ancient books and glinted on the curious artifacts. In the center, the statue of Humility still cast its gentle light, rendering the shop's shadows warm and welcoming. She felt a swell of gratitude and respect for this place and for the mentor who had guided them so faithfully. "We won't forget," she said softly. "Not this lesson, and not the ones to come. Every step we take shapes who we become, and we'll carry these truths with us."

Cornelius's smile deepened. He moved to the door and opened it, gesturing for them to go forth. Outside, the alley was quiet and empty, as if nothing unusual had happened at all. The only trace of magic was the subtle shimmer clinging to the threshold of The Six Statues, like morning dew catching the moonlight.

One by one, the six young wizards filed out, then turned to face Cornelius. They bowed in unison, a gesture of deepest respect and thanks. Cornelius returned the bow with a graceful incline of his head.

"Until we meet again," he said in farewell, his voice nearly blending with the night breeze.

They stepped back into Boston's embrace. The streets were just as they had been—old brick and iron under streetlamps, hushed in the late hour. But something felt different to the wizards. The intangible heaviness that had hung in the air earlier was gone. In its place was a sense of harmony, as if the city itself recognized that a positive change had come about this night.

Breezie drew in a deep breath and could have sworn the air even smelled sweeter now, carrying a hint of autumn leaves and chimney smoke instead of tension. "No illusions tug at us here now," he murmured, closing his eyes briefly. Indeed, when each of them attuned their senses, they felt only the normal, gentle hum of the city. Whatever small malicious presence had been lurking was dispelled—at least from this neighborhood.

Checkered gave Firee's arm a soft squeeze, and Firee flashed her a bright grin in return. They all felt it: relief, accomplishment, and the growing excitement of what would come next. Hazleton awaited, and with it a new mystery of the Orloj to unravel.

Blunt drew the travel crystal from its pouch and held it aloft. It pulsed in response, sensing that its bearers were ready. "Time to open our path," he said. The six formed a circle around him, instinctively taking one another's hands again.

At the edge of a quiet side street, Blunt focused on the crystal. Threads of silvery light spiraled outward from it, responding to his will and to the unity of the group. The threads wove together in midair, forming a shimmering doorway large enough for them to walk through. Through that forming portal they glimpsed vague shapes of another place—perhaps the hazy outline of a clock tower under a night sky filled with unfamiliar stars.

Just before they stepped into the glowing gateway, Breezie glanced over his shoulder. In the alley's shadows, Cornelius's traveling shop, The Six Statues, was fading from view, its form turning translucent. Cornelius himself was nowhere to be seen; the mentor had slipped away as mysteriously as he'd arrived. Only the faint silhouette of the hanging sign remained, and then it too blinked out of sight. Breezie smiled to himself. The gentle power of humility and wisdom still lingered in the air, even as the physical shop vanished to wherever magic would carry it next.

With hearts bolstered by the night's triumph, the six young wizards stepped forward into the portal's light. They carried with them the lessons of truth in humility, etched indelibly into their minds and hearts. As the world around them blurred and the comforting weight of Boston yielded to the unknown pull of distant Hazleton, they held fast to one another.

Together, they crossed into the next chapter of their journey— prepared to face new illusions, new clocks, and new lessons with unwavering resolve. The crystal's glow enveloped them completely, and in a flash of brilliance they were gone from

Boston, off to seek the Engle Monumental Clock and whatever challenges awaited in its ticking gears. Their ever-unfolding quest continued, guided by the virtues they would never again take for granted.

Chapter 3

The Engle Monumental and the Stará Bystrica Clocks — Breaking Stagnation's Hold

Arrival at the Engle Monumental Clock

The crystal's glow flared brighter, leading the six young Wizards to Hazleton, Pennsylvania, and the base of the famed Engle monumental Clock—a beacon of industrial daring. Though not an astronomical Clock, a mechanical marvel.

Twilight cloaked Hazleton's cobblestone square in dusky indigo and gold. At its center stood Stephen Decatur Engle's creation, once a marvel of American ingenuity. The towering clock frame cast a long silhouette against flickering gas lamps, dozens of mechanical figurines poised as if waiting for a cue that never came. Built in 1878, Engle's clock had showcased forty-eight animated statuettes marching, dancing, and pondering in a grand display of humanity's drive for progress. Bart's research had noted that decades later, the clock mysteriously ground to a halt during a local economic slump—perhaps an early hint that illusions of stagnation had touched it before.

Now, a heavy stillness clung to the square. Bronze gears that should have whirred with life instead glinted dully, grinding with a labored, uneven hum. A faint tang of cold metal and damp leaves hung in the air, as if the monument itself exhaled in weary resignation. Overhead, the carved figure of Father Time remained frozen mid-swing, his scythe arrested by some unseen burden.

From a dim alleyway, a subtle ripple disturbed the air as six Wizards emerged from a hidden portal. Blunt, Reddish, Firee, Checkered, Breezie, and Greenie stepped onto the quiet street. In a shimmer, their travel-worn clothes shifted into vibrant Harlequin cloaks that gleamed in the twilight. Each cloak's pattern pulsed softly, reflecting the group's heightened awareness of elusive magic at work.

Blunt's gaze traveled up the motionless clock face. "Something weighs this place down," he murmured. His water-blue eyes caught flickers of a slow-moving gray haze coiling near the exposed gears. Reaching out with his water-aligned senses, Blunt detected a discordant rhythm in the mechanism—like a melody trapped in an unending loop.

Breezie tilted his head, tuning his acute hearing to the drag in the clockwork. "It's not just slow," he whispered, voice taut. "It's stuck—repeating the same pattern over and over. No change, no growth."

Beside him, Firee narrowed his eyes. Through his enhanced sight he could make out faint ashen tendrils wrapped around the mechanical figurines, draining the vibrancy from their painted surfaces. "Illusions of inertia," he said under his breath, tension edging his words. "They're sapping the clock's spark… and the people's energy along with it."

Greenie shivered as a wave of lethargy radiated from the clock into the square. A few townspeople shuffled by, their expressions vacant and movements listless, as though weighed down by invisible chains. One grey-haired shopkeeper stood on a stoop, slowly sweeping the same patch of cobblestones over and over with his broom, the motion so habitual and sluggish that it seemed he'd forgotten why he was doing it. "They don't even realize it's affecting them," she murmured, empathy making her heart ache. "If this spreads, Hazleton's spirit could simply fade away." She knew instinctively that only a bold spark of change could break this gloomy spell.

Zeetrikus's Guidance

Reddish clenched her fists, a defiant ember flickering to life at her fingertips. "Then we act now," she said, fiery determination in her eyes. "Stagnation won't hold this city hostage any longer."

Checkered ran her fingers over one of the clock's brass plaques, noting the elaborate carvings of soldiers and scholars that had gone still. "Engle built this clock to inspire forward-thinking," she observed. "We might have to do the same—push the boundaries of its design to free it from this inertia." Engle's clock, a monument to bold invention, demanded equally bold reinvention.

Blunt's cloak rippled as he steadied himself. "We face this together," he affirmed, his voice calm and resolved. "New ideas, guided by the humility we've learned, will light our way." With that pledge, the six Wizards stepped forward as one, determined to rekindle the clock's long-dormant spark of innovation.

As they neared the base of the clock, its groaning hum deepened. Wisps of gray mist curled more thickly around the unmoving figurines. Suddenly, in the haze beneath the clock, a modest shopfront flickered into existence as if forming from the shadows themselves. The sign above the door glowed with gentle amber light, its carved lettering reading: The Six Statues. Through the windows, the Wizards glimpsed cluttered shelves and the glint of curious tools. A wave of warm oak-scented air and a faint hint of heated metal wafted out, reminiscent of a workshop coming alive.

Slowly, the shop's wooden door swung open. Lazarus Zeetrikus stood in the doorway, tall and lean in a dark, long coat. A bent hat shaded his keen eyes, which sparkled with knowing light. He offered the group a slight, cordial bow. "You feel it, don't you—the weight burdening this clock," he said in a low, steady voice, tinged with concern. Stepping aside to welcome them into the shop's glow, he added, "Stephen Engle's masterpiece once stirred imaginations. Now it decays under the spell of stale repetition." Outside, the air itself seemed to thrum with the clock's labored plea for renewal.

Blunt returned the greeting with a respectful nod. "We sense the problem," he replied. "It's as if this place is resisting any new energy or change."

Zeetrikus's eyes glinted approvingly. He allowed a thoughtful pause, letting the distant grind of gears underscore his words. "Stagnation thrives where old patterns refuse to budge," he said finally, each word measured. "To break it, you will need innovation—tempered by humility. Engle's design was bold for its time; you must be equally bold in your approach, but never let pride or impatience fracture your unity."

Inside The Six Statues, the lamplight revealed shelves crowded with mechanical oddities. Self-turning compasses spun in little glass cases, and gears with etched runes hummed softly with stored potential. Cryptic puzzle-boxes clicked open and closed of their own accord, reconfiguring their shapes as if teasing at solutions. In the center of the shop stood a bronze statuette of a robed figure holding an upraised torch. Its pose celebrated creativity's triumphant spark, yet its expression remained calm and grounded—a reminder that unchecked innovation could easily spiral into chaos.

Checkered stepped forward, her curiosity piqued as she examined a rack of clock gears that seemed to twist themselves into new alignments. "So, we need to modify the clock's workings from within?" she asked, already contemplating how they might update Engle's century-old mechanism.

Engle's Mechanical Heart

"Precisely," Zeetrikus replied. He moved behind the counter and retrieved a small case of enchanted tools—tiny wrenches engraved with sigils, vials of glimmering oil, and more. He spread them out carefully, the instruments gleaming with latent magic. "But remember," he continued in his calm, instructive tone, "one mind alone cannot outwit the stagnation here. Each of you must contribute. Pride and solo heroics will only play into the illusion's hands, whereas collaboration will confound it."

Reddish's flame-flecked eyes roamed over the tools and gears. She nodded, already thinking ahead. "Adapting the clock's gear alignment to something more flexible might be the key," she mused. The old mechanism was likely locked in a rigid sequence; a new configuration could introduce the spark of change it needed.

Zeetrikus picked up one item from the counter and approached Blunt. It was a slender brass compass, its glass face etched with a tiny rune that shimmered faintly blue. He pressed it into Blunt's hand. "This will guide you to the clock's heart," he said. The compass needle spun, then pointed unerringly toward the massive clock outside. "Follow it to the core of the mechanism."

Blunt accepted the enchanted compass with gratitude. With tools and newfound insight in hand, the six friends slipped back out of the shop's door and approached the base of the clock tower. A service hatch yielded to their gentle push, granting them entry into Engle's mechanical giant. They ascended a narrow spiral staircase within the clock's iron framework, boots clanging softly on metal steps. Dust motes swirled in the beam of Checkered's lantern, and the air smelled of aged bronze and machine oil.

At the top of the stairs, they entered the main gear chamber—the mechanical heart of the Engle Monumental Clock. Interlocking gears larger than wagon wheels surrounded them, many coated in a dull gray residue. Some gears were halted altogether; others juddered fitfully against misaligned pivots, producing an aching squeal with each attempted turn. Shadows leapt across the walls, thrown by the few flickering gas lamps that still burned in the chamber.

Blunt held the compass up; its rune pulsed brighter as they moved deeper inside. The needle tugged toward a massive central gear partially encrusted in that gray film. "That must be the core pivot," Blunt said. "Let's start there." The team spread out carefully along the platform encircling the central mechanism.

"Checkered, can your lens spot what's jamming things up?" Reddish asked, keeping her voice low. Checkered unclipped an enchanted monocle-like lens from her belt—an heirloom tool they'd picked up in an earlier trial—and raised it to her eye. Gazing through it at the machinery, she could see beyond the surface grime. Tiny hairline cracks and fractures glowed faintly along several key gear teeth.

"They've locked into an old sequence," Checkered reported. Her analytical mind quickly parsed the pattern. "The gears are trying to repeat the same motions without variation. It's rigid… inflexible." She lowered the lens and looked at the others. "We need to introduce a modular system—something that can adapt. Right now, it's like the clock is stuck playing one note over and over."

Breezie had already uncorked one of the shimmering oil vials that Zeetrikus had provided. A fresh, pine-like scent filled the air as he poured a few drops onto a smaller gear assembly that looked rusted in place. "This oil resonates with new energy," he noted, watching the liquid glow and seep into the corroded joints. The stuck gear gave a lurch as the oil worked its magic. "Maybe it can lubricate the old parts, help them move again without us having to rip them out entirely. We don't want to destroy Engle's design, just help it evolve."

A few feet away, Firee hovered beside a warped brass gear tooth that wasn't catching properly. He summoned a gentle flame in his palm, the fire dancing orange and steady. "I can try to soften and straighten some of these warped teeth," he offered. Leaning in, he passed the flame over the bent metal. Under his careful control, the brass began to heat and flex. "Easy does it… We can't break too much at once, or the whole structure might collapse," he added, sweat beading on his brow as he restrained the fire's intensity.

Greenie stood at the opposite side of the central gear, coaxing a couple of slender green vines from her satchel. The living tendrils twined around a cracked wooden strut that braced part of the mechanism. Infusing the vines with a soft healing glow, she used them as makeshift clamps. "I'll stabilize this section while you refit the gears," she said quietly. The others could feel Greenie's supportive magic spreading through the metal and wood, reinforcing weak points. Their teamwork sparked a gentle pulse in the chamber—a hopeful counterbeat to the sluggish ticking.

As they worked—realigning one gear, tightening another bolt—a faint whisper began to echo around them. Threads of gray mist snaked along the floor and wound about their ankles. The illusion's voice was soft and insidious, needling at each of their minds: Why risk new ways? it seemed to sigh. The old path is safer… simpler. The mist tugged subtly, as if urging each Wizard to step back, to abandon these experimental fixes and leave the status quo intact. Worse, Greenie felt it trying to sow distrust: a suggestion that each of them work alone, that too many hands might spoil the task.

Blunt felt the cold tendrils curling up his legs and concentrated. The compass's rune flickered, reminding him of their shared mission. With a deep breath, he summoned a gentle surge of water magic. A translucent ripple spread out from his feet in all directions, pushing the creeping gray mist back. "Don't listen to that voice," he warned his friends, his tone calm but firm. "We're redesigning this clock together. No illusion is going to divide us or make us give up now." In the damp air, Blunt's protective water aura glimmered, keeping the worst of the whispering doubt at bay.

The Rusted Sentinel

Under their combined efforts, one large gear groaned and shifted into a new alignment, then another. Slowly, the reconfigured assembly began to turn with a bit less resistance. Encouraged, the Wizards pressed on—each adjustment building upon the last in a careful, iterative dance of mechanical innovation. Checkered guided Blunt on which gear to tackle next; Breezie's enchanted oil smoothed a particularly stubborn axle; Reddish used a small, controlled flame to burn away an oily residue that Greenie's vines then brushed clean. With each tiny success, the gray illusions hissed and recoiled, repelled by the fresh energy of change flowing through the machine.

But the stagnation wasn't finished with them yet. As the team converged on the central gear, the surrounding gloom began to thicken and draw together. Scraps of corroded metal, broken springs, and discarded bolts skittered across the floor and clumped upright near the main cog, as if magnetized by some malicious force. In seconds, these remnants assembled themselves into a hulking figure: a rusted sentinel born of the clock's inertia. The guardian loomed a full ten feet tall, its body a patchwork of old clockwork and jagged scrap. When it moved, it did so with a painful grinding sound—every joint shedding flakes of rust that hissed against the floor. Two hollow eyes glowed dull red in its corroded head, and it raised one heavy arm like a hammer about to fall.

The metal behemoth issued a low, metallic groan and stepped forward with a thunderous clank, blocking access to the central gear. Each ponderous movement sent vibrations through the catwalk beneath the Wizards' feet. Gray fog clung to the sentinel's form, enshrouding it in the illusion's protective aura. One swing of that iron fist could undo all their careful work in an instant. Reddish's heart pounded, but she stood her ground, flames licking at her fingertips in readiness.

"We have to be careful!" Blunt warned, summoning swirling orbs of water around his hands. "Protect the clock's mechanism while we handle this thing. If the gears get smashed, all our efforts will be for nothing." Forming his water magic into a translucent shield, Blunt positioned himself between the sentinel and the delicate machinery.

With a determined cry, Reddish thrust out her palm and launched a bolt of crackling flame at the sentinel's shoulder joint, hoping to stagger the creature. The firebolt struck the metal plating with a shower of sparks. For a moment, a scorch mark glowed on the iron. But the gray mist surrounding the sentinel thickened at the point of impact, smothering Reddish's flames almost immediately. Her magic sputtered and died out against the cold, resistant haze. Reddish grit her teeth in frustration as the creature turned toward her. "It's dampening my fire!" she yelled. Indeed, she realized, the guardian seemed to snuff out any forceful magic directed at it. "This thing hates change—it's literally trying to smother anything that pushes it out of its old ways!"

The rusted sentinel answered with a guttural, grinding roar. It stamped one foot down, emitting a shockwave of stagnant energy. A heavy malaise fell over the chamber like a lead blanket. Breezie felt it hit him like a gust of foul wind—his limbs suddenly felt weighted and slow. Each breath became an effort, as though the air itself had turned to molasses. He stumbled, fighting against the enchantment. In desperation, Breezie mustered a countercurrent of fresh air. He exhaled a whip of breeze that spiraled around him and his friends, thinning the oppressive aura. "Stay alert!" he gasped, shaking off the lingering heaviness. "It's trying to bog us down, make us too sluggish to fight back."

Checkered pressed the enchanted lens back to her eye and scanned the hulking figure for any weakness. Through the lens, the sentinel's form was a maze of mismatched parts held together by thick knots of illusory fog. But there—a faint gap, right at the elbow of its raised arm—she spotted a badly corroded hinge connecting the forearm to the rest of the mechanism. The pin holding it in place was barely intact. "Its right arm's hinge is nearly rusted through!" Checkered shouted over the clanking din. "If we can break that joint, we can disable its arm." She caught Firee's eye across the chamber, pointing urgently. "Firee, think you can melt that spot precisely?"

Firee followed her gesture to the creaking elbow joint. He nodded, determination flashing in his eyes. "I'll hit it with a focused heat beam," he replied. "But I'll need cover—one hit from that other arm and I'm done."

"On it," Greenie responded at once. With a graceful sweep of her hand, she sent her protective vines snaking up from the floor. The enchanted greenery twined into a mesh shield, intercepting the sentinel's massive left fist as it swung toward Firee. The iron knuckles crashed into Greenie's barrier of vines and wood. The shield cracked under the impact, but it absorbed enough force to deflect the blow, buying Firee a precious second.

Seizing the chance, Firee dashed in. Under the cover of Greenie's vines, he thrust his hands forward, and a lance of intense, white-hot flame shot from his palms. WHOOSH—the pinpoint jet of heat struck the rusted hinge dead-on. For an instant, nothing happened. Then the corroded metal began to glow cherry-red, softening to liquid. Under Greenie's protective watch, Firee's flame burned true, unhindered by the mist. The pin holding the joint melted away, molten iron dripping in glowing rivulets. With a shriek of stressed metal, the sentinel's entire right forearm sheared off at the elbow and crashed to the floor in a burst of sparks.

The iron giant let out a deafening, metallic bellow that rattled the teeth in the Wizards' heads. It staggered, now missing one arm, and nearly toppled backward into the machinery. Reddish immediately sprang forward, hurling a ribbon of flame at the creature's feet to drive it away from the vulnerable gears. The sentinel recoiled, but the illusions around it surged in fury. Thick tendrils of fog gathered and began oozing over the gear assembly the Wizards had just repaired, attempting to corrode their fresh modifications with accelerated rust. The chamber quaked as the sentinel, regaining its balance, prepared another assault with its remaining arm.

Defeating the Sentinel

"We won't let you undo our progress!" Blunt shouted, resolve hardening in his voice. Thinking quickly, he reached into his coat and pulled out the flask of shimmering oil. With the sentinel distracted by pain and fury, Blunt darted to the central gear. He poured the remainder of the enchanted oil over the newly realigned cogs. The liquid metal-like substance coated the gears in a protective sheen, causing the fresh brass surfaces to glimmer. The creeping rust retreated wherever the oil spread, unable to latch onto the renewed parts.

While Blunt safeguarded the mechanism, Reddish planted herself in front of him, summoning a broad arc of flame. With a sweep of her arms, she sent a wave of fire washing over the floor, burning away the slithering tendrils of illusion that lunged toward Blunt's hands. Channeling her frustration into purpose, her flames burned brighter now—reinforced by the knowledge that her friends had her back. "Keep at it!" she encouraged over her shoulder. "Don't back down, not for a second!"

Checkered closed her eyes briefly, focusing her mind. When she opened them, they gleamed with a violet light. In front of the lumbering sentinel, a pattern of illusory figures shimmered into existence—phantom duplicates of the Wizards, taunting and darting. Checkered's magic wove cleverly around the creature's perceptions, confusing it. The rusted sentinel swung its remaining arm at one of these mirages, believing it to be Breezie, and overextended itself with a heavy crash against a support beam.

Breezie, capitalizing on the opening, drew in a deep breath and released another cleansing gale. The wind whipped around the sentinel, blowing away fragments of rust and illusion alike. Each gust swept aside more of the choking gray haze. He concentrated on directing the breeze to shield the vulnerable gear assembly as well. Tiny flecks of corrosive dust that had started to settle on the gears were whisked off and scattered harmlessly into the air.

At the same time, Greenie noticed one of the main pivots in the clock's mechanism wobbling dangerously from the sentinel's onslaught. If it buckled, the clock might collapse internally. Gritting her teeth, she guided her remaining vine magic to coil around the base of the pivot. The enchanted vines tightened like a supportive bandage, reinforcing the structure with living strength. Greenie's quiet resolve flowed through the wood and metal, holding the clock's heart steady through the chaos.

"Together now!" Blunt called out. Their window of opportunity had arrived—the sentinel was off-balance and the illusions around it were faltering. Blunt could feel the elemental magic of each friend building, resonating like chords in a single harmony. With a deep breath, he let his own water magic surge and acted as the conduit for them all.

In unison, each Wizard unleashed their power one last time. Streams of water, fire, wind, and living earth spiraled together, bolstered by Checkered's illusory light. The combined torrent of magic struck the rusted guardian square in the chest, a brilliant convergence of every element they commanded. The sentinel's glowing eyes flared in shock as the blast pierced the fog of stagnation protecting it. Under the concentrated, collaborative strike, cracks spiderwebbed across the creature's corroded torso. Its remaining arm jerked and fell limp. For a heartbeat the iron giant stood quivering, rent with fissures of light… then its eyes dimmed to black and it crumpled inward.

With a final echoing clang, the rusted sentinel collapsed into a heap of scrap and dissolved into a swirling cloud of gray dust. That dust itself quickly scattered, the illusion unable to maintain form under the assault of united magic. All that remained were piles of inert metal fragments and a fading haze where the guardian had stood.

A warm, resonant hum arose from the clock's core. Freed of the clutches of stagnation, the mechanism resumed motion with smooth, confident turns. Gears that had been frozen or grinding now rotated in perfect synchronicity. High above, one of the long-silent chimes released a clear, bright peal that rang out over Hazleton. The note echoed down into the chamber like a celebratory shout. The six Wizards stood amidst the settling silence, chests heaving from exertion but hearts swelling with triumph. They had met the challenge of Engle's clock and prevailed.

In the quiet aftermath, a gentle warmth suffused the gear room. Sunlight, growing stronger as dawn turned to morning outside, filtered through the cracks in the clock face and illuminated motes of dust dancing in the air. The once-gray, gummed-up gears now gleamed with healthy gold and copper tones, the enchanted oil making them shine as if new. The oppressive fog of illusion had lifted entirely. Overhead, the statue of Father Time resumed his ancient dance—scythe swinging in a graceful arc, each measured sweep a symbolic promise that time and progress were moving forward once more. It felt as though the clock itself sighed in relief, breathing freely for the first time in ages.

Greenie rested a gentle hand on one of the great gears as it turned. She closed her eyes and felt the vitality humming through the metal. "It's like the machine is breathing again," she said softly. A smile of contentment played on her lips as the last of her vines withdrew back into her satchel. "All that stagnation… it had drained the city's spark. Now Hazleton can breathe easy too."

Reddish wiped a few beads of sweat from her brow with the back of her hand, her cheeks flushed but proud. "Pushing the clock to adapt—that was the key," she agreed. "If any one of us had tried to force a fix alone, we might've just slapped on a patch that wouldn't hold. But together, we orchestrated real change." She exchanged relieved grins with Breezie and Firee, each of them realizing how much stronger their magic had been when combined.

From the far side of the chamber came the sound of slow, measured applause. Zeetrikus stepped out from a shadowy nook between two tall gears, his boots echoing lightly on the metal floor. He approached with a calm smile and tipped his bent hat in a gesture of approval. "Indeed," he said warmly. "You overcame inertia by embracing innovation as a collective. Stephen Engle would be proud to see his clock in such good hands." The mentor's eyes shone with pride in the young Wizards. They had passed this trial not through brute force or reckless spells, but through creativity, cooperation, and humility—just as intended.

Blunt surveyed the now-stabilized mechanism with quiet satisfaction. The little brass compass in his palm, which had been vibrating all this time, finally fell still. Its rune ceased glowing, as if declaring that its purpose here was fulfilled.

"The compass has gone quiet," Blunt noted. He looked to Zeetrikus, tilting his head curiously. "What comes next for us?"

A New Challenge Awaits

In reply, Zeetrikus reached inside his long coat and drew out a new object: a small brass lever, ornately crafted and marked by script along its side. He held it out for them to see. Curved in elegant cursive were the words "Innovare Contra Stagnatio" — Latin for "Innovate Against Stagnation." This lever, about the length of Blunt's forearm, hummed faintly in Zeetrikus's grasp.

"The guiding compass has done its part," Zeetrikus explained. "Now, this lever will serve as the key to your next destination. Engle's clock was only one side of the lesson on innovation." He swept his gaze thoughtfully around the gear chamber. "Another clock, far from here, shares a connection with this one. Its harmony has also been disrupted—entangled in illusions of stagnation. And if left unchecked, that entire region could slip into apathetic decline." His tone was grave yet even; he was careful not to sound dire, but the urgency of the situation was clear. Time was of the essence.

Breezie stepped forward and accepted the brass lever with reverence. The moment it touched his hands, the lever resonated with a gentle vibration, as if reacting to the Engle

Monumental Clock's restored energy. It almost felt alive—eager. "Where do we go?" Breezie asked, watching the lever's handle glow in rhythm with the ticking gears around them.

Zeetrikus's eyes drifted to the base of the clock tower, where shadows had begun to pool and twist into a circular shape. "A portal awaits," he said, a note of encouragement in his calm voice. "It will bridge Engle's invention here in Pennsylvania to its distant counterpart. Follow where the lever leads. Your synergy will be tested again in that new place, in a new way."

Even as he spoke, the lever pulsed in Breezie's hands, aligning itself with the swirling shadows. Far off, a responding pulse—almost like an echo—seemed to answer from beyond mortal sight. The connection was established; across continents, one great clock called out to another.

Firee took a long, steadying breath and exchanged looks with the others. A hint of weariness tugged at his features from the recent battle, but it was overshadowed by resolve. "We're ready," he affirmed quietly. He placed a hand on Reddish's shoulder, and she nodded. One by one, Greenie, Checkered, and Blunt all stepped forward, forming a determined circle. Their Harlequin cloaks, now a bit sooty and scuffed from the fight, nonetheless shone with renewed color. There was no mistaking the confidence in their stances.

Zeetrikus stepped aside, extending an arm toward the forming portal as the shadows widened into a gentle, spiraling vortex of light. He offered a reassuring smile. "Then step onward, my friends. You've proven that humility anchors your fresh ideas—carry that strength with you to the next clock." As the portal's light reflected in his eyes, he gave them a final look of trust. "I know you will keep complacency at bay and continue to meet each challenge with open minds. Go, and bring hope to the next place weighed down by these illusions."

With that benediction ringing in their ears, the six Wizards stepped forward into the swirl of magic. Hazleton's clock chamber, with its triumphant golden gears and tolling bell, fell away behind them. In its place came a rush of color and wind as the portal enveloped the group. The air itself seemed to change—charged with the promise of a new challenge and scented with possibilities unknown. Together, they plunged into the light, leaving Hazleton and the Engle Monumental Clock revitalized in their wake.

Portal to Stará Bystrica

A whirlwind of emerald, gold, and sapphire light carried the Wizards swiftly across leagues of land and sea. They traveled as if through a prismatic tunnel—nothing visible beyond shifting colors and the hum of arcane energy. After a few dizzying moments, the vortex gently deposited them on solid ground once more.

They found themselves standing in a tranquil village square under a powder-blue morning sky. Crisp mountain air filled their lungs, carrying the scent of pine forests and rich earth. The hush of dawn lay over the area; it was clearly early, with only a few birds chirping and no townsfolk in sight yet.

Before them stood a remarkable clock tower, unlike any they had seen before. This one was not made of stone or metal alone, but a fusion of finely carved wood and sturdy beams. The structure itself resembled a piece of art. Its façade was adorned with celestial blue and gold arcs denoting the movements of the sun, moon, and stars. Ornamental motifs of local rivers and towering Carpathian peaks were etched around the clock face. Above it all presided an intricately carved figure of a seated Madonna—the patron saint of this land—gazing serenely out over the square. An open gallery below the clock face held several wooden mechanical statues that should have been moving in a proud parade each hour. But just like Hazleton's clock when they first arrived, these figures were eerily still. Their painted eyes were dull, their limbs locked in place as if slumbering under the same gray lethargy that had plagued Engle's monument.

"Stará Bystrica," Checkered whispered in awe. She recognized it from photographs and Bart's notes. Her eyes roved over the beautifully carved wooden exterior. "I've read about this clock. It's the only astronomical clock in Slovakia—a local marvel handcrafted to reflect cultural heritage and cosmic harmony." She remembered something else from Bart's research and felt a chill of anticipation. Indeed, Bart's diaries had flagged this place: years ago, during a push for modernization in the village, this very clock had inexplicably fallen silent for a time—an omen that illusions of stagnation had crept in even here, testing the balance between tradition and progress.

Reddish stepped across the dewy cobblestones, her boots leaving prints on the faint sheen of morning moisture. As she approached the base of the wooden clock, she noticed wisps of ghostly mist clinging around the foundation, just like in Hazleton. "Stagnation… again," she muttered, a few embers crackling in her eyes. It was the same kind of gray illusionary fog, barely visible in the growing daylight but undeniably present. "Let's see how these illusions are hiding themselves this time," she said, rolling up her sleeves. There was a fierceness to Reddish's tone—born not of anger, but of confidence. They had beaten stagnation once; they would do it again.

The Wooden Clock's Stagnation

Greenie approached the wooden tower and gently laid her palm against its smooth, carved surface. The wood was cool to the touch and carried a certain living warmth beneath the gloom. Her empathic sense tingled as she closed her eyes and felt for the clock's essence. Faint images danced in her mind: she sensed generations of Slovak craftsmen who had poured love and pride into these carvings, embedding stories of the region's past in every inch. This clock was meant to unite past and future. "It's supposed to blend tradition with progress," Greenie said softly. Her hand traced a carved motif of wheat stalks and constellations intertwined. "I can feel how much pride is in its artistry… yet something is stifling that purpose." The wooden orloj of Stará Bystrica, steeped in local tradition, needed a delicate balance to function—a balance now clearly upset.

Firee narrowed his eyes and peered at the interface between moving metal parts and wooden carvings. With his heightened sight, he could make out the telltale wisps of illusions, much like in Hazleton. Here, however, they seemed to be threading themselves between old and new elements—between the traditional wooden statues and the modern clock mechanisms.

"I see similar illusions at work," he reported, voice low.

"They're twisting the synergy between the old craftsmanship and the newer mechanical parts. Those figurines should be moving in harmony, but it's like they're pinned down by outdated routines."

Breezie tipped his head to listen. A normal astronomical clock like this would play delightful folk melodies or chimes on the hour, a celebration of community and time. He heard none of that now. Instead, only a slow, uneven ticking emanated from within the tower—joyless and arrhythmic. He frowned. "No cheerful melody, not even a proper hourly chime," he noted. "Just that heavy tick… tick… tick over and over. The illusions must be sapping its vitality, just as they did in Hazleton."

Blunt withdrew the brass lever engraved with Innovare Contra Stagnatio from his coat. As he held it up, the lever began to emit a soft golden glow, pulsing in resonance with the wooden clock. When he brought it closer to the tower's base, it vibrated gently in his hand, confirming that this was indeed the connected site. "Zeetrikus warned we'd face more illusions tied to stagnation," Blunt said. The lever's reaction only reaffirmed it. He glanced at the others. "That means we adapt our strategy again. Let's head inside and find the mechanism driving this clock."

Before they could act, a familiar voice—rich and warm with the local accent—floated on the breeze. It seemed to come from everywhere and nowhere at once. "Your synergy restored Hazleton's clock," the voice observed. It carried the unmistakable cadence of Zeetrikus, though the mentor himself was nowhere to be seen in the square. "Stará Bystrica's masterpiece will similarly test your innovation and unity." Perhaps only his echo guided them now, offering a hint but leaving the task in their hands.

The Wizards exchanged resolute glances. The quiet artistry of Stará Bystrica deserved to be saved from this creeping stagnation. Hazleton had taught them that humility and teamwork could spark renewal; now, in this village, they would have to blend that spark with respect for tradition. Armed with that understanding, they approached a sturdy wooden door at the base of the clock tower. Blunt pushed it open, and with a collective deep breath, they stepped inside— ready to breathe life back into another slumbering giant before apathy could claim a second corner of the world.

Realigning the Astrolabe

The interior of the tower was dim, lit only by narrow shafts of dawn light filtering through small windows. A steep wooden staircase spiraled upward, its steps worn smooth by years of caretakers' feet. The group ascended carefully. The smell of polished timber and old machinery grew stronger with each step.

At the top, they entered a circular chamber that housed the clock's mechanism. Instead of the industrial iron grandeur of Engle's clock, this room was an elegant fusion of wood and brass. The focal point was a large astrolabe contraption: interlocking rings of brass and carved wood representing the sun, moon, and stars, all connected to the clock face and figurines outside. This astrolabe should have been turning in a graceful cosmic ballet, regulating the clock's movements. Instead, it creaked along at a sluggish pace. Several of its wooden and metal components were misaligned, and a familiar dull gray residue clung to joints and pivots like cobwebs.

Blunt held up the brass lever, and it reacted immediately— glowing brighter to illuminate certain parts of the mechanism. As he slowly moved the lever around, they could see glints of light highlighting where pieces had slipped out of place or seized up. "We'll likely need a similar approach as before," Blunt said, kneeling to inspect a gear that connected to the astrolabe's central ring. "Rethink the setup, clean it, push it to adapt." He ran a fingertip over a pivot the lever revealed—it was almost completely frozen in place by that gray gunk. "But stay alert. The illusions here might exploit a different angle than simple inertia. This clock mixes tradition with innovation, so the challenge could be… nuanced." The chamber almost seemed to pulse around them, as if acknowledging Blunt's words and urging them to proceed.

Reddish approached a carved wooden gear as tall as she was. Gently, she pressed her hand against it. The wood was beautifully carved with traditional Slovak patterns—flowers and stars—but the gear teeth were jammed against a bronze cog. "It was built with such love for tradition," she murmured. There was a pang in her heart, recognizing the passion the builders had put into it. "We have to update its function without destroying its heritage." The idea of simply tearing out the old wood and shoving in new parts felt wrong. They needed a solution that honored the craftsmanship.

Checkered raised the Hazleton lens to her eye again and peered at a cluster of brass gears mounted on a wooden frame. "Look at this," she said, pointing. Fine cracks ran through one of the major support beams; the lens made them glow a faint blue. "Hairline fractures, just like we saw in Engle's clock." She pursed her lips. "Time has been forcibly halted here too, by artificial means. It's like someone tried to freeze this clock in a particular moment." It gave her an eerie feeling—whoever cast these illusions was intent on halting progress in both places.

Greenie moved to a carved wooden beam that depicted a scene of the local mountain range. She laid a hand on it, closing her eyes to sense the emotions bound in the wood. "I feel so much pride in these carvings," she said. "The artisans wanted to preserve their culture and history in this clock." But then her expression fell. "Yet pride can become a double-edged sword… If it's too rigid, it refuses to let anything change. That kind of pride could be exactly what these illusions are feeding on—turning love of tradition into fear of progress."

Breezie flapped a hand in front of his face, stirring some of the stale air thick with the scent of neglect. Fine tendrils of gray illusion clung like dust in the gear teeth. "So, what's our game plan?" he asked. "Do we start by cleaning off all this gunk, or do we try to realign the gears to get things moving a bit first?"

Firee bent down by a particularly troublesome spot where a wooden gear was stuck against a metal one. Using a cloth, he wiped at the congealed grime, then snapped his fingers to summon a tiny flame. He carefully applied the heat to soften the hardened grease and dirt. "We take it step by step," he answered Breezie. "First clean, then reshape parts as needed, then realign the whole mechanism. Just like Hazleton—only we'll be extra careful not to damage these carvings." He gave

Greenie a small smile, acknowledging the importance of preserving the craft.

The Wizards set to work. Greenie and Breezie took on the task of cleaning; Greenie coaxed a small tendril of vine along the gears to absorb and gently scrape away the gray residue, while Breezie directed light puffs of air to blow the loosened grime out of crevices. Reddish and Firee focused on repairs: Reddish carefully tightened bolts and binding around wooden joints that had come loose, and Firee used controlled heat to bend warped metal back into shape. Blunt and Checkered oversaw the reconfiguration—every time something was cleaned or repaired, Blunt would use the glowing lever and Checkered the lens to adjust the astrolabe's rings closer to their proper alignment.

It was meticulous and delicate work, and for a few minutes the chamber was filled only with the soft sounds of tinkering. But the illusions lurking in Stará Bystrica's clock were not about to remain idle. Sensing their interference, the gray shadows lurking in the corners of the room coalesced and struck back.

A chill wind—not Breezie's—wafted through the chamber, carrying with it hushed voices that curled around each Wizard's ears. "Your changes will erase the past…" the disembodied whispers sighed, weaving through their minds insidiously. "True progress needs only tradition... Why change what already works?" Greenie winced; the voice was gentle, almost sad, as it preyed on her reverence for tradition. Firee felt a tug in the opposite direction: an urge to force the mechanism into a new shape quickly by himself, as if collaboration were slowing things down. The illusions were cleverly trying both tactics—tempting some of them to cling stubbornly to the old ways and others to push ahead recklessly and alone.

Blunt felt a creeping cold on his back, as if unseen hands were trying to immobilize him. He realized with a start that the illusions were trying to freeze them just as they had frozen the clock. "No you don't," he muttered. Channeling his magic, Blunt released a pulse of cool water in a sweeping wave at ground level. It wasn't aggressive; instead, it was calming, like a flowing river that refuses to freeze. The water washed over their boots and dispelled a thin layer of ice crystals that had begun to form from the illusion's breath. The sinister whispers faltered for a moment under Blunt's cool, grounding influence.

Across the chamber, a tendril of shadow had snuck up onto the astrolabe and begun re-forming the grime on a joint they'd just cleaned. Reddish saw it and flared with anger. Not this time. "We can't let it undo our work!" she shouted. Holding her wand like a baton, she sent a cascade of bright, crackling sparks across the astrolabe's surface. The sparks skittered and danced, driving the shadows back from the machinery. Reddish kept the barrage up, her fire a dazzling distraction. "Keep that specter busy while we secure the mechanism!" she cried, trusting her friends to carry on the adjustments as she dueled the encroaching illusions with flames.

"Watch the central hinge!" Checkered warned, her lens catching sight of movement. One of the astrolabe's main hinges—connecting a wooden ring to a brass axle—was fracturing under the strain of partial movement and the assault of magic. A thin split was snaking its way across the wood, growing by the second. If it snapped, a whole section of the mechanism could collapse. "That joint's splitting—Firee, fuse it now!"

Firee was already moving. He dashed to the astrolabe's center where the large wooden ring hung precariously. Pressing one hand against the cracked hinge, he summoned focused heat with the other. A bead of sweat rolled down his temple as he carefully fed warmth into the wood and metal interface. "I need to heat the metal pin and the wood just enough to bind them—too much and I'll scorch it," he murmured. A soft orange glow emanated from under his palm as the wood fibers and metal began to respond.

"Breezie, keep it cool!" Firee called out, voice strained. The temperature in the immediate area was spiking, and that could do as much harm as good. With a quick salute, Breezie swirled his hands and sent a controlled stream of cool air swirling around Firee's work area. The breeze carried away the excess heat in gentle puffs, preventing the wood from charring and the metal from warping further.

Despite the tension, Breezie couldn't help but quip, "Just another day, reengineering a centuries-old clock!" His lighthearted comment drew a quick laugh from Greenie and a smirk from Reddish, bolstering everyone's spirits. In moments like these, a bit of humor was a welcome antidote to the creep of despair.

With Firee's careful mending and Breezie's cooling touch, the crack in the hinge began to seal. The metal pin re-settled in its bracket, and the wood's fracture knitted together under a subtle sheen of magic. The astrolabe ring straightened, finally aligning correctly with its counterparts. Checkered's lens showed the once-glowing fissure fading to nothing. "That did it!" she said, giving Firee and Breezie an enthusiastic thumbs-up.

No sooner had she spoken than a new threat emerged. The gathered shadows at the edges of the room thickened and rose, drawn by the commotion and the Wizards' progress. From the darkest corner, a figure floated forward: a spectral guardian born of Stará Bystrica's stagnation. Unlike the hulking, rusty sentinel in Hazleton, this guardian was wispy and translucent—an apparition of a clockmaker perhaps, with long, gear-laden limbs and eyes like pale glass. Its form was outlined in pale blue light, and within its ghostly chest, wheels and cogs turned fitfully with a discordant clang. It moved as if underwater, slow but inexorable, and where it drifted, the air grew colder.

"You dare tamper with tradition," the specter intoned, its voice a sorrowful whisper that echoed as if in a cathedral. "Innovation erases heritage… Your meddling defiles the past. Yield and keep the old ways intact!" The voice carried a note of beautiful melody beneath the malice, as though it were the spirit of an old craftsman horrified at seeing his work altered.

The Spectral Guardian

Greenie's heart clenched at the words. As the empath of the group, she could sense the kernel of truth the illusion was twisting. There was genuine concern for preserving heritage—but the specter was using it as a weapon against progress. It was a false dichotomy, a cruel trick to stall them. Greenie steadied herself and stepped forward, eyes shining with tears she didn't remember forming.

"We hear your worry," she addressed the phantom gently, "but you're wrong to think it's all or nothing. We can preserve culture without halting growth!" Her voice trembled with emotion, every word laden with compassion.

As Greenie spoke, the specter paused, its head tilting in an almost human gesture of uncertainty. Her sincere care and respect for tradition projected outward like a warm shield. In that moment, the creeping illusions faltered—unable to twist Greenie's genuine love for heritage into fear. Her empathy anchored the team's resolve, forming a protective barrier that the stagnation's lies could not penetrate. For an instant, the chamber was filled with a golden light, the manifestation of Greenie's heartfelt magic pushing back against the specter's chill.

The guardian's eyes flared with a sudden, cold rage. Stymied in one approach, it tried another. The apparition raised a flickering arm and unleashed an invisible wave of force that pulsed through the chamber. Wooden support beams groaned loudly in protest, and the astrolabe itself shuddered violently. The careful alignment they had achieved began to waver as bolts loosened and gears edged back out of sync, threatened by the specter's attempt to literally shake the clock apart.

Blunt reacted swiftly, calling upon his water magic to dampen the shock. A dome of shimmering water appeared above the astrolabe like an inverted bowl, absorbing the brunt of the spectral wave. The wooden beams stopped groaning, and the mechanism settled back down before any serious damage was done. "Ignore its ultimatums!" Blunt called out. "It speaks in false extremes."

He knew the real battle here was ideological as much as magical—this guardian embodied the illusion that new and old could never coexist.

The specter's face contorted in a snarl, its once-melodic voice turning harsh. "You cannot sustain both tradition and innovation," it hissed, circling them menacingly. "One must dominate the other! Choose, or watch both crumble."

The apparition thrust its arms outward, and shadowy replicas of the clock's wooden Madonna and brass astrolabe appeared on either side of it. In one spectral hand, the ghostly Madonna icon cracked; in the other, the phantom astrolabe sparked and fractured. It was a cruel visual metaphor: If you try to have both, I will break both.

Doubt prickled in each Wizard's mind. Must we choose? The thought flickered—perhaps to save the clock they had to sacrifice either its historical beauty or its functionality. For a moment, even Checkered's logical resolve wavered, and

Reddish's fiery confidence faltered. That was the opening the specter sought.

But Blunt was not swayed. He tightened his grip on the brass lever—this artifact itself born from the melding of Engle's old clock and new magic. The lever's inscription, Innovare Contra Stagnatio, glinted as if in reminder of their purpose. Drawing a deep breath, Blunt stepped directly in front of the astrolabe's central pivot, confronting the spectral guardian. "We reject your terms," he said firmly. In one decisive motion, he jammed the brass lever into a notch where a wooden beam met a metal gear, bridging them. The runes on the lever flared bright white as it locked the old and new components together in perfect balance.

"Tradition fuels progress when they're in balance," Blunt declared, his voice ringing out clear and strong in the enclosed space. "We won't choose one over the other. We choose synergy!" At that word, a resonant tone hummed from the astrolabe, as if the clock itself agreed.

The specter recoiled, its false icons of Madonna and astrolabe flickering uncertainly. The notion of synergy—of harmony between old and new—was something it had no power over. Enraged, it gathered itself for a final attack. But the young Wizards were faster.

"Now!" Checkered shouted. Having regained her composure, she channeled her magic into a beam of purple light aimed at the specter's head, trying to distract and disorient it.

Drawing on every lesson from Hazleton and this trial, the team unleashed a coordinated surge of magic. This time, it wasn't a violent blast as much as it was a restorative wave. Reddish and Firee combined their flames into a radiant phoenix of fire that blazed toward the specter—fire symbolic of renewal rather than destruction. Greenie thrust out her arms and sent a ripple of emerald vines and leaves spiraling around the fire, representing nature and growth continuing through change. Breezie added a sweeping gust that carried the fiery, green-tinged wave forward, his wind lending it guidance and gentle control. Blunt's water arced in from the other side, a cool blue stream that encircled the collaborative magic, keeping it cohesive and balanced. And Checkered, focusing hard, infused the entire mix with clarifying violet light—an illusion to counter illusion, ensuring their attack struck true at the specter's core deception.

The combined magic, a kaleidoscope of color and energy, washed over the spectral guardian like a harmonious tide. The apparition writhed and tried to rally its illusions, but it was overwhelmed on all fronts. The warmth of innovation intertwined with the nurturing respect for tradition—this was something the stagnation illusion could not combat. Harmony was its bane.

The guardian let out a keening wail that slowly dissolved into a lament. "You… disrupt the balance… you claim to protect…" it moaned, as if in disbelief. Cracks of pure light appeared across its transparent form. With one final, haunting shriek, the specter of stagnation shattered into countless motes of light that quickly faded away, like ashes carried off on a breeze.

As the last echo of the phantom's cry died out, the chamber fell still. Then came a sound: tick… tick… tick… — steady and robust. The clock's heartbeat had been restored.

Restoring Harmony

A soft glow of morning light filtered through the patterned openings in the tower's wooden walls, painting the interior with beams of gold. The mechanism now turned with a smooth confidence, free of grinding and strain. Gears ticked in well-timed rhythm, and the astrolabe's rings rotated gracefully once more, charting the celestial path as they were meant to. The oppressive gray residue had vanished along with the illusions that created it. In its place, every cleaned and repaired surface gleamed.

A gentle ding resonated from overhead—the clock's subtle chime ringing out the quarter hour. The tone was clear and sweet, reverberating through the wooden beams as if announcing new life. The melody had not been heard in some time; now it spilled into the square outside, undoubtedly reaching the ears of early risers in the village with its pleasant sound.

Greenie stood before a carved panel depicting the high Tatra Mountains and traced her fingertips over the ridges and valleys etched there. She could feel the love of the craftsman in each groove and also the renewed energy now humming beneath. Tradition and innovation—both present, both respected. "Its heartbeat has returned," she said quietly. A soft smile spread across her face, illuminating her features with joy. "Heritage and innovation can coexist… beautifully, in fact."

Breezie looked up at the Madonna statue that peacefully presided over the room. Sunlight caught the Madonna's carved face, making it seem almost alive with serenity. The mechanical figurines in the open gallery below began to stir as well—wooden apostles and regional heroes slowly resuming their promenade now that the clock was free. Breezie's eyes shone as he watched them. "This place resonates with centuries of tradition," he murmured. "I'm glad we preserved that soul even as we opened the door to fresh ideas. The balance feels… right."

The six friends gathered together, forming a small circle amid the now-whirring machinery. They had done it—two clocks in two very different places, both liberated by the same virtues approached in unique ways. For a moment, they simply savored the victory, exchanging relieved smiles and embraces.

In that moment, they understood: stagnation's illusions had tried to pit the old against the new, but by honoring both, they had forged the true path forward.

From the edge of the chamber, a shimmer in the air caught their attention. Lazarus Zeetrikus appeared, stepping out of a fading shadow with his hands clasped behind his back. His bent hat was tilted at a familiar thoughtful angle as he regarded the restored astrolabe. "Indeed," he said, his voice carrying a subdued pride. "Stagnation loves to pit the past and future against each other. You proved that was a false choice. You dispelled an illusion that demanded either-or. In truth, progress honors where we come from while it forges ahead."

Hearing their mentor put it into words, the group felt a warm glow of accomplishment. They had not only solved the practical problem but grasped the lesson behind it. Firee exhaled and allowed the lingering tension in his shoulders to finally release. The last wisps of gray mist were evaporating in the strengthening daylight. "The clock is safe now?" he asked Zeetrikus, casting a final look around for any stubborn shadow.

Zeetrikus inclined his head. "Stará Bystrica's heart is free of stagnation—for the time being," he confirmed. Then, ever the cautious teacher, he added, "But remember, illusions are resourceful. Never assume they're vanquished for good. There may come a day when complacency or arrogance lets them creep back in." He gave them a reassuring smile, offsetting the warning. "For now, though, you carry something precious away from this place: the lesson of Innovare et Harmonia—innovation guided by shared purpose and harmony." The Latin phrase rolled off his tongue with reverence. It was an evolution of the motto engraved on the lever from Hazleton. Engle's credo had been about fighting stagnation; this new one focused on balancing innovation with harmony. The trial here had added depth to the lesson they began learning in Hazleton.

Blunt adjusted his grip on the brass lever, which now glowed with a gentler, fulfilled light. He then realized something: nestled between two of the astrolabe's gears was a small wooden disk etched with runes that hadn't been visible before. As the mechanism completed its first full, healthy cycle, the disk rotated into view. Checkered's keen eyes caught a quick flash of text on it—likely the hidden clue Zeetrikus intended them to find here. Blunt gently plucked it out and the group gathered around. Arcane runes on the disk glimmered faintly, spelling out a brief message that Zeetrikus translated aloud:

"When culture changed, this clock froze—a warning to all. Boston's heart nears the same fracture."

Zeetrikus gestured to the wooden disk, confirming its meaning. "You've restored progress here. But Boston…" he paused, his face growing momentarily dark at the thought of their home city, "Boston stands on the brink of a great fracture. Each success you achieve arms you with new insight. You will need all of it for what awaits back home." The runes on the disk pulsed once and faded, their message delivered.

The six Wizards exchanged looks that were equal parts determination and concern. Their cloaks, catching the morning light, shimmered with the colors of resolve. They had twice confronted illusions of stagnation and twice found the means to break them—through humility, creativity, teamwork, and respect. But Boston… Boston was a sprawling metropolis with countless people and countless hidden corners for illusions to fester. The challenge there would be far greater than a single clock in a quiet square.

Still, seeing each other's faces, they found confidence. If they could unite industrial ingenuity with humility in Hazleton, and blend tradition with innovation here in Stará Bystrica, then whatever Boston required, they would adapt and overcome that too.

A small, proud smile tugged at the corner of Zeetrikus's mouth as he read the resolve in their eyes. "You have done very well," he said softly, his words for them alone. "Carry these victories with you as you face the next trial. May the balance of humility and boldness you've demonstrated continue to guide you, and keep any new illusions from taking root in your hearts."

He raised his cane and gave it a gentle twirl. In response, reality itself seemed to ripple near the chamber's wall. A round portal, shimmering with silver-blue light, spiraled open where moments ago there was only solid wood. Through it, they could discern the hazy outline of Hazleton's square and the Engle monumental Clock tower they had left behind. The scent of carved pine and the glow of morning in Stará Bystrica framed the magical doorway, reminding the Wizards of the place they were leaving—a village where heritage and progress now intertwined seamlessly. It was an example of harmony they intended to carry back with them.

Return to Hazleton

Blunt stepped toward the portal, the first to approach the threshold back home. He still held the brass lever firmly, its etched motto gleaming. He turned to Zeetrikus and bowed his head with gratitude. "Thank you, Zeetrikus," he said sincerely. "You showed us that we can merge creativity with tradition—and do it without letting arrogance or stagnation take hold. We won't forget that."

Zeetrikus returned the bow with a respectful tilt of his hat. His eyes were warm, proud. "Innovation is powerful only when balanced by humility," he reiterated gently. "Hold that truth close as you return to the city that needs you most. Boston's trial will be unlike these, but I have faith you'll meet it as gracefully as you have today."

One by one, they all thanked the mentor in their own ways— Reddish with a beaming smile and a salute of her wand, Breezie with a grateful bow, Greenie with a quick, impulsive hug that Zeetrikus chuckled at and returned kindly. He truly cut a different figure from when they first met him in Hazleton; gone was any stern urgency, replaced by calm guidance and pride in his pupils.

Reddish then turned toward the portal. She breathed in one last lungful of the crisp mountain air, letting the coolness soothe the remnants of battle-fueled adrenaline in her veins. The embers that always seemed to dance at her fingertips had settled to a gentle, warm glow. She was at peace, yet eager for what lay ahead. "Time to go," she said, her voice light but confident. A small smile played on her lips. "We've seen what happens when illusions pit old against new. Boston will be a bigger stage with different tricks, but we'll be ready for them." There was steel in her tone—born from hard-earned experience.

Checkered lingered a moment, letting her analytical gaze sweep over the restored clock's interior. Sunlight through the wooden slats cast dappled patterns on the floor. The feeling in here now was tranquil, balanced. The astrolabe shone in quiet equilibrium, dutifully charting the heavens once more. "I hope this village thrives for years to come," she said softly. "It deserves a future that echoes its rich past." She knew the townspeople might never learn of the strange battle that took place at dawn within their beloved clock, but they would certainly notice the difference: the clock would run true, its music returning to mark their days.

Greenie placed her palm on a polished wooden beam, eyes closed as she took in the gentle thrum of life now present. Where there had been tension and sorrow, she now felt peace and purpose flowing through the structure. "The villagers might not realize anything changed overnight," she murmured, "but they'll wake up to a clock that's alive and well again. And maybe that little renewed spark will inspire someone out there. Sometimes progress is as simple as restoring hope." She patted the beam fondly, as one might a living creature, then stepped back to join her friends.

Firee stood by the astrolabe for a moment, running a finger along one of the freshly cleaned brass arcs. His mind replayed the glowing runes on that wooden disk and the warning about Boston. "The message said Boston may face illusions even more widespread than what we've seen so far," he said quietly, as if to himself. The prospect was daunting, but then he looked around at his comrades and smiled faintly. "At least now we know how to confront them—together, with everything we've learned."

Breezie placed a reassuring hand on Firee's shoulder. "And if Boston's a bigger stage," he added with an easy grin, "we'll come up with some bigger ideas. We'll adapt, just like we did here… and in Hazleton… and everywhere else." His cloak fluttered with a conjured puff of wind—playful and optimistic.

Zeetrikus watched them with a fond twinkle in his eye. With their trials here complete, his role was done for now. He gave a final nod as the six Wizards gathered and, side by side, stepped through the shimmering portal.

In the blink of an eye, the quiet wooden chamber and the mountains of Slovakia vanished. The familiar outline of Hazleton's Engle Clock took shape around them. They found themselves standing once more inside the Engle monumental Clock's interior, right where they had been when they first departed Hazleton. But things had changed here too: the chamber was brightly lit with mid-morning sun pouring through the clock face, and the atmosphere felt lighter. The once-still figurines on Engle's clock tower were now in motion, restored by the earlier victory. Peering out a narrow maintenance hatch, they could see the tiny figures on the clock's facade far above joyfully going through their cycles—miniature scholars flipping the pages of their books, jesters executing jolly jigs, soldiers on parade. The Engle Monumental Clock was alive and well, a playful giant once more.

A collective sigh of relief and accomplishment went through the group. Both Hazleton and Stará Bystrica had been freed from stagnation's clutches. Each of them silently thanked Stephen Engle and the unnamed Slovak artisans whose masterpieces had guided them to these insights. In their mind's eye, Blunt and Checkered could almost imagine the ghost of Engle tipping his hat, and Greenie fancied the carved Madonna smiled a bit wider.

They carefully climbed down Engle's clock tower and exited to Hazleton's town square. The portal closed behind them with a soft pop, leaving only the clear late-morning sky above. The difference in Hazleton was immediate: the square was no longer weighed down by gloom. Townsfolk bustled about with fresh energy—some on their way to late breakfasts or opening shops, others gathered in small clusters pointing up at the clock tower's renewed pageantry. A few children clapped and laughed as the clock's figures did their hourly dance. The scent of bakery bread and autumn leaves drifted through the air, which felt crisp and full of possibility.

The Wizards stood together on the cobblestones, their Harlequin cloaks gently settling around them. The vibrant patchwork patterns of each cloak glinted in the sunlight, reflecting a quiet sense of completion and pride. Hazleton's ordeal had a happy ending, and they had been a part of it.

As they took in the scene, Blunt's sharp eyes noticed something new on the clock's base. "Look there," he said, pointing. Where once the stone was blank, now fresh lettering gleamed, as if etched by an invisible hand. The inscription read: Innovare Contra Stagnatio. The very same motto on their lever now adorned the Engle monumental Clock's foundation, commemorating what had transpired here. Right beside it was another inscription, intertwined elegantly: Innovare et

Harmonia. The two phrases shone together, a paired legacy of Hazleton and Stará Bystrica. Together they formed a tapestry of wisdom: Innovate against stagnation, and innovate with harmony.

Blunt ran his fingers over the Latin words carved into the stone, his touch reverent. He could almost hear Zeetrikus's echoing voice explaining each motto's meaning. Reddish stood at his shoulder, reading the inscriptions as well. A flicker of memory passed over her face—the illusions in Hazleton had nearly tricked her into trying to fix things with fiery force alone, just as the illusions here in Stará Bystrica had tried to make them choose tradition alone or innovation alone. She squared her shoulders. "We didn't fall for those traps," she said firmly. Then she added, thinking of what might come, "The illusions might try different tactics with other virtues next time."

Firee exchanged a glance with Breezie, both recalling the events back in Boston before they set out on this journey. Illusions had already been stirring there, causing apathy in some neighborhoods, aggression in others—signs of various virtues being tested or twisted. Firee gave a determined nod. "We've seen hints of what they can do in Boston—stirring up complacency, sowing discord. Next time, it might not be stagnation. But whatever it is, we won't be caught off guard," he vowed. There was a fire in his voice that had nothing to do with magic and everything to do with conviction.

Greenie pulled out her phone and quickly tapped out a message. She smiled as a reply came almost instantly. "I've let Antonella and Bart know we're on our way back," she said, sliding the phone away. "They might have dug up more clues about what's happening in Boston while we've been gone. We shouldn't lose any momentum—Boston needs us, and now we have a better idea of what to look for." Her emerald cloak swirled as if eager to head off immediately.

Checkered took off her lens and carefully polished it with a handkerchief. "No doubt the illusions in Boston will be more complex than what we faced here," she cautioned, always the strategist. "We'll need every lesson we've learned so far: everything from Bern, from Engle's Clock, from Stará Bystrica—perhaps even more." She listed their previous trials, thinking of each city's challenge they'd overcome. Each had prepared them for this moment.

Blunt looked around at his companions—his friends, his team—and felt a swell of gratitude and pride. They had grown so much together. He thought of the humility they'd gained in their earliest adventures, the inventive spark they'd nurtured here, and the balance they'd learned to strike. "We'll stick to what works," he said, eyes shining. "We'll face whatever comes with humility and with invention, side by side. As long as we stay true to our shared purpose, no illusion—whatever form it takes—will stand a chance against us."

The morning sun climbed higher, casting a hopeful light over Hazleton as the six Wizards turned to make their way toward the train station. Their steps were light, yet purposeful. Hints of color from their cloaks danced across the sidewalk—emerald, crimson, sapphire—like a promise of the magic and unity they carried with them. They each took one last glance over their shoulders at the Engle monumental Clock, now ticking smartly and shining in the sun. It was a sight that would forever remind them of what they had accomplished and what more they could do.

In that final moment in Hazleton, a quiet understanding passed among them. Ahead lay Boston, and with it challenges that would test everything—perhaps new illusions targeting compassion, honesty, courage, or more. But they would step into that fray as they had here: together. The stagnant gloom had been lifted in two corners of the world today. Buoyed by that knowledge, the six Wizards of Boston set off, renewed by one hard-won triumph and ready to spark the next, wherever the journey would lead them.

Chapter 4

The Old State House Clock — Innovation's Triumph

Decoding the Ancient Language

The Engle Monumental Clock's hum faded as the portal's glow delivered them back to Boston's twilight, calibrated to the same hour they had departed—when the city's pulse shifted between day and night. Dusk draped the historic district in lavender and gold. The Old State House mechanical clock's gilded face cast a faltering glow across the crowded plaza. Its weathered gears, etched with colonial motifs, strained beneath ornate engravings; their chimes—once a beacon of civic progress—now jarring and discordant, as if stagnation's weight had twisted their rhythm. Cobblestones gleamed under an eerily flickering torchlight—clearly an illusion overlaying the modern plaza with an old-time glow— where merchants and scholars mingled amid phantom vendor stalls, voices raised in rigid debates. A burly trader clung to outdated methods, dismissing a rival's new techniques, while a bespectacled orator scoffed at another's innovative theories.

The evening breeze carried sea salt and the buzz of city life, but an edge of tension cut through it—eyes in the plaza were dulled with resistance.

From the portal's soft radiance, six Wizards—Blunt, Reddish, Firee, Checkered, Breezie, and Greenie—stepped into the clock's looming shadow. Their Harlequin cloaks, normally vibrant, appeared subdued in the flickering glow, yet still pulsed softly in quiet defiance against the uneasy hush. Blunt's fingers grazed a brass gear etched with "Innovare Contra Stagnatio", the second artifact Zeetrikus had bestowed after Hazleton's lever—each piece part of a modular toolkit for innovation. Its warmth reminded them of their trials in Hazleton and Stará Bystrica. "We've seen innovation's power," Blunt said, his voice edged with resolve. "Now Innovare Contra Stagnatio points us to challenge Boston's inertia."

Checkered scanned the Old State House's brick façade, its tower slicing the twilight, each labored chime a cry for lost progress. "Stagnation is locking Boston's heart into rigid patterns," she observed, her analytical mind dissecting the plaza's tension. "The clue points here—where progress once thrived and is now twisted by old traditions."

Greenie extended her empathic senses into the crowd, feeling merchants' stubborn defenses and scholars' curt dismissals. Her cloak darkened in sympathy. "They're clinging to comfort, refusing new ideas," she whispered. "It's a city sinking into stagnation, like Hazleton was before we freed it." Yet even now, she sensed curiosity glimmering faintly among the people—a spark that could, if kindled, break stagnation's hold.

Firee's crimson cloak flared with vigilance as he recalled the illusions that had ensnared Hazleton. "Zeetrikus must be near," he said quietly. Boston's friction was no coincidence— the Old State House stood at a crossroads of old ideals and new voices.

Breezie noted the battered vendor stalls, the stiff postures of debaters fearful of change. "Innovation means adapting strengths to break inertia," he said contemplatively, recalling how Stará Bystrica's clockwork had thrived once they loosened its rigid gears.

Reddish's fiery resolve blazed at the sight of the bickering factions. Traders were locked in outdated practices; scholars scoffed at fresh theories. "Let's find Zeetrikus now," she urged, ember-lit eyes scanning the restless crowd.

Firee placed a cautionary hand on her arm. "If we rush, illusions could ensnare us," he said calmly, the lessons of unity from Hazleton guiding him.

Reddish drew a steady breath and banked the ember at her cuffs. "Right," she said, letting patience—not fire—take the lead.

Blunt looked at them both, his water-blue eyes steady. "We approach humbly, as a team," he affirmed. "The Old State House is our lead—Zeetrikus's shop awaits." Around them, the plaza's discord pulsed, urging their unity to prevail. With that, they wove into the deepening twilight, cobblestones echoing beneath determined steps, ready to spark progress where Boston's heart had stalled.

Decoding Innovare Contra Stagnatio

An oak-paneled library in Bart and Antonella's brownstone provided a brief sanctuary from the turmoil outside. Shelves sagged with well-worn tomes and leather-bound maps detailing the city's colonial roots. A carved globe stood by the fireplace, continents faded by years of study. Amber lamplight flickered against the walls, illuminating two artifacts resting atop a polished mahogany table: the brass gear from Stará Bystrica engraved with "Innovare et Contra Stagnatio", and the slender brass lever from Hazleton engraved with the original motto "Innovare Contra Stagnatio." Together, these gifts from Zeetrikus formed an evolving toolkit, each motto a philosophical anchor building on the last.

Outside, muffled voices carried from the streets—a jumble of heated arguments over new ideas. Blunt placed the Stará Bystrica gear at the table's center, letting its steady hum soothe his turbulent thoughts. "We need clarity," he said, recalling the tense swirl of energy near the Old State House. "Zeetrikus's clue, Innovare Contra Stagnatio—'Innovate Against Stagnation.' That's the key."

Checkered leaned in, tapping a finger on the gear's engraved runes. "That clock at the Old State House once symbolized forward-thinking ideals," she noted. "But the city's inertia has twisted it into a bastion of rigid tradition. I suspect that's where Zeetrikus's next test lies."

Breezie reclined in an armchair, eyeing an old engraving of the State House tower. "Innovation thrives only if people embrace change," he reflected. "Yet out in the plaza we saw merchants and scholars clinging to the past. Zeetrikus wants us to dismantle that mindset—just as we realigned clock gears in Hazleton."

Firee paced near a dusty bookshelf, unsettled by the echo of illusions that had nearly trapped them in Hazleton. "If illusions target Boston's very identity, we'll need caution," he warned, remembering how close inertia came to overwhelming them before. "Innovare implies we adapt our synergy again."

Greenie ran her hand over a centuries-old volume detailing revolutionary councils once held at the Old State House. She sighed softly. "It's tragic. A place that once championed new ideas has stagnated," she said, empathy coloring her voice. "Stará Bystrica taught us tradition can merge with progress. Maybe Boston needs that balance too."

Reddish's eyes glinted with impatience, embers flickering in the lamplight. "Then let's not linger," she urged. "The city's tension is rising—each moment, stagnation gains ground."

Firee raised a cautionary hand as ever. "Charging in blindly invites illusions," he reminded, his cloak dimming to reflect restraint. His vigilance, honed during their trials in Venice, guarded against illusion's subtle traps.

Blunt bridged their fervor with steady calm. "We'll find Zeetrikus's ephemeral store near the Old State House," he said, meeting each Wizard's eyes in turn. "We approach with humility and synergy—no illusion can stand if we remain united." The library's warmth steadied their resolve. Together, they answered the call to action.

Checkered gathered her notes, each line echoing Hazleton's hard-won victory. "Agreed," she said firmly. "It's time to face Boston's inertia head-on. Innovare Contra Stagnatio."

Seeking Lazarus Zeetrikus

Leaving the brownstone, they followed the clue's pull back to the Old State House Plaza. The atmosphere had grown even more charged. Stagnant arguments crackled in the air; voices carried harshly across the cobblestones. As the Wizards neared a familiar alley beside the old building, a shimmer of gray magic caught their eyes—a veil obscuring a humble wooden door. They recognized Zeetrikus's handiwork immediately.

Inside The Six Statues shop, twilight pooled in the corners, illuminating shelves lined with mechanical curios and weathered scrolls. Six statues—Innovation, Harmony, Knowledge, Courage, Resilience, and Humility—encircled the room, each carved from a different stone and glinting with enchantment. At the center stood Lazarus Zeetrikus himself, clad in patchwork robes and a bent top hat, leaning casually against the grand orrery dominating the shop's rear. Brass planets and gears turned in slow orbits above him, casting dancing reflections on the walls.

Zeetrikus greeted them with a subdued nod, eyes grave yet welcoming. "Boston's heart stagnates, bound by clinging minds," he said in confirmation, his tone calm and measured. "Have you brought the insights from Hazleton and Stará Bystrica?"

Blunt stepped forward and placed the two previous artifacts on the counter—the Stará Bystrica gear etched with "Innovare et Contra Stagnatio," and Hazleton's brass lever. "We have," he affirmed. "Hazleton showed us unity; Stará Bystrica taught us how to blend innovation with tradition. Boston seems to need both."

"Well understood." Zeetrikus allowed the smallest approving smile. "Tonight, this city's trial centers on breaking an impasse. Listen now. Two tales will guide you."

He gestured to a reading pedestal where two ancient scrolls lay waiting. "One fable, one poem," he explained. "They hold keys to unlocking Boston's stagnation. Who will read them?"

Breezie and Reddish exchanged glances. Together, they stepped forward, and each lifted a scroll from the pedestal.

A hush fell over The Six Statues shop as Breezie carefully unfurled the first scroll. Checkered's eyes brightened with intellectual curiosity, and Reddish leaned in, flame-tinged anticipation in her posture. Even Firee and Breezie himself relaxed slightly, recalling how Zeetrikus's prior fables and poems had cut through illusions in Hazleton and Slovakia. Greenie rested a gentle hand on the statue of Harmony beside her, feeling it resonate with the same synergy that had helped them overcome Hazleton's guardian.

Fable of the Lake

"Your voice suits the fable of the lake and the stream," Zeetrikus said softly to Breezie. "Show them how stagnation rots what should be alive."

Breezie nodded and held the scroll up to the lamplight. As he began to read, candlelight gleamed on the delicate script. The shop's instruments hummed softly in tune, as though the very words themselves carried transformative power. He wove a tale of stillness turning a beautiful lake stale, while a flowing stream thrived in renewal:

"The Lake and the Stream"

In the heart of a lush valley, there lay a beautiful, tranquil lake, fed gently by a lively, spirited stream. The lake was vast, reflecting the clouds and stars, admired by every creature nearby. The stream, though smaller and narrower, sparkled with ceaseless movement, dancing between rocks, its waters always clear and alive.

One day, the lake spoke to the stream with certainty, "Why do you rush so restlessly, dear stream? Look at me—I am calm, stable, admired by all who gaze upon my beauty. Your endless agitation seems foolish."

The stream chuckled gently, replying, "I must flow, for movement is my nature. Without it, I would lose all I cherish."

The lake laughed softly, dismissing the stream's words as restless folly. Years passed, and the stream continued to flow joyously, nurturing flowers, wildlife, and trees along its banks. It remained ever fresh and vibrant, admired for its crystal-clear waters.

But the lake, content in its stillness, gradually changed. Its calm waters slowly darkened, choked by weeds and algae. Fish began to avoid it, birds no longer nested along its shores, and animals ceased visiting. The stagnant waters, once so admired, turned stale and murky.

Eventually, saddened and puzzled by its solitude, the lake called out to the stream again, "Friend, tell me, why has the world turned away?"

The stream, still lively and fresh, replied softly, "Dear lake, beauty without movement fades into decay. You chose calm without growth, tranquility without renewal. Life thrives in motion."

Realizing the truth too late, the lake asked mournfully, "Is there hope left for me?"

The stream comforted the lake gently, saying, "It is never too late to renew. If you let me flow through you once more, perhaps together we can restore your vitality."

Humbled, the lake opened itself to the stream's refreshing waters, and slowly life returned. Fish swam, birds sang, and animals gathered once more. Though the lake never forgot the lesson of stagnation, it lived thereafter in grateful harmony with the stream—ever moving, ever growing.

A heavy hush followed the fable's final lines, as if the very shelves had absorbed the lesson. The Wizards exchanged thoughtful looks, hearts stirred by the echo of the stagnant debates outside. Hazleton's gears had once locked in old patterns; Stará Bystrica was nearly lost to apathy. Left unchallenged, stagnation decays even the grandest creation— just as Boston now risked losing its spark.

Breezie rolled up the scroll with care. "Beauty without motion turns to decay," he said quietly, summarizing the lake's late realization. "Boston's old ways mirror that lake."

Checkered nodded, tapping her chin. "It's easy to bask in past glory, being admired at first. But without renewal, everything goes stale," she reflected. "We saw it happen in Hazleton too."

Greenie shivered, recalling the friction in the plaza. "The people out there are locked in old beliefs—like the lake that refused the stream's help," she said softly. "We have to open them to change."

Zeetrikus inclined his head and gestured to the second scroll, this one glowing faintly with enchantment in Reddish's hands.

"Precisely. But note: stagnation isn't defeated by rejecting the old alone; you must also champion the new. Reddish, let your fire kindle the poem Dreamers Forge the World. Let them glimpse innovation's heartbeat."

Reddish took a steady breath and unrolled the scroll. The poem within described wanderers forging new horizons, unafraid of doubters and weaving the future from imagination's spark. Its verses danced with vivid imagery— dreams shaped into living truth, unstoppable invention, humble courage taking risks for the greater good. The lines conjured a meadow of wildflowers, each color representing a fresh idea pollinating the next, a vibrant counterpoint to the lake's stillness:

"Dreamers Forge the World"

We are the whispers in the dark,
The gentle sparks that light the flame,
We dare the unseen roads embark,
Inventing pathways without name.

With minds unbound, horizons wide,
In shadows deep we plant the seed,
Through possibility we stride,
For every need births greater deed.

A thousand roads before us part,
Yet courage guides our restless feet,

For innovation stirs the heart—
The music makers' pulse and beat.

We challenge comfort's sleepy reign,
In every limit, break the mold,
Transforming loss to hopeful gain,
Turning leaden dreams to gold.

We dwell where chance and vision blend,
Crafting future from desire,
Within imagination's bend,
We shape the world with endless fire.

Innovation, simply said,
Is daring thought made manifest,
Transforming visions in our head
To living truths, life's brightest quest.

We risk, defiant to the scorn,
Unshaken by the skeptic's call,
In faith of what is yet unborn,
Believing dreams despite them all.

Remember this, embrace the light—
Each dream pursued renews the earth,
For progress blooms from courage bright—
Innovation shapes rebirth.

So dream, create, and boldly strive,
Let courage write your lasting rhyme,
Through innovation we survive—
In changing, we defy all time, forevermore.

As Reddish's voice faded, the Harmony statue on the dais glowed warmly, as if the poem's creative energy had nourished it. A hush settled in the shop once again. Each Wizard took a moment to contemplate the synergy between the fable's warning against stagnation and the poem's call for bold creation. The poem had ignited an unmistakable spark of innovation—a beacon lighting the way for the challenge ahead. Zeetrikus folded his arms, a glint of resolve in his eyes.

Test at the Old State House

"Stagnation chokes the old clock outside," he said, calm and serious. "Your mission: dispel the illusions luring Boston to cling to comfort. Unite your powers—create solutions that fuse tradition with forward momentum. Innovare Contra Stagnatio."

Reddish set the scroll aside, embers dancing in her eyes. "Hazleton taught us synergy, Stará Bystrica taught us to merge heritage with progress. Boston demands we do both—again."

Firee gently touched a tuning fork displayed on a shelf, feeling it vibrate faintly. "We adapt, or illusions will drag us back into inertia," he agreed, recalling the crowd's refusal to change outside in the plaza.

Breezie inhaled and straightened, drawing strength from the poem's verses about courageous dreamers. "Then we blend hope with practicality—forge new gears for that old clock, metaphorically speaking," he said. He remembered how they had physically rebuilt cogs in earlier trials and knew now they must do so in spirit.

A rare, subtle smile crossed Zeetrikus's face. "Exactly. Prepare yourselves," he said. "The Old State House clock awaits your test. Remember: stagnation wields illusions of comfort—only true innovation shatters it."

At Zeetrikus's final word, the silver walls of The Six Statues shop trembled. "Confront stagnation's illusions—forge innovation's triumph!" his voice resonated, and the shop's glow swelled around the Wizards. In a dizzying blink, the cozy interior melted away, depositing them directly into the sprawling city plaza around the Old State House.

They stood once more under the clock tower, but now the plaza was draped in phantasmal echoes of the past. Dim, illusory torches flickered where modern lamps had been, bathing the scene in a ghostly antique glow. Rust-coated magical tendrils coiled around the clock's exposed gears high above, freezing them mid-chime.

All around, traders and scholars argued as before, each stubbornly defending archaic practices. The once-unified square was splintered into factions: "We don't need new methods!" one man shouted. "Don't fix what isn't broken!" cried another. Their defiant words echoed the fable's still lake. Overhead, the clock's great face shone an eerie, sickly gold. Even its quarter-hour bell tried to ring, but the note came out jarring and off-key, as if the clock itself were groaning in pain from the crowd's refusal to adapt.

No sooner had they gotten their bearings than a swirl of illusions assaulted the Wizards' minds. Each whisper was a honeyed voice promising the comfort of tradition. Blunt felt a sedating wave urge him to preserve Boston's heritage at all costs and ignore any newfangled ideas. Recall Hazleton, he told himself fiercely, shaking off the false nostalgia. He summoned a shimmering water ward that sliced through the mental fog. "We stand for progress," he reminded his friends, voice steady and clear.

Reddish gritted her teeth as an illusion crowned her the grand protector of the old ways, tempting her with pride and authority if she'd only stop pushing for change. She scoffed aloud, remembering Stará Bystrica's lesson that progress and tradition must balance. "We push forward!" she insisted. With a flourish of her hands, she released a burst of innovative flame that burned away rust clinging to the edge of a frozen gear above.

Checkered blinked rapidly as a comforting vision swam before her: a grand archive filled with dusty tomes that urged her never to alter a single page of knowledge. Her analytical lens flared, detecting the stagnation lurking in that message. "Knowledge must evolve," she snapped. With a sharp gesture, she conjured a complex false gear pattern in the air. An ensnaring iron tendril chasing it was led away from the clock's mechanism, momentarily freeing a jammed pivot.

Greenie staggered under a wave of fear that rolled out from the crowd's collective unconscious. For an instant, she heard a phantom chorus praising her for "keeping us safe" if only she upheld the status quo. She closed her eyes and let empathy guide her to the truth. The fable's stream flowed in her memory. "Safety isn't found in stasis," she whispered. She wove out tendrils of vine magic, and they nudged a second seized gear into alignment with gentle, persistent pressure.

Firee felt his danger sense spike as an illusion promised him glory if he would champion tradition and crush dissent. He exhaled sharply, heart pounding. Don't fall for it. In one swift motion, he traced a rune of heat in the air. A precise jet of flame lanced out and burned away the sticky residue binding a delicate cog, allowing it to spin freely once more.

Breezie, ever gentle, faced a whispered offer of peace: a quiet, comfortable life with no more battles, if only he defended ancient customs. He inhaled the cool night air and blew it out slowly. With a sweep of his arm, he summoned a controlled gust. The fresh wind cleared the cloying illusion from his mind. "Progress needs fresh wind," he said. He directed that breeze upward, keeping a loosened gear turning with careful, supportive currents.

Then, from deep within the clock's tower, a grinding roar reverberated. Gears heaved and an enormous shape tore free from the machinery with a shriek of metal. A towering guardian made of rusted iron took form before their eyes. Its joints were fused with corrosion, its eyes glowing dull gold through the grime. "Innovation is chaos!" it roared, each word a grating rasp. "Stagnation is order!" With that, the giant swung a massive, corroded arm toward the Wizards. Each step it took left patches of frost-like illusion on the ground, and its iron tendrils still tethered into the clock's works, threatening to lock everything solid.

Townsfolk continued their quarrels, oblivious to the spectral struggle now unfolding in their midst.

For a heartbeat, the arguments braided into a lulling certainty for Checkered—an easy promise that if the gears simply froze, the shouting might finally stop. The glamour gilded stillness as mercy. She touched the edge of her monocle, whispered *"Veritas in humilitate,"* and let the lie pass like breath on glass.

Blunt reacted instantly. He thrust out both hands and a dome of water sprang up, shimmering blue, to deflect the guardian's slow yet crushing fist. The impact rippled across Blunt's ward, but he held firm. "We unify or we fail!" he called out, voice resolute. "Innovation only thrives if we blend our powers!"

At his side, Reddish darted in low. She snapped her fingers and sent sparks dancing along the guardian's flank, each spark infused with a bit of mechanical insight gleaned from the poem's imagery. The glittering sparks sought out hinges and joints. "We can't let it freeze this clock," she warned, driving a focused lance of flame into a rusted hip joint. The creature hissed, swiping at her; illusions flared in angry halos around the damaged joint.

Checkered, staying back, raised her monocle and scanned the thrashing guardian up and down. Her keen eyes found the weakness: "Right there—its middle gear is misaligned!" she shouted, pointing to a large cog visible in the creature's chest. "Cripple that pivot!"

Firee heard and understood. Planting his feet, he summoned a white-hot flame to his palm. With a precise flick, he sent the narrow jet of fire streaking toward the misaligned middle gear.

Metal began to glow orange. "Stand by, Breezie!" Firee warned, not taking his eyes off the heating cog.

Breezie was already moving. He leapt upward and clapped his hands together, releasing a concentrated blast of wind. The gale struck the red-hot gear dead-on. A loud crack rang out as the abrupt cooling fractured the metal. The guardian bellowed in rage. It lashed out in desperation, slamming its remaining arm into the ground and sending a wave of stagnant illusion blasting outward. "Order demands no invention!" it howled, the cry echoing off brick walls.

Greenie raised her arms as if conducting. From the cobblestones beneath the guardian, thick green vines burst forth, summoned by her magic. They twined around the creature's straining arm and formed an ephemeral scaffold against the clock tower behind it, bracing a large gear the guardian had been trying to rip away. The creature roared and tried to tug free, but Greenie's vines held. She infused them with the calm, persistent energy of the flowing stream. "Stagnation suffocates; we must let fresh currents in," she intoned, voice steady. The guardian's frenzied onslaught faltered, its momentum ebbing under the combined restraint.

Seizing the moment, Blunt swept his arms in a wide arc. A surge of water magic swirled out and coiled around the guardian's legs like the crushing pressure of the sea. The rusted giant's movements slowed to a crawl, its feet held fast by Blunt's water wards. With a determined shout, Blunt solidified the water into bands of ice. The guardian was pinned in place.

Reddish and Firee didn't waste the chance. They met each other's eyes and nodded. Reddish summoned the fiercest flame she could muster in her hands, while Firee compressed his own fire into a sizzling lance. Together, with perfect timing, they unleashed twin blasts of heat straight at the guardian's chest. The combined strike hit the already cracked breastplate. Under the extreme temperature, the corroded iron split with a deafening crunch.

Checkered layered one final illusion over the staggering guardian's eyes—a sudden mirage of nimble foes darting at its flank. The rusted giant swung wildly at the empty air, overextending itself. "Now!" Checkered signaled.

With a mighty exhale, Breezie conjured a gale-force wind. The focused gust slammed into the guardian's exposed side. Off-balance and weakened, the hulking creature toppled backward with a crash that shook the plaza.

A ragged cheer almost escaped the Wizards' lips—but the fight was not over. From where it lay sprawled, the guardian's eyes flared once more with desperate light. Drawing on the last of its strength, it drove a colossal fist directly into the base of the clock tower. Gears deep within ground in protest. Instantly, an intricate web of gray magic crackled over the clock's mechanism. The guardian had triggered a final illusion: a spectral safety lock meant to protect the clock, now perverted into a trap.

That single breath of relief—too long—was all the failing giant needed. In that blink of celebration, it drove its fist into the tower and tripped the spectral failsafe.

"These new ideas will ruin our heritage!" the guardian shrieked, voice distorting as its body began to break apart. A crushing shockwave of magic exploded outward, slamming into the Wizards' combined defenses and driving them back a step. High above, the clock's great gear train shuddered. The delicate count wheel that governed the clock's chimes jolted and slipped out of sequence. A half-second later, the bells tried to chime an hour and a quarter-hour at once—an impossible, cacophonous overlap that rang out like a dissonant peal. Then…silence.

For a heartbeat, everything hung in eerie stillness. The clock's hands stopped moving. The overlapping strikes had triggered the clock's own fail-safe; in response to the mis-sequenced chaos, the magic of the place locked the mechanism entirely. What should have been a safety measure had become a spectral deadlock. Time itself felt frozen around the Old State House.

From the edge of the stunned plaza, a new sound suddenly rose above the silence. The bespectacled orator—the man who had been the most vocal opponent of change—cupped his hands around his mouth and shouted, "Stagnation leads to decay!" His voice rang out, startling those nearest to him. A merchant standing beside him, who moments ago had been arguing in favor of the status quo, took up the cry: "Only through renewal does life flourish!"

One by one, other townsfolk found their voices and began shouting variations of the fable's truth. "Innovation is hope!" called a young woman in scholar's robes. "New ideas, new growth!" yelled a street vendor, climbing onto his cart for all to see. The fervor spread through the crowd like wildfire. People who had been shouting against change only minutes earlier now spoke for it, as if awakening from a bad dream. Their collective conviction—born of a genuine realization— battered the lingering illusions from the plaza.

The effect was immediate. The guardian, already cracking, staggered under this onslaught of public will. Its illusory aura thinned and began to peel away as the citizens' cries grew louder and more confident.

Blunt's eyes shone at the sight: Boston's people were overcoming the illusion's spell on their own. "They're doing it…" he murmured.

Checkered's mind, however, was on the frozen clock. The guardian's dying trap still held the mechanism in a vice. She saw the main gear teeth grinding uselessly against each other, unable to turn. "The sequence is scrambled—the clock's stuck in a safety lock!" she warned sharply. "We need to realign it now, or all this will be for nothing!"

Blunt understood. "No brute force," he said. "We retune it—use the clock as our instrument." Together, he and Greenie dashed toward the base of the tower where the guardian had struck. Breezie, Firee, and Reddish fanned out around them, protecting the area as needed. Above, the clock's innards glinted in starlight, frozen by the spectral lock. The count wheel was indeed misaligned—a large notch that should have been centered under the chime hammer was off to the side, confused by the overlapping strikes.

With a flourish of his hand, Blunt directed a focused stream of water up into the tower's workings. The water flowed around the stuck count wheel, lubricating the mechanism and gently nudging it. Greenie extended a vine upward, its tendril wrapping delicately around a higher gear. She braced one foot against the tower's stone and pulled ever so slightly. Inside, metal softly clicked as the vine's tug helped the gear teeth slip back into proper alignment. Breezie added a precise gust of air to nudge a pendulum that had halted, setting it swinging in rhythm once more. They were mapping disciplines to function—water to loosen, earth to brace, air to restart the beat—turning the tower into an instrument rather a battlefield.

As the Wizards worked in concert, the spectral lock's gray sheen began to crack. One by one, the clock's gears gave a lurch and resumed their motion. The count wheel rotated to its correct position with a decisive clack. In that instant, the magical deadlock shattered—preservation and change finding balance as the clock protected itself and began to move forward again. It was an improvised harmonic reset, their spellwork keyed to the corrected cadence so the glamour had nothing left to anchor.

The guardian, deprived of both its illusion aura and its trump card, gave one last echoing wail. The six Wizards did not hesitate. They regrouped in a flash, each recalling the synergy they had perfected in Hazleton and abroad. Blunt anchored them with calm, fluid strength; Reddish poured fiery passion into driving momentum; Checkered's logic sliced through the final threads of unreality; Firee's precision burned away the last clumps of rust; Greenie's empathy knit their magic together in unity; and Breezie's guiding wind kept the combined spell focused and true.

"Now!" Blunt cried. In unison, they unleashed an innovative pulse of combined magic—fire, water, wind, illusion, and earth—straight at the reeling guardian's core. Timed to the clock's recovered rhythm. The spell carried the very cadence they had restored, innovation beating out stagnation's measure. The multicolored blast struck with the force of a cannon. Metal groaned and then gave way entirely. The rusted titan exploded into a burst of dull iron shards that rained across the cobblestones.

Unity had guided their synergy, forging innovation against inertia's chains. Overhead, freed of all restraints, the Old State House clock's gears spun into motion once more. They caught the restored rhythm and began to turn in smooth, balanced cadence. A heartbeat later, the clock's great bell pealed a clear, harmonious chime that echoed around the plaza.

All around, merchants and scholars halted their arguments and looked up in amazement. The heated debates that had filled the night fell silent. The previously bickering trader and scholar exchanged a tentative handshake, their ledgers pressed together like a truce; An outspoken street vendor tore a strip from his own handbill and, with a sheepish grin, pretended to chew it—eating his words to soft laughter; Two guild rivals reached for the same pen to amend a posted price, the left it resting between them like a signed peace; A bookseller and a sea-merchant, who'd been snapping at each other moments ago, tipped their hats at once and smiled at the coincidence; A bespectacled orator, who minutes ago was the loudest resistor, now found his voice rising in inspiration.

In the sudden calm, the clock tolled again, each note pure and resolute. Boston's oldest civic timekeeper was singing a new song.

Innovation's Triumph

As the shattered remnants of the guardian clattered to rest, the oppressive magic fogging the crowd's minds evaporated like dew in sunlight. Merchants who had been red-faced and shouting a minute ago paused, blinking in confusion at their own behavior. Scholars who had been stubbornly dismissing new ideas fell quiet, the weight of stale tradition lifting from their thoughts. Only now did any of them truly hear the Old State House clock ringing out in renewed harmony above.

A hush spread across the square—a breath of possibility. People traded startled looks and tentative smiles. The spell of stagnation was broken.

Blunt lowered his arms, finally dispelling his water ward. His heart was hammering in his chest, but triumph and relief rippled through his veins. "We did it," he breathed.

"For a moment I wanted the arguing to stop—even if the clock froze," Checkered admitted softly. "The glamour made stillness feel kind."

His water-blue eyes brimmed with pride as he surveyed the transformed plaza. He couldn't help but recall the gentle moral of The Lake and the Stream: stagnation's ruin had indeed been foretold—and narrowly averted here. Boston had escaped that fate.

Reddish exhaled, and the flames wreathed around her cloak dimmed to a warm, steady glow. She turned slowly, taking in the sight of townsfolk emerging from what felt like a dream. Many touched the sides of their heads or looked up at the clock in wonder. "Innovation overcame inertia again," she said, allowing herself a satisfied smile. "And not by forcing anyone—but by freeing the clock's voice so they could all hear it."

I almost rushed it at the start," she added, glancing at Firee. "Thanks for the hand on my sleeve."

Checkered stepped over a twisted shard of metal—the last flickers of the guardian's magic were fading from it. She knelt to inspect it briefly. "Stagnation can always reemerge if people refuse to adapt," she cautioned, ever logical. Standing, she dusted rust from her knees. "We've only opened the door to progress. They'll have to choose to walk through it."

"And we nearly stumbled by hesitating when the giant fell," Blunt said, not unkindly—an honest ledger entry the team would carry forward.

Greenie closed her eyes and sent her empathic senses washing gently over the plaza. What she felt now was vastly different from earlier: confusion, yes, but also relief, curiosity, even hope. She smiled softly. "At least they're not trapped in that rigid deadlock anymore," she said. She remembered Hazleton's celebration when their clock chimed purely again, and the awed hush in Stará Bystrica's square. Here in Boston, she sensed a similar turning point. "Maybe now they'll truly listen to each other."

Monticello's Call

A gentle ripple in the air announced the arrival of their mentor. Lazarus Zeetrikus stepped forth from behind a low stone wall at the plaza's edge, his bent hat angled jauntily and the corners of his mouth lifted in subtle approval. He crossed through the dispersing crowd toward the six, iron shards crunching softly under his boots. "You forged synergy once more," he said, voice low yet carrying in the expectant quiet.

There was calm pride in his tone. "You tested tradition with new ideas, refusing illusions that demanded static order."

Firee turned to face him, wand still in hand but lowered now. "Stagnation's illusions played on people's comfort—on their fear of losing identity," he noted, echoing what they had all witnessed. "But our innovative synergy gave them room to shake free and change."

Zeetrikus nodded in agreement. From the depths of his coat he drew out a small silver gear, freshly inscribed with elegant script. He held it up between thumb and forefinger. The new gear gleamed in the moonlight, engraved with the words "Innovare Est Virtus." Its faint, melodic hum matched the rhythm of the newly revived clock's ticking. "Take this as your anchor," Zeetrikus said, offering the silver gear to Blunt. "Collaboration shaped your victory here—remember that beyond Boston."

Blunt accepted the gear with reverence. He pressed it against the older brass gear from Stará Bystrica still strapped at his side. The engraving "Innovare Est Virtus" glinted beside "Innovare et Contra Stagnatio." Each motto-bearing artifact they'd earned had evolved from the last, he realized. To innovate against stagnation had led them here; now they held a new truth: To innovate is a virtue. "We'll carry these lessons forward," Blunt promised quietly. He looked to each of his friends in turn—Reddish's determined, fiery gaze; Firee's careful, thoughtful eyes; Checkered's bright, logical focus; Breezie's calm and kindly smile; and Greenie's warm, empathetic expression. They had grown through this trial, each and every one.

In the distance, the Old State House clock chimed again, echoing clearly through the night. The note was bright and confident. Around the plaza, clusters of citizens exchanged cautious smiles and began talking in softer tones. They were uncertain, yes—but visibly more open than before. A spark of curiosity glowed now where there had been only hostility. It was a small spark, but one that might blossom into true progress.

Zeetrikus cast a final sweeping glance over the plaza and the clock tower, ensuring no stray illusions remained. Satisfied, he gestured gently. The last translucent wisps of magic parted around the Wizards, drawing them all back into the soft silver glow of The Six Statues shop for a final word together.

They found themselves standing once more amidst Zeetrikus's curios. The shop's magical quiet had returned, broken only by the distant ring of the clock's liberated chimes outside. Dust motes shimmered in the lamplight, drifting near the statue of Innovation—its carved stone fingers intertwined in a gesture of unity, a silent reminder of their collaborative victory.

Zeetrikus stood by an array of mechanical trinkets on a shelf, his sharp eyes reflecting a grudging admiration. He inclined his head to the six Wizards. "You've broken stagnation's hold on Boston's Old State House clock," he said, his voice reserved but warm with respect. "Where illusions preached endless adherence to tradition, you championed forward motion. This city breathes freer air now, thanks to your synergy." You did not simply overpower a glamour," Zeetrikus added. "You recalibrated the clock and keyed your spell to its clear cadence—innovation practiced, not merely preached."

From the inner fold of his coat, Zeetrikus produced a small silver gear whose fresh-cut teeth gleamed. He turned it so the letters caught the light. "*Innovare Est Virtus,*" he said, and placed it in Blunt's palm; the gear thrummed in time with the clock's renewed cadence.

"Not merely victory," Zeetrikus said softly, watching the letters settle. "Revision."

Blunt held up the new silver gear—Innovare Est Virtus—feeling it thrum in his hand with energy that matched the unity among them. The earlier readings—The Lake and the Stream and Dreamers Forge the World—still lingered in his mind, a vivid contrast between stagnation's stillness and innovation's spark. "We learned to unify bold ideas," he reflected aloud, turning the gear so its inscription caught the light.

As the silver gear brushed the brass at his belt, warmth pulsed through the older metal. The inscription *Innovare Contra Stagnatio* shivered, strokes loosening and sliding into new lines until the words re-formed as *Innovare Est Virtus*. Their accomplishment had literally rewritten the message.

Checkered gave a small, satisfied smile. "And Monticello's the next step, isn't it?" she prompted. She recalled a cryptic line they'd uncovered earlier in their journey: Where curiosity ignites thought in ink and flame, seek the clock that guards a founder's name. It had puzzled them briefly, but now the meaning seemed clear.

Zeetrikus slipped a folded parchment from an inner pocket of his coat and handed it to Checkered. "Yes. Monticello stands where invention and philosophical pursuit once merged," he replied. "A place once alive with inquiry, now threatened by illusions akin to those you've faced here. You'll need all you've learned to keep stagnation at bay there." Monticello—Thomas Jefferson's historic Virginia estate, home to countless experiments—was calling to them, much as the Engle Monumental Clock in Hazleton had at the start of their quest.

Reddish's eyes sparked at the mention of a new challenge. She remembered how close illusions had come to turning her into an enforcer of old ways tonight, and how she had fought back. "We're ready," she declared, her spine straight with renewed resolve. "We overcame Boston's friction—Monticello won't break us."

Greenie let out a long breath, releasing the tension she had carried. Her empathic senses still tingled faintly with echoes of Boston's near-catastrophe. "Each place reminds us that progress is fragile," she said softly. "We have to guard it by staying open-minded and adaptive."

Firee's cloak settled into a calm, steady hue now that Boston's illusions were behind them. He nodded at Greenie's words. "Denying the new is all too easy," he remarked. "That's why illusions flourish where fear of change lingers. We'll be on guard."

Breezie reached out and gently tapped a mechanical quill on a nearby shelf, as if to affirm the spirit of invention that filled the shop. "We'll face Monticello together, forging our synergy again," he said confidently, his voice carrying a note of hope. The trials in Hazleton, Stará Bystrica, and Boston had honed them. Whatever Monticello held, he believed in their unity.

Zeetrikus stepped back and inclined his head in a fond, almost fatherly gesture. A small grin softened his usually stern features. "Go then—carry these truths onward," he said. "Stagnation lurks everywhere, waiting for comfort to triumph over curiosity. Your path leads next to Monticello's clock. Remember: humility, invention, and unity." With that final counsel, the Antiquarian of innovation lifted his bent hat in a subtle salute. In the next blink, he and his mystical shop faded gently into the city's shadows, as ephemeral as he had arrived.

The six Wizards turned to one another in the moonlight that now filtered into the empty alley. Their Harlequin cloaks glowed softly, reflecting the pride and camaraderie in their faces. They had stabilized Hazleton's industrious clock, revitalized Stará Bystrica's cultural treasure, and now freed Boston's revolutionary clock from the clutches of inertia. Soon, Monticello would call them to reaffirm that hard-won synergy once more.

A soft swirl of residual magic ushered them out of the hidden alley and onto a quiet side street. Boston's night air greeted them with a gentle breeze, no longer carrying the grating debates that had met them earlier. In the distance, the Old State House clock chimed the hour—clear, harmonious notes rippling across the cobblestones, hinting at a modest but significant shift in the city's collective mindset.

Still clutching the Innovare Est Virtus gear, Blunt felt its reassuring hum echo the unity of their group. He cast a glance up at the clock tower—an emblem of Boston's renewed willingness to adapt rather than cling to stagnation. "We've opened a door," he said softly to his companions. "Not everyone here will embrace change overnight, but illusions can't keep them stuck forever now."

Reddish let a small smile warm her features. An ember of her magic danced at her fingertips as she nodded. "Innovation overcame rigid tradition today. I'd say that's a win," she said. She couldn't help but recall how those sly illusions had tried to tempt each of them with power in stasis—and how they had all refused.

Checkered tucked her lens back into its leather pouch, her mind still turning over the lessons of Zeetrikus's readings. "The Lake and the Stream… Dreamers Forge the World," she mused. "Both remind us that growth comes from steady renewal and bold ideas." She looked toward the clock tower's illuminated dial. "Boston's clock just might keep chiming a clearer future now."

Firee exhaled, releasing the last of his tension into the cool night. "The townspeople might not remember exactly what changed or why," he said, watching a pair of merchants speak to each other in unusually civil tones across the way, "but they'll feel it. We gave them space to question their old assumptions. That alone could stir real progress."

Greenie drew her cloak around her against the slight chill, but mainly to savor the comforting spark of hope she still felt in the air. "From Hazleton's factory gears, to Stará Bystrica's carved wonder, to Boston's revolutionary heart—each place had a story about resisting new concepts," she reflected. She had no doubt this pattern would continue. "I suspect Monticello will present yet another kind of illusion for us to face."

Breezie gazed up at the night sky thoughtfully, listening as the clock's chimes mingled with distant harbor sounds. "Monticello… home to a founder's experiments in architecture and science," he murmured, recalling what he knew of Jefferson's estate. Then he smiled, his keen ears picking up optimism in the timbre of the clock's fading ring. "We'll see how curiosity is tested there by new illusions—but I believe we'll manage, together."

As they made their way along a lamplit street toward Bart and Antonella's brownstone, they noticed that the crowd they passed was subtly changed. Merchants were no longer shouting over one another; scholars spoke in measured, calmer tones; a gentle air of open-mindedness had seeped into many conversations. These were small signs of change, but promising ones. The Wizards' unity—forged through Boston's victory—carried them forward with unwavering resolve. Illusions might still reemerge on the road ahead, but for this moment, progress had found room to breathe in Boston.

They headed up the steps of the brownstone to rest at last, each step guided by the warm glow of streetlamps and the distant ring of a liberated clock. Inside, Bart and Antonella were waiting with anxious, excited faces. No sooner had the six crossed the threshold than Bart burst into an eager grin.

"You did it!" he exclaimed in a hushed whisper, mindful of the late hour. His eyes shone as he ushered them into the cozy front parlor where a fire crackled merrily. "I swear, the whole city felt something shift."

Antonella pressed warm mugs of spiced tea into their hands as they sank gratefully into cushioned chairs. "While you were out, we combed through some archives," she said, unable to contain her excitement. On the low table before them lay an open leather-bound journal dotted with scraps of yellowed newsprint. "We thought you'd be interested in what we found."

Bart flipped a few pages with reverent care to show them a newspaper clipping from over a century ago. "'Clock Malfunction Baffles City Officials,'" he read the headline, then tapped the article text. "This was 1877, during a big uproar when Boston was resisting a slew of new technological improvements. The Old State House clock suddenly stopped for two days straight. No mechanical cause ever found."

Antonella turned the page to another clipping, dated 1926. "Here—during the public outcry against a modern art installation in the city. The clock's hourly bell reportedly skipped strikes intermittently that week," she explained. "Again, no explanation."

Bart looked up at the Wizards, eyes twinkling. "In fact, every time the city leadership or populace vehemently opposed some new innovation, there are records of this clock acting up—stopping, chiming at odd hours, even running backward once." He closed the journal thoughtfully. "There are no such stories linking this clock to times of social injustice or disunity. Those troubles seem tied to other sites, other clocks, perhaps. But innovation paralysis? That has always been this clock's curse."

Blunt exchanged astonished glances with his friends. The trials truly were woven into the fabric of Boston's history. "So the Old State House clock itself rebelled whenever Boston tried to freeze progress," he said softly.

"Precisely," Antonella replied. "It's as if the city's timepiece knew Boston needed to keep moving forward." She gave a weary but delighted smile. "Thanks to you, it's in good health now."

A gentle silence fell as the Wizards absorbed this. Outside, the newly freed clock began to strike midnight, each bell note clear as a star. Reddish raised her mug of tea in both hands. "Innovare Est Virtus," she said, toasting in Latin with a grin.

"To innovate is a virtue," Bart translated warmly, lifting his own cup. The others followed suit, and the simple new motto passed appreciatively over their lips: "Innovare Est Virtus."

They sipped the sweet tea and let their fatigue start to ebb. Through the parlor window, they could see the clock tower in the distance, illuminated and peaceful. Boston's trial was over—and it had not been about justice or unity or any other abstract ideal, but squarely about the courage to change and innovate. The old clock had proven tonight that preservation and change need not be enemies: by correcting its sequence and honoring its design, they had restored safety and allowed progress.

As the six Wizards settled into much-needed rest, their thoughts drifted to the journey ahead. The silver gear engraved Innovare Est Virtus gleamed on the table beside Blunt's elbow, a reminder of the night's hard-won wisdom. In the comforting glow of Bart and Antonella's hearth, the companions allowed themselves to savor their triumph. Boston's venerable clock had resumed its faithful ticking, and the mood of the city had shifted with it.

It was only one chapter in a much larger quest, but it felt momentous. The Old State House clock—once silenced by fear of change—now rang out with renewed purpose. In time, its clear chimes would remind all who heard them: Innovare Est Virtus. Innovation is a virtue. And that truth, like the steady ticking of the restored clock, would echo far beyond this night.

United by innovation, the six young wizards had given Boston's old clock – and its people – a new lease on life.

Chapter 5

Quiet Progress – Mentor Guidance

Dawn's Charged Hush

Morning's first glow broke over Boston, gilding steeples and rooftops in a gentle hush. Down in the old colonial quarter, the air felt charged—soft stirring breezes hinting at recent upheavals. Cobblestones glistened with overnight rain, and faint chatter from merchant stalls drifted through the winding streets. Yet beneath the calm lay an undercurrent of tension: townsfolk moved hesitantly, as though lingering illusions still tugged at the edges of their thoughts.

Six young wizards—Blunt, Reddish, Firee, Checkered, Breezie, and Greenie—stepped into a narrow lane behind the Old North Church. A damp autumn chill hung in the air, carrying the earthy scent of rain-soaked cobblestones. It clung to their travel-worn cloaks, which were still damp and scuffed from two recent trials. Only days ago, they had confronted Tetragor's corrupting illusion in Hazleton and Zeetrikus's stagnation glamour in Boston—ordeals that had left shadows of fatigue on their faces. Yet beneath the weariness, they moved with a quiet, unbreakable unity forged by adversity.

"Feels calmer here than at the Old State House," Firee murmured, recalling how frantic illusions nearly engulfed them there just a few days ago. The memory clung to him like a layer of soot.

Greenie pressed a hand against the church's old stone foundation, sensing faint runic echoes. "But there's something watchful too," she added under her breath. She could almost feel the city bracing for the next wave of sorcery. The very air hummed with latent magic, urging them to stay sharp.

Into the Old North Crypt

The city's hum faded as they slipped into the church's shadowed crypt, seeking the Orloj's guidance. By a small arched door, Reddish exhaled and glanced up toward the bell tower. "This is where we always find him," she said quietly. "After facing two Antiquarians, it's time for our customary guidance, right?"

Checkered nodded, keeping her voice low. "Illusions in Hazleton and Stará Bystrica nearly broke our unity—first corruption, then stagnation—but humility and innovation saw us through. The Orloj should be here now to help unify those lessons."

Breezie brushed rain from his sleeves and motioned to the crypt's heavy oak door, flanked by old lanterns. "He'll be waiting," he affirmed. They could not afford any more slip-ups, not with new illusions surely lurking ahead.

As they drew near, the wooden door creaked open on its own, spilling warm light into the dim alley. A familiar voice—steady and fatherly—echoed from within. "Enter, Harlequins," it called kindly. "Your journey is noted. Let's talk."

Exchanging quick, resolute nods, the six friends stepped through. The muffled city noise fell away, replaced by quiet torchlight and the promise of further guidance from the being who had shepherded them through so many trials—Boston's Orloj.

They emerged into a hidden nook beneath the Old North Church. Its stone walls were etched with faint colonial runes. Flickering sconces cast dancing shadows across a low ceiling, revealing a curved wooden bench and a modest table set with warm pastries and steaming mugs—an inviting spread for weary travelers. By the far wall stood the Orloj of Boston, silver-haired and stout, radiating an air of gentle wisdom. His eyes gleamed like distant lanterns as he greeted them with a single welcoming nod. The Harlequins took their seats around the table, cloaks settling around them in the cozy glow.

What We Learned—And What's Missing

"You look drained," the Orloj observed gently, his resonant voice carrying concern. "Two Antiquarians faced, and each one nearly shattered your unity at moments."

Reddish winced and ran a hand through her hair, remembering how close she'd come to succumbing to those deceptions. Illusions had nearly turned her into a champion of outdated ways. "We overcame them," she said, a hint of regret in her tone. The victories felt hard-won.

"Barely," Blunt interjected, bowing his head in frank admission. "In Hazleton we hesitated too long and gave corruption an opening. Then at the Old State House we charged in too recklessly and almost fed stagnation's trap. Both times, the illusions nearly got the better of us." He looked around at his friends. "We have to find a better balance going forward."

The Orloj nodded and seated himself on the bench's edge, folding his hands calmly. "Balance—and speed," he emphasized. "Corruption and stagnation do not wait politely. You must address illusions instantly, or risk losing ground." His tone grew grave as he continued. "The Dark Harlequin lurks nearby, capitalizing on every lapse. It may be that he weaves all these illusions into a single trap, awaiting even the slightest pause from you."

A hush fell at the mention of this Dark Harlequin. Breezie drew in a slow breath; just hearing that name sent a chill through the crypt's warmth. Rumors painted the Dark Harlequin as a far more sinister presence than any Antiquarian they had faced. "We won't let illusions fracture us again," Breezie vowed quietly, clenching a fist at his side. Under stress, it had been all too easy for doubt and disagreement to creep in—but no longer.

Firee glanced between the Orloj and his companions, his eyes determined. "We can all sense it… a bigger threat is looming now, isn't it?" he asked. It felt as if the very shadows in Boston were growing bolder.

"Yes," the Orloj confirmed, a thread of fatherly concern weaving into his expression. "But first, you'll meet an old friend—Benjamin Franklin. I believe you've heard a tale or two of him." A small smile tugged at the Orloj's lips as the young wizards blinked in surprise. "We will visit a moment drawn from this city's revolutionary spirit to bridge your recent lessons. Then we'll speak further." He lifted a palm-sized lantern from the table; it glowed from within with a spark of caged lightning. "True synergy demands a clever mind," he added enigmatically.

Surprised glances shot around the group. Franklin? A historical cameo? Reddish's ember-orange eyes widened with curiosity. "Why Franklin?" she asked, tilting her head.

"You'll see," the Orloj replied. With that, he stood and raised the lantern high. Its electric glow intensified, washing over the crypt with a crisp, charged brilliance. A gentle pressure enveloped the Harlequins, as if the very air were folding around them.

Philadelphia, 1770s—Franklin's Workshop

In a heartbeat, the stone walls and flickering sconces of the crypt began to waver. Light and gravity shifted—and then, in place of the crypt, a new scene crystallized around them: a cobbled street in Philadelphia under roiling storm clouds.

Drizzling rain pattered on the cobblestones. The distant clang of a blacksmith's hammer and the rattle of wagon wheels echoed through the damp air. Directly ahead stood a tall brick building with a painted wooden placard swinging above its door: B. Franklin, Printer. A flicker of lightning lit up the sign's edges, and for an instant Greenie thought she saw faint magical runes woven into the curly letters. The six friends exchanged astonished looks as their cloaks adjusted themselves against the sudden wet chill. They remained instinctively alert for any illusion, unsure what this "timefold" might bring.

Checkered stepped forward under the eave of a nearby shop, her spectacles fogging slightly from the rain. "Benjamin Franklin…," she breathed, recognizing the name on the sign. She'd read so much about his inventions and boundless curiosity. "Are we really in his time? Is this some kind of historical overlay?"

The Orloj now appeared beside them on the rain-slick street, lantern in hand. He nodded reassuringly. "Yes. A time-folded cameo of the past—not true time travel," he explained. The rain ran off his silver hair as he spoke. "Franklin's wit helped shape this city's progress. Allow him to guide you now. He stands at the cusp of storm and solution—a mirror to your own challenge, where illusions must be met with swift, unified action."

Reddish pulled her cloak tighter, wiping raindrops from her brow. A spark of excitement lit in her eyes despite the drizzle. "So we're here to see how he handles a storm… the way we need to handle illusions," she said, a smile tugging at the corner of her mouth. The prospect of meeting Franklin and learning from him sent a thrill through her veins.

Greenie shivered pleasantly; even through the rain, her empathic senses absorbed the vitality of colonial Philadelphia. Vendors were shouting about pamphlets down the block, and children darted under awnings to escape the wet. "They're so alive here," Greenie whispered, half expecting an illusion to slither out from the swirling storm shadows. But everything felt historically real—an echo of the past brought vividly to life.

Blunt tipped his head toward the doorway of Franklin's shop. "Let's go inside," he suggested. He recalled that during past Orloj-guided cameos, valuable lessons often awaited them in the thick of the action. Firee was already a step ahead, wand tucked discreetly under his cloak as he eyed the darkening sky. He was prepared for any trick of illusion that might interrupt this lesson.

They pushed open the heavy wooden door and stepped into the workshop. A warm, bustling scene greeted them. Dozens of candles cast a gentle glow over shelves of leather-bound books, jars of ink, and neat stacks of freshly printed pamphlets. Amid the clutter, a portly man in colonial attire stood at a sturdy workbench. He was rummaging through an assortment of metallic rods and glass spheres. Sparks of static crackled around him each time his hands brushed a metal rod, and an apprentice scurried by with an armful of unusual contraptions.

"Harlequins, is it?" the man exclaimed, turning towards them with bright, inquisitive eyes behind wire-rimmed spectacles. Benjamin Franklin's face broke into a welcoming grin. He beckoned them out of the rain and into the heart of his workshop. "Quite the downpour brewing out there! But never fear—storms are splendid teachers for prepared minds." He gave a jovial wink, one hand still gripping a slender brass rod that glinted in the candlelight.

Checkered stepped forward first, completely enthralled by the array of contraptions spread across Franklin's bench. Tesla-like coils of copper wire, glass Leyden jars, kites and keys—it was like stepping into one of his famous experiments. She managed a polite bow. "Benjamin Franklin…," she began, half in awe, half remembering her manners. "We're honored. The Orloj sent us to seek a lesson in… in acting immediately, together."

Franklin chuckled, the sound warm and crackling like the sparks around him. He placed the brass rod in Checkered's hand—it tingled with static in her grip. "Then you've arrived at the perfect moment," he said with a delighted gleam in his eye. "I'm about to demonstrate how to coax lightning into cooperation." As if on cue, thunder rumbled outside, rattling the windowpanes. Franklin's apprentice peered nervously at the darkening sky while Reddish felt her heart quicken. The electric charge in the air set her embers aglow. So this was the "clever mind" the Orloj had hinted at. Whatever Franklin was planning, it promised to be a vivid demonstration of quick thinking and teamwork.

Catching Lightning

Lightning flashed, splitting the sky above Philadelphia with a jagged white streak. Inside Franklin's shop, the young wizards gathered around as he hastily assembled a makeshift apparatus on a cleared table. There were metal rods of varying lengths, a couple of glass spheres etched with symbols, and coils of copper wire. The very air in the workshop crackled with potential. It felt eerily reminiscent of standing in the grip of an illusion—but here the only magic was human ingenuity harnessing nature.

"Don't dawdle now—lightning doesn't wait," Franklin teased as he directed Reddish and Firee to fix two brass rods upright onto a wooden stand. They moved without hesitation.

Breezie braced the stand from the other side, one hand subtly channeling a steady breeze to keep the structure balanced. Greenie hovered nearby and closed her eyes for a second, feeling the hum of their cooperation. She could sense each friend's heartbeat picking up in unison at the thrill of trying to capture a lightning bolt.

At Franklin's instruction, Checkered carefully aligned a glass sphere at the apparatus's center, rotating it until engraved runes along its surface matched up with corresponding symbols on the rods. "Each symbol… it's like a puzzle piece," she murmured, eyes shining. The configuration would ensure the electrical charge flowed where intended.

Blunt oversaw their efforts, recalling the Orloj's warning that storms—like illusions—demanded swift, coordinated action. "We can't linger," he reminded, voice firm. "If we hesitate, the storm will strike on its own terms." The others nodded; there was no room for delay or second-guessing.

Franklin handed a spool of conductive copper thread to Firee. "Secure this to that metal plate by the window," he directed. "Make sure there are no gaps—lightning finds every little gap." Firee unfurled the wire and, with a touch of his heated magic, soldered it firmly to the plate. The plate was connected to a thick wire running out through a high window, disappearing into the raging storm. It looked like Franklin had rigged a path to invite a lightning bolt right into the apparatus.

Outside, thunder rumbled again—a vibrating call to action. The Wizards exchanged a single, silent glance, and at once each of them sprang to their final positions. Reddish's eyes flashed as she adjusted the last rod into place. Firee double-checked the copper thread, making sure the circuit was taut and unbroken. Greenie kept gentle pressure on the wires, her empathic senses tracking the group's unified focus. Breezie breathed a stabilizing breeze around the apparatus so nothing would topple at the critical moment. Checkered crouched to tighten the final clamp, peering through her lens to confirm there were no weak points. Finally, Blunt spread his palms and cast a faint blue ward over the entire contraption—a thin film of watery magic to dampen any stray sparks. In mere seconds, without a word spoken, they had coordinated perfectly.

A blinding fork of lightning crackled down, striking the roof of a building across the street. "All set!" Franklin's apprentice hollered as he hauled open a small skylight in the shop's ceiling. Rain sprayed in, and with it the charged night air. Franklin gave a satisfied nod and flipped a switch on the wooden stand. Suddenly the whole apparatus hummed and buzzed, arcs of static dancing between the rods. "Here comes the show!" he announced, a grin of anticipation spreading beneath his wiry mustache.

For an instant, everything seemed to pause—the Wizards held their breath as a tingling charge built in the air. Then a searing flash: lightning slammed through the open skylight, drawn by Franklin's device. The bolt funneled down the rods and hit the glass sphere dead center. The sphere blazed with brilliance, containing the raw power for a few heartbeats before dispersing it safely into the connected wires. The entire workshop lit up in stark white light. Apprentices ducked behind crates with wide eyes as sparks skittered in loops across the floor.

As the light faded, Franklin let out a triumphant laugh. He hoisted the now-glowing sphere off its stand, arcs of electricity still dancing inside the glass. "Innovation, harnessed swiftly!" he declared, clearly delighted by the success. "See how a unified, timely effort can tame nature's fury?"

Blunt and the others exhaled and broke into relieved grins. The parallel to their own trials was unmistakable. In that intense moment, they had acted as one and prevailed—just as they needed to against any illusion. Reddish gently elbowed Firee and couldn't help a quick laugh of astonishment. They were standing in Benjamin Franklin's workshop, having just helped him catch lightning in a bottle, or close enough. And beyond the thrill, the message of this demonstration blazed in each of their minds.

The lingering glow from the captured lightning danced around the apparatus, painting the workshop in pulsing arcs of blue-white light. Franklin's apprentices crept out from hiding, applauding and whooping in awe. Rain continued to drum on the roof, but its threat felt diminished now.

Back to the Crypt

The Wizards stepped back, hearts still pounding from the adrenaline. Outside, thunder boomed once more, but it sounded distant and harmless after the strike they had just weathered without hesitation. Firee wiped sweat—or perhaps rain—from his brow, and Greenie realized she'd been clutching Blunt's sleeve in the excitement. They all burst into breathless laughter, exhilarated and a little astonished by what they'd just done.

Franklin carefully set the electrified glass sphere aside on a padded crate. Faint tendrils of electricity snaked within it, casting playful shadows on the walls. He turned to the six visitors, his expression equal parts pride and professor. "You see?" he said, patting the sphere. "Nature waits for no one. If you hesitate, the storm will decide the outcome. But act swiftly, in unison, and you bend the storm to your benefit."

Reddish let out a low chuckle as she caught her breath. Her mind flashed to their near-disaster in Boston's Old State House when they had faltered. "Just like those illusions we faced," she murmured. "A second's indecision can be costly." If they had been even a heartbeat slower assembling this device, the lightning strike might have ended very differently. It was a lesson she would not forget.

Greenie nodded, a slight tremor in her voice. "We can't let the Dark Harlequin exploit even a moment of doubt among us," she said. The specter of that unseen foe made her stomach tighten, but Franklin's demonstration gave her hope that they could deny him any opportunity.

Franklin raised an eyebrow at the unfamiliar name. "Dark Harlequin, you say?" He didn't seem alarmed, more curious than anything. He regarded the group of soaked but determined youths with admiration. "Well, you lot are quite the traveling defenders—a bit like a lively thundercloud yourselves!" His grin returned, and he clapped Blunt on the shoulder. "I suspect that villain will find himself in trouble if you strike with a single purpose. A foe like that won't stand a chance against unified lightning."

Checkered was still inspecting the lightning apparatus, marveling at how each piece had fit together at the critical moment. She traced a finger along one of the rods where runic lines glimmered faintly. "Your method, sir, it fosters quick adaptation," she noted. "Every piece locks in place so fast." She exchanged a meaningful look with her friends. "Too often we've hung back waiting for the perfect alignment… and the illusions only grew stronger because of it. We can't afford that delay."

Franklin chuckled knowingly. He picked up a slender copper tool from his bench and twirled it between his fingers, sparks trailing its tip. "Perfect alignment is a fine ideal, but boldness in the moment is better," he said. "By all means be prudent—but never let caution paralyze you." He held the tool out for Firee to take; it was a curious object like a small lightning rod topped with a coil. "A half-second advantage can turn the tide in any confrontation, magical or otherwise. Remember that spark." Firee accepted the copper tool with a solemn nod, understanding that Franklin meant both the literal spark and the metaphorical one.

Just then, the rain-soaked street outside began to ripple and fade. The Orloj, who had been quietly observing, lifted the enchanted lantern once more. Its light swirled together with the misty air, bending the scene around them. The clamor of colonial Philadelphia softened. The brick walls of Franklin's shop and the workbenches wavered, dissolving back into the contours of the Old North Church crypt.

"Benjamin Franklin's cameo concludes," the Orloj announced, his voice gently drawing them back to the present. "He taught you the crux of this lesson: swift synergy. Immediate unity. A delay only gives strength to storms—and to illusions alike."

Reddish brushed a stray raindrop off her charred-orange cloak. She already missed the crackling energy of Franklin's workshop. "Franklin's lightning rod… that was exhilarating," she admitted, eyes still shining. "There wasn't time to second-guess—just action. Act, or the storm wins. We needed that."

Firee flexed his fingers, finally noticing how tightly he'd been gripping the copper tool Franklin handed him. He let out a breath and nodded. "A good reminder," he said quietly. "We've paid the price both for hesitating and for rushing in blindly before. Next time, we'll strike like lightning—no time wasted and no loose ends."

Breezie ran a hand through his damp hair and shut his eyes, recalling the way stagnation illusions had once pinned him in agonizing indecision. That feeling would haunt him no more. "I won't freeze again," he promised aloud, steel in his normally breezy tone. Franklin's spark had lit something in him—he could still feel it warm in his chest. "From here on, we keep our synergy immediate."

Checkered adjusted her spectacles, which were still slightly fogged from the sudden temperature shift back into the crypt. Her analytical mind was already cataloguing the parallels. "No more waiting for the perfect plan," she said firmly. She thought of how many times she'd overanalyzed while illusions multiplied around them. "Better to make one decisive move together than to let a dozen illusions swarm us while we debate."

Blunt took all his friends' words to heart. He gently set a hand on the engraved silver gear at his belt that read Innovare Est Virtus, and the charm pulsed faintly as if echoing Franklin's lesson. He met each of their eyes and gave a single resolute nod.

A brief silence fell as the group collectively absorbed their renewed resolve. They realized they were all smiling—tired, wet, but filled with fresh confidence. In that silence, they also recognized something else: how quickly they had come to an unspoken agreement.

Checkered broke into a grin. "Did you notice?" she said softly. "We pulled that together without a word—just a look."

Greenie giggled. "Honestly, I barely had time to think. We just… knew what to do."

Blunt's lips curved into a rare smile. "Then let's make it our habit," he said. "From now on, the moment an illusion shows itself, no one waits for an order." He glanced around at each of them. "One of us gives a quick signal—could be a nod, a word, whatever—and we all act at once. Agreed?"

Reddish responded by tapping the tip of her wand three times against her palm—thump, thump, thump—then pointing it outward as if at a phantom foe. "Three beats, then together," she suggested, eyes alight.

Firee cracked a grin. "Like a conductor giving us the count-in," he said. "I like it."

They all nodded, a new tactic set among them. The next time illusions struck, they would be ready with a single heartbeat of preparation—a silent count to synchronize their magic. In that small moment, the Harlequins felt more coordinated than ever.

Gradually, the final wisps of Franklin's timefold faded, leaving only the steady glow of the crypt's lanterns. They were fully back in the quiet undercroft of the Old North Church. Stone walls re-solidified around them and the scent of old dust and candlewax replaced the ozone of lightning. The oak door to the alley was shut once more, muffling the sounds of morning outside. The cameo was now just a memory buzzing in their hearts.

The Dark Harlequin Watches

Back in the crypt's stillness, the Orloj guided the young wizards to gather around a simple wooden bench. The old stones of the church arched overhead, emanating a cool calm. From beyond the closed door came the muffled rustle of the waking city. Morning had matured while they were away; the soft hush of dawn had given way to a mild bustle—reminding them that illusions never rest, even as life goes on.

As if on cue, a fleeting shadow flickered just outside the crypt's threshold. Greenie stiffened, sensing a presence, and in the same instant Reddish's wand hand twitched upward. Firee's palm ignited with a ready flame and Blunt half-rose from the bench, water magic at his fingertips. In the half-lit entryway there was nothing—only a pigeon fluttering off the steps into the sky. The six friends exchanged wary smiles as they eased back down. Without a single word, they had all reacted in unison. It was only a false alarm this time, but it showed how attuned they'd become. They would be ready.

The Orloj's eyes crinkled in quiet approval. He waited until all were settled again, then spoke. "Benjamin Franklin's cameo was your 'memorable event' this time," he began, meeting each of their gazes in turn. "He demonstrated how quickly you must unify in the face of a threat."

Greenie drew a deep breath. Her heart was still skittering from that sudden shadow, but she nodded firmly. "I felt it," she said. "There were no illusions to trick us in that storm, but the storm itself demanded immediate action, or we'd have failed. There was no room for doubt."

Checkered glanced around at the crypt's carved runes and recalled how, in previous trials, the Orloj had often taught them through riddles or fables. "No reading or fable from you this time," she noted with a small smile. "Just Franklin's direct demonstration."

The Orloj's stern face gentled into a wry smile. "Indeed. Tetragor and Zeetrikus each tested you in their way—through illusions and allegories. But now Franklin's cameo stands alone as your lesson from the Orloj. A purely practical example, reminding you to fuse what you've learned and do it swiftly."

Firee closed his eyes for a moment, releasing the last of his tension. "I have to say, I preferred the storm over more illusions," he admitted with a chuckle. "No twisted words or mind games—just raw nature. We either responded fast, or we got fried. Simple as that."

Blunt's gaze drifted to the crypt's floor, where a faint pattern of light from a high grate sketched shapes on the stone. "We overcame storms of corruption and stagnation in those first trials," he mused, thinking of Hazleton and the Old State House. "But the next illusions might be fiercer, right?" There was a note of concern in his voice. They all knew the Dark Harlequin would not be a simple foe.

The Orloj's eyes narrowed gravely. "Yes. The Dark Harlequin is weaving illusions beyond the scope of Tetragor or Zeetrikus. He will seize upon every idle moment you give him as an invitation."

Monticello Calls

The faintest hint of satisfaction warmed the Orloj's expression. "Another clock beckons you now," he said, his voice echoing gently off the crypt walls. "Monticello, in Virginia—a place of inquiry shaped by a founder's curious mind. There, questions will take the place of open attacks. They will still be illusions all the same, meant to mislead and confound you." He paused, surveying their faces. "You sensed Monticello's call last night, did you not? Franklin's lesson has shown you how to answer that call when it comes."

Reddish's eyes sparked at the mention of a new site. Monticello—Thomas Jefferson's home and his famous clock—the prospect was thrilling. "We'll handle it," she declared, embers of confidence flickering in her voice.

Firee's crimson cloak swirled as he squared his shoulders, the last of his fatigue falling away. The thought of a new challenge replaced it with resolve. "Monticello awaits, then," he said. The quiet nook around them almost seemed to breathe in agreement. By instinct, the friends clustered a little closer together, a six-pointed star of determination. The promise hung unspoken in the air: the next illusion they faced would meet a lightning-swift, unified front.

Soft lamplight guided them as the Orloj led the way deeper into the crypt's stone passages. A faint chill lingered in these corridors—the same hush that had greeted them upon arrival, now mixed with the lingering scent of rain they'd carried back from Philadelphia. Above them, the morning city bustled on—vendors opening their stalls, scholars climbing library steps—but down here time moved at the pace of whispering runes and heartbeat echoes.

At last, they reached a small chamber lined with colonial relics. Greenie's eyes darted around in quiet wonder. There was a cracked fragment of a bell set on a pedestal, an ancient lantern said to be one of the two hung for Paul Revere's ride, and a battered wooden sign painted with the image of a lightning bolt. The sign's paint was peeling with age, yet as the Orloj laid a hand on it, it glimmered with a faint enchantment—clearly a nod to the Franklin cameo they had just experienced.

"Boston has taught you to resist illusions of tradition—Zeetrikus's realm," the Orloj said, his voice low and reflective in the close space. "And now, thanks to Franklin, you've seen how quickly unity can channel the fiercest storm." The lightning-bolt sign under his palm gave a soft pulse. "Monticello is next. It will test you in a different way: a place where questions and doubts might distract or mislead you, if you're too slow to see through them." The chamber's relics seemed to hum in agreement. Franklin's lesson about acting swiftly anchored their resolve; they would not let Monticello's riddles trip them up.

Checkered stepped forward and gently ran her fingers over the cracked bell fragment. Faded runes were etched along its curve, almost worn smooth by time. "Questions," she echoed thoughtfully. "We've seen how illusions exploit hesitation. If Monticello challenges us with riddles or half-answers, that's another kind of delay—confusion. We'll have to be just as quick to cut through that."

Greenie moved closer to Blunt, drawing steadiness from the quiet confidence he exuded. She could feel his heart thumping in a calm, strong rhythm. It helped ground the rest of them.

Firee's eyes narrowed as he caught a subtle shift in the Orloj's expression. A shadow of worry crossed the old mentor's face at the mention of Monticello. "There's something else, isn't there?" Firee asked softly. "You're worried about… the Dark Harlequin?"

The Orloj inclined his head, not denying it. "He's not merely an illusionist," the Orloj said solemnly. "He's cunning. He will twist every virtue you have learned and turn it against you if he can. Corruption and stagnation may prove to be child's play compared to the snares he's laying now." His grey eyes swept over them with a fierce protectiveness. "Act with an unwavering bond, or his illusions will slip through the cracks between you."

Reddish felt a heat rise in her chest at his words. She tightened her grip on the hilt of her wand, her knuckles pale against the coppery wood. "No more waiting, no more reckless rushing," she vowed, her voice quiet but fervent. "From here on, we respond immediately and together." The others murmured their agreement, each recalling in their own way the sting of past mistakes and the promise of what they'd just accomplished in Franklin's shop.

At that, a faint golden glow rippled along the corridor walls. The crypt's ancient wards seemed to respond to the group's determination, reinforcing themselves with the magic of unity. The Orloj gave a small, tight-lipped smile. He looked proud.

"Good," the Orloj said, his voice resonant in the stone chamber. "You've taken Franklin's demonstration to heart. Carry that forward now." He gestured toward the shimmering lightning-bolt sign, which now illuminated a passage leading back toward the main crypt. The Orloj's eyes shone as he offered one final piece of guidance. "Go forth with speed and unity, dear wizards. Monticello awaits. Remember—illusions will not stand idle, and neither can you."

With that clear directive ringing in their ears, the six Harlequins prepared to depart. The Orloj lingered at the threshold of the passage, watching silently as each young wizard straightened their cloak and set their shoulders. There was no hesitation in any of them now. They felt as if they shared one heartbeat, rapid and ready.

Wordlessly, the six friends moved with swift, synchronized purpose. Checkered gathered up a map from the table and handed it to Breezie, who slipped it neatly into his satchel. Reddish quietly stacked their empty mugs and passed them to Greenie, who returned them to the tray beside the remaining pastries. Firee retrieved Franklin's copper rod from where he'd tucked it at his belt and passed it to Blunt, who stowed the new tool safely beside the silver gear charm under his cloak. Even the act of Greenie quietly pulling open the crypt's heavy oak door for their exit seemed perfectly timed. In the dim torchlight, the engraved gear at Blunt's hip glinted with a soft, brief glow, as if acknowledging their silent harmony.

As they climbed the steps back toward daylight, they carried Franklin's lightning-swift unity with them. In their minds they could almost hear the crack of thunder and see the glow of that captured bolt. Together, they were resolved to meet the Dark Harlequin's next illusions head-on, without an instant's hesitation.

Chapter 6

Thomas Jefferson's Clock at Monticello and the Horologium of Lund – The Lantern of Inquiry

Under the Skylight: The Clock That Hides Answers

The dawn's golden rays cascaded over Monticello's rolling hills, bathing Thomas Jefferson's red-brick estate in a warm glow that danced across ivy-clad columns and blooming dogwood. The morning air hummed with dew's crisp freshness, laced with a faint metallic tang, as if the estate itself exhaled secrets of inquiry. A restless magical pulse prickled at the young Wizards' senses, stirring the serene morning.

Blunt, Reddish, Firee, Checkered, Breezie, and Greenie emerged from a swirling portal into Monticello's entrance hall, a cool dawn breeze accompanied their arrival, stirring their Harlequin cloaks softly around them. In front of them stood Jefferson's restored astronomical clock, its polished brass gears ticking with a low, deceptive hum. Each celestial dial, etched with zodiac arcs and lunar phases, gleamed beneath the high skylight. The engravings, wrought in 1806 to track Virginia's skies, whispered of Jefferson's relentless curiosity, yet a faint distortion across its starfield dial hinted at hidden mysteries.

Morpheus Rubicom—the Antiquarian who conjured illusions of ignorance—had clearly woven a glamour into this place. That subtle hum carried his signature: a distortion that offered only half-answers and hid the rest.

Blunt stepped forward first, letting his fingers glide over the clock's cool, smooth brass casing. A subtle vibration pulsed through his hand, making him inhale sharply. The sensation echoed in the innovation gear tucked inside his cloak—Zeetrikus's gift inscribed Innovare Est Virtus ("To Innovate Is a Virtue"). "Jefferson's mind crafted this," Blunt said, voice calm but intent as his eyes traced the dial's precise arcs. "A tool of curiosity… but that hum, it's obscuring something." The gear at his side pulsed in agreement, reminding him of the teamwork that had seen them through Boston's earlier trials.

Reddish edged closer, one hand hovering near a brass gear as if tempted to jostle it into honesty. Her amber eyes flared—sparks dancing to life—when she caught a deceptive quiver in the clock's humming. It reminded her of a truth half-hidden in shadow. "It's blinking at us—like the constellations are skipping half their stars," she said sharply. Her fiery resolve, tempered by the unity they had forged, kept her from blasting the clock then and there. Instead she balled her fist against her side. The metallic tang in the air sharpened in that instant, a bitter taste that brought Morpheus Rubicom's nature to mind—he was the embodiment of ignorance, and this hum was his doing.

Greenie closed her eyes and let her empathic senses sweep through the hall. She absorbed lingering traces of Jefferson's legacy all around them: telescopes mounted by tall windows, well-thumbed journals on a side table, ingenious inventions resting under glass. "He lived to know," she breathed, her cloak's green hues brightening with reverence. "This clock— built for his almanacs to chart a young nation's stars— breathes with that same need to understand. But this distortion… it's veiling a truth from us." A shiver ran up her arm as she touched the clock's frame, her cloak pulsing in quiet warning. She remembered Tetragor's lesson of humility steadying her heart; only a humble mind would sense there was more to learn here beyond the illusion.

Checkered's analytical gaze roamed over the exposed gears, noting a faintly uneven rhythm in their turnings. She adjusted her monocle lens over one eye. "A marvel of the Enlightenment," she remarked crisply. "Refurbished to honor his science, yet it's… uneasy. It wants us to ask more questions." Indeed, as the others watched, a tiny gear skipped a beat and then resumed ticking, as if the mechanism itself begged for deeper inquiry. The six friends exchanged knowing looks. Their Harlequin cloak patterns pulsed in unison—a silent vow of unity ready to unravel whatever cryptic glamour plagued Jefferson's clock. Bracing themselves, they prepared to meet Morpheus's test head-on, curiosity awakening against the looming shadow of ignorance.

Where the Starfield Lies

Early sunlight slanted through the skylight, refracting into prismatic colors across Jefferson's Astronomical Clock. Its brass gears continued their furtive cadence, each rotation tinged with a deceptive quiver. The Wizards clustered close now, their Harlequin cloaks softly pulsing in resonance. The metallic tang in the hall grew stronger, hinting that some illusion lurked behind the clock's outward brilliance.

Firee knelt by the clock's base, his crimson cloak grazing the polished floor. With gentle precision, he ran his fingers along the exposed gears, noting that each cog was etched with tiny lunar crescents. "Jefferson's precision is remarkable," he murmured in subdued awe while examining the interlocking brass teeth. "Every turn tracks the heavens—brass capturing curiosity." Yet even as he admired the craftsmanship, his vigilant gaze caught a faint tremor along the zodiac dial. One engraved constellation—Virgo—wavered as if seen through heat haze, and the moon-phase disc beside it lagged nearly half a day out of step. Something in the mechanism was being subtly thrown off.

Checkered leaned in next to him, monocle lens held before one eye. Her mind sparked with analytical focus as she hovered over the celestial dials. The engravings of stars and figures on the clock face shimmered oddly under her lens. "It's extraordinary," she allowed, "but the motion feels… off. Like it's masking its own rotation." As if to confirm her suspicion, a delicate equation-of-time pointer stuttered at the quarter mark before resuming its sweep—a telltale quirk of the glamour at work. The clock's hum seemed to intensify under Checkered's scrutiny, as though the illusion resented being observed so closely.

Nearby, Greenie rested her palm on the clock's wooden frame, letting her empathic magic stir to life. In that moment she could almost sense Jefferson's restless pursuit of knowledge echoing from the very gears. She pictured his almanacs and star charts, each discovery feeding the next question. "This clock breathes with his questions," she said softly. "But that tremor… it's stifling something deeper." Her cloak fluttered in quiet alarm, the distortion pricking at her empathic sense. Greenie bit her lip, worried that if they didn't act, the unanswered questions lingering here might never come to light.

Checkered suddenly darted to a side table where a rolled star chart lay among Jefferson's notes. Swiftly unfurling the yellowed parchment, she held it up beside the clock's starfield dial and peered through her monocle. Her pulse quickened. One constellation's position on the chart did not match the dial's reading. "These stars don't line up…" she said, voice tight with realization. "It's like a parallax error—the chart and the dial are out of sync."

Breezie edged closer, his Reality Sight cutting through the illusion. He saw a faint overlay of true starlight hovering askew from the dial's display, as if the clock showed the heavens from a warped angle. "You're right," he said, heart thudding. "The dial's lying about the sky. The real stars are in a different spot."

Blunt's eyes narrowed as he recalled Jefferson's meticulous astronomy logs. He stepped to Checkered's side, glancing between the chart and clock. "Jefferson's own calculations would never be off by this much," he affirmed. A steely resolve settled in his chest. "The illusion is twisting the heavens' truth."

Just then, Breezie's eyes flashed as his Reality Sight revealed a faint shimmer across the starfield dial. He raised a hand toward it. "A portal is forming," he announced, his usually calm voice edged with urgency. A faint bronze light now laced itself through the turning gears—an unmistakable sign of illusion magic coiling for a new move. "It's tied to curiosity's path, but it's deceptive—like it means to leech away knowledge if we're not careful." The air pressure in the hall dipped as that bronze glow swirled, hinting at a doorway opening just out of phase with reality.

Blunt narrowed his water-blue eyes, catching sight of an engraving emerging along the clock's edge. New Latin words had appeared within the metal: "Scientia Lucem Affer; Ignorantia Tenebras Praebet" – "Knowledge brings light; ignorance brings darkness." He recognized the phrase at once as a warning—the very motto of their challenge. "So that's the lesson… our curiosity must push us to dispel this ignorance," he said, resolve hardening in his voice. Even as he spoke, the innovation gear inside his cloak hummed, urging them onward.

As Blunt finished reading the Latin motto, Checkered sucked in a breath. Her lens caught an additional detail glinting just beneath the glowing inscription. Carved beside the Latin script was a small symbol—a rune in an unfamiliar script, its sharp lines and curves distinctly Norse. It gleamed for an instant with otherworldly light, then faded as quickly as it had appeared. Checkered exchanged a quick, bewildered look with Blunt. Why would a Scandinavian rune be etched into Jefferson's clock?

She shook off the distraction for now and raised her chin. "This is a challenge," she declared, refocusing. "We need to uncover the truth together—no half-measures." Her words recalled the vow of synergy they had all sworn.

The six Wizards' cloaks brightened in unison, each of them remembering how swiftly they had torn through illusions in previous trials by acting as one. The clock's deceptive hum rose to a crescendo; the starfield dial flickered erratically as the portal on its face began to stabilize. The bronze glow intensified around the forming doorway. They could all feel it now—a beckoning pull beyond the bounds of Monticello. An illusion was waiting on the other side of that portal, daring their curious minds to follow.

Arc Opened: Path to Lund

Monticello's entrance hall glowed in the strengthening sunlight, Jefferson's Astronomical Clock casting a golden shimmer across the oak floor. Its deceptive hum grew louder by the second, an unseen tension coiling in the air. The six Wizards stood resolute around it, cloaks flaring with shared purpose. The lesson of the Latin motto burned in each of their minds like a lantern in the twilight, urging them to drive away the encroaching darkness.

Greenie's hand hovered near the starfield dial where the constellation Virgo still trembled. Her empathic senses felt the distortion pulsing with restless magic. "It's beckoning us," she murmured, her cloak deepening to a verdant shade as the energy tugged at her. Beneath her fingertips, the brass felt warm and alive, emitting a low, evasive whine reminiscent of a question left unanswered.

All at once, the starfield dial quivered and began to split apart, unveiling a swirling portal edged in bronze and azure light—like liquid starlight spilling forth. Blunt recognized the telltale glow of his innovation gear (Innovare Est Virtus) resonating in response. "Curiosity opens a path," he affirmed, voice steady. With a sweep of his arm, he cast a gentle watery ward to steady the portal's oscillating edges, countering the stubborn hum that resisted their entry.

The portal's whine rose in pitch, as if the lurking illusions resented the Wizards' unified front. Undaunted, Reddish stepped forward and pressed her palm flat against the portal's shimmering boundary. Fiery embers wreathed her fingers, reflecting her unwavering resolve. "To Lund," she declared, her eyes alight with certainty. The strange Norse rune they had glimpsed moments ago left little doubt in her mind—it had to be pointing them to the medieval clock in Lund, Sweden. "No hesitation this time."

As if in answer to her boldness, a gentle shimmer took shape beside the portal. A translucent figure appeared—the familiar mentor spirit Mrs. V. Her half-cape fluttered in an unseen breeze as she surveyed them with proud warmth. "Curiosity seeks truth, but humility must guide your steps," she advised softly, her voice carrying the tone of a patient teacher. "And beware: if any illusion offers easy ignorance, ignore it. Press deeper." With this timely reminder, Mrs. V's form dissolved into motes of silver light, urging them onward.

Exchanging determined nods, the young Wizards tightened their formation and stepped toward the portal as one. Their Harlequin cloak patterns pulsed in synchronized rhythm. Breezie summoned a steady wind at their backs to shepherd them through. Firee shot a last glance around Monticello to be sure no stray illusion lingered. Checkered adjusted her grip on the monocle, lens ready, and Greenie drew a calming breath as she steeled her heart. At Blunt's signal, all six plunged into the corridor of swirling, star-flecked brightness.

They tumbled through a prismatic passage of light, ears filled with the distant tick of unseen gears. After a heartbeat suspended in cosmic hush, the magic corridor deposited them onto cold, damp stone. Monticello's warmth vanished; in its place came the chill of an underground crypt. The faint glow of candlelight revealed vaulted stone arches around them, and the air smelled of old incense and moisture. Greenie took in a sharp breath—she knew this place from historical accounts. They all did.

They had arrived in Sweden's ancient Lund Cathedral. At the crypt's far end stood a towering wooden clock, Horologium Mirabile Lundense, its aged oak frame adorned with carved saints and celestial markers. Though still at first glance, the clock emitted a low hum of its own—an illusion lying in wait. The young Wizards gathered themselves, curiosity unbroken and courage undimmed. They were prepared to pit the power of their united inquiry against ignorance's most seductive shadows.

The Horologium's Second Thought

As the portal's bronze-and-azure glow faded, the Wizards found themselves standing in the dim crypt of Lund Cathedral. Flickering torches cast long shadows along the vaulted stone arches, throwing just enough light to reveal the ornate wooden clock towering ahead of them. Horologium Mirabile Lundense, crafted in 1425, dominated the crypt with its presence. Carved Biblical figures of angels and kings encircled an astrolabe-like clock face etched with zodiac signs. Each wooden figure was frozen in a silent tableau of reverence, as if waiting for centuries to speak again.

Everything here felt markedly different from Monticello. The air was cool and damp with hints of incense, and a distant chant-like chime echoed from above, though it kept slipping a beat out of sequence—as if the automata's normal procession had been thrown off. Beneath the cathedral's ancient grandeur lurked a familiar distortion: a subtle hum, like the one they'd heard at Monticello, now emanating from deep within the wooden gears of Lund's great clock. The starfield dial on this Horologium glowed faintly but its patterns flickered incomplete. Blunt stepped forward cautiously, the innovation gear in his cloak pulsing a warning. "This medieval marvel once taught people to question time and faith," he said under his breath. "Now illusions are trying to stifle that curiosity."

Reddish paced beside him, embers crackling at her fingertips. The humming here was sharper than it had been at Monticello, almost aggressive. "Morpheus's ignorance is thicker here," she murmured, narrowing her eyes. "I can feel it. We'll get no half-measures in this place."

Greenie closed her eyes and let her empathy reach out. She caught faint echoes of scholars and astronomers who had once gathered in this crypt centuries ago to calibrate the clock— seeking knowledge by the light of its stars. "The Horologium used to champion inquiry," she whispered sadly. "Now illusions shroud it. We'll have to question everything to break through."

Checkered raised her monocle and inspected the clock's face carefully. The zodiac rings and carved scenes around the dial were subtly out of alignment. "Some of these engravings have shifted," she noted, her analytical voice hushed. "It's as if the illusion has rewritten parts of the design." The thought made her jaw tighten; someone had tampered with this historical treasure's truth.

Breezie drew in a slow breath, tasting the crypt's stale air on his tongue. "It's just as we suspected—when people accept things blindly, illusions thrive," he remarked. He recalled how at Monticello the clock's trickery had nearly fooled them with partial information. "We beat that by acting together without delay. We'll do the same here."

Firee ran a gloved hand a few inches above the stone floor, sensing for any traps. A gentle heat wafted from his palm as he scanned the base of the clock. "Everything feels unsettled," he muttered, his brow furrowing. "If we rush in blindly, whatever illusion is lurking might lash out." He glanced over at Blunt, who nodded in agreement—they would proceed with both curiosity and caution.

A sudden flicker of motion in a dark corner of the crypt caught their attention. A lean figure stepped out from behind a crooked pillar: Morpheus Rubicom, at last in plain view. His ragged antiquarian's cloak hung off his shoulders, and a collection of tarnished trinkets and keys clinked at his belt as he moved. His eyes were puffy and fever-bright in the torchlight. "You simply couldn't resist the beckon of a mystery, could you?" he said, his voice like a dry rustle. A thin smile curled on his lips, but it held no warmth. "Tell me, young ones, would not a blissful ignorance have spared you all this trouble?"

Blunt moved in front of his friends, chin raised. "We prefer truth, even when it's hard," he answered, steadfast. "We won't abandon our questions—no illusion will go unchallenged."

Morpheus arched a brow, his grin twisting. He spread his hands in a mocking gesture of welcome toward the looming clock. "Then by all means, continue your noble inquiry… and face the illusions of ignorance I've prepared." His tone was silky, almost conversational, but undertones of menace lurked beneath. "Consider this: if the light of your curiosity falters for even an instant, what do you think will happen?" His question hung in the cold air for a heartbeat. "It will be snuffed out," he continued softly, answering himself. "And my illusions will devour you in the dark." With a snap of his fingers, the Horologium's great dial gave a sickly groan—its painted starry arcs warping under the pressure of unseen forces.

The challenge was laid bare. The six Wizards fanned out subtly, cloaks flaring as they summoned their courage. Each of them recalled how, back in Monticello, their united curiosity had banished the darkness that Morpheus cast over Jefferson's clock. They would not let any illusion here stifle their questioning or obscure the truth.

Morpheus, Master of Ignorance

Within the crypt's lantern-lit hush, Morpheus Rubicom circled near the base of the Horologium, his puffy eyes flicking from one young wizard to the next. His tattered cloak bristled with tarnished trinkets and scraps—rusty keys, half-burnt maps, frayed scrolls of cryptic writing. Each artifact hanging from him seemed to thrum with a fragment of incomplete knowledge, woven together into a ragged tapestry of ignorance that clung to his form.

"You cling to your questions," Morpheus said, his voice dry as rustling parchment. "But tell me, do you know when illusions truly flourish? It's when you're satisfied with half an answer." He lifted one of his ring-laden hands and whispered an incantation. In response, a section of the Horologium's dial twitched and twisted outward, revealing a few fleeting star-shapes that danced and then vanished.

Checkered's monocle flashed as she quickly tracked the subtle phantoms creeping around the gear's edges. "Ignorance feeds on our willingness to accept easy conclusions," she agreed coolly. "We learned that in Monticello."

Greenie's emerald cloak glowed softly. Through her empathic gift, she could sense a quiver in Morpheus's aura— a kernel of fear buried beneath his bravado. Perhaps he feared that if they questioned everything, his illusions would unravel. "If illusions thrive on apathy and shallow acceptance," she said gently, "then our unity must remain unwavering."

Firee edged forward on Morpheus's flank, his wand at the ready and red cloak flickering with heat. "We've seen illusions of corruption, and illusions of stagnation," he said, invoking the names of Tetragor and Zeetrikus from their past trials. "Now we face illusions of ignorance. The remedy is the same: we question everything."

Morpheus smirked, dragging the toe of his threadbare shoe across the stone floor with a grating scratch. "Corruption and stagnation… yes, those falsehoods are obvious enough to be noticed. But ignorance?" He gave a low, contemptuous chuckle. "Ignorance hides in plain sight. People rarely even think to suspect they're in the dark. One moment of complacency, one convenient half-truth accepted… and an illusion slips by as your 'truth.'"

Reddish stepped forward, embers swirling around her fists. "Not with us," she shot back, her voice sharp. "The instant an illusion rears up, we cut it down. We refuse to accept partial information."

Blunt felt Zeetrikus's innovation gear throbbing against his side in agreement with the clock's distortion. He leveled a firm look at Morpheus. "Your illusions can't win as long as we keep digging for the full truth," he said. "We won't ever settle for your half-truths."

A dry, scratchy laugh escaped Morpheus's throat. "Then let's put those bold words to the test." From within his cloak he flicked a small tarnished key into his palm—a key engraved with strange swirls and suspicious runes. He turned it in the air, and suddenly the Horologium's wooden figurines gave a jerk, as if something unseen had seized their strings. The carved angels and saints twitched in their niches, poised between motion and stillness. Morpheus's eyes gleamed. "Curiosity or complacency—which will it be?" he challenged, holding the key aloft. "Show me you can resist the illusions that aim to bury your questions."

A tense silence settled over the crypt. The six Wizards braced themselves, cloaks flaring with a unified glow as they steeled their resolve. Breezie's calm voice finally broke the hush: "We'll challenge every illusion the moment it appears."

At that, the very air of the crypt thickened with tension. Wisps of illusion began to coil around the carved saints and prophets on the clock, making shadows jump eerily in the torchlight. Morpheus's puffy eyes glittered with anticipation. "We shall see," he whispered, stepping back into the darkness between two pillars. The Horologium's dial flickered chaotically as the magic within it stirred. Illusions were gathering for an assault—but the Wizards stood ready, determined to pierce through ignorance's veil with unified urgency.

Chimes That Ask Back

A tremor coursed through the crypt as the Horologium's dial began to glow fiercely, its starfield arcs warping under the strain of burgeoning illusions. Wooden figurines of angels and prophets jerked and contorted in their alcoves, driven by ephemeral apparitions of false knowledge. From the shadows, Morpheus subtly spread his fingers and twitched them, goading the illusions to ensnare any wizard who might accept an easy answer.

Checkered was the first to strike. Through her monocle she scanned a swirl of illusory shapes coalescing into a luminous scroll in midair. Ornate script on the scroll proclaimed, "All cosmic secrets—no effort needed." She snorted, immediately recognizing the trap: a promise of knowledge with no work, a classic ploy of ignorance. "No shortcuts," she said sharply, casting a focused beam from her lens. The scroll crumpled and dissolved into wisps of light.

Greenie stepped up next to a cluster of ghostly images that hovered before her, depicting Monticello's clock miraculously fixed by a single, simple question. "Nothing else required," the illusions whispered enticingly. But Greenie knew better—true understanding had taken all of them working together and asking many questions. "One shallow question solves nothing," she declared. Vines of green magic snaked from her fingertips, wrapping around the vision and tearing its comforting façade to shreds. The illusion popped like a bubble and vanished.

Nearby, a thick tome bound in gilded leather appeared in Reddish's path, its cover emblazoned "Total Lund Chronology — No Need to Investigate." Reddish could see its pages were blank behind the glow. She let out a derisive laugh. "We learned to dig deeper," she said, hurling a controlled bolt of flame that set the false book alight. As it burned to ash, she added coldly, "Ignorance thrives on complacency."

Firee found himself facing a whole workshop of half-finished contraptions conjured out of thin air. Each bore a little label that read, "Sufficient if you trust us." His innate danger sense prickled; these mirages conveniently avoided showing any critical details. "No illusion stands once we press further," he growled. A thin jet of flame shot from his wand, cutting cleanly through the workshop scene. The deceptive images sputtered and collapsed into a cascade of sparks.

Breezie hesitated for just a heartbeat as a cluster of hovering lights chimed around him in a hypnotic rhythm. They offered "the gist" of the Horologium's secrets—supposedly enough knowledge to move on without digging deeper. He felt a brief temptation to accept, but then Franklin's earlier lesson echoed in his mind: act together, act now. "Not enough," Breezie said, coming to his senses. He summoned a gust of wind that swept through the chorus of half-truths. The illusory lights guttered and went out with a faint hiss.

Finally, Blunt confronted an illusion in the shape of an elderly scholar, beckoning him with an antique manuscript. "Here lie Jefferson's missing pages," the figure promised, "if only you stop all these tiring questions." Blunt's eyes narrowed at the offer. "No deals," he said firmly. With a broad sweep of his arm, he sent a wave of water magic crashing over the scholar's form. The illusion sputtered and dissolved into nothing under the deluge. Blunt stood tall, steam rising around him from the heated battle. "We question everything," he affirmed.

In a matter of moments, all of Morpheus's conjured illusions lay in tatters. As each deception cracked under immediate scrutiny, the Horologium's distorted dial began to steady itself. The off-tempo chimes rejoined their proper rhythm. From his darkened corner, Morpheus's puffy eyes narrowed. His illusions were unraveling far faster than he had anticipated. A reluctant sigh escaped his lips. "So," he murmured, "curiosity proves mightier than ignorance… once again." He stepped out from the gloom with hands lowered, conceding this round. As the last remnants of false starlight faded, the crypt returned to its natural hush and the Horologium's starfield dial realigned to its truthful configuration. The young Wizards exchanged relieved, triumphant looks—their quick, united inquiry had carried the day.

Return Portal & Departure

With the illusions thoroughly dispelled, Lund's great clock regained its peaceful countenance. The Horologium's dial shone with a calm luster, and the wooden saints and angels around it returned to their tranquil, reverent poses. Not a hint of distortion or hum remained in the crypt; ignorance's fleeting hold had been vanquished.

Morpheus Rubicom stood in the center of the quiet crypt, his hood hanging askew and his posture slumped in defeat. Still catching his breath, he regarded the young victors with a puffy-eyed resignation. At length, he reached into his tattered cloak and produced a small, tarnished key engraved with intricate swirling runes. He extended it toward Blunt. "You've bested ignorance today," Morpheus muttered. His voice was subdued, but there was a strange, distant respect in it. "Perhaps this will aid you in the questions yet to come."

Blunt stepped forward and accepted the key with a polite nod. As he did, he felt the familiar pulse of Zeetrikus's innovation gear humming approvingly inside his own cloak. "We'll continue to question every illusion we encounter," Blunt promised. "Ignorance can't thrive as long as we stay united in curiosity."

At those words, Morpheus's tense shoulders eased slightly, as though in grudging acknowledgment of their resolve. He hesitated, the corners of his mouth twitching as if weighing one last piece of advice. "Be on your guard," he finally cautioned, raising a trembling hand toward the Horologium. "Ignorance has a way of creeping back in… given the smallest chance." With that, he swept his hand in an arc. A portal swirled into existence beside the ancient clock, its edges glowing with familiar bronze light. "Go now. Monticello awaits your final check."

Reddish stepped up to the portal, her eyes still glowing with embers. She hadn't forgotten the faint distortion they'd sensed lingering in Jefferson's clock when they left. "We'll make sure Monticello's clear of all illusions," she assured Morpheus with a determined nod. "No half-answers left lurking."

Greenie lingered a moment, looking at Morpheus as he withdrew toward the shadows. In his weary eyes she sensed a flicker of something almost like longing—a wish, perhaps, that he himself could escape the very ignorance he spread. "Ignorance chains everyone it touches," she said to him softly. "We choose knowledge and questions to keep us free." Her cloak glimmered with gentle green light, as if offering him a sliver of empathy, before she turned away.

Checkered gave the Horologium one last, careful examination through her monocle. No illusion—however small—went undetected by her keen eye. "All clear here," she reported briskly. Satisfied that Lund's clock was truly free of any lingering glamour, she traded relieved smiles with Firee and Breezie.

"Time to head home," Firee said, already conjuring a small flame in his palm to help stabilize the waiting portal. Breezie summoned a final guiding breeze that caused the portal's bronze edges to dance and widen invitingly. Together, the six Wizards stepped through in single file.

A familiar weightlessness enveloped them as they traveled back through the glowing corridor of magic. In the blink of an eye, the cool darkness of Lund gave way to the gentle warmth of Monticello. The Wizards found themselves once more in Jefferson's entrance hall, now dim in the violet shades of late twilight. The oppressive brassy hum that had greeted them at dawn was gone—only a crisp, pure ticking remained, echoing honestly in the quiet hall.

"Jefferson's clock stands untainted," Firee said softly, breaking the silence. He gazed at the restored clock face, which now reflected the deep indigo of the evening sky outside. The estate's hush felt comforting and clean, as if Monticello itself breathed easier now that the illusion had been lifted. Blunt slipped Morpheus's gifted key into a pocket of his cloak, his heart buoyed by the hard-won victory. With the darkness dispelled and truth shining through once more, they prepared to ensure that Monticello would remain at peace.

Monticello's Clock Freed

Twilight shadows lengthened across Monticello's entrance hall, painting the redbrick walls in subtle purples. Jefferson's Astronomical Clock stood at the center, its brass gears ticking harmoniously, freed from the stifling hum. The Wizards—Blunt, Reddish, Firee, Checkered, Breezie, and Greenie—took in the sight with quiet relief.

Checkered stepped nearer, lens stowed but ready. "No illusions remain. The star dials reflect precise data again—no false glimmers or partial arcs," she said decisively.

Greenie, placing a hand lightly on the polished brass, felt only calm inquiry instead of discord. "It's as though the clock breathes Jefferson's spirit again—questing, eager, unafraid," she observed softly. The ephemeral tension that once crawled beneath the surface had lifted.

Reddish's embers subsided to a gentle glow, her earlier tension melting into a satisfied grin.

"All stable," Firee confirmed after a final sweep of the area. "Seems Monticello's knowledge thrives again."

Blunt approached the side table, noticing star charts and half-finished notes. Now they appeared corrected, as though illusions had previously scrambled them. "Facts fall back into place once illusions vanish," he commented, setting down Morpheus's tarnished key. "Ignorance's hold on this place is finally broken."

Outside, the estate's hush merged with cicadas singing in the oncoming dusk, the day's final glow brushing across the west windows. Monticello seemed at peace, as if grateful that no glamour marred Jefferson's legacy of curiosity.

Greenie turned to face the group, a gentle smile warming her features. "I guess that's it—Monticello stands inquisitive once more, no illusions thwarting truth." Her cloak pulsed softly, reassurance sinking in.

Reddish flicked an ember from her fingertips, letting it dissipate. "We'll have to stay on guard," she reminded them. "Morpheus might try something else down the line, but at least here we've sealed the breach for good."

Blunt nodded, his water-blue gaze steady with resolve. "We remain vigilant. For now, Monticello's clock runs true and honest. Curiosity has brought light to this place, and the shadows of ignorance have faded."

Nearby, the Latin motto engraved along the clock's rim seemed to gleam with approval in the dim light: Scientia Lucem Affer; Ignorantia Tenebras Praebet—"Knowledge brings light; ignorance brings darkness." The young Wizards exchanged smiles as its meaning resonated in their hearts. In that moment, each of them understood that it was the humility to keep questioning—never to assume they knew everything—that would keep that light shining as they moved forward.

Reflecting on Lessons

Night settled fully over Monticello by the time the six Wizards reconvened in the grand foyer. A few oil lamps cast a mellow glow across Jefferson's portraits and the clock's polished brass, which gleamed anew. A gentle hush prevailed as they all took a moment to reflect on how dangerously close ignorance had come—and how their persistent questioning ultimately routed those illusions.

Reddish leaned against the banister of the staircase, eyes on the clock's zodiac dial now spinning free and clear. "Those ignorance illusions in Lund were pretty cunning," she remarked. She remembered the seductive feeling of being offered an easy shortcut to knowledge. "They almost had me thinking I could skip doing the work. Good thing we knew to push deeper and not fall for it."

Greenie twirled a small vine between her fingers, recalling how each illusion had tried to present an incomplete solution that a less wary person might have accepted. "Half-truths can be so soothing," she said softly. "They lull you if you're not careful. In the end, only steady, consistent inquiry can break that spell."

Checkered let her monocle dangle on its chain as she thought back to the illusory cosmic "revelations" they had faced. "Illusions rely on people not double-checking," she said crisply. "Whenever one appeared, we cut it off before it could take hold."

Firee crossed his arms over his chest, his face thoughtful. "Corruption illusions tried to warp our morals, stagnation illusions stalled our progress… and ignorance illusions hid behind our willingness to accept things easily," he said. "No matter the type, our unity and quick action saw us through. We just never accept an illusion at face value."

Blunt stood a little apart from the others, hands resting on the back of a settee as he replayed the night's events in his mind. He realized that in the fight at Monticello's clock, not one of them had hesitated—the moment an illusion appeared, they all reacted in sync. The memory reminded him of Franklin's lightning-quick guidance during their trial in Boston. "Not one of us hesitated when an illusion appeared," he said, looking around at his friends. "Our unity in that instant made the difference."

Breezie exhaled and allowed himself to relax into one of the armchairs, the tension in his posture finally unwinding. "It feels good how well we handled things," he said contentedly. "If only every challenge went this smoothly."

Greenie's expression grew more serious at Breezie's comment. Her empathic intuition carried a note of warning. "We have to remember not every illusion will be so isolated," she cautioned. "They might combine tricks next time—ignorance mixed with something else. We'll need to stay flexible and ready for anything."

Checkered nodded firmly at that. She tucked her monocle away and squared her shoulders with resolve. "We have to keep every lesson we've learned at the ready," she said. "Humility, innovation, curiosity—each virtue we've gained so far. We might need them all together for whatever comes next."

Reddish's eyes flashed in agreement, a determined grin spreading on her face. "That's our game plan then," she agreed. "Maybe the Dark Harlequin out there will try to throw every illusion at us at once eventually—but we'll throw every virtue right back."

A comfortable silence fell among them. In the distance, they heard a pair of footsteps echo briefly down a side corridor—likely a caretaker making late rounds—but nothing disturbed the peace of the foyer. No stray flicker of illusion remained. The clock's steady ticking filled the hall with a soothing, honest rhythm. The six friends exchanged looks of confidence. They had faced ignorance in its many guises and prevailed without losing themselves. Together, they silently renewed their vow: whatever illusions might come, they would stand unified, inquisitive, and humble—ensuring falsehoods would find no foothold in the light of their shared wisdom.

A Subtle Clue for Future

They lingered in the foyer a while longer, savoring the hard-won tranquility. The last rays of sunset painted the redbrick walls in a mellow copper glow. As Blunt moved to wind the clock gently, Checkered's gaze caught on a scrap of paper pinned behind a stack of old star charts on a side table. Frowning, she slid the brittle paper free and held it to the lamplight. Faded scribbles became just legible: "Horologium: Past, Present, Future… Seek synergy in the Founders' shadows."

"Another riddle," Reddish sighed, peering over Checkered's shoulder at the cryptic note. The firelight from her cloak made the curling script stand out slightly more. "Looks like these illusions always leave a breadcrumb leading to the next challenge."

Greenie gently plucked the note from Checkered and studied it, her brow furrowed in thought. "It mentions Horologia—clocks," she translated softly, recognizing the Latin plural. "Past, present, future… Founders' shadows… It's hinting that other historic clocks might face similar illusions."

Blunt exchanged a knowing glance with Greenie. It seemed their work might not be done. He exhaled slowly. "We can't run ourselves ragged chasing every hint," he said, feeling a mix of resolve and fatigue. Still, the restored Monticello clock in front of them was proof that following the clues had been worthwhile. "But we'll stay watchful for any sign that ignorance is creeping up again."

Firee carefully folded the tattered note and tucked it into a pocket beside Morpheus's tarnished key. "If more illusions do show up, we'll piece these clues together then," he said matter-of-factly. He shared Blunt's wary optimism—they wouldn't obsess over every hint, but they wouldn't ignore them either. And if ignorance tried another trick, he felt confident they could handle it. "Whatever happens, it won't catch us off guard for long."

Breezie picked up an old quill from the side table, idly twirling it between his fingers as he pondered the possibilities. He could almost picture new half-truth illusions stirring in some distant city. "At least Monticello's safe now," he said quietly. A tired but content smile crossed his face. "Jefferson's legacy is intact—no lies lurking in these halls."

Checkered nodded and adjusted her cloak, already thinking ahead. "When we get back to Boston, we should cross-reference this clue," she suggested. "Maybe in the Orloj's hidden library or another archive. The Orloj might even guide us directly. One way or another, we'll fit these puzzle pieces together soon."

Reddish stepped away from the clock, stretching her arms overhead until her cloak flared out behind her. "We took down these illusions once we understood the threat," she said, reflecting on their victory. "Feels good to see Monticello's clock shining free of any trickery now."

Greenie brushed a lock of hair behind one ear and smiled serenely. "Knowledge is thriving here again," she agreed. She had no doubt that any future illusions would prove just as fleeting as this night's challenge—provided they remained as united as ever. After all, in both Lund and Monticello the enemy had tried to isolate them with easy lies, and each time the plan failed when they stood strong together. "Whatever comes next will unravel just as easily if we keep our unity and curiosity," she added, confidence soft but unshakable.

A comfortable silence fell. In that moment, it felt as if Monticello itself heaved a contented sigh of relief. No shadows lurked in the corners of the foyer; only the gentle tick of the clock and the faint chirr of cicadas could be heard through the open window.

Brief Interlude: Monticello's Twilight

Night had fully descended by the time the six friends stepped beyond Monticello's doors. A gentle twilight hush wrapped the estate in a soft purple glow, the tall columns and trellises of Jefferson's home cast into peaceful shadow under the first stars. The Wizards walked the flagstone path toward the main drive, each footstep light with hard-earned confidence from their swift victory. Flickers of fireflies were beginning to dot the lawns—tiny golden sparks dancing among the trees, as if mirroring the united spark that had driven out ignorance's darkness in an instant.

Chapter 7

Old North Church Clock –
When Questions Win

The Steeple's Whine

Mid-morning sunlight filtered through Boston's Old North Church, casting a soft glow over the dusty stones of its colonial crypt. Ancient runes glimmered faintly on the walls, and the air carried the mild scent of candle wax mingling with aged wood. Yet beneath this tranquil façade, a restless pulse stirred—a deceptive hum pricking at the six young Wizards' senses.

In a subtle rush of energy, guided by the pull of Morpheus's enchanted key, Blunt, Reddish, Firee, Checkered, Breezie, and Greenie emerged from a bronze-and-azure portal into the crypt, fresh from their Monticello victory and Franklin's electrifying lesson in unity. Their Harlequin cloaks flickered softly in the dimness as motes of dust swirled in the air. The mild aroma of wax and old timber grounded them in the reality of the crypt even as magic tingled at the edges of their awareness. Above them, the Old North Church's clock—a relic of 1723—ticked steadily high in the steeple. Its brass gears, etched with tiny lantern motifs, turned methodically, but a faint whine underscored each tick, as if something unseen wove incomplete answers into every motion.

Clutched in Blunt's hand was Morpheus's tarnished key from Lund, its Latin inscription "Quaestio Veritatem Revelat" ("Questions Reveal Truth") still faintly aglow from their last triumph. Tucked inside his cloak was Zeetrikus's innovation gear, "Innovare Est Virtus" ("To Innovate Is a Virtue"), which pulsed in quiet resonance with the key. "Curiosity lit Monticello's path," Blunt murmured, recalling their recent victory, "and now this clock demands deeper questions."

Reddish's amber eyes narrowed, sparks flickering across her cloak's fabric. She caught a subtle discord in the clock's whine, reminiscent of the half-truth glamours they had dispelled before. "This presence is evasive," she said, scanning the crypt's shadows. A faint metallic tang hung in the air, making her grit her teeth. "It's like the truth here is being smothered—kept just out of reach." The sensation immediately brought Morpheus Rubicom's trickery to mind, hanging in the air like acrid smoke.

Greenie closed her eyes and sent out a gentle empathic sweep. In her mind's eye she glimpsed echoes of April 1775—

Paul Revere's lantern signals glowing in the steeple above, an entire city awakened by urgent questions. "This place once birthed a nation's inquiries," she whispered, her cloak's green patterns pulsing with emotion. "But now a veil of ignorance hangs here, just like at Monticello all over again."

Checkered adjusted her monocle and surveyed the church clock's pendulum, noticing an irregular sway that no mere mechanical flaw could explain. "A colonial masterpiece," she said crisply, one hand hovering near the ancient gears. "Built to track time for an age of enlightenment—yet it's restless, urging us to dig deeper." Through her magnified lens she caught a faint ripple in the air beneath the pendulum: some intangible force tugging at the clock's rhythm. "Definitely magical, not mechanical," she confirmed as a tiny swirl of phantasmal energy glinted under her monocle, revealing that unseen forces were indeed at play in the clock's workings.

Firee gently laid his fingertips against the clock's wooden frame. A slight tremor vibrated under his touch. "The pendulum's off-kilter," he said in a low, vigilant tone. He'd faced similar disturbances in Lund and Monticello—this felt the same. "Ignorance might be muting its true motion." As if in reply, the whining note in the clock's tick sharpened for an instant, a petulant squeal from the old mechanism.

Greenie let her empathy trace the outlines of the crypt, attuning to the disturbance. She sensed how this clock had once measured out the moments before revolution—timing questions that challenged an empire. "It once marked crucial instants of inquiry," she breathed, "and now it's tangled in mirages of ignorance."

A bronze glow flickered in the gloom as Breezie peered at the pendulum through his Reality Sight. "A portal is forming," he noted calmly. A swirling oval of light coalesced just at the pendulum's nadir—a doorway tied to curiosity's pursuit. But tendrils of illusion clung to its edges like dark vines, trying to obscure the portal's presence with half-answers and doubt.

Blunt ran his hand along the base of the clock and felt new engravings raised under the patina. "Quaestio Veritatem Revelat," he read aloud, fingers tracing the Latin script. "Questions reveal truth." He exchanged a knowing look with the others. This was Morpheus's signature challenge: a puzzle of false fronts that would yield only if pressed by true curiosity. The innovation gear at Blunt's side hummed in agreement, sensing the unity of purpose growing among them.

Checkered leaned in to magnify the inscription's edges. "It's a direct challenge," she agreed. "Either we question everything, or the illusions stand unopposed." She knew from experience that only thorough inquiry could shatter such deception.

The Wizards steeled themselves. One by one, their cloaks glimmered as each internalized that resolve. The clock's faint whine rose to a piercing whirr, as though resisting their combined insight. The modest clock face above them almost seemed to watch, its pendulum lurching unevenly. The call was unmistakable: press forward or accept the half-truths lurking here. In unspoken accord, they braced for another test from Morpheus Rubicom, determined to protect the Old North Church's legacy of truth-seeking from the creeping hush of ignorance.

Through the Pendulum

Under the crypt's vaulted ceiling, the bronze glow at the clock's base flared brighter. The pendulum shuddered and, with a flash of azure light, a swirling portal unfurled beside the clock's foot. Static energy crackled along its edges—the same distortion they had seen when illusions tried to bar their way in Monticello. Blunt's water-blue eyes narrowed as he stepped forward. "Curiosity opens paths," he reminded them, echoing an earlier lesson. With a fluid sweep of his hand, he cast a gentle, flowing ward of water magic that stabilized the portal's oscillating rim.

Reddish pressed her palm near the forming vortex, embers dancing in her gaze. "We go through," she said firmly. "No ignorance can hide if we question it at once." Her confidence was bolstered by the memory of Monticello, where their swift unity had unraveled every deception in their path.

As the portal widened, a spectral shimmer took shape beside it. Mrs. V—their mentor spirit—materialized briefly, her half-cape drifting around her shoulders. "Curiosity reveals truth, but illusions will deter deeper queries," she cautioned gently, her voice echoing in the crypt. "Stay unified, as Tetragor taught you." With a reassuring smile, the apparition burst into motes of silver light, urging them onward.

United in purpose, the six Wizards moved as one. Breezie summoned a steady breeze to reinforce the portal's boundary. Firee cast a watchful glance behind them to ensure no stray phantasm lingered in the crypt's shadows. Checkered held her lens at the ready for immediate analysis, while Greenie's empathetic sense tingled with anticipation of whatever lay beyond. At Blunt's brisk nod, they stepped into the portal's bronze-blue glow together.

A chorus of ticking gears and rushing starlight enveloped them as they crossed the threshold. For a heartbeat, they were weightless in a corridor of cosmic hush. Then, with a gentle thump, the portal ejected them onto damp earth. Morning mist curled around weathered gravestones as they regained their footing.

The Wrong Question

Blunt took a few careful steps forward through the swirling mist, immediately noting a wrought-iron gate ahead of them. Arching over the gate was a modest clock embedded in the stonework—darkened with age, yet faintly humming with the same dissonant note they'd sensed in the crypt. A few yards away, a weathered headstone stood out among the rest, its chiseled epitaph softly illuminated by a lingering trace of enchantment.

Without pausing, Blunt raised his voice into the quiet graveyard. "What secrets are you hiding here?" he called out, directing his challenge at the clock and the unseen forces around it. His tone was firm, edged with the presumption that something in this burial ground was deliberately concealing truth.

The effect was immediate and jarring. The Granary Clock answered with a discordant clang, as if a bell inside it had mis-struck the hour. The harsh, off-key peal reverberated through the burying ground. At that same moment, the gentle glow on the nearby epitaph sputtered and died—the engraved letters sank into darkness, their faint light snuffed out. It was as though Blunt's forceful question had caused the very essence of this place to recoil, obscuring rather than revealing its secrets.

Checkered's eyes widened behind her monocle. "Careful!" she hissed, moving to Blunt's side. Through her lens she saw the magical aura around the clock jitter and flare chaotically in response to his demand. The way you asked... it forced the illusion to react. She realized a leading question—one that presumed an answer—was only emboldening the glamour. "You're feeding it by phrasing it like that," Checkered warned. "It twisted your words into more confusion."

Greenie hurried to the dimmed headstone, resting a hand on its cold, mossy surface. She sent out a pulse of empathic magic, probing the emotional spike that Blunt's challenge had provoked. "I sense frustration… and fear," she reported softly. The illusion blanketing this graveyard felt almost like a living thing, now spooked and bristling, lashing out because it felt cornered. Greenie turned her earnest gaze to Blunt. "Try a different approach," she urged gently. "Ask with curiosity, not accusation. Invite the truth out—don't demand it."

Blunt's cheeks flushed as he recognized his misstep. Taking a steadying breath, he nodded. They needed to embody the very virtue they championed. He stepped forward again, closer to the archway's clock, and this time placed his palm flat against the cool stone beneath the clock face. In a calm, clear voice, he spoke into the mist, framing his words with genuine curiosity: "What truth do you guard here?"

For a heartbeat, all was still. Then the Granary Clock responded. Its pendulum, which had been lurching irregularly, steadied into a smooth, even swing. The dissonant hum underlying its ticking faded to a quieter, more natural rhythm. From deep within the clock's workings came a single, low bong—not a harsh clang, but a resonant chime that seemed to acknowledge the correctly phrased question.

Across the way, the inscription on the headstone began to glow once more. The carved letters rekindled one by one until the entire epitaph gleamed clearly again, as if rejuvenated by the respectful inquiry. And high above, behind the clock's face, a bronze gear hidden in shadow briefly glinted with warm, golden light.

Checkered adjusted her monocle and watched in satisfaction as the web of magic around the clock began to relax rather than tighten. "That's more like it," she murmured. The distortion in the air was easing; the illusion, soothed by the well-asked question, was no longer thrashing against them.

Greenie let out the breath she had been holding. She felt the earlier tension lifting from the graveyard, the angry static in the atmosphere dissipating. "The illusion is relenting—at least for now," she confirmed softly. The oppressive feeling that had choked this place moments ago was retreating, calmed by the power of a genuine question.

Blunt stepped back toward his friends with a small, relieved smile as the clock's single chime faded into silence. "How a question is asked…" he began thoughtfully.

"…can be the difference between fog and clarity," Checkered finished, returning his smile. Her monocle caught a last flash of the bronze gear's glow before it dimmed once more.

Greenie's eyes lingered on the re-illuminated epitaph and the now-steady clock. A gentle peace had settled over the graveyard again. "We have to remember that," she said, her voice full of meaning. The bronze glint behind the clock face had been like a wink from the mechanism itself—a promise that in this trial, as ever, the right question would light the way.

Reinvigorated by this small victory, the Wizards pressed forward through the thinning mist, moving under the arch and into the heart of the cemetery.

At the Gate of Names

Now fully within Granary Burying Ground—Boston's iconic colonial cemetery and resting place of rebels and heroes—the Wizards took in their surroundings. Tall oak and maple trees loomed overhead, their late-summer leaves filtering the pale morning light. Crooked headstones jutted from the soil at odd angles, each etched with centuries-old names. A faint breeze whispered through the misty rows of graves, stirring a few fallen leaves and carrying the distant sounds of the waking city.

Near the iron gate behind them, the modest clock embedded in the archway ticked onward. This hidden "Granary Clock," dating back to 1713, was not marked on any map or tourist guide; it was an occult timepiece silently watching over the dead. Though Blunt's well-phrased question had calmed it momentarily, the clock's hands still moved with a subtle, uneasy rhythm. A low hum lingered beneath each tick—a slight tremor that felt eerily familiar, as if the spirit of ignorance were still trying to whisper over the sound of time.

Blunt stepped up to the clock once more and ran his fingers over its tarnished brass face. "Built in 1713, marking time even for a city of restless ideas…" he murmured, recalling a scrap of history even as he sought new clues. The metal was cool under his palm, but an unnatural vibration throbbed beneath the steady tick. "Like the Old North Church clock, its rhythm isn't pure," Blunt noted quietly. It was as though a shadow of falsehood still lay across the clock's workings. His synergy gear gave a sympathetic thump at his side. He glanced at his companions. "No illusion will stand if we act in unison—just like always."

Reddish felt embers stir in her cloak as she surveyed the silent ranks of tombstones around them. "This has Morpheus's mark all over it," she said in a low, fierce voice. The air here held the same charged hush of half-answers that they remembered from Monticello. She tightened her grip on her staff, small tongues of flame flickering at its tip. "If these graves—if Boston's very history—is being muffled by phantasms, we'll uncover it fast."

Greenie closed her eyes and let her empathetic awareness ripple outward over the cemetery. Faint impressions of the past rose up to meet her: passionate debates at patriots' gravesides, defiant vows whispered over victims of the Boston Massacre. "They questioned tyranny here once," Greenie breathed, her heart echoing with those old reverberations. "Now a glamour of ignorance is trying to smother that spirit— like a damp veil over a fire." Her cloak's verdant pattern glowed softly as she spoke, Tetragor's lesson of humility steadying her resolve to listen to even the faintest voices of truth.

Checkered peered at the hidden clock's weathered edges through her monocle. Subtle auras danced in every hairline crack between the stones. "It's a sturdy relic," she noted, her tone as brisk and analytical as ever, "but something is making it stutter." Indeed, through her lens she observed the second hand twitching unevenly with each tick. The deceptive hum vibrated through the iron lattice of the gate. She recognized this pattern from their earlier trials and clicked her tongue in annoyance. "We'll have to unravel this quickly, before it spreads further."

Breezie watched a coil of mist slide beneath a nearby headstone. "This ground holds countless questions from Boston's origins," he mused, keenly aware of the historic curiosity that lay interred here. His eyes narrowed at the thought of that legacy being obscured. "If any fog of deceit settles here, we'll blow it away," he said, raising his hand. His cloak shimmered as he summoned a light breeze, ready to disperse whatever mirage might creep forth from the lingering mist.

Firee drew a slow, calming breath, his eyes scanning the perimeter of the graveyard. He could see tendrils of illusion hovering at the edge of sight, melding with the natural morning haze. He tightened his grip on his wand. There would be no half-measures today. He knew from experience that ignorance grew best in darkness—when left unchallenged. At the first sign of any deceit here, they would respond without hesitation.

Suddenly, a flicker of movement skittered at the corner of their vision. The Granary Clock's gentle hum spiked into a sharper note, each tick now coming faster than the last—as if provoked by their very presence. The Wizards tensed, hearts pounding, instincts honed from many prior battles. They knew this feeling all too well: the charged air before a final test. Morpheus Rubicom's trial in Boston was about to reveal itself.

Morpheus's Half Answers

A cool gray mist clung to the edges of the burying ground as a gaunt figure stepped out from behind a crooked tombstone. Morpheus Rubicom emerged at last—tall and cadaverous in a tattered antiquarian's cloak, his eyes puffed and shadowed from ages spent poring over forbidden tomes. Creaking trinkets dangled from his belt, each perhaps a reliquary of half-truths. He regarded the young Wizards with a crooked sneer.

"So, you've returned," he rasped, his voice threaded with a dry, agitated hiss. "Boston's thirst for knowledge is legendary… yet knowledge is fragile. Given the chance, comforting illusions will cradle the mind if no one thinks to dig deeper." Bitterness dripped from his words, as though he resented that these children refused to settle for the easy lies he offered.

Blunt squared his shoulders, feeling the gentle pulse of the synergy gear through his cloak. "We've come across your illusions before," he replied, meeting Morpheus's bloodshot eyes evenly. "Monticello, Lund—each time we refused your partial truths, and each time we prevailed. We're not stopping now."

Morpheus's gaze flicked toward the Granary Clock behind them, then back. "Ignorance thrives when you accept incomplete realities," he murmured, his gnarled fingers twitching at his sides. "Here in Boston's hallowed ground, unanswered questions give my phantoms strength. Dare you press on and strip them bare?"

Checkered lifted her chin, lens in hand. "We've beaten every falsehood by digging until the truth showed itself," she said confidently. Not a quaver marred her voice—she had absolute faith in the process that had carried them this far. "No deception can withstand thorough inquiry."

Greenie's heart ached as her empathic magic perceived the twisted longing woven through Morpheus's tone. A part of him almost wanted them to succeed, she realized—yet he couldn't relinquish the power he drew from ignorance. "Even if illusions comfort those who fear the unknown," she said softly, "Boston's spirit deserves better. We won't abandon curiosity, not here."

Reddish stepped forward, embers dancing along her sleeves. "Your illusions might promise easy knowledge or convenient stories," she said sharply, "but they only keep people in the dark. We'll face them together—no hesitation."

Determination burned in her eyes like hot coals.

Morpheus's gaunt face twitched—a flicker of annoyance, but also a glimmer of reluctant respect. Slowly, he drew out a dusty leather-bound tome from within his ragged cloak. "Bold words," he croaked. "If it's true that you seek answers in every shadow… then let's test the depths of your curiosity." He gestured to one side, and the mist before the Granary's gate swirled, reshaping itself.

To the Wizards' surprise, the fog congealed into the outline of an old wooden table surrounded by six empty chairs. A warm golden lantern flickered to life at its center, casting dancing light over several ancient scrolls and books strewn across the tabletop. Morpheus shuffled toward this uncanny reading nook and beckoned them curtly. "Come," he said, voice gentler than before but laced with challenge. "Indulge an old librarian's habit. Read… and tell me what you learn. Perhaps you're right—perhaps curiosity will reveal all."

Two Lamps for One Question

Wary but intrigued, the six friends slowly took their seats around the conjured table. Their Harlequin cloaks fell still about them, the vibrant colors dimming respectfully in the lantern's golden glow. This felt less like a battle and more like a strange seminar in the mist—a brief, uncanny truce in the heart of a haunted graveyard. Morpheus remained standing at the far side of the table, one skeletal hand resting on the open tome. In the silence, his demeanor had shifted from foe to instructor.

"Curiosity dislodges illusions," Morpheus muttered, as if quoting a proverb they all knew. His tone took on a measured, lecturing cadence. "Yet even then, shadows remain—unless you shine the light fully." He ran a finger down a yellowed page and, with an oddly gentle motion, slid the tome toward the group. It lay open to a short fable titled "The Owl and the Shrouded Forest." The cramped ink illustration at the top of the page glinted faintly in the lantern-light as the Wizards leaned in to read:

"The Owl and the Shrouded Forest"

In an ancient forest veiled in endless twilight, shadows whispered softly, weaving tales of fear and ignorance. Trees stood solemn and silent, their branches heavy with resignation, their roots bound by apathy. They spoke as one: "The dark has always been our home. To question is perilous; better to accept what is known."

Yet amid this dimness lived Lira, a curious owl with feathers like silver moonlight and eyes bright as stars. Restless and unafraid, she peered into the gloom, her heart burning with a single question: "Why must we dwell forever in darkness?"

The forest groaned dismissively, leaves rustling in disdain. "Curiosity brings danger. Do not disturb what has always been."

But Lira could not silence the yearning that stirred within her. Driven by the need to understand, she spread her wings and soared into the very heart of darkness, deeper than any creature had dared to go. There, hidden behind tangled branches and ancient thorns, she found a secluded glade illuminated by the faint glow of a solitary star.

In the glade lay a shroud woven thickly from threads of ignorance and fear, pulsing like a living entity. As Lira approached, shadows hissed fiercely, "Accept the darkness! Return to safety!"

Yet Lira's curiosity was stronger than fear. Determined, she called out to the creatures of the forest, urging them to share her question. Foxes crept forward bravely, hares stepped forth with wary hope, and ravens descended from their high perches, driven by a newfound hunger for truth. Together—paw by claw by wing—they began to unravel the shroud.

Slowly at first, then faster, the threads of ignorance loosened and fell away. With every thread removed, more light poured *into the glade, spreading warmth and illumination throughout the forest. At last, brilliant sunlight broke through, bathing the trees in golden radiance.*

Awakened from their long, passive slumber, the trees stirred in awe, leaves shimmering in wonder. They whispered softly to Lira, "We were wrong to fear questions. You have taught us to seek, to learn, to illuminate our world."

Perched on a branch in the heart of the forest—now vibrant with life and light—Lira gazed upon her community renewed. "Curiosity," she declared softly yet firmly, "is the beacon that dispels darkness. Together, our questions become the light by which truth is revealed."

Morpheus watched them read in silence, and when the final line had been absorbed, he closed the tome softly. "Reflect on Lira's search," he instructed, breaking the quiet. "Is that not the very method you yourselves employed in Monticello—unmasking ignorance by refusing to accept half-answers?"

Blunt nodded slowly, understanding dawning in his eyes. "At Monticello, we shattered ignorance by questioning everything—just as Lira refused to accept eternal darkness," he said. "Ignorance survives only when no one asks questions."

Without a word, Morpheus turned a few crackling pages, then produced a rolled scroll from beneath the tome. He handed it to Reddish. The title on its vellum read "The Lantern of Inquiry," and Reddish's fingertips glowed faintly as she unrolled it. Morpheus's challenge continued: "Read, and see how a shared flame can banish shadows."

Clearing her throat, Reddish began to read aloud. The scroll's verses told of a humble lantern of inquiry that ventured through darkened halls, gathering people together in a common search until dawn's first light triumphed. As she recited, the lantern on the table bobbed and flared as if stirred by the poem's tale. At the end, another moral glimmered into view across the page:

"The Lantern of Inquiry"

In a realm of shadowed halls,
where whispers cloaked the light,
a lantern burned, its flame so small,
yet piercing through the night.

It sought the hidden, the unseen,
through corridors of doubt,
each question a spark, a glowing gleam,
to drive the darkness out.

The shadows hissed, "Accept our shade!"
but the lantern's flame grew bold,

The final lines of the poem faded into the lantern's gentle glow. The Wizards looked up from the scrolls, their hearts kindled by the twin lessons. Checkered realized with a start that Morpheus's stance had shifted while they read. The hostility in his face had been tempered by a strange, grudging respect. In this moment he stood less as an enemy than as a stern teacher. These readings underscored a truth they all held dear: united curiosity could topple any deceit.

Morpheus's eyes flickered, and a hard edge crept back into his voice. The interlude of learning was over. He snapped the tome shut and tossed the scroll aside, retreating a few steps into the drifting mist. The warm glow of the reading nook began to wane. "Curiosity or complacency," he challenged, spreading his arms wide as shadows began to pool around him, "let's see which will prevail now."

Even as his words echoed, the comforting lantern light vanished. The graveyard plunged back into gloom as a swirling cloud of half-truths and phantoms erupted around the Granary Clock. Illusory shapes coiled and lunged in the air—each a tantalizing snippet of knowledge riddled with lies. Morpheus's form melted into the background darkness, leaving only his bitter laugh hanging in the air. The true confrontation had begun.

Checkered reacted first. Before her, a luminous signboard flickered into being, proclaiming in grand gilt letters: "Complete Boston Secrets — No Effort Required!" It was an illusion tailor-made to tempt a scholarly mind like hers. For an instant, the promise of quick, easy knowledge tugged at Checkered's curiosity and her heart skipped a beat at the idea of gaining insight without struggle. But she narrowed her eyes and lifted her monocle to scrutinize the glowing sign. "No, you don't," she muttered, refusing to accept the offer at face value. As she probed deeper with her truth-sight, the grandiose signboard began to waver. It hissed at her in frustration, then crumpled into tatters of light, revealing nothing but empty air behind it.

Greenie staggered back as another specter swooped toward her—a ghostly historian drifting above a gravestone, offering a neat, packaged narrative of Boston's past. "Trust the official story," it whispered soothingly. The suggestion was almost comforting in its simplicity, and for a heartbeat Greenie felt the urge to simply nod and let the matter rest. But she shook her head, recalling the messy, passionate reality of history. "History isn't that simple," she countered, voice firm. The specter's tale was too tidy, too sanitized—devoid of the passion and grit she knew the truth held. Planting her feet, Greenie extended her empathy like roots into the soil beneath her. She could feel the gaps and omissions in the specter's tale, the hollowness behind its comforting narrative. Vines of green magic unfurled from her cloak and wrapped around the false historian. With a resolute tug, Greenie peeled away the illusion's layers. The polished narrative disintegrated into wisps of black smoke, unable to withstand deeper questioning.

Not far away, a cluster of spectral documents swirled around Firee—pages promising to reveal all of Boston's knowledge compiled in a single, definitive volume. Firee's pulse quickened at the sight; what scholar wouldn't be enticed by such a trove? He snatched one parchment out of the air. It appeared impressively detailed; for a moment, he almost believed the illusion's promise. But then Firee's innate danger-sense prickled at the back of his neck. He realized the page was hollow—nothing but a pretty cover concealing emptiness. "A slick trick," he growled. With a sharp gesture, he sent a precise burst of flame from his wand, igniting the deceit. The false records shrieked as they burned away to ash, leaving only a lesson drifting in the air: real understanding had no shortcuts.

Nearby, Reddish found herself facing a beckoning mirage of her own: a glowing red door that materialized in midair, through which she glimpsed towering stacks of books and glittering artifacts. A honeyed voice from beyond the threshold whispered, "All Granary's lore can be yours… just take the quick path." Reddish's heart pounded. For a moment, her competitive instinct—her desire to claim victory swiftly—flared at the tantalizing prospect of an easy win. She took a half-step forward, fingertips reaching toward the door's handle as the illusion sensed her wavering and glowed brighter.

But then a line from the poem flashed through her mind: "the lantern's flame grew bold, its curious light refused to fade."Reddish halted. This beguiling offer of a shortcut was exactly the kind of shadow the Lantern of Inquiry had warned against. Gritting her teeth, she drew back her hand. "Curiosity doesn't take shortcuts!" she shouted, her voice ringing across the graves. With a sweep of her arm, she summoned a surge of fiery magic. The mirage-door burst into a cloud of embers and vapor, the whispering voice cut off in a strangled hiss.

A swirling aurora of cosmic light descended around Breezie, coalescing into an illusion that pleaded in a soothing chorus, "Stop searching—be content with what you know." The shimmering lights were beautiful, almost hypnotically so, and for a second Breezie felt a blissful urge to rest, to simply accept things and cease his quest. But he shook off the trance, remembering Lira's courage and how the forest creatures united to tear down the shroud. Breezie's eyes hardened. "No stagnation," he murmured. Spinning his staff overhead, he summoned a roaring gale. The comforting aurora couldn't withstand the wind—shreds of false serenity were torn apart and scattered like glittering dust. "Truth can't flourish if we stop seeking," he said, as steady as the breeze now rustling the leaves.

Finally, an imposing silhouette loomed before Blunt: an elderly scholar in colonial attire who emerged from the mist holding a massive leather-bound ledger. "All the knowledge of every soul buried here, yours for the asking," the phantom promised in a gentle, avuncular tone, "if you will only cease your relentless questioning now." Blunt felt the weight of years in that offer—the temptation to possess complete knowledge without all the struggles. For a single heartbeat, he yearned to accept. But then he caught a faint, sickly scent emanating from the phantom's ledger: the odor of old paper and stagnation, of knowledge long sealed away and left to rot. It was the smell of curiosity's death. Blunt's stomach turned. He raised his palm and conjured a broad shield of rippling water between himself and the spectral scholar. "We will never stop asking," Blunt declared. The watery shield surged forward like a cresting wave, crashing over the false scholar. The ledger dissolved in an explosion of waterlogged pages, and the phantom sputtered before bursting into vaporous mist.

One by one, the glamours fell apart under the Wizards' onslaught of questions and unwavering resolve. In mere moments, the graveyard fell quiet once more. Only the steady tick of the Granary Clock remained—and even that was now settling into a clear, honest cadence. A cool breeze swept through the cemetery, dispersing the last wisps of illusion like the final smoke from a guttered candle. Off to the side, Morpheus stood in a weak halo of gray morning light, his expression unreadable and his shoulders sagging.

The trial of curiosity was over. Surrounded by the headstones of Boston's truth-seekers, the six Wizards had met ignorance in its own lair and cast it out. For a long moment, the only sound was the Old North Church's clock far above, ticking away in peaceful accord—each tick an affirmation of knowledge reclaimed.

A gentle clink drew their attention. Morpheus stepped forward from the thinning shadows, his breathing ragged. The fight was over for him—curiosity had triumphed here. With trembling hands, he reached into his cloak and drew out a small bronze gear, ornately wrought and edged with green patina. Etched along its circumference was the phrase "Quaestio Iterum" — Latin for "Question Again." The gear glinted in the pale light as he offered it to Blunt, a token of their victory.

"Where progress stirs in mechanical hearts," Morpheus mumbled cryptically as Blunt accepted the gear, "seek the clock that curiosity restarts." It sounded like a riddle—and indeed a hint of another site. This was his final half-answer to them. Morpheus's puffy eyes blinked, a mix of relief and defeat crossing his features. He had lost here, but his words suggested that ignorance might yet take root elsewhere if left unchecked.

Blunt closed his hand around the bronze gear. The metal was warm, resonating with the power of their combined inquiry. He met Morpheus's gaze and nodded. "We won't let ignorance thrive in any corner," Blunt vowed quietly. The others gathered around him, their cloaks still faintly luminescent from the synergy of victory.

Reddish exhaled, a satisfied glow on her face. She gently tapped the edge of the new gear in Blunt's hand, sending a tiny ember dancing across its surface. Another victory—another lesson learned.

Greenie placed a gentle palm against the Granary Clock's now-steady surface. All she felt was the normal, reassuring tick of time. "Boston's spirit of inquiry breathes freely again," she murmured. The oppressive hush that had blanketed this place was gone, lifted as surely as Lira's shroud had been in the fable. "Morpheus can't dim it any longer."

Checkered adjusted her monocle and scanned the air one last time. Not a flicker of illusion remained. "All falsehoods are dispelled," she reported softly. In the growing sunlight, nothing lurked in the cemetery's corners anymore. "Not a half-truth lingers."

Morpheus drew his tattered cloak tighter around himself. His expression was weary, but oddly at peace. "Go," he said hoarsely. "Your unity of purpose outstrips my illusions. But remember—ignorance, once scattered, can return wherever questions cease to be asked." With that final counsel, his figure dissolved into the morning mist. A faint swirl of red and black flickered, then vanished, leaving only silence where the antagonist had stood.

From a shaft of sunlight near the gate, a familiar silhouette emerged as if carved from the light itself. Mr. M., the genial mentor spirit in the half-cape, appeared to greet them. "Curiosity conquers ignorance," he praised, his voice warm and proud. "Another triumph on your journey! But never grow complacent—ignorance never sleeps. Keep your synergy strong and question everything, just as you did today." He gave them a wink and a tip of his tricorn hat before his form evaporated in a shower of golden sparks.

The six Wizards exchanged relieved smiles, hearts buoyed by the praise. They had done what they came to do. Blunt carefully tucked the Quaestio Iterum gear into an inner pocket alongside their other hard-won tokens. As a group, they turned away from the Granary's gate. Already, a subtle rumble in the air signaled that their portal was re-forming to carry them back.

They stepped through the veil of magic and reappeared in the cool shadows of the Old North Church crypt. Above them, the old clock's pendulum swung in perfect, honest rhythm once more. Its deceptive whine was gone, replaced by the simple ticking of a well-tuned clock. Sunlight filtered through the trapdoor leading up to the chapel, illuminating motes of dust in the now-tranquil crypt.

Blunt drew out the new bronze gear one more time and read its inscription aloud: Quaestio Iterum. A smile touched his lips. Like the other gears they had collected, it bore a Latin motto—another link in the chain of their quest. This token's message was clear: there would always be another question, another mystery, another clock to set right. "On to our next lead," he said softly.

As they prepared to depart the crypt, Checkered's eyes caught a glint behind a dusty candlestick on a stone niche. She walked over and retrieved a small metal plaque hidden in the shadows. The others gathered around as she brushed away the cobwebs. It bore a faint engraving in Latin: "Quaestio Prodevit: Mortifer Artifex?"

"Another clue, perhaps," Reddish said, translating roughly. "It means 'A question emerges: deadly craftsman?'" The phrase was cryptic. Greenie ran her fingers over the etching and sensed a lingering trace of the same illusion magic they'd just dispelled. "We should take this with us," she suggested. "It might be pointing to something—or someone—we'll encounter next." Firee nodded and tucked the mysterious plaque safely away with their other curiosities.

With the Old North Church's secret now safeguarded and new clues in hand, the Wizards climbed the steps out of the crypt. The world outside awaited, full of new questions ready to be asked.

After the Bell

Outside the Old North Church, Boston's late-morning light spilled across the cobblestone streets. The everyday world bustled on—vendors opened their stalls, horses clopped by pulling delivery carts, and a few early tourists wandered with guidebooks in hand, blissfully unaware that anything unusual had just occurred beneath their feet. The crisp air carried a briny hint of the harbor, mingling with the aroma of fresh-baked bread from a nearby bakery. Everything was as it should be.

Blunt led the group down the brick pathway from the church, the Quaestio Iterum gear tucked safely in his cloak. He glanced back up at the steeple where, moments ago, a hidden battle for knowledge had raged. Now the only sound from above was the honest toll of the church's bell marking the hour. He marveled at how swiftly ignorance had been vanquished here. "Each time, it seems faster," he mused aloud. "Monticello, Lund, now Boston's heart—ignorance never stood a chance."

Reddish nodded, letting her gaze drift over the historic buildings lining the street. "We've really honed our approach," she agreed. "The moment any mirage rose, we united and brought it down. They simply couldn't take root." There was pride in her voice, but also a note of caution—she knew they would have to stay sharp for whatever came next.

Checkered walked alongside with her monocle tucked away and a contented smile on her face. "Ignorance tried to feed us shallow answers, but we never let it finish a sentence," she said. She had already catalogued each illusion they'd dispelled: every false claim had crumbled to ash under the force of their rigorous questions. "It's starting to feel like second nature."

Breezie inhaled deeply as they passed a street vendor arranging an array of pastries. The sweet smell and the calm morning scene felt like a well-earned reward. "I think Monticello taught us speed and unity," he reflected. "By the time we got here, we gave ignorance no time to dig in. It's… reassuring, actually, how quickly those phantasms fell apart."

Firee walked a step behind, turning the enigmatic plaque from the crypt over in his hands. "We've seen corruption illusions, stagnation illusions, and now ignorance illusions all defeated," he said quietly. His eyes flickered with a determined light. "The Dark Harlequin won't sit idle after this. He may try combining those strategies next time, or push something we haven't seen yet. We need to be ready."

Greenie reached out and gently squeezed Firee's shoulder. "We will be," she assured him, her voice warm and steady. No matter what form ignorance or any other shadow took, she had faith they would face it the same way—together and without delay. She looked around at Boston's lively streets and smiled softly. "This city's spirit of inquiry lives on in each of us."

They walked on in companionable silence for a while, simply enjoying the brightness of the day. Another wave of ignorance had risen and broken against them, like dark water crashing against a steadfast lighthouse. The synergy gear in Blunt's pocket pulsed with gentle warmth, reminding them of the united strength that had carried them through once more.

Latinate Breadcrumbs

A few blocks from the church, the group paused by a modest bronze statue of Paul Revere on horseback. Sunbeams slanted across the famous patriot's determined face—a symbol of Boston's revolutionary curiosity. As Breezie admired the statue, Reddish noticed something affixed to its base. Nestled near Revere's bronze stirrup was a small, weather-worn plaque, almost invisible to a casual passerby.

"There's writing here," Reddish called, crouching down. The others gathered as she wiped away a layer of grime. The text was etched in a florid, antiquated script: "Chronos taceo, Hazleton vocat?"

"Latin again," Checkered murmured, adjusting her glasses. "Roughly… 'Time is silent, Hazleton calls?'" She exchanged a glance with Blunt and Firee. The name Hazleton rang a bell from their studies and prior clues.

"Hazleton… that's where the Engle monumental Clock stands," Blunt said, recalling an earlier reference in their quest. The Engle monumental in Hazleton, Pennsylvania was a 19th-century clocktower known among clockworkers—and a likely target for whatever the Dark Harlequin planned next. "This can't be a coincidence."

Greenie laid a hand on the plaque, sensing faint magical residue. The phrase "time is silent" gave her a slight chill. "It looks like Morpheus—or one of his ilk—left us a breadcrumb," she said softly. Perhaps something, or someone, was muting that clock in Hazleton, much as ignorance had tried to mute this one.

Firee carefully pried the plaque loose from Revere's statue and placed it with the one they had found in the crypt. "Two Latin clues in one morning," he remarked. "Our adversary certainly loves his riddles." He straightened and looked around at his friends. "It appears Hazleton, Pennsylvania is calling us next."

Breezie rolled his shoulders as if already preparing for the journey ahead. "If ignorance or any other darkness has crept into Hazleton's clock, we'll handle it," he said calmly. The morning sun gleamed on the edges of his cloak—another day, another city's secrets to safeguard.

Reddish grinned and gave her staff a playful twirl. "Let them try whatever they want in Hazleton. We'll do exactly what we did here," she declared. "Hit them fast, hit them together, and ask the questions that burn away the shadows."

Checkered carefully tucked the two clue plaques into her satchel. "We'll have time on the trip to parse every nuance of these phrases," she said eagerly. Already the itch of a new mystery was forming in her mind, invigorating her. "If there are answers hidden in them, we'll find them."

Quaestio Iterum

With the Old North Church clock restored and the Granary's secrets laid bare, the Wizards knew they had once again defended Boston's light of knowledge against encroaching darkness. Morpheus Rubicom's latest campaign of ignorance had been thwarted here by their unwavering curiosity and unity. Every half-truth and convenient lie he had conjured up faltered under the simple act of asking the next question.

They strolled through Boston's historic North End, the weight of this victory gradually giving way to a lightness of heart. The city's inquisitive legacy—born from midnight rides and lantern signals—remained safe and vibrant. Overhead, the Old North Church's bell tolled noon, each peal a celebration of truth ringing free. No secret murmurs haunted its notes now.

From this adventure, the friends carried new wisdom and new clues. The bronze gear engraved Quaestio Iterum in Blunt's pocket was more than a trophy—it was a reminder that the journey of questions never truly ends. The cryptic Latin phrases they'd gathered hinted that the next chapter awaited in Hazleton. Perhaps the Dark Harlequin would send another emissary, or weave ignorance together with his other dark threads of corruption and stagnation. Whatever lay ahead, the Wizards felt ready.

Their triumph in Boston had reinforced how powerful a united pursuit of truth could be. Still, as they left the North End behind, they remained alert and humble about the challenges to come. In their wake, the Old North Church clock ticked on in peaceful honesty, and Boston's bustling streets hummed with the casual conversations of a free people. Curiosity had prevailed here. The six friends stepped forward toward the horizon, hopeful that their united light would guide them through any shadows that loomed ahead.

Chapter 8

Wanamaker and Rostock Clocks – Compassion's Triumph

Court of Tin Hearts

Late morning light poured through the lofty atrium of Philadelphia's Wanamaker Grand Court, bathing the Wanamaker Grand Court Clock—a towering antique masterpiece—in a warm, golden glow. The intricately designed gears, once celebrated for inspiring compassion, now thrummed with a cold, callous energy. Dozens of mechanical figures—soldiers, scholars, jesters—stood locked in distant poses, their motions slowed by a palpable lack of empathy. Even the clock's famed automata that normally enliven each hour remained eerily still: a Father Time figure that usually turns his hourglass and rings a bell at each quarter-hour was frozen mid-stride, and a skeleton meant to toll the hour hung motionless, bony arm forever poised to strike a skull that never sounded.

At the court's edge, Blunt, Reddish, Firee, Checkered, Breezie, and Greenie materialized from a bronze-and-azure portal, their Harlequin cloaks—emerald swirls, crimson flames, sapphire waves—glowing softly. The faint tang of damp stone and machine oil greeted them, but a deeper chill prickled at their senses – a latent undercurrent of indifference radiating from the clock.

Clutched in Blunt's hand was a bronze gear engraved with "Caritas Veritatem Revelat" – "Compassion Reveals Truth." He recalled their prior victory in Boston. "Curiosity unveiled truth there," he murmured, referencing how they had dispelled the illusions of ignorance. Tucked inside his cloak, Zeetrikus's innovation gear – "Innovare Est Virtus" – hummed in quiet agreement, reminding him of their combined strength. "Now we face illusions that feed on apathy – illusions that seek to snuff out compassion itself."

Reddish swept her amber gaze across the clock's silent tableau, the embers in her eyes catching a faint, unnatural glimmer in its metal. "It feels distant," she observed, noting how each mechanical figure's emptiness reflected an imposed lack of concern. She recognized the telltale whine of sorcery – illusions often manifest as subtle distortions. "Something's actively stifling empathy here."

Greenie closed her eyes and extended her empathic senses over the court, catching flickers of John Wanamaker's philanthropic vision that once animated this machine. "This clock used to stir heartfelt connections," she whispered. Now she felt only a cool remoteness in its hum. Her cloak's greens swirled resolutely as she braced herself; the warmth of community the clock once radiated had been leeched away.

Checkered approached the base, her analytical eyes noting tiny mechanical imbalances. "It's a century-old marvel," she said crisply, "crafted to promote kindness and unity. Yet an icy haze of magic clings to it. This isn't a mechanical failure at all – it's deliberate." Memories of prior illusions flickered in her mind; each had been undone by swift, united action, and this would be no different.

The Wizards' cloaks glowed in unison as each recalled how quickly illusions crumbled when confronted without hesitation. In answer, the Wanamaker clock gave a sullen, intensified hum, as if the lurking enchantment recognized their defiance. The glass eyes of several figures glinted with an unnatural emptiness, almost seeming to track the newcomers. Some deeper illusion was indeed testing compassion here—no doubt the handiwork of the newest illusion guardian they'd heard named: Paulina Tetrikus, the rumored Antiquarian of Compassion.

Quietly, the six friends gathered closer to the Wanamaker Astronomical Clock, prepared for whatever phantom thrived on apathy in this place once dedicated to compassion. Where the Grand Court's showpiece had once forged community warmth, an illusion now sought to harden hearts. So began a new quest in this court of tin hearts.

What the Gears Remember

Golden light drenched the Wanamaker Grand Court as the team commenced a careful inspection of the Wanamaker Clock. Its brass gears churned with a hollow, dispassionate rhythm that undercut any notion of warmth. Blunt, Reddish, Firee, Checkered, Breezie, and Greenie spread out around the clock's pedestal, Harlequin cloaks pulsing softly as each attuned to signs of sorcery. A pungent metallic tang hung in the air, as though the essence of empathy had been stripped away, leaving the machine's movements oddly heartless.

Firee knelt by a set of tarnished cogs, his crimson cloak pooling on the polished marble floor. He pressed a palm against one large gear. "These figures usually enact little dramas of compassion—miniature scenes of caring," he murmured. Typically, on the hour, the clock's mechanical cast would come alive: a scholar might tip his hat to a soldier, a nurse tend to a patient, a farmer share harvest with a beggar— each vignette a lesson in empathy. "But now they're all frozen stiff. Arms locked, no unity among them."

Checkered raised her gleaming monocle and let it hover over the interlocked gears. Tiny Latin etchings and decorative motifs glinted under her lens. "It was built to symbolize neighborly empathy," she reminded them, recalling historical notes. "If it's seizing up like this, it's because an illusion is sapping its spirit. Mechanically it's fine; something magical is making it run cold."

Greenie hovered near a statue of a schoolteacher that had ceased offering its usual gentle gesture. Her empathic sense confirmed what her eyes saw: each mechanical character that once interacted warmly with its neighbor now stood isolated and inert. "They've lost their connection to each other," she said softly. It reminded her of illusions that foster isolation. "It's like they no longer care at all."

Breezie paced around the base, stirring a light breeze with a subtle motion of his hand. The air against the clock felt heavy and stagnant, resisting even his gentle wind. "We countered ignorance illusions in Boston with immediate action," he noted, casting his mind back to their recent triumph. "This wave seems to starve compassion—trying to keep every heart cold and apart." He frowned as his breeze died against an unseen weight.

Blunt's fingers traced a faint engraving newly revealed on the clock's stone pedestal. The letters glowed with a cool blue light as he brushed aside grime: "Caritas Contra Calliditas" – "Compassion Against Callousness." He exchanged a knowing look with Checkered. "Paulina Tetrikus's mark, I'll bet," Blunt said. Every illusion guardian left clues to the virtue needed to overcome their trials. Tetragor had emphasized humility; Morpheus, curiosity. Now Paulina had literally inscribed compassion versus callousness into the scene.

Reddish's flames rippled along the hem of her cloak as she straightened with determined resolve. "If illusions here aim to freeze hearts," she said firmly, "we'll answer with immediate compassion. No hesitation." She remembered how in previous challenges any delay had given illusions a foothold. They would not allow it here.

As if on cue, a subtle swirl of energy gathered around one of the squeaking gears overhead. The clock's hum deepened into a low drone, as though aware that foes of indifference had arrived. The mechanical figures' painted eyes seemed to glint with lifeless challenge, daring them to intervene. Without another word, the six Wizards formed a focused half-circle at the clock's base, each drawing on their unique gifts to probe for unseen glamours.

Checkered's lens glowed violet as she attuned it to scan for lingering illusion magic clinging to the metal. Firee's wand ignited in a steady flame at his side, ready to burn away any phantasms that took shape. Greenie closed her eyes to better feel for hidden sorrow or pleas in the court, while Blunt centered himself, the synergy gear tucked in his cloak pulsing in time with his heart. The clock's unnaturally cold hush thickened, as if the illusion recognized their unity and bristled.

Suddenly, a sharp jolt ran through the central gear. Greenie gasped, stepping back as a narrow seam of light split across the clock's face. The hum modulated into a discordant whine. Illusions were stirring, acknowledging the challenge. A swirl of bronze-and-azure magic coalesced at the foot of the monument—exactly where Blunt had touched the inscription.

A portal was forming.

The conjured corridor of light spun itself open with a crackle of energy. Blunt narrowed his eyes at the shimmering doorway and lifted his hand. "Compassion forms the path," he intoned. Indeed, each virtuous triumph so far had literally opened new doorways for them. Without missing a beat, he summoned a tendril of water from the air and wove it around the portal's edges. The watery ward stabilized the gateway's flickering frame into a steady oval.

The illusory hum around them pulsed angrily, as if trying to dissuade the Wizards from stepping through. Reddish strode forward first, embers flaring bright in her eyes. "We go now," she insisted, her voice cutting through the eerie noise. "If something is blocking compassion, we'll tear it down the instant it appears."

As if in response, a faint silhouette shimmered into being beside the portal—a familiar maternal figure in a modest half-cape. Mrs. V. materialized with a comforting smile. Her spectral presence had guided them before in trials of humility and curiosity. "Compassion fosters unity, but illusions breed indifference," she said gently, her voice warm with encouragement. She reminded them of Tetragor's lesson: illusions feed on cold hearts. "Stay true. Callous illusions rely on you to turn away—do not give them that chance."

Mrs. V. dissolved into sparkles of light, the portal's glow reflecting in her kind eyes until she vanished completely. The way was clear. The six companions shared a brief look of unified resolve. Breezie sent a buoying current of air swirling around them, and Firee's vigilant flame curled protectively along his wand. Checkered clutched her notebook to her heart, Greenie took a steady breath, and Blunt extended his arm toward the portal, leading the way as the synergy binding them flared in unison.

One by one, cloaks streaming and hearts resolute, they stepped into the molten starlight of the portal.

Ancient Constellations, Frozen

A heartbeat later, the Wizards tumbled out of the swirling vortex onto the cold stone floor of a vast Gothic church. They found themselves inside St. Mary's Church in Rostock,

Germany. Pale morning light filtered through the high stained glass windows, illuminating one of the world's oldest astronomical clocks towering before them at the back of the nave. This medieval marvel, a treasured piece of German heritage built in 1472, consists of three partitions: the top features an Apostle-go-round – twelve apostle figurines that normally cross in front of a figure of Jesus for a blessing (with the last figure, Judas, shut out); the middle tier holds a colorful astrolabe dial displaying the Sun and Moon moving through zodiac constellations; and the bottom tier houses a calendar disc that charts the date across centuries (recently updated to extend far into the future). Normally, the church's bells would ring to accompany the apostles' procession each hour, drawing awe from all who gathered to watch.

But now, all was silent and still. The Astronomical Clock's gilded dials and carved figures were dimmed under a pall of cold, unnatural hum. The zodiac dial crept along sluggishly, its constellations barely shifting as if weighed down by invisible frost. A chill blue haze clung to the clock's façade and the surrounding stone pillars. Illusions of callousness had clearly taken root here as well, draining the warmth and communal spirit that usually radiated from this beloved timepiece.

Blunt took a step forward across the damp flagstones, recognizing the locale from a previous visit. "We've been here before," he murmured, recalling how a different kind of illusion had once tested them at this very clock. Now the same site was under siege again, this time by apathy. He laid a hand on the smooth wooden frame of the clock's base. "This clock embodies community spirit," Blunt said quietly. His synergy gear hummed as it resonated with faint magical vibrations in the wood. "Illusions are choking that spirit—hampering empathy among these people."

Reddish drew her cloak tighter against an unnatural chill in the mist. She sensed an aura of isolation emanating from the clock, as if discouraging anyone from reaching out to others. "We overcame ignorance illusions by uniting immediately," she mused, thinking of Monticello's library and Boston's crypt where swift teamwork dispelled falsehoods. Her breath puffed white in the cold morning air. "Likewise, these callous illusions must be shattered the instant they appear—one genuine act of care might break them."

Greenie walked beneath the now-motionless figurines of the twelve apostles that were set in the clock's upper tier. Normally those apostles would process out of their little doors each hour to the music of the bells, reminding the faithful of hope and fellowship. Now their wooden faces seemed forlorn.

Greenie's empathic senses tingled with an unpleasant numbness; she could feel how the townspeople's hearts were being magically nudged apart. "This clock used to unite neighbors in pride and prayer," she said softly. Her cloak's verdant patterns swirled with determined energy. "Now an illusion is pushing them apart, freezing their hearts in place."

Checkered let her monocle sweep across the astrolabe and the surrounding Gothic carvings. The normally vibrant artwork and intricate details looked subtly warped and muted, as if even the craftsmanship suffered under the spell. "The details are distorted," she noted, frowning. A painted numeral on the calendar dial was misaligned, and the face of one carved apostle appeared faded. "This isn't weathering – it's the illusion tampering with reality." She glanced back at the team. "We'll push back with compassion, just like we did minutes ago in Philadelphia."

Breezie stepped through swirling wisps of mist, circling the clock. He summoned a playful breeze that made the candles on a nearby altar flicker and a hanging church banner flutter. When that breeze reached the clock, however, it died to stillness. "It's resisting any warmth," he murmured, recalling that illusions often feed on negativity like cynicism. The wood and metal of the clock felt inert even to his elemental touch. "This apathy feeds on itself… but we won't let it."

Firee moved to the front of the clock, listening to the faint ticks of its mechanism. They were irregular and shallow, like a faltering heartbeat. He placed one hand on the wooden panels, sharing a pulse of his inner warmth as if offering encouragement to a sick friend. "We ended the last illusion wave almost instantly," he said, looking to each of his comrades. "Let's do it again. The second anything appears, we act in complete unity." A small flame danced at his fingertip, eager to burn away whatever chill lay ahead.

As if on cue, the clock's low hum deepened ominously. The painted stars on its zodiac dial briefly flashed with a frosty sheen. The illusion acknowledged its challengers. This ancient clock—usually a vibrant focal point of community life—had been drained of its warmth, its heart held in icy stasis. The six Wizards knew a trial was about to commence. And given where they stood, they had a strong hunch who would preside.

Greenie's eyes drifted to a pair of carved wooden angels flanking the clock. Their expressions, once gentle, looked almost mournful in the gray morning light. Each detail of the scene seemed to plead for the return of compassion. We won't keep them waiting, she thought. The Wizards quickly drew together and advanced to the center of the nave. They had no intention of hesitating. Each recalled how illusions of vanity, corruption, even stagnation had all crumbled under the full force of their synergy. Illusions of callousness would be no different.

"We bring genuine care, swift and unified," Blunt affirmed, drawing his wand. They formed a tight ring, back to back, facing outward. Elements began to gather subtly around them—water, flame, wind, earth, light, and empathy. "No false front trying to sever our bonds will stand for long." The team steeled themselves. A wisp of icy fog snaked across the flagstones, heralding the illusion's onset. They were ready.

Paulina's Gentle Ultimatum

From the mist-shrouded edge of the nave came the soft tap… tap… of measured footsteps. A tall figure emerged between two stone columns, wrapped in a flowing robe of silvery-gray that caught the weak morning light. Her face was illuminated by a gentle radiance. The air itself warmed slightly at her approach, though swirls of the lingering fog clung at her feet.

It was Paulina Tetrikus, the Antiquarian of Compassion. Unlike the restless, bitter presence of Morpheus Rubicom, Paulina carried herself with a calm grace. Each of her fingers bore a ring that hummed with subdued warmth. As she neared, the very illusions coiling in the church seemed to retreat slightly, swirling around her hem but not daring to touch her.

She stopped a short distance from the group and offered a soft, sympathetic smile. Her voice rang out melodically in the hush, carrying both kindness and gravity. "You've come to free this clock from apathy," Paulina said. Her tone was inviting, but her words were a solemn acknowledgment of the crisis. "Callous illusions have trapped hearts here, halting the clock's spirit of unity."

Blunt stepped forward and inclined his head respectfully. Despite the tension in the air, he recognized in Paulina the same type of guiding presence they had encountered before in Tetragor and Zeetrikus. "We overcame ignorance illusions in Monticello," he replied, water-blue eyes steady. "Now empathy is being hampered in Rostock. We stand ready to help." The others fanned out beside him, six cloaks gently billowing in the light breeze.

Paulina's eyes sparkled with sad understanding. She could sense their sincerity. "Exactly. Callous illusions lure good people into ignoring each other's needs," she explained, clasping her hands before her. "Only genuine compassion— swift and without reserve—dissolves them." She turned slightly and gestured toward the silent Astronomical Clock, whose great dial trembled as if in pain. "My illusions will test your willingness to connect," Paulina warned gently.

Reddish stepped forward, a small orb of flame hovering above her palm. "We've seen illusions that push people apart before," she said, recalling prior scenarios where division and isolation were the goal. Her embers flared in determination. "We respond the same way every time: together. We'll offer help the instant it's needed."

Greenie felt waves of emotion emanating from Paulina—sorrow, hope, and empathy all intertwined. It was comforting, even as the fog of indifference thickened around the nave. "Ignorance illusions withheld knowledge from us," Greenie said softly, remembering how Morpheus's riddles tried to deceive. "Callous illusions withhold compassion from those who need it. We won't let that stand, not here." She set her jaw, her heart open and resolute.

Checkered's lens hovered beside her, focused now on Paulina's feet where faint tendrils of dark fog curled. She analyzed the patterns calmly. "So you'll create scenarios of coldness or distance," she inferred. Illusions often followed patterns; she was already anticipating them. "We'll break each one by immediately bridging the divide—no hesitation." She clicked her monocle once in readiness.

Paulina raised one graceful arm, her silver robe catching the morning light with a shimmer. Though her expression remained compassionate, a note of stern challenge entered her eyes. "Prove it," she said simply. The two words hung in the air like a gauntlet. "Accept the illusions that hamper empathy… or tear them down with genuine care." She swept her arm toward the clock, and as she did, cracks of spectral light spiderwebbed across the clock's large circular dial. Her warm countenance bore a hint of urgency now. "This clock thrived on communal bonds; illusions twist that into apathy. Show me that your compassion can untwist it."

Firee inhaled deeply and braced himself. He knew what came next—an onslaught of illusionary scenes designed to ensnare them. "Then let these glamours come," he declared, his cloak's red flames flickering with anticipation. "We'll unify our compassion at the first sign of any need." He gripped his wand, a ribbon of fire twining around his arm, ready to act.

Paulina offered the smallest smile of approval and stepped aside. With a gentle wave of her hand, she revealed the Astronomical Clock's face now fracturing with ghostly lines of light. This is your trial, her eyes seemed to say. "Callous illusions loom. Let your hearts connect swiftly," she whispered, as the thick fog around the nave began to coalesce and form shapes. Paulina's figure grew indistinct among the swirling mist, watching quietly from the sidelines with hope in her eyes.

No further words were needed. The six Wizards drew close, forming a tight circle shoulder-to-shoulder. Their cloaks flared with inner light as each focused on the virtue they represented. They caught each other's eyes briefly, sharing a nod of unwavering resolve. Monticello, Lund, Boston, Philadelphia… in each place, illusions had been dispatched almost instantly by their synergy. This would be no different. Compassion would be their shield and sword here.

A low hiss snaked through the mist as the illusions struck. The thick fog around the clock twisted itself into distinct phantasms, forging frigid scenes of indifference in the space around the Wizards. Paulina Tetrikus's form became a pale silhouette observing from a short distance, her hands clasped as if in prayer. The surroundings dimmed, reality half-giving way to illusion.

Each Wizard quickly found themselves confronted by a personal trial:

Checkered saw an elderly villager apparition struggling to carry a heap of firewood far too heavy for her thin arms. The woman stooped and gasped, dropping sticks as she went. Around Checkered, a whispering voice coiled: "Not your concern… keep moving." It was an invitation to indifference. Checkered's analytical mind recoiled at the cold suggestion. No, she thought, we help immediately. "We help at once," she declared aloud, her decision instant. In her mind she rushed forward, taking part of the burden from the old woman. At that moment, the illusion cracked—literally. The image of the firewood and the struggling villager split like brittle ice, revealing nothing but mist behind it. The false burden evaporated, and the path before Checkered was clear.

Greenie found a small child clutching a tattered doll standing in her way, crying for her mother. The illusion tugged at Greenie's heart even as it tried to fool her mind: "Someone else will help… this isn't your problem," a disembodied murmur suggested. Greenie's nurturing instincts flared hot against that cool temptation. "We stand together. No one is abandoned," she said firmly. She extended her arms and imagined wrapping the lost child in a comforting embrace. A soothing green glow emanated from her cloak as vines of empathic magic wove around the little figure protectively. The crying ceased—and then the child's form faded to smoke within Greenie's gentle hug. The glamour couldn't hold once met with genuine concern.

Reddish was encircled by an illusion of two townsfolk locked in a vicious argument. A man and a woman shouted at each other, voices rising with anger and hurt. Ghostly onlookers stood by and did nothing. An insidious whisper drifted toward Reddish: "Don't interfere… it's their issue, not yours." She felt the temptation to remain an uninvolved bystander, but only for a split second. Not a chance, Reddish thought. She calmly stepped between the two quarreling figures. With a gentle push of her hands, she released a pulse of warm, calming magic—her embers casting a soft glow that bathed both combatants. "No more callousness here," she said softly. The illusory man and woman slowed their shouting, faces relaxing—then they vanished entirely, melting away into ribbons of mist. The conflict was gone as though it had never been, and the space was quieter for it.

Firee was confronted with an illusion of a shivering beggar boy sitting on a church's steps, ignored by dozens of prosperous townspeople passing by. The boy reached out pleadingly, but every passerby turned away with a huff or an excuse. A cold voice whispered to Firee: "You can't help them all… move along." Firee's eyes narrowed. Perhaps he couldn't help everyone, but he could help this one right now. "We do not stand aside," he growled. With a sweeping motion, Firee summoned a controlled blaze of warmth that whooshed across the scene. The golden fire wasn't to burn – it radiated comfort and hope. It engulfed the beggar and the aloof townsfolk alike in a bright glow. When the flames cleared, the church steps were empty – both the begging child and the indifferent citizens were gone, the cruel mirage dispelled by a wave of compassion.

Blunt found an entire tableau spread before him: a line of weary villagers outside a shuttered clinic, knocking for aid that wouldn't come. Inside, an official in a fine coat shrugged and closed the blinds, turning his back on the sick and injured. "Nothing to be done," a cynical voice sighed around Blunt. "Not your role to fix this." Blunt's heart surged with righteous anger on behalf of the forsaken villagers. "Compassion must unify communities," he proclaimed, raising his wand high. From its tip burst a cascade of pure, clean water that swept gently through the scene—washing over the waiting villagers and right through the clinic's doors. Instead of drenching them, the water carried a sensation of shared understanding and collective care. The illusory official sputtered and vanished under the wave; the villagers' desperate faces flickered out one by one. When the water subsided, Blunt stood alone on wet cobblestones, the oppressive scene gone like a bad dream.

Breezie's illusion was quieter but no less poignant: a lonely elderly woman called out feebly for companionship, but no one came to her. Doors and windows around her slammed shut one by one. A dismissive thought drifted into Breezie's mind: "She's not family… you have other things to do." Breezie felt a pang in his chest. Instead of turning away, he strolled directly toward the forlorn figure. "Why care?" a disembodied voice hissed. Breezie answered by gently kneeling at the woman's side and offering her a friendly arm to lean on. He summoned a tender wind that carried the sound of joyful laughter and the comforting scent of fresh-baked bread – memories of companionship. "You are noticed and loved," he said kindly. The old woman's face lit up just as her form dissipated into the soft breeze. The vision of shuttered homes around them melted away into the mist, the final illusion having fallen.

As each Wizard enacted an immediate gesture of compassion, the frigid phantoms fell apart. Within barely a minute, all six illusory scenarios of isolation had been utterly demolished. The biting cold that had gripped the space lifted. The gray fog lightened and began to evaporate, dawn sunbeams piercing through the stained glass above. Overhead, the church bells gave a single, jubilant peal. The frozen astrolabe wheel resumed its smooth rotation, and the apostle figurines high above began to move along their track once more, their carved eyes suddenly looking more hopeful.

Paulina Tetrikus stepped forward through the last wisps of dispersing mist. She was smiling radiantly, her eyes damp with happy tears. "You overcame callous illusions with swift compassion," she called to them, her voice ringing with approval. One hand rested over her heart as she regarded them with genuine pride. All around, the Astronomical Clock's figures were moving once more. The little automatons on the façade—the Apostles and the central figure of Christ—resumed their gentle motion, and the harsh cold hum was gone, replaced by a warm, steady ticking. Rostock's proud timepiece was alive again with communal spirit.

Paulina approached the group with graceful steps, her silver robe swishing softly over the stone floor. In her palm, she conjured a new object: a bronze gear about the size of a saucer, intricately engraved. She offered it to Blunt with both hands. "Your synergy reawakened empathy here," Paulina said, her voice melodic and firm. The gear's inscription glinted: "Caritas Est Finis" – "Compassion Is the End." "Wherever illusions feed on callousness, carry this symbol. Let it guide you on the road ahead."

Blunt accepted the bronze gear reverently, reading its inscription and feeling the gentle warmth that pulsed from the metal. "Thank you," he replied earnestly. Greenie leaned in at his side to touch the gear as well, and felt that pleasant warmth radiating care. "We'll make sure illusions of indifference don't thrive," Greenie promised, closing her fingers around the gear's edge with a smile. Paulina nodded, clearly satisfied with that answer.

With a small flourish of her hand, Paulina then conjured a swirling portal near the clock's base – their doorway back to Philadelphia. The edges of the portal shimmered in golden-white, showing the faint outline of the Grand Court beyond. It was time for them to return and ensure the Wanamaker Clock was fully freed.

Reddish's eyes glowed like coals in the dawn light as she reflected on their rapid double victory. "Let illusions try anywhere else," she said, chin lifted proudly. "We'll respond with compassion, without delay, every time." There was a confident fervor in her stance, embers dancing along her cloak's trim.

Firee took one last sweeping glance around Rostock's now-brightening church. The church's caretaker and a couple of early worshippers were peeking in from a side door now, their faces curious but noticeably kinder than before. No shadows of illusion lurked. Firee breathed out in relief. "All clear here," he affirmed, dispelling the lingering ember at his wand's tip. "Time to return to Philadelphia and check on the Wanamaker Clock's final state."

Checkered peered at the new bronze gear in Blunt's hand, tilting her head as she mentally cross-referenced it with their growing collection of clues. "Caritas… bridging hearts," she murmured, running her finger over the Latin phrase. "Another key to illusions undone." She recalled how each virtue they'd gathered – humility, innovation, curiosity, and now compassion – had been instrumental in unraveling waves of deception. This new piece clearly fit the puzzle of the Dark Harlequin's overarching scheme.

Breezie was first to step into the gently swirling portal. "No illusions remain here," he observed with a satisfied grin. "Rostock's clock stands free and warm again." He gave Paulina a polite bow. She returned it with a gracious smile as, one by one, the rest of the team followed Breezie into the portal's embrace. Paulina watched them depart, silver robe shimmering in the new daylight, before she too vanished – a guardian pleased with the triumph of compassion she had just witnessed.

In a flash of light and a familiar stomach-turning twist, the Wizards traversed the star-flecked pathways between worlds and emerged back in Philadelphia's Grand Court under a dusky violet evening sky. It was as though no time had passed at all here – dusk had deepened to early night.

The Wanamaker Grand Court Clock greeted them with its dignified silhouette at the center of the hall. Immediately the six noted the difference: its mechanical figures were gently moving, not frozen. The entire clock exuded an aura of calm. The bitter chill that had earlier seeped from it was gone, replaced by a mild, pleasant hush. People strolled by with easy, welcoming manners – a few glanced curiously at the clock's now-animated tableau and at the reappearing Wizards in their colorful cloaks, but continued on with warm smiles and friendly nods to one another. The oppressive sense of apathy that had gripped the Grand Court was nowhere to be felt.

Blunt still held Paulina's bronze gear from Rostock. He cradled it carefully, its warmth bleeding through his gloves. As he looked up at Philadelphia's freed clock, he thought of how swiftly they had undone the illusions there and abroad. "We overcame illusions of callousness," he said quietly, confirming to himself that their earlier efforts here had succeeded. "The Wanamaker clock should be stable now."

Reddish stepped forward, her boots tapping the marble tiles that only hours ago felt unnaturally cold. Now the air was still and temperate. She inhaled deeply; the atmosphere even smelled different, carrying a hint of perfume and polished brass rather than that prior staleness. "No illusions hamper empathy here anymore," she announced, a faint, satisfied grin gracing her lips. Each Wizard took a moment to attune their senses. Indeed, the Grand Court's mechanical marvel once again radiated a gentle spirit of compassion. The subtle shift was almost palpable – like a weight lifting off the entire hall.

Night settled fully as they observed the transformed scene. Dusk's last golden glow had faded, giving way to soft lamplight that illuminated the Wanamaker Clock in shades of silver and blue. Philadelphia's clock was freed. Each of its mechanical figures—soldiers, scholars, jesters—moved with renewed grace and purpose, exactly as John Wanamaker intended when he unveiled it over a century ago. The Wizards gathered quietly at its base, savoring the gentle tick and whirr that now sounded comforting and warm.

Checkered activated her monocle one more time to scan for any lingering traces of illusion magic. She circled the clock slowly, lens gleaming as it found nothing but clean, normal energy. "All clear," she reported, her voice tinged with relief and fatigue. "Its compassion is intact—no more icy hum." The haunting vibration that had set everyone on edge earlier was completely gone.

Greenie placed her palm tenderly against a bronze figurine of a scholar offering a helping hand to a poor man—one of the clock's many little scenes. The metal felt gently warm to her touch. She closed her eyes and sensed only the benign intention of the design, the caritas that Wanamaker meant to inspire. "It's warm again," she said softly, smiling. Her empathic intuition picked up no lingering malice, only the honest emotions of people going about their evening. "No illusions hinder it now."

Reddish's cloak of flames had dimmed to a comfortable glow. She ran her fingers through her hair, which sparkled faintly with soot-like magic. "They tried to freeze hearts here," she reflected, remembering how a cold apathy had almost settled permanently. The thought made her shiver – only now in retrospect. "We overcame them so swiftly." She looked at her friends, pride shining in her ember-bright eyes. In Rostock and Philadelphia alike, their synergy had made those illusions vanish almost the moment they appeared.

Breezie chuckled, a gentle breeze lifting the edges of his cloak as if in celebration. He playfully ruffled one of the decorative banners hanging from an upper balcony. "It was the same approach as Monticello and Boston," he remarked. "Illusions appear, we unify—illusions end." He snapped his fingers, and the banner fluttered. "Compassion overcame callousness in a heartbeat this time."

Firee scanned the hall, where a few late passersby were now pausing to admire the Wanamaker Clock's gentle motion. A small cluster of children in the Grand Court pointed and laughed as one figure—a court jester—tipped his hat on the quarter chime. An elderly couple stood near the great bronze eagle statue at the court's center, watching with contented smiles. Firee nodded in satisfaction. "They sense no tension here now," he observed, meaning not just the onlookers but the city as a whole. The illusions had never gotten a chance to truly take root and sow distrust. "We didn't give those phantoms any time to dig in."

Blunt turned slowly, gazing over the softly lit Grand Court. He recalled how in earlier adventures they had sometimes struggled to identify or agree on how to defeat an illusion. But here—and in Rostock—they had acted without a second's doubt. "We're getting better at this," he said quietly, almost to himself. "At the first hint of an illusion, we act. We don't wait or second-guess anymore." He allowed himself a small, pleased smile. It was true; their growth was evident.

Checkered slipped her notebook from a pocket and scribbled a brief final note: Philadelphia – Compassion triumphs, illusions 0. She snapped it shut and sighed contentedly. "And because we refused every attempt to make us apathetic, no illusion survived more than a moment," she said. "They rely on people just accepting the situation or hesitating. We gave them none of that." She tapped the notebook for emphasis.

Greenie let her attention wander to the street outside, visible through the Grand Court's doors. A few families were still chatting under the shopfront awnings, and bright laughter drifted from a nearby café where a group of friends lingered. A soft sense of peace settled in her chest. "Philadelphia's clock stands for compassion again. Wanamaker's vision is alive and well," she said. Indeed, John Wanamaker's hope of a community brought together by the gentle lessons of this clock was fulfilled once more tonight.

A profound hush fell over the hall then, but it was a peaceful one, resonant with the quiet whir of gears no longer corrupted by any dark influence. The Wizards took a collective breath and recognized the tableau for what it was: another illusions wave ended, another city's legacy saved. They had united swiftly and compassionately, ensuring that no deception found footing in hearts that refused to grow cold.

After a moment, they regrouped with the unspoken understanding that their work here was done. As the Wanamaker Clock began to chime the hour – a sweet, mild tune that floated through Philadelphia's twilight – the six lingered at the monument's base, reflecting on how this chapter of their journey had unfolded.

Each of them couldn't help but think back to illusions from earlier challenges: corruption in Monticello, stagnation in Lund, ignorance in Boston. Now they had confronted callousness here in Philadelphia (and its mirror in Rostock) and dismantled it just as swiftly.

Reddish allowed her inner flame to dim to mere embers. "Those compassion illusions were easier than I expected," she admitted, breaking the silence. She realized with some surprise that it was true. "They tried to lure us into indifference, but we spotted it immediately and refused."

Greenie's cloak glowed a gentle green in agreement. "We recognized each scenario: someone needed help and the illusion whispered 'do nothing.' The moment any of us stepped in, the illusion unraveled completely," she said. It warmed her to realize how automatic it had become for them to respond with care.

Checkered flipped back a few pages in her ledger, scanning their past encounters. "Yes. In Monticello and Boston, we learned that acting together at once made those illusions fail. Here, illusions of callousness collapsed as soon as we extended a hand or a kind word," she noted, capping her pen with a decisive click.

Firee gave a relaxed, boyish grin – a rarity during their intense travels. "Our synergy basically means illusions never get to take root now," he said. "Whether it's a single conjured scene or an entire wave across a city, these phantoms fade under immediate response." He twirled his extinguished wand with a flourish.

Blunt crossed his arms and considered the pattern of their trials thoughtfully. "We've seen illusions test moral virtues, intellect, emotions… The Dark Harlequin might attempt to throw all of them at us at once eventually," he mused, thinking aloud about the rumored master orchestrating things from the shadows. "Ignorance, corruption, callousness – perhaps even more. But each time, we respond together at the first sign, and illusions crumble." He nodded firmly, as if convincing himself further.

Breezie folded his arms and let a gentle breeze swirl around the group in the hall's warm lamplight. "So I guess we just keep doing exactly that," he said lightly. "Until even the most cunning illusion can't muster any effect on anyone." He gave a playful shrug. "Tonight we pretty much made illusions disappear in seconds again."

A sense of calm pride suffused them. Each remembered early in their quest when illusions sometimes confounded or delayed them. Now those same tricks barely lasted a heartbeat under their united front. They had become adept – forging an unstoppable synergy. Monticello's corruption illusions had been snuffed out quickly, Boston's ignorance illusions even faster, and now callousness illusions in Philadelphia and

Rostock had evaporated almost immediately. The six of them together were simply too swift and too cohesive for any lie to hold.

Greenie exhaled a small sigh of relief. "It feels right," she said softly. "If illusions return in new guises, we'll meet them the same way. That's our formula now: immediate, unified action."

Checkered tucked her hair behind one ear and smiled wryly. "Illusions rely on hesitation or doubt," she said. "We give them none. It's no wonder they fall apart instantly." She pocketed her lens; there was nothing more to analyze here.

Above, the Wanamaker Clock's mechanical figures continued their gentle cycles of movement, each one now once again a little portrayal of compassion in action. A soldier figurine raised his sword in salute to a scholar, who tipped his book in return. A tiny family tableau showed a mother hugging a child. All around the dial, these symbols of empathy rotated faithfully. The Wizards watched for a quiet moment, taking satisfaction in having preserved this iconic piece of Philadelphia's heritage.

At length, Checkered's keen eyes spotted something half-buried among a few fallen autumn leaves near the clock's pedestal. "What's this?" she murmured, stepping over and crouching down. Blunt joined her, brushing aside the leaves.

There, glinting in the lamplight, was a small brass plate covered in engraved letters. Time and weather had worn it, but they could just make it out: "Humanitas Sive Nexum: Rises?"

Blunt read it aloud slowly. "Humanity or Connection: rises?" he translated roughly, brow furrowing. It sounded like a riddle or motto. Greenie leaned over his shoulder, her empathic sense flickering with a faint unease as she regarded the cryptic phrase. "Likely another illusions breadcrumb," she guessed. They all remembered that after each victory, some clue had been left behind – a hint of the next challenge to come.

Reddish folded her arms, a spark of frustration in her eyes. "So the mastermind is laying out the next test," she said. "Illusions plan something bigger, maybe trying to unify themes. It's like they're teasing what's ahead." She huffed, then managed a grin. "Whatever it is, we'll handle it the second it starts. We've shown we won't give them any chance to build."

Checkered had already drawn out her notebook and carefully copied the Latin words. "Humanitas sive nexum…Humanity or connection," she mused as she wrote. "It might hint at the next illusions wave – perhaps another historic site or clock that deals with uniting people." She underlined nexum, thinking of bonds or perhaps networks of people.

Firee gently took the brass plate from Blunt and slipped it into his satchel for safekeeping. The metal was cool now, inert, but who knew what power the clue held for the future. He gave a reassuring smile. "We overcame illusions in Monticello, Boston, Philadelphia, Rostock," he recounted. "Wherever this next hint leads – even if illusions try combining everything – we'll be ready."

Blunt nodded and felt the synergy gear under his cloak pulse softly in agreement. "We'll stay prepared," he affirmed. "Whenever illusions reappear, we respond as we do now: immediate, unified, thorough. That kills illusions on contact, every time."

Breezie cast a gentle breeze to scatter the remaining leaves around the clock, making sure nothing else was hidden. The air was clear; no trickery lingered. "All's quiet now," he confirmed contentedly. "If the next illusions wave is bigger or more complex, we're ready for it." He felt it in his bones – they all did. They had become a formidable force for truth and virtue.

Greenie slipped her arm through Checkered's in a gesture of sisterly pride. "If the illusions try to combine ignorance, callousness, or whatever else, we'll just unite all the virtues we've learned – compassion, curiosity, humility, innovation – without delay." She looked around at her friends. They each carried a piece of that puzzle within them now.

Checkered stifled a yawn – the long day and evening were catching up to her at last. She slid her pen back into its loop and placed a hand on the now-benign clock base. "At least for now, Philadelphia's safe," she said softly. The bronze felt normal, even pleasantly warm under her fingertips. "The clock breathes empathy again." She allowed herself a smile. "Let whatever illusions come next do their worst – we know exactly how to handle them."

That settled, the six took a final, loving look at the Wanamaker Grand Court Clock. Its melodic chimes were just dying away, echoing through the quiet hall. The time was nearing midnight; the Grand Court was nearly empty save for them and the statues.

Reddish conjured a tiny flame at her fingertip and idly flicked it into the crisp night air beyond the doors. It winked out harmlessly, symbolizing the final extinguishing of this wave of illusions. "We'll decipher that plate's meaning when the time comes," she said, glancing in the direction of Blunt's satchel where the clue now rested. "Meanwhile, this city is free of callous illusions." She flashed a grin, acknowledging the small yet important victory they'd earned.

Blunt drew in a deep breath and then let it out slowly, his shoulders relaxing for what felt like the first time that day. He looked fondly at each of his companions – his friends – in turn. "Then we move on," he said decisively. "If callousness or any other illusion crops up somewhere else, we'll quell it just as we did here. Another job well done." They exchanged nods and small smiles. The adrenaline of battle was ebbing, replaced by a warm glow of accomplishment and camaraderie.

Above, a few stars were beginning to peek out between sparse clouds, visible through the atrium's glass ceiling. Outside on Market Street, the city had returned to its normal calm state – the last shop lights were going dark, and only the streetlamps burned. The Wizards gathered themselves and stepped out of the Grand Court, heading toward the road that would lead them to their next destination – wherever that might be.

At the corner, they paused beneath a wrought-iron streetlamp where Market Street began again. Its glow cast long shadows behind them – six silhouettes united as one. They took in the peaceful city scene one last time. Another wave of illusions had been faced and defeated. Synergy had prevailed once more.

They knew not to get complacent, of course. New signals would come – the magical Prague Orloj that had first set them on this quest would surely call on them again soon, or perhaps that cryptic brass plate would guide them. But they also knew that wherever illusions might next appear, they would respond instantly with compassion, with curiosity, with every virtue they had earned – in short, with synergy. They would let no veil of deceit fester in any heart or any historic clock across the world.

With that silent promise among them, they ventured off into the moonlit city beyond. The Harlequin wizards – Blunt, Reddish, Firee, Checkered, Breezie, and Greenie – moved as a relaxed unit, cloaks shimmering softly against the darkness. They talked quietly of Paulina's kind eyes, of how swiftly they'd dispatched the illusions, and of what the Dark Harlequin might try next.

Their voices faded into the distance as Philadelphia's great clock chimed a final gentle quarter-hour behind them, a soft benediction on the night. "Compassion's Triumph," indeed, had been achieved here. The spirit of empathy was unbound and shining.

Thus, the Wizards' latest quest ended in quiet victory. Philadelphia's venerable clock ticked on in harmonious serenity, once more a beacon of community care. The six friends marched onward into the night, illusions undone in minutes and their synergy truly unstoppable – each step drawing them nearer to the grand climax of their illusion-quelling journey.

Chapter 9

Rostock's Trial – Compassion's Final Test

Answering the Wooden Clock

A lonely hush draped the world as twilight fell. The lantern's flame bent eastward in the breeze, drawing the young wizards along frost-silvered roads toward the Baltic port. They entered the market square of Rostock just as day's last golden light met the edge of winter. Locals moved about their market stalls with mechanical routine. Each greeting and footfall was muted, as if a cold haze had settled over the town's usual warmth. Blunt, Reddish, Firee, Checkered, Breezie, and Greenie gathered at the square's center, Harlequin cloaks shimmering faintly in the amber glow. They had triumphed over a wave of callous illusions in Hazleton that morning, yet an intuition—like a lantern's subtle pull—had led them here to complete compassion's final test. This was compassion's final trial—the very challenge quietly foreshadowed on their path. Now, as they surveyed the scene, a frosty breath of indifference hung in the air, stilling voices and chilling the late autumn breeze.

Greenie drew her cloak tighter, her empathic senses reaching into the quiet. Beneath the clatter of hooves on cobblestone and the vendors' subdued chatter, she felt tension and isolation: neighbors who should be jovial kept to themselves, eyes averted. This town thrives on unity, she thought, yet something is smothering its heart. Indeed, where laughter or friendly banter might normally echo, there was only muffled silence – as if compassion here had been frozen under glass.

Checkered's keen gaze flicked from one clustered group to another. At a corner stall, two townsfolk argued over produce prices while others passed by without so much as a consoling glance. Across the way, an old man dropped a sack of kindling and struggled, ignored by those next to him.

For a heartbeat, none of the onlookers moved to help—but Greenie did. Without hesitation, she slipped through the chill and knelt at the old man's side, gently gathering the scattered kindling back into his sack. The elder started in surprise at this sudden kindness, then managed a grateful, trembling smile as she offered him a steady arm to regain his feet. Breezie quietly retrieved a stray stick that had rolled away, placing it atop the pile with a reassuring nod. Around them, the other townsfolk carried on, scarcely noticing even this act of care. As the old man shuffled away with his bundle clutched to his chest, Blunt cocked his head at a faint sound from above. The wooden clock tower's next tick came a breath late, as if the timepiece's heart had faltered. An instant later, another tick followed—stronger and truer—slipping subtly back into rhythm, as though the clock itself were heartened by the timely act of care.

"Paulina Tetrikus must be near," Checkered murmured, recognizing the pattern of apathy that had plagued Hazleton. Illusory tendrils of callousness were winding through the city, coaxing everyone to mind only their own affairs. A pine-tinged mist curled around her feet as she spoke, the air's bite pricking at her nose. Callous illusions feed on people turning away, she reflected, lips set in determination.

Reddish stepped up beside Checkered, her amber eyes catching a warped reflection in a shuttered window. A thin film of ice clung to the glass, distorting the faces of a mother and child inside who sat back-to-back, each unaware of the other's quiet despair. Reddish's heart twinged at the sight. "It's strangling their bonds," she said softly. A lick of crimson flame danced at her fingertips in answer to her rising resolve. Though she spoke quietly, the promise in her voice was clear: they would thaw this unnatural frost. Compassion will find a way through. Her flickering ember cast a gentle glow on the snow-dusted sill, a tiny warmth against the encroaching chill.

Breezie exhaled and a breath of wind spiraled outward, stirring the mist that clung to the ground. In that swirl he glimpsed the same unsettling stillness—neighbors failing to meet each other's eyes, doors closing where help might have entered. "A coldness is creeping in," he observed under his breath. Even as he spoke, his breeze swept past a lamppost, and hoarfrost crackled on the iron as if to affirm his words. Breezie closed his eyes, feeling the unusual heaviness to the air. Empathy is being stifled here, undone by something heartless. The six friends exchanged knowing looks. However subtle this illusion of indifference was, they had seen its like before. In unison, their cloaks pulsed with gentle light, remembering how swiftly a genuine act of care had shattered similar glooms in the past.

Blunt stepped forward, planting his staff firmly in the cobblestones. "We've seen what apathy can do," he said quietly, recalling Hazleton's haunted square at daybreak. His hazel eyes traveled up the road toward an old wooden clock tower silhouetted against the dimming sky. The carvings on that clock were just visible—a procession of wooden figures now motionless in the gathering dusk. Blunt felt a faint vibration in the air, as if the clock itself were calling out to them. "Another challenge awaits in the heart of that clock," he continued solemnly. Around them, the evening deepened and the city seemed to hold its breath. The six Wizards nodded to one another. In that silent accord, compassion kindled between them like a shared flame. No matter how frigid the illusion that gripped this place, they would answer it with warmth. Together, they pressed inward toward the clock tower, every sense on alert. The air grew colder with each step, a frosty gloom thickening as if to meet them – but the young wizards carried a lantern of empathy in their hearts, and its glow would not be denied.

Across Market and Mist

Rostock's narrow lanes lay under a veil of unnatural stillness. Normally, warm lamplight and friendly gossip would cozy the twilight, but now each alley felt dim and estranged. The six companions fanned out gently across the square, moving as silent sentinels. A fleeting motion caught Greenie's eye: down one cobblestone path, a woman in a silver-grey robe slipped between market stalls, her form half-lost in swirling fog. Paulina Tetrikus—the Antiquarian of Compassion—glided at the edge of sight. Though the mist distorted her outline, an aura of gentle sorrow radiated from her, like moonlight behind clouds. She was leading them, intentionally or not, toward the old churchyard beyond the square.

Blunt motioned with two fingers, and they followed in formation. The last rays of dusk clung to the red-brick rooftops as they passed shuttered shops and silent doorways. The closer they drew to Paulina's path, the stronger the chill became. Thin rimes of ice crystallized along wrought-iron railings and the edges of windowpanes. Breezie drifted to the front, raising his hand. A soft wind gusted forward at his command, pushing aside tendrils of mist curling through an alley. By the light of a solitary streetlamp, they saw Paulina's silhouette pause at the far end, beside a wrought-iron gate that led toward the Astronomical Clock. She's guiding us to the clock tower, Blunt thought, heart steady.

From nearby lanes, the illusion's influence pressed in, testing their resolve even as they walked. Greenie's empathic magic spread like unseen vines along the ground, sensing ripples of discontent. Through cracks beneath stout wooden doors, she caught fragments of petty quarrels and muffled sobs. "Neighbors are bickering over trivial matters," she whispered, "and no one stops to soothe them." She could feel how these small abandonments fed the greater illusion, like dry kindling to a fire.

Reddish's eyes narrowed as she scanned the deepening shadows. By a shuttered bakery she spotted a pale figure huddled on the stoop—a young illusion of a child, head in hands, that vanished the instant someone might have noticed. Across the lane, another phantom flickered: an old woman struggling with a heavy bucket while passersby—real and illusion alike—turned aside. Reddish's auburn curls crackled with static as her anger rose. "If the illusion urges us to ignore a cry for help," she said under her breath, "we'll answer by reaching out." Her resolve glowed in the coals of her wand. There would be no hesitation—she was already preparing to act.

Checkered's monocle gleamed as she focused on a faint shimmer near a lamppost. Two ghostly townsfolk stood there in heated argument, while around them other silhouettes walked past with noses in the air. The scholar in Checkered bristled at the obvious pattern: these were tests, conjured scenes to provoke indifference. "They're traps for the heart," she warned quietly. "Illusions to see if we'll walk by. We must not let them anchor." As if in agreement, Firee's ruby cloak flared behind her. "Not a single one," he muttered. A spark snapped at his fingertips, reflecting his impatience to confront the invisible foe. They all remembered Hazleton's lesson: the instant compassion was shown, the illusion of apathy had cracked. Here and now, they intended to do the same without delay.

The group pressed on through the labyrinth of cottages and shops, alert and united. With each turn, a new scene of quiet despair or discord appeared—apparitions cast like bait into the twilight. And at each step, the Wizards answered with living empathy. Checkered broke away briefly to lift that phantom bucket from the elderly woman's grasp, offering a gentle smile before both woman and burden faded into fine mist. Not a heartbeat later, Reddish knelt beside the mirage of the crying child, wrapping the little figure in the comforting heat of her cloak. "You're not alone," she whispered, and the child's sobbing silhouette dissolved into light. Breezie sent a bracing current of wind between the two arguing specters by the lamppost, clearing their heated voices into silence; in the sudden calm, the quarreling illusion lost all substance. At the same time, Firee came upon an apparition of a shivering elder slumped against a wall. Without a word, he shrugged off his own cloak and draped it over the faint form, conjuring a gentle warmth that melted the ice from the cobbles beneath the old man's feet. A grateful smile creased the illusion's face an instant before it vanished like breath on a mirror.

Each compassionate act was simple and small, yet in those moments the oppressive haze recoiled. The illusions that prowled these lanes had no answer for such immediate kindness. One by one, they flickered and died, leaving only faint traces behind—a single dry tear warming on the stone, a glimmer of light where there had been shadow. As the six friends regrouped near the churchyard gate, the air around them felt ever so slightly lighter. Kindness, however brief, had begun to thaw the frost. Even the townsfolk hidden behind closed doors seemed to stir with a bit more empathy, as if unconsciously touched by the gentle ripple the Wizards sent through the night.

A wrought-iron gate creaked open ahead. Paulina Tetrikus stood just beyond, in the broad yard of the church where the great wooden clock tower rose. She turned her veiled face toward the six, her eyes sorrowful but proud. The final vestiges of mist swirled about her feet. Beyond her, the Astronomical Clock inside St. Mary's Church in Rostock waited in eerie stillness. Its carved constellations and figures were already dimmed under a glaze of rime, the entire tower exuding a chill. Paulina lifted one slender hand, beckoning them through the gate. The time for subtle tests was over; the heart of the illusion lay here, bound into the ancient clock, and it was here that compassion would face its ultimate trial.

The Kindness Trial

Inside the churchyard, an uncanny quiet reigned. Twilight had faded to night, and a few snowflakes drifted in the lantern light as if time itself had slowed. Rostock's famed

Astronomical Clock towered before the Wizards, its carved figures and intricate dials silenced under an enchantment of ice. For five centuries, since the clockmaker Hans Düringer built it in 1472, this timepiece had faithfully marked the hours — until tonight. Normally, at noon each day, the clock's carved figures would spring to life: a skeleton representing Death would toll a bell, and the twelve apostles would parade out before a central figure of Christ who raised His hand in blessing for each – all except the last apostle, Judas, for whom the door would remain closed. It was a centuries-old ritual of time and faith that reminded the city of life's precious brevity. But now the clock stood silent and still. No figures moved in their alcoves, and no cheerful chime rang out—only the distant rustle of barren branches broke the silence. The sight sent a pang through Greenie's chest. This timepiece had guided the city for generations; seeing it so stilled felt like beholding a heart turned to stone.

Paulina Tetrikus stepped forward beneath the clock's great zodiac dial. In the gloom her silver-grey robes caught the lantern glow, shimmering as if woven from the very mist. Her gentle face was partially obscured by a hood, but the concern etched there was evident. At her feet, faint spectral scenes continued to flicker—illusions of townsfolk in need, replaying and multiplying as the source of the magic fought to keep hold. Paulina's voice was soft and clear, carrying across the cold air: "Callous illusions creep here, severing hearts from one another." As she spoke, one phantom tableau beside her showed two neighbors turning away from each other with folded arms and cold eyes. Paulina swept her arm sadly through it, and the vision scattered into icy motes. "Left unchecked, this apathy would spread until no one feels another's pain."

The six Wizards formed a half-circle facing her, their breath rising in pale puffs in the frigid night. They understood well – this was the very illusion they had battled earlier, now concentrated and desperate. Blunt could feel the lingering malignance like pins and needles on his skin. But more powerful was the warmth glowing in his chest: the unshakable knowledge of what must be done. "We will not let it take root," Blunt vowed quietly. Reddish placed one hand over her heart, her wand hand already igniting in a calm, steady flame. "No hesitation," she affirmed. Firee clenched a fist and nodded. Checkered adjusted her monocle, eyes bright with resolve; Greenie and Breezie exchanged a reassuring glance. One after another, each of the six pledged in their own few words or determined silence the very same promise: that at the first sign of need, they would respond with genuine compassion. No whispered lie or chilling glamour would tempt them into indifference. They were here to care, immediately and wholeheartedly, until this illusion broke like thawing ice.

Paulina's solemn expression softened at their declarations. Her eyes gleamed with a mix of sorrow and hope, as if she carried both the weight of those still suffering and the belief that these brave souls before her could lift that weight at last. For an instant, she simply looked at them—six young faces set with courage against the dark. In their determined stance she saw the reflection of every virtue they had gathered on their journey: humility in their lack of boastfulness, innovation in their creative approach to each rescue, curiosity in how they sought out every hidden hurt, perseverance in the way they never gave up—and now compassion shining as the sum of all those lights. Paulina exhaled, a puff of silver mist leaving her lips. Satisfied by their resolve, she inclined her head. "Let the test begin," she said softly.

With a graceful turn, Paulina led them toward a low stone bench at the base of the clock. A dim lantern hung there on an iron hook, its flame quivering against the surrounding cold. Beside the lantern sat a small wooden table dusted with snow, and on the table lay two rolled parchments secured with simple ribbon. The scene was oddly intimate: an impromptu study set in the shadow of the towering clock, as if a teacher had prepared one last lesson for her students before the final exam. The Wizards gathered around, the lantern's light painting gentle highlights on their cheeks. Its orange glow revealed warm hope in some eyes, steely determination in others, and in all of them, the reflection of that tiny flame steady against the dark. Paulina stood across from them, hands lightly resting on the parchments. "Compassion is nurtured by understanding," she said quietly. "Before you face these illusions fully, remember the lessons that guide you."

She picked up the first scroll and passed it to Greenie. "We begin with a tale you've heard before—The Sparrow and the Valley of Stone. We read it in Hazleton this morning, but under this night's silence its truth may shine anew." Greenie accepted the parchment reverently. Though she knew this fable, she understood why Paulina wanted it revisited: some lessons deepen each time they are reflected on. Greenie carefully unrolled the scroll across the table. The parchment crackled slightly, releasing the faint scent of aged ink. Everyone drew closer, shoulders nearly touching, as Greenie's soft voice rose to read by lanternlight.

"The Sparrow and the Valley of Stone"

In the Valley of Stone, sunlight burned relentlessly, leaving the earth cracked and lifeless. Here dwelled creatures whose hearts had long ago dried into hard shells of indifference.

Lizards basked alone on brittle rocks, coyotes prowled in bitter solitude, and even the cacti stood rigid, their spines sharp and unyielding. "It has always been so," they murmured, resigned to a world drained of tenderness.

Yet into this parched land fluttered Elara, a small sparrow with feathers the color of dawn and a heart radiant with compassion. Wherever she flew, she spread whispers of hope, but they scattered on deaf ears and closed hearts. Undeterred, Elara searched tirelessly, sensing a hidden truth beneath the barren land.

The hot winds mocked her efforts, hissing cruelly through the valley, "Give up, foolish bird. Compassion cannot soften stone."

Still, Elara refused to yield. One starlit night, guided by her unshakable empathy, she felt a pulse beneath the valley's crust, like the distant heartbeat of the earth itself. Landing softly, she pecked gently at the ground. Soon, a trickle emerged, tiny but miraculous—a secret spring concealed deep below.

The creatures watched skeptically. "It will vanish," hissed the lizard. "It is nothing but trickery," growled the coyote. Yet day by day, Elara continued her humble work, carefully widening the tiny stream with tireless effort.

Gradually, curiosity softened the valley's hardened inhabitants. The cactus leaned closer, offering shade to the tireless sparrow. The lizard, intrigued by her perseverance, cleared loose pebbles from her path. The coyote, moved by her gentle strength, dug into the hard earth beside her. Through shared purpose, claws and spines, paws and feathers united in harmony—each creature contributing what it could.

Finally, the spring surged forth, clear and abundant, cascading joyously into the valley. Life blossomed rapidly, softening not only the land but also the once-callous hearts of those who lived there. Flowers bloomed where despair had taken root, laughter echoed where silence had reigned, and the formerly solitary beings discovered the warmth of community.

Elara, her mission fulfilled, perched contentedly upon a flowering branch. "Compassion," she sang gently, "is the hidden water that nourishes all life. Together, we flourish. Divided, we wither."

And from that day forward, the Valley of Stone was remembered not for its callous past, but as the Valley of Renewal—where compassion flowed as freely as the waters that restored their world.

Greenie's voice trailed off, and for a few breaths the only sound was the quiet sputtering of the lantern. She held the parchment tenderly, as if feeling the weight of Elara's journey settle into her own heart. "Even a desert of indifference can be restored," Greenie whispered. The image of that tiny sparrow pecking persistently at stone seemed to hover in the cold air around them. She thought of Hazleton's illusions that morning, how a single act of reaching out had started to crack the ice of apathy. "Elara brought everyone together to help," Greenie continued, eyes shining. "The moment someone dared to care, the illusion of a lifeless valley lost its hold." And indeed, in Hazleton they had witnessed the same truth: one spark of compassion had rallied many.

Paulina nodded, a gentle smile warming her features. "Exactly so." With great care she took the first scroll from Greenie and drew out the second one. This parchment's edges gleamed with a faint hoarfrost in the lantern's glow, as though it had been waiting for a winter night such as this. She placed it into Reddish's eager hands. "And now The Shroud of Indifference," Paulina said. "A poem to reinforce compassion's quiet magic. Read it aloud, and let each verse remind you how empathy thaws what is frozen."

Reddish unrolled the scroll and cleared her throat softly. A chill breeze sighed across the churchyard as if listening. In a clear, low voice, she began to read the poem's title and lines, the lantern light winking with each measured word.

"The Shroud of Indifference"

*In winter's grip a **shroud** was spun,*
A veil of ice concealing pain,
Where hearts lay encased in silent frost,
Each plea in darkness cried in vain.

Silent suffering lingered unseen,
Cries hung like breath in frigid air,

Cold indifference gripped the land,
No one remembered how to care.

Yet deep within the brittle chill,
A single spark began to glow—
The quiet warmth of tender care,
A seed of kindness in the snow.

It spread gently from heart to heart,
Melting bitter ice with grace,
Until compassion thawed the frost,
Revealing truths time can't erase.

As warmth dissolved the icy veil,
Illusions shattered, clear and bright:
When hearts unite in empathy,
They bring the world from dark to light.

No cruelty stands where love abides,
No frost remains once kindness grows;
Gentle warmth heals the deepest wounds,
And through it, humanity flows.

Reddish let the final verses echo into the silence. The imagery of the poem lingered like a breath visible in the cold—fading slowly, but not before everyone had felt its truth. Breezie closed his eyes, picturing that "veil of ice" splitting apart under the force of many caring hands. Firee's fingers drummed lightly on the table, each line stirring memories of illusions they'd defeated: ignorance's shadows, injustice's storms, and now this chill of apathy. They all sensed the gentle power woven through the poem's rhymes. Compassion did not arrive as a roaring fire or a sudden thunderbolt; it started as a spark, a small steady glow that spread from one person to the next, melting even a vast frozen gloom.

"For when hearts unite, no illusion endures," Reddish said under her breath, almost as if to herself. The lantern's flame quivered, and in that moment each of them absorbed the poem's promise: No frost remains once kindness grows. Blunt exhaled a breath he hadn't realized he was holding. He thought of the Dark Harlequin—the faceless puppeteer behind these trials—and felt a quiet confidence take root. Whatever final illusion that foe might weave, it could be unraveled by the same patient warmth described in these lines.

A hush fell over the group after the reading. Paulina closed her eyes as if in brief prayer, then opened them with renewed clarity. "You hold the lessons now," she murmured, her voice reverent in the wintry stillness. "A sparrow's hope, a lantern's glow, a thawing shroud—each teaches the choice before you." Slowly, she rolled up the frosted scroll and set it aside. When she looked at the Wizards again, her demeanor had changed subtly. The kind mentor was still there, but in her poise was also the firm resolve of an antiquarian about to administer a final examination. "Compassion or callousness," Paulina said, raising one hand. "Show me which prevails." In response to her words, the surrounding air trembled, and out of the corners of the yard the spectral figures of indifference began to gather once more. The trial's last wave was imminent.

The six friends straightened and squared their shoulders. They could feel the illusion's power eddying around them now, drawn to Paulina's summons. Checkered quickly tightened her ponytail, her analytical mind already anticipating the patterns these tests might take. Greenie placed a calming palm against her own chest, centering her empathic energy and preparing to project it outward at a moment's notice. Firee and Reddish each let a trickle of elemental magic—warmth and flame—flow through their wands, ready to deploy kindness in any form needed. Breezie and Blunt exchanged a final look of steady assurance. They had done all this earlier and would do it again, as many times as it took. In their minds echoed the refrain: no hesitation, only heart.

Paulina swept her arm in a gentle arc and stepped back. The lantern on the table fluttered and dimmed as the chill in the yard intensified. "Stand fast," she said softly. Her silver figure seemed to blur into the background as the true test began. "Show these illusions the warmth that dwells in you. Show them now, or be lost in the frost." At her final word, a sudden gust howled through the churchyard, carrying with it a flurry of snow and six distinct scenes of need that surged toward the young wizards from every direction.

Scenarios of the Heart

A cluster of spectral images burst to life around the clock tower, each one a moving tableau of loneliness or strife, each demanding immediate empathy. In the first, a middle-aged man sat on the ground a few paces from Checkered, face buried in his hands. Though just a phantom, he radiated despair so palpable that Checkered felt her throat tighten. As she took a step toward him, a hissing whisper curled around her ear: "Keep walking—this isn't your concern. You have more important things to do." The voice was thin and needling, an illusion's last attempt to seed doubt. For the briefest heartbeat, Checkered's rational side nearly agreed; they were in the middle of a critical trial, after all. But then she remembered the fable of the sparrow and the poem's vow. Nothing is more important than a single act of compassion when it's needed. Casting aside the poisonous thought, Checkered strode through the gust of snow and knelt beside the hunched figure. She rested a steady hand on the man's shoulder. "I'm here with you," she whispered. Her words were simple, but she poured all the gentle immediacy she had into them. At once, the phantom man lifted his head; his hollow eyes sparkled with a sudden glimmer of comfort. The illusion quivered under Checkered's touch, cracks of light forming along its outline. In the next blink, the sad figure evaporated into a swirl of snowflakes, leaving only the warmth of Checkered's hand touching the empty air.

On the opposite side of the yard, Greenie confronted a second apparition. A newcomer to the town—discernible by a travel-stained coat—stood timidly at the edge of a small crowd. The townsfolk in this illusion turned their backs, speaking in harsh tones about "outsiders" while the newcomer's face crumpled in hurt. Greenie's heart throbbed with empathy; she could feel the sting of rejection as keenly as if it were her own. A cold voice drifted from the illusionary crowd: "Stay out of it. This isn't your problem." Greenie's eyes flashed determination. She would not be a bystander to cruelty. With a graceful sweep of her arm, she sent out a wave of emerald light. From the snow at her feet, tendrils of soft green magic sprouted and twined around the villagers in the vision, gently turning them back toward the newcomer and linking their hands in a chain of ivy. "We welcome you," Greenie said, her voice gentle but firm. The spell of isolation broke in an instant: the hostile faces in the crowd softened, and one by one they reached out to the newcomer as friends.

A collective sigh of relief seemed to emanate from the illusion as it shattered into a thousand motes of emerald light, like leaves carried away on a breeze. Where the phantom townsfolk had stood, Greenie now faced only falling snow and felt the thankful warmth of a dozen hearts finding acceptance.

Reddish, her senses honed for any spark of suffering, caught sight of a third phantom near the old stone well. A young child staggered and fell in the fresh snow, crying out in pain. Around the child, figures walked past, noses in the air and expressions blank—no one stopped, no hand reached down. Reddish didn't even hear the whisper that tried to dissuade her; she was already moving. "Oh, you poor thing," she murmured, rushing across the yard. She swept the little boy into her arms without hesitation. The child's form was light as air—only a specter—but he clung to her neck, sobbing into her shoulder as if real. Reddish's crimson cloak flared and cast a halo of warmth around them both, melting the snow where they knelt. She rubbed the child's back soothingly. "It's all right. I've got you." The illusions of indifferent passersby stopped in their tracks, each frozen figure dissolving into mist when confronted with the undeniable evidence of compassion. The boy's crying quieted. He peered up at Reddish with eyes full of wonder and gratitude before his small shape glowed and vanished like a spark rising into the dark. Reddish remained on one knee a moment, smiling softly at the empty space in her arms that moments ago held a child in need. A single tear—no longer cold—wet the corner of her eye, and she let it fall.

Firee squared off against the fourth illusion as it pushed toward him in a whirl of sleet. An elderly man appeared on a bench, arms wrapped around himself, teeth chattering from an invisible cold that none of the townsfolk around him seemed to notice. The old man's spectacles fogged as he looked around pleadingly, but people hurried by, heads down. A voice needled at Firee: "You can't help everyone. Leave him be." Firee's response was to generate a gentle flame between his cupped hands, the fire casting a dancing glow on his determined face. He approached the bench and knelt. Without a word, Firee extended his hands toward the shivering elder, offering the gift of warmth. The illusionary man's eyes widened behind his glasses as the golden heat enveloped him. Slowly, his rigid posture relaxed and a faint color returned to his cheeks. Firee met his gaze and spoke softly, the steam of his breath mingling with the cinder-sparks from his palms. "You haven't been forgotten," he said. "I am here." The old man gave a slow, grateful nod as tears of relief glinted in his eyes. In that moment, the lonely bench was bathed in a glow that no winter wind could dim. The entire scene then faded into a fine vapor, the last wisp of the man's grateful smile lingering an extra second before disappearing into the night. Firee rose to his feet, the snow at his boots melted in a perfect circle. He pressed one warm hand over his heart, which beat steadily with compassion and pride.

A roar of angry voices drew Breezie to the fifth illusion near the lychgate. Two groups of townsfolk—translucent as smoke—faced off, yelling accusations about a trampled garden. Others stood around watching, arms crossed in disinterest, while the argument escalated toward a physical fight. This was a perfect breeding ground for apathy: a conflict that everyone deemed "not their problem." Breezie felt a familiar tug of temptation in the air: Better not to interfere; what difference can you make? But Breezie had long ago sworn off such cynicism. He summoned a sweeping breeze that rushed between the feuding parties. The sudden wind startled them, tugging at coats and hats. It carried with it a soothing scent—pine needles and hearth smoke, the comfort of home—and wrapped the arguing figures in an airy embrace. Breezie stepped between them, his cloak billowing like a gentle flag of truce. "Peace," he whispered, as if to the wind itself. The swirling air responded by spiriting away the harsh words on everyone's lips. The phantom villagers blinked in confusion as anger drained from their faces, replaced by sheepish compassion. One man stooped to pick up a scattered sheaf of papers for the other; a woman brushed snow from her neighbor's shoulders. The crowd of apathetic onlookers flickered out of existence at once—there was nothing for indifference to feed on here anymore. With a final whoosh, the entire conflict—people and all—blew apart into fine glittering snow. Breezie smiled and let his wind subside. Where the quarrel had been, two real townsfolk across the yard suddenly paused mid-stride and shook hands for no apparent reason, as if touched by the ripple of harmony Breezie had set free.

The sixth and final illusion lunged toward Blunt. Two spectral neighbors stood outside the church, face-to-face, shouting angrily over a property line marked in the snow. Other town figures walked past, shrugging, "Not my concern," on their lips. Blunt felt the illusion tug at him to do the same—just walk on and leave them to their fight. But he had already tightened his grip on his staff, resolve flooding through him. As Reddish helped the phantom child nearby and Firee warmed the elder, Blunt stepped directly between these two feuding phantoms. He raised his free hand, and from his fingertips a soft blue radiance unfurled like a ribbon of water. The soothing light wove itself around the arguing neighbors, forming a gentle bridge of illumination between them.

"Enough," Blunt said, quietly but with authority. "Look to each other." The two ghostly neighbors fell silent, peering through Blunt's veil of light. In the glow, their expressions softened from rage to remorse. One reached out a tentative hand to the other in apology. Blunt nodded, guiding their hands together within the cerulean haze. Compassion fosters resolution, he thought as he watched their misunderstanding melt away. The bitter cold fueling their argument evaporated, and with it the entire illusion burst like a bubble. Snowflakes cascaded to the ground where the angry neighbors had stood, now nothing more than harmless crystals dissolving into the wet earth. Overhead, the great clock's star-carved arch glinted, catching the reflection of Blunt's blue light as it faded.

For a beat, none of the Wizards moved. Small puffs of breath rose from each of them as they stood in the aftermath of their immediate, selfless actions. Around the churchyard, the phantasms of apathy had all been dispelled almost as soon as they appeared. Six trials, six instant responses—compassion offered without hesitation to every fleeting need. The young wizards exchanged glances of quiet triumph. In each pair of eyes was the same realization: the illusion never had a chance. Deprived of the indifference it required, the magic of callousness had withered like frost under a spring sunrise.

A low, harmonic hum began to emanate from the base of the clock. The enchantment freezing its gears was breaking. Firee, still standing near the bench where the elder had been, looked up to see the Astronomical Clock's face start to glow with a gentle golden light. One by one, the clock's mechanisms resumed motion. A small door above the dial opened, and out stepped the carved skeleton of Death, striking its bell in a solemn rhythm. At the same time, the procession of apostles resumed: each apostle figurine glided forward in turn, and the central figure of Christ slowly raised His hand in blessing. Even the painted calendar disk at the clock's base began to turn once more, quietly counting days and years yet to come. The entire clockwork came alive with grace and purpose, freed from the icy enchantment. A hearty, warm tick-tockechoed through the yard – the first true sound of time moving forward that the city had heard since the illusions fell—time and life, restored in harmony.

Paulina Tetrikus lowered her arms, the last remnants of conjured frost evaporating around her in silvery wisps. Her face shone with gratitude and quiet wonder as she surveyed the transformed scene. "You've proven your care," she said, voice ringing with gentle pride. All around, the menace of indifference had been banished by the unstoppable embrace of empathy. No shrieking fanfare announced the victory—only a deep, settling peace, the kind that creeps in when a nightmare ends and one realizes the dawn is near.

The Clock Breathes Warmth

The ancient clock tower glowed now with a kindliness that could almost be felt. Rostock's ancient astronomical clock, moments ago entombed in ice, radiated a soft heat like sunlit oak. The lantern's flame on the table brightened of its own accord, as if fed by the compassion saturating the night. Beneath the clock, Paulina stood with her hands pressed together over her heart, taking in the sight of her beloved city reawakening. The carved figures on the clock continued their gentle motions, turning toward each other in poses of friendship and concern. It was as though the clock itself was breathing once more—each tick a heartbeat of communal spirit returning to the town.

Across the square, a few townsfolk had emerged from their homes, drawn by the strange calm that had settled. They did not know of the phantoms that had swirled around them minutes before; they saw only their familiar clock shining warmly and a handful of strangers in colorful cloaks standing in the churchyard. Yet something subtle had changed in their behavior. Two neighbors who had avoided each other all day now exchanged smiles and walked arm-in-arm down the lane. A passerby paused to help an older woman carry her firewood, and they continued on together chatting amiably. Laughter, soft and sincere, drifted from the direction of the reopened tavern as friends greeted friends. Without knowing why, everyone in Rostock suddenly felt a little more generous, a little more aware of one another. The chill that had hunched their shoulders all day was gone. In its place flowed a quiet ease, like a thawed river moving gently after a long freeze.

Blunt stepped back from the clock tower and let his gaze wander over the serene city scene. He realized his fists were still clenched from the trial; slowly he unfurled them, feeling the cold night air nip at the sweat that had gathered in his palms. In one hand he still held his oaken staff, but in the other he found a small object he didn't remember grasping during the flurry of action. Surprised, Blunt opened his fingers to reveal a bronze gear, no larger than his palm. Its surface was embossed with ornate patterns of stars and vines, and though a thin layer of frost clung to it, the metal beneath glinted invitingly. He suddenly understood—it must have been nestled among the clock's wooden carvings and shaken loose when the enchantment broke. A token of the trial's completion. As the remaining frost melted away from the gear's edge, letters became visible, etched in a graceful circle. Caritas Veritatem Revelat. Blunt's lips moved silently over the Latin, and he felt the translation in his heart as clearly as if someone had spoken it: "Compassion reveals truth."

He held the bronze gear up reverently, and its engraved words caught the lantern glow. This was the very phrase that had guided them here, the virtue that bridged their past victories to this moment. Greenie and Checkered stepped closer to see the gear, and their eyes widened at the sight. The inscription seemed to pulse with a gentle light of its own, as if acknowledging that compassion's truth had indeed been revealed this night. One by one, the others gathered around Blunt, forming a small circle under the clock's benevolent gaze.

Greenie gingerly ran her fingertips over the inscription. The bronze was warm to the touch, almost alive. "The next link in our chain of virtues," she said softly. In her mind's eye she saw the progression of their journey: from humility's humble seed in ages past, to the spark of innovation that Zeetrikus had kindled, to the probing light of curiosity they wielded against ignorance, to the steadfast fortitude and perseverance that had carried them through every hardship—and now to compassion, gentle and radiant, bringing all those threads together. Each virtue had led naturally to the next, forging an unbreakable bond among them. Greenie's throat tightened with emotion as she realized how far they had come.

Blunt nodded, cradling the gear against his chest. Inside his cloak, another artifact—a silver innovation gear given by Zeetrikus long ago—hummed in sympathetic harmony. The new bronze gear's motto felt like both a promise and a revelation. Compassion had literally uncovered the truth here: that the callous chill was an illusion and the real heart of this city was still beating, warm and kind, underneath. Blunt turned toward Paulina, who watched them with tears of joy glistening on her lashes. "Thank you," he said earnestly, and though he addressed Paulina, his words seemed to encompass the entire lesson, the fable, the poem, and the trial they had just shared.

Paulina approached the group, folding her hands over Blunt's to enclose the bronze gear between them. For a moment, she said nothing, letting the quiet speak. In the background, the clock's restored tick-tock was as soothing as a mother's heartbeat in a lullaby. When Paulina finally spoke, her voice was low with gratitude. "Where compassion stands, illusions fail," she said. She looked at each of the six in turn, pride and affection shining through her gentle demeanor. "Carry this wisdom forward, my friends. Not all trials will announce themselves as clearly as this one—but a caring heart will always reveal what falsehood hides."

The Wizards bowed their heads slightly in acknowledgement. They understood well: whether in a mystical illusion or in everyday life, acting with kindness would illuminate the path ahead. Breezie stepped forward, removing his velvet cap in a courteous gesture. "We won't forget," he promised quietly. Around them, snow began to drift down again, but this time the flakes were large, soft, and harmless, blanketing the churchyard in a scene of pure tranquility.

Paulina gave a last, long look at the rejuvenated clock and the peaceful city beyond. Her role here was done. With a smile as serene as moonlight on snow, she pulled her silver hood back over her dark curls. "Your journey carries you far from here now," she said. "Across lands and ages… and back to where it began." Her eyes twinkled knowingly, hinting at truths yet to unfold. Greenie felt a slight shiver—not of cold, but of anticipation—at those words. Back to where it began. Was it possible Paulina knew about Boston's hidden Orloj, the ancient halls waiting for them there? Before Greenie could ask, Paulina took a graceful step backward.

"Safe travels, brave ones," the antiquarian blessed them. She raised one hand, and starlight seemed to gather at her fingertips. In a slow sweep, she drew a symbol in the air: a delicate outline of a heart that glowed, then gently drifted down over the six like falling snow. The symbol of Caritas—compassion—imbued into the night. With that, Paulina Tetrikus's form began to dissolve into the same silvery mist from which she had emerged. Reddish hastily wiped a happy tear from her cheek and called out, "We'll do you proud!" Her voice echoed softly against the stone church. Paulina's fading figure gave a final warm nod. Then she was gone, leaving only a few shimmering motes that mingled with the snowflakes descending from the sky.

In the silence that followed, the Wizards realized they had been holding their breath. They let it out in unison, and a sense of profound peace filled the churchyard. Above, the Astronomical Clock chimed a single, clear note as the carved figure of Death appeared and struck its bell, marking the passing of the trial. Compassion's glow would reside in this place for a long time to come.

Reflection in the City Square

For a few minutes, none of the six moved to depart. They wandered through the now-tranquil square, letting the experience sink in. Snow gathered on their shoulders and eyelashes, but they scarcely felt the cold. Greenie closed her eyes and extended her empathic aura outward in a gentle sweep. All she sensed now was the normal, healthy emotion of a community at peace: mild contentment, a touch of weariness at the end of the day, but underneath it a renewed current of neighborly affection. Families were indoors sharing meals, friends were exchanging greetings on their way home, and not a trace of malice or despair tainted the atmosphere. Greenie smiled to herself. As if the earlier gloom had never been. In a way, that was the greatest triumph—they had set things right so swiftly that no scar remained.

Nearby, Checkered leaned against a lamppost, turning over the night's events in her analytical mind. A soft golden halo from the lamp fell on the snow at her feet as she replayed each illusion scenario. Every one of them had been a variant of the same theme: someone in need, and others tempted to ignore them. And each time, the Wizards had answered immediately, uniting action and empathy without delay. She gave a small, satisfied nod. "It's consistent," she murmured into the quiet, her breath forming a brief cloud. "If compassion comes at once, the illusion of indifference simply cannot take hold." In that realization lay a profound encouragement: they had found a formula to defeat this vice as surely as a proven theorem. Checkered allowed herself a rare grin, feeling pride in how far their understanding had come.

Firee, meanwhile, wandered past the market stalls they'd seen earlier, now shuttered for the night. He ran a gloved hand along one snowy counter, recalling how illusions in their earliest adventures would sometimes linger and resist. Not tonight. Even a combined wave of callousness had melted almost instantly under their concerted compassion. He looked up at the distant outline of the city's red-brick towers, then beyond them in his imagination to Boston, where more trials certainly waited. A soft chuckle escaped him. "Illusions that once took us hours to unravel," he said to no one in particular, "now barely last a minute." There was no arrogance in his tone—just a kind of astonished laughter, as one might have at realizing they'd grown taller without noticing. Firee felt a deep confidence glowing inside him. They were quicker now, wiser and stronger together, like a well-practiced orchestra that could play any piece flawlessly on the first sight.

Breezie drew in a long breath of the cold, crisp air, savoring the clean feeling of a world scrubbed free of shadows. The scent of pinewood fires and fresh snow filled his lungs. As he exhaled, he sent out a playful wisp of wind to dance among the churchyard's yew trees. The branches whispered softly as if thanking him. Breezie's thoughts flitted back to Concord, to Monticello, to every place they had visited on this journey. A pattern was clear: when they hesitated, even for a moment, illusions found footing. But when they acted as one, straight from the heart, those illusions collapsed immediately. "Immediate compassion, immediate results," he said under his breath, echoing the simple truth. A quiet pride settled in him. It wasn't that they were stronger or faster than before in any muscular sense—rather, they had learned to trust the importance of now. A kindness delayed was kindness potentially lost; a kindness given at once was a seed that could save a life.

As Breezie's gentle breeze circled back to the group, carrying with it a flurry of snow that sparkled in the lamplight, Blunt cleared his throat to gently call everyone together. They had a habit after each trial of sharing a final reflection, and old instincts drew them into a close huddle. Their breath and body heat formed a cozy pocket in the cold night. No words were necessary at first—they each saw their own sentiments mirrored in one another's eyes. Relief. Accomplishment. Determination for what lay ahead. Greenie gave Blunt's shoulder a little squeeze, and he returned it, acknowledging all that she had done with a single gesture. Firee offered a light fist-bump to Reddish, who met it with a grin, both recalling how swiftly she had cradled that illusory child. Checkered adjusted her monocle and gave Breezie an appreciative nod for his deft handling of the quarrel. In the silence, their unity was reaffirmed more strongly than any spoken oath.

Departure from Rostock

At length, the six friends knew it was time to move on. Night had fully fallen, and a silver crescent moon peeked between snow-laden clouds, illuminating their path out of the churchyard. Before they left, they gathered at the foot of the Astronomical Clock for one last look. The clock tower stood tall and proud, each of its restored figures glowing softly as they continued their gentle procession on the hour. Lamplight and new-fallen snow lent the whole square a storybook charm. "They'll be all right now," Blunt said quietly. In the stillness, his words carried weight. Rostock was safe from apathy's grip once more.

Blunt slipped the bronze gear with Caritas Veritatem Revelat into an inner pocket of his cloak, close to where he kept the other tokens of their journey. The gear vibrated softly, as if content. He felt a similar hum resonate through his own synergy gear—an artifact bestowed when their fellowship was first formed. The two items seemed to acknowledge each other, bronze and brass, compassion and unity, pulsing in harmony. Blunt smiled at the comforting rhythm against his chest: a job well done.

The city gates were open and unguarded, welcoming the travelers to depart just as warmly as they had arrived. As they crossed beyond the last cottage, Firee turned for one final glance. The clock tower's face was just visible above the rooftops, its gilded hands reflecting moonlight. Earlier that evening, those hands had been frozen; now they moved freely, keeping perfect time. Firee gave a satisfied nod and murmured, "Illusions rely on our hesitation to survive—and tonight we gave them none." Checkered, walking beside him, added under her breath, "Not a second to latch on." The two shared a knowing look. It was a reassuring thought to carry with them into whatever darkness might come: they would not allow evil even an instant's head start.

Once past the city outskirts, the road descended through a grove of slumbering pines. The heavy boughs bent low with fresh snow, forming a natural archway. Breezie paused, sensing something on the wind. He closed his eyes and reached out with his magic, sifting through the night breeze as if through pages of a book. When he opened his eyes, they were sharp with information. "All clear here," he reported softly. The last wisps of Paulina's illusion had fully dispersed; nothing malign lingered in the vicinity. Breezie then sent that same breeze skipping ahead down the road, east to west. It returned with the faintest hints of salt and chimney smoke—scents of the distant city by the sea that they called home for now. Breezie grinned. "Boston's calling," he said, his voice carrying a note of excitement. "I suspect its ancient halls have kept something waiting for us." Perhaps another trial, or perhaps a confrontation long in the making—either way, their journey was curving back to Boston, where it had begun.

Blunt's eyes lit up at the mention of Boston. He drew the bronze gear out again for a better look in the moonlight. Sure enough, along with the Latin motto, the gear bore tiny symbols around its rim: an astrolabe, a set of scales, a quill pen, a lantern. He hadn't noticed them in the churchyard's dimness, but now he recognized those icons – each tied to a virtue and a location they had encountered. And there, just beside the engraved word Veritatem, was a minute etching of a familiar spired building: Boston's Old State House, or perhaps the Old South Meeting House – one of the colonial halls that housed the city's oldest clock. Blunt couldn't be certain which, but it was enough of a clue. Boston's ancient corridors, as Paulina hinted, were indeed beckoning. "We'll investigate every old hall and hidden clock in Boston if we have to," Blunt said with quiet resolve, carefully pocketing the gear again. "Whatever illusion or adversary awaits us there, we'll be ready." He felt the comforting weight of all their collected tokens and lessons resting against his heart. Each one would guide them now.

Reddish walked a few steps ahead, her boots crunching in the new snow. She glanced over her shoulder at her comrades, the ends of her red scarf fluttering in the night breeze. "Let illusions gather all they want," she said, not with arrogance but with a kind of bright eagerness. Sparks of scarlet danced at her fingertips briefly, reflecting her fiery spirit. "We'll face them as we always have—together and without delay." In Reddish's mind, she was already imagining the final showdown that surely loomed: if the Dark Harlequin intended to merge all the vicious tricks they had defeated—ignorance, corruption, stagnation, callousness, and perhaps more—they would counter with the merged virtues they now embodied. Her eyes glowed like embers at the thought.

The companions fell into an easy stride as the road opened up before them, stretching westward under the moon. The snowfall had ceased, leaving the landscape draped in pristine white. Their silhouettes cast long shadows on the glimmering blanket of snow, six dark shapes surrounded by a faint aura of light reflecting off their enchanted cloaks. They did not speak much; words weren't needed to acknowledge what each felt. In the silence, the soft crunch of their steps seemed almost loud, and above them the stars shone crisp and clear in the black sky.

Contemplating the Merged Virtues

As they traveled westward beyond the Hanseatic city's outskirts, Reddish found herself listing in her mind all the illusions they had faced so far. Ignorance, injustice, stagnation, apathy… Each one had tried to fracture them or slow them down, and each had failed faster than the last. She bit her lip in thought. If these moral flaws were pieces of a grander puzzle the Dark Harlequin was assembling, then perhaps a final test would involve all of them at once. The idea was daunting—a single illusion embodying every vice they'd seen—but Reddish felt no fear. Instead, a curious calm came over her. We already know the antidote, she mused. Act with virtue immediately, act as one. She glanced around at her friends trudging through the snow, each lost in similar reflection. Checkered caught her eye and gave a small affirmative nod; she clearly shared Reddish's train of thought. The two women fell into step together, and though neither spoke, both took comfort in the unspoken fact that when virtues combined, their power didn't just add up—it multiplied.

Insight on the Upcoming Boston Clue

Hours later, as the sky in the east began to pale with the approach of dawn, the Wizards paused at a lonely roadside inn that stood dark and closed at this early hour. They gathered under the eaves to rest briefly and plan. Blunt drew out the bronze compassion gear once more and held it up for all to see in the dim blue morning light. The Latin inscription around its edge glinted: Caritas Veritatem Revelat – "Compassion reveals truth." Blunt's thumb ran over the etched words thoughtfully. "This token carries Paulina's parting lesson," he said. In the silence of the sleeping inn yard, his voice was steady. "Somewhere in Boston's old quarters, another clock, another truth waits to be revealed."

Greenie pulled her traveling cloak tighter as a gentle cold wind blew by. Her breath puffed white as she spoke. "Perhaps the final illusion will try to hide behind every lie and darkness we've seen so far," she wondered aloud. "Ignorance, fear, hatred—all woven together." The prospect might have made her tremble once, but now she merely set her jaw. If that was what awaited them, they would meet it with everything they had become.

Firee placed a hand on Blunt's shoulder, drawing warmth from the red aura that still clung to him from the night's exertions. "Whatever comes," Firee said, completing Greenie's thought, "we'll shine the combined light of all our virtues on it. Compassion first and foremost." He glanced at the gear in Blunt's hand. It almost seemed to shine brighter at his words. "We'll reveal the truth behind any illusion," Firee added with a confident smile. One could have mistaken his certainty for bravado, but each of them felt the same confidence welling up. It wasn't that they believed themselves invincible—only that they believed wholeheartedly in the principles guiding them. That belief, they knew, made all the difference.

With the first faint rose of sunrise touching the east, they stepped away from the inn and back onto the road. The city of Boston lay far beyond the horizon, but in their minds it loomed near and dear. Checkered pulled her cloak around her against the early morning chill. "Ancient halls… ancient clocks," she murmured, recalling Boston's many historic sites. "We'll start at the oldest and work our way through. The clue will make sense when we find the right place." The others agreed. It was a sensible plan. And if the Dark Harlequin intended to confront them there, so be it. They carried humble courage from Concord, innovative wit from Zeetrikus's teachings, relentless curiosity from Monticello, and now, from Rostock, the gentle, unyielding fire of compassion. United, these virtues would guide them to truth as surely as the North Star guided sailors home.

Compassion's Triumph

Thus, as dawn broke, Chapter 9 of their journey came to a quiet close. The trials of compassion in Hazleton's square and Rostock's clock had been like two movements of the same symphony, each reinforcing the same refrain: a caring heart, shown without delay, can disperse even the deepest shadows. In Hazleton, they had rekindled warmth in a community nearly lost to apathy. In Rostock, they proved that even an enchantment freezing an entire city's spirit would shatter under immediate, unified kindness. The bronze gear inscribed Caritas Veritatem Revelat was both proof and reminder of these victories—a small, shining piece of the truth they were uncovering step by step.

Under the gentle light of early morning, the six Wizards walked on, leaving fresh footprints in the snow. Behind them, Rostock began to stir under the protection of its restored clock, the townsfolk waking to a new day filled with unknowing tenderness for one another. Not a single person in that city would realize how close they had come to losing their communal warmth to an unseen chill the night before; life would simply feel a little sweeter, a little more hopeful, as if kindness had gotten a head start on the day.

Blunt looked around at his companions as they traveled. Reddish was humming a lullaby under her breath, a tune she had picked up from the Hazleton antiquarian, Paulina, perhaps. Breezie was twirling a tiny vortex of snow in his palm absentmindedly, a boyish grin on his face. Firee marched with a lightness in his step, periodically tossing a spark into the air that burst into a mini-firework before fizzling out. Checkered walked slightly apart, scribbling in a small notebook even as she kept pace—no doubt recording insights from the night's events while they were fresh. And Greenie… Greenie was gazing ahead down the road, a faraway look of contentment in her eyes, as if she could already glimpse the next needy soul they would help, the next illusion they would dispel with love.

The Dark Harlequin's presence was still a distant thundercloud on the horizon of their story, but none of the six showed fear at the prospect. If anything, the idea of a final confrontation brought them a sense of calm readiness. They suspected that all the scattered threads of deception they'd encountered—ignorance in Monticello, injustice in Boston, stagnation in Hazleton, callousness here in Rostock—might soon be woven by that unseen adversary into one daunting tapestry of illusion. But if that were to happen, the young wizards felt a quiet certainty that the virtues they carried, interlaced and immediate, would be enough to tear right through it. Humility had taught them to listen and learn; innovation taught them to adapt; curiosity taught them to seek truth; perseverance taught them to stand firm; and compassion, most of all, taught them to reach out to each other and to those in need without a second's doubt. Together, these lights formed a single flame that no darkness could withstand.

As the sun's first rays broke free of the horizon, painting the snow with a blush of pink, the six friends quickened their pace. Their long shadows fell behind them, pointing back toward the East and the trials already overcome. Ahead, to the West, lay Boston and whatever final challenge awaited in its oldest halls. The morning was silent save for the crunch of their steps and the distant call of a winter bird, yet in that silence each of them felt the same vow taking shape: that when illusions rose anew, as they surely would, they would answer as they had done here—immediately, with unity and love, as constant and bright as the dawn. In the still air, their determination shone unspoken, a compassionate light guiding them onward. And so they journeyed on, toward truth, toward hope, and toward the awaiting chimes of the Orloj of Boston.

Chapter 10

Concord Reflection – The Seeds of Synergy

The Silent Watcher's Warning

Twilight's soft glow seeped into the Old North Church crypt, where centuries-old stones were etched with faint colonial runes that pulsed gently—an undercurrent of magic humming through Boston's historic heart. Candlelight flickered against weathered arches, casting elongated shadows that danced like spirits from 1775. From a bronze-and-azure portal stepped Blunt, Reddish, Firee, Checkered, Breezie, and Greenie, their Harlequin cloaks—emerald swirls, crimson flames, sapphire waves—glimmering in the dim light.

Blunt held a bronze gear inscribed with "Quaestio Veritatem Revelat," still faintly aglow from their Monticello triumph. The Latin motto—"Question Reveals Truth"—evoked how curiosity had shattered the illusions of ignorance in that trial, earning them Morpheus's key. Equally fresh was the memory of illusions of callousness recently undone by compassion in Stará Bystrica. He now sensed a new call from the Boston Orloj—an energy not demanding battle but reflection. Its subtle hum, resonating through the crypt's runes, felt like a welcoming beacon.

Reddish surveyed the hushed crypt, embers in her cloak tempered by prior lessons of empathy and curiosity. "Feels sacred," she murmured, noticing that any lingering haze of illusion had receded. Greenie's empathic senses brushed the old stones, catching faint echoes of Revere's legacy—lanterns signifying inquiry and unity. "The Orloj wants us in a calmer stance," she observed softly, Tetragor's humility steadying her.

Checkered's analytical mind traced faint magical currents etched across the crypt's floor, remnants of enchantments once fought here. "No direct illusions," she said crisply. "More like a reflective invitation." Firee exhaled, tension easing. "Let's respond as we always do—together," he added, referencing their hard-won synergy.

Breezie exuded an even deeper calm, recalling prior arcs: the ignorance deception at Monticello, the callous ruse at Hazleton. "We're forging ahead," he said softly. The only shadows around them came from candlelight; no new deception stirred in the sacred calm.

The crypt's dome shimmered then, forming the celestial outline of the Boston Orloj—starlight and gears melding into a radiant figure whose eyes burned like lanterns. Its voice, a gentle cosmic hum, filled the air. "Harlequins," it intoned, "you've vanquished illusions, yet the Dark Harlequin stirs.

Reflect on your journey—embrace transcendence's light." The group's cloaks pulsed at the words, each recalling illusions undone by their swift unity. Another step called them, not to a fight, but to introspection, the crypt's sanctity a shield for the next level of moral clarity.

The Orloj's Lantern Sermon

At the Orloj's gentle beckoning, a pocket of warmth formed around an oak table lit by soft candlelight. The Wizards—Blunt, Reddish, Firee, Checkered, Breezie, and Greenie—settled on its worn benches, cloaks glowing in the hush. The Boston Orloj, manifest as a shimmering figure of starlight and interlocking gears, stood at the table's head, cosmic eyes gleaming like colonial lanterns.

A single bronze gear inscribed "Quaestio Veritatem Revelat" rested on the table beside a runic teapot that exhaled aromatic steam. Flickers of scenes from earlier lessons played in the steam's swirls: Monticello's illusion of ignorance, Hazleton's illusion of callousness—each undone by the Wizards' united effort. The Orloj's voice, soft but resonant, broke the silence: "You've triumphed through curiosity, compassion, unity. But the Dark Harlequin's illusions unify moral flaws—reflect now, so you stand unbreakable."

Blunt nodded, remembering how every illusion fell as soon as they responded as one. "Curiosity steered my leadership," he admitted, referencing the ignorance illusion they overcame. "I did hesitate at first, but deeper questions bonded us."

Reddish's embers flickered. "I used to charge blindly," she confessed, recalling how illusions once exploited her impulsivity. "Innovation taught me to craft, not just destroy." Her tone carried relief as well as renewed purpose.

Checkered fiddled with her lens. "I nearly faltered under illusions of partial knowledge," she said crisply. "But synergy overcame them in time."

Greenie's empathy glowed as she thought of deceptions that tempted her to disconnect. "I was almost fooled into apathy," she said softly. "Compassion and curiosity anchored me." She recalled how they bridged hearts in Hazleton and Stará Bystrica.

Firee, watchful yet calmer now, added, "My own fear was turned against me, but together we snuffed every illusion out," he said.

Breezie's gentle voice sealed their reflection. "Together, we extinguish any darkness," he concluded quietly. "We rely on each other's spark."

The Orloj's eyes brightened at their responses. "Your virtues converge—humility, innovation, curiosity, compassion," it said approvingly. "The Dark Harlequin may yet strike by combining all failings at once, but if you respond without delay, his illusions will have no chance to take hold." The runic teapot's steam shifted to hint at future arcs—Sedona's desert Orloj, Morpheus's lurking ignorance—signs that the Wizards must not waver. They exchanged resolute glances as the crypt fell silent again; in that calm, their bond felt truly unbreakable. Another stage concluded, the Orloj's cosmic hum guiding them to new heights of clarity in transcending illusions.

A Constellation of Clocks

As this reflection settled, the crypt's stone arches glimmered with new light, starlight weaving across the runic engravings. The Boston Orloj lifted an ethereal hand, projecting cosmic images that danced along the walls. Galaxies, gears, and faint silhouettes of distant clocks swirled in a grand tapestry—some known, like Monticello and Hazleton, others unnamed—each shining with a different virtue. The Wizards gazed in awe, their cloaks shimmering in response to the Orloj's cosmic hum. As it raised its hand higher, the candle flames guttered low—briefly dimming as if an eclipse had passed—before spectral visions swirled into view.

First, a windswept desert scene appeared—Sedona's Orloj among red rocks, with tendrils of ignorance twisting around Morpheus Rubicom's silhouette. "Curiosity stands," the Orloj intoned, highlighting how inquiry would dispel deception.

Blunt recalled Monticello's lesson and nodded at the desert vision. "Our path awaits in Sedona," he murmured.

Next, a futuristic tower soared into view—the Long Now Clock, each gear representing centuries of stewardship and generosity. Paulina Tetrikus's silver-robed figure hovered there, illusions pitting generosity against greed. "Compassion defies apathy," the Orloj said. Reddish's embers flared, remembering Hazleton's test of empathy. "We won't hesitate," she asserted, determination in her voice.

Then a majestic department store timepiece—the Wanamaker Clock—emerged, symbolizing harmony over fractious division and hinting at Tetragor's domain. "Unity silences division," declared the Orloj. Checkered's lens glinted as she recalled how those divisive illusions had been overcome. "We stand ready," she said crisply.

Greenie felt a wave of empathy wash through each vision. "Each clock challenges a moral flaw," she said softly. Firee recognized the pattern—humility versus arrogance, innovation versus stagnation, curiosity versus ignorance, compassion versus callousness—challenges they had repeatedly dispelled with synergy.

At last, the cosmic mosaic faded, returning the crypt to flickering candlelight. The Orloj's gaze turned solemn, conveying a clear warning: the Dark Harlequin would try to unite ignorance, greed, and division all at once, and only immediate unity would prevent those shadows from deepening. The Wizards' cloaks pulsed as each of them remembered how quickly they'd shattered illusions by responding instantly. The crypt's runes glowed brighter, Boston's centuries of inquiry fueling their unity. Another step of reflection concluded. The Orloj's grand vision had bolstered their readiness for the trials to come.

Walking with Emerson

As the cosmic vision dissipated, a swirling portal opened in the crypt's corner, weaving bronze-and-azure threads reminiscent of previous cameo visits from Franklin and Tetragor. Mrs. V., the Concord antiquarian whose half-cape always caught the slightest breeze, glided forth. "A sage beckons," she said gently. Without hesitation, Blunt, Reddish, Firee, Checkered, Breezie, and Greenie stepped into the swirl behind her. Colors spiraled and starlight flickered until they emerged in Ralph Waldo Emerson's Concord study, circa 1841.

The walls were lined with books, a crackling hearth exuding warmth, quills and manuscripts scattered on an oak desk. Emerson—lean and sharp-eyed—broke from his writing to survey the visitors. His presence brimmed with thoughtful introspection, reminiscent of Franklin's cameo yet deeper in philosophical nuance. "Travelers," he greeted them in a melodious voice, "you bring inquiry. Tell me—what is curiosity to you?"

Blunt, the synergy gear humming beneath his cloak, met Emerson's gaze. "Seeking truth through shared questions," he answered readily. "We found that as soon as we united, any illusion would collapse." Emerson's thin smile reflected approval. "A shared mind, then," he mused. "Illusions root in unasked queries."

Reddish stepped forward, embers respectfully subdued. "We used to fight illusions with raw fire," she said. "Now synergy and craft unmask them." Emerson's grin broadened. "Fascinating—nature's Over-Soul at work in harmony," he remarked, gesturing them nearer.

Greenie's empathic sense brushed his aura, feeling a quiet but immense intellectual warmth. "We overcame illusions in Monticello, Hazleton, Stará Bystrica," she said softly. "Curiosity anchored us each time." Emerson's eyes sparkled. "Curiosity births transcendence," he intoned, pleased.

Checkered's lens flickered over his scattered papers. "We unify each time an illusion appears," she said crisply. Emerson lightly tapped a manuscript titled Nature. "Indeed. Thorough unity dispels illusions—shadows of the unexamined self," he remarked calmly.

Firee, recalling Franklin's stormy lesson and Tetragor's trials, found Emerson's tone more contemplative. "We can't tarry," he said with concern. Emerson nodded. "Precisely—delays feed illusions." Breezie gave a measured nod that sealed their shared resolve.

Thus, they settled into chairs by the hearth, Concord's wooden floor gently creaking underfoot. "Let's craft an essay," Emerson proposed, quill in hand. "Weave your synergy with the Over-Soul's gift—nature's universal connection. A bulwark against illusion." The Wizards' cloaks pulsed in agreement. Another cameo lesson began, forging deeper moral clarity in the gentle hush of Emerson's study.

Transcendentalist Lesson

Emerson's study glowed with hearthlight, reflections dancing off runic manuscripts. The Wizards gathered around a broad mahogany desk, each contributing lines to a new essay on synergy and transcendental curiosity. Emerson oversaw their work, quill tapping lightly, the runic ink shimmering with intangible warmth.

Blunt recalled illusions undone in Monticello, Boston, Hazleton—each deceptive wave battered down by instant unity. He wrote: "When illusions knock, we answer in unison, posing questions that no half-truth can withstand." Emerson nodded approvingly.

Reddish's embers flickered as she penned lines about turning raw energy into creative empathy. "Once I burned illusions blindly," she admitted on the page, "but synergy taught me to transform chaos into mindful care." Emerson's gentle smile confirmed the insight.

Greenie, empathy swirling, framed her lines around bridging hearts. "Illusions isolate," she wrote, "yet synergy extends a hand. Compassion reunites what illusion would sever." She remembered how the callous deception had folded instantly in Hazleton.

Checkered's monocle hovered over the text for clarity. "No illusion survives immediate scrutiny," she added crisply. "Hesitation only lets falsehood spread." Emerson praised her logical precision, reminiscent of Franklin's methodical lessons.

Firee set his wand aside, carefully inking a caution about fear. "Fear thrives in corners of doubt," he wrote. "So we bring it into the light at once." Emerson nodded again, the quill dancing as their collective insights grew.

Breezie orchestrated a final weaving of their lines, evoking an image of a sunlit meadow from earlier in their journey. "Our synergy is the Over-Soul in miniature," he concluded softly. Emerson, reading the compiled essay, murmured,

"Marvelous. Your unity channels nature's own spirit. This stands as a testament to illusions undone."

The completed manuscript glowed, faint wisps of ignorance and apathy rising from the pages—but the Wizards responded as always with unified resolve. Any lurking shadows vanished, the essay's light triumphant. Emerson set his quill aside and locked eyes with the group. "Hold this synergy dear," he said earnestly. "The Dark Harlequin is cunning, and he will unify moral flaws if given the chance. Do not hesitate—unite at the first sign, and his illusions will vanish." The hearth's flames flickered as they all sealed that vow. Another cameo lesson concluded, forging a deeper moral clarity—transcendental insight to fortify them for trials to come.

Concord Walk & Departure

Soon after, under a silver moon, Emerson led them along Concord's hushed lanes, a torchlight gently illuminating fences and budding trees. The Wizards trailed behind, each quietly soaking in the peace of the New England night. Mrs. V. walked with them, her half-cape fluttering as if in silent encouragement. The intangible calm mirrored earlier adventures—no immediate illusions, just a faint tension testing their vigilance.

Emerson paused on a small stone bridge spanning a placid stream. "Nature reveals unity—ignore it, and illusions fester," he said reflectively. "Fear, ignorance, callousness—such shadows starve in the face of unwavering unity."

Greenie's cloak glowed softly, her empathic senses picking up the mildest whiff of doubt drifting through the night air. She sensed a subtle test forming, as if the darkness itself were probing them. Reddish's embers sparked as she eyed a faint wisp of mist curling off the stream. "Probably just fog," she murmured, almost dismissively.

But even as she spoke, the mist thickened unnaturally near the water—clearly an illusion taking shape. Blunt's wards flared, curiosity sharpening his focus. "What illusion lurks?" he challenged, scanning the gloom. Firee ignited a small flame in his palm, dispelling a fleeting shadow—perhaps one last spark of ignorance daring to show itself. Checkered's lens captured the dark wisp briefly before it dissolved in a single unified breath. "Gone," she reported crisply.

Emerson's eyes shone with satisfaction. "You see? When you act as one without delay, illusions have no chance to take hold," he said as he stepped off the bridge. Breezie sent a breeze that scattered the final wisps of mist. "We never let them settle," he confirmed quietly.

They soon reached a crossroads by a cluster of old houses. Mrs. V. halted, her half-cape fluttering as a portal swirled open beside an elm. "Your time with Emerson closes," she said kindly. "Return now to Boston's crypt." Emerson offered a gracious bow, tipping an imaginary hat. "Ever question, dear travelers," he encouraged them. "No illusion can endure against your unity."

Parting Chimes

With that, the Wizards stepped into the portal, bronze and azure light enveloping them. The hush of Concord fell away, illusions left with no foothold. Moments later, they stood once more in the Old North Church crypt, runes along the walls softly aglow. Emerson's cameo had ended—no illusions remained, and their synergy felt more refined than ever. This peaceful encounter had advanced their moral clarity, preparing them for the greater trials yet to come. The Boston Orloj's cosmic silhouette awaited them by the runic table, its starlit gears humming softly. The Concord reflection had solidified their unity, and now the Orloj itself seemed poised to offer a final word of guidance.

Twilight Beneath the Elms

Not long after, the group emerged under the twilight sky of Boston Common. The city's lanterns glowed along winding paths, late passersby strolling peacefully among old elms and oaks. The calm here contrasted sharply with the turmoil of their earlier trials—no swirling illusions, just a gentle, reflective hush in the warm evening air. They paused on the grassy lawn, remembering Emerson's words and the Orloj's cosmic revelations, recalling how ignorance had been dispelled at Monticello, callousness at Hazleton, and division at Stará Bystrica.

Reddish inhaled deeply, her cloak's embers softened by introspection. "That felt less like a fight and more like a lesson," she said, gazing at the peaceful park. "No illusions challenged us—Emerson's cameo simply raised our synergy to a new level."

Checkered adjusted her monocle thoughtfully. "Our unity is stronger than ever now," she ventured. "Nothing can even gain a foothold if we act at the first sign of trouble."

Breezie listened to the mild night breeze and felt only peace. "Yes," he agreed, "the city is quiet—this cameo was about growth, not conflict."

Blunt stood a step apart, quietly reflecting on how far they had come. Challenges that once took them hours to unravel now fell before them in mere moments. Their unity reaffirmed, the cameo's moral clarity lingered as they strolled along a winding path through the Common. Each Wizard held Emerson's transcendental perspective close. Another lesson had concluded, forging a deeper spiritual anchor for the battles yet to come. No shadows harried them this night—the city rested under a star-flecked sky, all prior illusions long undone and their synergy shining bright.

Meeting at the Frog Pond

Crossing through pools of lamplight on the Common's paths, the Wizards converged at the Frog Pond, its still water mirroring the starlit sky. A gentle hush blanketed the area; a few late strollers passed by with friendly nods. There was no trace of illusion here—only the soft hum of the city beyond. The bronze gear in Blunt's cloak pulsed faintly, a subtle echo of the cameo's spiritual afterglow.

Reddish leaned on the pond's low iron fence, her embers reflecting off the water's calm surface. "The Orloj's cameo really re-centered us," she said quietly. "We overcame all those illusions before—maybe it's preparing us for one final wave."

Firee's eyes scanned the moonlit surroundings for any sign of trouble. "All's peaceful," he reported. The only ripples on the pond came from the night breeze. "Even if something tries to strike now, we're beyond ready."

Blunt ran his fingers over the Quaestio Veritatem Revelat medallion at his chest, the inscription warm with meaning. "We'll carry these lessons forward," he said softly.

"We must stay true to the virtues we've cultivated." Each virtue—humility, innovation, curiosity, compassion—had been proven in their recent trials, and he knew they would guide them ahead.

Breezie flicked a gentle ripple across the pond's surface with a tiny gust of air, watching the water settle back to glassy stillness.

Across the pond, city noises lulled—a reminder that no darkness lurked tonight. The team sensed they'd reached a new plateau of unity—no future deception could truly challenge them if they remained steadfast. With the cameo behind them, they were confident that tonight's lesson had taken root. Another step in their journey concluded, leaving no lingering deception in its wake. Their synergy remained undiminished as the Frog Pond calmly mirrored the stars above.

Debriefing the Cameo

Eventually, beneath a venerable oak at the Common's edge, the Wizards gathered in a half-circle to discuss the evening's revelations. Night insects hummed softly, unaccompanied by any illusory whispers. The faint glow of Blunt's synergy gear was like a nod of approval from the Orloj itself.

Greenie opened the conversation, her cloak's emerald hues shimmering. "Emerson's cameo was so… peaceful," she said softly. "No attacks, no chaos. Pure reflection." She marveled at how previous arcs had demanded battle, yet this one had been gentle.

Reddish crossed her arms, thinking back to fiercer trials. "We smashed those callous illusions in Hazleton pretty fast," she noted. "Maybe the Orloj knew we didn't need another fight tonight."

Checkered fiddled with her lens. "Perhaps," she agreed. "Each cameo had its purpose—some made us confront illusions head-on, others refined our unity. This one sharpened our introspection, pushing our synergy onto a more spiritual plane."

Firee gazed at a nearby lamppost, its light steady and unthreatening. "We'll stay alert," he said confidently. "Just because this cameo was peaceful doesn't mean nothing will test us soon."

Blunt tapped the bronze medallion from Emerson's study that now hung around his neck. "Exactly," he said. "Tonight proved we have to stay quick and united—just as we have been."

A contemplative hush fell as each Wizard reflected on what they'd learned. This time with Emerson felt like a spiritual pivot, carrying them beyond scattered individual illusions toward the possibility of one culminating wave. They knew the Dark Harlequin might soon attempt to gather every lingering vice at once, but they stood unwavering. Their synergy was stronger than ever.

Greenie smiled gently, sensing no lurking darkness around them. "We'll hold to this approach," she said, breaking the silence. They let that resolve settle among them—the fruit of this calm interlude. Every past illusion had been undone in a flash, and this reflective cameo had only steeled them for what lay ahead. Their synergy soared to new heights under the quiet boughs of the old oak.

Faint Hints of Sedona

After a time, the Wizards drifted toward a quieter corner of the Common. There, at the edge of their vision, a subtle swirl of desert imagery danced—flickers of orange buttes and swirling sunbeams in the dark. Blunt recognized it at once as a glimpse of Sedona, perhaps heralding Morpheus Rubicom's next move involving illusions of ignorance.

Reddish narrowed her eyes at the ethereal swirl near a lamppost. "Sedona's call," she muttered, recalling their victory over ignorance in Boston's earlier trial. "He might try that trick again out there."

Checkered adjusted her lens, noting faint gear-like motifs spinning within the mirage of red rocks. "If that is Morpheus, illusions of ignorance are brewing," she said crisply. "And we know how to handle those."

Greenie gently reached out with her empathic sense, tracing the edges of the flickering vision. "Desert winds…" she whispered. "It could be Sedona's Orloj merging cosmic elements. Another wave coming?" She remembered how partial knowledge had tested them in Monticello and wondered if a combined challenge was ahead.

Firee's caution flared as he studied the mirage. "Ignorance might join forces with other flaws this time," he warned under his breath, flames reflecting in his vigilant eyes.

Breezie sent a mild breeze toward the vision. It passed straight through—intangible, a mere premonition. "No illusion has actually formed," he said calmly. "This is just a mirage of what's to come—a warning from the next site."

Blunt felt the synergy gear throbbing subtly at his side and understood the Orloj's intent: to ensure no illusion ever caught them off-guard again. "We'll stay vigilant," he said firmly. "Sedona may bring new illusions soon, but we'll be ready for whatever arises."

Soon, the desert mirage faded, leaving only an ordinary lamppost flickering in the quiet city night. Nothing had truly manifested—just a hint of events on the horizon. Buoyed by the confidence gained from their introspective cameo and all their past victories, the Wizards carried on through the resting city. The night remained quiet and clear, their unity unshaken—a living testament to how far they'd come. No challenge confronted them in this moment—only the silent promise of Sedona awaiting beyond the darkness.

Night's Calm in the City

As midnight neared, the Wizards walked a tranquil route along Beacon Street, each recalling lessons from prior adventures. Some of those trials had been intense, but all were ultimately resolved by their synergy. Now no shadows dogged their steps. The cameo's moral resonance lingered, strengthening their resolve under the dim glow of old streetlamps.

Reddish rolled a small ember between her fingers, its glow gentle and steady. "We've come a long way—from me charging in with raw aggression to all of us responding in instant unity," she murmured. "No trick can exploit me now when we stand together."

Checkered nodded at that, remembering how some illusions once demanded multiple attempts to defeat. "It's true. We used to stumble and regroup," she said. "Now even a complex illusion can collapse with a single combined effort."

Breezie cast a light breeze down an empty sidewalk, stirring a few dry leaves. "Nothing lurking at the edges," he reported with a satisfied smile. "We can rest easy for now."

They paused at a corner where an old lamppost flickered, recognizing that perhaps a final, combined wave of illusions might eventually gather—but none of them felt any fear at that prospect. Their quest at this stage was ending not with a climactic battle, but with an absence of threats and a deeper sense of unity. In fact, this peaceful cameo had even defeated an intangible foe—hesitation—without any new illusion needing to appear. The Wizards left Beacon Street with hearts calm, all past illusions long undone, their unity unshaken under the starry canopy.

Frog Pond Revisited

At last, drawn again to a familiar spot—the Frog Pond—the Wizards found it deserted at this late hour. The water lay smooth as glass, reflecting faint starlight and the dark silhouettes of surrounding trees. They lingered by the railing, recalling how in earlier days, illusions would sometimes ambush them in unsuspecting corners of the city. Now, no such darkness arose; the clarity gained from Emerson's cameo seemed to have dispelled even the possibility.

Reddish folded her arms on the iron railing, her embers now faint and calm. "We keep reaching across every divide," she said, the night's lesson fresh in her mind. "One spark— and poof—the darkness is gone."

Firee tapped the rail thoughtfully, his cloak's crimson quiet. "We'll remain vigilant," he replied, resolve in his voice.

Breezie sighed contentedly, a reassuring breeze ruffling the pond's surface. "We've become a force to be reckoned with," he said calmly. "This cameo made that clear."

Blunt, his synergy gear humming softly, placed a hand on its runic inscription. "Emerson's wisdom, the Orloj's vision, Franklin's storm, Tetragor's guidance," he said quietly, thinking of all their allies. "All of it points to one thing: the need for swift unity. We'll carry that forward."

They stood for a moment in reverent silence, gazing at the tranquil pond. Every prior illusion was now just a memory, and this reflective night had refined their synergy even further. They understood that everyday fears could no longer threaten them—only the promise of one final test remained on the horizon. Whenever any new illusion might rise, they would respond at once. With that silent resolve, the Wizards left the Frog Pond under the midnight sky, no shadows trailing behind, their unity shining unwavering and bright.

Completing the Night's Lesson

Long past midnight, the Wizards finally reconvened near the crypt's entrance, each quietly absorbing the night's significance. No threats had surfaced; no direct conflict had been needed. Instead, they had gained a deeper moral anchor.

The synergy gear in Blunt's cloak glowed softly, as if confirming the peace of the hour.

Checkered broke the silence. "Our time with Emerson reaffirmed our need for unity," she said succinctly. "And the Orloj gave us glimpses of challenges to come. We saw that if the Dark Harlequin tries to unleash all those flaws at once, our synergy can counter him in an instant."

Greenie nodded, thinking of Monticello, Hazleton, Boston. "We overcame every illusion he threw at us," she added gently. "Now we know we can handle any final wave together."

Firee glanced around the crypt's dim nook, confirming all was calm. He grinned wryly. "Looks like the cameo preempted any trouble tonight," he quipped. "I bet the next time we see an illusion will be in Sedona—or whatever final act that Harlequin has planned."

Reddish's embers glowed softly as she smiled. "We stand prepared," she agreed. "Emerson's cameo gave us a deeper perspective—illusions can't blind us now."

Without needing to speak, each of them felt the same steady confidence building. Blunt closed his eyes for a moment, attuning himself to the gentle hum of their combined strength. "All right," he said at last. "Let's rest. If any illusion appears, we'll face it together." Each Wizard nodded at that—there were no doubts left, no lingering fears. The cameo was complete.

They stepped away from the crypt, the Old North Church cloaking them in a gentle, final reassurance. The clarity and unity gained tonight would carry them forward into new adventures. Each of them anticipated that the Dark Harlequin might yet attempt to unleash every vice against them at once—but none of them doubted their ability to meet that challenge together. This encounter had ended not in battle but in enlightenment. The silent streets of Boston welcomed them as they walked out into the pre-dawn calm, no shadows in sight, their bond as strong as ever.

Transcendence's Light

The night enveloped Old North Church, its colonial crypt resting in peaceful silence. Where once illusions had threatened the city's iconic clocks—with stagnation, ignorance, and callousness—none now stirred. The Wizards realized that this encounter had not been a battle at all, but a reflective cameo conjured by the Boston Orloj. In the crypt's hush they had examined how curiosity, innovation, and compassion shaped their unity, forging a shield no illusion could breach.

Guided by the Orloj's cosmic hum, they had glimpsed broader historical and future arcs: cameo visions of other clocks, each site representing a virtue tested by deception. In the same breath, the Orloj made clear that any delay would allow illusions to take root, whereas a response in unison would snuff them out before they spread.

Their time with Ralph Waldo Emerson became a spiritual pivot. Instead of fighting swirling phantoms, they had collaborated peacefully in his Concord study, writing about synergy and the Over-Soul. No hordes of illusions swarmed them there—only a brief trick of mist on a bridge, dispelled the instant they acted together. Emerson's cameo recalled earlier lessons from Tetragor and Franklin as well, each forging a deeper layer of unity. By the end of their walk through Concord's moonlit lanes, any stray shadow fled within seconds, reinforcing the strength of their bond.

Returning to Boston, the cameo ended quietly. The Orloj acknowledged their readiness, advising them to carry this transcendent light of unity into their next trial—perhaps at Sedona's desert Orloj, or wherever the Dark Harlequin would strike next. Transcendence's Light was the name and gift of this new plane of unity: a moral and spiritual strength that no illusion could tarnish.

Thus, the Wizards' second encounter with the Boston Orloj drew to a close with their unity deeper than ever. They stepped out of the Old North Church crypt as night waned, into the city's calm. Not a single illusion lurked in the shadows. The cameo's gift—immediate, unwavering synergy—remained their cornerstone for any challenge ahead. And if the Dark Harlequin dared to unleash a final wave of every vice at once, the Wizards' transcendent bond would ensure that his grandest illusion crumbled into dust. The stage was set for the next arc—Sedona and beyond—wherever new illusions might rally anew. The Wizards would be ready, their unity shining with transcendence's light.

Chapter 11

Sedona's Orloj & Eise Eisinga's Planetarium – Justice Prevails

Arrival at Sedona's Orloj

Midday sunlight poured across Sedona's red-rock desert, illuminating a modern Orloj of crimson stone and bronze gears—a breathtaking blend of ancient design and Southwestern art. Yet its celestial dials turned with a skewed, off-kilter rhythm, as though injustice itself weighed on the clock's balance. From a swirling bronze-and-azure portal, Blunt, Reddish, Firee, Checkered, Breezie, and Greenie emerged with harlequin cloaks softly glowing in the dry heat.

Blunt gripped a runic medallion engraved with "Aequitas Est Virtus." It was a token earned during their reflective cameo with Emerson, and its presence steeled him now. "Ignorance and callousness tried to sway justice before," he said, listening to the Orloj's off-kilter hum, "and now injustice itself lurks here." Inside his cloak, Zeetrikus's "Innovare Est Virtus" gear vibrated in agreement—a reminder of the synergy forged through all their trials.

Breezie lifted a hand to test Sedona's desert breeze, catching faint murmurs from passing tourists. "People are whispering about unfair practices—local disputes shadowed by something unreal," he reported. The pattern felt familiar: in previous trials they had swiftly dispelled illusions before harm could be done. "I suspect these phantoms center on injustice," he added, calm but alert as the wind itself.

Reddish's ember-like eyes narrowed as she scanned the trembling Orloj dials. The carved constellations and desert creatures etched there quivered out of sync. "The mechanism is skewed," she muttered. "This clock was built to symbolize fairness—like the old-world Orlojs. Something's obviously twisting it." The memory of Hazleton's clock flashed through her mind; they had put that one right before any lasting damage was done. She set her jaw, tiny flames licking at her fingertips. "We'll do the same here."

Greenie closed her eyes and extended her empathy into Sedona's famed mystical aura. Usually this land's energy brimmed with unity, but now she felt a faint distortion—like a vortex of spirit turned sour. "This place is known for its spiritual vortexes," she said softly. "But I feel them warping toward bias. Injustice is in the air, and we can't let it linger." Checkered hovered her monocle-like lens over the Orloj's exposed gears, each tooth and tick visible to her trained eye.

"What craftsmanship," she murmured, noting the precision of the design even as it shuddered under unseen strain. "Yet it's being distorted by injustice. I see illusions feeding on every biased judgment and shred of favoritism in the area." She recalled Monticello's clock tower, where ignorance-fueled mirages had tested them as well. They had overcome that together, and she had no doubt they would unravel this distortion, too.

Firee placed his palm on the warm stone base; the desert heat pulsed through him in time with the clock's uneven heartbeat. "Illusions feed on hesitation," he said, his voice low but fervent. "We won't give them that chance." A familiar determination flared in his chest. "We move as one and act fast." Around him, his friends nodded in agreement. Experience had taught them that a swift, united strike could break any mirage before it took hold.

Without another word, the six wizards advanced toward Sedona's Orloj. The closer they came, the more the great clock's humming intensified, as if urging them to confront the injustice disrupting its gears. They answered that call without fear. Each of them was poised to unleash their unique virtue at the first sign of falsehood. In the desert stillness, they resolved that no deception would be allowed to root itself here.

Discovery & Inspection of the Clock

Sedona's Orloj towered in the center of a sunlit plaza ringed by towering red rocks. Up close, its intricate gears—engraved with cactus blooms, canyon ridges, and cosmic spirals—gleamed with artisan pride, yet they shuddered under a strain that shouldn't be there. A shrill, discordant whine emanated from deep within the mechanism, a sound that set the wizards' teeth on edge. It was the unmistakable keening of injustice disrupting what should have been perfect harmony. The six companions spread out around the clock's base, their cloaks catching the midday light as they moved into position.

Checkered adjusted the focus of her lens and peered at the main dial. The bronze hands jerked in fits and starts, the entire clock face quaking as though conflicted. "The craftsmanship is excellent," she observed in a hushed voice. "This clock wants to run true, but something is forcing it off-balance." She pointed toward a ring of tiny painted planets set into the dial; even those miniature orbs trembled out of their paths. "It's just as we thought—some unfair influence is twisting its motion."

Firee pressed a gloved palm against one of the larger exposed gears. He could feel it trying to turn steadily, only to jolt under an unseen pressure. "It's like the mechanism is straining to move fairly," he said, brow furrowing, "but an outside force keeps tilting it astray." The sensation reminded him of Hazleton's courthouse clock, where an illusion of bias had threatened to jam the works—until they had joined forces to set it right. Drawing on that memory, Firee's grip tightened with resolve. "We've corrected this kind of imbalance before," he muttered, more to himself than anyone.

Greenie inhaled and extended her awareness into the bustling plaza around them. Normally Sedona's energy felt uplifting, but now she sensed irritation and discontent. A couple nearby grumbled about "unfair fees," and two others argued over a trivial slight. This haze of petty resentment was not typical of Sedona's wonder. "There's injustice hanging over this place," Greenie said softly, opening her eyes. Concern rippled in her voice. "People are already on edge. We need to right this before it festers."

Breezie summoned a gentle breeze that spiraled around the clock's bronze base, stirring the desert dust. Even the air current met resistance near the Orloj, as if the very mechanism pushed back against the concept of impartiality. He could feel it in the way the wind eddied oddly around the gears. "The whole device is straining under bias," he noted, his usually carefree face drawn serious. He would not let that bias harden. "It won't remain crooked for long. Not if we have anything to say about it."

As Blunt circled the base, something new caught his eye. Along the pedestal of the clock, lettering had begun to glow with ethereal light. He knelt to read the Latin inscription now visible on the stone: "Aequitas Est Virtus; Iniquitas Est Vitium." The phrases alternated on either side of the dial like the balancing arms of a scale. "Equity is virtue; injustice is vice," Blunt translated under his breath. He recognized this signature immediately. "This has Lettizia Dillettante's mark all over it," he called to the others. Lettizia was one of the Antiquarians who set forth moral trials like this. "It's a test of fairness versus unfairness."

Reddish moved to Blunt's side, her fiery hair and cloak casting a warm glow as she read the motto. Her embers smoldered in anticipation. She understood exactly what kind of trial this was: illusions of injustice would try to trick them, and even a second's hesitation could let those falsehoods spread. She squared her shoulders. "We'll give them no time at all," Reddish said, her voice firm. A small flame danced across her knuckles, ready to ignite. "The instant an illusion appears, we hit it together and snuff it out."

No sooner had she spoken than the Orloj's humming whine rose sharply in pitch. The six friends drew back to regroup at the foot of the clock. Above them, the air shimmered with the first hints of distortion, like heat waves coalescing into shapes.

416

A few tourists glanced around, perplexed by a sudden flicker of motion they couldn't quite see, then shrugged and moved on—blissfully unaware of the phantom injustices taking form overhead. But the wizards saw everything. These twisting shadows and half-formed figures were signs they knew too well: an illusion wave was building.

Blunt and the others tensed, exchanging quick, resolute looks. They had encountered such gatherings of falsehood before, and they understood what had to be done. Each of them drew on their particular strength—light, flame, wind, water, empathy, insight—and prepared to act in concert. Whatever injustice meant to show itself here, they would strike it down before it could fully take shape. Steeling themselves, the six stood ready to deliver swift, united justice once more.

Scales in the Red Rock

A hazy image of a great balance scale flickered into being above the Orloj. One pan hung significantly lower than the other, burdened by some unseen weight of injustice. As the spectral scales hovered, a phantasmal scene took shape on the plaza floor beneath: townsfolk appeared, shouting in a heated dispute. In the illusion, an innocent traveler was being accused and condemned by an angry mob while the true wrongdoer slipped away with a smug grin.

The six friends exchanged a glance of recognition—this scenario was exactly the sort of unfair outcome they were here to stop. Yet Greenie felt a tight knot form in her stomach as she watched the distorted drama unfold. What if this injustice is more stubborn than the others? she wondered for a split second. The sight of the helpless stranger facing punishment tugged at her empathic heart, and a sliver of doubt tried to creep in. But then she caught Reddish's fiery, determined gaze and Blunt's steady nod. Each of her companions stood unwavering, ready to act. Greenie drew in a breath and steadied herself; they would not allow this travesty to play out, not even for another moment.

"Justice requires truth!" Checkered shouted, wasting not a heartbeat more. She thrust her lens forward, and a beam of clarifying light shot out, slicing through the mirage. The glowing beam illuminated the cowering figure of the real culprit hiding at the edge of the scene, revealing the deception for all to see. Overhead, the ghostly scales of justice trembled, the weighted pan beginning to rise.

Seizing the opening, Reddish stepped forward with her cloak swirling around her. "No more injustice!" she declared. With a sweep of her arm, she unleashed a rolling wave of crimson flame. The magical fire washed over the crowd scene, not harming the innocents but burning away the lies. The false angry townsfolk, the unfair verdict—every element of the illusion ignited in a brilliant flash and then evaporated into sparks of golden light.

In the span of a single breath, the vision was gone. The scales above the Orloj faded into mist, their balance restored. From within the clock came a reassuring tick as its disrupted cadence leveled out, freed from the bias that had plagued it. Sedona's Orloj was itself again.

The wizards had only a moment to exchange satisfied, relieved smiles when a new surge of magic crackled in the air. From behind the Orloj's main dial, energy began to gather, swirling like a mini-whirlwind of silver and onyx. Blue sparks snapped at the edges of a circular portal as it opened, as though tearing a hole between this place and somewhere far beyond. Sedona's immediate crisis was resolved, but their mission was clearly not finished. This portal felt like a doorway stitching two distant sites of justice together—and it was beckoning them onward without delay.

Portal Activation & Journey to Franeker

A low thrum of magic vibrated through the ground beneath the Orloj as the very air in front of the clock began to crackle with energy. From behind the main dial, a portal spiraled open—silver and onyx swirls spinning outward like the gears of a cosmic clock. Electric sparks danced around its edges.

The six wizards gathered before this gateway, exchanging resolute nods. They had seen portals like this before, linking one troubled timepiece to another across the world. Injustice was beckoning them to a new battleground.

Greenie stepped closer to the portal's shimmering surface, feeling her fingertips prickle with the familiar sensation of nearby wrongdoing. "I can sense more injustice on the other side," she murmured. An image fluttered at the edge of her mind—painted planets and a wooden ceiling. "It's connected to this clock… I'd bet it's Eise Eisinga's planetarium calling to us." She remembered their previous leaps between far-flung clocks and trusted her intuition.

Blunt's synergy gear, tucked in his cloak, began to hum in resonance with the portal's power. He drew a steadying breath. "It looks like the injustice here is trying to spread outward," he said gravely. "We'll answer it with fairness, immediately and decisively." He recalled how in earlier trials they had needed to strike swiftly, before any falsehood could solidify into a real threat. This would be no different.

Reddish placed her hand against the portal's rippling side. Her palm glowed with a soft red heat as she steadied the magic for their passage. "Same drill as always," she said, her embers dancing eagerly. "We go in fast and hit hard. They won't get a foothold on our watch."

Firee twirled his wand once and squared his shoulders, preparing himself mentally for whatever lay beyond. "Illusions feed on delay," he agreed. "We won't leave them a moment to exploit."

Checkered peered through her lens at the portal's interior, but all she could see was swirling light. "No sign of any illusions on this side," she reported. She clicked the lens back into place over her eye with a firm snap. "Which means they're waiting for us on the other side."

Breezie exhaled and centered himself, feeling the dry Sedona air give way to the portal's cooler breeze. "The plan doesn't change, no matter where we step through," he said calmly. "The second we spot an illusion, we all act together, without hesitation."

United in purpose, the six companions stepped forward and entered the portal as one.

At once, they were swept up in a vortex of light and motion. Sedona's blazing sunshine and red cliffs vanished behind them, replaced by a rush of cool darkness spangled with stars. For a dizzying moment, it felt as if they were tumbling through the night sky itself. The air turned from desert-dry to woodsy and rich with the scent of old paper, ink, and candle wax—a library warmth that curled around them as they hurtled onward. All around, they heard a rhythmic ticking that grew louder with each passing second, like a giant clock measuring their journey.

In the heart of that transit, a hushed whisper of bias brushed against their minds, an echo of the injustice ahead trying to seep into the void. But the wizards had come too far to be so easily swayed. As one, they pushed back with their collective will—a burst of silent resolve that shattered the whisper into nothingness before it could form into a coherent lie.

Moments later, the swirling lights around them abruptly parted. The team found solid ground beneath their boots and stumbled forward into gentle lamplight. They had arrived intact, together, and ready in a cozy living room half a world away.

Arrival at Eise Eisinga Planetarium Clock

They found themselves standing in an 18th-century Dutch parlor. The walls were lined with books and a small hearth crackled in the corner, perfuming the air with woodsmoke and old paper. Overhead, an elaborate wooden model of the solar system—the famous Eise Eisinga planetarium—spanned the timber ceiling. It normally ran like a perfectly ordered cosmos, but now a faint off-key hum vibrated from its gears, echoing the imbalance they'd encountered in Sedona. The companions gathered under the slowly circling planets, their cloaks casting soft multi-colored light on the cozy room as they took in this subtle wrongness.

Checkered's gaze was immediately drawn upward to the drifting planets overhead. She flipped her monocle lens into place and examined the model with keen interest. "Absolutely fascinating," she breathed, marveling for a moment at the centuries-old engineering. Her admiration quickly turned to concern as she noticed a jitter in the movement of Jupiter's wooden sphere. The planet jerked and stuttered in its orbit, its path elongating unnaturally whenever a hidden gear stuck. "Something's not right… illusions are meddling with the orbits," Checkered concluded, eyes narrowing behind her spectacles. Indeed, faint wisps of silvery magic clung to some of the gear teeth like cobwebs, interfering with the motion. "There's injustice at work in this mechanism."

Firee's eyes followed the wobbling path of Saturn and Mars above. He knew clockwork and he knew chaos, and this pattern was familiar: a system designed to run fairly and accurately was being pushed off course by an outside force. "We've seen this kind of imbalance before," he said quietly. "A fair device being skewed unfairly." He recalled the courthouse clock in Hazleton—they had managed to set that right swiftly once they combined their efforts. Buoyed by that memory, Firee set his jaw. "We can fix this one too. Just like before."

Greenie closed her eyes and let the room's aura speak to her. Beneath the pleasant aroma of the books and the calm crackle of the hearth lay a current of unease. It was as if the very air still remembered the fear this planetarium was built to dispel. "This home was created to replace fear with understanding," she murmured. "Eisinga wanted knowledge to triumph over panic. But now I sense that very reason being twisted by illusion—turning understanding into prejudice." She opened her eyes, resolve shining in their emerald depths. "We have to restore the balance here, for the sake of truth and knowledge."

Breezie wandered closer to the fireplace, feeling the difference in temperature and atmosphere from the Arizona desert they'd left behind. He gently blew a puff of air upward, sending it wafting toward the hanging model. Instantly, he felt resistance as the planets above lurched; the entire contraption seemed to shudder at even that slight disturbance. "They're trying to unravel fairness in these movements," he said, frowning. "Little lies, half-truths, prejudice—the illusions are threading them into the clockwork." His expression hardened from wonder to determination. "We know how to answer that.

However they try to twist things, we'll meet it together and set it straight before it can do any real damage."

Blunt walked toward one wall where a brass plaque gleamed in the lamplight. Etched upon it were Eisinga's own words celebrating cosmic harmony and order. But right beside this plaque, Blunt noticed fresh symbols glowing with a pearly luminescence. He recognized the phrase at once: "Aequitas Est Virtus; Iniquitas Est Vitium." It was the very same motto that had appeared in Sedona. It hung here like a direct challenge, letters shimmering in and out as if alive. Blunt's synergy gear vibrated at his hip in response to the magic. "That confirms it," he called out to the others, pointing at the Latin words. "Lettizia Dillettante has set this challenge for us as well." The Antiquarian's signature was undeniable. "Another test of justice—equity versus inequity—underway."

Reddish stepped beneath the gently swaying model of the sun, her fists clenched in readiness. The memory of Sedona's victory was fresh in her mind; barely minutes ago they had snuffed out the last phantom injustice in that plaza. Her blood was still up. "We just finished putting an injustice to rest," she said, her voice passionate and her cheeks flushed from the residual heat of fire magic. "We're not about to lose momentum now." She glanced around at the others, her eyes alight like coals. "Biased rulings, partial truths—whatever form these phantoms take, we'll extinguish every last one of them."

Antiquarian Encounter – Lettizia Dillettante

Overhead, the wooden gears of the planetarium gave a low, mournful groan—the only warning before the trial manifested in full. The six companions drew together beneath the slowly orbiting planets, forming a tight circle of resolve. Each prepared their heart for what was to come, standing shoulder to shoulder with unwavering determination as the forces of injustice gathered invisibly around them.

From a dim alcove beside the hearth, a graceful figure stepped forward. She moved into the light with calm purpose—a woman in an antique gown of deep blue, its fabric threaded with silver filigree that glittered in the lamplight. This was Lettizia Dillettante, one of the enigmatic Antiquarians. Her eyes were serene and kind, yet the atmosphere around her crackled with the weight of judgments yet to be rendered. Tiny flickers of apparition flitted at the edges of her presence: ephemeral images of scales tipping unfairly, judges with blindfolds askew, scrolls of unjust decrees curling in ghostly hands. Each of these pale visions represented a biased verdict or a moral failing, half-formed and awaiting a chance to ensnare the unwary.

"Welcome, travelers," Lettizia greeted them, her voice as gentle and melodious as a lullaby, though her words carried the gravity of the challenge. "Injustice has crept into this clock, threatening to pervert Eisinga's pursuit of reason." She swept an elegant hand upward. In response, the wisps of illusion clinging to the planetary model glowed more distinctly. The wizards could make them out clearly now: phantoms of unfair rulings, of favoritism granted and voices silenced—each a distortion of justice entwined with the turning of the gears.

Blunt stepped forward from the group, offering Lettizia a polite bow of acknowledgement. Though respectful, his voice was steady and sure. "We only just finished cleansing Sedona's Orloj moments ago," he informed her. "We're prepared to do the same here." There was no bravado in his statement, only the quiet confidence of someone who has prevailed before and fully intends to prevail again.

Lettizia inclined her head in return, her expression gracious but resolute. She moved closer, the glow from the hearth catching the silver patterns on her gown as she drew a rolled parchment from her sleeve. "Injustice thrives only where hearts allow unfairness to take root," she said, her tone at once didactic and encouraging. With a quick motion of her wrist, she unfurled the scroll. The parchment seemed to come alive, its text shining and shifting. The team could see entries and notes flashing by—records of judgments marred by bias, decisions warped by favoritism, evidence ignored and guilt misassigned. "Show me your commitment to true fairness," Lettizia challenged, "or these accumulated illusions will hold sway over this place."

Reddish answered by letting her inner fire blaze a little brighter, the flames around her shoulders casting dancing reflections on the walls. She recalled the burst of triumph she'd felt in Sedona when they erased the false scene in an instant. Drawing on that strength, she fixed Lettizia with a determined smile. "We stand together in this," Reddish declared, conviction ringing in her words. "Joined as one, we won't allow a single lie to prevail."

As if on cue, new flickers of movement appeared near the rafters where the gearwork hung. Checkered pushed her spectacles higher on her nose, already strategizing. "We'll intercept every illusion the moment it appears," she said crisply. "No hesitation. No mercy for falsehoods."

Greenie's emerald cloak rippled gently as she attuned herself to the emotional undercurrents in the room. Her sensitive heart picked up faint echoes—perhaps the residual cries of those who had been wronged in the cases described on Lettizia's scroll. She placed a hand over her heart and nodded. "We will bring back balance," she promised softly. Though her voice was quiet, it was rich with compassion and resolve. "Whatever injustices have taken hold here, we'll set them right."

Firee lifted his chin, and the tip of his wand ignited with a pure, white flame. "Not long ago, a trial like this might have lasted all night for us," he said, meeting the Antiquarian's gaze with steady eyes. "But we've learned and grown. Now we see through illusions as soon as they surface. They won't find any foothold here." The quiet power in his statement left no room for doubt.

Breezie rolled his shoulders back and let out a calming breath. The air around the group stirred slightly, as if responsive to his confidence. "We're ready, Lettizia," he said, his voice polite but unyielding. "Test us as you will. We'll meet every injustice you summon with swift and unwavering fairness."

Lettizia's gentle smile transformed into a look of fierce approval. "Then let justice guide you," she declared, raising both arms.

With a sudden rush, those silver strands shot outward and took shape across the planetarium. Scenes crystallized in midair—temptations to accept biased outcomes, to stay silent at wrongdoing, to choose loyalty over fairness. The Wizards knew this ploy; they tightened their formation, each prepared to counter the coming illusions without delay.

Orbits of Equity at Eisinga

Lettizia swept her arms in a commanding arc, and silvery strands of magic unfurled from her like a spider's web cast across the room. Almost immediately, scenes began to crystallize in the air amid the dome of stars overhead—each one a test, a temptation to choose wrong over right. The Wizards tightened their formation, shoulder to shoulder. They had trained for exactly this: confronting whatever moral illusions were thrown at them without delay or doubt.

The first vision emerged in the space above the rotating planets. In the dim light, they saw the outline of a courtroom drama gone awry. A lone figure—the scapegoat—stood condemned before a judge, while off to the side the true culprit watched with a smug smile. The scales of justice beside the judge teetered unnaturally, weighted by deceit.

Checkered reacted instantly. "Justice demands the truth!" she cried. Her monocle flashed, projecting a lance of pure illumination straight into the phantom trial. The beam cut through the shadows obscuring the scene, revealing the guilty party for all to see. Under that uncompromising light, the false judgment shattered with a crack. The entire illusion broke apart in an instant, like glass blown to dust by a sudden gust.

Even before those glimmering shards faded, a second illusion flared to life near the model orbit of Mars. This time it was a personal quarrel: two friends stood back-to-back, their faces twisted in anger. A crowd of onlookers pressured the Wizard in the middle to take a side unjustly—favoritism rearing its head. Greenie's heart surged at the sight of friendship being distorted by bias. "No favoritism here," she declared. She extended her hands, and gentle green tendrils of empathic magic coiled around the arguing figures. Her power soothed the tension and illuminated each friend's perspective equally. "Fairness sees all sides." In the blink of an eye, the two friends in the vision reconciled and the entire scene blinked out of existence, gone as swiftly as it had come.

A third illusion sparked by the wooden sun at the center of the model. Reddish found herself face-to-face with a mirage of a shadowy figure offering her a heavy pouch of gold and a scroll of influence—if only she would endorse an unfair decision. Greed and personal gain personified. Reddish's eyes narrowed to embers. "We reject your bribe," she said icily. With a flick of her wrist, she sent a crimson ribbon of flame slicing through the temptress figure and the glittering bribe. The false gold coins melted into slag and the scroll curled into cinders, both burning away to nothing within a few heartbeats.

The illusion of the corrupt deal evaporated in a wisp of oily smoke.

Not a breath later, another scene coalesced near the model of Saturn with its rings. A pompous judge stood atop a dais, pronouncing two different sentences for two defendants who had committed the same crime—one lenient for a favored person, one harsh for someone he disliked. Firee stepped forward, righteous anger flashing in his eyes. A thin flame danced along the length of his wand. "One law for all!" he challenged, drawing a fiery sigil in the air. The blazing symbol of equity sailed forward and branded itself across the vision. At once, the duplicity was laid bare: the two sets of scales the judge held—one for each defendant—fused into one honest balance. The unjust judge and his uneven scales burst apart like a spray of sparks, the illusion consumed by Firee's flame and gone.

A subtle motion drew their attention to the great pendulum that hung from the ceiling, swinging slowly through the air. Around the pendulum, a curling wisp of illusion tried to take shape. Blunt squinted and saw an image of himself being encouraged to stay silent—an illusory colleague whispering in his ear to ignore a wrongdoing for the sake of loyalty. His blue cloak surged as he raised one hand. "No," Blunt said firmly, his voice echoing like a gavel strike. "Wrong is wrong, no matter who commits it." A wave of shimmering water magic rushed out from him in a broad arc. It crashed over the pendulum and the deceitful whisperer alike. The entire scene was drenched and doused, dissolving the moment it was submerged. The watery curtain fell away to reveal nothing behind it—the illusion had been washed clean from the air. Overhead, the wooden gears of the planetarium creaked and then glowed with a healthier golden hue, as if even the mechanism itself felt relief at the truth proclaimed.

Finally, a faint cry echoed from a far corner of the dome, where the lamplight barely reached. An apparition of a council chamber flickered there: a lone figure struggled to speak at a podium while the council members turned their backs, pointedly ignoring the pleas for justice. Breezie felt a pang in his chest at the sight of someone's voice being smothered. "No voice goes unheard!" he boomed. He inhaled deeply and then exhaled a steady, powerful gust of wind toward the tableau. The breeze swept through the council hall illusion, scattering the papers and blowing open the closed windows of those phantom councilors' minds. The council members in the vision wavered, then vanished one by one, carried off by the wind like dandelion seeds. In seconds, the final phantom was gone, leaving only silence—and justice—hanging in the air.

For a moment, stillness fell. The six Wizards stood amidst the gentle ticking of the model planets, victorious. It seemed they had met every challenge Lettizia could conjure. But the Antiquarian's eyes narrowed thoughtfully; she was not finished with them yet. These young heroes had dispatched each obvious injustice with ease—perhaps too much ease. With a subtle gesture of her hand, Lettizia gathered the lingering mists in the center of the room, weaving them into one last test. This final illusion swirled bigger and denser than the ones before, its color tinged with a deep twilight blue. Immediately, the team sensed it carried a different weight, and each of them felt their heart catch in their throat.

The mists parted to reveal a familiar figure robed in magistrate's robes: it was Morpheus, one of the Wizards' own beloved mentors. His wise face looked down on them from a judge's bench as if presiding over a trial. Before him knelt two people. On the left was a young wizard—a favored protégé whom all of them recognized as one of Morpheus's star pupils. On the right was a stranger to the team, a person unknown and unremarkable. In this illusory tribunal, Morpheus struck his gavel and solemnly declared the protégé innocent, despite evidence of that individual's clear guilt shimmering in the air. At the same time, he pronounced the stranger guilty of all charges, condemning the blameless party without a second thought.

Firee felt the fire in his wand falter and dim. The sight of their esteemed mentor delivering such an obviously biased judgment was almost unthinkable. He took an uncertain step backward, eyes wide. "Morpheus would never... do this," he whispered, his voice strained. "Maybe... maybe he knows something we don't?" In Firee's heart, respect for his teacher warred with the shock of witnessing such unfairness. He desperately wanted to believe there was a hidden reason, some piece of evidence or wisdom that justified Morpheus's ruling, yet the scene before him looked undeniably wrong.

Beside Firee, Greenie's hands clenched at her sides. Her empathetic senses recoiled at the raw injustice playing out. She could almost feel the despair and betrayal of the falsely condemned stranger as if it were a physical weight in the room. Tears pricked the corners of Greenie's eyes. "Who is being harmed by this?" she asked softly, her voice trembling with emotion. "An innocent stranger is about to suffer, while the guilty walk free—that can't be right." Her voice gained strength as she spoke, indignation overriding sorrow. "We love Morpheus, but even the best of mentors can falter. And if he's wrong this time... this injustice cannot be allowed to stand."

Blunt's jaw tightened like a vise. He recognized the trap hidden in this illusion: it was pitting their loyalty to a beloved figure against their commitment to justice. His heart ached to see Morpheus—whom he admired deeply—seemingly fall from grace, but his mind zeroed in on the truth that transcended any one person. "It doesn't matter who delivers an unjust verdict," Blunt said, raising his voice so that it rang across the phantom courtroom. "Wrong is wrong—even if a friend or mentor is the one committing it." He stepped between his teammates and the illusory judge, planting himself firmly on the side of fairness.

For a moment, the phantom courtroom seemed to grow even more solid. The ghostly onlookers depicted in the illusion murmured in agreement with Morpheus's pronouncement, their faces set in obedient acceptance as if this outcome were simply the way of the world. That sight, combined with Morpheus's authoritative tone, made Firee's resolve waver further. A cold trickle of doubt crept into him—what if their mentor did have a greater plan? What if defying him was a mistake? Firee's shoulders sagged as he wrestled with the idea that perhaps, somehow, this injustice could be justified.

Then—tick. A sharp, singular sound cut through the thick silence. One of the clock's gears above skipped against another, producing a misstep in the otherwise smooth ticking that should not have been possible in Eisinga's precise model. The aberrant tick echoed like a warning shot. Checkered's keen eyes darted upward behind her lens, immediately catching sight of a tiny wooden planet veering out of its ordained orbit on the ceiling mechanism. That planetary model drifting askew was a clear signal: the very stars in Eisinga's clockwork heavens were rebelling against Morpheus's pronouncement.

"Even the stars contradict this verdict!" Checkered shouted, thrusting an accusatory finger towards the errant planet overhead. Her voice pulsed with fervor and certainty. "Not a shred of real evidence supports such a judgment, and the cosmos itself shows it's wrong!"

Lettizia's illusion flickered at this bold declaration of truth. The ghostly spectators that had been nodding along began to waver, their unanimous murmurs breaking into confusion. On the judge's bench, Morpheus's stern expression faltered; uncertainty rippled across his familiar features, as if the figure within the illusion was doubting the fairness of his own decision.

Seeing the enchanted glamour lose its grip on reality, the young wizards felt a surge of hope—and shame for ever doubting. They straightened their backs and shrugged off the last remnants of the illusion's emotional pull. Firee's eyes blazed with resolve once more, and Greenie dashed away a stray tear, her face hardening with purpose. One by one, each of the six stepped forward and raised their wand, staff, or hand toward the image of Morpheus.

Reddish's voice was gentle but firm as steel. "Forgive us, teacher," she addressed the apparition quietly, "but fairness must prevail."

At her signal, the six friends unleashed everything they had learned in a single, unified strike. A dazzling burst of energy roared forth—a spectrum of virtues entwining together. Emerald empathy and sapphire truth, ruby conviction and golden integrity (and the cool shimmer of water and the invisible force of the wind)—all melded into one harmonious beam aimed straight at the heart of the illusion.

The illusory Morpheus raised an arm as if to defend his false verdict, but the combined light of their virtues slammed into the image of their mentor with righteous force. He recoiled, the confident facade on his face evaporating into mist. The entire phantom tribunal shook under the impact. In a breath of silence, the vision exploded into motes of light. Morpheus's figure and the two kneeling forms beside him disintegrated together, fading into nothingness side by side.

For a single heartbeat, the planetarium's parlor was utterly still. Only the normal ticking of the real clock mechanism remained, and even that seemed momentarily hushed, as if the room itself were processing the profound truth that had just been reaffirmed. The six wizards stood breathing hard, their emotions swirling—relief, sadness, resolve—at what they had just done. They exchanged quiet, sober looks. The weight of this final lesson settled heavily on them: true justice must stand, even when it means challenging someone they hold dear.

Then, gradually, the great planetarium clock resumed its perfect rhythm. One by one, each painted planet on the ceiling slipped back into its proper orbit, the earlier discord corrected. The wooden gears turned seamlessly once more, and the faint off-key hum that had plagued the room was gone, replaced by a gentle, harmonious ticking. The trial of justice had been passed.

The Aequitas Coin & the Boston Call

As the last wisps of the Morpheus illusion evaporated, a calm fell over the parlor. Eisinga's planetarium began to run smoothly again: each painted planet gliding along its track in perfect harmony, the discordant whine from the gears replaced by a gentle, confident ticking. Lettizia stepped forward toward the six victors, a proud, gentle smile gracing her features. Resting in the palm of her hand was a bronze coin that glinted in the mellow light, engraved with the motto "Aequitas Est Virtus."

"You have restored justice here," Lettizia said softly, her words warm with gratitude. She extended the bronze coin toward Blunt. "Carry this token forward — your next challenge lies ahead."

Blunt bowed respectfully as he accepted the coin from the Antiquarian. The metal felt weighty and significant in his grasp. His own synergy gear hummed faintly, still charged with the energy of their victory. Blunt turned the coin between his fingers and read the Latin inscription. They had seen those words before, but each time they carried new meaning. "Most of those illusions never even fully formed before we dispelled them," he observed, marveling at how far the team had come. Closing his fist around the inscribed coin, he added firmly, "We'll stay on guard for whatever comes next."

Lettizia followed Blunt's gaze upward to the now gently turning orrery overhead. "Eise Eisinga built this wondrous clockwork to dispel fear with understanding," she said, her voice echoing slightly in the high-ceilinged room. "Today, your unity and vigilance ensured that the illusions of injustice found no foothold here." She then swept her arm toward the hearth on the far side of the room. Before their eyes, the flames in the fireplace twisted and expanded, transforming back into the familiar swirling portal. Within its shimmer they could see a hint of Sedona's red rock vistas. "Now, return to Sedona's Orloj," Lettizia instructed kindly, ushering them home.

Greenie stepped forward and gave the Antiquarian a polite, grateful nod. "Thank you, Lettizia," she said earnestly. "We won't let injustice take hold anywhere we go. That's a promise."

Reddish allowed herself a small, confident grin. The coals in her eyes reflected the portal's light. "After what we just faced," she added, "I don't think any illusion out there stands a chance against us." The warmth in her tone made it clear this was less boast and more steadfast conviction.

Checkered flipped down her lens one last time and scanned the living room, which now looked perfectly ordinary and peaceful. "All clear here," she confirmed, jotting a final note in her ever-present notebook. Off to the side, Firee and Breezie exchanged a satisfied glance, the former twirling his wand once before holstering it, the latter letting out a contented breath of relief.

Lettizia stepped back with a serene smile, her hands clasped before her as she watched the young wizards gather themselves. Blunt tucked the bronze Aequitas coin safely into an inner pocket of his cloak. With their heads held high, the six companions stepped into the waiting portal together. In the blink of an eye, the cozy lamplight of Franeker gave way to blinding Arizona sunshine. The team found themselves standing once more in the open plaza of Sedona, the dry desert air replacing the Dutch parlor's warmth. They had returned exactly to where they had left, beside the great crimson clock, and now all was as it should be.

Sedona Orloj Freed

Back in Arizona, the six wizards took a moment to appreciate the sight that greeted them. Sedona's Orloj was moving exactly as it was meant to. The mechanical figurines of Southwestern lore—scorpions and jackrabbits, cacti and cosmic arches—paraded around the clock face in smooth, flawless synchronicity. The midday sun bathed the red stone tower in radiant gold, a shining testament to justice restored. Checkered stepped forward and swept her lens across the Orloj's dials and gears one final time. She saw nothing but clean, precise motion—no shimmer of distortion, no lingering magic except the benign enchantments that powered the clock. "All clear. Not a single distortion remains," she reported with a satisfied nod. It was as they had hoped: every illusion was truly gone. "We took care of the trouble here just as thoroughly as anywhere else," she added, snapping her notebook closed with a triumphant little tap.

Greenie closed her eyes and reached out with her empathic sense. The oppressive psychic weight that had earlier hung over the plaza was lifted entirely. In its place she felt only relief, fairness, and the usual gentle awe that Sedona's vortex-like energy imparted to visitors. "The balance is back," she said softly, opening her eyes and smiling. "Those illusions fell apart before they could ever really take hold. Sedona's clock stands for equity once again."

Reddish let the flames along her shawl subside to a gentle, contented glow. She rolled her shoulders, finally allowing herself to relax. "That does feel good," she admitted. She couldn't help but recall how, not so long ago, a battle against injustice might have raged for hours before they found a solution. Now, by contrast, their foes had been vanquished almost as fast as they appeared. "A year ago, this kind of fight would have worn us ragged. Now injustice disappears in mere moments. Our teamwork has become something special."

Nearby, Blunt turned the bronze Aequitas coin over between his fingers, watching how the desert sun caught its engravings. "Aequitas Est Virtus," he read to himself, running his thumb thoughtfully over the Latin words. Every time they earned one of these tokens, it felt more significant than the last. "Same motto," he mused aloud, "but each time we prove it, the meaning deepens." He looked around at his friends, his expression fond but serious. "We can be proud, but we also have to stay vigilant. Different kinds of wrong can still come together if we ever let our guard down."

Breezie fished out a similar bronze coin from the pocket of his cloak—a prize from a prior trial—and flipped it playfully before catching it. He compared the inscription on his coin to the new one glinting in Blunt's grasp and broke into a breezy grin. "They'll never get that chance," he said confidently. Turning to the group, he clapped Blunt on the shoulder. "Not if we have anything to say about it. We won't hesitate, not now, not ever."

A light desert breeze swept through the plaza then, ruffling their hair and tugging at their cloaks, as if the land itself agreed with their resolve. The Orloj's crimson stone seemed to glow with renewed life, and its metal gears caught the sunlight with a brilliant sheen. The dark wave of injustice that had threatened Sedona had come and gone in a flash, swept away by the light of their combined virtues. The great clock chimed the hour with a clear, melodious tone, ticking along in perfect harmony once more. For now, at least, no new threat cast a shadow on the horizon.

Debriefing Franeker Encounter

As the sun dipped low and painted the sky in shades of orange and purple, the friends regrouped in a loose circle on a broad, flat slab of rock near their overlook. Blunt held up the bronze coin Lettizia had given them, watching it catch the day's last rays. In the glow of twilight, they began to discuss the whirlwind sequence of events they had just navigated.

"Think about it," Blunt said, turning the coin thoughtfully in his hand. "We went from Sedona's modern Orloj to an 18th-century Dutch parlor and back again all in one afternoon—and we didn't let injustice fester in either place for more than a few seconds." The others murmured in agreement. It was a remarkable fact: in both locations, they had struck so fast that the malign influences barely had time to put down roots.

Checkered adjusted her monocle and flipped to a fresh page in her ledger to jot down this concluding thought. "Those illusions in Franeker tried to form, but we jumped on each one and poof—gone," she said, tapping her quill pen against the page for emphasis. It was almost comical how quickly each phantom had met its end once exposed. Checkered gave a satisfied little nod, as if punctuating the memory with a period in her notes.

Greenie wrapped her arms around her knees, recalling how the oppressive feeling in Eisinga's parlor had lifted the instant they intervened. "I remember the atmosphere in that planetarium changing as soon as we acted," she said. "Once we stepped in, there wasn't a trace of tension left hanging around." She smiled, the memory of that warm, peaceful living room returning. "Our unity wiped out every distortion on contact. It was like clearing smoke from a room—all that remained was clarity."

They all agreed that the illusions had never stood a chance. They reminisced about how, not so long ago, a single illusion might have exhausted them for an entire day. Not anymore. They knew now how to stop these falsehoods before they even really got going, never allowing a lie to dig in. Only one thorny dilemma in Franeker had made them hesitate at all—Morpheus's phantom—but even that had ended with truth and unity restored.

As dusk continued to gather, the six climbed down from the rocky perch, hearts both proud and peaceful. They knew the Dark Harlequin, or whatever other adversaries lurked in the shadows, would surely concoct new trials. But after today's triumphs, the Wizards felt more prepared than ever for any scheme that might unfold.

Hints of Another Illusions Site

Toward evening, the six friends wandered beyond the town limits of Sedona, following a winding trail into the open desert. The sun had nearly set, and the landscape was cast in velvety purple shadows. They ascended to a high ridge that offered a sweeping view of the valley below, now tinted with the dusky colors of twilight.

Greenie, walking a few paces ahead, suddenly stopped and squinted at the horizon. "Do you see that?" she asked, pointing toward a ripple in the distance. The others gathered around, following her gaze. There, shimmering in the heat haze far away, was the faint outline of a tower. For an instant it sharpened into the image of a clock tower with elegant, perhaps Moorish, arches and hints of turning gears. Then it wavered, becoming translucent against the dusky sky.

"Likely another clock in need of us," Checkered said, immediately pulling out her lens to get a better look. Through the magnifying glass, she caught a brief glimpse of intricate stonework and a distinctive blue-and-gold facade before the mirage flickered. "Interesting... that architecture isn't from around here," she murmured, mostly to herself. The image began to dissolve, and Checkered lowered her lens. "Illusions clearly aren't bound by distance or time," she noted. "It looks like they might be linking across continents now."

Reddish crossed her arms over her chest, and a few sparks of excitement escaped her cloak. This was a new twist: illusions from different places potentially joining forces. Instead of intimidating her, the prospect made her blood race. "If they're planning to team up their tricks," she said with a fierce grin, "we'll just have to be one step ahead of them." There was zero doubt in her voice.

Firee tapped the end of his wand against his boot as he scanned the horizon. By now, the mirage of the distant clock tower had already begun to fade back into the ordinary shapes of mesas and clouds. Only the normal desert dusk remained. "Nothing pressing right this moment," he observed pragmatically. He slipped his wand back into his belt. "But that doesn't mean we can relax. We'll stay ready."

Breezie closed his eyes for a second and felt the gentle night breeze that was beginning to stir. He could sense change on the wind, but it was impossible to tell if the next call would come minutes from now or days. "Maybe an hour from now, maybe a day," he mused. "Whenever the next summons comes, we'll answer at once. No new illusion will get any time to grow on our watch." He opened his eyes and smiled at the group, the wind lightly tousling his hair. His calm certainty was infectious.

Blunt watched as the last glimmer of that mysterious distant clock tower vanished into the twilight. The desert around them was quiet and still again, as if nothing unusual had happened. He set his jaw and gave a firm, single nod. "We remain vigilant," he affirmed softly. "Whatever that was and wherever it is, if injustice is brewing there, we'll bring our answer to it — even faster than we did here."

They lingered a moment longer on the ridge, but the horizon revealed no further signs. The six turned back toward Sedona, the first stars of evening beginning to peek out overhead. As they hiked down in the final light of dusk, the sky above blazed orange and pink behind the dark silhouettes of the red rocks. They all understood that more trials lay ahead—possibly challenges greater and more complex than any before. But after the victories of this day, their resolve was only strengthened. Together, they felt equal to any task the future might hold.

Desert Evening Calm

Night fell gently over Sedona's red rock country. The six wizards found themselves strolling once again through the plaza, past the now-restored Orloj, as the first stars pricked the sky. Townsfolk were lighting lanterns along the walkways, and a handful of late tourists meandered by, completely unaware that their peaceful evening had nearly been disturbed by forces of injustice. Blunt's synergy gear remained silent against his cloak—no alarms, no urgent vibrations. For the first time in a long while, the team could savor a victory at sunset without immediately rushing off to the next crisis.

Greenie slowed her pace to admire the bands of red and violet still fading in the western sky, the jagged silhouettes of Sedona's rock formations standing dark against the twilight. She breathed in deeply, enjoying the tranquility. "Not even a scuffle this time," she said, half marveling. She was thinking of how seamlessly they had resolved the conflict in Eisinga's planetarium, and how in Sedona they had snuffed out the illusions almost before anyone knew something was wrong. "We banished those illusions before they could cause any harm at all."

Checkered scribbled a final line in her ledger, then snapped the book shut with a contented thump. "Injustice never had a chance tonight," she stated matter-of-factly. She adjusted her spectacles and looked at her friends. "We act before a problem can grow—that's exactly why it disappears so quickly." It was their formula, simple but unwavering: see the problem, unite, solve it. Every time they followed it, the outcome was the same.

Firee caught a whiff of mesquite smoke from a nearby hearth fire, which made him smile as he remembered some of the tougher battles now behind them. He raised an eyebrow and added, "Same pattern every time now. If an illusion even dares to pop up, we knock it right back down." He mimed a hammering motion with his fist into his palm, eliciting a small laugh from Breezie.

Breezie's face was relaxed and content as he listened to the nighttime sounds of Sedona—distant music, laughter from a cafe patio, the chirp of a cricket. "And we won't let any little evil join up into something bigger, either," he said, picking up where Firee left off. He spread his hands wide as if encompassing all their past foes. "Our bond is too strong for that now." Each small challenge would be snuffed out before it could ever combine into a larger threat; he was sure of it.

As they walked, Blunt felt a gentle pulse from the synergy gear hidden in his cloak, almost like a cat settling into a comfortable purr. It reminded him of the vow they all shared. He reached out and laid a hand on the Orloj's outer railing as they passed by it. The metal was cool now, calm—just like the situation. "We'll keep that promise," Blunt said softly, his eyes on the stars beginning to emerge overhead. "No matter what comes, we won't let it overshadow what we've achieved here tonight."

They paused for a moment near a low adobe wall at the edge of the plaza, collectively taking in the scene. Sedona's Orloj glowed gently in the darkness, its clock face illuminated by lantern light, the hands moving with steady, reassuring purpose. The timepiece was entirely free of corruption, ticking away like a guardian of the night. Another challenge had been met and overcome; their teamwork had proven unbreakable once again.

Without another word, the six turned and departed the plaza, their silhouettes melting into the deepening twilight. The desert night was cool and still around them as they headed off to find rest. The trials of this day had ended in decisive victory, and tomorrow's challenges had yet to announce themselves. But under the vast canopy of stars, as they guided themselves by the coin's quiet promise and the strength of their unity, they were confident that whatever new dawn brought, justice would prevail wherever their journey led next.

Debriefing Eisinga's Influence

Later that night, the wizards made camp under a blanket of brilliant stars. As they rested beside a small fire, they realized that justice—like Eisinga's cosmic clockwork—required constant balance. It wasn't just their swiftness in action, but the virtues guiding those actions, that kept injustice at bay. Not long ago they might have wrestled with illusions until dawn, but now their clarity and unity caused falsehoods to collapse in mere moments. They had learned to see through deceit immediately and respond as one at the first hint of trouble, leaving no chance for any illusion to take hold.

They vowed to remain just as vigilant moving forward. If the Dark Harlequin or any adversary ever tried to combine all these moral failings into a single overwhelming trick, then the six of them would unite every virtue they had cultivated and meet it head-on. Nothing, they agreed quietly under the sparkling Sedona sky, could outmaneuver the power of their unity.

Nightfall in Sedona & Aftermath

By the time the moon was high, Sedona's red cliffs had become dark silhouettes outlined against a tapestry of stars. The six friends found themselves drawn back to a familiar overlook above the quiet town. From this vantage point, they could see Sedona's Orloj below, its clock face faintly illuminated and peaceful.

Greenie settled on a smooth ledge of rock and gazed upward, softly ticking off a list of names on her fingers. "Monticello, Hazleton, Boston, Stará Bystrica, Sedona, Franeker…" she murmured, naming some of the places where they had dispelled illusions over the past months. "We've set things right in every one – and faster every single time."

Reddish lowered herself onto a boulder with a contented sigh. She picked up a small pebble and tossed it into the darkness, listening for it to clatter below. "Not so long ago, we'd be nursing wounds and second-guessing ourselves after a day like this," she said, recalling the early days of their quest when victories were hard-won and their confidence was still fragile. She shook her head in wonder at how far they had come.

Checkered polished the lens of her eyepiece with a corner of her cloak, reflecting on Greenie's list of conquered trials. "It's funny," she said thoughtfully. "Every illusion we've encountered was tied to some moral failing… ignorance, fear, cruelty, injustice. But our combined virtues cut through them every time. It's almost... routine." She chuckled softly at that word, because none of them had ever imagined their extraordinary adventures could feel routine. Yet here they were.

Firee stood a few paces away at the very edge of the overlook, the silver moonlight catching in his hair. He looked up at the vast night sky. "If someday all those failings came at us at once—every last one of them—I think we'd be ready," he said quietly, conviction in each word. He turned back to face his friends, the moon reflected in his eyes. "We'd unite everything we've learned, all our virtues, and face it head-on."

Breezie, for once, found he had nothing to add. He simply exchanged a series of knowing smiles with the others, each of them acknowledging the quiet truth of Firee's statement. They all felt it: even if a final, grand confrontation awaited them, they would face it side by side, without hesitation.

Blunt remained silent a moment, letting the night wind play about them. The synergy gear in his cloak pulsed with a slow, steady light, like a heartbeat at rest but ever watchful. At last, he spoke, his voice firm in the darkness. "We'll remain ready," he said, and the certainty in his tone made everyone look his way. Blunt's eyes traveled over each of his comrades, full of pride and affection. "The next site, the next villain—whoever or wherever it is—we'll meet them just like we did today: together and without delay."

With that vow reaffirmed under the stars, the six young wizards rose as one and began the short hike back down from the overlook. The desert night was cool and still around them, and the silhouette of Sedona's Orloj stood guard over the sleeping town. The challenges of this chapter of their journey had ended in triumph. Tomorrow's challenges had yet to reveal themselves. But guided by the quiet gleam of the Aequitas coin and strengthened by the unbreakable bond between them, the Wizards of Virtue walked on—confident that as long as they stood united, justice would continue to prevail wherever their path led next.

Chapter 12

Rittenhouse and Jens Olsen Clocks – Justice's Triumph

The Coin's Call

Night fell gently over Sedona's red rocks as the six Wizards gathered their wits after the Arizona trial. In Blunt's hand glinted a newly earned bronze coin from Lettizia Dillettante – its Latin inscription, Aequitas Est Virtus ("Fairness is a Virtue"), still warm from dispelling Sedona's injustice illusions. The coin tugged at Blunt's palm with a subtle, insistent pull. Reddish's eyes narrowed in curiosity. "It's drawing us northeast," she noted, watching the coin glow softly. Checkered spread a map on a sandstone boulder, and the coin's glow intensified over one spot.

"Philadelphia," Checkered said, tracing the location. "Home of the American Philosophical Society... and David Rittenhouse's famed astronomical clock at Drexel." A spark of recognition lit her monocle-covered eye – Rittenhouse, patriot-scientist and clockmaker, had championed reason in the young republic. Greenie smiled determinedly. "Fairness guided by reason – that must be our next trial." Blunt nodded and raised the coin. In response, the bronze token emitted a shaft of pale light. The very air shimmered, forming a portal ringed with faint constellations. Trusting the coin's call, the Wizards stepped through together.

They emerged in the hush of a darkened gallery. Moonlight filtered through tall windows, illuminating the David Rittenhouse Astronomical Musical Clock standing proudly at the room's center. The clock was a mahogany tall-case masterpiece, its Chinese Chippendale carvings ornate yet dignified. Six tiny planets of brass orbited a painted sun just above the clock face – an elegant orrery demonstrating the solar system known in 1773. Around the dial, gilt zodiac constellations twined in a circle. Even in stillness, the clock exuded an air of reasoned order: it kept not only time, but also the positions of heavenly bodies and the month and day. It was said to even play ten different tunes on its chimes, though now it ticked in solemn silence. Breezie drew a breath at the sight of the craftsmanship. "Truly a triumph of reason… the most important clock in America, they called it," he whispered. Firee ran a hand along the mahogany case, feeling the weight of history. "Built in the Revolutionary era, when fairness and freedom were new ideals," he murmured. "Rittenhouse was a friend of Franklin and Jefferson – men who tried to wed governance with enlightenment." The team exchanged knowing looks. This clock, a blend of science and art, symbolized knowledge guiding justice.

A faint shimmer of illusion clung to the clock's dial like morning frost. The bronze coin in Blunt's hand grew warm, warning of an injustice lingering here. Checkered flipped down her monocle, the enchanted lens revealing wisps of oily darkness coiling around the orrery's planets. "There's bias in the gears," she alerted softly. As if on cue, the long-case clock gave a shuddering tick and the orrery began to spin out of alignment – Mars and Jupiter jarringly stopped in retrograde, the Moon halting in its orbit. Greenie winced, sensing a pang of imbalance in the air. "An illusion is trying to form," she warned.

Without further prompt, a phantom scene materialized around them in the gallery. The scent of lamp oil and old books wafted by. Ghostly figures in 18th-century attire appeared, arranged as if in a colonial court. At the center stood Rittenhouse himself, recognizable from portraits: a dignified man in a wool coat, holding a sheaf of astronomical charts. Opposite him rose a figure in a judge's robe and white peruke, slamming a gavel. "Superstition and fear have no place here!" Rittenhouse's specter declared firmly, confronting a murmuring crowd. The judge's apparition scowled. "Your scientific toys challenge tradition," it barked, pointing a finger at the splendid clock behind Rittenhouse – the very same orrery now glowing with an inner light. Some phantom onlookers nodded in fearful agreement, casting suspicious looks at the mechanical planets and gears. The atmosphere bristled with a familiar injustice: prejudice against knowledge and truth.

Checkered stepped forward into the illusion's midst, her cloak's sapphire hues catching the flicker of illusory lamplight. This was a test of justice through reason. "You accuse what you don't understand," she said sharply to the ghostly judge, raising her wand like a professor brandishing a pointer. "Show evidence of harm in this device or this man's work – if you cannot, your judgment is baseless." Her logical words rang out crisp and clear. The judge's form wavered uncertainly, mouth opening and closing without rebuttal. Emboldened, Reddish added, "Knowledge isn't heresy. It's illumination! Our nation was founded on truth, not fear. We will not let ignorance condemn an innocent man." Flames danced at her fingertips, casting chasing shadows that caused several phantom townsfolk to step back in awe. A few in the crowd started to murmur assent, their expressions softening as if waking from a spell of fear.

But not everyone was convinced. A panicked shout rose from the back of the hall: "Witchcraft!" cried one spectral townsman, his eyes wild with fear. "Smash that infernal clock!" another voice snarled, shaking a fist. Sensing the resurgence of dread, the ghostly judge banged his gavel again and jabbed a finger toward Rittenhouse. "Seize the heretic and his contraption!" he commanded. With a roar, several phantom figures lunged forward, determined to silence this "dangerous" knowledge by force.

Firee moved in a flash. He planted himself before Rittenhouse and the orrery, sweeping his arm in a wide arc. A sudden curtain of incandescent flame roared to life, drawing a bright line between the advancing mob and the clock. "You will not touch this symbol of truth!" Firee thundered, his voice blazing with righteous fury. The wall of fire billowed outward, circling protectively around Rittenhouse's creation. The leading phantoms recoiled with cries of alarm, stumbling back from the searing heat. Even the judge staggered, his certainty faltering in the face of the Wizards' fierce defense.

Beside Firee, Greenie stepped forward with both palms raised—not to strike, but in appeal. Her emerald cloak swirled in the heat as she met the wide eyes of the panicked colonists. "Please, listen!" she implored, her tone gentle yet carrying through the hall. "This clock was built to enlighten, not to curse. Knowledge is not your enemy—your fear is. Don't let ignorance blind you to the truth!" Her compassionate words washed over the crowd. A few ghostly townsfolk faltered, lowering the torches and clubs they had imagined wielding. Uncertainty flickered across faces that moments ago burned with hatred.

A cool gust of wind followed, sweeping through the gallery to chase away the last shadows of fear. Breezie stepped forward next, guiding a cleansing breeze with a subtle motion of his wand. The gentle gale snuffed out the lingering embers of Firee's flames and peeled back the oily black mist clinging to the judge's form. "Think, all of you," Breezie said, his voice calm and clear. "Would you punish what you haven't even tried to understand? True justice seeks understanding, not blind destruction." His words, carried on fresh air, wove through the assembly. One by one, the colonists' enraged cries died down. The mob's unified front broke apart as shame and second thoughts took hold. The judge's spectral arm—still raised to incite violence—wavered and slowly lowered as the illusion's fury drained away.

As silence fell, Rittenhouse's apparition stepped forward from behind the clock. He stood straighter now, shoulders lifting as relief glinted in his eyes.

Blunt seized that hopeful moment. He strode to the orrery and gently placed a hand on the model sun. "Truth and fairness move in harmony," he said, his voice low but resolute. With a slight push of Blunt's hand—empowered by the coin's guiding virtue—the mechanical planets resumed their orderly motion. The celestial model realigned itself with a satisfying click, each planet finding its proper path once more. At that instant, the illusory judge's gavel splintered and broke in two with a sharp crack. The oppressive shadows around the judge evaporated. The entire colonial courtroom scene dissolved like mist in sunlight. In the hush that followed, the Rittenhouse clock chimed once, a single clear tone echoing through the gallery as if declaring its approval.

The six friends exhaled, hearts still hammering. That injustice had fought hard, but in the end it was banished. "Fairness through reason," Checkered affirmed, resting a hand on the clock's cool brass dial. Greenie closed her eyes and found only clarity where confusion had lurked moments before. Indeed, once faced with evidence and their unity of purpose, the illusion had finally collapsed – a testament to how far they had come. Blunt held up the bronze coin; its glow was steady, contented. "Onward," he said, feeling the coin tug at him again. A new portal irised open above the clock, swirling with cold, starlit blue light. The coin's next call had awakened – and it pointed across the ocean.

Without hesitation, the Wizards stepped through the portal's blue haze. A brisk night breeze met them on the other side.

They found themselves in a spacious hall of stone, the air cooler now and tinged with the scent of old metal and oil. Tall windows revealed a European cityscape beyond – they had arrived in Copenhagen, inside the City Hall. Before them loomed an enormous, gilded contraption of wheels and dials: Jens Olsen's World Clock. Greenie's breath caught at the sight. The clock was a marvel of modern horology – fifteen thousand interconnected parts of brass and gold leaf, all polished to a gentle gleam. Multiple faces and sub-dials crowded its front, each measuring a different cycle: the local time, the exact time in cities around the globe, the positions of planets and constellations, sunrise and sunset times, the date and even the future dates of eclipses and holidays. All of these disparate indicators ticked in synchrony, an intricate harmony of mechanisms. The entire clock was designed to run for 2,500 years with weekly winding – a true Verdensur(World Clock) that balanced the celestial and the earthly. Its golden surfaces reflected the Wizards' awed faces back at them.

"This is… spectacular," Breezie whispered, running a hand through his airy silver hair as he eyed the myriad moving hands and stars on the dials. Checkered adjusted her monocle to take in fine details: delicate gears within gears turning with mathematical precision. "Olsen devoted his life to this masterpiece," she said softly. "A clock to unify all the world's times and heavens… every system in balance." Reddish's normally fierce demeanor gentled as she regarded the clock's silent poetry of motion. "Balance across all systems," she repeated. "If any part fell out of sync… the whole would suffer." A sense of gravity settled on them. This clock's very purpose resonated with the principle of justice they cherished: fairness that accounted for everyone, for the entire whole, not just one piece.

No sooner had that thought crossed their minds than the World Clock's great gears groaned. The central time dial began to spin erratically, and several smaller dials representing cities around the world flickered at conflicting hours. The harmony of ticking mechanisms faltered; in its stead rose a discordant whir. Greenie gasped, pressing a hand to her heart as an overwhelming sensation of disharmony struck her empathic senses. "Something's wrong… I feel voices clashing," she said. Wisps of silvery illusion magic seeped out from the clock's works, coalescing into translucent shapes around the hall. The team formed a circle, instantly alert. They recognized the creeping fog of a complex illusion taking shape – one of Lettizia's signatures, perhaps.

Figures emerged from the mist: an assembly of ghostly silhouettes representing people from many lands. Some wore the draped silks of the East, others the somber suits of the

West; some appeared as humble farmers, others as officials with scrolls in hand. Their faces were etched with frustration and desperation. Immediately a cacophony of overlapping pleas filled the hall in a dozen languages. Though the tongues differed, the sentiment was the same: "It isn't fair! Hear us – our needs must be met!"

A burly specter in a miner's cap slammed his fist into his palm. "Our village labors day and night, yet we have no bread while others feast!" he thundered. Across from him, a dignitary in a judge's robe retorted, "Order must be maintained! If your village gets more grain, another must starve – that is the cost!" A woman in humble clothes stepped forward with tears in her eyes, clutching an empty basket. "My children go hungry," she pleaded, voice quavering. "Who decides which of us eats?" Behind her, a growing chorus echoed: "Who decides? Who decides?"

The illusion presented a global clamor of competing voices – each with a valid need, each fearful of being overlooked. The Wizards stood in the eye of this storm of grievances, feeling the tide of discord threaten to wash over them. This was a trial of justice's balance: could they find a fair harmony among so many clamoring needs? Firee's fists tightened, the fiery glow around him pulsing as he fought to keep his own emotions in check against the wave of despair and anger. Breezie closed his eyes briefly, focusing on the coin's calming weight in Blunt's hand and the memory of the World Clock's intended harmony.

Blunt took a step forward and raised the bronze coin overhead. Its inscription glowed brighter, casting a warm amber light that cut through the cold blue mist. The disparate voices quieted a fraction at that golden glow. "Listen to us!" Blunt called out, his voice carrying authority. "We hear each of you. All of your lives matter, and true justice will not sacrifice one people for another." The crowd of phantoms wavered, uncertain. A gaunt man in the garb of a scholar pushed forward, eyes desperate. "Our libraries are shuttered to fund their granaries," he cried, pointing at the miner. "Is that justice? Must knowledge starve so bodies can live?" Immediately an angry rebuttal rose from the miner and those behind him.

Before the factions could collide, Greenie stepped between them. She extended her arms, emerald cloak flowing like calming water. "Hurt and want exist on all sides," she said, her voice gentle yet carrying to every corner of the hall. "Please – instead of shouting against one another, look." She waved her hand, and the golden light from Blunt's coin refracted into a broad beam that illuminated the World Clock behind them. In that radiance, the clock's many dials became clearly visible to the crowd: one for each time zone, one for the planets, one for the calendar, and so on. All were interconnected. "This clock carries many faces, yet they are part of one creation," Greenie spoke, eyes shining. "Your concerns are no different – many facets of a single world. Justice means no voice is forgotten."

Breezie took Greenie's side, his wind magic swirling the lingering mist into gentle ribbons. "Justice isn't a tug-of-war where only one side wins," he added, looking from the hungry mother to the robed scholar and the weary miner. "It is a covenant that all are due fairness. If one part of the system fails, the whole suffers." As if to illustrate his words, Checkered directed her wand at the clock's mechanism. She muttered an incantation, and one rebellious gear that had been spinning erratically began to slow. Instantly the clattering of mis-synced parts eased. Encouraged, Firee unleashed a controlled pulse of flame at another grinding cog – its sudden jolt brought the cog back into rhythm with the others. Bit by bit, gear by gear, the six worked in concert to restore the mechanism's equilibrium.

The effect on the hall's illusion was profound. The furious delegations fell silent as they watched the Wizards methodically right the clock's operation. The scholar lowered his accusatory arm, brow furrowing with thought. The miner unclenched his fists, casting a wary glance at the mother with the basket. In the new quiet, the only sound was the steady tick, tick, tick of Olsen's World Clock gradually synchronizing – a thousand tiny clicks merging into a steady hum. Checkered spoke into that calm: "Resources, knowledge, order – all are important. We do not deny one need for another; we find a way to uphold them together." She stepped over to the phantom mother and gently placed a conjured loaf of bread into her empty basket. At the same time, Breezie summoned a quill and ledger before the scholar, symbolically reopening the library he feared losing. "There is enough, if we cease to fear one another," Breezie said softly.

From the crowd came a tentative voice: "Can we truly find balance?" It was the dignitary in judge's robes, his stern face now etched with vulnerability. Reddish stepped forward, lowering her wand. The heat in her aura subsided to a warm glow rather than a blaze. "We can," she affirmed. "Justice means each gives a little so that all may thrive. Strength tempered by compassion, law guided by equity." She lifted her chin, her voice swelling with conviction. "No more 'us versus them.' We choose together."

A murmur of agreement rippled through the specters. The judge slowly nodded, lowering his head in acceptance. The miner placed a gentle hand on the scholar's shoulder, while the mother clutched her bread and wept tears of relief. The disparate groups that had been ready to tear each other apart now mingled, their outlines already fading as the illusion's energy dissipated. United understanding had undercut the injustice at its source. Above them, the World Clock chimed sweetly – all its dials now aligned and clicking in perfect concert. Midnight struck in Copenhagen; the great bells of City Hall tolled with deep, melodious peals. The illusionary assembly bowed their heads in gratitude as they melted away into motes of light, leaving the hall silent and still once more. At the base of the clock, a small compartment popped open with a soft click. From it rolled an object onto the floor – a tiny silver key glinting in the faint light. Breezie retrieved it, holding it up between thumb and forefinger. The key's bow was wrought in the shape of balanced scales. "A parting gift from Jens Olsen?" he wondered aloud. Checkered peered at the object, noting delicate runes along its shaft. "More likely from Lettizia," she said with a half-smile, sensing a familiar virtuous enchantment on the key. "A token of balance… to use when the time comes." Blunt placed the key safely in his cloak next to the bronze coin. The others exchanged looks of satisfaction – they had passed the global trial of justice. Now only one destination beckoned.

Greenie pointed toward a grand oak door that led out of the clock room. Through its glass inset, they could see a new portal shimmering to life in the hallway beyond, its surface rippling with the image of an old brick meeting hall. "Boston," Greenie breathed. Indeed, the coin's pull now resolved in that direction, confident and steady. With renewed determination, the six companions stepped through the portal, the silver key and bronze coin in hand.

They emerged on a quiet street under a misty pre-dawn sky. Towering before them was the historic Old South Meeting House of Boston, its brick walls and white steeple dimly visible in the bluish early light. A large round clock face was mounted high on the tower, faintly illuminated by a nearby gaslamp – its hands showed that dawn was fast approaching. The square around the Meeting House was deserted at this hour, lending the scene an otherworldly calm. Yet the Wizards immediately sensed they were not alone. A prickling haze of magic hung in the air, tinted with the unmistakable chill of injustice illusions. The bronze coin in Blunt's pocket pulsed urgently, and the silver key gave a single warm thrum as if in warning. Reddish drew her wand, a tongue of flame flickering at its tip to light their way. "Lettizia is here somewhere," she muttered. The coin had guided them here for this very confrontation – the final test of Justice's virtue was at hand.

The six moved as one toward the Meeting House's entrance, but before they reached the door, a lithe figure stepped out from the shadows of a nearby gaslit alley. Clad in a flowing silver-gray robe with a diaphanous veil of stars trailing behind, Lettizia Dillettante appeared like a wraith of moonlight. Her serene face regarded them with gentle, knowing eyes. In the dim glow, wisps of illusory fog swirled at her feet, coiling across the cobblestones. Faint distortions gleamed within that fog – Checkered lifted her monocle and saw flashes of scenes inside it: images of partial verdicts, mobs with torches, scales tipping unjustly. Lettizia's presence was unmistakable; this was her trial to oversee.

"Welcome, travelers," Lettizia greeted softly, her voice melodic and calm. "Injustice gathers here like dew before sunrise. Will you help dispel it?" Without waiting for an answer – she knew it already – Lettizia turned and glided toward a small side door on the Meeting House. A sign above it, swinging gently in the breeze, identified it as The Six Statues. The door appeared to be locked tight, secured by an iron padlock. Lettizia paused on the threshold and glanced back at the companions, a challenge in her eyes. "Do you seek fairness," she asked, "or will you cling to comforting illusions?" With that, she passed through the door; the mist around her form made it unclear whether she opened it or simply drifted through like a ghost. The door thudded shut behind her.

Blunt stepped up and grasped the iron padlock. It was real and very solid. Reddish's flame cast dancing shadows over its rusted surface. "It's shut fast," Blunt growled, tugging. But Breezie was already at his side, producing the silver key they'd earned in Copenhagen. "Perhaps a key gifted for balance will also grant us entry," Breezie said, sliding it into the lock. The fit was perfect. With a satisfying click, the padlock opened and fell away. The Six Statues shop beckoned from the darkness beyond. Sharing a resolute nod, the Wizards pushed the door open and entered.

The Six Statues: Scales in Lamplight

Inside, the shop called The Six Statues was lit only by a few low oil lanterns, their flames painting long shadows across shelves of curios and old books. The space was hushed and close, smelling of aged paper, brass, and a hint of incense. As their eyes adjusted, the team saw six marble statues arranged in a semi-circle at the far end of the shop. Each statue depicted a robed figure representing a virtue – Courage with a sword, Compassion with an open hand, Wisdom with an owl, and so on. At the center stood a taller statue of Justice, unmistakable with her blindfold and balanced scales. Those marble scales, however, were swinging gently as if disturbed by an unseen breeze. The Wizards could feel latent magic in the air thickening. Lettizia Dillettante stood near the base of the Justice statue, one graceful hand resting on the pedestal. In the lantern glow her silver robe shimmered, and her expression was calm, almost tender.

"This shop is dedicated to fairness," Lettizia said in a low voice, "yet even here, illusions creep in to distort truth." She nodded toward the Justice statue, whose scales were now tilting unevenly from side to side of their own accord. "Show me your commitment to true justice. Set these scales right again." As she spoke, the last lantern flame flickered and died, plunging the shop into a dim twilight broken only by the faint aura emanating from the statues themselves.

The Wizards stepped forward cautiously, spreading out in a semi-circle. Their harlequin cloaks pulsed in a gentle rhythm, the only movement in the shop's expectant hush. The air felt charged yet strangely still; no illusion had fully materialized, but something unseen hung here like a held breath. Blunt's synergy gear vibrated faintly against his chest, attuned to the latent magic drifting about. "Injustice is gathering here," he whispered. The pricking tension reminded him of other enchanted places they'd been — Sedona's astronomical clock, Franeker's planetarium — sites where illusions lingered, waiting to be confronted.

Greenie drifted alongside a shelf of old artifacts. She ran her hand lightly over a row of brass weights and measures, and her empathic intuition caught fine threads of strain in the atmosphere. "I feel bias hiding, ready to twist the truth," she breathed. Her fingertips tingled as they passed a dusty ledger on the shelf; faint impressions of partial verdict illusions clung to it. "They're lurking just out of sight — half-formed judgments like the ones we've dispelled before, waiting for a chance to tip the scales."

At that moment, the marble Statue of Justice almost seemed to stir. The scales in her hand began to tilt, one side dipping as if some invisible weight had been added to the pan. Around the statue's base, shadows pooled in unnatural dark swirls. From behind the statue, Lettizia emerged like a figure stepping out of a painting. Her expression was calm and authoritative, and in the low lantern-light her gray eyes glinted with purpose. "Welcome, seekers," she greeted them, voice low and melodious. "This shop is dedicated to fairness — yet even here, illusions seep in to tip the scales with partial truths and hidden bias."

Reddish's fiery hair swayed behind her as she turned, tracking the shifting shadows that crept along the floor. She held her staff at the ready, flames already licking along the haft. "We know these tricks," she said, her voice steady and bold. "No matter what trickery tries to tip those scales, we'll set them right."

Checkered moved to one of the tall silver mirrors lining the wall. Instead of her own reflection, for a split-second she glimpsed a phantom image: a judge's bench with scales weighed down heavily to one side. She clicked her tongue in distaste and snapped her lens shut. "We'll counter every imbalance," she declared. "No illusion born of bias will hold sway while we stand watch."

Breezie inhaled slowly, attuning himself to the faint stagnation in the air. As he exhaled, a soft breeze stirred through the shop, making the remaining lantern flames flicker. Though he said nothing, his calm stance spoke for him — they had never ignored a distortion before, and they weren't about to start now.

Lettizia gave a slight nod, as if satisfied by their responses. Her eyes flashed as subtle phantasms of biased judgment drifted among the shelves like wraiths waiting to pounce. "Then prove your fairness again," she challenged. With a graceful flourish, she raised one slim hand.

At Lettizia's gesture, the shop itself seemed to come alive. The bronze lanterns dimmed, their flames guttering as an unnatural shadow thickened in every corner. The marble statue's scales began to seesaw up and down, as though an unseen hand kept adding then removing weight. The shelves rattled and the silvered mirrors fogged, smoky images writhing on their surfaces.

Another wave of illusions gathered, swirling through The Six Statues like a rising storm of whispers. The Wizards felt a familiar pressure building around them — the test was beginning in earnest. Instinctively, they drew close together in a defensive circle beneath the statue's impassive gaze. They had faced countless illusions before, usually snuffing them out within moments by standing united. This time would be no different... or so they believed.

Pages that Weigh the Heart

In a niche off to one side of the shop, near Justice's pedestal, a cozy reading alcove beckoned. A round wooden table stood surrounded by high-backed chairs, and a bronze lamp hanging overhead cast a steady golden glow. Neat stacks of scrolls and leather-bound folios were arranged on the tabletop. The air here was rich with the scent of melted wax, old leather, and parchment. At Lettizia's gentle invitation, the six Wizards took their seats around the table, their cloaks rustling and then falling quiet around them. Lettizia remained standing at the head of the table. With deliberate care, she opened a massive leather-bound tome that lay before her.

"Justice triumphs over illusion," she intoned softly. There was a reverence in her voice that hushed even the anxious shadows flickering at the edge of the lamplight. "Before you face the heart of this trial, hear these lessons." From the pile of manuscripts beside her, Lettizia drew forth two aged scrolls. She offered the first one to Greenie with a solemn smile. "Two short readings," Lettizia said, "to remind us how fairness disarms falsehood."

Greenie accepted the scroll with steady hands. Her empathetic gift often attuned her to the deepest meanings hidden in such tales. She unrolled the parchment carefully, smoothing it flat on the table. The others leaned in, their eyes on Greenie as she began to read:

"The Tree of Echoes: A Fable of Injustice and Hope"

In a valley nestled between two great mountains stood the Village of Mirrors, where villagers lived in harmony, reflecting kindness to one another. At the heart of this village grew the Tree of Echoes, its silver leaves whispering truths and its golden fruits nourishing fairness.

One day, a shadow fell upon the valley—a traveler cloaked in darkness named Injustice. He carried a staff carved from deception, and wherever he walked, flowers wilted and voices that spoke truth were silenced.

Injustice approached the Tree of Echoes, disturbed by its ceaseless honesty. He struck the trunk with his staff. Cracks raced along the bark as silver leaves fluttered to the ground, turning to ash at his feet. "Your fairness is a burden," he hissed. "I will silence your echoes."

The villagers gathered, alarmed, but fear gripped them into silence. Each waited for another to stand up, and in their hesitation the shadow's grip tightened.

Blunt's fist clenched under the table; he knew well how darkness feeds on the silence of the good.

The once-radiant valley dimmed; its mirrors tarnished, reflecting only confusion and doubt.

Yet beneath the fractured roots of the great tree, a single golden seed remained. A young girl named Aletheia, who had watched truth be struck down and fairness wounded, gently scooped up the seed. Guided by quiet courage, she planted it at the valley's edge and nurtured it with her tears and hopeful whispers.

Over time, a new sapling emerged—a humble tree, resilient and steady. Its bark was scarred but strong, its fruits modest yet sustaining. When the villagers cautiously tasted this new tree's fruit, their lost voices were restored—soft at first, then clearer and braver. Strengthened by even this small taste of truth, they united and confronted Injustice.

"You fed on our silence," Aletheia proclaimed, standing tall despite her trembling voice. "But truth cannot be destroyed. Even from the smallest seed, justice will rise again."

Overwhelmed by the unified voices and the return of truth's light, Injustice retreated, slinking away beyond the mountains.

From that day on, the villagers cherished the new tree that had grown from the tiny seed. They learned that justice thrives not through grand displays of power, but through the quiet, unwavering bravery of those willing to speak up—even when their voices shake.

A heavy hush followed the fable's final lines, as if the very shelves had absorbed the lesson. The Wizards exchanged thoughtful looks, hearts stirred by the echo of the stagnant debates outside. Hazleton's gears had once locked in old patterns; Stará Bystrica was nearly lost to apathy. Left unchallenged, stagnation decays even the grandest creation— just as Boston now risked losing its spark.

Greenie lowered the scroll slowly, her eyes shining with emotion. The tale's echo of courage in the face of oppression resonated deeply with her—Sedona's ordeal had been much the same. "Aletheia refused to stay silent, just as we've refused to give any ground to illusions," Greenie said softly. "Even one voice speaking the truth can start to undo great injustice." Lettizia inclined her head in approval, a gentle smile on her lips.

Next, Lettizia handed the second scroll to Reddish. "This one," she said, "speaks of balance."

Reddish unfurled the parchment, her fiery hair casting a soft copper glow on the aged paper as she began to read:

"The Lake of Fair Reflections"

In a land veiled by mist lay a hidden lake, its waters pure as crystal and mirroring only truth.

At the lake's edge gathered three creatures—Fox, Raven, and Deer—each seeking justice, for bias had spread like a plague through their homeland.

Fox spoke first, smooth and cunning. "Justice favors the clever," he purred. "The wise outsmart the strong." Yet when Fox peered into the lake's mirror-like surface, his reflection quivered and distorted, revealing a sly grin hiding deeper deceit.

Then Raven cawed, sharp and harsh: "Justice belongs to the loudest, those who claim it first." But upon the water, her image twisted, stretched thin by the weight of arrogance.

The Wizards exchanged uneasy glances as they listened. Checkered's lips thinned at Fox's smooth falsehood, and Reddish's eyes flashed at Raven's brazen claim—cunning tricks and loud boasts, they all knew, did not make true justice.

Finally, Deer stepped forward, gentle eyes wide and clear. "Justice is neither cunning nor loud," she said quietly. "It listens patiently and speaks softly. It walks humbly, but stands firmly when it must."

As Deer gazed down, the waters stilled; her reflection remained steady and undistorted.

Then the lake spoke, its voice calm and deep, echoing across the mist: "True justice reflects not the loudest cry, nor the cleverest mind, but fairness—an honest mirror free of bias. Justice is an impartial light of truth, rooted in fairness, equality, and integrity. It ensures each voice is heard and every action weighed without prejudice.

Justice is balance, a careful weighing of right and wrong. It knows no favorites, no ranks, no disguises. It seeks truth over comfort, and clarity over noise. Justice is the courage to stand for another's truth as staunchly as for one's own."

When the voice fell silent, Fox and Raven bowed their heads, chastened. Side by side with Deer, they departed, each carrying away a newfound understanding: justice is brightest when the scales are balanced and every voice—even the softest—counts.

Reddish gently rolled up the second scroll, the story's words still echoing in the hush of the alcove. She thought of how, time and again, illusions of injustice had withered whenever they stood unwavering for what was fair. "No illusion of injustice can withstand true fairness," she said, her voice fierce with conviction.

Lettizia's eyes glowed with satisfaction. "Precisely," she replied, clearly pleased with their understanding.

Even as she spoke, the lamplight overhead flickered. The friendly glow turned dim and uncertain as shadows began pooling once more at the edges of the alcove. Blunt felt a sudden vibration through the table as his synergy gear responded to a swell of magic in the air. His muscles tensed. "Something's coming," he warned under his breath.

Checkered flipped her monocle back down; its lens pulsed with alert light as she scanned the darkening corners. "Illusions," she confirmed sharply. "They're gathering again."

Firee and Breezie traded resolute looks — this was the moment Lettizia had prepared them for.

Lettizia gently closed the large tome in front of her. "You have read of justice," she said softly, sliding the heavy book aside. Her gaze lifted to the encroaching darkness. "Now, face the trial of justice once more."

The lanterns around the shop dimmed further, their flames shrinking to pinpoints. A low rumble shuddered through The Six Statues as if the very building were holding its breath. Illusions of bias and unfairness — emboldened by that pause for reflection — now burst forth in earnest. All at once, the silver mirrors on the walls clouded over, each revealing a different scene of injustice playing out like a ghostly film. The marble Statue of Justice trembled on its pedestal, and one of its bronze scale pans sank dramatically, weighed down by unseen prejudices.

"Prove fairness, or injustice stands!" Lettizia challenged, her voice cracking through the air like a judge's gavel. In an instant, the Wizards tightened their formation beneath the statue. Six colorful cloaks brushed together as they closed ranks, shoulder to shoulder.

At first the illusions attacked as they often had in previous trials — splintering into multiple smaller phantoms that tugged at each of them individually, trying to divide their focus:

From a mirror to Checkered's left, a ghostly courtroom swelled into view around her. A robed judge leaned forward on the bench, whispering insidiously in her ear: he offered her a hefty bribe in exchange for ruling in favor of a wealthy defendant over a poorer plaintiff. Checkered recoiled in disgust, her monocle flashing. "Truth demands equity," she snapped, her voice cracking like a whip. She thrust her lens forward, and a beam of light lanced out. The illusory judge shrank back, hissing, before the beam seared straight through his form. With a howl, the corrupt phantom shattered into wisps of smoke. Above Checkered, the statue's scales creaked — its heavier pan rising slightly as the bribery illusion's weight disappeared.

On the opposite side, Greenie confronted a vision of two villagers locked in a petty dispute — one villager was Greenie's longtime friend, the other a stranger. The illusion slyly urged her to side with her familiar friend, regardless of who was truly at fault. Greenie's heart held firm against that pull. "We must remain balanced," she whispered to herself. She extended her empathic magic outward like gentle vines curling around the two spectral villagers. In a soft rush, insight blossomed between them; each villager was suddenly made to feel the other's perspective and pain. Understanding kindled where bias had been. The urge to favor one over the other dissolved, and the quarrel resolved itself into mutual apologies. A soft breeze wafted through the shop as that illusion faded, and the statue's tilted scales tipped closer toward even.

Next, a flicker in the air before Reddish solidified into a tempting parchment contract, its text glowing with promises of personal gain — if only she would ignore a certain wrongdoing. Reddish's eyes blazed like hot coals at the very idea. "No reward built on injustice will tempt us," she declared. She swept her hand through the floating contract, a trail of fire following her fingertips. The illusory document erupted in a burst of embers and vanished. High above, the flames briefly bathed the bronze scales in light; one of the heavy pans glowed and lifted, as if a great burden had been removed from it.

Not far away, Firee found himself facing an apparition of a mob of townsfolk encircling a lone, frightened figure. The mob's angry murmurs filled the air — they demanded someone to blame for a recent misfortune, and an unlucky scapegoat stood in their midst. The illusion insinuated that the simplest solution was to sacrifice the one for the contentment of the many. Firee's face hardened; he had seen this cruel logic before in other forms. "No scapegoats!" he thundered. The passion in his voice sent a visible ripple through the smoky mob. From his cloak burst a plume of red fire. It roared outward, not to burn, but to form a protective ring around the outcast at the center of the crowd. The specters comprising the mob recoiled from the searing barrier. Their outraged cries faltered, then fell silent one by one as the entire hateful scene evaporated into a fine mist. Above, the scales of Justice swung back toward balance by another degree.

From behind the group, Blunt suddenly felt an oppressive weight press down on his shoulders. An illusion had coiled around him: a vision of himself standing in a grand council hall while a cruel decree was passed. A disembodied whisper urged that staying quiet would be safer — it insisted someone else might object if he did not. Blunt's jaw set in grim determination. "Silence abets injustice!" he bellowed, his voice echoing off the rafters. Raising his wand high, he brought it down like a gavel. A tidal surge of water magic cascaded forward, blue and gleaming. It crashed through the phantom council chamber that had sprung up around him, washing over the dais and benches. The wave swept away the oppressive hush, and in its wake the silenced councilors in Blunt's vision found their voices, rising in a chorus of dissent against the cruel decree. The false council hall collapsed into nothingness, leaving Blunt standing firm as water rained down in glistening droplets.

At the same time, Breezie — at the very center of the Wizards' circle — detected a final subtle deceit creeping through the cracks. This one slithered directly into their minds: a sly insinuation that perhaps the Wizards did not truly trust one another, that each harbored secret doubts or biases about the others. It was an illusion of mistrust, attempting to coil around their hearts and pit them against themselves. Breezie closed his eyes and exhaled a long, calming breath. A cool, cleansing wind radiated outward from him. "No half-truth can break our unity," he intoned gently. Opening his eyes, he swept his arm in a wide arc, guiding the breeze through and around his friends. The unfounded doubts were caught up like dust and whisked away. In moments the final tendrils of that isolating illusion unraveled and blew out, leaving the circle of friends unbroken.

Together, the Wizards had countered each trick almost as quickly as it appeared. Within the span of a minute, the shop fell silent again save for the sound of six steady breaths. Overhead, the bronze scales of the Justice statue still swung, but now their arc was slowing; balance was nearly restored. The lantern light brightened slightly, revealing a space largely cleared of shadows.

Suddenly, the scattered phantom remnants around them began to draw together, merging into one grand illusion that encircled the Wizards on all sides. The true heart of the test was coming into play. Every silver mirror in the shop glowed in unison, projecting a single seamless scene that overlaid itself onto reality. The walls of The Six Statues seemed to melt away, and the Wizards found themselves standing in a ghostly reimagining of the Old South Meeting House itself – or rather, an illusion of it.

Verdict at Old South

They recognized the high vaulted ceiling and wooden pews. It was as if time had slid back two and a half centuries: the hall was packed wall-to-wall with ghostly townsfolk in colonial garb, faces contorted in anger and fear. Lit lanterns cast a wild glow across the scene. At the front, where the pulpit would be, stood an austere magistrate and a trembling young man in chains. The youth knelt, bound and wide-eyed with dread. The magistrate's spectral face was twisted in a triumphant sneer. "Guilty of witchcraft and treason!" boomed a disembodied voice – a blend of many voices speaking as one. The mob of onlookers roared in agreement, their collective fury pressing in like a physical weight.

The Wizards realized this was the first illusion's form: majority tyranny. A terrified innocent was about to be condemned simply to satisfy the mob's fear. Greenie's empathic heart almost buckled under the onslaught of the crowd's emotion – she staggered, feeling the tidal force of terror and wrath bearing down on that lone youth. But she recalled the story that had guided her moments before: the fable of the Tree of Echoes, where an entire village remained paralyzed by fear until one brave voice spoke truth. Drawing on that inspiration, Greenie pushed back against the psychic pressure and stepped forward. She raised her voice, clear and unwavering: "Where is the proof?" Her words cut through the din as she placed herself protectively in front of the shackled young man. "We will not condemn an innocent soul just to appease a frightened crowd."

The ghostly congregation hissed at her defiance, their outcry redoubling. The magistrate's form swelled larger, looming over Greenie with eyes blazing. "They demand a verdict!" the many-layered voice bellowed from the rafters. The crowd's chant rose: "Verdict! Verdict!" The chained youth squeezed his eyes shut in despair as the magistrate drew a long illusory sword to execute judgment.

Not a single Wizard hesitated. Reddish sprang to Greenie's side, embers flying from her fingertips in defiant sparks. The sight of a howling mob poised to sacrifice a blameless boy ignited righteous anger in her chest. "We won't trade away fairness to calm your panic!" she shouted, her voice crackling with passionate fury. "Scapegoating this boy will not bring peace – it will only heap injustice upon injustice!" Each of Reddish's sparks erupted into a tiny flame hovering in the air, illuminating shocked and guilty faces in the mob. The crowd recoiled slightly from her blazing wrath.

Meanwhile, Checkered's analytical mind raced. She peered intently at the magistrate through her monocle and spotted it – a greasy darkness clinging to his outline like ink. Bias and deceit, nearly invisible except to one trained to see truth. "This trial is a sham!" Checkered declared, pointing her wand at the magistrate like an accusatory finger. A beam of prismatic light shot forth, revealing stains of falsehood all over the judge's robes. "The evidence is tainted by prejudice. We won't follow a howling crowd or a lying accuser over actual truth!" Her words rang like hammer blows. The magistrate staggered as if struck; uncertainty flickered across his rigid face.

Yet the mob was not so easily swayed. A ripple of outrage went through the assembled colonists, their murmurs swelling into an angry roar at the Wizards' resistance. The entire meeting hall trembled under the force of that collective fury. Cracks snaked across the wooden floorboards. The air itself quaked with the threat of violence about to erupt – it felt as though the illusion would tear the world apart to get its way.

At that critical moment, Blunt advanced and planted himself firmly between the furious mob and the shackled prisoner. He threw out his arms, one hand gripping his wand and the other clutching the bronze Aequitas coin in his pocket. The coin seared hot against his palm, empowering his voice as he thundered, "Justice is not a vote of the majority, nor the whim of the powerful!" The sheer force of his declaration sliced through the cacophony like a blade. Silence fell, shock rippling through the ghostly townsfolk. Blunt's eyes blazed with integrity. "We stand for what is right – even if we must stand alone against all of you." Conviction rolled off him in an almost visible wave.

For a heartbeat, nobody moved. Then, with a metallic creak, great scales of Justice appeared, hovering between the magistrate and the accused youth. A collective gasp rose as those phantom scales – which had been heavily tilted toward the magistrate's side – began to level out. The imbalance was correcting itself. The magistrate's sword arm quivered and lowered slightly. Down on the floor, the imprisoned young man felt his chains loosen of their own accord. A glimmer of hope lit his tear-streaked face as he realized the execution had been stayed.

The oppressive weight of majority tyranny was lifting. But the test was not over. Lettizia's dual illusions always struck twice – two faces of injustice. As the crowd's angry shouts faded into uneasy murmurs, a swirl of dark smoke enveloped the scene. The magistrate and the mob dissolved into vapor, along with the young prisoner. The lantern-light dimmed and shifted. It was as though a coin had been flipped to its opposite face, heads to tails. The Wizards braced themselves, knowing another challenge was coming.

When the smoke cleared, a new tableau had formed in the meeting hall. This time, a weeping woman stood where the youth had been, clutching a thin, frightened child to her chest.

Opposite her loomed a stern town constable with a drawn sword. His face was impassive, merciless. The blended disembodied voice spoke again, now with a sly, cajoling tone: "If you refuse to punish the innocent… will you punish the guilty?"

The constable's boots thudded on the wooden floor as he stepped forward. "This woman," he pronounced, gesturing at her with his blade, "stole bread to feed her starving child. The law demands punishment — a hand for a loaf. Many go hungry; justice calls for an example, lest others also break the law." Behind him, ghostly townsfolk flickered into being once more. But unlike the first mob, these faces were conflicted. Some nodded grimly at the constable's decree, echoing "The law is the law." Yet others looked pale and aghast, whispering that the punishment was far too cruel for a desperate theft. Sympathetic eyes fell on the sobbing mother and her thin child, but those kindly voices were hushed and hesitant.

The Wizards understood: this was the misguided mercy dilemma. Earlier the illusion pushed cruelty; now it pushed excessive harshness, testing whether they would be so soft-hearted as to ignore justice entirely. Bias had changed its guise, from callousness to undue rigidity, to tempt them into abandoning fairness under the sway of pity. True justice, they all knew, walked a razor's edge between heart and principle.

Breezie felt his gentle heart ache at the sight of the poor mother shielding her child. The entire illusory courtroom weighed heavy with sorrow and moral complexity. Slowly, Breezie approached the woman, lowering his wand. He placed a comforting hand on her shoulder; though she was but an illusion, his compassion was sincere. Speaking clearly, he addressed both the constable and the crowd. "We hear her plea. Justice isn't blind to suffering – mercy has a place," he said, voice calm and soothing. "But true justice cannot turn a blind eye to the law, either." The weeping woman looked up into Breezie's kind face, hope and confusion mingling in her expression.

Firee stepped forward next, the flames that normally wreathed him subdued to a steady, gentle glow. He had fought many dark illusions before, and he recognized this battle was not about defeating a clear evil, but about balance. "No one is above the principles of fairness," Firee declared, his tone measured and firm. "Her reasons for stealing are heartrending and understandable. But if we ignore the theft entirely, what of all the others in town who are suffering? What stops the next desperate soul from turning to crime and meeting the same fate? We must find a solution that protects the community and shows compassion."

Greenie knelt by the illusory child, brushing a tear from the little one's cheek. The child's fearful eyes met her warm, green gaze. "Justice balances compassion with accountability," Greenie said softly, squeezing the child's hand in reassurance. She then rose to face the constable. "Yes, a law was broken – but it was born of desperation, not malice. The answer isn't to maim this mother, nor is it to pretend nothing happened. The fair path is to address the cause of her crime. Help her rather than harm her. Ensure no one in this town must steal just to survive."

Checkered, ever pragmatic, fixed the constable with a sharp look. "Isn't the purpose of law to uphold the common good?" she asked pointedly. "What good comes from cutting off a mother's hand for trying to keep her child alive? A just society would rally to support this family, not brutalize them and call it 'justice.'" Her logical challenge hung in the air, confronting the black-and-white harshness of the decree with practical wisdom and humanity.

Their collective reasoning and empathy gave even the stern illusion pause. The constable's sword arm wavered. Doubt flickered in his cold eyes. Behind him, some phantom townsfolk started nodding in agreement with the Wizards' words. The balance of opinion in the hall was visibly shifting:

hardened faces softening, angry whispers turning to thoughtful murmurs.

Sensing its control slipping, the disembodied voice of the illusion hissed furiously, making a last desperate stand. "The law must be upheld!" it shrieked. The constable's form flickered, torn between solidifying back into uncompromising hardness or dissolving into yielding light. "Will you defy the letter of the law? What message does that send?" the voice challenged, wavering.

Blunt stepped forward to answer, his posture radiating calm authority. He placed himself squarely between the constable and the mother and child, meeting the phantom officer's gaze unflinchingly. "We uphold the spirit of the law," Blunt said, each word measured and resolute. "The true purpose of law is to create a just and harmonious society – and there is no justice in cruelty." As he spoke, the small silver key of balance in his cloak pocket began to emit a soft glow, reminding them all of the hard-earned lesson of Copenhagen: justice must temper law with humanity. Blunt lifted his wand high, addressing the specter of the constable and the whole hall of onlookers. "Our verdict is this: fairness with mercy. The wrong will be righted without spilling blood."

Blunt's pronouncement echoed like a clarion call. At that instant, Breezie's keen eyes caught a gleam on the judge's bench behind the constable – something new had appeared there. It was a single golden seed, pulsing with gentle light. Breezie recognized it at once: a seed from the fable of the Tree of Echoes that Greenie had read. Their courageous voices of reason and compassion had caused it to sprout here, a symbol of truth taking root. As the seed glowed, even the ghosts of the angry townsfolk now bowed their heads, shamed into understanding. The collective stance of the illusion had irrevocably changed.

Blunt brought his wand down in a broad sweeping motion. A surge of silvery-blue light flowed forth like a wave. It washed over the entire hall, cleansing every corner of shadow and injustice. The stern constable staggered back as the light broke over him; his figure cracked and then dissolved into motes of shimmering dust. The mother's tears of terror transformed into tears of relief. The deadly blade poised to maim her faded away into nothingness. Her child blinked in disbelief and then broke into a bright smile, pointing upward. "Look!" the child cried.

Above the vanishing judge's bench hung a clock – the Meeting House's old gallery clock – frozen at an impossible hour: thirteen o'clock. Now, before their eyes, its long-stalled hands began to move. With a loud tick… tock…, the hour hand slid back into its rightful place and the minute hand swept forward, correcting the time. The clock face now read 5:59, on the cusp of dawn. A breath later, the clock's bronze bell tolled a single clear chime to mark six o'clock. The sound was pure and resolute, echoing through the hall as if announcing the final verdict: Justice has been served.

As the bell's echo faded, the entire phantom courtroom evaporated like morning dew under the sun's first rays. The Wizards found themselves standing once more in the quiet lantern-lit confines of The Six Statues shop. The ghostly spectators, the constable, the grieving mother and child – all were gone as if they had never been, leaving only the soft flutter of the lantern flames. Above, the marble Statue of Justice reappeared in its place, looking down at them impassively. Its scales, which had been swinging wildly before, now hung perfectly still and level, each side equal. A gentle golden glow suffused those scales for a moment, then faded, as if the virtue of their fair decision had been acknowledged and sealed.

For a long moment, none of the six spoke. Hearts pounding, they each took in slow breaths. The trial they had just endured had tested them as never before – not their magical prowess or physical courage, but their judgment, unity, and moral integrity. They glanced at one another, and a silent understanding passed between them: this victory was not about vanquishing an enemy, but about affirming what was right. It was a triumph not of might, but of true justice.

A soft sound broke the silence – gentle laughter, warm and approving. Lettizia Dillettante emerged from behind the Justice statue, clapping her hands quietly in praise. Her eyes shone with pride. "Justice's triumph," she said, and her voice was rich with satisfaction. "Achieved not by force of arms, but by wisdom, compassion, and unity of heart. You have done well." The antique shop seemed to brighten as Lettizia's illusions fully dissipated. The last wisps of dark haze melted into nothingness, leaving only the warm glow of lantern light and the dusty comfort of old shelves.

In the silvered mirrors along one wall – mirrors that moments ago reflected scenes of injustice – the Wizards now glimpsed their own reflections. They looked weary, yes, but also proud and steadfast, gathered together as an unbreakable circle. In those same mirrors new images appeared, superimposed beside their faces: visions of balanced scales set right, of open hands offering mercy, of wrongs being redressed. Fairness restored. The six friends realized these were not illusions but gentle affirmations conjured by the virtue they'd upheld.

Lettizia moved to the base of the Justice statue, trailing her fingers along its marble pedestal. The stone was unmarred and cool; no trace of shadow remained. Satisfied, she turned to the

Wizards with a serene smile. "Tonight, you have reaffirmed fairness," she said softly. There was deep respect in her eyes now.

Blunt exhaled, a long release of tension. He placed a hand on the statue's pedestal, as if to reassure himself that it was solid and real. Beneath his cloak, his synergy gear gave a steady, contented hum – like a heartbeat returning to a calm rhythm. "Those illusions tried hard to throw us off balance," he said, looking around at his companions. "But we didn't waver when it truly mattered."

Greenie nodded. She wandered to a nearby shelf and ran her fingertips over it – it was layered only in benign dust motes now. That same spot had held a lurking phantom of injustice when they first entered; now nothing remained of it. "Illusions like these feed on people's fears and biases," Greenie observed. "Tonight, we gave them nothing to latch onto. We refused to accept either extreme the illusions offered."

Checkered tucked her monocle away, a rare, bright satisfaction on her face. "Even when the illusions tried to overwhelm us all at once, we found the answer together," she said. The analytical scholar in her couldn't help noting the strategy aloud. "Partial truths, loud lies, hidden cruelty, or misplaced pity – we unraveled every one of them as a team."

Breezie grinned, feeling the lingering adrenaline ebb into contentment. "It helped that we confronted justice from multiple angles before we got here," he added. "In Philadelphia, Rittenhouse's clock reminded us to trust reason and evidence over clamor. In Copenhagen, Olsen's World Clock showed us how to keep everyone in mind. We brought those lessons with us." He nodded gratefully toward Blunt's cloak, where the bronze coin of Sedona and the silver key of Copenhagen were safely stowed. Fairness through reason, balance across voices – those insights had been their lanterns in the dark.

Reddish twirled a leftover spark between her fingers and laughed softly. "It's true. Each stop prepared us for this final test," she agreed. "No single perspective – neither cold law nor raw emotion – could sway us, because we knew justice needs both heart and mind." She reached out and gave Firee a playful nudge. "Not even a mob of illusions could bully us into a wrong choice."

Firee chuckled, rubbing his shoulder as if the nudge had hurt (though his grin said otherwise). "They certainly tried," he said. He glanced to the now-perfectly balanced scales held in the statue's hand. "But in the end, justice won out." His flame-hued eyes flickered toward Lettizia. "Thanks to the challenges you set for us."

Lettizia inclined her head graciously. "Indeed, justice has prevailed here." With a sweep of her hand, she beckoned the Wizards closer. From a pocket of her robe, Lettizia drew out a small object that glinted in the lantern light. It was another bronze coin, identical to the one they had earned in Sedona – inscribed with Aequitas Est Virtus. She handed it to Blunt, who accepted it with a respectful bow. The coin felt warm and reassuring in his palm. "Take this token of Justice's triumph," said Lettizia. "May it remind you that fairness, once won, must be continually upheld."

Blunt closed his fingers around the coin. He could feel the two identical coins now side by side in his pocket – twin reminders of the battles for justice they had fought. "Thank you," he replied earnestly. "We won't forget this lesson." The others murmured agreement, each standing a little taller than before. Outside, through the shop's window, the first golden rays of sunrise crept over Boston's skyline. Night had given way to dawn. Lettizia's eyes seemed to shine with the same morning light. "Your journey continues, my friends," she said softly. With a gentle gesture, she indicated an object on a nearby table that hadn't been there before: a weathered, leather-bound journal emblazoned with the image of a bell and a cracked Liberty Bell emblem. The spine read Independence Hall Log – 1776.

Checkered picked up the old journal, and as she did, a vision bloomed in her mind – of Philadelphia's Independence Hall and a great clock tower overlooking it. A new trial, the virtue of Fortitude, awaiting them there… She met Blunt's gaze and nodded. "Our next destination reveals itself," she said. Blunt smiled and turned to thank Lettizia, but the Antiquarian had vanished as quietly as she had arrived.

The six Wizards stepped out of The Six Statues shop into the crisp morning. Boston's Old South Meeting House stood peacefully before them, its clock tower now showing the correct time in the brightening sky. In that dawn light, the friends felt the weight of the night's trials lift, replaced by a sense of hard-won peace and confidence. Justice had been tested and had triumphed – not by any single one of them alone, but by all of them together, their virtues combined like the interlocking gears of the finest clock.

"Onward, then?" Breezie asked, flipping the bronze coin and catching it with a grin.

Blunt tucked the coin and the silver key safely into his cloak beside the first coin. He looked around at his companions – Greenie, eyes shining with compassion; Checkered, monocle glinting with insight; Firee and Reddish, flame and ember both burning with courage; Breezie, the morning breeze stirring his cloak, carrying hope. Blunt felt pride well within him. "Onward," he agreed. "Wherever the next clock leads, whatever trial awaits – we will meet it, together."

Unified, the six Wizards departed down the awakening Boston street, the bronze coin already beginning to glow with the promise of the next adventure. Justice's triumph here would light their way forward. And as they vanished around the corner, the Old South Meeting House clock tower rang out the hour of six, each peal a reassurance that, so long as wisdom and virtue guided them, justice would continue to prevail.

Chapter 13

From Independence Hall to Gdańsk Astronomical Clock: Fortitude's Trial

Independence Hall at Midnight

Midnight starlight draped the clock tower in a tempered glow. The colonial brass—greened by a century's breath—caught moonlight in thin seams, as if the metal remembered vows. A hush settled over the square; even the bell's last echo seemed to lean its shoulder on the brick and listen. From a bronze-and-sapphire fold in the air stepped Blunt, Reddish, Firee, Checkered, Breezie, and Greenie, Harlequin cloaks whispering color—emerald in slow eddies, crimson banked like coals, sapphire in clean, wave-bright arcs.

Blunt's fingers found the runic pendant at his throat—Fortitudo Vincit Timorem—the award from a night when courage had weighed more than spectacle. Beneath his cloak, the synergy gear inscribed Innovare Est Virtus gave a quiet, recurrent hum that matched the clock's pulse. Those same runes had winked at them before—in the Zytglogge's patient stone, in Stará Bystrica's carved orbit—threads of one pattern stitched across cities. Tonight the thread tightened. The motto under his thumb seemed to warm, as if the tower recognized it.

Breezie lifted his chin and let Reality Sight rake the tower's base. The pendulum's motion snagged on something not mechanical—a hitch, a tremor that didn't belong to brass. "There," he said, voice low but certain. "The beat stumbles— fear has wedged itself between the ticks." He exhaled, and a mild current parted an invisible film clinging to the dial face, the way breath clears glass.

Firee set a palm to the masonry and felt a heat that was not heat so much as friction—like metal protesting an ill fit in the forge. "The whole frame's bristling," he murmured. "Not flame—resistance. Something's grinding the courage out of the works." Reddish's eyes found the pendulum slot and held there, embers soft in her hands—not a blaze, but the attentive glow of resolve. "Then we give it no slack to seize," she said. "Not one heartbeat."

Greenie, tuned to the human air, felt it before she saw it: a ripple of nameless alarm skating the edges of the square. A pair of late walkers tightened their coats without knowing why. A cab's yellow light jittered. "Dread without a name," she said softly. "It feeds on what isn't checked." Checkered's lens, held to the silver stillness, flashed once—an ephemeral ripple near the upper gearing, almost a suggestion of shadow trying to become fact. "It wants hesitation," she said, crisp as a surveyor. "We'll deny it the map."

A small inscription revealed itself at knee height, letters soot-dark against pale stone—Fortitudo Vincit Timorem; Timor Est Vitium. The phrase matched Blunt's pendant stroke for stroke. The runes on the metal answered with a faint line of light, and for an instant the brass hands above seemed to catch the gleam—a thread of gold tracing a seam in the night. "Anchor text," Blunt said, half to himself. "Same handwriting across the clocks." The line of light did not flare; it thinned and lengthened—as if drawing a hair-fine compass bearing eastward, hinting at a gate not yet opened but already choosing a direction.

The hum spiked. A middle-aged man on the far curb stumbled off his path, eyes gone wide under an unnamed pressure. Reddish reached him before the thought of falling finished in his body. She set a steady palm on his sleeve; the ember in her other hand cast a quiet circle of warmth, light enough to be ordinary. "You're all right," she told him, her voice a steady metronome that lent him its count. The man blinked; his breath found itself; whatever had been spooling him from the inside loosened its hold. He nodded—

embarrassed, grateful—and hurried on, unaware of how precisely his panic had been kept from making a story of itself.

Around the tower's face, a new surge gathered—more suggestion than force, a borrowed gloom trying to muscle into shape. The six closed ranks without fuss. Checkered's lens settled; Breezie's hands floated, shaping the air to clarity; Greenie named the plain facts in a whisper—brick, lintel, dial—giving the scene edges. Firee's palm stayed to the stone, reading strain; Reddish's embers held their patient burn. Blunt's hand tightened on the pendant, the gear's hum steadying to the clock's intended rhythm.

"We act together," Blunt said, not loud but final, "and fear finds no place to hide." The shadow-impression wavered. It didn't pop like a bubble or blink like a trick; it thinned the way mist thins when the sun is not argued with—slow enough to see it leave. The brass above found one clean swing, then another. The square breathed.

Blunt glanced again at the inscription—Fortitudo Vincit Timorem; Timor Est Vitium—and felt the runes in the pendant answer with a soft pull toward dawn. The memory of previous clocks rose not as triumphs tallied but as steps rehearsed: find the name, keep the count, lift the courage, step through when the path declares itself. Somewhere ahead, that path would sharpen into a gate. He could almost hear a distant mechanism align—another dial waiting, patient as a harbor light.

"Hold to the beat," Checkered said, eyes still on the gearing. Breezie nodded, easing the last cling of haze. Greenie's attention lingered on the passersby until their shoulders settled. Firee withdrew his palm; the masonry's protest had slackened. Reddish's ember dimmed, not extinguished—kept ready, like a spark held at bay. The six looked up together.

"We don't flinch," Blunt said, and the line of light along the runes steadied, as if agreeing. "That is enough." The tower answered with the plain tick of a clock that knows its work. And somewhere just beyond the square's far edge, the air held a seam as fine as a drawn thread—direction chosen, not yet traveled.

The Gate Takes a Bearing

Under the shuddering gears, a low luminance gathered—first a vein of blue fire along the base stones, then a thread that drew a clean circle in the night. The inscription there—Fortitudo Vincit Timorem—answered itself in light, and a bronze-and-sapphire whirl opened in silence. Blunt felt the hum of his synergy gear climb to meet it, the pendant at his throat sending a small rippling ward over the team as if testing the seam for snags. "Same hand, same pattern," he said, thinking of the other clocks whose runes had stitched cities together. "Philadelphia's fear is tugging on another gear."

Greenie set her palm near the threshold; the air beyond pressed back with a steady, unshowy dread, like a crowd holding its breath. "Real fear waiting," she said, voice even. "Not rumor." Breezie teased the portal's edge with a draft; it curled inward and returned, as if recognizing discipline. Checkered's lens hovered and caught faint angular marks turning within the swirl—coordinates braided with prayer. "Direction's fixed," she said. "Gdańsk's clock." Reddish flicked a patient ember across the seam; it didn't vanish so much as pass into a deeper blue and keep going. Firee pinched a spark from nail to thumb, reading the portal the way a smith reads heat: no burn, only the feel of tempered metal asking to be worked.

They did not waste the certainty. Cloaks whispering, they stepped through—the ward from Blunt's pendant spreading like rings from a cast bell—into stone-cool air that tasted of wax and old ash. Far off, bells answered with a sober interval count. The whirl sealed, leaving only the impression of a circle that might have always been part of the floor.

Under St. Mary's: The Bell at the Hinge

The nave of St. Mary's received them with shadowed ribs and a breath of centuries. A handful of candles leaned in their cups, light pooling along pews rubbed smooth by prayer. The Astronomical Clock rose like a wooden city—saints, astronomers, kings—and high on its face the carving of Death held a bell mid-strike, as if the moment before sound had been stretched taut and tied off. The mechanism was fifteenth-century work, a craft begun around 1460 and stubborn as oaken beams; yet beneath that durability, a tremor traveled the gears, a low hum of fear trying to rewrite the beat.

Checkered's lens steadied over the trembling cogs, mapping the shiver the way a surveyor maps subsidence. "Disruption in the train," she said. "Not failure—interference." Greenie's gaze moved to an elderly caretaker sweeping near a side altar. The woman's hands shook in tiny, unbecoming loops, the broom sketching half-circles on stone. "It's leaking into people," Greenie murmured, and let her breathing fall into a count the room could borrow. Reddish took a step nearer the base; the ember in her palm wasn't for show, only a private compass of warmth that neither wavered nor grew. "We hold," she said. "That's the work."

Firee laid two fingers to a carved saint; the wood gave a forge-floor heat, not burning but the remembered temperature of labor. "Grind, not blaze," he reported. "Something's forcing the teeth to bite off tempo." Breezie drew a breath, and the haze that clung to the lower dial parted by degrees, the way cool air coaxes a kiln toward clarity. Blunt traced the postwar plaque with his eyes—Fortitudo Vincit Timorem; Timor Est Vitium—and the gear at his chest clicked once, like a tool seating true. "This city has named fear before," he said. "The clock knows the difference between courage and noise."

Another pulse came—not the wavering veil they had dismissed in other halls, but a thicker working of shadow arrested in the wood grain, trying to anchor in the carvings themselves. The six closed ranks, every motion unhurried on purpose. Breezie's draft cleared space. Checkered's lens held the line of measurements. Reddish's ember kept its quiet light. Firee listened for the anvil-note inside the tremor; the heat there wasn't blaze but friction, and he waited it out like a smith saving steel from warping. Greenie stayed with the caretaker until the woman's sweep recovered a steady arc. Blunt lifted the pendant; the ward skimmed the metal's face, gentle as a sigh.

The first swell receded—but not to nothing. It thinned, gathered, and pressed again, testing their steadiness the way a tide tests a jetty. The team did not trade proclamations for proof; they gave the room count, edges, names. A second receding—then another return, this one clinging to the carved Death's bell. The figure seemed to lean, less frozen than before, as if the clock itself were caught between strike and silence and wanted them to choose. "It's learning our rhythm," Checkered said, not alarmed, simply noting that this would not be a single-breath task. "Good," Blunt answered. "So will we."

They advanced to the base, and Blunt reached toward the plaque again, not for portent but for plainer anchoring—the cold of metal under hand, the serif bite of letters, the way the screws sat flush in the wood. Each fact held. Somewhere above, a cog found one clean mesh. Dust lilted from the gearing and settled. The caretaker's broom traced full circles now, and she did not look up from her work.

Lucrecia Van Egmond watched the near strike soften, not gone, but taking a step back from presumption. "Better," she said, and closed her hand; the skeins of shimmer dissipated like dust into light air. "Again—and again—until the clock remembers that fear has no authority here." She inclined her head toward the plaque. "The words are not a charm," she added. "They are a practice."

Her cloak turned a deeper blue as she moved to stand beside the base. "When the next pressure comes, you will let it announce itself fully," Lucrecia said. "You will give it its proper name, and then you will refuse it its room. The bell will strike when it is time—not because fear shook it." The nave held its breath. The six prepared, not for a trick to pop, but for a habit to be retrained.

Lucrecia's Counsel

"Seekers." The voice carried from the transept, calm without softness. Candlelight ran along the midnight-blue cloak as Lucrecia Van Egmond stepped from between two pillars, her posture calm and sure. Authority traveled with her, unspoken but steady; no flourish, only a presence that had never failed. She lifted one hand. Between her fingers, thin skeins of shimmer gathered—no theatre, rather a measured demonstration of the substance that had been worrying the gearing. "You've met its cousins," she said. "Here it wants to sit on the bell."

She took in the clock with a librarian's assessment—saints, dial, strike train, plaque—and then the six, one by one. "Fear isn't loud here," Lucrecia said. "It is habitual, almost polite. That is why it is effective." The faint threads between her fingers shaped themselves into the notion of a crack where none existed; she allowed it, then unshaped it, and the wood remained whole. "You know how to refuse panic. Good. Tonight requires something steadier."

Greenie's attention flicked to the caretaker; Lucrecia followed the glance and nodded. "Start with what can be tended," she advised. Reddish's ember showed as little more than a pulse behind her knuckles; Lucrecia's eyes marked the discipline and approved without a word. Firee, reading heat in the timber, met Lucrecia's look and inclined his head; he recognized in her poise the strictness of a master smith's hand. Breezie kept the space clear. Checkered's lens wrote its quiet geometry. Blunt, the inscription under his fingers, felt the pendant's ward rise and fall like a tide bound to the moon.

Another swell crept through the carvings, this one bold enough to attempt a tremor in the bell at Death's shoulder. The figure did not move; the sound did not ring; but the prospect of the strike threaded the air. The team answered not with declarations but with placement: Greenie spoke to the caretaker until her sweep became the metronome the nave needed; Breezie shored the stillness that the clock's face was asking for; Firee's palm steadied on a panel where the heat of friction wanted to overtake the craft; Reddish held the ember to the level of a small, relentless star; Checkered's measurements gave the tremor a box to be measured by and therefore limited; Blunt let the ward pass over the bell's metal without forcing it either toward silence or sound.

Lucrecia watched the near strike soften, not gone, but taking a step back from presumption. "Better," she said, and closed her hand; the skeins of shimmer dissipated like dust into light air. "Again—and again—until the clock remembers that fear has no authority here." She inclined her head toward the plaque. "The words are not a charm," she added. "They are a practice."

Her cloak turned a deeper blue as she moved to stand beside the base. "When the next pressure comes, you will let it announce itself fully," Lucrecia said. "You will give it its proper name, and then you will refuse it its room. The bell will strike when it is time—not because fear shook it."

The Hinge's Question

A hush gathered beneath the vault as a darker seam drew itself along the Astronomical Clock's base. The air thickened with the kind of counsel that comes without a face—turn back, grow small, make no sound—and the carved Death above, bell poised, seemed to listen for which way their courage would lean. Lucrecia's midnight cloak took the candlelight and made a cloak of it. She lifted one hand; faint skeins coiled between her fingers, the very threads that had been worrying the strike. "Well then," she said, not unkindly. "Fortitude—or fear?"

The six answered with practice rather than pronouncement. Breezie's palm coaxed a draft through the nave that gave the haze fewer corners. Checkered fixed the tremor in a frame of measurements so it had a size to lose. Greenie let her breathing find a count the room could borrow; the old caretaker's sweep steadied as if someone had kindly taken her hand and matched

516

it. Firee set two fingers to the wood and listened for the anvil-note inside the shiver; the heat there wasn't blaze but friction, and he waited it out like a smith saving steel from warping. Reddish held an ember no larger than a thumbjoint, not to scorch, only to keep a center warm. Blunt brought the pendant up and a ward rippled from it—element unnamed—smoothing the first surge without fuss.

Whispers tested every seam they could find. You'll fail slid toward Checkered; she did not argue. "We endure," she said once, and in that single word the lens steadied, the taunt unthreading into nothing useful. A lighter voice braided itself around Greenie's shoulder—they doubt you—and met the quiet answer of her count until it ran out of numbers to steal. A tidy temptation tipped Reddish toward comfort—let go, be safe, no one will know—but the ember in her palm didn't flare or dim; it kept the temperature of resolve and the offer had no purchase. A larger picture tried to throw itself at Firee—ruin, futility, a future already broken—and he looked at the carved saint beneath his hand the way a craftsperson looks at grain: "The work holds," he said, and the image, denied spectacle, found itself small. Breezie swept one last curl of dark and it thinned obediently, dust showing where air had been confused.

For Blunt the push came quiet and domestic—your synergy won't hold; this is where it frays—the sort of sentence that unpicks itself if you touch it wrong. The pendant answered with another outward ring, a steadiness that didn't force or smother but refused to wobble. The pressure fell back a step. Around them, the clock remembered one honest mesh, then another; the nave took a modest breath.

Not everything yielded. A hairline insistence remained at Death's bell, a seam of almost-sound clinging to the hinge, returning each time they smoothed it—patient, well-mannered, and therefore stubborn. Checkered's figures boxed it in; Breezie cleared the air around it; Firee cooled the friction from heat to labor; Reddish's ember proved attention could outlast appetite; Greenie held the caretaker's new tempo as a metronome for the room; Blunt let the ward pass over the metal without forcing silence or strike. The seam receded, yes, but refused a final step. Lucrecia watched the restraint with approval. "Better," she said. "And exactly right. What shows its face to pressure is not the whole of it." Her hand closed; the loose skeins she'd drawn from the air fell back like dust settling into corners. "We will not bully a bell into courage."

The fear that had spread like damp had been pulled back and named by its limits; the clock's hum steadied to a workable evenness. Yet the hinge-shadow at the bell remained, not a threat, not a triumph—a question left where it belonged until they had a truer answer to give.

A Key That Opens What's Ready

Lucrecia's gaze flicked to Blunt and Reddish. "Courage, meet precedent," she said softly. From her palm she produced a small silver key, cool as a thought well kept; the bow bore the motto cut in bold letters—Fortitudo Vincit Timorem, trimmed in Oxford blue. "This is not a prize," she said. "It is a reminder—and it opens only what is already ready to open."

Blunt palmed the key; the runes along its edge felt like a promise that refused to overstate itself. "We'll return when we've got the right word for what clings at the hinge," he said, meaning neither hurry nor delay. No one answered with slogans. Checkered tapped the closed spine of her notebook once. Breezie's breath matched the tower's count. Greenie's attention stayed lightly on the street, confirming that no one nearby borrowed fear they didn't need. Only then did Blunt give it voice, once and only once: "We're ready." The clock answered with a tick that sounded like agreement rather than applause.

"They're ready," Breezie repeated, and then: "We can step through."

They stepped through together. The portal closed with a quiet click, and the square at Independence Hall received them with its own plain night: streets emptied down to their bones, a breeze with the smell of brick and a hint of iron, the tower above ticking in a rhythm that no longer staggered. What pressure had bled from Gdańsk no longer pressed here; the colonial brass—greened where history insists—held its swing without asking for help. Blunt weighed the key in his palm. He slid it inside his cloak. "We hold to the beat," he said, meaning neither haste nor delay. No one answered with slogans. The clock's steady count did the talking, and they let it.

The Clock Resumes Its Ordinary

Independence Hall's great clock was at peace again. The faltering beat it had carried melted away, and the familiar tick-tock asserted itself in the quiet of early morning. The six young wizards stood before it, shoulders easing. Breezie sent a gentle current through the plaza air, and the dusk seemed to let go of its tension. Checkered scanned the clockwork with her lens and found nothing ominous – only the brass hands swinging true. Greenie closed her eyes and felt the emotions of the few passersby: calm curiosity, nothing more. Even the breeze across the square felt free of the charge it had borne.

"That was fast," Reddish whispered, embers flickering low in her palm. She remembered how, on countless nights, they had undone fear without ever letting it take hold. Firee simply nodded, a quiet warmth behind his eyes, as he flipped a spark between his fingertips and let it die out. Blunt rested a hand on the silver key at his throat – a cool weight that seemed to agree: act immediately, name the truth, and the darkness vanishes. They shared no speeches; there was no need. Philadelphia's colonial streets were empty now, the clock restored, and the lesson was written plainly in the night.

They turned away from the hall under moonlit sky. No lullabies had been sung, no flourishes needed – the clock was ordinary again and so were they. As the first wisps of dawn approached, footsteps rang out softly on the cobbles. Ahead, a dark-cloaked figure moved with purpose just beyond an alleyway. It was Tetragor – or rather, the shape of him under the streetlamp's halo – and three muted harlequin masks stepped into the light behind him. With barely a glance back, the figure in the inkdark coat cut into a narrow passage. Instinctively Blunt gave the signal.

Old City, Thin Ovals

Moonlight fell in thin ovals on the wet slate as the team followed. A service door clanged somewhere nearby, its hinge giving a quick apology into the quiet. Blunt's gaze never wavered: a man in an inkdark traveling coat had just slipped through. That had to be Tetragor. Three masked pursuers –

muted in their motley chevrons – fell in behind him, bound by some sinister purpose.

"On him," Blunt murmured. Six cloaks flowed into the lane after Tetragor, keeping pace with the clock's restored beat.

The first harlequin hissed an illusion underfoot – the cobblestone ahead seemed to disappear. Checkered's lens was sharp: she saw past the trick. "Stone," she noted softly, and the hole filled with hard ground. At the next step, a figure lunged; Breezie released a breath that slipped down the street. The second harlequin wavered off balance. Reddish exhaled a bloom of warmth around the corner, and a chill clutch in the air faded. Firee's hand swept across a nearby lamppost; its metal frame hummed in gentle protest and set a firm boundary the third mask could not cross. Greenie extended a calming thought into the block, steadying the beating hearts of a few late sleepers who otherwise would have shuddered.

Tetragor almost reached a seam in the brickwork. He rapped a sequence on a narrow door – three-two-one – and slipped through as it quietly gave way. The six reached the gap in a flash of footsteps, but the bolts slammed shut behind him with old metal's honesty. Dust drifted down from the rafters, settling as though the shop, now closed to the night, was relieved of its burden.

Inside, the air smelled of paper and binding glue, midnight-colored slipcases lining narrow shelves. Tetragor hung his cloak by the door, unhurried. He turned to face them as they stepped in. "Good," he said, voice pitched low as ink on paper. "You kept your count while being asked to spend it. Fortitude, not flourish – you'll need that for what still clings to a hinge."

He placed a small steel tuning fork on the counter. Its surface caught the meager light like a careful thought. "The lesson tonight is one piece," Tetragor continued. "A fable and a pocket poem – two faces of the same coin."

He opened an old, thin book. Everyone gathered around to listen. Tetragor scanned their faces with quiet intensity. "Listen well," he said softly, "this story will show you how truth can shrink even the greatest of shadows."

"The Tuning Fork and the Shadow"

A traveler carried a tuning fork tucked behind the ear, for rumor said a Shadow lived in the next square. "Don't make a sound," one door advised. "Silence will save you."

"Run," said another. "Outpace what you fear."
The traveler walked instead.

In the square, the Shadow rose – taller than roofs, broader than alleys.

"Lower your noise," it breathed. "Do not strike your note. Listen to me, and I vanish."

The traveler did not argue. The traveler struck the fork – a clear, steady tone that asked nothing and agreed with nothing false.

With nowhere vague to borrow from, the Shadow shrank to the size of a stray cat and hid behind a rain barrel.

"Name yourself," said the traveler.

A voice, thin as thread, answered from the dark. "I am Suppose. I live on what you do not measure."

The traveler held the fork over the stones until the tone touched every corner. Having no room left to swell, Suppose became a smudge where two cobbles met. The traveler stepped over it and went on.

Tetragor closed the book. "Fortitude is not a louder heart," he said. "It is a truer pitch – and the habit of naming what hisses in vagueness."

He let the words settle over the group. Greenie lifted her eyes and asked softly, "Does that mean if we name a fear, it becomes smaller?" Tetragor gave a faint smile. "Precisely," he replied. "You've grasped the heart of the story." Tetragor nodded approvingly. "Good," he said. "Now listen to this."He turned the page and slid out a single heavy sheet, its surface almost rigid.

"Note of the Steady Hand"

When windows rattle, strike – not hush – your note;
name chair and lintel, ledger, clock, and coat.
Breath finds its count while you list what is true;
doubt loses math when the facts number you.

Grasp not for thunder – set your pitch instead;
step through the hush with unembarrassed tread.
Courage is not how loud the banners fly –
courage is staying while phantoms pass by.

Let hands be steady; let the count be plain;
hear each small tremor, but do not refrain.
When whisper says "Suppose," hold the tuning high –
shadows grow smaller when truth is the sky.

Tetragor let the final line linger. Breezie's brow furrowed and he whispered, "Why list so many objects?" Tetragor met his gaze. "Because by naming the world around you, you anchor yourselves in reality," he explained. "Now, practice the steps."

"Practice the steps," Tetragor instructed, setting the tuning fork back between them. "Name. Breathe. Lift. Step. When fear insists on being large, make the room specific until it runs short of places to stand.”

Reddish whispered the words under her breath. Checkered scribbled them onto a corner of her leather-bound ledger and did not need to underline. Breezie counted the syllables on his fingers, letting his breathing follow the rhythm. Greenie pointed around the room and named the simple facts – oak, varnish, ink – until every edge was pronounced. Firee felt the tug to raise his voice and chose instead to keep silent, steady and patient. And Blunt palmed Lucrecia’s silver key from beneath his cloak; even the gear at his chest clicked quietly, like a tool seating true.

Tetragor nodded once, clearly pleased. “Well done,” he said quietly. “You’ve practiced well tonight. Carry this steadiness with you whenever darkness looms.

Outside, muted footfalls faded to the ordinary murmur of Philadelphia’s streets. Tetragor lifted the latch. “Transitions matter,” he said. “Go out the way you mean to go on: pitched, lettered, ready to call things by their names.”

They stepped into the night air. The heavy panel of the door slipped shut and resumed its disguise, looking once again like nothing that had ever opened. Blunt’s gear throbbed in his cloak – subtle, as if echoing a distant clock.

Dawn at the Tavern Eaves

By the time the first pale thread of dawn stitched the far seam of sky, they had come upon a colonial-era tavern. Its wooden shutters looked like half-closed eyelids, beginning to admit morning. The air was hushed. A faint pulse from Blunt's gear hinted at a pattern deep below their work, but all six paused in stillness. At the tavern's eaves, where the old beams curved into the street, something like a face played on the dawn – an outline of gears, a suggestion of a bell hinge.

Checkered lifted her lens for a moment and saw a single flicker of geometry in the air – there, then gone – as if an unfamiliar mechanism had briefly taken measure and decided to wait. "A call, not a demand," she observed softly, lowering the device. "Possibly the next clock reaching out to us." She did not write that down; some tests preferred to be earned.

Greenie closed her eyes for a slow count and breathed in the ordinary morning: the tavern sign, the barrel by the door, the thin strip of sky everyone shared. "Let's give the moment its real names," she said quietly. "That will be enough." As she spoke, a wisp of something under the eaves tried to form again. Reddish's gentle ember and Breezie's steady breeze left it nowhere to gather; it thinned to nothing in the cool light. Firee, watching, allowed himself the smallest, almost shy smile as sunlight crept up the street.

Breezie gave his staff a quiet twirl, a habit more than performance, and the hint of breeze settled without drama. "Pattern holds," he said, voice a soft lift. "We keep our pitch." Blunt closed his fist around the silver key in his palm and felt no tug toward haste. "When it calls, we'll answer," he added. "For now, let the city finish its breath."

They stepped off again at the same even pace they had moved through the night, neither hunting for portents nor running from them. The colonial lanes remained narrow and honest, leading wherever the day might lead. Underfoot, the brick and cobblestone drew their own straight lines. And with each step, any flicker of darkness dissolved quietly.

Philadelphia, Steady

By early afternoon they let the city's older streets set the pace – brick underfoot, sunlight on windowpanes, the hush that comes when work has been done well. If a thin worry tried the corner of a shop window or the seam of an alley, it found itself outnumbered by facts: lamp, lintel, curb. The group walked on, together but unhurried. They exchanged no fanfare and little talk; the ordinary rhythm of Philadelphia was its own reward.

Checkered closed her lens and gave a single, measured survey of a worn brick facade – once was enough. "Clean," she said softly, letting the word stand for an entire page of observations. Greenie kept an easy watch on passing pedestrians. When she finally spoke, it was only, "They'll sleep fine," and the city itself seemed to agree.

Nearby, Firee leaned a knuckle to an iron fence and felt only the honest cool of metal – no residue of the earlier friction. "Craft holds," he remarked quietly, as satisfied as a smith whose blade has cooled in perfect form. Reddish circled a small ember in her palm and let it dwindle, not to extinguish anything, only to show warmth need not flare to be true. "Little pockets of chill, that's all," she murmured, watching one shadow slip into a corner.

Breezie lifted a trickle of breeze to stir the dust on the pavement and then let it fall back where it belonged. The distant flag on the hall's roof no longer felt asked to shiver. Blunt rolled Lucrecia's key between his fingers; the gear under his cloak offered a quiet click of assent, the sound a mechanism makes when perfectly aligned.

They turned onto the wide street leading back toward the square. Storefronts showed their sleeping glass to the hour. Occasionally a stray wisp of shadow scratched at an edge – the way a half-formed thought scratches at your mind – but the wizards simply named what was truly there: mail slot, bell pull, a chalked special on a sidewalk board. The shadows had nothing left to claim. A late bus sighed away down the avenue, and somewhere a distant siren chose another road.

Breezie cocked his ear to the street's ordinary draft. "Square," he said simply – meaning, the air, the moment, the measure. Reddish answered with a small, pleased breath. Checkered smiled and set down one final tally in her ledger: Philadelphia, steady. She didn't underline it. Greenie looked around at the calm faces of the city's inhabitants and felt their shoulders relax; no one was borrowing dread they didn't need. Firee let the last trace of heat in his hand slip back into the ironwork and felt no pull in return. "We don't have to make the note louder when it's already true," he said.

Blunt said nothing more. He simply reached toward the plaque on Independence Hall as they walked past, feeling the solid certainty of the letters under his hand – Fortitudo Vincit Timorem; Timor Est Vitium. He didn't tally their victories; he didn't need to. "We act together – and fear runs out of places to hide," he said quietly to the empty air, then let that truth stand. The gear at his chest hummed a contented chord under his cloak, a quiet witness to their resolve.

And so they walked on. The city's old bones kept pace with them. Where earlier in the night the air had tried to borrow shape faster than anyone could name it, now it needed more space than the facts would allow. A faint tremor under a stoop dwindled when Greenie called it by its materials – brick, lime, grit – and Breezie lent the scene its proper temperature. Reddish kept a thumb-sized ember alive at the edge of her sight – attention, not appetite. Firee listened for any friction in the world and heard only the cooling echo of honest labor. Checkered counted the streetlamps – not for omen but for order. None of them hurried; the hour did not need hurrying.

Fortitude's Work

Evening drew the edges of the brickwork into relief like ink on a plate. They took one last turn past the tower that had steadied them in the early hours, then let the square release them to its ordinary citizens – people who would never know how carefully they had been kept from an unnecessary story. A trolley clattered on by, a late walker cut across the plaza; no one sensed the near miss of panic. Reddish thought of the rooms behind them – Monticello's patience, Hazleton's grit, Boston's clean measurements, Sedona's dry light, Gdańsk's bell waiting for the exact word – and felt only the quiet pattern those trials had made. It was not a tally she recited, only the sense that each place had asked the same question in a different way. "Some work," she said softly, "asks you to stay." Greenie nodded; she understood that staying had proved a craft of its own, not a stumble. Firee gave a satisfied smile, the way a smith smiles when a blade cools straight.

They did not recount their victories aloud. They let the day's tests settle into them, and then simply walked. The key rode in Blunt's palm like a silent promise – not something to flaunt, but something to trust. He did not need to announce how quickly any future trick would fall. Instead he said only, "If all the failings gather, we'll keep our pitch." That was all that needed to be said.

Breezie's staff turned once in his hand, and the air folded itself back into its familiar lanes. Checkered, ever precise, allowed herself one indulgence: a final look up at the tower. Its hands held the hour without wobble; its face did not strain to look important. "All right," she whispered to the night, more to herself than anyone. They were unnecessary now. Together they stepped off the last curb as the first stars pricked the dusking sky.

By the time the second-floor lights blinked on in nearby windows, any leftover whisper of fear had forgotten its lines. If even a smudge of shadow tried to linger under an eave, Reddish's quiet ember and Breezie's steady breeze left it nothing to stand on. Greenie still named the ordinary things – sign, barrel, hinge – until the street had no appetite for drama. "We don't flinch," Blunt said once, and that was enough.

A soft breeze braided past the tower and out into Market Street as they walked on. Checkered's ledger stayed shut and silent. Greenie's shoulders softened. Firee's hand left the railing with a satisfied ease. Reddish let her ember sleep. Blunt closed his hand around Lucrecia's silver key and felt the gear under his cloak answer with a modest, contented click – as if to say the pieces sat true.

Philadelphia, steady, allowed them to go.

Chapter 14

Great Historical Clock of America and Ulm Clock – Fortitude's Fire

In Search of Purpose

Twilight blanketed Boston's Beacon Hill in a hush of gaslit fog. Lanterns glimmered along narrow brick sidewalks, their light dancing across ornate iron railings. Footsteps echoed off cobblestones polished by centuries of history—whispers of revolution and resilience. Into this tranquil tension stepped Blunt, Reddish, Firee, Checkered, Breezie, and Greenie, emerging from a swirling bronze-and-sapphire portal at the edge of Louisburg Square, drawn here by the faint tug of a silver key. Their Harlequin cloaks—emerald, crimson, sapphire—flickered with subdued brilliance as they stepped fully into Boston's embrace. And in Blunt's hand, the silver key awarded by Lucrecia in Gdańsk glowed softly, its edge etched in fluid Latin with "Fortitudo Vincit Timorem" — fortitude conquers fear — a reminder of the courage that had banished despair in that distant city and a beacon for the challenge now unfolding on these storied streets.

A brisk wind shivered through the maples. Passersby hurried home under the yellowish haze of lamplight, eyes averted, tension bristling in the air. It felt as though fear had crept into the city, darkening windows and stirring anxious murmurs on doorsteps.

Greenie closed her eyes, sensing an undercurrent of worry pulsing beneath Beacon Hill's regal façade. "There's a trembling spirit here," she whispered. "Something gnaws at Boston's courage. It's as if illusions linger, feeding on hidden dread."

Blunt exhaled, the key's hum resonating with his own resolve. "We faced illusions in Philadelphia," he said quietly, recalling how unwavering belief had pierced falsehoods. "If fear threatens this place, we stand against it."

Reddish stepped forward, flames flickering in her amber irises. A memory flickered too — days ago she had overcome an ordeal by holding fast to unity over isolation. She felt that same fire kindle now. "Where do we begin?" she asked.

From behind a swirling patch of fog, a figure moved like a shadow across the cobblestones — a silent hint of midnight-blue cloth. Lucrecia Van Egmond. Her presence radiated purpose and challenge. The silver key brightened in Blunt's hand, as though drawn toward her mysterious aura.

Chase Through Beacon Hill

Lucrecia vanished around a corner, cloak trailing through gaslit mist. Instantly, the young wizards followed, their strides echoing off the timeless architecture. Firee's senses prickled, half expecting illusions to twist the alleys — he'd learned how cunning fear could be from prior encounters.

The gentle slope of Beacon Hill rose before them, crowned with lampposts that stood like sentinels. At one intersection, Checkered paused to study a flickering glow. Her lens glinted as she scanned for hidden runes or deceptions carved into the bricks. "Something here…" she murmured.

Blunt lifted the silver key. The inscription "Fortitudo Vincit Timorem" pulsed with a faint rhythm, as if urging them onward. "Lucrecia is leading us," he said, voice hushed. "But is she guiding us or testing us?"

Breezie's wind magic rustled the branches overhead, stirring the scent of damp leaves and old wood. He cast out a soft current to part the fog. "Maybe both," he replied. "Her illusions in past trials taught us to see beyond surfaces."

They rounded a wrought-iron gate into a quieter lane lined with towering brick houses. Lantern glow cascaded over the group, revealing spectral shapes behind them — brief apparitions rippling at the edge of Firee's vision. He stiffened, then realized it was only residual magic left in Lucrecia's wake. "We can't let fear sink into these streets," Greenie whispered, noticing a young couple slip inside their home, bolting the door as though pursued by phantoms. "Boston has always been a place of defiance. Let's keep it that way."

Up ahead, a star-shaped rune shimmered on a lamppost. Its outlines glowed faintly, reminiscent of a celestial clock design rumored to be linked to an ancient Orloj crypt. Blunt's eyebrows rose. "Look," he said softly, placing his hand over the symbol. "It's pointing us further uphill."

A swirl of midnight-blue fabric caught their eye again — Lucrecia disappearing behind a row of tall hedges. With shared nods, they pressed on. The chase quickened, every footstep punctuated by the quiet drumbeat of their determination.

Mist clung to fences and window boxes as the wizards followed Lucrecia deeper into Beacon Hill. Each alley they crossed felt narrower, each turn revealing more of Boston's historic soul — a tension-laced blend of defiance and dread. Reddish's embers flared against the moist air. She recalled how illusions once nearly shattered her confidence. Now she moved with steadiness, letting the warmth of her cloak drive away lingering anxiety. "I see her!" she called, pointing to a fleeting glimpse of Lucrecia's cloak at the far end of the lane.

Suddenly, a surge of eerie stillness fell over the street. The gaslit lamps flickered unnaturally, their flames bending as if buffeted by invisible winds. Checkered raised her lens, suspicious. "Anyone else feel that?" she asked, a note of dread creeping into her voice. A swirl of phantasms sprang up: walls seemed to crack, paving stones threatened to collapse, and frightened cries echoed in the haze. Firee extended his hand, sparks dancing around his fingers. "Stand together," he urged. "Don't let the visions scatter us."

Breezie exhaled, conjuring a gentle gust that peeled back layers of phantoms. "There are real people in these homes — imagine their terror." With slow, steady determination, he guided the specters away from a doorstep where an older resident had peered out with wide eyes.

Greenie focused on the empathy coursing through her. She felt hearts beating rapidly behind closed shutters, their fears tangible. Summoning a soothing aura, she let hope radiate, offering the neighborhood a balm of calm.

Blunt pressed the silver key to his chest, summoning a faint protective ward that rippled through the alley. Transparent ribbons of blue light nullified the illusion of crumbling brick. As the street's solidity returned, a fleeting silhouette of Lucrecia watched from under a distant lamppost. A half-smile flickered across her face before she vanished into the fog once more.

"Her mirages feed on fear," Checkered said, stepping over where the phantom cracks had been. "But we can show Boston how resolve cuts through terror."

With determined strides, the six wizards pressed on, hearts united against the conjured gloom. Another turn beckoned — a courtyard tucked behind tall row houses, known in local lore as Lamplighter's Court — and they sensed this test was far from over. Their pursuit halted where history itself stood watch.

Lanterns flickered overhead, their glass panes etched with archaic patterns. In the courtyard's heart stood a lamppost of polished brass, its surface so smooth that it distorted the glow around it, faintly mirroring the six cloaked figures in a ghostly panorama. Intricate runic inscriptions glowed along its column, radiating an aura both welcoming and daunting.

Lucrecia waited there, midnight-blue cloak settled around her like the hush before a storm. "Boston's spirit stands on centuries of courage," she said softly. "Fear is cunning. It saps unity if you let it."

Blunt approached, holding the silver key aloft. The lamppost responded to its presence, runes flaring with renewed brilliance. "We've seen illusions tear at communities," he answered, recalling how false visions once led to chaos in Gdańsk. "But we also know unity's power."

Lucrecia's gaze traveled over each young wizard. "You have strengthened your hearts against deception," she acknowledged. "Yet fortitude must also be tested. Fear is not just an illusion in the streets — it preys on the unspoken doubts within."

Checkered studied the runic lamppost through her lens. Intricate symbols, including a faint star motif, aligned in geometric perfection — patterns resonating as if even time itself had been etched into the design. "These markings resonate with a deeper magic," she mused, "like a sentinel reminding us that, in the darkest night, steadfast resolve guides the way."

Greenie laid a gentle hand on the lamppost's base. The brass was warm to the touch, a subtle vibration humming beneath her fingers. She sensed a powerful undercurrent of solidarity, recalling how patriots once gathered in secret within Boston's narrow lanes, steeling themselves for adversity. "Fortitude overcame oppression then. It can do so again now."

Reddish lifted her chin, embers flickering in her eyes. "We stand for those who can't fight illusions alone," she declared. She glanced at Firee, who nodded in silent agreement.

Lucrecia reached into her cloak and drew forth a worn, leather-bound tome. "Then let us read," she said, opening the book to a marked page. "In knowledge, we glean perspective. In perspective, we find clarity. And in clarity, we discover true fortitude."

A hush fell over the courtyard as the six friends gathered close in a circle beneath the gentle glow. Beyond the ivy-covered walls, the faint hum of Boston's nightlife seemed to fade, leaving them in a space where only courage or fear would prevail.

The lamppost's runes cast steady light across the cobblestones, banishing the last of the lingering shadows. The young wizards stood shoulder to shoulder in that pool of golden light as Lucrecia ran a finger along the tome's runic text. "Fortitude conquers fear's illusions," she said, her voice low yet resolute. "Two short readings will illustrate how resolve dispels panic."

Their group closed ranks. Beacon Hill might have shed its eighteenth-century battles long ago, but tonight it stood poised for a new trial of fortitude. With the lamplights wavering against the deepening twilight, they braced themselves, hearts steady, ready to dispel whatever illusions lurked in these historic streets.

The lamplight trembled, and the fog that clung to Beacon Hill began to shift, swirling inward as though drawn by invisible hands. The silver key in Blunt's grasp glowed, its Latin inscription pulsing with soft radiance.

From that glow, Lucrecia emerged—midnight cloak shimmering with quiet authority, her eyes reflecting both pride and purpose. "Boston's courage endures," she said. "But tonight, your strength is needed where the nation's memory sleeps—in the halls of its history."

She extended her hand, and light gathered before her in spirals of bronze and sapphire. Within it shimmered fleeting images—columns of marble, the glint of brass, and the faint outline of a colossal clock turning beneath glass. "The Great Historical Clock awaits," she said gently. "Go forth and steady its heart."

Just then, the door of a nearby townhouse opened and a middle-aged man stepped out, gazing at the six cloaked figures in surprise. Only minutes ago the neighborhood had been in the grip of fear; now all was quiet. The man looked around, noting nothing amiss beyond this unusual group. "Everything all right out here?" he called, his Boston accent colored with mild concern.

Reddish stepped forward with a reassuring smile, subtly drawing her cloak tighter to dim its magical glow. "All clear, sir," she replied warmly. "Just a bit of strange fog earlier, but it's passed now."

He studied them for a moment, then nodded, satisfied by her calm confidence. "Strangest thing — we thought we saw… well, never mind. Good that it's cleared. You folks take care now." With a polite wave, he tugged his cardigan close and retreated indoors.

As the door latched, Breezie released a breath he hadn't realized he was holding. "Fear's hold is weakening," he observed softly. Beacon Hill might just sleep easier tonight.

The six wizards stood together as one. The air vibrated; the world folded.

Bronze light swept through the street, and the fog became a bridge of stars.

When it cleared, Beacon Hill stood empty once more—its lamps burning steady, its courage passed onward to another city, another test.

Portal Arrival at the Smithsonian

Night had fallen over Washington, D.C., draping the National Mall in a serene hush. A swirl of bronze-and-sapphire light unfurled in front of the Smithsonian's National Museum of American History, depositing six cloaked figures onto the deserted sidewalk. Blunt, Reddish, Firee, Checkered, Breezie, and Greenie stepped forward as one, their Harlequin cloaks—emerald, crimson, sapphire, and more—gently luminescent in the glow of a nearby streetlamp. In Blunt's hand, a silver key pulsed and shimmered, its edge etched in flowing Latin script: "Fortitudo Vincit Timorem"—Fortitude conquers fear. This was the very key bestowed by Lucrecia in a distant trial, and its gentle tug had guided them here. Blunt could feel the inscription's truth humming against his palm—a reminder of how courage had dispelled fear in Philadelphia and beyond, and a beacon for the challenge now awaiting them on American soil.

They approached the museum's grand entrance, the city silent around them. The glass doors yielded to a subtle unlocking charm from Checkered. Inside, the vast atrium was dim, illuminated only by security lights that cast long shadows across exhibits of the nation's past. The air was cool and reverent. Marble floors echoed their footsteps as they moved with purpose, each wizard instinctively alert for any sign of illusion. It was after hours, yet an unnatural stillness pervaded the hall—a feeling that something, or someone, awaited them in the dark. Greenie closed her eyes and reached out with her empathic sense.

"Something stirs here," Greenie whispered. Her heart quickened as she felt it: an undercurrent of worry thrumming in the emptiness. "An anxiety… as if the very building holds its breath." She could almost taste the tension, like static before a storm.

Reddish stepped forward, her chin lifted. In the faint light, her amber irises flickered with tiny flames. "We've felt this before," she murmured, recalling how fear's illusions had once gripped a city street until they stood united to break them. The memory ignited a steady fire inside her. "If fear lurks here too, we'll face it—together."

Blunt nodded firmly. He brushed his thumb over the Latin engraving on the glowing key. "We have stood against illusions of terror in other places," he said quietly, confidence resonating in his voice. "Philadelphia, Gdańsk, Lund… each time, unity and courage carried us. If fear threatens this museum—threatens America's historical heart—we stand against it now." His declaration settled over them, and each wizard drew their cloak a little tighter, fortifying their resolve.

A sudden clink echoed from deeper within the museum. Breezie flicked his wrist and summoned a whisper of air to scout ahead, the breeze carrying the scent of old parchment and brass. The faint wind brushed past a towering exhibit in the shadows: the outline of a giant clock. Checkered adjusted her spectacles, and even without full light she recognized the shape from her studies. "The Great Historical Clock of America," she breathed. High in the gloom, the contours of an enormous 13-foot-tall timepiece loomed, crowned by a miniature Statue of Liberty. Even dormant, its presence was commanding.

They advanced towards the clock's exhibit hall, the key in Blunt's hand glowing brighter with each step. As they entered the space, moonlight filtered through a skylight, illuminating the clock's gilded frame. The Great Historical Clock of America stood encased in glass but visible in all its intricate glory: carved scenes of battles and reunions, a golden zodiac ring at its center, and rows of figurines—minutemen, presidents, pioneers—poised to march through dioramas of the nation's triumphs and trials. Even now, past midnight, the clock face showed the correct time, and the astrological dial below glinted with cosmic symbols.

Greenie's breath caught at the sight of the figures frozen in mid-story: tiny sculpted soldiers huddled on one side, a painted Niagara Falls on the other, Paul Revere on horseback, and allegorical statues of the stages of life. It was as if the soul of America's history had been distilled into a clock. But something was off. The usually proud Statue of Liberty figurine at the clock's crown was dim—its torch unlit. And the glass case that should shield the clock from harm was…open. A hairline fracture zigzagged across it, as if forced by some magical tampering.

Checkered peered through her runic lens. "This isn't right. The case has been broken from within," she noted, her voice hushed. Tiny motes of illusory magic danced around the clock's base, detectable to her trained eye. It was as though the clock had been agitated by a bad dream. "Illusions have breached this display."

At her words, a low creaking groan emanated from the clock's mechanism. Firee and Reddish immediately stepped in front of their friends, each raising a hand defensively. The creak turned into a whir of gears. Without warning, the Great Clock came alive in the darkness. Normally, it would play cheerful folk tunes and parade its historical figurines in celebration. But now the chimes that plinked out were discordant, warped by illusion. George Washington's tiny figure jerked forward from a domed tower, as if to begin his procession, but where a dignified nod was meant to be, his wooden face twisted into a mournful frown. The procession of presidents that should follow him remained frozen, their painted eyes suddenly etched with anxiety.

A projected tableau sprang up behind the clock, startling the young wizards: a phantom image of a battlefield, Revolutionary War soldiers wavering as though uncertain of victory. An ethereal chorus of voices echoed through the hall—whispering in despairing tones. Breezie's sharp ears picked out fragments of their lament: "too hard... can't go on... all is lost..." The voices of patriots and pioneers from the clock's dioramas were being distorted into tones of surrender.

Greenie winced, feeling the wash of hopelessness these illusions cast. The Clock of America, meant to inspire, was having its stories turned against themselves. "They're trying to erode our collective resilience," she said, eyes shining with compassionate outrage. Personal or collective, resilience is under attack here, she realized. It wasn't just about scaring individuals; it was about sapping the fighting spirit of a people.

"Not on our watch," Blunt growled. He could sense the same insidious magic at work here that they'd battled before—fear and despair given shape. The silver key's glow intensified, reacting to the challenge.

Illusions in the Hall of History

Before Blunt could step closer, a tremor ran through the floor. The museum's banners and flags, hanging from the ceiling, fluttered though there was no breeze. In the eerie half-light, the great American flag exhibit on the far wall—an enormous banner with stars and stripes—seemed to waver and dim as if a shadow had been cast over the nation's hope. The illusion was spreading.

Without needing to be told, the six wizards tightened formation around the clock's exhibit. Crash! A sudden jolt shook the hall as one of the clock's glass panels cracked further and a shard fell, shattering on the marble. At that sound, the illusions fully sprang forth: spectral figures emerged from the clock's dioramas and flooded the hall. Ghostly minutemen stumbled out with rifles drooping, their spectral faces etched in doubt. Pioneer families made of mist huddled as if the light of their courage was dying. A translucent figure of Lady Liberty herself flickered to life beside the real clock, her torch hand quivering as though the weight of it had become too great.

"Stand together! Don't let the visions scatter us!" Firee shouted over the rising cacophony, echoing the rallying cry he had learned in earlier trials. A swirl of phantasmal smoke tried to separate him from the others, but Breezie sent a steady breeze through the hall that pushed the choking fog back. The six closed ranks in front of the clock, presenting a united front amidst the ghosts of surrender.

One particularly large illusion leapt from the clock's base: a galloping black horse carrying a figure of General Sheridan from the Civil War tableau. But instead of charging forward bravely, the phantom horse reared and threatened to trample a group of cowering apparition civilians. Reddish reacted instantly, darting out with a fiery glint in her eyes. With a sweep of her hand, she conjured a controlled burst of flame across the marble floor. It wasn't meant to burn, only to corral and redirect. The sudden brightness startled the spectral horse, and it veered away from the illusory victims, dissolving into smoke with an echoing whinny.

Checkered adjusted her lens and scanned the swirling illusions. Amid the chaos, her keen sight caught glimmers of runes flashing on the clock's turning zodiac dial. Someone or something is powering this, she thought. "There!" she called, pointing to the golden zodiac ring at the clock's center, where the figures of the zodiac should cycle calmly. Now, however, the ring of zodiac symbols—a lion, a bull, a scorpion, and others rendered in gilt—spun erratically. Each symbol glowed malevolently as it passed the top. The normally benign signs of the stars were being twisted to fuel fear. "It's focusing the illusion through the zodiac," Checkered deduced. The clock itself had become a conduit of magical attack on morale.

Blunt met her gaze and understood. He had an idea. Fortitude's fire isn't about quick victory, he reminded himself. It's about endurance and unity. "Buy me a moment!" he urged. Clutching the silver key, he leapt onto the exhibit platform, positioning himself right before the spinning zodiac dial. The clock's towering façade loomed over him, its decorative columns and gilded sculptures casting long shadows.

At once, the illusions seemed to sense his intent and converged on the platform to stop him. A pair of ghostly colonial-era women, faces twisted in panic, rushed toward Blunt as if to beg him to share their terror. Breezie intervened with swift compassion—he swept in front of them and breathed out a cool, soothing gust. The phantom women paused, their forms flickering as the calming wind dispersed the edges of their fear. Greenie followed, stretching out her hand and emanating a gentle wave of reassurance. "You are not alone," she whispered, not just to the phantoms but to whatever real spirits of history might linger. The ghostly women's frantic expressions softened; they looked at one another as if remembering the strength they once had. In a wisp of light, they vanished, their energy dispelled by empathy and solidarity.

Firee and Reddish stood guard at Blunt's sides as he pressed the silver key against the zodiac dial's glass. The dial fought back; a bolt of illusory lightning crackled across its face, nearly knocking Blunt from the platform. Reddish quickly planted her feet and caught Blunt's arm to steady him, her other hand raised outward. The embers in her eyes flared to life. Boom! Another shock of magic from the clock burst forth, but Reddish absorbed the brunt of it, her fiery aura dissipating the blow in a shower of harmless sparks. She gritted her teeth, the heat in her blood unwavering. "Not this time," she growled at the manifestation of fear.

Meanwhile, Firee focused on the Statue of Liberty figure atop the clock. Its bronze torch was dark, symbolically snuffed out by the illusion. Firee's heart clenched—he felt the import of that image. He raised his wand and, with a careful stream of magic, lit Lady Liberty's torch anew. A tiny flame, no bigger than a candle's, flickered to life in the statue's hand. It cast a warm glimmer across the clock's face. The real-life statue had once greeted the tired and poor with hope; now even this replica could shine. "Stay lit," Firee whispered, pouring his determination into that little flame. It was a defiant spark in the darkness.

The effect was immediate. Some of the nearest illusions— woeful soldiers and weeping settlers—shied away from the torch's golden light as if it pained them. Encouraged, Blunt pressed the silver key harder against the zodiac ring, closing his eyes to concentrate. He remembered how in Gdańsk, confronted with despair, Lucrecia had challenged them to hold fast. He summoned that same resolve now. The key began to glow brighter, channeling his will. Fortitudo Vincit Timorem.

Checkered climbed up beside Blunt, flipping through a small notebook of glyphs with one hand while holding on to her hat with the other as another gust of chaotic magic swirled by. "Almost… got it," she muttered, locating the rune she sought. With a decisive motion, she traced a symbol of steadfastness on the clock's glass casing, right above where Blunt pressed the key. A cool blue rune flared to life, anchoring Blunt's protective magic to the clock.

The zodiac dial shuddered and then ground to a halt, pinned by the combined force of the key and Checkered's rune. In that moment, the hall fell eerily silent. The remaining illusions hesitated, forms wavering as if unsure whether to attack or retreat. The tiny flame in the Statue of Liberty's torch burned steadily on, unthreatened.

Greenie and Breezie moved together to capitalize on the pause. Greenie spread her arms wide, eyes closed, sending out a ripple of compassion and encouragement into the space. She thought of all the real people who had once stood strong in this city—civil rights marchers, suffragettes, soldiers and nurses—souls who endured fearsome times with fortitude. Drawing on that collective strength, she projected a calming empathy that flowed through the hall like a reassuring embrace. Breezie, sensing her intent, guided her aura with a gentle breeze, carrying it to every corner, every quivering phantom.

One by one, the ghostly figures stopped trembling. The minutemen who had faltered now straightened their translucent backs, recalling their bravery. The pioneer family illusions released their fear and held each other sturdily before fading away. Even the phantom of General Sheridan on his horse reappeared momentarily at the edge of the exhibit, not as a threat but as a proud silhouette saluting the group, before dissolving into harmless mist. The malevolent magic infecting the clock had been broken; only the echoes of America's true history remained, watching in silent gratitude.

On the platform, Blunt opened his eyes as the silver key cooled in his hand. The zodiac dial was frozen at a peaceful alignment—the golden sun at its apex, signifying a new dawn. The Great Historical Clock of America stood still and quiet once more, its figures now calm. The Statue of Liberty's torch continued to glow gently, a tiny beacon of hope in the dark hall.

"It's done," Checkered whispered, adjusting her lens to verify that no illusion magic lingered. All she saw were ordinary traces of long-settled dust and the faint natural aura of this magnificent timepiece. She let out a breath of relief.

Reddish hopped down from the platform, helping Blunt and Checkered safely to the floor. "We did it—at least for this place," Reddish said softly. She ran a hand over her hair, smoothing stray strands that had escaped during the fray. Her cheeks were flushed, but not from exertion—from pride. The illusions had tested their collective resilience, and they had answered with steady resolve.

Firee stood gazing up at the now-quiet clock. The little flame in the torch he'd lit was finally flickering out, having fulfilled its purpose. "That was only the first wave," he murmured, sensing in his gut that their trial of fortitude was not yet complete. The silver key in Blunt's hand, though dimmer now, still emanated a subtle tug—as if pointing beyond these museum walls, to another challenge yet to come.

Breezie nodded in agreement with Firee. He could almost hear a distant sigh, like the turning of a great page in history. "The fear here has been quelled," Breezie said, feeling the atmosphere in the museum lighten. The great flag on the wall hung still and proud once more. "But something tells me our test isn't over. There's more to face, somewhere else."

As if in response, a gentle footfall sounded from behind them. From the shadows at the hall's edge, a tall figure stepped forward. The six friends immediately turned, though not in alarm—for Blunt's key pulsed in recognition. A woman in a midnight-blue cloak emerged into a shaft of moonlight. Her hood was drawn back just enough to reveal a resolute, familiar face framed by silver-streaked hair. Lucrecia Van Egmond.

Lucrecia's dark eyes gleamed with approval and purpose. "You've done well here," she said, her voice low and clear in the hush. It was the same voice that had challenged them before in distant Gdańsk, where she first presented the silver key now in Blunt's grasp. "The clock's illusions fed on the collective fear of failure—on the nightmare that fortitude would fail when history needed it most. But you showed that resolve and unity can turn back even such despair." Lucrecia swept an arm gently toward the Great Historical Clock. The air around it shimmered briefly, and the glass case repaired itself with a soft chiming sound, sealing the precious artifact safely once more.

Greenie stepped forward, relief and curiosity mingling on her face. "Lucrecia… this trial, it's not finished, is it?" she asked. "I can sense it—like an unfinished story." Her empathic intuition told her that the fear they'd vanquished here was only one chapter of the test of fortitude.

Lucrecia inclined her head. "Correct. Fortitude must shine in more than one realm." She reached out and touched the rim of the giant clock's case thoughtfully. "In the young nation of

America's history, you have reignited a spark of hope. But another place calls out, a far older place, where fortitude's flame must also be defended." As she spoke, she drew back her cloak, revealing an ancient leather-bound tome tucked under her arm.

Checkered's eyes lit up at the sight of Lucrecia's tome. She remembered the wisdom and stories it contained from their last encounter. Lucrecia continued, "We stand now in a hall of democracy and memory. Next, you will journey to a hall of centuries-old wisdom and faith—to confront illusions that prey on endurance in another form. But before you go…" She gently opened the book to a page marked with a silken ribbon. "…you must remember what true fortitude means."

The six wizards exchanged anticipatory glances and gathered around Lucrecia as she moved to a nearby exhibit bench. The museum hall was quiet now, and in the faint glow of the clock's gilding, they felt as if they sat at the hearth of an ancient storyteller. Lucrecia placed the tome on her lap, its weathered pages catching the light. "Fortitude is not just physical bravery or a moment's courage," she said softly, looking at each of them in turn. "It's the sustained fire within that outlasts the cold of fear. Stories and fables have long been used to kindle that inner fire. Listen now, and remember."

A hush fell over the hall of history as Lucrecia began to read. The young wizards formed a semicircle at her feet, cloaks pooling around them on the marble floor. Overhead, the moon slipped behind a cloud, and for a moment the only light was the soft golden aura emanating from Blunt's key and the quiet determination in Lucrecia's eyes.

"The Raven and the Shattered Cliff"

In a village cast in the long shadow of a jagged cliff, fear ruled as a sovereign. Every creak of stone and every gust of wind sparked dread among the people, who huddled in silence, whispering of collapse. Legends turned the cliff into a monster—not of rock, but of imagined doom. Their trembling hearts fractured the ground more than time or tremor ever could.

High above them, in a pine that leaned bravely into the sky, lived Veyra, a lone raven with feathers like storm-slick stone and eyes dark with insight. She watched as fear wrapped itself around the villagers like fog, thickening each day. "Why," she asked the wind, "do they fear what they've not dared to know?"

The villagers rebuked her calm. "To be afraid is to be safe," they chorused. Yet beneath their words, the earth groaned—less from the weight of the cliff than from the weight of worry. In tiptoeing away from danger, their retreat loosened the very soil beneath them. Veyra took flight.

She did not flee, but flew closer—to the cliff, to the truth. Through biting winds and echoing warnings, she circled and descended on a jutting ledge, scarred yet firm. Her wings furled and her gaze unwavering, she stood sentry as the night howled. One by one, villagers looked up.

Not all at once, but in small ripples of courage—hearts stirred by Veyra's defiance of dread. A young shepherd was first to climb, then a stonemason, then a widow with shaking hands. Together, they joined her on the ledge—not because it was safe, but because it was solid, and because their unity made it stronger still.

With each step taken in courage, the cliff ceased its moans. The ground quieted. The wind, once fierce, now carried the song of a people no longer hiding.

They rebuilt—not beneath the shadow, but beside the strength. And at the cliff's foot, where fear once ruled, rose a gathering of souls, brave not because they felt no fear, but because they chose not to bow to it.

And so it was that Veyra, the raven of the unshaken pine, taught a trembling world that fortitude is not loud, but luminous. It does not roar; it perches. And it waits—not to be followed, but to be understood.

When the reading stopped, a profound silence embraced the museum hall. For a long moment, none of the wizards spoke. They could almost hear the imagined wind from the fable, feel the weight of that village's fear, and then the relief of standing firm on solid ground. A faint, reverent breeze—perhaps conjured unconsciously by Breezie—stirred the edges of Lucrecia's cloak and rustled the pages of the tome, carrying the fable's wisdom into the very walls lined with American memories.

Blunt was the first to break the silence. He bowed his head, the tale resonating deeply. "Veyra showed them the cost of panic," he said softly. In his mind's eye, he pictured the villagers' trembling hearts, and remembered moments in their own journey when fear had nearly driven them apart. "That same panic nearly consumed us once—until we stood side by side, like those villagers on the ledge." His gaze drifted to each of his friends, gratitude and determination evident on his face.

Checkered's monocle glinted as she blinked away a mist of emotion. She recalled how, not long ago in Lund, illusions had nearly convinced some of them that trust was broken and each was isolated. "Fear deepens every crack," she said quietly, echoing a lesson they all knew too well. Her analytical voice was gentle now. "But when we dared to unify, the cracks mended and the illusions lost their power."

Greenie reached out and ran her fingertips over the silver key in Blunt's hand, tracing the etched word Fortitudo. The key thrummed as if alive with the story's energy. "Every community can splinter under fear," she murmured, thinking of the villagers, of Boston in the grip of terror earlier, of any tight-knit group of friends. "Unless we remember Veyra's example: stand firm, stand as one. Fear may howl, but we do not have to face it alone."

Lucrecia gave a small, approving nod. With a quiet rustle of paper, she turned to another marked page in her tome. "One more tale awaits," she said, her voice warm with encouragement. "Another lens through which you can glimpse the nature of fear and fortitude—this time, in verse." She carefully lifted a folded parchment that had been tucked between the pages. It unfurled to reveal lines of elegant script. A subtle pulse of magic emanated from it, stirring Reddish's elemental senses.

Reddish accepted the scroll with reverence. The moment it touched her hands, she felt a soft thrill—a tingling of embers as if the parchment itself carried a living warmth. "Let's see what more we can glean about courage," she agreed. Stepping a pace away, she unrolled the scroll. The others watched as a subtle glow of red-orange light reflected off Reddish's face, as though the words on the page were written in fire. Indeed, as Reddish began to read, tiny embers danced along the hem of her crimson cloak, matching the quiet passion in her voice.

"The Flame of Resolve"

In lands where silence stifled breath,

and stars withdrew in fright,

where dread distilled the scent of death

and day dissolved to night,

there stirred a flame no storm could snuff,

no whisper could dismay—

a sovereign spark, though small enough,

it would not turn away.

It shimmered on a shattered wall,

where once bold voices spoke;

it dared to rise though fears would crawl

and cloak the air in smoke.

The void hissed threats in every gust—

"Extinguish! Or obey!"

But fire, when born of sacred trust,

will never turn to gray.

Through thunder's wrath and shadow's leer,

it danced in calm defiance—

not loud, but deep, not loud, but clear—

a flame of self-reliance.

Its glow did not demand a throne,

nor wait for tides to shift;

it lit the path for those alone,

a bridge, a buoy, a gift.

One watched. Then two. Then throngs drew near,

each soul with burdened eyes,

yet in the flame's unblinking cheer,

they saw their own arise.

The timid hand, once clenched in fright,

now reached to shield the flame;

each breath it drew gave birth to light,

and none remained the same.

The darkness, vast as ocean's hold,

now thinned with every gleam—

for fire that's shared grows not old,

but lives in shared esteem.

And so the cliff did cease to crack,

the wind no longer moaned;

for hearts alight will not fall back

when fear stands not alone.

Now etched in stone where once was dread,

these words in embers burn:

"Let courage walk where fear once tread—

and hope will not adjourn.

When Reddish finished, her voice tapered off into the silence, as soft as a dying ember yet as potent as a bonfire's core. She lowered the scroll slowly, her eyes shining with awe and the afterglow of magic. The words of the poem seemed to hang in the air like the final notes of a song. In that vast museum hall filled with relics of resilience, the poem's imagery of a single flame igniting the hearts of many resonated powerfully.

"Courage spreads like that spark," Reddish said, breaking the silence. She exhaled, her breath steady, and one could almost imagine the little sovereign flame from the poem reflected in her eyes. "Once lit, it won't be snuffed out by mere specters." As someone who carried literal fire within her, Reddish felt a kinship with the flame of resolve. It was not a roaring blaze, but a steady light—just like the inner strength she aspired to.

Firee had crossed his arms tightly over his chest at some point during the poem. Now he relaxed them, feeling those verses coil with warmth inside him. He remembered past illusions all too well—how cunning they were at turning friends against themselves, at sowing silence and compliance. "When even one of us resists the shadows," he murmured, "it emboldens the rest." He thought of how Blunt's refusal to yield to despair in Philadelphia had galvanized them all, or how Reddish overcoming her inner fire's fear had inspired him. Each individual's courage was a spark; together, they were a bonfire.

Breezie let out a breath he didn't realize he'd been holding. With a gentle sweep of his hand, he circulated a balmy breeze around their circle, easing any lingering tension from the intense stories. He smiled as the moving air mimicked soft applause for the poem's truth. "Fear isolates," he said, recalling the void in the verse where darkness tried to divide and conquer. "But fortitude draws people together, fueling a common flame." How many times had he seen that now? A single act of bravery—one flame—uniting many. The thought filled him with quiet hope.

Lucrecia rose from the bench, closing her tome and carefully tucking the scroll back between its pages. Her midnight-blue cloak shimmered as she moved into the center of the group.

The golden light from the great clock's gallery reflected off her, giving her an almost otherworldly aura. She regarded the six young mages with clear, proud eyes. "Remember the raven's ledge and the flame's brilliance," she advised gently. "Fortitude is not merely withstanding fear. It's forging a unity that outlasts any illusion. It's the fire kept alight in each other, especially when nights grow long." They all absorbed her words, standing a little straighter as they did.

For a moment, a strange stillness settled. It felt as though the whole museum—and maybe the spirits of history within it—were holding their breath alongside them, contemplating the profound courage and unity these tales extolled. The Great Historical Clock of America was silent but present, its repaired glass reflecting the group like a ghostly echo of Washington, Franklin, and others who had once banded together for a greater cause. The flame of fortitude glowed in each wizard's heart now, kindled anew by story and verse.

Lucrecia gently snapped shut her book, and the sound seemed to signal the next movement in their journey. As if on cue, the silver key in Blunt's hand and the runes on Lucrecia's tome both emitted a soft pulse of light. The time for reflection was over; the time for action had come again. Lucrecia stepped back, and with a graceful sweep of her arm, she drew a circular shape in the air. Wisps of sapphire light trailed from her fingertips, lingering and connecting, until a large oval portal materialized before them. Through it swirled mists of magic and a glimpse of starry sky.

"Your next trial awaits beyond," Lucrecia said, her voice echoing slightly as the portal widened. "Far from here—across the sea in a place of ancient timekeeping. The Ulm Astronomical Clock in Germany has stood for centuries, a testament to human curiosity and faith. But tonight, it will test your fortitude in new ways. Steel yourselves. What you faced here in the hall of history was but one facet of fear. In Ulm, the illusions will strike at the personal doubts and the endurance of an entire community's spirit. Remember: not speed or strength, but sustained resolve will see you through."

The six friends drew close, peering into the swirling portal. They could not yet see Ulm, but they felt the cool whisper of European night air and the faint toll of a distant bell. One by one, with Blunt leading and Lucrecia following behind, they stepped into the magical gateway, leaving the quiet museum and the Great Historical Clock behind. The portal's light enveloped them, and in a blink, Washington D.C. was gone.

Arrival at Ulm Town Hall

The young wizards emerged on the other side of the portal into crisp night air and found themselves standing in a wide cobbled square. Overhead, the sky was a tapestry of stars, and the moon hung low, bathing the town in silvery light. They were in Ulm, Germany—an old city at the crossroads of history and myth. All around the square stood picturesque, half-timbered houses and shops shuttered for the night. But the most arresting sight was directly in front of them: Ulm's Rathaus, the famed Town Hall, adorned with lavish painted murals and crowned by an astronomical clock that quietly dominated the façade.

Greenie drew in a soft breath as she spun in a slow circle, taking in their surroundings. The Rathaus was like something out of a storybook. By moonlight, she could make out murals painted in rich blues, reds, and golds covering the building's walls—scenes of virtues and vices, commandments and fables, all interconnected. High above, at the center of the ornate eastern façade, the astronomical clock gleamed. It featured a large circular astrolabe dial about two dozen feet across. At its heart, an intricate arrangement of celestial symbols indicated the positions of sun and moon. Concentric rings marked the hours in bold numerals and the zodiac in a ring of golden sculptures. Even in darkness, some of the gilded figures caught the moonlight: she spotted a shining Leo the lion, a Virgo maiden, a Sagittarius archer poised to loose his arrow among others, all forming the zodiac wheel around the dial.

"So beautiful," Checkered whispered, entranced. She adjusted her goggles to zoom in on the clock's detail. Inscribed around the dial's edge were Latin mottos and tiny pictograms for the days and planets. A 24-hour chapter ring in the outermost circle glinted faintly, and just within it, a revolving golden ring depicted the zodiac, much like a cousin to the one on the clock they'd just left in Washington. But this one was older, heavier with centuries of meaning. At the clock's top, figures of medieval knights stood guard, and just beneath, a small window likely hid automatons or bell-strikers waiting for the hour to chime.

Breezie drew his cloak around himself as a cool wind came off the nearby Danube River, which he could smell but not see in the darkness. "This place… it's seen ages of turmoil and rebirth," he said quietly. The murals across the façade indeed depicted scenes that looked instructive: to one side, personifications of the Seven Virtues (he recognized symbols of Courage wielding a sword and Justice with scales), and opposite them the Seven Vices with ghastly, distorted features. Latin inscriptions ribboned through the artwork, warnings and wisdom both. Breezie's eyes were drawn to one painting in particular—a portrayal of Fortitude as a woman in armor, calmly holding a tower on her shoulder while around her demons of fear broke their claws against her feet. It gave him confidence.

They stepped further into the square, their boots making soft clacks on the ancient stones. It was late—somewhere past midnight by the feel of the air—so the square was empty, save for their party and Lucrecia who now moved ahead of them with purpose. In the stillness, they could hear the rhythmic ticking of the clock's mechanism echoing through the quiet. The pendulum inside swung faithfully, a metronome for the city's heartbeat.

Lucrecia stopped at the foot of the Town Hall's steps. "Ulm's Astronomical Clock," she announced softly, "installed in the 16th century and still guiding eyes to the heavens." Her gaze rose to the clock face towering above. The moonlight caught carved figures around the dial—perhaps the Four Evangelists or local historical figures—and cast a spiderweb of shadows across the astrolabe's surface. "For generations, this clock has weathered storms and even war. In 1944, the interior of this very building was gutted by fire," she added solemnly, "yet the clock and the outer walls survived. Ulm rebuilt, restored the paintings, and the clock ticks on—a testament to resilience."

As her words faded, a faint rumble disturbed the air. Firee tensed, half-expecting another portal or some physical threat, but it was only the clock's machinery engaging. The wizards realized the hour was about to turn. A moment later, the clock began to chime midnight. A deep, sonorous bell from the clock tower tolled twelve times, each chime rolling out across the deserted square. With each peal, the automata of the clock came to life: small doors above the dial opened and painted figures of kings and prophets processed out in stiff, ancient motions. Normally, it would be a charming display of medieval pomp and faith for onlookers by day. But here in the middle of the night, under uneasy stars, it felt decidedly more ominous.

On the twelfth and final chime, something in the air snapped. The automaton figures halted abruptly mid-procession, their wooden faces locked in uncanny stares. The last reverberations of the bell dissolved into an unnatural hush. Greenie pressed a hand to her heart. "Do you feel that?" she whispered. Indeed, a prickle ran up all their spines—a feeling of being watched by unseen eyes, as if the painted Virtues and Vices around them had suddenly come alive with hostile intent.

Checkered raised her lens to scan the area. For an instant, the square looked normal—just an empty plaza under moonlight. Then, at the very edge of her magical sight, she caught a distortion: the silhouettes of the Rathaus's murals flickered. The Virtues painted on the wall—Prudence, Justice, Temperance, Fortitude—each shimmered, and their eyes glinted. The Vices—Envy, Greed, Pride, Fear and the others—seemed to writhe in their painted forms, their grotesque features sneering. "Illusion magic… saturating the facade," Checkered warned, voice tight. "It's seeping out of the paintings!"

No sooner had she spoken than the first illusion fully broke free. With a sound like cracking plaster, the mural of Fear peeled itself off the wall. The vice was depicted as a gaunt, hollow-eyed creature clutching at its heart, and now it descended onto the square in three-dimensional form, towering twice the height of a man. Its painted face became a lifelike mask of terror and malice, and it let out a silent scream that sent ripples through the air. Close behind, other vices dragged themselves from the wall—Despair, in a shroud of gray, and Doubt, depicted as a pale, two-faced imp, leapt down and began circling the heroes with uncanny speed.

The six wizards backed up automatically, forming a protective ring with Lucrecia at their center. Firee's palms burned with a ready flame, and Reddish's fingers twitched, small embers trailing from her hair. Blunt lifted the silver key he still carried; its glow now returned, casting a blue halo around them. The key's magic clearly recognized this challenge: illusions borne of humanity's oldest inner enemies, given shape by the enchanted clock's domain.

Lucrecia's midnight-blue cloak fluttered as the illusions prowled at the edge of their circle. Her face was calm but stern. "Face your hidden fears," she intoned, echoing the challenge she'd voiced earlier. "Fortitude blossoms only when tested." With that, she stepped back toward the Town Hall steps, deliberately removing herself from their immediate fight. This was their test to pass.

The vice-phantoms wasted no time. Despair struck first: it skulked forward, a swirling mass of charcoal gloom, and enveloped the group in a freezing shadow. In each of the wizards' minds, Despair's magic sought out their personal doubts and magnified them.

Blunt staggered as a vision gripped him—a sudden horrific flash of their mission ending in failure. He saw his friends scattered, the Dark Harlequin (their distant nemesis) victorious, and Boston—his beloved home—submerged in a sea of despair. His heart clenched painfully, and for an instant cold fear whispered that all their efforts might be futile. But beneath that, something burned: the steady flame of resolve. He clutched the silver key until its ridges pressed into his skin, using the slight pain to anchor himself. "No," he growled under his breath, teeth clenched. The nightmare vision wavered. He focused on what was real—five friends around him, standing firm. He thought of Philadelphia again, where false terrors had melted when they believed in each other. "We do not stand alone," Blunt reminded himself, and the doubt gnawing at him shrank back. The silver key pulsed, projecting a wave of protective blue light that pushed Despair's shadowy tendrils off of him.

Checkered felt a sudden chill as well. In her mind's eye, Doubt and Fear together conjured a terrible scenario: she saw her friends turning away from her, accusing her of failure, her careful logic helpless to save them. It was an illusion of betrayal, of her keen mind unraveling when it was needed most. A strangled gasp escaped her—almost a sob. But no, this wasn't real. She forcefully slid her goggles down over her eyes, the lenses flashing with determined magic. Through them, the illusions' true nature was laid bare: ugly, hollow, without foundation. "Lies," Checkered hissed, her voice cutting through the silent scream of the fear-phantom. With a sweep of her hand, she banished the phantom images of her friends abandoning her. The truth shone through her lens—her companions were right here, facing the fight with her. "These nightmares have no root in our bond," she declared. Her lens glowed bright, emitting a beam of clarity that sliced across the looming specter of Fear. The tall, gaunt creature recoiled as if burned, its hollow eyes blinking in surprise at her fierce resistance.

Greenie's empathic heart was under siege as well. The Despair illusion wrapped around her like a smothering blanket, isolating her senses. She felt utterly alone—cut off from the warm thread of her friends' feelings that she always could sense at the edge of her mind. To her horror, a vision bloomed: a future where each of her companions succumbed to their weaknesses and left her one by one, until she stood solitary against the darkness. A hot tear slid down Greenie's cheek at the overwhelming loneliness of it. Is this my fate? a tiny voice in her wondered. But another voice, gentle and resolute, answered from within: No. Reach out. Greenie inhaled deeply, steadying herself. She closed her eyes and sought the life around her—not the false lifeless despair, but the true pulsing hearts she knew so well. She found one: a wind-borne spark of worry from Breezie, right beside her. Then another: the fiery defiance in Reddish, and the steadfast courage in Blunt, the analytical focus in Checkered, the fierce loyalty in Firee. One by one, Greenie reconnected with each of her friends' heartbeats as if weaving threads into a tapestry. The empathic bonds between them glowed in her mind's eye, vibrant and unbreakable. With a cry that was half sob, half laughter, Greenie flung her arms out, pushing a wave of connection against the darkness. The sense of isolation shattered; the phantom Despair faltered as Greenie's magic asserted the truth: they were together, and she could feel them, everyone.

A swirl of black smoke lunged at Reddish next. Within that smoke, vivid as a lightning flash, Reddish was made to relive her worst memory: the moment her uncontrolled flames once raged out of fear and nearly hurt those she loved. The illusion whispered to her that she was a danger, that her temper was a ticking bomb, that she would fail her friends when it mattered most. Reddish's hands shook as she recalled that perilous moment from her past—how close she'd come to disaster. For an instant, the phantom's words stung like salt on an old wound. But then Reddish remembered the fable of Veyra on the ledge, and how unity gave courage. She remembered the countless times since that dark moment when her friends' understanding, and her own growth kept that fear at bay. She squared her shoulders, planting her feet firmly on Ulm's cobbles. "I accept that part of me," she whispered to the smoke, her voice steady. "But I am more than my anger. I'm not alone with it anymore." As if in answer, a gentle green aura—Greenie's empathy—enfolded her, and a crisp breeze—Breezie's reassurance—brushed her cheek. Reddish opened her palm, and a controlled flame blossomed in it, bright and confident. Her ember eyes flashed. The black smoke creature shrieked silently, rushing her like a furious wraith. Reddish thrust her palm forward, and the flame in her hand expanded into a wide arc of cleansing fire. It wasn't a wild blast, but a deliberate burn of courage. The arc sliced through the smoke, burning the specter of her self-doubt to ash. The cinders blew away over the square, and Reddish stood unscathed, fire crackling in her hair like a crown.

Nearby, Breezie himself faced a phantom as well. The vice of Doubt flitted around him as a pale imp, whispering a cold thought that seeped into Breezie's mind: "Your voice is too soft to ever be heard. In the end, you'll be left yelling into a void." Breezie stumbled as the illusion conjured a howling emptiness around him—an echoing chasm where his calls for help vanished into the dark, unheard by anyone. It was a primal fear of insignificance and abandonment that he rarely acknowledged, yet there it was. But even as the hollow wind of the vision roared in his ears, Breezie's mind caught hold of a line from the poem they'd just heard: "one flame, one spark, can ignite many." In that void of the illusion, he imagined a single candle lighting another, then another—just as one calm breath can give life to a fire. He realized with a calm certainty that his gentle nature was not a weakness; it was the breeze that fanned their collective flame. He closed his eyes, steadied his breathing, and summoned a focused current of air from deep within. "We are with each other," he intoned, almost in prayer. The breeze he cast was not a violent gust but a steady wind carrying reassurance. It blew through the mental void, and as it did, he felt the presence of his friends around him in reality, anchored by Greenie's empathic thread. The terrifying emptiness was revealed for what it was—an illusion. Breezie opened his eyes, and with a firm flick of his wrist, he sent his conjured wind outward. The impish Doubt creature was caught in the stream and dissipated like a wisp of cloud under a rising sun.

Firee's trial came last and all at once, like a flashover of flame. The vice of Fear, though wounded by Checkered's light beam earlier, had circled around and now struck directly at Firee's heart. A chorus of mocking voices hissed in his ears, illusions dredged from his own anxieties: "They will abandon you. In the end, you'll stand alone. Why keep fighting with them?" Firee's temper sparked—he recognized the venom of those words. He had seen illusions like these drive wedges between good people in previous cities, turning insecurity into self-fulfilling prophecy. His fists clenched, fire licking between his fingers. The voices grew louder, sneering that his friends' loyalty was only temporary. Anger flared hot in Firee's veins—not at his companions, but at these cowardly phantoms daring to suggest such lies. And beneath the anger, hurt. Perhaps once, in his darker moments, he had feared being left behind. But not after all they had been through. He recalled nights on their journey where he'd stood watch till dawn, only to find each friend still by his side when morning light broke. They had never abandoned him, nor he them. What was there to doubt now?

"Enough!" Firee shouted, and his voice echoed off the stone walls. In that instant, a corona of flame erupted around him, bright and furious. The fear-phantom that loomed over him shrieked, raising shadowy arms to shield itself from the heat. Firee's eyes blazed as he unleashed a focused torrent of fire straight through the apparition. "We've walked too far together for fear to wedge us apart now!" he roared. The flame punched through the phantom, which exploded into a burst of smoky fragments that were quickly swept away by Breezie's lingering breeze. Firee stood panting, the firelight fading from around him, leaving only the gentle glow of nearby lampposts on the square.

With the personal illusions shattered, the six friends regrouped instinctively, backs to one another in a circle, facing outward. The Vice illusions had been beaten back, but the trial wasn't over. Above them, the entire facade of the Town Hall quaked, as if the building itself resented their victory. The painted murals of Virtues and Vices flashed with alternating light and shadow. Then, with a grinding roar, cracks of light splintered across the front of the building—not actual physical cracks, but rifts in the illusion. All the negative energy coalesced into one massive specter that slithered free of the facade and thudded onto the cobblestones.

In form, it was monstrous: a towering amalgamation of Fear, Despair, Doubt, and every other discouragement, woven together into a giant humanoid silhouette that blotted out the stars behind it. This final illusion was the embodiment of collective defeat—a vision of an entire city, an entire people, succumbing to hopelessness. It had hollow eyes like dark moons and a mouth that opened to a voiceless wail. The six could feel waves of intimidation radiating from it, pressing at the edges of their minds with the weight of utter failure.

For a heartbeat, none of them moved. This was the most formidable illusion they had ever faced: the sum of all fears. The golden runic inscriptions on the Town Hall's walls and clock flickered erratically, as if questioning whether the youths could stand against so great a horror. The enormous phantom raised an arm and the air itself grew heavy, gravity doubling as if to force the heroes to their knees.

But fortitude had been growing in each of their hearts all night, and now it blazed forth. Blunt, Reddish, Greenie, Firee, Checkered, and Breezie exchanged a single silent glance. In it was a vow: We do this together. Simultaneously, they stepped forward in unison, forming a line of resolve facing the towering mirage.

Each wizard summoned their magic, not separately, but in concert. Reddish planted her feet and let the embers in her core surge—she became a beacon of crimson fire. Firee mirrored her on the opposite end, flames licking around his arms. Together, their fires twined and spiraled upward, casting a warm light that illuminated the square. Greenie stood beside Reddish, her empathy flowing into the flame, giving it purpose and heart—tiny vines of green energy laced through the fire, symbolizing life and hope. Checkered was next to Firee; she raised both hands and projected a beam of brilliant white clarity from her lens, the light of truth focusing the flames into a coherent force. Breezie stepped up behind them and lifted his arms, pouring a steady, guiding wind into the mix, shaping the fiery light into a spearhead. At the center, Blunt held the silver key aloft between both hands. The key blazed with blue radiance, activating the protective ward and uniting all their contributions into one magnificent spell.

The phantom colossus swung its massive arm down, as if to crush them in one blow. But at that exact moment, the six released their combined magic. A brilliant wave of light — multi-hued, roaring silently—shot forth from the united wizards and met the descending arm. Sparks erupted at the point of contact. The giant's arm, composed of shadow and fear, began to vaporize under the onslaught of that fortitudinous light.

Emboldened, the friends pressed forward together, each matching the other's step. Their cloaks billowed, each shining with its signature hue: red, blue, green, gold, checkered patterns and silvery moonlight. The fused beam of fire, wind, empathy, clarity, and courage drove straight through the phantom's center. Cracks of pure radiance spread through the dark form, spiderwebbing across its chest and limbs. The giant reeled, staggering back without a sound. Through the cracks in its form, they could see the outline of Ulm's Town Hall behind, as if the creature were nothing but a hollow shell.

Step by step, united, the wizards advanced, pushing their magic harder. The great specter of defeat tried to rally—it raised both shadowy arms and mustered a final wave of dread that rolled towards them like a black tsunami. For a breath, their forward movement halted as the pressure of that despair hit. Greenie's knees buckled slightly, and Firee's flame faltered. But Blunt ground his teeth, and from the very front of their line, Reddish let out a determined shout, reigniting her flame hotter. Breezie increased the force of his wind at her cry, blasting the wave of dread with fresh air. The others followed: Firee's fire blazed back to life, Greenie pushed more loving energy into the beam, Checkered's lens burned like a star.

With a last concerted effort, they broke through. Their radiant magic overwhelmed the wave of dread and smashed into the phantom's core. The colossal illusion gave a final, soundless shriek, a mouth open in agony, as the light spread through it completely. Then the towering figure shattered into a thousand shards of shadow that quickly evaporated into thin mist. In the space of a heartbeat, the monstrous shape was gone, dispersed on the night breeze.

Silence fell over the square once more. The murals on the Town Hall's façade stopped flickering and returned to their painted stillness—Virtues and Vices now just art, nothing more. The astronomical clock resumed its gentle ticking, the crisis passed. The lampposts around the plaza, which had dimmed during the confrontation, now glowed steadily again, their warm light revealing six young heroes breathing hard but unharmed at the center of the square.

They had done it. Together, they had faced down the worst fears and emerged not just intact, but stronger.

Lucrecia stepped forward from the shadows of the steps, her eyes shining with pride and relief. She said nothing immediately—no words were needed. The faintest of smiles played on her lips as she regarded the exhausted but elated group. Actions had spoken louder than any voice: fortitude, in its truest form, had triumphed here tonight.

Above, the Ulm clock's astrolabe dial gently chimed the quarter hour, as if applauding in its own way. The runic patterns hidden in the facade's artwork glowed briefly, then settled, as if the ancient building itself acknowledged that the trial was passed.

Fortitude's Triumph and a New Path

A soft wind whispered through Ulm's Rathausplatz, clearing the last wisps of illusionary fog from the air. The six friends gathered near Lucrecia at the foot of the Town Hall steps. For a moment none of them spoke, each reflecting on the battle and its lessons. The square around them felt imbued with calm. It reminded Blunt of how Beacon Hill in Boston had felt after they dispelled the fear there—like the very stones sighed in relief. Here too, Ulm's old souls seemed to exhale, a collective breath of gratitude that courage had won out over fear.

Lucrecia finally broke the silence. "Your fortitude has carried you far," she said quietly. Her voice was both gentle and strong, like distant thunder on a clear night. "You have defended not one, but two great clocks tonight, spanning continents and centuries of meaning. Where fear sought to take hold—in America's hopeful past and Europe's steadfast heritage—you rekindled hope and held firm."

Her role in this trial was at an end. Lucrecia's midnight-blue cloak settled around her as she reached within its folds and produced something that glinted in the lamplight. She extended her hand toward Blunt and opened her palm. In it lay an ornate runic pendant on a silver chain. The pendant was round, fashioned of aged pewter or iron, and engraved with a circular design reminiscent of a clock face. At its center, shining clearly, was the inscription: "Reflectio Est Virtus" — Reflection Is Virtue, etched in flowing script around a small mirror-like gemstone. The symbol was unmistakable: their next guiding principle.

"With both hands, Lucrecia offered the pendant to Blunt. "Wear this as proof of your stand against fear," she said. Her tone carried respect; this was a badge of honor and a tool for trials to come. Blunt bowed slightly and accepted the pendant with reverence. As the cool metal touched his skin, he felt a gentle warmth emanate from the inscription, similar to the comforting hum of the silver key. It was as if the pendant recognized the fortitude they had demonstrated and responded with its own quiet strength.

Blunt fastened the pendant chain around his neck. The metal disk settled against his chest, still warm. He gently covered it with his hand and felt the faint pulse of magic within. It resonated in harmony with the key he still held in his other hand. Key and pendant, fortitude and reflection—two lessons earned through hardship, two artifacts to light the way. "Thank you," Blunt said to Lucrecia, his voice thick with gratitude. He knew that this token was not lightly given; they had earned it through every act of courage and unity this night.

Lucrecia allowed herself a small smile, one of quiet satisfaction. "Fortitude overcame the illusions here, as it did in Beacon Hill," she affirmed. Her eyes drifted to each member of the group, and they could see a thread of emotion there—pride, yes, but also something like farewell. "You have proven the strength of your resolve. But new challenges lie ahead." She inclined her head toward the pendant resting over Blunt's heart. "Once fear no longer clouds your vision, reflection can lead you to hidden truths. The next virtue you must master is hinted by that inscription."

Checkered stepped closer, curiosity tempered by respect. She leaned in to inspect the runic pendant's markings. By the moon's glow and the lamplight, she saw an etching around the edge: a tiny pattern of interlocking stars and hourglasses. At the center, the small circular gem gleamed like an eye. "This design… it echoes the star motif we saw earlier," Checkered noted, recalling how in Washington the zodiac and here in Ulm the starry patterns had played a role. Indeed, the pendant bore a tiny, subtle engraving of a star at its top, much like the star runes they'd seen guiding them uphill in Boston's Beacon Hill or carved into Ulm's lampposts. "Perhaps it connects to an ancient Orloj crypt rumored to test reflection," she mused aloud. She had read whispers of such things in arcane tomes— secret places where time and introspection intersect.

At this, Lucrecia gave a single nod of confirmation. "In a place where old stone meets the hush of time, you'll find a clock whose secret can only be unraveled by those who look within," she said enigmatically. Her words conjured an image in each wizard's mind: a silent crypt, dust motes dancing in stagnant air, and an ancient clock hidden under centuries of history. "Let this pendant guide you. It will know when you are near, and its virtue will protect you in the trial to come."

Reddish turned the pendant's Latin phrase over in her head: Reflection is virtue. She thought of Veyra's fable, of the villagers who had to confront their unfounded fear. Reflection was an inward courage, perhaps even harder than outward bravery. "When fear is stripped away, clarity remains," Reddish said, almost to herself, but loud enough for all to hear. Her amber eyes glowed softly, not with fire now but with thoughtful light. "Maybe the next path is about that clarity… about facing truths we've avoided." She recalled how she'd admitted her fear of her own temper to her friends earlier on the bench in Boston. It was reflection that led her to that strength. A new path indeed—one that might require even deeper honesty.

Greenie gently brushed her hand along a trailing vine of ivy that clung to the Town Hall's stone. The leaves were cool and damp with dew. She felt the steady thrum of the earth beneath Ulm's square, ancient and patient. "Then we press on, unified," Greenie said, finishing Reddish's thought with a confident serenity. She looked around at her comrades, her family in all but blood. They had weathered so much, but likely the greatest tests would be the ones inside them. Still, she felt no apprehension, not after tonight. Whatever came, they would share the burden and thus lighten it.

Lucrecia stepped back, her silhouette melding once more into the shadows near the base of the Rathaus. Her role as the guide of fortitude's trial was completed, and the next steps would be for someone else to lead. "You have done well, my friends," she said softly. "Boston rests easier because of you, and now Ulm's night is calm again." Indeed, as she said this, they noticed a few windows of nearby houses cracked open— curious townsfolk perhaps awakened by the bell and sensing the strange disturbance had subsided. A distant clock tower (perhaps Ulm's cathedral) chimed a quarter past midnight, perfectly normally. The world, it seemed, was resuming its usual course.

With a parting smile touched with both pride and a hint of sorrow, Lucrecia's form wavered. A thin mist rolled through the square (Breezie wondered if he felt Lucrecia's magic or just natural fog from the river), and in that moment, she was gone. Perhaps she stepped back through her own portal, or perhaps she simply faded into the air. The six young wizards were left standing in the gentle glow of Ulm's street lamps, victorious and alone together.

For a short while, none of them moved or spoke. They simply absorbed. The brass hands of the Ulm clock above ticked softly, the only sound aside from their breathing. Ulm's Town Hall, moments ago a battleground of illusions, now appeared as just an exquisite old building again, its painted façade benign under night's gaze. The astronomical clock's dial reflected the moon, as if winking at them knowingly.

Blunt finally broke the silence. He lifted the pendant from his chest and held it up so that it caught the light. "Reflectio

Est Virtus," he read aloud, translating it silently and nodding. In his pocket, the silver key gave a gentle pulse, as if in response—as if saying, yes, fortitude leads to reflection. Blunt looked around at the empty square. "No illusions here now," he said with a small smile. "Not in D.C., not in Ulm. We've dispelled them all tonight." There was no arrogance in his tone, just contentment.

Firee rolled his shoulders, easing the last bit of tension from them. His cloak, which had been flickering with residual flames, finally calmed into its normal crimson fabric. "Lucrecia's test here is complete," he confirmed. His voice was modest but there was a note of pride. He glanced at the murals on the wall, now still. The painted figure of Fortitude in armor almost seemed to nod at him approvingly. Firee grinned and added, "The vices didn't last long against us, did they?"

Checkered chuckled, pushing her goggles up onto her forehead. "They certainly tried," she said. Her analytical mind replayed the sequence of their battle, and she found herself impressed by how seamlessly they had worked in concert. We truly are a team now, she thought. "Fear's immediate grip on these places is broken." She tapped her temple, where the memory of the illusions lingered only as a warning. "And we learned a lot about ourselves in the process."

Greenie stepped away to the center of the plaza, where an old stone fountain stood dry for the night. She ran her hand along its edge and then pressed her palm flat against the cool cobbles of the ground. She could sense the history here—how many times this city had faced calamity (fires, floods, wars) and rebuilt anew. "Ulm has seen its share of trials," she said softly, echoing her earlier words in Boston. "Yet it endures. Resilience is in its very foundation." She stood, turning her gaze to the clock face above, where now the astrolabe showed the moon's phase and the zodiac wheel pointed to Libra—the scales, a sign perhaps that balance had been restored.

Reddish wandered a few steps from the group, scanning the perimeter of the square. She thought she saw the curtain of a house shift slightly—maybe a resident peeking out to be sure all was well. She gave a small wave and the curtain quickly closed; whoever it was likely saw nothing more alarming than six travelers enjoying the night. Reddish closed her eyes for a moment, letting the night's calm settle in her bones. She remembered how earlier in the night—was it only hours ago?—they had stood in Boston's Common after quelling fear there. She had felt then, as now, that their unity was their greatest asset. "We have each other," she said quietly as she returned to her friends. Her face was flushed with contentment, her earlier fears thoroughly dispelled. "That's our shield against whatever shadows come next." They all voiced soft sounds of agreement at that.

Breezie inhaled deeply, savoring the cool air. It carried the faint smell of the Danube and the greenery of distant parks. Somewhere, a night bird sang a single note. All signs of a peaceful night regained. He turned to Blunt and the others, a boyish grin on his face. "So… where to now?" he asked, letting a bit of excitement creep into his voice. They had the key, they had the pendant. The next destination beckoned, and he, for one, was eager to keep momentum.

Blunt lifted the silver key and the new pendant together, holding one in each hand. As he brought them close, a fascinating reaction occurred: the key and pendant glowed in unison, projecting a slender beam of light between them. Where the beams met, a faint swirl of light began to coalesce—a hint of another portal forming, though not yet fully realized. It swirled with images of stone steps and ancient books, then dissipated. The artifacts were giving a clue, not opening the way just yet.

Blunt smiled and lowered his hands. "Lucrecia gave us a hint, back in Boston," he said. He remembered her parting words from Beacon Hill clearly: Where wisdom weighs in historic halls, seek the clock. He shared this with the group, voice thoughtful. "A place of wisdom, historic halls… and a hidden Orloj." He turned slowly to face west, where across the ocean Boston awaited their return. "I suspect our journey comes full circle," Blunt continued. "Back to Boston—beneath Old North Church, perhaps, or another sanctum where time and knowledge intertwine. An Orloj crypt." The silver key in his hand tugged ever so gently, confirming his intuition.

Their eyes drifted upward one last time to Ulm's grand clock. It was nearly time to depart. The portal would soon be ready, likely taking them home to prepare for the next challenge. But none of them felt rushed; they had earned this quiet victory lap in Ulm's moonlit square.

They gathered themselves and began to walk across the plaza, leaving the Rathaus behind. The pendant's gentle glow provided enough light to see their path. As they moved away, a few local stars seemed to twinkle extra brightly, as if winking farewell. Perhaps it was an illusion of the night, or perhaps the city truly was grateful.

Exiting the square, they passed under an old stone arch. On the other side lay the mouth of a narrow street leading toward where they knew a portal could safely open. The streets of Ulm were utterly still. As they walked, they could hear the soft lapping of the river on the quay and their own footfalls. The adrenaline of battle was ebbing, leaving behind a pleasant fatigue and a deeper understanding of themselves.

Checkered adjusted her spectacles and spoke up as they navigated the winding lane. "Reflection…" she mused. "If that's truly our next trial, it might be the hardest yet." She had a far-off look as she imagined what it might entail. "Illusions thrive on doubt, we know that now. Reflection could mean facing doubts we carry within—without any monster to fight but our own selves."

Greenie reached out and squeezed Checkered's hand gently. "We'll face it the same way we face everything," she said with a warm smile. "Together." Checkered returned the smile, the worry in her eyes easing.

They rounded a bend and came to a small stone bridge overlooking the dark ribbon of the Danube. The water reflected the moon in long, shimmering columns. Here, in the open, Blunt sensed was as good a spot as any to open their portal home.

He stopped and turned to his friends. "Fortitude, justice, compassion, curiosity… all the virtues we've encountered— each trial has given us something," he observed, holding up the key and pendant. "A key, a coin, a gear, and now a pendant. Pieces of a larger puzzle." He knew they all felt it:

they were closing in on something big, something at the heart of all these Orloj clocks and illusions.

Reddish brushed back a strand of red hair and looked at her reflection ripple in the river below. "I have a feeling," she said quietly, "that the next challenge won't be as… external. We might have to face ourselves in ways we haven't yet." There was no fear in her voice now, only resolve.

Breezie let the night breeze swirl around them playfully, fluttering their cloaks. "If reflection demands honesty," he said, picking up the thread, "then we have to be ready to confront truths we usually turn away from." He took a deep breath of the cool air. "But after tonight, I'd say we've got a good start on that. We've each admitted something painful and overcome it." He gave Reddish a reassuring nod, and she returned it gratefully.

Firee patted Blunt on the back. "And whatever we find in ourselves," he said, flashing a grin, "we'll handle it, as we always do. With trust and a bit of flair." There was a spark in his eyes—not of anger now, but of eagerness. Firee had learned to trust the group deeply, and that freed him from many of his old fears.

Blunt looked at each of them in turn, pride swelling in his chest. From the anxious encounter in D.C.'s hall to the fierce battle in Ulm, they had proven themselves once more. And more importantly, they had grown. "Reflection awaits, then," he said softly. He raised the silver key and the pendant together. The artifacts responded, shining brightly now in tandem. The portal's swirling light blossomed before them, illuminating the bridge and their determined faces. Through the misty gate, they glimpsed the familiar outline of Boston's skyline under a predawn sky—their next destination and home base.

One by one, the six wizards stepped into the portal, leaving Ulm's quiet beauty behind. As the last of them vanished into the ether, the first hints of early dawn touched the eastern horizon over Ulm, and the astronomical clock chimed softly, as if in gentle congratulations.

They emerged on the other side in a secluded corner of Boston, the world they knew best, carrying with them the hard-won wisdom of fortitude's fire. The portal had folded not only distance but the hour; Boston met them again at the edge of dawn. The night in Boston was beginning to wane, and the lamplights were still aglow, casting long shadows over the cobblestones of home.

They reached a small park near the hill's crest — a tiny refuge of green behind an iron fence. Beneath old oak trees, a few wrought-iron benches invited them to rest. The six companions sank onto the seats, grateful for a brief respite.

Gas lanterns along the fence cast shifting shadows across the ground, flickering gently in the night breeze.

Blunt placed the new pendant in his palm, letting a nearby lamplight play off the script: "Reflectio Est Virtus." He thought back to the trial of justice in Philadelphia, how illusions there had been dispelled by unwavering truth. "Fortitude, justice, reflection — each trial has given us a piece of a larger puzzle," he observed quietly.

Checkered folded her arms, her lens resting in her lap. "We've learned that illusions thrive on doubt," she said. "Reflection will demand we confront not just external tricks, but the insecurities within ourselves."

Greenie nodded from the next bench. "Standing before that lamppost tonight, I felt a flicker of what Boston's early rebels must have felt facing their oppressors," she said. "They had to reflect on whether their cause was just — and in doing so, they found the courage to persist."

Beside Greenie, Reddish traced a finger along the embroidered edge of her cloak, her eyes downcast as embers danced softly within them. "I used to fear my own temper," she admitted in a low voice. "I was afraid it would consume me or drive all of you away." She managed a small smile as she looked around at her friends. "But through our unity, I learned that accepting our flaws can become a strength, not a weakness."

Breezie let a gentle breeze stir the oak branches above. Leaves whispered against one another, a soothing sound. "We've come far," he said softly. "But a greater trial might yet lie ahead. If reflection demands honesty, we need to be ready to face truths we've avoided until now."

Firee exhaled, a faint spark escaping his lips into the cool air. "We overcame illusions here by trusting each other," he said, his voice firm. "That same trust will be our best weapon for whatever comes next."

They sat in thoughtful silence a moment longer, each turning over memories of illusions conquered in places like Gdańsk and Lund — each keenly aware that the hardest illusions to dispel might be the ones lurking inside themselves. When they finally rose, the path ahead seemed a bit clearer: find the hidden clock, heed the call of reflection, and rely on the unbreakable bond they had forged.

Leaving the little park behind, they wound their way through Beacon Hill's maze of brick sidewalks and graceful stoops. The silver key in Blunt's pocket continued to emit a soft guiding glow, tugging them gradually downhill. Occasionally, they paused by the old lampposts at each corner — more than once, Checkered pointed out faint runic carvings spiraling around a post. Each was inscribed with words of perseverance or riddles about the flow of time.

At one such lamppost, Checkered halted. She lifted her lens toward an engraving of a stylized star and compass rose near the top. "This is the same motif," she remarked, "like a guiding star pointing toward something central."

Greenie brushed her fingertips over a weathered groove in the carving. "It's similar to those ancient designs we found in the hidden archives," she agreed. "Symbols linking celestial cycles with mortal resilience. A trail of stars, perhaps, leading somewhere important."

As they continued, a pair of local residents strolled by walking a dog, offering polite nods. The wizards returned the gesture with warm but unassuming smiles, noticing how calm these late-night walkers appeared compared to the frightened faces from earlier. Perhaps the miasma of fear truly had receded from Beacon Hill.

Firee crouched by the next lamppost, discovering a small bronze plaque set into its base. The words were worn by time, but leaning close he could discern references to an "underground chamber" once used by revolutionaries for secret gatherings. "This might be part of the route to that crypt we're seeking," he speculated, tracing the etched letters with a careful finger.

Breezie looked up toward the glimmer of the Charles River visible between rooftops, then further out to the twinkling lights beyond. "Boston is layered with hidden corners and secrets," he mused. "We might find an entrance to this crypt somewhere near the city's historic heart."

Blunt felt a gentle pulse from the pendant against his chest, as though it resonated faintly with the star symbol on the lamppost. "It's drawing us toward the city's historic heart," he said. "An Orloj-like clock concealed in a place older than we realize."

Satisfied that they were on the right track, the group carried on through the winding lanes. Each step brought them closer to understanding how the next virtue — reflection — would shape their forthcoming challenge. Behind them, the lamppost's engraved star dimmed and its runes faded, as if content that its guidance had been received.

As they caught their breath and reoriented themselves, the six friends instinctively formed a small circle. Above them, the last stars of night twinkled as if in encouragement. Blunt held up the runic pendant and silver key together; both artifacts gleamed in unison, two guiding lights joined. He looked around at his companions — tired, perhaps, and a bit travel-worn, but eyes alight with conviction.

"Our next step," Blunt began, "lies where wisdom weighs in historic halls. We will seek this Orloj crypt." He smiled knowingly at Breezie and Checkered, who both nodded, recalling Lucrecia's clues. "There, reflection will test us in ways no illusion could — by turning our gaze inward. But however sharp the truths we uncover," he placed a hand at the center of their circle, and one by one each of his friends did the same, stacking their hands in a gesture of unbreakable fellowship, "we will face them together. Just as we always have."

In the east, beyond the awakening city, the sky began to lighten, a promise of dawn. Boston's historic halls and hidden crypts awaited the trials of reflection. But in this moment, on the cusp of a new day and a new chapter, the six young wizards stood united, their hearts fortified by the flames of fortitude. Fear was behind them, reflection lay ahead — another adventure, another chance to illuminate the darkness with the enduring light of their friendship and courage. And as they set off down the quiet street, their laughter soft and their resolve steeled, it was clear that no illusion, however cunning, would ever dim that light again.

Chapter 15

Willard and Zimmer Clocks – Reflection's Reckoning

Beneath Old North: The Orloj Wakes

Dawn's gentle light seeped into the Old North Church crypt, illuminating weathered stones etched with colonial runes. A swirl of bronze-and-sapphire light announced the arrival of Blunt, Reddish, Firee, Checkered, Breezie, and Greenie. Their Harlequin cloaks—emerald swirls, crimson flames, sapphire waves—caught the glow of the scattered candles.

Blunt held aloft a runic pendant inscribed "Reflectio Est Virtus." The residual warmth from their last trial had quietly led them to this hidden sanctum. He recalled how they'd recently stood firm against illusions threatening Beacon Hill. Now, in this subterranean refuge, the hush felt almost sacred.

Along one crypt wall, a thin wire arched overhead, flickering with static sparks. It was a curious detail—something mechanical or even telegraphic in nature. Perhaps it was a preserved conduit from a 19th-century caretaker's telegraph experiment, oddly present in a colonial crypt. Breezie noticed it first. "Never seen an installation like that in a place so old," he murmured, as the wire's faint buzz added to the crypt's mysterious aura.

Reddish swept her gaze around the chamber. "No illusions swirling this time," she observed, embers in her eyes flickering at the memory of how illusions once plagued them. "It feels more like a place to pause and think."

Greenie pressed her palm against the carved runes on the wall. She felt echoes of Boston's heritage—brave souls who met danger with contemplation instead of panic. "It's meant for reflection," she whispered.

Behind them, Checkered examined a carved arch bearing the same words as Blunt's pendant. "Everything here points to seeing our own truths clearly," she noted. Her lens glinted with practiced curiosity, as though half-expecting some hidden illusion—but none materialized.

Suddenly, the crypt's domed ceiling shimmered. A silver-haired silhouette, outlined in ghostly clockwork, coalesced overhead. The Boston Orloj—an embodiment of historical knowledge and mechanical magic—took form and spoke in a gentle tone that reverberated through the stone chamber.

"Welcome, Harlequins," the Orloj greeted. "Fortitude opened one door; now reflection stands at the threshold of another. Prepare yourselves, for new trials approach—ones solved less by dispelling illusions and more by understanding hidden mechanisms."

The hum in Blunt's cloak intensified, reminding him of the hard-won synergy forged through countless challenges. He nodded and met the Orloj's gaze. Whatever trial awaited next, they would face it together in the calm stillness of dawn.

Rule of Two: The Pairs of Clocks

The Orloj's presence lingered in midair—silver hair gleaming, clockwork eyes turning like meshing gears. Candlelight danced along the crypt walls, and even the telegraph wire crackled softly, as if echoing the Orloj's words.

"Harlequins," it began warmly, "you have known illusions that fed on fear and bias, and you shattered them by standing united. Now, reflection leads you forward. The next challenges revolve around pairs of clocks—puzzles more intricate than any fleeting glamour."

Blunt bowed his head in quiet respect. He remembered recent illusions in Philadelphia and Boston that had nearly unraveled each city's peace. "We've proven we can stand firm under threat," he said. "But if illusions are gone, what stands in our way now?"

"New tests demand deeper insight," the Orloj answered. "Mechanical riddles, historical codes—each clock holds secrets that only collaboration will unlock."

Reddish's embers flared gently, far more subdued than in any heated battle. "We'll face them one pair at a time, then?" she asked.

"Yes," the Orloj affirmed with a knowing gleam in its clockwork eyes. It raised one translucent hand, and the crypt seemed to hold its breath. Two ghostly clock faces materialized in midair—one glowing brightly, its twin barely visible in shadow. A thin tendril of pale light arced from the Orloj to the overhead wire, which began to crackle in a measured pattern of short and long sparks—like a silent Morse code message. At each pulse, the dim clock face briefly glowed to mirror its bright twin, then faded once more. The six friends exchanged astonished glances as the meaning crystallized: only by linking each pair of clocks—making them beat as one—would their secrets be revealed.

As the phantom clock faces winked out and the wire fell silent, Checkered adjusted her lens thoughtfully, scanning the air for any lingering glimmers around the Orloj's form. "Any clue about where we should begin?" she ventured.

"Seek out a Simon Willard artifact," the Orloj replied. "There, you'll find the first puzzle. Once you solve it, look to its companion overseas, in a tower of many dials. Complete both to progress."

Firee's eyes narrowed with vigilance. "And if illusions do resurface while we're at it?" he asked warily.

A gentle laugh flickered through the crypt's shadows—perhaps a lingering Harlequin echo from long ago. "Illusions can appear when you least expect them," the Orloj admitted. "But these tasks will challenge you more through cunning mechanics. Stay alert."

Greenie felt a steady calm radiating from the Orloj's presence—a reassurance that reflection itself would guard them. "We won't take this peace for granted," she promised softly.

The Orloj nodded. "Go now. Each puzzle you solve will reveal the next. Trust in your synergy, and let reflection guide each step."

With that, the crypt's golden glow began to dim. The Orloj's silhouette dissolved into swirling motes of light, leaving behind a reverent hush that invited introspection—and a new journey hinging on the secrets of those paired clocks.

In the lantern-lit stillness that followed, the young wizards gathered around a simple oak table near the crypt's far wall. The runic pendant engraved Reflectio Est Virtus (reflection is virtue) rested between them, its surface still faintly aglow. Sensing the moment was right, Blunt cleared his throat and unrolled a small scroll he had discovered in an antique journal.

It was a short tale he thought would crystallize the power of reflection for them.

"The Council of Mirrors"

In an ancient city veiled in perpetual fog, where light struggled to pierce the gloom, a solemn council of elders convened in a marble hall. Each elder carried a mirror—ornate, silver-framed, and untouched. They had been given these mirrors not for vanity, but for wisdom. Yet none had dared to gaze into them.

The city had grown restless. Whispers turned into accusations. Blame passed from mouth to mouth like a torch, burning bridges between neighbors. In their great chamber, the elders quarreled. "You've sown the seeds of discord!" cried one. "It is your ambition that darkens our streets!" barked another. And always, their mirrors remained veiled in cloth, hidden away in fear.

One evening, a traveler entered the city—cloaked not in silk or armor, but in clarity. He listened in silence, then spoke not with judgment but with calm:

"You speak of shadows, yet none of you has faced your own."

He gestured toward their covered mirrors.

"You carry the light you deny yourselves."

His words stung—not with cruelty, but with truth. Unease swept the chamber. One elder—a once-proud woman whose voice had grown sharp—was first to uncover her mirror. She gasped, not at the lines of age, but at the anger etched into her eyes. Another elder followed, and another. One by one, they dared to look. And what they saw was not guilt, but grief. Not malice, but misunderstanding. Their own reflections revealed truths they had long buried beneath the clamor of certainty.

Tears fell—quietly, without spectacle. And as they wept, something miraculous occurred: the fog outside began to thin. Light filtered into alleys. Windows gleamed again. Laughter returned to the courtyards.

The council did not declare a victor. They embraced silence, then forgiveness. For the first time in generations, each elder saw the others not as foes, but as mirrors—each reflecting the potential for both fracture and healing.

From that day forward, whenever discord threatened the city, the council did not raise voices. They raised mirrors. And in the stillness of self-recognition, they found peace.

Blunt set down the scroll. "In our battles with illusions, we had to see falsehoods for what they were," he said softly. "Now we're facing riddles that demand we look inward— patiently and without fear."

Greenie's eyes glistened, touched by the fable's lesson. "Like those elders, we must be willing to see ourselves clearly," she murmured.

Reddish whispered, "And each puzzle we confront might reveal more about how we function as a team. Reflection could unify us even more deeply."

Firee crossed his arms, his expression thoughtful. "In some of our earlier challenges, mirror illusions tried to tempt our pride or stoke our fears," he noted. "But in this story, the mirrors helped an entire community find truth and heal together."

A quiet hum emanated from the pendant on the table, as if affirming their resolve. Outside, daybreak was brightening the sky. Firee and Breezie exchanged determined nods. These new challenges wouldn't rely on brute force or trickery; they would hinge on knowledge, cooperation, and honest self-examination.

"Let's find Simon Willard's Astronomical Clock," Checkered said, her lens gleaming with resolve. "Time to see how well we've learned the council's lesson of mirrors."

They left the crypt just as dawn spread golden light across Boston's narrow streets. The city was already stirring to life—shopkeepers unlatching their doors, carriages clattering over cobblestones. Overhead, faint telegraph wires stretched from spire to spire, reminders that inventions like Morse's telegraph were reshaping communication. Blunt glanced up thoughtfully at the crisscrossing lines, wondering if the quiet hum they'd heard in the crypt was an experimental conduit linking Old North Church to another site — a hint that knowledge here was meant to connect far and wide.

Greenie walked beside him, recalling how she once felt isolated by her empathic gift. Illusions had tried to twist those feelings into despair, convincing her she was alone. But now she found strength in honest reflection. Embracing her powers openly had soothed her doubts — and drawn her closer to her friends.

Breezie exhaled, releasing a small, calming breeze that settled around the group. "We face mechanical obstacles ahead. People here may not realize how these old clocks could stir up trouble. Let's stay focused," he advised.

Grafton Parlor: The Mirror Clock's Test

Late morning light filtered through antique glass windows as Blunt, Reddish, Firee, Checkered, Breezie, and Greenie stepped into the parlor of the Willard House & Clock Museum in North Grafton after a brief journey west from Boston. The room smelled of old varnish and history. On the mantel stood their quarry: Simon Willard's Astronomical Shelf Clock, a modest wooden case with a round brass dial. To a casual eye it looked like any colonial-era timepiece, but the six young wizards knew better.

Checkered adjusted her lens with a scholarly glint. "This is one of only two ever made," she whispered, reverently running a finger near the dial (but careful not to touch). Through the wavy glass door, the dial's fine engravings were visible. "Willard built this around 1780 as a sort of home planetarium," she explained. "It can track the day, date, even tides and star positions—a tiny orrery on a shelf. Paul Revere himself engraved some of these parts, like the almanac scales." Breezie let out a low whistle as Reddish's eyes widened at this blend of patriotic craftsmanship and scientific curiosity.

They circled the clock, cloaks brushing against creaking floorboards. Greenie could almost feel the intent within the mechanism—a quiet hum of purpose, as if the clock knew they had come. Blunt produced the runic pendant from around his neck, the one inscribed Reflectio Est Virtus (reflection is virtue). Its faint warmth, a remnant of their last trial, had led them here, and now it pulsed gently in his palm, syncing with the subtle tick of the clock.

Without warning, the clock's long hand jerked forward on its own. Click. The time was not quite noon, but the clock chimed softly anyway—an ethereal, bell-like tone. A hush fell. The sunlight in the room dimmed as if a cloud passed overhead, yet outside the summer sky was clear. Greenie inhaled sharply. "Do you feel that?" she murmured. A prickle of magic crept along the walls: something unseen, like a mirror catching light, flashing at the edges of their vision.

Each of the six suddenly found themselves standing not in the cozy museum parlor, but seemingly alone in a gray, misty space facing… themselves. Or rather, a distorted reflection of themselves. The museum around them faded; only the clock remained, now glowing with a silvery sheen. Reddish blinked and steadied herself. No, she was still in the room—she could see the vague outlines of her friends around the clock—but it was as though each friend was encased in a bubble of illusion, confronted by a personal mirror-image.

Firee's hand went instinctively to the hilt of a wand hidden in his cloak, but he hesitated. His mirror-self stepped forward from the clock's reflection. This doppelgänger's eyes were wild, ringed with sleepless shadows. It wore Firee's face but twisted into an expression of doubt and fear. "You always expect the worst," it hissed at him, voice low and trembling. "All your vigilance, and still you failed to prevent past hurts." Firee felt his heart pound—memories of a previous illusion in Prague where his caution had briefly wavered flooded back. A flame flickered at Firee's fingertips, but he remembered their purpose here was reflection, not combat. He clenched his fist, snuffing the flame, and met his double's eyes quietly.

Nearby, Reddish confronted a fiery apparition with her own features. Her mirror-self's hair crackled like embers, eyes glowing hot. "Your anger defines you," it snarled. "Without it, who are you? Weak, or worse—irrelevant." Reddish felt heat rise in her chest; the urge to argue flared. But she noticed the edges of the illusion warping in tandem with her temper. She forced a slow breath, recalling the gentle stillness of the Old North Church crypt they'd recently left. "I am more than my anger," she answered steadily. The ember-eyed double wavered, its ferocious stance faltering as Reddish's calm took hold.

Elsewhere in the hazy chamber of the mind, Breezie faced a wraithlike copy of himself that flickered and shifted like an unsteady breeze. It whispered of inaction – all the times he'd held back out of fear of causing storms. "You let others lead. You drift, contributing little," it sighed, voice like a lonely wind. Breezie's eyes stung at the accusation that echoed his own private misgivings. He remembered a critical moment in Paris when his reluctance to act nearly cost them a victory until he finally mustered courage. He straightened now, summoning a gentle breeze that swirled around both him and the phantom. "I move when it matters," he said, offering a small smile. The breeze carried away the whispery figure's doubt like smoke on the wind.

Greenie's mirror-self had tears streaming down its face, vines crawling up its arms. "You feel too much," it sobbed, voice choked. "Every hurt, every loss – it paralyzes you.

Wouldn't it be easier to shut it all out?" Greenie swallowed hard. There was truth in those words – her empathy was both a gift and a burden. But through reflection she had learned that feeling deeply was also her strength. Gently, she reached out and clasped her double's hands. "My feelings connect me to others. I won't abandon them." The vines around the mirror-Greenie withered and the tears dried as the double gazed back with a gentle, albeit sad, smile before dissolving into motes of light.

Checkered's apparition stepped out from the clock face carrying an exaggerated version of her signature lens. Its eyes were cold behind the glass, voice clipped and analytical to a fault. "Logic over all," it droned. "Friends are variables, equations to be solved. You hold your heart in check, lest it lead you astray." Checkered bit her lip. She had often taken refuge in reason during chaos, sometimes to the point of shutting others out. With a trembling hand, she lifted her own small lens to her eye and peered straight at the illusion. In its reflection, she saw not a calculating automaton, but a frightened girl using logic as armor. "I can be logical and caring," Checkered whispered. A warm light glinted off her lens—and the stern double crumbled into fragmented patterns, like broken facets of a prism yielding to light.

Lastly, Blunt confronted a towering silhouette of himself, arms crossed in stern judgment. This mirror-Blunt radiated stoic hardness, his face etched as stone. "You must be the rock, the leader with no doubts," it boomed. "Vulnerability is weakness. Hesitation will destroy your team." Blunt felt the weight of every decision he'd made for their group, the pressure to be unflinching. Indeed, he often hid his own fears to keep the others confident. But he had learned that honest reflection and admitting doubt could forge stronger unity. He stepped forward and met the giant's stony gaze. "A true leader learns from his own flaws," Blunt said quietly. "I don't have all the answers—and that's okay." He gave a slight, genuine smile. The giant mirror-self fissured with a thunderous crack, then bowed its head in respect before shattering into dust.

One by one, each young wizard's acceptance and clear-eyed response caused their mirrored adversary to dissipate. The silvery haze in the parlor cleared. They found themselves standing together around the Simon Willard clock once more, breathing hard but unhurt. The entire confrontation had taken only moments, though it felt much longer. The clock's hands were now precisely at noon. With a final resonant ding, the clock fell silent. Its brass pendulum, which had been still during the trial, resumed swinging gently as the normal sunlight returned to the room.

Greenie released a breath she didn't realize she'd been holding. "They were our reflections —exaggerated, diminished… but us," she said, voice hushed. In the quiet that followed, each of the six absorbed what they had seen: private strengths highlighted, regrets laid bare, blind spots exposed. Reddish gave a shaky laugh. "Facing a dragon would've been easier." But her smile was grateful. "In a way, I'm glad. I feel… lighter." She touched her own face as if confirming she was truly herself.

Firee nodded, brow knitted in thought. "Reflection," he murmured, recalling the virtue's mantra. "To see oneself clearly, without distortion. That was the only way to dispel them." His eyes, normally burning with battle-ready intensity, were softer now.

Checkered's gaze drifted to the Willard clock. She noticed something new: the glass over the dial, once dusty, had been polished to mirror brightness during the illusion. It now reflected their gathered faces. Where moments ago, phantoms loomed, now only the true young wizards stared back. And just at the clock's crown, a small, engraved word glinted— Lier. Checkered's heart skipped. Was it there before? Perhaps revealed only now. "Lier," she read aloud, pointing. As the others leaned in, the clock emitted a soft mechanical whir. Its hour and minute hands spun of their own accord, faster and faster, until they became a glowing circle of light. Whoosh—with a gentle rush of air, the circle expanded beyond the clock's face, hovering in the room like a portal window. Through it they glimpsed a cobbled square and a tall stone tower with a magnificent multi-dial clock on its facade.

Breezie grinned, recognizing the image. "That's the Zimmer Tower in Lier, Belgium, isn't it? The Jubilee Astronomical Clock." The portal view was unmistakable: a large central dial encircled by numerous smaller dials set into an old tower wall. The very sight of it made Checkered nearly vibrate with excitement. "The counterpart!" she said eagerly. "It has to be. Remember the Orloj's hint about pairs of clocks? We've linked the first pair by overcoming this test, and now the second of the pair calls to us."

Blunt closed the cover of the Willard clock's case, securing it respectfully. Their reflections were done here, and they had what they needed. Tucking the glowing runic pendant back under his cloak, he looked around at his friends. All bore expressions of renewed determination. "We face the next reflection," he said, gesturing to the portal. The six formed a circle and, hand in hand, stepped forward into the light.

Lier, Belgium: Twelve Faces of Reflection

The Harlequins emerged on the other side of the portal into the open air of a small Flemish city square. Dusk was settling over Lier, painting the sky in lavender and rose. Before them stood the Zimmer Tower, its 14th-century stonework and brick glowing in the last light of day. High on the tower's face was the astonishing Jubilee Clock: a large central clock dial surrounded by twelve smaller dials, each displaying a different cosmic cycle. A life-sized statue of Saint Gummarus stood guard above the arched doorway below, and above the dials a great golden globe representing the sun caught the light. Even at rest, the tower felt alive with knowledge – a cathedral of time.

"This tower was once a medieval fortification," Checkered recounted softly as they approached, recalling her notes. "In 1930, astronomer-clockmaker Louis Zimmer transformed it by installing this very clock to celebrate Belgium's 100th year as a nation. It turned the whole tower into a public time museum." Greenie gazed up at the array of dials encircling the main face, each marked with intriguing symbols. "All those smaller clocks…" she began.

"…Show different scientific times or cycles," Checkered finished, eyes shining. "Moon phases, tides, zodiac signs, the calendar dates—so much. They call it the Wonder Clock here. And inside," she added, pointing to an adjoining pavilion building at the tower's base, "inside is Zimmer's even more complex masterpiece: the Wonder Clock with 57 dials and a planetary orrery. One of its hands takes 25,800 years to complete a revolution!" Her voice was reverent. "Even Einstein congratulated Zimmer on that creation," Breezie chimed in, remembering a tidbit. Clearly, this place was a pinnacle of reflective horological art — perfectly suited for the trial of reflection.

The square was quiet at this hour, nearly empty save for the six travelers. As Blunt stepped forward, the pendant under his cloak gave a gentle pulse, as if to affirm they were in the right place. They expected perhaps a caretaker to appear or the pavilion door to open for them, but nothing of the sort happened. Instead, the Jubilee Clock itself began to stir. The central dial's hands, which showed local time, started to move erratically—minutes skipping forward and back. The twelve surrounding dials glowed one after another, as if each were waking. The great gilded globe at the top (symbolizing the sun) emitted a warm light, while the blue rotating Earth model at the bottom of the clock started to spin in fits and starts.

Reddish tensed. "Everyone, stay alert. We may be in for another illusion… or something different." The square's light dimmed, twilight suddenly deepening unnaturally fast. The street lamps flickered on, and their elongated shadows wavered as if alive.

Without warning, bell tones rang out from the tower – seven chimes, though it was not yet the top of an hour. With each peal, a different one of the small dials flashed brilliantly. On the seventh chime, beams of colored light burst forth from seven of the dials, converging on the square before the wizards. The lights swirled, forming into vague human shapes—six shapes. Breezie's breath caught. Not again…

Indeed, the lights coalesced into six spectral figures, each one taking on the face and form of the young wizards – but not identical copies as before. These were warped amalgamations, shifting through various versions of their subjects. Blunt's form was sometimes tall and imposing, then suddenly hunched and weary. Reddish's specter flickered between a roaring flame-haired warrior and a dim, ash-covered silhouette. Each of the six apparitions cycled through exaggerated and diminished embodiments of the person they reflected. It was as if the tower's many dials were cycling through possibilities – the phases of their inner selves – like the phases of the moon or the turning of seasons displayed on the clock.

Greenie felt a chill as she watched her doppelgänger swing from sobbing uncontrollably to standing serenely indifferent, as if her empathy was being dialed up and down by an unseen hand. "These aren't separate illusions for each of us," she warned, recalling how isolated they had been in Grafton. "This time we're seeing all of them, together." Indeed, they stood in a circle back-to-back, facing outward as their six warped reflections paced around them in the square. It was a true council of mirrors – a collective confrontation.

The ghostly Reddish stepped forward first, eyes blazing one moment and dull the next. In a taunting voice that alternated between a furious hiss and a monotone drone, it addressed the group: "You think you've mastered your temper, little spark? Look how easily you still ignite and fade." The real Reddish bristled but set her jaw, refusing to be goaded.

Next, the false Blunt loomed, then shrank, then loomed again, speaking in echoing tones: "Strong leader one minute, paralyzed by doubt the next. Will your indecision doom your friends someday?" A muscle in Blunt's cheek twitched, but he kept his composure, recalling how he faced the giant earlier.

One by one, the specters voiced insidious doubts and questions not just to their counterparts, but loud enough for all to hear. Firee's apparition crackled: "Ever-vigilant, or just afraid of the dark? Your caution could cripple you when bold action's needed." Breezie's specter whispered through wind: "Peacekeeper or coward? Will you vanish when conflict comes?" Checkered's double oscillated between calculating and confused: "All your knowledge—what if it fails you?

Without it, are you worth anything?" Greenie's phantom asked in a plaintive chorus: "Your heart aches for all... But what of when it breaks? Wouldn't it be easier to harden it?"

The six friends pressed their backs closer together, ringed by these accusations. The words stung because they all knew each other's struggles intimately by now. Hearing them spoken aloud by these distorted selves threatened to unravel the confidence they'd just built. Firee's fingers sparked unconsciously; Reddish's palms glowed with gathering heat. It was tempting to blast these ghosts with magic and be done with it.

But Checkered's voice cut through the rising tension: "Remember the fable!" she cried. "The Council of Mirrors – how did they find peace?" Her lens caught a glint of the tower's light as she turned slowly, making eye contact with each friend. In that tale, the council's salvation was not in shouting down the accusations, but in listening and accepting truth. They had raised mirrors to themselves.

Blunt was first to act. He unclasped the pendant from around his neck and held the small reflective disc toward the phantom Blunt. In its polished surface, his own face and the ghost's appeared side by side. "I see you," Blunt said steadily to his specter. The towering-shrinking figure halted its tirade, uncertain. "You are a part of me—my pride and my doubt. I acknowledge you." As he spoke, the pendant glowed and the phantom Blunt's shifting stabilized into a single form: a calm, life-sized mirror-image looking back at him with a faint, approving smile. Blunt exhaled, then gently inclined the pendant mirror. The specter copied him, bowing respectfully before dissolving into a stream of silver light that flowed upward into one of the tower's dials. High above, the dial marked with the Dominical letter and solar cycle gleamed, as if recording a victory.

Encouraged, Reddish took out a metallic compass from her satchel – its cover was mirror-polished brass. She faced her raging/waning double and opened the compass, reflecting the apparition's fiery eyes back at itself. "I'm not afraid of what I see anymore," Reddish said softly. "Rage and vulnerability— I have both, and I grow from both." The ghostly flames around her mirror-self cooled to gentle embers. Two Reddishes, real and reflected, exchanged understanding nods. The phantom then burst into a swirl of embers that flew upward. A dial depicting the phase of the Moon pulsed with light as the embers merged into it.

Around the circle, the others followed suit. Breezie summoned a miniature whirlwind in his palm, its surface spinning to a glassy sheen. Confronting his wavering specter, he spoke as one would to a scared friend: "I accept my quiet nature and my power when needed. I will not disappear." The whirlwind briefly reflected Breezie's gentle smile back at the ghost, who then vanished in a soft gust. Overhead, the Seasons dial (winter to spring) twinkled.

Firee drew a polished steel striker from his cloak (a tool from a past fire-making lesson). Holding it as a mirror to his crackling double, he admitted, "Yes, I am cautious, and sometimes afraid. That caution has saved us—but I won't let fear rule me." The specter's formerly wild eyes gained a measure of peace. It saluted him briefly before dissipating in a shower of sparks. The Tides dial on the tower front glowed with a cresting wave symbol.

Greenie reached up and gently plucked a fragment of glass from a nearby lamppost's broken light (perhaps shattered by a stray bit of magic earlier). In that shard, she met the tearful eyes of her phantom. "My sensitivity is my strength," she said, voice calm and full of compassion. "I won't ever completely seal my heart, even when it hurts." The ghost's tears turned to sparkling droplets of light, and with a grateful smile, it too melted away, its droplets flying up to the Globe dial (the Earth) which glimmered warmly.

Lastly, Checkered faced her double. She held up her own silver-rimmed monocle lens, now functioning like a mirror.

"Logic and intuition, analysis and heart—I need them all. I won't deny any part of me," she proclaimed. The phantom Checkered regarded her with a quizzical expression that softened into a proud grin. It touched its forehead in a gesture of respect, then disintegrated into gleaming puzzle pieces that rose toward the dial of the Metonic cycle and Epact (symbols of long-term calculation), lighting it up in acknowledgment.

As the last illusion ascended and slotted into the great clock, a profound silence fell over the square. The young wizards slowly lowered their makeshift mirrors. Each felt a strange internal lightness and unity, as if previously fragmented pieces of their spirits had clicked into alignment—gears meshing in a well-tuned clock. Above, all twelve dials of the Jubilee Clock were now illuminated, shining in the dusk like a crown of stars around the central face. The main dial struck the hour with a harmonious chime. It was 9 o'clock local time, and this time the bell rang true and normal.

With the illusions dispelled, the door of the Zimmer Tower's adjacent pavilion creaked open of its own accord. Exchanging hopeful glances, the friends climbed the few steps and entered the dimly lit museum. Inside, the air was cool and smelled of aged wood and clockwork oil. At the center stood the legendary Wonder Clock on display – Louis Zimmer's magnum opus. It was a gigantic, ornate clock mechanism mounted in a mahogany frame, covered in dials upon dials. Even in stillness it was breathtaking. As they approached, the Wonder Clock whirred to life in greeting: planets of a built-in orrery began to orbit, tiny moons circling their globes. Gears turned behind 57 different displays of celestial and calendar data. On one dial, a nearly imperceptible hand inched forward – the one that would take millennia to complete a turn. The six wizards stood in awe, reflections of myriad tiny dials glinting in their eyes.

Greenie clasped her hands to her heart. "It's beautiful," she breathed. The moment felt sacred – as if the clock understood the significance of their triumph. On a nearby plaque, Breezie noticed a quote from Einstein praising the Wonder Clock's design, and he couldn't help but smile at the full-circle feeling of learning and wisdom present in the room.

Suddenly, a soft metallic clink drew their attention. At the base of the Wonder Clock's case, a hidden compartment had opened. Within lay a small object, gleaming with reflected light from the dials. Blunt reached in and carefully lifted it out for all to see. It was a finely crafted hand mirror. The back was engraved with ornate patterns of stars and waves, and in the center, it bore an inlay of two interlocking clock faces – one design reminiscent of the Willard shelf clock's dial, the other a miniature of the Zimmer Tower's display. The symbolism was unmistakable: two clocks, two realms of reflection, united as one. Around the rim, in flowing script, was engraved the same Latin motto as their pendant: Reflectio Est Virtus.

"A new artifact," Checkered whispered, eyes wide. Greenie ran her fingers gently over the inscription. The mirror's surface shimmered, and for a moment the six could see themselves within it – not distorted as before, but as they truly were: young, a bit worn from trial, but resolute and shining from within. Firee cleared his throat, his voice thick with emotion. "This will remind us, whenever we doubt, to look at ourselves honestly." Blunt wrapped the mirror carefully in a piece of velvet and stowed it safely. It was a treasure not of power, but of wisdom.

They exited the pavilion into the night. The tower clock had dimmed back to its normal gentle glow. High above, only a few dials—the moon phase, the globe—still twinkled as if winking at them. Lier's quiet streets were empty, but the six friends felt the presence of the town's history watching over them kindly. In the distance, the bells of Saint Gummarus Church tolled the hour, a comforting sound.

"This kind of trial calls for a steadier kind of courage," Reddish said, embers glowing with quiet pride.

Firee nodded in agreement, gazing at the quiet clock tower. "No sinister illusions attacked us at every turn," he said, his voice thoughtful. "But we can't underestimate these trials. Each solution might grow more cryptic than the last."

On the cobblestones of the square, the group huddled together in a spontaneous embrace. No words were needed; the bond between them had grown stronger in this chapter of their journey. They had confronted the illusions within and emerged whole. Each felt more themselves than before: Blunt's steady leadership tempered with openness, Reddish's fire gentled by understanding, Firee's caution balanced with bravery, Breezie's calm fortified with resolve, Checkered's intellect fused with intuition, and Greenie's empathy guarded by inner strength.

As they prepared to depart, Blunt produced the old scroll he had shown them earlier in Boston – the fable "The Council of Mirrors." By the light of the lantern hanging by the pavilion door, he read one line again quietly: "You carry the light you deny yourselves." Greenie smiled at the truth of it. They each carried a light now a little brighter for having been honest with themselves. Reflection's reckoning had left them quieter, wiser, and more introspective indeed.

Greenie sank onto a bench by the tower wall, feeling the night breeze on her face. "Nothing's preying on our fears now," she said softly, meeting each friend's eyes. "Just like the elders in the story, we faced ourselves... and we're still together."

Reddish nodded, resting a hand on Greenie's shoulder. "I guess reflection can be a friend, not an enemy," she mused, echoing a lesson hard-won. Each of them felt it – a lighter heart, a quieter mind.

Breezie glanced at the runic pendant and the new mirror artifact Blunt held. "Where to now?" he asked softly. Over their heads, a few stars had begun to appear in the night sky, twinkling in patterns that hinted at distant horizons. Reddish looked up at the constellation and then at each of her companions. "Wherever the next trial calls," she said. There was no fear in her voice, only conviction.

Checkered consulted her ever-present chart, which now had fresh notations from Grafton and Lier. "We've balanced reflection and action here," she noted. "Whatever comes next, I suspect we'll need to give of ourselves in new ways." A feeling of gentle anticipation passed among them, as if they could sense that the virtue of generosity – of spirit, of knowledge, of heart – would soon be tested.

Blunt extended his hands, and the others took them, forming their circle once more. The mirror of reflection was safe in his satchel, its weight reassuring. Greenie closed her eyes, centering herself on the calm they now shared. The trials ahead were sure to be challenging, but the hardest battle – the one within – had been fought here and won.

"Ready?" Firee asked quietly. They all nodded. In unison, the six young wizards stepped forward, their cloaks swirling. Behind them, the Zimmer Tower's great clock ticked softly, a guardian of time and truth. Ahead, the portal shimmered into being – a doorway shaped by newfound clarity. One by one, they vanished into the light, carrying reflection's lesson with them. And as the square fell silent once more, the clocks of Lier and Grafton beat in gentle harmony, marking the end of one chapter and the hopeful beginning of whatever new dawn awaited them.

Chapter 16

Clock of the Long Now and Wells Cathedral Clock – Generosity's Triumph

The Ten-Thousand-Year Pulse

Midnight's stillness settled over a vast subterranean chamber deep inside a remote desert mountain near Van Horn, Texas, where the Clock of the Long Now rose in towering splendor. This was no exhibit, but a deliberate sanctuary built to house the millennial timepiece far from the hurried world above. The colossal clock spanned a vertical shaft carved into the mountain's heart. Giant interlocking gears and ringed wheels lined the rock walls, and massive stone counterweights hung poised in the darkness overhead. High above, great bronze chimes hung silent, engineered to ring a melody that would never repeat itself in ten thousand years. Yet for all this grandeur, its steel gears—designed to mark ten millennia— turned with a subtle, off-kilter hum, as though greed had seeped into the mechanism and dulled its grand rhythm.

A swirl of bronze-and-sapphire light appeared near a stone archway, revealing Blunt, Reddish, Firee, Checkered,

Breezie, and Greenie in their Harlequin cloaks, newly arrived via a magical portal. Each cloak—emerald, crimson, sapphire—caught the faint radiance of this futuristic space. Breezie adjusted the strap of his satchel, ensuring the precious reflection mirror they'd earned in Belgium remained secure inside. In Blunt's hand, a runic wire labeled "Donatio Est Virtus"(Generosity Is Virtue) pulsed like a guiding beacon. Paulina had gifted him this very wire in Boston—a token of the lamppost's magic meant to guide them through the trials ahead.

Blunt recalled a moment of self-doubt from a previous trial, when illusions had nearly overwhelmed him. Back then, forging unity with his friends had dispelled those phantoms. Now, with that memory fueling his resolve, he said quietly, "We've seen what illusions can do when fear or greed take hold. Let's see how generosity restores this clock." Checkered peered at the clock's lower gears, each carved with cryptic inscriptions. "Look—something's interfering with the core mechanism," she observed. "It's as though the clock is starved of the spirit it was built to share."

A curious echo drifted through the air, faintly resembling a distant, mocking laugh from an older trial. Reddish stiffened at the sound, embers flickering in her eyes. "Wherever we go, it seems shadows still lurk," she muttered. Greenie laid a hand on the steel casing, feeling its weight beneath her palm. She sensed that this clock had been designed to benefit future generations—time measured not for personal gain but for the collective good. She whispered, "Greed threatens this clock's legacy. We need to free it."

In the distance, a figure emerged, a shawl draped over her shoulders. It was Paulina Tetrikus, exuding a gentle warmth that cut through the mechanical chill. She beckoned them forward. "Welcome to the Long Now," she said in a low, inviting voice. "Its gears feel the strain of selfish hoarding, but generosity can right what's gone astray." The group exchanged determined glances, hearts united against the weight of greed. They stepped deeper into the chamber, ready to prove that generosity—shared freely—could restore the clock's intention to stand for all humankind ten thousand years into the future.

Steel, Runed

They followed Paulina through a narrow passage leading to the clock's central shaft. Overhead, steel beams intersected in graceful arcs, shining under discreet lights. A quiet hum filled the air—part mechanical pulse, part intangible tension. "We designed it for the long haul," Paulina said softly, placing her palm against a massive gear. "Humanity's future, measured in centuries. But greed gnaws at its purpose, weakening each gear's synergy."

Blunt moved closer, noticing a faint glimmer tracing along the gear's rim. Embedded in the metal were shapes reminiscent of medieval runes—an unexpected clash of eras, as if the high-tech steel had revealed a hidden palimpsest of ancient symbols only under the clock's strain. One symbol flickered with an otherworldly light, hinting at something ancient bridging them to Wells Cathedral far across the ocean.

Firee knelt and studied the gear's pivot with narrowed eyes. His trap-sense tingled. "There's a microfracture here," he murmured. "If we don't address it, the clock's entire sequence could jam." The possibility of failure was grave: a stoppage here might even desynchronize the other regional time beacons connected to this mechanism. Illusions had once attacked more directly, but greed's subtle sabotage felt just as menacing.

Checkered adjusted her monocle, scanning the rotating runes. "These inscriptions might connect to an older design— maybe a 14th-century invention," she observed. "A link to some companion clock in Europe?" Paulina nodded. "You may be right. The Wells Cathedral clock stands among the oldest of its kind, echoing a centuries-old generosity. If we can heal both clocks, we preserve the spirit of giving across time."

Breezie noticed Reddish's shoulders tense, the embers in her eyes flaring. He gently placed a hand on her arm, letting a calm aura flow through his touch. "We'll solve this piece by piece," he murmured. "Anger won't help us here." She exhaled and her embers receded to a soft glow, and she gave a grateful nod. Each friend sensed how their strengths fit together—logic, empathy, vigilance, reflection. They all served generosity's higher calling.

For a moment, Reddish's fingers twitched at the sight of the runic wire in Blunt's hand. The temptation to seize its power—just for herself—was almost like a pulse in the air. In that instant, the large gear beneath their feet groaned as if aware of her passing impulse. Breezie squeezed her arm gently. "Remember why we have it," he reminded softly. Reddish blinked, letting the notion of selfish claim fade. She reopened her hand and drew a steadying breath.

An uneasy quiet swept the chamber. Despite the hum of steel and ozone, something like a hidden hiss of greed coiled around them, urging each to claim personal gain. But the young wizards stood firm. "Let's fix the fracture," Blunt said, tapping the runic wire in his hand. "And see if it reveals a path to Wells." The notion of bridging centuries—mending a futuristic clock in the mountain clock site near Van Horn, West Texas, and a medieval clock in England—hung in the air. Their mission was clear: where greed had divided, generosity would unite.

Rune-Flare to Wells

As Firee carefully eased open an inspection panel on the clock's foundation, a sudden flare erupted from the medieval rune etched in the steel. A swirl of violet sparks danced through the vaulted chamber, and a faint chime echoed like a distant cathedral bell. Paulina drew back, adjusting her amber shawl. "The clock is responding to your presence. It knows you've come to restore its altruistic purpose," she said with quiet conviction. Her nurturing energy felt almost palpable.

Greenie's empathic senses tingled. She felt a strange link forming—part Long Now, part something older. "There's a thread connecting us to another place," she whispered, carefully holding her hand above the swirling glow. "A 14th-century memory… an old cathedral—" Before she could finish, the swirl expanded, revealing a hazy image: tall stone pillars and candlelit arches. Wells Cathedral, centuries away, beckoned. An inscription flickered along the metal rim: "Avaritia Est Vitium." Greed is a vice. Reddish inhaled sharply. "So that's our next step after we stabilize things here—heading across the sea?"

Checkered peered through her lens. "Likely. The melding of runic codes suggests these two ancient clocks share a spiritual bond. One can't fully heal if the other remains tainted." Blunt recalled a grim moment from a prior ordeal—illusions had once lured him with false promises of personal glory, and he had overcome them by focusing on the communal benefit. That memory flared now, urging him to remain steadfast. "We have to show generosity in action, here and at Wells." Breezie rubbed the runic wire gently. "All right. Let's keep working on the gear fracture, then see how we transition overseas. This portal-like phenomenon might guide us, but we should be sure the Long Now is stable first."

A soft laugh—the kind that wavered between comfort and mischief—drifted from the swirling image. Whether it was the Harlequin's echo or the clock's own voice, none could say. Paulina, undaunted, offered a wise smile. "We'll secure this clock's spirit," she said, "and I'll help you harness the portal. Greed has no place in a legacy meant for every generation to come."

At Paulina's nod, the six sprang into action. Blunt and Checkered clambered onto adjacent platforms to inspect the faulty gear, while Firee and Reddish braced the surrounding cogs with steady magic. Working in unison, they gently redistributed the clock's burden across multiple gear trains, treating the mechanism as a shared commons rather than isolated parts. At Checkered's direction, Breezie released a controlled gust to slow one spinning flywheel, allowing Blunt to wedge the runic wire against the fractured gear like a clamp to reconnect a broken circuit. Firee applied a focused lick of flame to seal the microfracture, while Reddish channeled warmth into a stubborn linkage until it loosened. Bit by bit—a borrowed surge of torque here, a relieved weight there—the Long Now's components began to move in balance once more.

At last, the damaged gear shuddered and then turned smoothly in alignment with the others. A slow, triumphant tick rippled through the clock's frame—the ten-thousand-year heartbeat returning to its rightful cadence. Relieved of strain, the great mechanism settled into a steady rhythm, each cog again sharing the load of time as it was always meant to. With the clock stabilized, the violet sparks around the rune subsided, leaving only a faint vision of medieval stone arches hovering in the air. In that charged hush, the friends felt time itself bridging centuries—generosity the unseen keystone linking past and future.

A Lamppost Called "Donatio"

With their task complete, a flicker of portal light beckoned them onward. One by one, they stepped through and emerged beneath the streetlamps of Boston's North End, an old waterfront district of winding alleys and worn cobblestones.

Night stretched overhead, the moon casting silvery pools across narrow lanes. Yet something felt off: an undercurrent of greed haunted these corridors, manifesting as illusory whispers of quick wealth and hidden hoards. Passersby seemed on edge, eyes darting at every shadow.

"We'd better move," Blunt murmured. "Paulina said she'd meet us here if the Long Now was stabilized." He glanced around, searching for the flicker of her shawl. Firee's trap-sense prickled—someone, or something, lurked a few streets away. "Watch out," he said quietly, gently tugging Reddish's cloak. "I sense illusions. This place is thick with greedy temptations."

Sure enough, faint shapes shimmered at the edges of their vision, whispering, "Keep it all… don't share…" These phantoms cloaked the truth, urging solitary gain. Reddish kindled a low flame in her palm, ready to strike, but Breezie stepped forward and calmly rested a hand on her shoulder. "Let me clear it first," he said, releasing a tranquil gust. The dark mirages ebbed, revealing a simpler reality of old brick walls and wrought-iron balconies. "No need to scorch the entire district," he added, and even Reddish had to grin at that.

They caught a glimpse of Paulina's shawl vanishing around a corner. Embers dancing in her wake, Reddish took the lead. Checkered followed close, monocle glinting as she searched each corner for hidden runes. Blunt and Greenie hung back briefly to reassure a startled resident of the alley's safety, while Firee scanned every stone and shadow for further traps, vigilance unwavering. As they wove deeper into the North End, a mocking cackle skittered between the buildings—perhaps the same Harlequin presence they'd sensed by the mountain in West Texas. It rattled the windows like a sudden gust of wind. Still, they pressed on, drawn by Paulina's steady presence.

At last, they reached a small courtyard at the end of a secluded lane. Paulina stood beside a dim old lamppost whose base glowed with an amber rune, beckoning them forward. This was more than an ordinary streetlight—Boston's lamppost of generosity, the sole safe conduit linking the modern city and medieval Wells. Breezie's earlier breeze had thinned the darkness; now the lamppost's gentle radiance melted away the last of those greedy mirages. "Generosity must be tested here," Paulina said simply, her shawl rippling in a subtle breeze. "Only then will we open the way to Wells."

Light Shared, Fear Unclenched

The lamppost's light revealed a swirl of shifting inscriptions under Paulina's touch. She raised her palm, and runic light fanned out, illuminating the entire courtyard in a soft golden hue. The effect was mesmerizing—warmth that felt both physical and spiritual. "This place was once a haven for sailors who shared what little they had," Paulina explained. "It stands now as a testament to how generosity binds a community."

Greenie watched in awe. She sensed the sincerity in Paulina's actions: the energy flowing from the woman's shawl and fingertips was not an illusion, but a genuine offering of solace. Through her empathy, Greenie could feel how that gift eased the tension of locals peering out from shuttered windows. A small cluster of onlookers gathered silently at the edge of the light. One woman nervously approached, eyes filled with worry over her dwindling savings. Paulina extended both hands in a calming gesture, letting the golden light wrap around the woman like a protective mantle. The woman closed her eyes and let out a slow breath of relief.

Checkered observed how the crowd's demeanor shifted from anxious to hopeful. This was generosity in motion—no grand speeches or forced charity, just a quiet willingness to share. Even Reddish, typically fiery and combative, felt her embers softening in that glow. Firee stood watch at the courtyard's edge, scanning for any lingering illusions. Breezie hovered nearby, ready to soothe the air again should more phantoms surge, though none did.

Blunt watched Paulina's display with growing respect. For an instant, old self-doubt flickered in him—he remembered a time he'd hesitated, fearing any show of weakness. But seeing Paulina's selfless act reminded him that even vulnerability could foster unity. When Paulina finished sharing her runic light, the courtyard felt renewed. Neighbors murmured gratitude, and even the night breeze blew more softly. "Let's continue," Paulina said, meeting the young wizards' gazes. "The path to Wells Cathedral is now open." The lamppost's base glowed brighter for a moment, as if acknowledging her words.

Paulina produced a small leather-bound tome from beneath her shawl. "Before you depart for Wells Cathedral," she said, "hear this tale of generosity. It may guide your hearts when greed whispers false promises." She opened the book to a passage titled *"The Well That Shared Itself."* Clearing her throat softly, she began to read:

"The Well That Shared Itself"

In a sun-scorched land, a community found its single source of water in a deep stone well. Drought loomed, and each family feared losing what little remained. In desperation, some tried to hoard containers of water, hiding them behind locked doors. Others sabotaged neighbors' buckets, hoping to conserve more for themselves.

One scorching morning, a young child stumbled to the well, parched and weak. Though her family had tried saving water, they had exhausted their ration. Seeing her desperation, an elderly man who had a few extra scoops left offered them willingly. Witnessing this generosity, others stepped up to share, first timidly, then with unguarded hearts.

Despite the drought, the well's supply endured longer than anyone expected. With each shared scoop, gratitude replaced fear, forging bonds where suspicion had festered. When precious rainfall finally returned, the entire village celebrated not just water, but the generosity that had saved them from despair.

From that day forward, the well was never hoarded again. Each villager remembered that when one among them thirsted, all were at risk of withering. And so they passed along this lesson: in giving, we preserve life; in hoarding, we sow desolation."

Paulina closed the tome. A reverent silence lingered, broken only by the lamppost's soft hiss. The tale's meaning settled over them like a soothing warmth—potent and undeniable. Paulina's expression softened. "Take that spirit with you," she said, "for the journey to Wells may test your generosity in ways you don't expect."

Afterglow of the Well

A light night breeze rustled the courtyard trees as the fable's lesson sank in. Each of the six wizards stood quietly, turning the story over in their hearts and measuring the weight of generosity in their own lives. Greenie recalled a past trial where illusions preyed on her empathic nature, nearly driving her to hide her gift. "Like that well that shared itself," she said quietly, "empathy only works when offered freely. Holding it back made me feel alone." Reddish let a small ember dance across her palm. "I once thought raw strength was enough," she admitted. "But I see now it's generosity, not force, that breaks cycles of fear. If everyone clutches what they have, we all suffer."

Firee was the first to break the silence that followed. "Illusions always tried to push me into thinking only of myself," he said in a low voice. "Maybe that's why this step in our quest wasn't about a fight at all, but about proving we could give." Checkered placed a hand on the lamppost's metal, the analytic light in her eyes gentled by reflection. "These clocks we're protecting—they're built to outlast any one of us, but only if their gift of time is shared," she noted. "Resources, knowledge, even time itself… they have to circulate, like the water in that well."

Blunt nodded thoughtfully and ran a finger over the runic wire coiled in his palm. "When darkness nearly overtook me before, it was your shared strength that pulled me back," he said to his friends. "Generosity takes many forms." Breezie's eyes gazed back toward the quiet street. "Even a small act of giving can change the whole tide of events," he added softly.

"That one old man's compassion saved a child—and inspired a village."

Paulina approached as they finished sharing their thoughts, her shawl stirring in the breeze. "Wells Cathedral awaits," she said, "the clock there resonates with this same theme—ancient gears requiring a collective spirit to function properly. If greed is left unchallenged, that clock's significance will erode as well." The group collectively exhaled, strengthened by the fable's lesson. The lamplight brightened for a moment, as if recognizing the depth of their resolve. They would leave Boston behind for the medieval grandeur of Wells, guided by the story's lesson in their hearts.

Bridge of Gift

Paulina stepped forward and laid her palm on the lamppost's base. A low hum reverberated, and the inscriptions around its circumference began to rotate, coalescing into a spiral of light. "By embracing generosity here," she said, "you've opened the way to Wells. Be warned: greed's influence lingers in that ancient place. The clock has endured since the 14th century, but it's not impervious to corruption."

The spiral of light expanded, revealing a fleeting glimpse of stone arches and glowing candles. Faint echoes of distant choral song filtered through, as if the cathedral itself were calling out across time. Reddish took a step closer, her embers softly illuminating the swirling portal. "This is no ordinary travel," Paulina continued. "You'll cross thresholds of both era and perspective. Trust what you've learned: in giving, there's safety."

Greenie looked around at her companions—Blunt with the runic wire in hand, Checkered ready with her lens, Firee poised to sense any traps, Breezie calm at the fringe, and Reddish with resolve flickering in her eyes. A wave of gratitude for their collective synergy washed over Greenie. Then, with a final flourish of light from the lamppost, the portal solidified. Arcs of medieval runes danced in the air, forging a luminous bridge. A faint whiff of candle wax and ancient stone wafted through, and the sound of water trickling—as from a distant fountain—echoed softly.

No illusions sprang forth to stop them; perhaps the Harlequin's malice lay elsewhere or bided its time. Either way, they stepped boldly into the swirling gate. Paulina's final words lingered in the crisp air: "May generosity shape your path forward." The long gear sighed; a bell in Somerset answered. A brief surge of energy enveloped them. The lamppost's courtyard vanished, replaced by the dim hush of a hallowed space centuries older than the Boston streets they had just left.

Stone, Incense, Time

Silence fell as the swirling portal dissipated, leaving the young wizards in Wells Cathedral's dimly lit nave. Towering columns framed the central aisle, candlelight pooling across the ancient stone floor. The 14th-century astronomical clock stood along one wall, its zodiac dial and little jousting knights eerily still. A chill tinged with old incense drifted through the arches. Breezie's breath caught in his throat—this place exuded a solemn reverence. "Feels like stepping back in time," he whispered, mindful of the centuries layered within these walls.

Checkered lifted her lens toward the high rafters. "That clock is one of the oldest of its kind," she said softly. "Crafted in the medieval era, it once symbolized a communal sharing of knowledge about the heavens. If greed tarnishes it, we risk losing a living piece of history." Firee ran his hand along the edge of a carved pew, half expecting an illusion to surge. Instead, he sensed something more pervasive—a low, discordant hum that hinted at avarice. "We've seen greed sabotage mechanical wonders before," he murmured. "I'd wager it's doing the same thing here."

Indeed, a faint disharmony vibrated from the clock's gears, as if it longed to chime but was stuck in the grasp of selfish energy. Reddish stepped closer, eyeing the knight figurines that traditionally jousted every quarter-hour. Now they stood rigid, locked in a tension that suggested the hoarding of something intangible. Blunt gripped the runic wire. "We overcame illusions with fortitude and reflection," he said. "Let's see if generosity can unbind these gears." He recalled Paulina's fable and how a single act of giving could transform an entire community.

Greenie extended her empathic sense into the cathedral's atmosphere. She felt it thrumming with ancient devotion. "Wells has always been a place where pilgrims gave of themselves—labor, coin, prayers. Maybe that spirit still lingers." As they converged at the clock's base, a whisper emanated from the dial: "Avaritia Est Vitium… Donatio Est Virtus." Greed is vice; generosity is virtue. The words crackled like a quiet warning. The friends exchanged determined looks. They had come prepared to restore what centuries of devotion had built, refusing to let greed lay claim to this medieval masterpiece.

When Knights Lay Down Lances

A sudden mechanical lurch rattled the clock, and the knights' figures jerked to life. But instead of their usual playful joust, they advanced in a menacing march, each brandishing a lance. Candle flames guttered, casting exaggerated shadows along the stone walls. Blunt stepped in front of the group. "They're twisted by greed," he muttered, recalling how illusions in earlier trials had corrupted otherwise benign figures. He raised a protective ward—a shimmering barrier of water-like light—between them and the oncoming knights.

Reddish, embers pulsing at her fingertips, prepared to strike with fire. Yet she hesitated, sensing these animated figures were part of the cathedral's long heritage. She didn't want to destroy them—only to free them. Breezie swept forward, extending a calm breeze that wafted around the knights' clockwork forms. "We come to share, not to hoard," he called out in a steady voice. "Lay down your weapons and return to your rightful motion!"

The knights trembled, as if battling the very grip of avarice. One lurched forward, clanging its lance against stone. Firee tensed, scanning for a deeper trap in the mechanism. Sure enough, he spotted a jammed rod behind the clock face, pulsing with the same runic malignance they'd seen in West Texas. "I see it!" he shouted, pointing for Checkered. Checkered rushed behind the clock's housing, lens in hand. There, a chunk of corroded metal locked a critical gear in place. Inscribed upon it was "Avaritia" – Greed. "This is what's twisting their purpose," she said, carefully prying at the corroded piece.

Reddish channeled her empathy outward, imagining how this clock once delighted onlookers with its cheerful displays. "Be free of this corruption," she whispered, sending vines of gentle green light to twine around the knights' arms. Gradually, the tension in the mechanism eased. Checkered dislodged the corroded chunk, and Firee unleashed a searing flash that dissolved the malignant fragment without harming the sacred space. The knights staggered back into position, their mechanical jaws opening in silent acceptance. A soft whirring sigh signaled the gear's release.

As the mechanism reset, a clear chime rang out through the cathedral. The knights resumed their proper dance, elegantly jousting in harmless spectacle as they had for centuries. Quiet returned to Wells Cathedral, now suffused with relief. Reddish lowered her hand, her flames dying to embers. "They're back in alignment," she whispered, exhaling deeply. "Greed lost here." Blunt bowed his head in quiet gratitude. The ancient clock, turning freely once more, stood as proof that what was meant to be shared could never be held by greed for long.

Candles flickered anew as the clock's chime faded. The etched zodiac dial glowed faintly, revealing a hidden compartment beneath an engraved lion—an emblem from the 14th century signifying both regal authority and communal stewardship. Checkered and Greenie exchanged looks. Greenie's eyes widened. "I sense something new—something needs to be shared," she murmured.

Greenie glanced at the tarnished brass coin still in Blunt's hand. It bore the inscription "Donatio Est Virtus." Heavy and cool in Blunt's palm, the coin's weight felt portentous. "The pilgrims who once gave coins to maintain this clock," Greenie said softly, "their generosity kept it running for generations." Checkered tapped the coin's edge with her thumbnail. It seemed to pulse with potential energy.

"Maybe this is what completes the mechanism," Checkered said. Without hesitation, she placed the Donatio coin into a recessed slot at the base of the clock, right under the lion carving. The moment the coin clicked into place, the zodiac dial flared brilliantly. With a soft mechanical groan, a panel slid open. Inside lay the small star medallion, its surface cool and smooth, etched with constellations reminiscent of the Long Now's design. Blunt carefully lifted it out, feeling a subtle warmth spread through his fingers as if the artifact recognized their unselfish efforts.

The implication was clear: the coin had completed the Wells mechanism. The way was now open to fully link back to the futuristic design they'd left behind. Blunt held the star medallion up, light catching on its polished face. "It seems we're bridging two worlds: medieval and modern," he said, voice quiet with wonder. The choir stalls rustled in a gentle draft—whether literal or spiritual, no one could say. But the message was clear: generosity had restored Wells Cathedral's clock. The next step—linking fully back to West Texas' Long Now—awaited.

Steel Breathes Easier

Paulina stood near the Long Now's primary gear shaft, her shawl caught in the subdued glow. As the group reappeared in the underground chamber, she broke into a bright smile. "You've freed Wells from the grasp of avarice?" she asked, hope in her voice.

"We have," Checkered confirmed, holding up the star-marked medallion. "That clock runs on its proper cycle again. Greed no longer claims it." Reddish smiled and lowered her hand, feeling embers cool to a gentle glow.

A low vibration coursed through the Long Now's apparatus, as though responding to the triumph at Wells. Firee felt a shift in the gear alignment and realized the earlier microfracture was smoothing itself out—symbolically, perhaps—now that both clocks resonated with the spirit of generosity. Greenie pressed her palm to one of the large steel supports. "I sense less tension… like it's breathing easier," she said with a soft smile. She recalled the fable of the well that shared itself:

when water flowed freely among the thirsty, it sustained everyone. Here, time and generosity had flowed across centuries to mend both clocks.

A fleeting cackle—echoing the Harlequin's mockery—broke the momentary peace. Reddish narrowed her eyes. "That presence again," she hissed, embers flaring. But the sound quickly slithered away, leaving only the steady hum of clockwork. "It won't give up easily," Blunt muttered, recalling how illusions had nearly consumed them in the past. "But we'll face it the same way—standing together and sharing what we have."

Paulina guided them to an open panel near the clock's center. Inside was another compartment, glowing with the same star emblem. "You bridged the gap between old and new," she said warmly. "The Long Now can function as it was meant to—an enduring gift to humanity." Checkered stepped forward with the star medallion in hand. For a moment she hesitated—this relic's ancient design was a trove of knowledge she yearned to study. But it was meant to be shared, not hoarded. Steeling herself, she fitted the medallion into place. A satisfying click echoed, and the system's hum grew steady and confident. A faint swirl of runes—half medieval, half futuristic—shimmered along the metal. "It's complete," she whispered.

With the Long Now clock fully restored, Paulina gathered the wizards around the main gear. A radiant circle of runic light rose from the panel, forming a mosaic of cosmic patterns and archaic symbols beneath their feet. Her voice carried the calm assurance of one who had seen greed's worst but believed in humanity's best. "By acting generously here and in Wells, you've proven how greed can threaten time's legacy. Left unchecked, it would poison any clock or community it touches." She paused to let her words sink in. The group remembered how illusions had preyed on their insecurities, nearly fracturing their unity. Greed was simply another face of that same darkness—one that could erode entire civilizations if unchallenged. Paulina continued, "Your success means these two clocks will now endure for future generations. But it also signals new trials ahead. The Harlequin's mischief remains—lurking in illusions and subtle manipulations, ready to feed on anyone who hoards rather than shares."

Breezie folded his arms and traded a glance with Firee. "So we move on to the next link in this chain of timepieces?" he asked.

"Yes," Paulina affirmed, brushing back a lock of hair. "Each clock you restore repels another shadow of greed. That is the power of generosity."

Greenie felt a subtle weight settle on her shoulders, as though each step forward carried greater responsibility. "We stand ready," she said softly, recalling the small child in the fable who had nearly perished from thirst. "If generosity saved that village, it can save countless others." Reddish clenched her fist, embers glowing with resolve. "No illusion, no greed, no phantom laugh will stop us," she said. Paulina offered a proud smile. "Then you will continue," she said, gesturing toward the swirling mosaic. "The path extends beyond this chamber. Find the next clock. Defend it. Show that generosity triumphs over every form of avarice."

A faint rumble shivered through the floor, as if the Long Now itself approved. The lights beneath them flickered, hinting at a nascent portal to some future challenge. The friends exchanged steeled nods—there was no turning back now.

Provisioning the Gift

The main gear gradually slowed, releasing a final, resonant chime through the cavernous space. Paulina led them away from the machinery to a quieter alcove lined with archive boxes and old sketches—plans for future expansions of the Long Now clock. "You'll need a moment of rest," she said, offering them water and small parcels of food. Even generosity, she knew, required tangible nourishment now and then. Each of them gratefully accepted, mindful that giving and receiving were part of the same cycle.

Blunt gazed down at the runic wire in his hand. "We carry these tools for a reason," he reflected, toying with its length. "They're not for personal gain, but to connect us with others who need help." Firee, sipping water, thought about how illusions once twisted his vigilance into paranoia. "If I keep my senses open not just for myself, but for everyone's well-being, maybe no illusion can snag me again," he said quietly. Checkered nodded. "And my lens—at first I only used it to gather data. Now I see it's meant to decipher illusions and inscriptions that benefit more than just my curiosity." She remembered scanning the medieval runes in Wells and unlocking a piece of history many had forgotten.

Reddish leaned against a stone pillar, her embers still flickering gently. "We beat illusions by uniting, and we beat greed by sharing," she said wryly. "I'm definitely noticing a pattern here." Greenie set aside her empty water cup and closed her eyes, breathing in the stillness. "Generosity may be a simple idea," she said softly, "but it's the hardest thing for the selfish to grasp. We'll carry that spirit with us wherever we go."

Paulina's shawl caught a faint draft, swirling around her ankles. "Whenever you're ready," she said gently, "follow the path that forms from this vantage point." She nodded toward an open archway where a soft light shimmered—a new portal blooming to life. It beckoned toward Argent Keep, the hidden sanctuary high in distant mountains that the orb's clue had named. What once seemed a mere metaphor was about to become a very real stronghold—and the site of the next clock. The six rose, cloaks swaying. No illusions prowled these halls now—greed had been banished from the Long Now and from Wells. But the road ahead was long, and they would journey onward, trusting that each step taken in generosity would dispel whatever darkness waited in unseen corners.

Coda: Two Clocks in Concord

A final silence fell over the underground chamber as the young wizards gathered beside Paulina. Beyond the archway, a shimmering tunnel of light flickered, promising passage to yet another clock-bound destination—one that would surely test their unity and generosity in new ways. Paulina's kind gaze swept over each of them, her shawl glowing with the same warmth that had calmed the North End crowd. "Remember the fable of the well that shared itself," she said softly. "It's the essence of all you've done here—when one person gives, it inspires others." She didn't need to spell it out any further; the lesson was clear.

Blunt stepped forward, taking her hand in gratitude. A memory of his past self-doubt flashed through his mind, but standing here now, he felt none of that weight. "Your guidance helped us see how future and past can share time's gift," he said. "We'll keep forging ahead." Reddish and Greenie joined in, each offering quiet words of thanks. Firee, Breezie, and Checkered likewise voiced their appreciation, acknowledging that Paulina's nurturing influence had not only mended clocks but also smoothed out their own rough edges.

A faint echo of the phantom laugh still hovered at the back of their minds—a lingering reminder of the Harlequin's influence. Yet it no longer felt threatening, merely a distant cackle drowned out by the warmth of their collective purpose. Paulina gave a final, proud nod and stepped aside. The swirling portal beyond the arch pulsed in beckoning arcs of pale blue and gold. Steeling themselves, the six friends exchanged resolute glances. One by one, they crossed the threshold, cloaks shining in the half-light as they vanished from the Long Now.

The moment their figures disappeared, the chamber's stillness deepened. An almost musical resonance spread through the great steel gears, as if the entire clock recognized their selfless act. Ten thousand years of ticking lay ahead, sustained by the spirit of generosity.

Back in Wells Cathedral, the ancient clock chimed with renewed vigor, its knights once again jousting playfully for the delight of visitors. Across an ocean and across centuries, two clocks—one medieval, one futuristic—now moved in quiet concord. Each tick was a living testament to what the wizards had accomplished. Thus ended their confrontation with greed at the Long Now and at Wells Cathedral. The young wizards' journey continued—ever watchful for illusions that preyed on fear and avarice, ever faithful that the flame of unity and generosity would guide them through whatever darkness lay ahead.

Chapter 17

Adler Planetarium and Münster Clock – Justice's Balance

Chicago Under the Scales

A crisp Chicago night sky shimmered over the domed silhouette of Adler Planetarium, where a celestial clock stood silent and askew. Commissioned when Adler opened in 1930 to demonstrate cosmic harmony, its starry gears—usually humming in tune with the heavens—now emitted an unsettling, off-kilter rhythm. To anyone attuned to magical interference, it felt like injustice warping the universe's natural balance—turning the very hourglass of the cosmos on its head.

From a swirl of bronze-and-sapphire light, Blunt, Reddish, Firee, Checkered, Breezie, and Greenie stepped into the grand hall. Harlequin cloaks—emerald, crimson, sapphire—caught glimmers of overhead exhibit lights. In Blunt's hand, a sigil inscribed with Aequitas Est Virtus pulsed, guiding them forward.

Firee glanced around, recalling how illusions once preyed on their vulnerabilities in a previous city. "No glamours swirling yet," he murmured. "But the energy here feels… skewed."

Checkered pressed her lens to the planetary clock's base, reading an engraved motto: "Justice Is Virtue; Injustice Is Vice." She spotted a faint distortion in the brass orbits. "Something is pulling these cosmic paths out of alignment," she said softly, "like a moral imbalance given physical form— truth suspended in starlight, awaiting balance."

Greenie closed her eyes, sensing the unfulfilled dream of the clock—stars bridging humanity in fairness. "It was built to show unity under the cosmos," she whispered, "but something is dividing it."

Reddish's embers flared at the thought of oppression. She remembered illusions that once forced entire communities into isolation. "If injustice can twist starry arcs," she said, "we need to restore this machine's fairness."

A subtle radiance emanated from the dais. Lettizia Dillettante, calm and statuesque, emerged near a cluster of antique displays. Her serene gaze carried the promise of a test, yet also an air of reservation. "Adler's clock stands for universal justice," she explained. "Biased forces have sabotaged its heart."

Blunt tightened his grip on the sigil. Past lessons—generosity, fortitude—burned in his memory. "We overcame illusions by standing united," he said. "Here, we ensure justice triumphs over division."

Lettizia's eyes narrowed slightly, as if weighing their resolve, then she inclined her head. "Prepare yourselves. Only a shared commitment to fairness can unlock the clock's mechanism and lead us to Münster, where further challenges await."

Gears that Tilt the Sky

The vast hall darkened slightly as the Wizards approached the clock's central apparatus. Around them, star charts and model solar systems cast faint reflections across polished floors. Silence fell, broken only by the insistent ticking of misaligned gears.

Checkered crouched beside a panel where several brass rods converged. "Each rod directs a different orbit," she explained. "They're usually balanced, but one is forcing them to tilt—like a moral imbalance given physical form." She remembered how relying on pure logic once caused her to overlook an important emotional clue, and she vowed not to repeat that mistake. This time, she would fuse careful analysis with empathy.

"I sense a fracture inside," Firee said quietly, brushing metal with a gloved hand. His heightened trap-sense sparked, as if illusions might be lurking behind the clock's sleek façade. "If we let it fester, the entire star map could seize up."

Greenie rested her palm on an inscription depicting constellations meant to represent global unity. "This place was designed to show we all share the same sky," she murmured, "and a common responsibility beneath it. Injustice tears that unity apart."

Nearby, Breezie observed a small group of late-night visitors who strayed too close, enthralled by the clock's grandeur. He offered them a calm gesture, ensuring no illusions startled or harmed them. The visitors soon retreated, leaving the hall quiet again.

A faint hum beneath the floor signaled deeper energies. Blunt traced the glowing sigil in his hand: Aequitas Est Virtus. He recalled how illusions of greed once threatened a different clock near Van Horn in West Texas, only to be dispelled by a united front. Now, it was injustice—a subtler but equally corrosive force.

Reddish watched as a swirl of cosmic light danced overhead—an echo from the exhibit's star projector. "If bias can misalign orbits," she said, "we'll align them back. Let's see if Lettizia can guide us to the root of this sabotage."

From behind a bronze column, Lettizia stepped forward. Her gown caught the overhead constellations, turning her silhouette into a living tapestry of starlight. "Follow me," she said softly, beckoning them to a hidden hatch near the clock's base. "We must confront injustice at its source, or this celestial map will remain twisted."

Lettizia's Scale of Justice

They descended a short ladder into a maintenance alcove rarely visited by the public. Brass wiring and star-shaped cogs lined the walls, originally meant to replicate cosmic movements. However, each component vibrated with an undercurrent of tension.

Lettizia paused before a pedestal bearing a small set of runic scales—one side dipped drastically lower than the other. With steady hands, she lifted it into view. "This scale was designed to reflect cosmic equilibrium. Yet see how it tilts?"

Reddish furrowed her brow, embers glowing. "It's like it's weighed down by something intangible."

"Injustice," Lettizia replied, gently placing a faintly glowing feather onto the higher side. "When decisions, resources, or opportunities favor one group at the expense of others, the universe's moral fabric distorts."

In that moment, wisps of smoky energy surfaced around the pedestal, coalescing into half-formed phantoms—weighted shadows of privilege and bias urging certain cogs to spin faster than others. Within the swirling mirage, a ghostly council chamber flickered into view: one faction of phantoms clamored for exclusive rights and privileges, while across from them another faction cried out against exploitation. Accusations overlapped in a discordant clamor, neither side heeding the other's words. Lettizia's gaze never wavered.

"I restore balance by recognizing each person's equal stake," she continued, channeling a subtle wave of magic into the scale. This conjured a soft shimmer of fairness that dispersed the illusions in swirling motes. The scale's pans leveled out, if only for an instant.

Greenie felt a gentle pulse of empathy emanating from Lettizia's demonstration—her vow to see the powerless included. Meanwhile, Firee's trap-sense flared again. He noticed flickers of illusory hands trying to tip the scale back down. "They're persistent," he warned.

Breezie stepped behind Reddish, softly placing a hand on her shoulder when he sensed her frustration rising. "Let's stay calm," he said, voice soothing. "We learned from illusions past that fear or anger can feed them."

Reddish exhaled, letting the embers recede. She knew that fighting illusions with pure rage often backfired. "Right," she said, nodding at Breezie. "Steady as we go."

With a final surge of purpose, Lettizia balanced the runic scale once more. This time, the illusions vanished entirely. A hidden gear behind the pedestal clicked into motion, signifying partial restoration of the clock's cosmic harmony. High above, one of the planetary rings that had been askew shuddered and slid back into its proper groove, as if the heavens themselves acknowledged the regained equilibrium.

Lettizia allowed herself a relieved smile. "Justice starts here," she said softly, lowering the scale. "But we'll need to take that principle beyond Adler—into Münster, where an older clock also struggles under bias's weight."

A Spire of Stars

A subtle hum grew beneath their feet, resonating with the newly balanced scale. Lettizia led them back into the main hall. A silver gear—the heart of Adler's clock—now hovered under the dome, glowing with renewed power. Its light bent eastward across the projected night sky, sketching the outline of a distant spire among the stars. Overhead, the usual constellations gleamed, but now one flickered and reformed into a medieval cathedral spire etched into the dome.

"There's your path," Lettizia said, pointing to the glimmering outline. "Münster's 1540 Astronomical Clock shares a bond with Adler's. Both were designed to unify people's gaze upward, yet injustice has corrupted them."

Blunt watched as the starlit spire glowed with swirling runes. "A cathedral rune flared," he observed, marveling as an ephemeral pattern arced across the dome—a shimmering bridge linking Chicago's cosmos with the German city. He felt the weight of a new test summoning them.

"Injustice threatens cosmic balance," Greenie murmured, quietly recalling how illusions once cloaked truth in times before. "We can't leave it unresolved."

The hall fell quiet, as though the planetarium exhibits themselves sensed a transition. Reddish noticed the ghost of a shadowy laugh echo around the dome—perhaps the Harlequin's mocking presence. She gritted her teeth, remembering illusions that once tried to drive them apart. "We'll face that laugh if it returns," she vowed.

Checkered glanced at Breezie, recalling how earlier illusions once rattled the group. "We'll stay calm," she said, referencing the moment when pure logic once failed her. Now, she understood that empathy and fairness worked alongside analysis.

Firee nodded. "So the portal forms in synergy with the clock's partial restoration. Let's ensure we fix every gear before we jump."

Lettizia moved toward the central dais, placing one hand upon an orrery that spun a golden ring around Earth's miniature sphere. "Adler's system is stable enough to allow passage," she confirmed. "But Münster awaits the same cleansing from bias. Otherwise, the cycle remains incomplete."

A swirl of cosmic wind rushed through the exhibit. The starlit outline above suddenly flared into a brilliant comet streaking across the dome. In an instant, the comet's tail unfurled into a luminous hand of stardust that plunged downward toward the Wizards. Reddish instinctively stepped forward as the radiant hand closed gently around them all. With a swift tug, the comet-hand yanked the six off their feet and into the glimmering spire of light. As the world dissolved into a blur of stars, Lettizia's voice echoed after them: "Bring justice to Münster's ancient clock. Only then will true balance return."

Angels Ask for Balance

Emerging from the cosmic whirlwind, the Wizards found themselves in a candlelit nave. High Gothic arches soared overhead, light dancing across carved pillars. At one side rose the 1540 Astronomical Clock, with zodiac angels and lunar saints perched on rotating tiers. Yet the mechanism jerked erratically, as though some hidden force tugged at its gears.

A faint smell of candle wax mixed with centuries-old stone, heightening the sense of solemn history. Greenie shivered at the tension in the air. "Münster has endured many trials. Now it faces illusions of injustice."

Checkered adjusted her lens, scanning the clock's outer ring. "Centuries ago, this clock symbolized communal unity," she noted softly. "People came from all around to see its cosmic display—a reminder we share one sky—and a common responsibility beneath it."

Reddish noticed certain figures—angelic statues holding gilded scales—tilted out of place. "Something is twisting them. They look almost… resentful."

Firee stepped closer to the mechanical underpinnings, searching for traces of sabotage. "I sense a trap forming," he warned, picking up faint pulses of negative energy behind the dial. "A portion of the clock's rods is about to snap if we don't stabilize them."

Breezie caught the flutter of robed phantoms at the edge of his vision—spectral judges and clerics, illusions suggesting hierarchical favoritism fueling the injustice. He noticed Reddish's fists clench as anger flashed in her eyes. Meeting her gaze, he gave a subtle nod and exhaled slowly, projecting a calming presence. Reddish drew a deep breath of her own, feeling her racing heart steady at his silent assurance. "Stay steady," he whispered. They both knew they couldn't allow these illusions to bait them into rashness.

Blunt nodded, feeling the Aequitas Est Virtus sigil pulse with renewed urgency. He recalled the moment in Chicago when they saw how a single unbalanced gear could undermine an entire system. "Münster's clock is likewise compromised," he said softly. "If we restore it here, the synergy with Adler will be complete."

As if on cue, the zodiac angels trembled to life, brandishing starry orbs. A biased hum reverberated in the cathedral's hush, urging favoritism for some figurines while isolating others. The group exchanged firm glances—they were ready to confront illusions that fed on division.

When Angels Tilt

A sudden jerk rattled the cathedral clock. The angels—once symbols of unity—were now contorted, tilting their orbs as though ready to strike. At the same time, lunar saints scowled from their perches, hoarding small star emblems.

Blunt stepped forward, calling on a ward of watery light to shield his companions. "Justice endures!" he shouted, recalling how illusions of fear once shattered under shared determination.

An angel flung an orb at the group, only to have Reddish deflect it with a controlled swirl of embers. She channeled her frustration into a focused flame, mindful not to scorch the ancient relic. "Balance, don't divide!" she snapped, scattering the glamours swirling around the angel's wings.

Greenie's empathic senses pulsed. She felt a crowd of minor illusions lurking in the shadows—flickers of congregants who once deemed themselves superior or unworthy, now feeding the clock's bias. "Fairness binds us all," she murmured, weaving a gentle vine of energy that calmed the clock's mechanical thrashing.

Firee pinpointed the trap he had sensed: a cluster of half-real cogs jammed under a carved saint's foot. "These illusions have hardened into something physical," he said. With a precise burst of flame, he incinerated the corrupted metal.

Checkered's lens glowed, highlighting runic inscriptions that writhed across the clock: Iniquitas Est Vitium. She steadied her mind, refusing to be swayed by the insidious whispers. Drawing on both reason and compassion, she deciphered how the illusions had skewed each figure's motion. "Truth aligns!" she declared as the hidden pattern became clear.

Breezie summoned a steady breeze that swept aside the last ephemeral shapes clinging to the zodiac angels. One by one, the celestial figures returned to their rightful motions, no longer pinned by illusions of favoritism. Silence settled, broken only by the soft ticking of gears resetting.

Mrs. V.'s maternal spirit flickered near a candlelit alcove, offering a gentle affirmation: "Justice defeats bias." Then she faded, leaving the group with a sense of calm triumph. The mechanical hum of Münster's clock softened, as though exhaling relief after centuries of tension.

For a brief moment, one of the zodiac angels slowly rotated back to its upright stance, lifting a tiny golden scale in a gesture of restored balance. Nearby, a carved saint beside the dial slid back into its alcove with a soft click as a delicate chime sounded—subtle signs that order had been restored to the ancient clock.

Heritage of the 1540 Clock

With the illusions dispelled, the 1540 Astronomical Clock resumed a graceful dance of celestial figures. Candlelight glistened on gilded details, revealing the artistry of those who first fashioned it nearly five centuries ago.

Checkered read a small plaque at the clock's base. "In 1540, local artisans completed these rotating angels and saints to remind everyone of cosmic fairness," she said reverently. "No single group overshadowed the others—each carved element contributed to the grand design."

Greenie touched the smooth stone of a nearby pillar, sensing echoes of past congregants who once marveled at the clock's daily performance. "They came to see how the heavens moved in tandem, reflecting a moral order," she whispered. "Injustice was never meant to tarnish it."

Firee exhaled, releasing the last of his tension. "It's stable now. If illusions try to return, we'll sense them. But I think we broke their hold."

Breezie nodded, noting how Reddish's embers had cooled to a gentle glow. He offered her a small, reassuring smile. "We can stand down," he said quietly, remembering how close anger had come to consuming her. "The danger's passed."

Blunt pressed the Aequitas Est Virtus sigil to a newly revealed notch on the clock's side. With a mechanical click, a hidden panel slid open, unveiling a cipher-coded disc. "Looks like Münster's final secret—maybe a link to yet another location?"

A soft voice echoed from the darkness behind them. Lettizia's presence shimmered briefly in the candlelit shadows. "You've brought justice here," she said quietly. "Adler's cosmic map and Münster's historical device both reflect fairness returned. But there is more to discover."

The group exchanged knowing glances. They had conquered illusions that peddled bias, bridging two clocks across continents. Yet the path to restoring every magical timepiece still lay open.

In the silence that followed, a gentle whisper rose from the shadows of the nave, as if a lingering echo of the dispelled illusions were speaking:

"How can you govern fairly if you refuse to hear each other's plight?"

After a moment's calm, Lettizia beckoned them toward a carved choir stall. From within her robes, she withdrew a small parchment. "Before you move on, hear this," she said softly. "An old fable about a divided city council that learned the meaning of impartial justice."

Clearing her throat, she began:

"Voices Divided"

A prosperous city became mired in dispute when half the council demanded exclusive rights to new lands, while the other half insisted such grants would exploit the poor. Meetings turned heated, each side casting accusations.

In the midst of this uproar, a wise mediator arrived with a single question: "How can you govern fairly if you refuse to hear each other's plight?" The council laughed at the notion of listening to opponents. But the mediator stood firm, proposing a day for each side to speak uninterrupted while the other listened in silence.

Reluctantly, the council agreed. By day's end, both factions realized they misunderstood each other's fears and hopes. The wealthy feared losing established privileges, while struggling families feared permanent disenfranchisement. With the mediator's guidance, they drafted a charter ensuring reasonable land access for all—a balance preserving the city's prosperity without trampling the vulnerable.

Once the charter passed, tension ebbed. Residents found renewed trust in their leaders, and the city thrived. The council, though still opinionated, embraced a rule: no law could pass without hearing each voice in turn. Fairness prevailed over division.

Lettizia finished reading, then lowered the parchment.

A soft hush fell around the choir stall. For a moment, none of the Wizards spoke as the question echoed through the air. Blunt finally broke the silence, his voice thoughtful. "Fairness isn't just an ideal," he said quietly. "It's something we practice—by hearing every voice and pausing our own judgments. Division turns to harmony only when we truly listen—just as we've learned to do with one another."

Lettizia's eyes sparkled with quiet approval. "Well said. Your unity thrives when each voice is heard—no illusion can tear that apart."

Back to Boston: The Unbalanced Harbor

A subtle swirl of magic engulfed them, triggered by Münster's clock reactivating. Blunt felt the Aequitas Est Virtus sigil grow warm, urging them onward.

"Adler is stable, Münster is stable," he said, noticing the familiar tug of teleportation magic. "But I sense another call—something pulling us back to Boston before the next horizon."

Lettizia stepped aside, and near the base of the cathedral's side altar a portal shimmered into being. "One more thread remains in Boston," she said. "A place where injustice lingers. Only by cleansing it can you claim the final piece to unlock future clocks."

One by one, they stepped through the glowing doorway. A brisk breeze greeted them as stone walls gave way to open night and the smell of brine. They emerged on a moonlit waterfront, the outlines of historic vessels and drydocked ironclads looming in silhouette.

Salt and tar tinged the cold air. The quiet was broken only by the creak of wet ropes and the faint lap of harbor water against wooden pilings.

Charlestown Navy Yard sprawled before them—an expanse of docks, ropewalks, and ships preserved from another era. Ghostly illusions skirled over the water's surface, casting warped reflections that cloaked truth in shimmer. It was as though the very sea glinted with half-truths, fed by unresolved bias.

Breezie inhaled the salty wind, sensing lingering tensions among the bobbing masts. "Ships shimmering with illusions," he murmured, eyes tracking ephemeral shapes dancing atop the waves. "We'd better stay alert. These illusions may be craftier than most."

Reddish let her embers rise just enough to cast a warm glow along the wooden planks. "Injustice threatens cosmic balance," she reminded quietly, recalling an old oath that even a small bias could warp entire worlds. "We can't let it anchor itself here."

Checkered raised her lens and scanned the dim yard. "Illusions of unfairness could easily fester around contested sites like these old battleships," she said. "They're symbols of power—and power often breeds bias if left unchecked."

Greenie squared her shoulders, remembering the lesson that every voice must be heard. "Whatever illusion appears," she said, "we'll confront it together—justice as our anchor."

Illusions on the Tide

They ventured deeper into the Navy Yard. Old cannons lined the docks, and moonlight glinted off the steel hulls of decommissioned ships. The site was silent at this late hour—

no tourists or workers, only the drip of brackish water and the scrape of rope against metal.

Suddenly, Firee halted and held up a hand. His trap-sense flared. "Watch out," he hissed. "There's a cluster of illusions swirling near that old submarine's hatch." He pointed toward a shadowed vessel moored ahead. "They're weaving visions of partial truths—promises of favor for some, neglect for others."

As the group approached, spectral shapes flickered into view atop the submarine's deck: uniformed officers pinning medals on certain sailors while pointedly ignoring others. Reddish's embers surged. "Injustice at sea," she muttered, bracing herself as if facing an old foe.

Before anger could overtake her, Breezie glided close and rested a steady hand on Reddish's shoulder. The memory of the whispered counsel—of patience and listening—rose in Reddish's mind. She drew a slow breath, banking down her flame. "Easy," Breezie whispered. "Don't give them what they want." Reddish exhaled, nodding. "You're right. I won't let them manipulate me."

A swirl of phantom medals drifted temptingly through the air, but the Wizards did not take the bait. Checkered's lens confirmed the illusion's lure: special privileges offered to some at the cost of others—a direct echo of bias. She pursed her lips, remembering how a misjudgment once cost them precious time. "Not this time," she said, pressing forward with resolve.

Greenie closed her eyes and extended an empathic wave, encouraging the illusions to dissolve in the face of shared fairness. Firee followed up with precise bursts of flame, burning away each illusion's anchor. Blunt stood guard over the group, holding the Aequitas Est Virtus sigil aloft like a beacon.

Gradually, the phantasms thinned and finally vanished, leaving the submarine's hatch and decks empty and still. The group pressed on, hearts steady in their unified stand.

"Injustice can seduce with half-truths," Blunt observed as they regrouped, "but we see beyond its glamour. We won't be split."

The Medallion of Balance

They continued along a row of aging warships, guided by faint runes now glowing on nearby crates and mooring lines. A soft silver light beckoned from beneath a rusted iron anchor mounted on the pier. As they neared, Lettizia Dillettante emerged from the shadows, her flowing gown tinged with the navy yard's blue-gray gloom.

"Injustice seeps even into places long at peace," she said quietly, turning to face them. Her tone was calm, but a note of relief underlay it. "Your resilience here proves you refuse to let illusions twist who deserves respect."

Greenie gazed around at the silent ships. "We've driven the illusions from these docks," she said, "but the stains of past bias still lie in their history."

Checkered thought of a wise mediator who had once bridged two hostile sides. "We have to be that mediator wherever we go," she added softly. "Never letting one perspective dominate unfairly."

At those words, the faint runes around them swirled and coalesced. A slender medallion emerged in Lettizia's open palm, forming from the very silver-blue light of the harbor. Etched on it was a pair of balanced scales. The medallion glowed with a pure silver-white radiance, distinct from the amber and bronze hues of the tokens the Wizards had claimed before.

Lettizia offered the runic medallion forward in silence. Its luminance bathed the group in a gentle glow, as if acknowledging their hard-won unity. "This symbolizes what you've earned," she said at last. "Justice isn't a one-time verdict—it must be woven into every act, every place you touch."

A few stray wisps of illusion quivered at the edge of the pier, but at the medallion's radiance they melted away. Breezie sent a final breeze through the yard to dispel any lingering shadows. Reddish's flames danced low and steady, no longer stoked by anger but by resolve.

"Charlestown lies quiet now," Reddish said softly, scanning the moonlit yard. "No illusions stir. We've kept bias at bay."

Blunt stepped forward to accept the medallion. He felt it resonate with the sigil already in his grasp, the two shining in harmony. "We've dispelled illusions in futuristic halls, ancient cathedrals—now even an old navy yard," he said, the medallion's silver light reflecting in his eyes. "Justice endures because we carry it within us."

Lettizia bowed her head, satisfied. "Adler's cosmos and Münster's clock are at peace again. But your journey continues. The cosmic design calls you onward, each new challenge demanding justice's unwavering light."

At her feet, a familiar swirl of runic light began to gather— yet Lettizia held up a hand. "Before you depart, take a moment," she said, gesturing to a makeshift seating area of old crates nearby. "Justice reaches beyond dispelling these illusions. Allow me to share one more story—one that shaped my own devotion to equity."

The Wizards settled on the improvised seats as Lettizia opened a weathered journal and began to read:

—

"The Two-Factions"

A great city was split into two factions: the High Terraces, where nobles dwelled, and the Low Fields, home to laborers. The nobles passed laws favoring only themselves, and the laborers seethed at the injustice.

One day, a traveling judge arrived, answering the Low Fields' desperate pleas. She convened both sides in an open forum, placing a single chair at the center. "None may speak unless seated in this chair," she declared. The crowd stirred curiously, for the seat was too small for any one person to claim entirely.

The nobles tried to sit first, but the chair tipped whenever they refused to share. The laborers, attempting in turn, found it equally unsteady alone. At last, one noble and one laborer approached together, each taking part of the seat. To their surprise, it balanced beneath them.

The judge proclaimed, "Justice requires no side to tower above the other. Only when we share the space of debate can we stand firm." Realizing this truth, the factions rewrote their laws—addressing privileged concerns and common hardships alike, forging solutions that benefited all.

Henceforth, the city's council sessions always included a balanced seat at its center to remind everyone: if one side claims it all, both sides fall.

Closing the journal, Lettizia folded her hands. "That traveling judge became legendary," she added. "Many say her balanced seat shaped the city's destiny for generations."

The Wizards sat quietly, the lesson sinking in. Each of them saw themselves in the tale's mirror: times when pride or fear had nearly tipped their own balance. Blunt rose from his crate, the new medallion of Justice glinting silver-white in his hand. "Your traveling judge's chair, Lettizia… it echoes your scale demonstration at Adler," he said thoughtfully. "Both taught that justice thrives only when every voice has space and no one stands above the other."

Lettizia's reserved demeanor finally melted into a warm smile. She had seen the proof of their understanding. "Your insight honors the judge's legacy," she replied. "Carry that lesson into every place illusions seek to breed bias."

With the fable's wisdom absorbed, the runic light behind Lettizia flared brighter, signaling that the time had come to move on.

Return to Adler & Münster

A final whirl of shimmering light rose from the Charlestown pier and swirled around them, whisking the Wizards back to the Adler Planetarium in Chicago. They arrived to find the celestial clock's orbits perfectly steady, starry gears humming with renewed clarity. As they watched, a comet-shaped hand swept gracefully across the clock's face, and a delicate chime rang out from deep within the mechanism—signs that the timepiece was thriving once more. A faint cosmic breeze whispered, "Aequitas Est Virtus," as if the very stars acknowledged their triumph.

Lettizia stood by the central dais beneath Adler's great dome, her expression serene. "Injustice sought to fracture Adler's cosmic map and Münster's ancient clock," she said. "You restored both by rejecting every false verdict of bias. Now each gear and figure moves in rightful harmony."

Blunt stepped forward under the dome's glow, holding the silver-white medallion of Justice. He took a steady breath, looking from the restored cosmic clock to his companions gathered around. "We've overcome greed's illusion before, and now injustice," he said, his voice echoing in the hushed hall. "Harder trials await, but we face them together."

As Blunt spoke, the others drew close in silent solidarity. Greenie's eyes shone with hope as she gazed up at the balanced stars overhead. Reddish rested a calm hand on the hilt of her wand, her ever-burning embers now a gentle warmth at her core. Firee twirled his staff once and let it settle, content that no traps lurked in the shadows. Breezie stood at Reddish's side, a grounding presence, while Checkered polished the lens that had shown her the importance of empathy alongside logic. In their own quiet ways, each affirmed Blunt's words: they were ready for whatever came next, their unity forged stronger by justice's light.

Lettizia approached and laid a gentle hand over the medallion in Blunt's palm. "You carry the spark of justice with you now," she said. "Beyond these two clocks, other trials await your intervention. The tapestry remains incomplete until every site is free of illusion."

At her words, the planetarium's star projector brightened, casting a ghostly image of another grand spire into the dome— a hint of some distant clock tower, perhaps Salisbury or Strasbourg, beckoning on the horizon. A faint laugh— distinctly the Dark Harlequin's mocking undertone—rippled through the air, but it faded quickly beneath Adler's cosmic hum.

"Go forth," Lettizia said, her voice kind and resolute. "You have balanced injustice here; carry that hard-won fairness forward. The Orloj's grand design still calls, and each clock you restore brings us closer to a future free from the illusions of division."

With those final words, the six Wizards stepped toward the forming portal, Harlequin cloaks fluttering in the renewed cosmic breeze. Justice had prevailed in Chicago and Münster—its silver-white token secure—and the journey

pressed on. New virtues awaited discovery, new illusions
hungered to be dispelled, and the pendulum of conscience
swung onward as they ventured forth to weave a brighter
tapestry of unity across ages and continents.

Chapter 18

Salisbury and Strasbourg Clocks – Courage's Fire

Moonlight Over the Oldest Clock

Moonlight filtered through the high Gothic arches of Salisbury Cathedral, illuminating the ancient clock dated to 1386—a marvel recognized as the world's oldest working mechanical clock. Its weathered oak gears spun in stuttering motions, as though courage itself had fled. A tense hum lingered in the nave, carrying the chill of centuries past.

Blunt, Reddish, Firee, Checkered, Breezie, and Greenie emerged from a swirl of bronze-and-sapphire light, Harlequin cloaks—emerald, crimson, sapphire—catching the moon's glow in subtle flashes. In Blunt's grasp, a runic medallion inscribed with "Fortitudo Est Virtus" throbbed faintly, reflecting the charge that had guided them here from a recent victory in Chicago. That stand of courage, though outside the Orloj's clock trials, had prepared them for the challenge ahead.

The silence felt charged with unspoken fears. Cowardice hung over Salisbury's sacred legacy, poised to stall the clock's timeless service to faith and history. Checkered, peering through her specialized lens, spotted an inscription on the base:

"Fortitudo Est Virtus; Timiditas Est Vitium"
(Courage Is Virtue; Cowardice Is Vice).

Reddish's amber eyes shimmered in the half-light as an intangible dread settled on her chest. "This place shrinks from its own power," she murmured.

Greenie gently brushed the clock's wooden frame, feeling the deep devotion of medieval craftspeople. "Salisbury has stood strong for centuries—its tower soared above storms and wars," she said. "Yet fear can erode even the strongest foundation."

Firee ran a careful hand along a large gear, noticing a subtle tremor as if the mechanism hesitated. "It's like a quiet voice urging this clock to stop," he observed grimly.

Blunt tightened his hold on the medallion. "Courage is the test," he said quietly. "We stand firm or yield to fear. The choice shapes what happens next." A faint echo, perhaps the clock's ancient tick, answered him from the gloom.

Their cloaks flared in unison, each color brightening as if the clock recognized allies in its silent fight. Morpheus

Rubicom, the one rumored to test them here, was nowhere in sight. Yet his presence felt near—like an uneasy quiet in the far corners of the nave, as if an unseen guardian of cowardice skulked in the shadows, radiating paralyzing dread.

Whispers in the Gears

Torchlight flickered against the carved stone walls as the Wizards moved deeper into the nave. Each echo of their footsteps merged with the uneven grind of the 1386 clock. Greenie sensed it exuding a silent plea for rescue: centuries of faithful service now overshadowed by a creeping timidity that stole the machine's will.

Checkered knelt near the exposed framework, the metallic tang of old gears hanging in the air. Through her lens, she saw a delicate interplay of cogs, each etched with devotional symbols—a testament to medieval craftsmanship that had defied centuries of upheaval. "This clock withstood the test of time," she noted. "Why yield to fear now?"

Firee's crimson cloak fluttered in a faint draft, and he pressed a hand to one shuddering gear. "I sense illusions or sabotage warping its tempo," he said. "If we let cowardice fester, the entire mechanism could stall."

Reddish recalled a moment from an older test when she nearly hesitated at a critical juncture because illusions of failure clouded her mind. Now, she recognized that same subtle chill trying to infect Salisbury's clock. "Not this time," she muttered, amber sparks dancing in her eyes. "We've learned to stand firm." At her words, the cold presence in the nave recoiled slightly.

From overhead, a faint glow flickered around a hidden dial—an unexpected swirl of runic shapes that cast dancing lights upon the stone floor. Breezie tilted his head. "Look there—a portal forming," he whispered.

Within that luminosity, a single French rune gleamed in the swirling sapphire vortex, hinting at a cathedral beyond England's borders. Blunt tightened his grip on the "Fortitudo Est Virtus" medallion. "This must be the path to Strasbourg," he surmised. "The next test of courage awaits in that French city."

An uneasy tremor coursed through the clock's gears, as though the same hidden foe opposed their discovering this route. The runes shimmered, mingling with echoes of centuries-old chanting. Cowardice threatened to derail Salisbury's legacy, and a parallel fear whispered in the flicker of that French rune—foretelling what might lurk in Strasbourg.

With a resolute nod, Blunt turned to his friends. "We'll stabilize Salisbury first. Then we follow that portal to

Strasbourg Cathedral, where another clock needs courage's spark."

Behind them, the clock emitted a low, uneven groan. The challenge had begun, and each Wizard felt the faint tang of anxiety in the air. If they failed here, the ancient timekeeper might forever succumb to dread.

A sudden rush of cold air swept through the nave, and the clock's hands faltered as if an invisible weight pressed upon them. From the shadows above came a sibilant whisper: "Give up... let it fall silent..." The words slithered into their minds, igniting flickers of doubt. Checkered's eyes narrowed behind her lens. "Morpheus," she hissed, recognizing the cunning undertone of the voice.

Blunt stepped forward and raised the medallion, its runes glinting. "We will not yield," he declared, the phrase "Fortitudo Est Virtus" glowing brighter against the trembling gloom. The inscription on the clock's base responded in kind, letters illuminating as courage flowed from the Wizards into the mechanism.

At once, Reddish swept her arm toward the largest gear, sending a gentle spray of ember-light to chase away the creeping frost forming on its iron teeth. Firee pressed both palms to the clock's frame and murmured an incantation, channeling warmth—the gear that had nearly frozen groaned and inched back into motion. Breezie summoned a focused gust that whooshed through the clock's inner workings, scattering a cluster of illusory cobwebs that had tangled around the escapement. Greenie laid a calming hand on the oak frame, pouring steady resolve into the timbers as if soothing a panicked creature.

A contorted shadow—like a clawed hand of darkness—peeled away from the pendulum and writhed in protest. Checkered spotted it through her lens and swiftly signaled. With a sharp nod from Blunt, Firee unleashed a ribbon of flame. The phantom recoiled with a voiceless shriek and dissipated into motes of black mist.

Gradually, the clock's tick began to strengthen, a steady tick-tock supplanting the erratic stutter. The chill in the air receded. For an instant, high in the rafters, a cloaked silhouette flickered into view. Reddish caught the gleam of two watchful eyes. But as soon as she blinked, the presence was gone, leaving behind only the fading echo of a low, mirthless chuckle.

Salisbury's trial of courage was won. The 1386 clock now beat with a restored rhythm, each swing of its pendulum more confident than the last. Overhead, the portal's glow flared brighter, fully unfurled in sapphire luminescence—a doorway beckoning them onward.

Blunt exchanged determined looks with the others. "Salisbury stands safe," he affirmed quietly. Holding the medallion aloft, he stepped beneath the swirling runes of the portal. One by one, the six Wizards moved with him, resolve in their stride, and together they vanished into the sapphire light.

Strasbourg: Courage Stalls at Noon

A swirl of radiant magic enveloped them, and in a heartbeat, they stood beneath the soaring vaults of Strasbourg Cathedral. Candlelit shadows danced on imposing columns, the air heavy with melted wax and ancient dust, revealing the renowned 1842 Astronomical Clock in all its ornate glory. Yet something was off: the heavenly cherubs and planetary knights, meant to illustrate cosmic harmony, jerked in fits and starts, as though gripped by unseen terror.

Blunt clenched the medallion. "Cowardice is poisoning this sacred legacy—it's freezing the flow of time and faith," he said quietly. "We've got to reignite its fire."

Greenie caught the stillness among the flickering tapers. "The cathedral's history is rich—these walls stood firm through revolutions and wars," she murmured. "Fear shouldn't take root here, of all places."

Firee pressed forward, scanning for illusions with his sharpened senses. He recalled a moment of near defeat once, when false visions almost caused him to freeze. That memory fueled him now. "We'll break any enchantments that strangle the gears," he promised.

Meanwhile, Breezie approached a twisted cherub figure. Its carved expression, meant to be joyful, was now contorted in trembling dread. "It looks as if something spooked them mid-celebration," he observed, voice tinged with concern.

Checkered studied an inscription near the base of the clock face:

"Fortitudo Est Virtus; Timiditas Est Vitium."

Courage is virtue; cowardice is vice.

She brushed a hand over the text. "This clock symbolizes bold innovation," she noted. "Strasbourg's heritage was meant to inspire awe, not timidity."

Their cloaks flared in unison, each Wizard steeling for confrontation. The hush shifted wood and metal creaked. From behind the clock's massive dial, ephemeral shapes flitted: fear-fed apparitions, ready to turn the cathedral's proud legacy into a cautionary tale. This was fear on full display—unlike the subtle dread at Salisbury, here the phantoms openly sowed chaos.

Blunt raised the medallion, voice resolute. "Cowardice can't stand against unity. Let's spark courage for Strasbourg's sake—and for Salisbury's clock, too."

A tense beat followed before the apparitions struck. From the dial lunged Strasbourg's fear guardian—a nightmarish specter exuding overwhelming panic. The cathedral's great clock shuddered under the assault—its gears grinding to a halt at the cusp of noon, as if time itself refused to advance. Greenie staggered back as a wave of cold panic washed over them. But Firee reacted instantly, unleashing a ribbon of flame that tore through the phantom's form, while Breezie summoned a sharp gust that sent the remaining wraiths skittering backward. Still, the heavy clock hands remained frozen in place, quivering under the weight of the lingering terror.

The planetary dial shuddered—and held. Checkered drew a breath and tilted the medallion's light into the clock's shadowed recess. For a heartbeat, nothing. Then the gilt knight at the hour gate lowered his trembling sword and stepped forward, the cherub above him releasing a steady belltone that cut clean through the hush. The procession of figures resumed, not loud but unwavering. Courage, at last, was moving again.

The Athenaeum Trial

No sooner had they quelled the immediate threat in Strasbourg than a tug of magic pulled them back to Boston. This time, they emerged in the quiet grandeur of the Boston Athenaeum, an institution renowned for its historic collections. The air smelled of leather bindings and old parchment. Moonbeams fell through tall windows, illuminating rows of ancient tomes.

But something churned the stillness: illusions whispered among the shelves, shimmering across the pages and drifting like ghostly script overhead. Morpheus Rubicom was said to roam these halls tonight, testing whether they'd cower before hidden knowledge or face it bravely.

Firee sensed a potential trap: some illusions manifested as swirling glyphs that threatened to distract the group or bury them in half-truths. "Watch out," he cautioned. "These deceptions feed on confusion—promising safe ignorance but sowing deeper dread."

Breezie noticed Greenie's shoulders tense, her empathy picking up on the unsettled atmosphere. Gently, he touched her arm. "Stay calm," he whispered. "We've already seen illusions try to separate us. Courage means facing them together."

A fleeting shadowy laugh echoed between the shelves, chilling the lamplit corners. Reddish tightened her fists, recalling phantasms in an earlier library that once made her question her own fire. "We stand, not flee," she muttered, turning a corner in pursuit.

They glimpsed Morpheus's cloak vanishing behind a massive reading desk. Ink-stained manuscripts rippled with illusions. Blunt gripped the runic medallion inscribed with "Fortitudo Est Virtus." "Morpheus is testing our nerve," he said. "We can't falter, because the path to sustaining courage crosses these uncharted stacks."

Checkered's lens caught glimpses of ghostly inscriptions swirling overhead—reflections of readers' doubts or hidden knowledge that once intimidated them. "Facing the unknown is half the battle," she remarked, weaving among the shelves.

A cluster of spectral figures rose in front of them, shaped like robed scholars urging retreat, their hollow voices hissing, "It's safer not to learn… safer to turn away…" Firee's flames flickered, Breezie readied a gentle breeze, Reddish stoked her embers, Greenie summoned empathy to reassure any onlookers, and Blunt steadied the ward. Together, they advanced.

Rounding the final row of towering bookcases, the Wizards spotted Morpheus Rubicom standing under a stained-glass skylight. Moonlight cast dancing patterns across his trinket-laden cloak—a patchwork of small relics and charms that clinked in a restless rhythm. In his grasp, he clutched a runic scroll defiantly, eyes flickering with an odd mixture of challenge and vulnerability.

"Cowardice lurks in every unwritten page," Morpheus said, voice low. "Will you flinch from knowledge that threatens comfort? Or will you seize it?"

Reddish's embers flared. She remembered a time she once acted rashly out of fear she'd fail if she hesitated. Now she steadied herself. "We've faced illusions fed by greed and fear," she replied. "We won't let ignorance overshadow what we can learn."

Greenie felt a tremor in the air, as though unseen phantoms in the stacks behind them were trying to coax her into fleeing. Breezie noticed her stiffen and whispered a reassuring note: "Courage isn't never feeling fear—it's refusing to yield to it." She exhaled, remembering how similar illusions had once cornered her in a distant city and forced her to stand or succumb.

Firee's gaze locked on a swirl of illusions creeping along the floor. He recalled how a single moment of indecision once nearly cost them a crucial victory. Determined, he let a measured flame burn the illusions away. "If knowledge reveals new threats," he said quietly, "we face them, not hide."

Morpheus's posture relaxed a fraction, the runic scroll glinting in his hand. "Your words ring true. Courage is more than bravado—it's acknowledging fear, then pressing on." His trinkets clinked again, each seeming to echo some past defiance.

Checkered thought of a logical puzzle she once failed because she was too afraid to trust her intuition. "Morpheus, we stand ready," she declared, lens bright in the dim library. "We'll open every page, no matter how daunting."

A swirl of illusions shaped into timorous silhouettes behind Morpheus. He glanced at them, then back at the Wizards. "So be it," he said. "Show me that your resolve doesn't quiver in the dark."

Morpheus stepped to a wide oak table, setting the runic scroll at its center. "Before we finalize this lesson," he murmured, "hear a fable of courage—one I found scrawled in a battered journal centuries ago."

"The Stormbound Guardian"

A coastal city built its timekeeping tower on a high bluff, reliant on a single clock to warn sailors of the tides. One fateful year, a fierce tempest loomed—thunder roiled, lightning split the horizon, and monstrous waves surged. In panic, most fled inland, abandoning the clock.

Yet a solitary guardian remained. Despite the howling winds and lashing rain, she refused to leave her post, knowing that if the clock failed, ships at sea would have no signal of safe harbor. Fear clawed at her mind, urging her to retreat to shelter, but she steadied her trembling hands.

Hour by hour, she reinforced the tower's beams, shielding the clock's mechanism from raging waters. Lightning scorched the sky, debris hammered the walls, yet she persevered. When dawn broke, battered and soaked, she rang the bell—alerting ships to return home. The city realized her courage saved hundreds of lives. Ever after, the townspeople told of the guardian who stood unyielding, reminding all that real bravery isn't the absence of terror, but the triumph of resolve over surrender.

A hush followed the reading. The Wizards exchanged thoughtful glances, each resonating with the fable in unique ways.

Blunt let out a contemplative breath. "That guardian risked everything to keep the clock running. It mirrors how we stand our ground—even when illusions shriek at us to retreat."

Reddish's embers glowed. "I can relate—once, I almost hesitated at a critical moment. The guardian's unwavering stance reminds me we have no time for second-guessing when others rely on us."

Checkered nodded, lens softly reflecting the lamplight. "Her logic might've said run, but she balanced it with courage. Like us, she refused to let illusions of safety overshadow real responsibility."

Breezie exhaled calmly. "And in the morning, she wasn't just heroic—she was a beacon. We can be that beacon in every place illusions darken."

Morpheus rested a hand on the runic scroll. "You see, the city thrived because one person didn't cower. Courage held them together. Are you ready to stand as that guardian, no matter the cost?"

In unison, they gave a resolute nod. The lingering illusions wavered under the combined force of their agreement.

Cipher & Role of the Next Clock

With the fables fresh in their minds, Morpheus gestured to the runic scroll on the table. "It's not just a story," he said. "This scroll contains ciphered coordinates, linking the Salisbury and Strasbourg clocks to another site—Greenwich and beyond."

Blunt placed a hand on the scroll. "We've been following these clock pairs. Each location had illusions warping a fundamental virtue—generosity, justice, and now courage." He recalled how each victory opened the path to the next.

Firee leaned closer, scanning the scroll's swirling glyphs. "The Orloj's design weaves each clock into a single tapestry. If we decode this, we'll know where perseverance stands."

Checkered agreed, her finger tracing a line of text revealed under her lens. "Our friend with an inventive mind once hinted that Greenwich's tidal flows were vital to the Orloj's final steps. This cipher might confirm that."

Reddish gazed at the last wisps of illusion dissipating from the shelves. "So the message is simple," she said. "Master courage here, carry the lesson to the next challenge."

Morpheus tapped the parchment gently, a subtle restlessness in his movements. "Greenwich and, possibly, Ulm in Germany—both symbolic sites for perseverance. Cowardice would unravel the entire sequence, but your stand in Salisbury and Strasbourg proves you won't let fear decide."

Breezie inhaled, catching the faint must of old tomes. "So do we decode it now, or does it need the final synergy from the clocks we just rescued?"

With a faint grin, Morpheus shrugged. "You'll see. Courage forging onward is half the key." He turned to Blunt, giving a slight nod. "Open the path as you did for the other clocks. Show me that no storm can break your circle."

Deciphering the Scroll: Courage in Unison

They spread the scroll across a desk, lamplight washing over lines of archaic script. Glancing from the runic medallion to the text, Blunt recognized repeating phrases that matched inscriptions in Salisbury Cathedral.

Checkered ran a fingertip along the parchment, her lens revealing hidden connotations. "Some glyphs reference fortitude, others speak of fear's illusions. If we layer them, we might see the final message."

Firee used a subtle flame to warm parts of the parchment, exposing faint ink patterns. "Like an invisible code," he noted. "Knowledge usually demands we step beyond comfort."

Greenie picked up a quill, lightly tracing empathic energy into the symbols. "Courage doesn't always roar," she quoted softly. "But it breaks illusions' hold all the same."

Breezie provided a gentle breeze to lift the edges of the scroll so they could examine each portion. Reddish steadied the corners with a tiny burst of embers, ensuring no stray flame would consume it.

Gradually, an underlying diagram emerged—a stylized set of tides referencing Greenwich's prime meridian, overlaid with a vaulted structure that could only be Ulm Cathedral's famed spire. The words "Perseverantia Est Virtus" shimmered faintly, bridging both sites.

Blunt tapped the final sigil. "That's it. Greenwich for perseverance, and another clock across the sea in Ulm. We anchor one to unlock the other—just as we did here."

Morpheus's restless eyes softened. "Good," he rasped. "You decode not just words, but the spirit behind them. Courage stands."

Confrontation of Illusions: Final Test in the Athenaeum

A sudden gust of frigid air swept through the Boston Athenaeum. The illusions that had lurked among the shelves returned in a last, desperate surge. Silhouetted forms rose from behind reading desks, each shaped by half-seen anxieties— threads of doubt that could unravel the group if they yielded.

"You've done well so far," Morpheus intoned, stepping back. "But illusions dig in hardest when cornered. Show me if your courage truly holds."

Reddish felt a swirl of gloom press at her chest, whispering old insecurities about acting too hastily and failing. She clenched her fists, remembering how the stormbound guardian never surrendered to her fear. "Not now," she snapped, letting embers burn the doubt away.

Greenie staggered as waves of anxiety drifted toward her— threatening to overwhelm her empathetic heart. Breezie noticed her strain and conjured a soothing breeze to envelop her in calm. Greenie inhaled deeply, summoning the memory of how a single beacon flame had endured a long night's gale. If one light could defy the darkness, she told herself, so could their united courage. "I won't collapse into fear," she vowed.

Checkered intercepted illusions that tried to warp logic into panic. "Facts remain facts," she declared, lens flaring. "I refuse to let lies twist them into dread."

Firee stepped forward, recalling a near-disaster in an old conflict where indecision almost cost them victory. He projected steady flames that incinerated illusions creeping across the floor. "I learned from that moment," he said quietly. "Hesitation yields ground to fear—but not here."

Blunt raised the medallion overhead, its runes shining. "Courage is not about never trembling," he said firmly. "It's about standing in spite of it."

One by one, the cornered illusions cracked, disintegrating into wisps of faint light. Quiet returned—the library once again a safe haven of knowledge rather than a maze of intimidation.

Morpheus's Approval & Transfer of the Gear

Morpheus exhaled, tension easing from his frame. The final barrage of illusions had tested their collective resolve, yet they stood unbroken. With slow steps, he approached Blunt and retrieved a small gear from within his cloak—a piece etched with bold runes. Its surface gleamed as though forged from starlight.

"This gear embodies the essence of Perseverantia Est Virtus," he explained. "Carrying it marks your triumph over cowardice, linking Salisbury and Strasbourg to the next stage."

Blunt accepted the gear, feeling an electric hum in his palm. "Your illusions tried to push us into hiding," he said softly. "But we faced them."

Morpheus's restless eyes flicked over each Wizard—Reddish with steady embers, Greenie radiating calm empathy, Checkered's lens bright, Firee's flame unwavering, Breezie's breeze gently stirring the air. "You've proven that courage can banish the impulse to flee or cower," he said, his voice rasping with sincere approval. "In ancient times, timidity often destroyed great works. Let it not destroy these clocks."

A stillness settled as the last spectral remnants dispersed, leaving only the comforting smell of parchment and the warm radiance of lamplight. The final shade of fear seemed to recede from Morpheus's expression. "Let no storm push you from your watch," he murmured, recalling the guardian's tale.

In that moment, the synergy among the Wizards felt absolute. Another virtue had been claimed from illusion's grasp.

Courage Rings the Hours

Having sealed their success in Boston, they felt the tether pull them back to Salisbury Cathedral. A familiar swirl of light enveloped them, and once more they stood in the silent majesty of the 1386 clock's domain. The gears turned with renewed steadiness—faint yet unmistakable.

Morpheus appeared beside them, the restless flicker in his eyes partly calmed. He set a hand on the old oak frame. "Salisbury's clock now breathes courage. The silence of fear is broken; no illusions remain to paralyze this ancient marvel."

Checkered smiled, observing how the mechanism no longer rattled with timid vibrations. "A place that survived centuries of storms shouldn't be undone by cowardice," she said. "We've restored its rightful spirit."

From behind the centuries-old dial, a faint French rune glowed again, reaffirming the portal to Strasbourg. A final wave of reassurance swept through the cathedral, as if acknowledging the group's victory.

Greenie placed a gentle touch on the clock's wooden housing. "We stand as that guardian in the fable, ensuring the clock's survival so others may keep time and faith."

Breezie tilted his head at Morpheus. "And Strasbourg's clock stands aligned too. You guided us there. Is our part done?"

Morpheus exhaled, a quiet acceptance in his nod. "For now, yes. Another pair of clocks awaits. The path leads to Greenwich, where perseverance will be tested. Carry forth the gear—and may your courage remain unbroken."

Reddish glanced at Blunt, who still held the shimmering gear. "We've seen illusions undone before. Let's keep the flame alive for whatever challenge Greenwich holds."

The Guardian Flame

A gentle ray of moonlight settled across the cathedral floor as Morpheus stepped away from the clock, resting his cloak against a pillar. For a moment, his features—those weary, puffy eyes—reflected a deeper gratitude than words could convey.

"You never truly conquer fear once and for all," he observed softly. "It resurfaces in new forms—illusions, storms, unsettled hearts. But each victory steels you for the next."

Blunt inclined his head, the gear in hand humming faintly, bridging time and place. "We'll remember that. Courage is a choice renewed at every test. We can't let illusions catch us off guard."

Reddish's embers flickered, recollecting her own near missteps. She had once burned with impulsive fire, but ironically, fear had also held her back on other occasions. "I won't forget the guardian's watch," she said, voice low. "Nor how Morpheus forced us to face illusions in Boston's library."

Firee stood by the clock's base, scanning one last time for any remnants of sabotage. "All seems clear," he concluded. "No illusions cling to these gears now."

Greenie gently closed her eyes, sensing the cathedral's pulse. "Salisbury can once again mark the hours without trembling. That's all we needed to ensure."

Morpheus gave a faint smile, pressing a small silver trinket into Reddish's hand—perhaps a personal token to remind them of the test they passed. "Farewell. Let your boldness guide the next challenge."

Meridian's Call

An ambient hum filled the nave, blending the clock's steady tick with a subtle magical resonance. In Blunt's hand, the runic gear etched with "Perseverantia Est Virtus" glowed softly, as if pointing the way toward Greenwich's prime meridian. The Wizards exchanged determined glances, steeling themselves for the trial of perseverance that lay ahead.

Far away, beneath the lofty vaults of Strasbourg Cathedral, its astronomical clock now ticked in peace, free of cowardice at last. Yet high among the rafters, a patchwork shadow flickered and vanished—a silent hint that the Dark Harlequin's influence had not fully departed.

Blunt drew a steady breath and met his friends' eyes. "Courage holds," he affirmed quietly.

Chapter 19

Greenwich and Messina Clocks – Perseverance's Triumph

Prime Meridian, Fading Pulse

Even as the echoes of Salisbury's triumph faded, an ambient hum began to rise around them, carrying the strength of their courage into the next trial. The swirling bronze-and-sapphire light of the portal dissipated, revealing the Greenwich Observatory under a calm moonlit sky. The Courage gear pulsed east-west, bending time itself to the Prime Meridian. Moonlight bathed the Royal Observatory in Greenwich. Perched above the tidal Thames, the historic 1852 Shepherd Gate Clock—a fixture of global timekeeping—gleamed softly. Yet its brass gears ground in protest, as though a bleak hush threatened to stop time itself. Blunt, Reddish, Firee, Checkered, Breezie, and Greenie stepped out together, their Harlequin cloaks flickering with subdued luminescence.

Clutched in Blunt's hand was a runic gear etched with "Perseverantia Est Virtus"—a guiding artifact from their triumph over fear in a distant cathedral. Now they faced a new ordeal: the test of perseverance against despair. Checkered surveyed the clock's base, where an inscription read:

"Perseverantia Est Virtus; Desperatio Est Vitium."

(Perseverance Is Virtue; Despair Is Vice).

A chill undercut the air, making each breath feel oddly heavy. Reddish's amber eyes glimmered as she sensed an unnerving hum coursing through the mechanism—like a lament that sapped the will to continue. She clenched her fists, recalling the fortitude they had mustered before. "It's like this clock is giving up," she muttered, embers dancing in her eyes.

Greenie stepped forward, laying a gentle hand on the clock's wooden frame. "This place anchors global time," she said softly. "If despair takes root here, it undermines the world's heartbeat." Firee ran a careful finger along a large brass cog. "We overcame illusions of fear once," he pointed out. "Now we must face illusions shaped by hopelessness."

From within the observatory's shadows, a faint silhouette stirred—Lazarus Zeetrikus, reputed to be the final mentor of perseverance. His presence was stern, an undercurrent of relentless will in his posture. Blunt tightened his grip on the runic gear, his expression steeled. "Let's see if we can spark this clock's resilience," he whispered.

The quiet gloom pressed in on them like an invisible weight. In earlier struggles, illusions had thrived on fear or injustice.

Now the threat was deeper—an urge to abandon hope altogether. The group exchanged solemn looks; each resolved not to back down. A new test beckoned, and they would face it as one, no matter how the darkness pressed in.

Gate of the Meridian Star

Inside the observatory chamber, flickers of lamplight revealed the Shepherd Gate Clock's elaborate brass frame. Shadows danced on the stone floor, and a dull hum vibrated through the air—a menacing pulse chipping away at fortitude. Breezie's calm voice broke the uneasy silence. "We have to see where this despair is coming from. This mechanism was known for unwavering precision."

Checkered knelt to examine the slowing gears. Each cog bore the hallmark of 19th-century craftsmanship, an era that codified global time standards. Yet the apparatus faltered, as though the intangible weight of hopelessness had lodged in its heart. Her fingers trailed along one gear; something felt off. A glint of engraving caught her eye. "Desperatio Est Virtus"— the twisted script read. She felt a chill. "That's not right," she whispered. "Despair is vice, not virtue. This gear is a lie."

Realizing the Harlequin had sabotaged the clock, the Wizards sprang into action. Firee and Reddish steadied the clock's frame while Blunt and Checkered pried at the false gear. With a metallic screech it came free, falling to the floor.

The clock shuddered as if coughing, then settled into motion. For a heartbeat nothing happened. Then, very slowly, the hands began to turn again, one by one. The hope that had been strangled began to return. Reddish's embers flared warmly. "Sabotage by the Harlequin," she said grimly. Blunt offered a hand to steady the mechanism. Greenie closed her eyes and extended empathy into the clock's brass; the dark hum faded away.

Just then, a faint portal shimmered beside the clock's central axle. The swirling energy carried threads of arcane bronze and sapphire, but one detail stood out: an italian rune glowed in the vortex. Blunt narrowed his eyes. "That must be our route to Messina," he said. He ran a hand over the runic gear in his grip. "It brought us from the old cathedral that taught us courage. Now it urges us onward."

Firee noticed the remnants of gloom intensify as soon as they recognized the portal. "Whatever's feeding this despair must sense we're about to disrupt it," he said, flame sparking in his palm.

A resonant voice cut through the hush—a stern timbre of unshakable resolve. Zeetrikus stepped into view, his bent hat slanted low yet dignity unbowed. "Persevere," he commanded. "Follow the portal, or watch this place succumb to oblivion."

With a measured exhale, Blunt led the others to the shimmering gateway. The gear in his hand pulsed in rhythm with the clock's revived beat. "Let's see if we can save Greenwich," he said. "But if Messina also calls, we won't shirk that duty." Nods rippled through the group. Breezie took one last look at the Shepherd Gate Clock. Greenie placed her hand once more on its face; the second hand made a reassuring tick. "Greenwich's time is safe now," she said softly.

The six companions stepped into the portal's sapphire light. The Italian rune in the vortex glowed brighter, beckoning them toward the next battle against creeping despair.

Gate of the Sicilian Star

A brassy peal rolled over the harbor as they stepped from the portal into Messina's cathedral square. The Duomo's clock tower loomed against a violet sky, its astronomical dial dimmed by a sapping hush. Above, the great tower-show—lion, rooster, apostles—should have promised noon's spectacle; instead, a pall of finality hung in the mechanism, as if Despair itself had lodged in the works and was teaching the city to give up.

The clock's dial trembled as though on the brink of collapse. A bitter hum pervaded the air, thick with the sense of giving up. Firee's eyes darted around—he recalled a time in an old conflict when his flame nearly guttered out because he doubted himself. That memory stung, fueling his resolve to act now.

Blunt stepped forward, gripping the runic gear inscribed with "Perseverantia Est Virtus." The obligation to rescue another clock burned in him. "We can't let hopelessness overwhelm this place," he said, voice resolute. "Messina's clock has endured centuries. We'll help it endure centuries more."

Reddish sparked faint embers around her fists and scanned the ancient carvings. She thought of how she once faced illusions that preyed on her rash instincts—over time she had tempered that fire without losing her passion. "Despair wants us to bow out," she muttered. "But we've learned to stand firm."

Greenie let her empathic senses flow over the trembling tower automata and orbs. She felt fear lurking—a creeping notion that everything would crumble, making any effort pointless. "We overcame illusions that fed on fear," she recalled softly. "Now we face illusions telling us it's not worth trying at all."

A sudden shriek split the air from the clock's center. The carved seraph figures, animated by twisted magic, unleashed starry tempests that crashed into the Cathedral of Messina's clock tower. Firee tensed—his earlier brush with doubt echoed in his mind—but he forced his flame to intensify. "Not this time," he vowed, conjuring a shield of fire that deflected a barrage of swirling lights.

Breezie summoned a steady gale. The wind spun around Reddish's embers, keeping them blazing without harming the hallowed walls. Checkered's lens glowed as she recognized the pattern in the madness. "They're conjuring illusions of finality," she said. "Like everything's already lost, so why keep fighting?"

Blunt raised a water ward, forging a shimmering barrier around the group. "Messina's clock once symbolized unwavering faith," he said. "It won't break to despair—not if we stand with it." At his nod, each Wizard took a firm stance, bracing to quell the onslaught. The hum of hopelessness pressed in, but they'd seen illusions crumble before. Firee let his flame burn bright, lighting the darkness, and so the battle for Messina's clock began in earnest.

At the quarter, the lion's jaw trembled and the rooster's crest twitched—but the rhythm faltered. From the astronomical face a squall of false endings spilled outward: stutters, reversals, the taunt of "too late." Across the zodiac and calendar trains, a chill spread as if time itself were tiring. Checkered's lens caught faint runes around a seized pinion—

there, buried in the train, a lying gear engraved "Desperatio Est Virtus" throttled the advance.

When the Tower automata Waver

The swirling illusions collided with the Wizards in rapid succession, star-laced energies lashing out from the animated tower automata and luminous orbs. The entire clock tower seemed to seethe under a storm of defeat trying to weigh them all down. A crack of phantom thunder boomed overhead, rattling the ancient vaults. Reddish swept a wave of embers through a crossfire of distorted light, forging a path toward the clock's heart.

Greenie's empathic vines spiraled through the gloom, seeking to calm each frenzied illusion that fueled tower automata's barrage. She found in every phantom a kernel of sorrow, as if someone—something—had convinced itself there was no point in continuing. "We've seen illusions twist justice and courage," she said. "But despair… it's more silent, more absolute."

Checkered focused on the gilded clockface with her lens, hunting for runic inscriptions to counter the enchantment. "There," she called, spotting faint sigils carved near the astronomical dial and calendar train. "We can reset the clock's alignment by illuminating these symbols."

Blunt turned to Firee. "We'll hold back these illusions while you finish the enchantment," he said. Firee hesitated only a moment—old doubt flickering like a dying ember—before recalling a distant battle where unity had saved them. He forced the doubt away and unleashed a precise column of flame that cut through the swirling mirage around the sigils.

Breezie conjured another gust, pushing back a new wave of starry tendrils. He anchored Reddish's embers so they burned fiercely, illuminating Checkered's lenswork. He would not let this darkness splinter them.

Gradually, the illusions weakened. Greenie locked onto each seething shape and unraveled it with her empathy. Checkered's lens flared brighter as she completed the final strokes on the astronomical dial and calendar train. A surge of hope broke through the gloom—no longer the moan of despair, but the rumble of a will reclaimed.

The tower automata and orbs froze mid-attack, uncertainty flickering on their carved faces. With a final concerted push, the Wizards banished the illusions entirely. A hush fell, leaving only the faint ticking of a freed clock, its gears alive once more. Firee exhaled, tension melting from his shoulders. For a moment he allowed himself a relieved grin—despite the paralysis that had threatened him, he had persevered. And so had Messina's clock.

At that instant, the clock's new heartbeat grew strong. One of the great bells above stirred to life and tolled a deep, resonant note that rolled through the clock tower. In the sleeping city beyond, a few lights blinked on as the sudden peal cut through the darkness, awakening those who had known only silence.

An elderly abbot emerged from a side chapel, drawn by the miraculous renewal. Lazarus Zeetrikus stepped forward too, his eyes reflecting the gentle glow of the restored dial. He found a gap where a gear had been shattered by despair and, taking the runic gear from Blunt, pressed it into the empty space. A spark of magic flared at his fingertips, fusing the new piece into harmony with the ancient brass works.

As the final gear clicked into place, the clock shuddered and the bell pealed once more in triumph. The abbot crossed himself reverently. Placing a trembling hand on the newly forged gear, he whispered, "Perseverantia Est Virtus," consecrating the mechanism with the old credo. A warm golden light suffused the gear, which then released itself from the clock's embrace and floated gently back into Blunt's palm. In that moment, the astronomer's craft and the abbot's faith had united to rekindle the clock's enduring heartbeat.

From high above, another bell tolled long and true. The fresh sound echoed through the Cathedral, affirming that hope had won.

The calendar clicked forward; the astral hands flowed in steady arcs. Above, the tower-show at last found its voice—no roar of triumph, only the confident cadence of a clock that refuses to quit.

A familiar sapphire glow coalesced at the center of the clock tower, forming a portal home. The Wizards gathered their hard-won tokens—the runic gear now humming with renewed power, and a small star-shaped relic dislodged from the zodiac dial. Greenie held the star up to her face and, in its shifting light, thought she saw something remarkable: the jagged silhouette of Boston's Custom House Tower on the horizon, winking like a distant promise. In that vision, home and destiny converged.

With grateful nods to the abbot, Zeetrikus and the six companions stepped into the portal's light and vanished, leaving Messina in peace once more.

Back to Boston: The Stacks Stir

A swirl of arcane light carried them from Messina back to Boston in a single breath. The cold stone air of the church yielded to the warm glow of lamplight and the faint must of old pages as they found themselves standing in the hushed grandeur of the Boston Public Library's historic reading room. High arches, polished marble floors, and shelves lined with age-old volumes lent the atmosphere both solemnity and quiet hope.

Flickering lamps cast elongated shadows across the stacks. Nearby, Lazarus Zeetrikus moved between desks piled with books, his bent hat etched with faint runic scars that hinted at past endurance. The silence felt heavy with despair-laced illusions, as though the library's knowledge threatened to drown in hopelessness.

Greenie inhaled, remembering illusions that once toyed with her empathy in a similar labyrinth of books. "Despair might feed on the notion that learning or effort is pointless," she whispered, scanning the dusty volumes. Reddish nodded, recalling a time she had charged ahead too impulsively and nearly lost a vital clue. Now she recognized the need for steady perseverance in pursuit of knowledge.

They glimpsed a flicker at the far end—a swirl of shadowed shapes drifting among the shelves. Breezie tensed, a pang reminding him of times he had felt isolated from the group. But he steeled himself and sent a gentle wind to scatter the lingering darkness. They had overcome illusions that tried to break their resolve before, and he silently vowed they would not falter now.

Firee cupped a guarded flame in his hand, mindful of the library's flammable pages. The uncertainty he had conquered in Messina now kindled deeper resolve. Illusions of despair might whisper that nothing mattered, but he was determined to prove the opposite—their perseverance would burn away that lie.

Checkered raised her lens and spotted subtle runic markings along the shelves. "Zeetrikus is definitely testing us," she murmured. "He's left a trail, so we have to follow it."

Blunt silently gripped the runic gear stamped "Perseverantia Est Virtus." The memory of Greenwich's battered clock urged him on. They had revived a mechanism that anchored global time, and Messina's ailing clock had likewise been freed. Giving in now would undercut everything they had fought to protect.

A subdued but ominous laugh, reminiscent of the Dark Harlequin's meddling, echoed through the aisles. The gloom thickened, illusions swirling among the dusty tomes. Reddish's embers glowed gently, ready to ward off any attempt to bury them in hopelessness. Step by step, they pressed deeper into the reading room, determined not to let despair overshadow knowledge or sabotage their final mission.

The illusions that once hovered in the library corners resurged, perhaps seeking a final stand. But the Wizards moved with purpose. Breezie's calm wind parted the swirling gloom near the exit, and Checkered's lens banished any ghostly whispers of "Why bother?"

Greenie guided anxious onlookers—late-night researchers who had glimpsed the supernatural. She reassured them, her empathic aura spreading hope. "Your pursuit of knowledge won't be stifled by illusions," she promised. Reddish stood nearby, her embers pulsing gently, ensuring no phantom threat encroached from behind the shelves.

Firee weaved between clusters of specters seeking to rekindle old fears. His flame, now brimming with confidence from the Messina battle, made short work of them. "We won't bow to despair," he murmured, each word fueling his defiant spark.

Zeetrikus lingered near a marble pillar, arms folded, observing their efficiency. After a moment he gave a single nod. "This location is secure," he pronounced. "The illusions can't rally here any longer."

With that, Zeetrikus gestured toward the library's ornate doors. "You've learned the watchman's lesson: do not pause while the storm still rages," he said. "Now take that star and see this through."

With minimal fuss, the Wizards cleared the last illusions from the reading room. A hush returned, warm with relief rather than stifled by gloom. As they left, Blunt caught a flicker at the edge of his vision—a fleeting shadow, perhaps a Harlequin echo, slithering out of sight. A final reminder that the ultimate battle lay just ahead, where perseverance alone might not be enough. They would need unity.

What We Carry Forward

As they walked under the late-night sky toward their next trial, each Wizard reflected quietly on lessons learned. Reddish found herself recalling a reckless moment from her past—charging into a maze of illusions, trying to extinguish them by sheer force. She had nearly isolated herself from the group and almost doomed an entire mission. "I see now how perseverance means more than charging ahead blindly," she said softly. "It's pressing on wisely, letting your allies support you."

Breezie nodded. "I used to worry I'd fade into the background," he admitted. "That fear once made me question my place. But I see how each of us stands for something. My winds calm the tempest, your embers ignite hope. We all persevere together."

Greenie placed a reassuring hand on Breezie's shoulder. "We overcame illusions that tried to wedge us apart," she reminded him. "We're stronger for it."

Firee exhaled a gentle flame, mindful of the city street ahead. "And we'll need all of that solidarity in what's to come," he said. "Even if despair or a stronger threat tries to sever our unity."

Zeetrikus, strolling just ahead with his bent hat, looked back over his shoulder. "You see? Perseverance isn't a solo act. It thrives in a group that refuses to let any member falter."

Blunt chimed in, recalling the battered clocks they had rescued. "We've endured illusions because we trust each other," he said. "No single spark or gust stands alone."

The six walked on through the quiet square, prepared to face whatever came. At their backs, Salisbury's ancient clock chimed softly into the night, as if blessing their departure. Across the water, Strasbourg's great clock continued its rhythmic procession—unburdened by fear now. No illusions reigned there anymore; only the quiet triumph of courage. A patchwork shadow flitted across the cathedral's tall dome and vanished, hinting that the Dark Harlequin still lurked unseen.

Thus ended their confrontation with cowardice, bridging two venerable clocks across England and France. The Wizards' next horizon lay beyond a swirling sea of trials. But they carried a flame unquenchable, akin to the guardian's light in the fiercest storm. Courage had been proven—now perseverance must be claimed.

Poems for the Long Night

The autumn night air cooled their flushed faces as the six gathered in a small, lamplit square. Zeetrikus unrolled a tattered scroll with reverent care. In a steady voice, he began to narrate one last tale, and even the darkness around them seemed to pause and listen.

"The Windswept Beacon"

In a rugged coastal region, a colossal beacon tower once guided ships through relentless storms. When a cataclysmic gale struck, the keeper faced floodwaters racing in, threatening to drown the machinery that operated the beacon's revolving light.

For two days the keeper fought exhaustion, manning a manual crank whenever the engine sputtered. Rain battered his every breath, salt spray stung his eyes. More than once he nearly collapsed, but he recalled the ships depending on that glow to find safe harbor.

At dusk on the second day, the storm peaked, slamming the beacon with waves tall as houses. Despite trembling hands and a battered body, the keeper refused to abandon his post. He cranked again, sweat and rain mingling on his brow. Finally, at dawn, the storm lifted. The beacon still turned, and countless vessels had avoided disaster.

From then on, local lore held that no gale could break a spirit fused to a greater cause. Where hopelessness demanded surrender, the keeper persisted—his light never fully dimmed.

Silence settled after Zeetrikus finished the reading. Each Wizard absorbed the fable's lesson in his or her own way. Blunt recalled how, when saving a battered clock in a European city, he had nearly lost hope to overwhelming illusions—yet pressed on, knowing entire communities relied on him.

Greenie thought about how empathy demanded constant care. She had once been tempted to shut out others' pain to avoid heartbreak, but recognized that keeping the heart open was essential to keeping the beacon shining for those in need.

Checkered likened the keeper's manual cranking to her own use of logic and reason. It could feel tedious, but stepping away would let illusions win. So, she continued to parse every puzzle, no matter how weary her mind grew.

Reddish empathized with the keeper's battered body. She felt the ache of pushing her fiery powers to their brink yet refusing to quit. Firee saw parallels in how he had overcome self-doubt to sustain his flame. Breezie connected it to his gentle breezes that persisted quietly, even when overshadowed by storms. Zeetrikus's eyes shone with fierce approval; the fable's lesson had taken root.

Now, with the story still in their hearts, the group turned their attention to the star they had carried from Messina, resting on a nearby bench. Checkered aimed her lens at the small runic star. Its intricate engravings glowed along the edges, forming celestial lines like a partial map. "This star might link all our efforts," she observed, voice alight with curiosity.

Blunt held out the runic gear stamped "Perseverantia Est Virtus." "We saw something similar in a previous clock," he recalled. "Each gear or star we've collected leads us to the next location."

Greenie traced a fingertip over the star's shimmering surface, feeling a faint pulse. "It's as if these runic artifacts form a code that unlocks the final piece—something about unity in a Boston tower," she said softly.

Zeetrikus nodded. "The cipher draws on each virtue we've reclaimed: generosity, justice, courage, perseverance. By combining these patterns, you'll find the tower where the Orloj's final secret awaits."

Reddish let out a steady breath, embers pulsing in unison with the star's glow. "All these illusions we've shattered—

fear, greed, bias, despair—tie into the Harlequin's plan to break us," she said quietly. "But we keep moving."

Checkered's lens revealed a phrase carved in faint light: "Unitas Est Virtus; Divisio Est Vitium." Beneath it, a simpler line read, "Custom House Tower," though illusions once tried to bury that clue. The star brightened, and a swirl of magic formed.

"A portal's forging," Breezie said softly, feeling the gentle wind swirl at his heels. "Unity or division—this is the last step."

Zeetrikus touched his bent hat, silent runic scars glinting in the lamplight. "Go, secure the tower," he urged. "Bring that watchman's spirit with you. Let no tempest or gloom break your stride."

The Watchman's Dawn

In a thunderous pulse of arcane wind, the star lifted from the bench and hovered between them, radiating a gateway of luminescent energy. The library's lamplit exterior seemed to flicker beneath the swirling portal, which revealed glimpses of a tall structure rising over the city skyline. There, no doubt, the Harlequin's illusions gathered, eager to sever the final link in their chain of virtues.

Blunt drew the runic gear stamped "Perseverantia Est Virtus" from his cloak, pressing it gently against the star. A perfect resonance bloomed, brightening the swirl of color into a blinding light. He turned to Zeetrikus, who watched with unwavering eyes. "We won't let despair or any illusions keep us from finishing what we started," Blunt said. "Not after seeing how the watchman refused to let the storm claim his beacon."

Zeetrikus inclined his head. "Your perseverance stands proven. Take that spark of endurance, combine it with all you've learned—courage, justice, generosity, empathy, and more. Only unity can seal this quest."

Reddish recalled the anxious moment in Messina when she nearly faltered, and the times Firee had doubted his flame. She saw how each of them had grown, forging an unbreakable circle of resolve. "We go together," she declared, stepping boldly toward the portal.

Greenie steadied Breezie's hand. Illusions loved to exploit doubt, but they had all embraced the watchman's lesson: keep going despite battered spirits and raging storms. Breezie, inspired by their empathy and teamwork, nodded confidently. "We face the Harlequin as we faced every threat: side by side," he said.

Checkered took one last glance at her lens. No illusions hovered now—fear, despair, hopelessness had receded under the power of perseverance. "This is the cusp of the final clock," she murmured. "Boston's tower, the Orloj that ties it all together. Let's end this."

With a collective breath, they entered the swirling light. The night air shifted into a cosmic vortex, and the star's brilliance enveloped them in a wave of unbreakable will. Each carried the watchman's fable in their hearts, a testament to the strength found in unwavering resolve. On the other side, the Custom House Tower in Boston awaited, the Harlequin's final stronghold. They emerged with hearts aflame—because perseverance had guided them here, and their unity promised a final triumph over any storm that raged.

So concluded Perseverance's Triumph—a victory that bridged Greenwich and Messina in a harmony of time and faith resonating across continents. The path to unity lay open, and the group's resolve blazed as they soared toward the tower, runic star in hand, unflinching in their stand against despair's darkest illusions. The watchman's dawn awaited, a promise of victory just beyond the horizon.

Chapter 20

The Grand Test – Unity's Eternal Flame

Into the Orloj's Maw

Beneath Boston's Custom House Tower, the Orloj's hidden gearworks groaned under strain. Ancient cogs clicked unevenly, their teeth slowly prying apart as if an unseen force were pulling them in different directions. Each massive wheel protested the tug, squealing like tortured metal. The very air crackled with tension. Ghostly apparitions flickered at the edges of the darkness — half-formed echoes of old faults and regrets. Whispered accusations and glimmers of past quarrels drifted among the girders, baiting the wizards with familiar doubts.

In a bronze-and-sapphire shimmer, Blunt, Reddish, Firee, Checkered, Breezie, and Greenie arrived at the tower's base. In the gloom their Harlequin cloaks glinted white and black like storm clouds lit from within. Blunt held in his hand the star-shaped runic artifact, pulsing steadily: a metronome of unity against the chaos. Its glow throbbed in time; each beat a reminder of Unitas Est Virtus — Unity Is Virtue. The Wizards exchanged determined looks.

"All the clocks we've saved have led to this," Blunt murmured. "Our final test." He recalled how in a distant observatory they had faced despair itself and forged an iron resolve. Now, a darker challenge loomed: the Dark Harlequin was tearing at the seams of Boston's heart.

Then, without warning, a static-laced gust knocked at their robes. Ghostly silhouettes swirled around them — visions of betrayal, of friends walking away, of trust shattered. Firee's jaw clenched as he flashed back to earlier phantoms that preyed on his self-doubt; tonight those doubts danced alive again.

Greenie's empathic sense flared in response. She felt the Orloj's anguish — a machine built for cooperation that now threatened to splinter. Quietly she said, "The Old Clock's gears cry out for unity. We withstood the Harlequin's greed and fear before — together, we'll stand firm against division."

Checkered's lens glowed in the darkness as she scanned the shadows. "These illusions are potent," she warned. "They feed on every hateful whisper we've ever heard." Breezie felt a cold finger of fear as phantoms twisted through the machinery. He had once felt himself fade into the background, but not again. Steadying himself, he let a small breeze rustle the nearby cogs. "We're not alone here," he whispered to his friends. "We face this as one."

Broken Teeth of Time

A thunderous rumble exploded from deep within the tower. Blunt tightened his grip on the star. Even above them, the city seemed to hold its breath — waiting to see if unity could quell the Harlequin's final onslaught. Resolute, the Wizards pressed forward into the iron maw of the Orloj, footsteps echoing in the mechanical gloom. Each gear they passed jiggled and shuddered under some uncanny force; arcs of twisting light leaped between teeth, as if trying to drive them apart.

Beyond a massive iron door they entered the Orloj's hidden labyrinth. Instead of the neat hum of clockwork, the chamber was fractured. Colossal cogs that once turned in perfect harmony now tilted at awkward angles. Gaps gaped where wheels no longer meshed. An acrid stink of burned oil and ozone hung in the air, as if the clock's own heart were being strangled.

Breezie halted, instincts warning him. "Something's here," he murmured, every hair on his neck rising. Checkered crouched to adjust her lens, confirming his fear: a coalescing swirl of inky darkness churned not far away. At its center was a half-formed vortex — a nightmarish embryo of the Dark

Harlequin, edges shimmering with malignant potential. It hung just above the broken gears, silent but laughing at them.

Firee gasped. "The Harlequin's true form," he whispered, flame dancing in his palm. His friends flinched as the vortex's gaze seemed to latch onto them, twisting their worst regrets into shadowy faces that peered from its depths.

Greenie pressed forward on the balls of her feet. The Harlequin feeds off their fears, she sensed — each vision aimed to isolate them. "It seeks to turn us on each other," she said softly. "Divide and conquer." Reddish's hands curled into fists, embers sputtering at her fingertips. She thought of her own impatience, the mistake that once cost them dearly. "Not this time," Reddish murmured. "No trick will break this circle."

Metallic screeches suddenly burst from the ceiling — the Orloj itself crying out. Faint inscriptions ran along the iron girders, speaking of revolution and alliance, of old and new eras joined. The runic star in Blunt's hand throbbed with energy. Blunt felt it tug toward the heart of the machine. "Let's keep moving," he said, voice steady despite the tremor of machinery. "Every gear must rejoin, or we lose everything."

Stakes Engraved in Brass

They climbed onto a raised metal platform at the chamber's heart. Steam hissed from colossal pistons in the walls, and the ground vibrated beneath their feet. In the center of the platform lay a huge brass dial, etched with runic letters around its edge. The writing glowed faintly. Breezie stepped forward and squinted at the inscription.

Blunt read over his shoulder: "Division threatens the Orloj's cosmic balance, unraveling reality." A chill ran down his spine. The fate of Boston — perhaps the entire world — balanced on this moment. If the Harlequin succeeded in driving them apart, reality itself could fray.

Blunt drew a slow breath, clutching the pulsing star. "This is bigger than just one city," he murmured. "If unity fails here, everything we've fought for collapses."

Greenie gently touched the brass rim of the dial. The metal was cold and slick with oil, and she felt a subtle vibration under her fingertips — the heartbeat of a world at war with itself. "It's like time and space converge in these wheels," she observed. "If the Harlequin severs them, reality will fray." She recalled how, once, her own empathy was twisted to isolation by a similar trick. She wouldn't let it happen again.

Reddish's eyes narrowed at the shadows creeping around them. Dark tendrils formed flickering mockeries of their teammates — whispered voices crying "They'll betray you." Each vision tried to pit one wizard against the others. Remembering how quickly it once worked on her impatience, she stood taller. Sparking embers danced along her arms. "We hold to unity," she said calmly. "We will not let anything come between us."

Breezie let a calm current of wind flow around them, a protective aura. "We've defeated every illusion so far — fear, despair, envy, selfishness," he said softly. "This is no different." His eyes met each friend's in turn. "Together, we can face whatever comes."

Unifying the Virtues – Collective Stand

Just beyond the brass dial, a network of metal walkways radiated like spokes from a wheel. Each path glowed with a faint light — a hue corresponding to a virtue they had reclaimed: courage, justice, generosity, perseverance, and more. It felt as if the Orloj itself demanded that the Wizards bind their lessons into a single, unbreakable synergy.

Blunt raised the star high, its radiance flaring. "We always stood together," he said, remembering battered clocks and far-flung towers where friendship had prevailed. "Our bond is our strength."

Reddish closed her eyes and let the memory of her earlier haste stir her resolve. Flames wound around her arms as she whispered, "We're each a piece of a bigger puzzle. Together we are strong."

Greenie felt the Orloj's hum deepen, as if the air itself sang of unity. Each past virtue — compassion, curiosity, humility — intertwined like threads in a great tapestry. She knew that when her empathy was tested in isolation, trusting her friends had pulled her through. "Every time one virtue fell, another held us," Greenie murmured. "We learned that side by side, we can carry them all."

Checkered knelt by the dial and let her lens scan the swirling runes. Lines of cosmic text wound around the metal like river currents. "The Orloj is telling us to merge every virtue into one," she translated. "To combine our gifts, or see reality tear itself apart."

Firee clenched the star tighter. Every trial they had passed — battles in fog and fire, feats of bravery and sacrifice — had been faced as a team. "We fought fear and despair together. We stood against greed and hate together," he said firmly. "Division won't stop us now."

Breezie opened his cloak and let a breeze spiral upward, rustling their robes. "We each hold a different key," he added. "Courage, wit, kindness, understanding — it all fits only together. We move forward as one, or not at all."

At once, the platform underfoot rumbled. Streams of runic light snaked up from beneath the brass spokes, connecting each Wizard's Harlequin cloak into a shining chain. The chaotic distortions around them hissed and recoiled. The star blazed with approval, and a path opened deeper into the labyrinth. Gears clanked in rhythmic unison, the fake shadows wavering before their combined strength. Together, they stepped forward, unwavering, into whatever trial awaited next.

Personal Trials — Firee & Breezie

As they entered the next chamber, the luminous ring of voices cut off, and a chilling silence fell. Suddenly the air around each Wizard shimmered and coalesced into personal nightmares, tailored to strike at their own weaknesses.

Blunt saw his reflection on a dais of cosmic splendor, the Orloj bending to his command — a vision of absolute power. Normally he might have been tempted, but humility anchored him now. He let the star's soft glow steady his gaze until the illusion crumbled.

Checkered faced a shifting maze of lies and half-truths, whispering promises of an easy path if only she'd turn a blind eye. She raised her lens steadily and cut through the deception with patience and logic. "No shortcuts," she murmured, and watched the phantasms scatter.

Firee's trial flickered to life as a memory: the day he lost control of his fire, flames leaping wildly towards his friends. His stomach lurched; once, that memory had almost crushed him. But now Firee felt control in his fingertips. He whispered, "I won't let old fears reignite," and with a controlled breeze guiding his palm, he snuffed out the hallucination.

Breezie's own trial took shape as harsh, disembodied whispers swirling around him: "Your winds are small… You are nothing." He recalled the nights he felt insignificant. Now, letting confidence fill him, Breezie released a steady wind that encircled the hall. "I'm part of something bigger," he said, and the accusing voices blew away.

Personal Trials — Reddish & Greenie

The darkness swirled fiercely at Reddish's and Greenie's feet. Each felt a cold touch: illusions formed that targeted their very selves.

For Reddish, the vision was heartbreakingly familiar: she was back at the moment of her own anger nearly derailing a plan, flame suddenly scalding an ally. The hall filled with heat and her past impatience, as if she could still hear the anger in her own voice. Pain pricked at her chest. But Reddish took a deep breath. Remembering how she had learned to temper her blaze with strategy, she let cool embers stream along her arms.

"I am with them, not against them," she assured herself. The illusion of betrayal wavered and flickered out like ash on the breeze.

Greenie's trial took shape as an uncaring world: voices insisted empathy was futile, that a giving heart would only be trampled. She recalled times she had felt empathy ignored — a past trial's deceit that tried to isolate her compassion. But she also remembered how strongly she'd learned to trust her friends. A calm smile formed. She raised her hand and conjured a gentle swirl of vines and light. The world around her blossomed green as the phantoms recoiled. "Compassion never fails — not when we face it together," Greenie said softly.

An Epic for Unity

The corridor opened onto a grand chamber. The runic star in Blunt's hand flared brightly, as if it knew this was the Orloj's final chamber. Around them, the gearworks twisted into a spiraling dais circled by colossal cogs. Above, the Dark Harlequin's vortex churned into a roiling column of black and purple light. The whole room thrummed with tension — reality's core seemed on the verge of cracking.

Greenie sensed the Orloj itself pleading through the magic, as if the clock were begging them to prove unity stronger than division. Breezie watched the swirling chaos overhead and whispered, "It's like the final storm about to break."

Reddish shut her eyes, recalling a mentor's lesson that synergy needed an anchor in story. "We've always used stories or poems to bind our lessons," she said. "Why not for unity as well?" Checkered nodded. "The star's urging us to something greater. Maybe an epic that ties all virtues into one tapestry," she said, scanning the dais's runic script. "If we can recast our journey as one story, maybe we'll finally seal the Orloj's power."

Firee gently stroked the star. "We had short fables for each virtue before. Maybe now we need a proper epic for unity — to show how all the virtues merge into something unstoppable."

Blunt looked up at the swirling shadow. The Harlequin's roar was building, but it was not complete. "We have one moment," he said quietly, "one chance to do this right. The Orloj was built for our coming — maybe for something like this."

The chamber fell silent except for distant echoes. Blunt's mind flickered on Zeetrikus's words from earlier trials: "Remember how perseverance overcame despair — let unity do the same for division." Drawing strength from the memory, the Wizards moved to the center of the dais and formed a ring with the star glowing between them. The dark phantoms above paused uncertainly. The moment had come to give voice to the final epic of unity.

Unity Epic

Greenie took a trembling breath and placed her hand on the runic star. In a hushed voice that seemed to answer the Orloj's silent plea, she began to speak the words that rose to her mind, an epic given to them as if by destiny:

"The Celestial Weave"

In an age before clocks and compasses, twelve shining virtues danced among the stars—courage blazed bright as dawn, justice balanced the heavenly scales, generosity gave a nurturing warmth, and perseverance refused to yield.

Compassion bound broken souls, curiosity lit unknown roads, fortitude withstood every storm, while humility kept pride at bay.

Yet these virtues spun alone, each a separate orb adrift in cosmic void.

Twisting shadows crept between them, sowing discord in every heart.

With no unity to brace them, the shining orbs began to splinter, lost in endless night.

Then from the darkness came one lonely star. It gazed at the splintered lights and felt their pain.

Slowly, each virtue heard its call. Courage embraced justice's balance, generosity soothed resentment, and

Silence fell as Greenie's last word echoed. The star in Blunt's hand pulsed one final time and then glowed steadily. Blunt exhaled. "That epic shows us the truth," he said softly. "Each virtue shines alone only in pockets of the world, but when joined together they dispel any darkness."

Reddish opened her eyes, remembering her earlier impatience. "I almost burned too fiercely once, but channeled by unity our fire brings warmth instead of ruin," she said, embers dancing along her arms.

Greenie's eyes glistened as she thought of the illusions that once preyed on her empathy. "I stand for compassion," she whispered, "but only in a circle of trust can it change the world."

Checkered tilted her head, recalling how raw logic had failed her when it stood alone. "Logic and curiosity by themselves are strong, but united with the others we discovered answers far beyond what I could find by myself," she said quietly.

Firee, still holding the star's glow, added softly, "I found strength by leaning on all of you. That's the real power."

Breezie smiled as dawn seemed to press in at the edges of the chamber. "I used to wonder if I was irrelevant," he said gently. "Now I know: every breeze I give is part of something greater."

As each Wizard spoke, the darkness above seethed in anger. The Harlequin's half-formed shape quivered, rings of void-eyes gleaming cruelly. The swirling shadows above them wavered, threatened at last — their final confrontation was coming.

The Harlequin Unmasked

Even as those final words faded, the chamber erupted. A blast of seething darkness exploded from above. The half-formed vortex flared into the Dark Harlequin's full, nightmarish shape — an immense swirl of shadow ringed by twisting gears. Hundreds of void-eyes opened in its form, each eye reflecting the worst flaw of whichever Wizard it focused on. Reddish's temper, Breezie's fear of being small, Firee's hesitation — all leered back at them, magnified and mocking.

And then a voice, cold and metallic, cut through the chaos. It was low and hollow, as if spoken from deep within the iron.

"Foolish mortals," it hissed. "Do you think unity makes you strong? I was once like you — part of a band of brothers bound by loyalty. But unity failed me. I was betrayed by trust and left empty. So, I embraced division, and I found clarity. Alone, one need make no compromise."

A sound like shattered glass snapped in the air — the Harlequin's laugh, raw and malicious, roaring to life. The vision above them seemed to feed on it, growing larger and more twisted.

Breezie's cloak billowed as he braced himself. "They called us dreamers," the voice continued, echoing through the chamber. "I'll show you what reality is."

A wave of malicious laughter reverberated, sharpened by the illusion's power. Breezie shivered as he felt a flicker of his old fear. But he had come too far to crack now. He summoned a steady wind, deflecting the swirling onslaught and refusing to be pushed aside again.

Greenie saw countless shadows pushing her to abandon compassion. She whispered, "We are that star," and wove her empathic vines outward. They snaked around her friends' forming wards — linking with Breezie's protective wind, Reddish's embers, Blunt's ward, Checkered's lens — knitting the Wizards into one unbroken circle.

The Harlequin's gaze snapped to Greenie, and for a moment the chamber froze. But Reddish was already reacting. An old memory hissed at her — her own blaze nearly harming her allies — and for an instant doubt crept in. She tightened her teeth against the whisper and fed her measured embers into the defense. "You will not ruin us," she snarled, burning away the lie.

Checkered steadied her lens against the tumult. Data and whispers attacked her mind, but she cut through them with calm focus — each phantasm shattering under her strike.

In the center, Blunt planted his feet and held the star aloft. Around him, the other Wizards poured their synergy into its light. The Harlequin's vortex shrieked as reality began to warp — but the star's runic energy flared back. This final battle was underway.

Chain of Light

The gear-laden floor trembled as phantasms hammered at them from every side. Reddish's controlled fire flared wildly as a vision tried to isolate her. Greenie felt icy apparitions attempting to suffocate her compassion. Breezie's wind wavered as dark voices claimed he was insignificant. But none fought alone this time.

Blunt summoned a boundary of water that surged around the circle. "We unify now or never," he called out, voice resonant over the clamor. Checkered's lens glowed as she saw each friend's strength. Breezie's wind reinforced Greenie's empathy, Reddish's embers stabilized Firee's flame, and Blunt's wards guided all of them. "This is the final chord," she said, steadying their bonds.

Greenie took a deep breath, feeling the gale of synergy at her back. "We've defeated every illusion before," she declared, voice calm. Reddish's fire flickered in agreement, each flicker a symbol of her restraint. Together their energies intertwined at their feet, forming a glowing circle of light.

As one, they reached out to the star and poured their combined will into it. The runes on the artifact flared fiercely: "Unitas Est Virtus." Blunt felt arcs of brilliant light leap from the star to each of them, forging an unbreakable chain. The darkness clashed against that brilliance, but it held fast. The chamber was lit in a ring of rainbow radiance — their unity against the void.

Crown of Fractured Virtues

Suddenly, the ground lurched. Above them, the swirling chaos coalesced into a towering vortex, jagged like a shattered crown. Each spike seemed to mirror a corrupted virtue — generosity twisted into greed, courage collapsed into cowardice, and so on. At the center gleamed the Harlequin's void-eyes, each orbiting with malevolent glee as phantoms surged forward.

A final wave of illusions rushed in. Blunt saw a vision of himself seizing the Orloj's power — absolute control. Reddish saw herself unleashing wildfire in anger, destroying what she swore to protect. Firee saw his flame snuffed out by his own hesitation. Breezie felt himself shrinking, swallowed by the shadow. Checkered was lost in an endless maze of lies.

For a heartbeat, the shadows succeeded in sowing terror. Blunt's ward flickered and Reddish's flame wavered. Breezie staggered as an unseen force tried to tear him away. The circle quivered, unity nearly broken.

But those doubts had been tested before. The Wizards inhaled deeply. Blunt summoned a tidal wave of wards fused with Reddish's controlled fire. Greenie's empathic light spiraled outward, linking them in warmth. Firee focused his flames into precise bursts, shattering the nearest echoes of doom. Breezie held the center with a calm, persistent breeze. Checkered's lens projected the remaining strength into clear purpose.

At last, they channeled everything into the runic star. "Unitas Est Virtus," they shouted together. The artifact erupted in a blazing corona, shooting arcs of brilliant color to each Wizard. The phantasms screeched as each dark reflection was pinned by a ring of light — their negative images exploding into harmless motes.

A thunderous groan ripped through the vortex as it began to unravel. The Dark Harlequin's monstrous swirl collapsed inward on itself. There was no crack in the Wizards' bond. Reality snapped back — the shadows dissolved into nothing, leaving only battered gearworks and a profound hush.

The Orloj Restored

For a moment, the chamber was silent. Then the star's light dimmed to a gentle glow. Relief washed over Greenie, and Reddish let out the breath she hadn't realized she was holding. The Harlequin's final onslaught was over — undone by unity.

The battered gearworks quieted to a steady pulse. Above the dial, the runic star hovered on its own, awaiting the final step. One by one, the Wizards stepped forward and placed their hands on the brass. Invisible pulses of energy rippled outward, realigning the cogs and threads of cosmic power. The dissonance melted away; harmonious light returned.

Finally, Blunt guided the star into a vacant slot in the Orloj's core. It fit perfectly, each etched rune on the star matching grooves on the dial. For a fleeting second, the star's runic symbol blazed, its light forming a crown-like halo above them as if hinting at a greater destiny to come. A final click resonated through the tower. The entire structure trembled — this time with relief rather than terror.

Lights flickered across every gear and axle. Projections glowed on each cog: images of Boston's centuries — revolutionaries, 19th-century builders, modern dreamers — all merging into one tapestry of unity and purpose.

The Orloj itself seemed to sigh in gratitude. A gentle mechanical chime rang out, as though the clock were offering a benediction. In the silence, a faint chorus of voices — Paulina, Morpheus, Zeetrikus — seemed to murmur their approval. This cosmic clock, lost to chaos for so long, now stood restored by synergy. The fusion of all virtues had overcome even the Dark Harlequin.

The chamber floor steadied. No trace of illusion remained. Their journey's end felt in sight, though each Wizard sensed that a new dawn might also bring new challenges. For now, they simply breathed deeply, letting the resonance of unity fill the tower's iron bones.

Rooftop Benediction

Outside, dawn found them atop the Custom House Tower. They emerged from the secret chamber into the cool morning air, Boston's skyline glowing in golden light. A brisk harbor breeze tugged at their cloaks. Far below, the Orloj hummed quietly, each cog turning with confident purpose at last. In the center, the star had settled into the machine's core, pulsing gently — a silent testament to unity made real.

For a moment the Wizards circled each other, silent and awed by the new day. Firee spoke first: "I remember the illusion that preyed on my fear of failure," he said softly, watching the sunrise. "I realized that fear was an ember that needed friends' air to burn safely. Now it feels so distant."

Breezie nodded, eyes on the awakening city. "I used to think I was the weakest breeze," he said quietly. "Now I see: every wind, no matter how small, helped free the gears of this tower. I have my place."

Reddish tilted her head to feel the sea air. "I used to see my flame as a wild thing," she said, smiling. "I almost burned all of us by myself. Now I know it warms everything it touches."

Greenie exhaled in calm satisfaction, sensing the city's peace. "We saw compassion mocked below," she said, eyes glistening, "but our compassion was woven into something powerful. That illusion is gone."

Checkered's lens caught the morning sun on their faces. She whispered, "Seeking truth with all our hearts led us here. We faced lies and shadows together — and emerged stronger."

Blunt stood at the center of their circle and bowed his head briefly. The memory of each clock they had restored — each virtue they had proved — coalesced into a single triumph.

Unity had become the keystone. He lifted his gaze to the dawn as a gentle wind swirled around them. Boston was waking below, blissfully unaware of the cosmic conflict it had just survived. The Orloj's steady hum was their reward: each echo a reminder that they had succeeded. Whatever the Harlequin's final gambit had been, it had found no purchase against a united front.

They lingered a moment longer, letting the sunrise fill them with warmth. Unity had prevailed. The young Wizards had not only confronted darkness — they had proven that together, they were unstoppable. A new day had dawned on Boston, and they faced it as one.

Chapter 21

Final Confrontation – Unity's Cosmic Victory

Shadow at the Crown

A hush of charged air enveloped Boston's Custom House Tower as Blunt, Reddish, Firee, Checkered, Breezie, and Greenie emerged from a vortex of bronze-and-sapphire light. As the portal sealed behind them, the runic star at their feet unfurled into a crown-star—the form unity takes when wielded by many. Their Harlequin cloaks flickered beneath the structure's hidden cosmic core—Boston's secret engine of harmony—where gears infused with old colonial icons churned under unnatural strain. Time itself felt stretched thin.

Blunt grasped the runic crown-star engraved with Unitas Est Virtus—the final relic proving their mastery of unity. He recalled how illusions around the world had tested their synergy; now the last trial loomed. Reddish peered into swirling shadows, catching a fleeting shape of a tall figure. For an instant it resembled an old wizard's robe but stained in living darkness. A faint, corrupted aura flickered around it.

Breezie tensed. "There was rumor of a hidden Harlequin leader—maybe a once-noble wizard," he whispered. "Looks like those rumors hold truth."

From behind the main gear assembly came a hiss of phantoms, their whispers dredging up flickers of old mistakes and half-forgotten regrets—remnants of past battles meant to unsettle them. Firee's flame quavered as he recognized illusions like those that had once gnawed at his courage. "We overcame illusions of greed, despair, division," he muttered, steadying himself. "If there's one last foe, we face it united." Greenie extended her empathic sense, feeling the Orloj's pulse throbbing in desperation. She sensed a razor edge of panic— as though the city's very unity were threatened by a single malignant presence. "We can't let illusions fracture the final anchor of synergy," she said quietly.

Checkered's lens glowed as she scanned inscriptions carved into the tower's cosmic engine. "These runes speak of forging the final bond," she murmured. "If that wizard's truly corrupted, he'll exploit every flaw we overcame." Yet each haunting image around them only reminded the Wizards that their unity had kept them whole through every trial. Blunt inhaled deeply. "We hold the key to unity," he said, lifting the crown-star. "No illusions can stand once we rally as one."

In the far corner, a low laugh echoed—a sinister hint of the Harlequin's presence. The group steeled themselves, remembering how illusions had nearly broken them before but always failed in the face of combined strength. Flickers of starlight danced off the gear-laden walls, each rivet etched with faint motifs of Boston's 1849 expansions. The tower's proud heritage felt dimmed by the encroaching darkness. Resolute, they stepped forward, prepared to see if their unity could banish the final vestiges of chaos lurking in the roiling gloom ahead.

Into the Gearheart

Deeper into the tower, the gearworks opened into a vast cosmic chamber—a tapestry of cogs and drifting star-fields. Each gear bore traces of Boston's Revolutionary spirit, but arcs of chaotic energy now threatened to warp them out of alignment. A menacing hush settled, as though the entire contraption teetered at the edge of reality. A faint draft sighed through the chamber, carrying the scent of aged oil and dust from long-still gears.

They heard it again: a harsh laugh echoing from the chamber's heart. It spiked adrenaline in everyone's veins, reminiscent of the illusions they once battled—fear, greed, injustice—but with an extra touch of malevolence. Reddish's embers crackled in response. "That must be the Harlequin's leader," she said. "He's grown bold if he's letting us hear him now."

Checkered's lens gleaned spectral shapes in the rafters—fragmented images of betrayals and failed missions. "He's harnessing illusions we already overcame, trying to stoke old doubts," she observed. Breezie conjured a gentle wind, blowing back creeping shadows that threatened to separate them. "No illusion can break us if we stand firm," he whispered.

Firee felt a flicker of tension in his flame. In the past, illusions had thrived by isolating him from the group's synergy. This time he steadied his breath, letting the warmth of unity overcome any lingering fear. Meanwhile, Greenie perceived the intangible pulse of the Orloj's cosmic heartbeat—a rhythmic call urging them to unify before illusions could fracture time itself.

Blunt brandished the runic crown-star. "We bind these cogs in synergy," he said, recalling how in prior cities their enemies' deceptions nearly caused entire cosmic systems to unravel. "Let that laughter echo. We've proven illusions can't sever true bonds."

A swirl of shadow parted near the center, revealing the faint silhouette of a tall figure. Black robes flickered with arcs of corruption as the group caught a glimpse of sallow skin and burning eyes. The rumors were confirmed: a once-noble wizard, now consumed by the Harlequin's divisive power. A shiver swept through them, but none stepped back.

The path ahead glowed with arcs of amethyst and sapphire light, beckoning them deeper. They advanced, each recalling the illusions that had tested them individually—moments of near betrayal or despair. But synergy had overcome every threat. With a new wave of determination, they braced for the cosmic maelstrom the corrupted wizard was about to unleash, certain that unity was their unbreakable shield.

Cloak of Contradictions

A swirl of illusions erupted from the wizard's tattered cloak, racing across the gear-laced floor. Each illusion took shape as a twisted reflection of the Wizards' own virtues: humility warped into arrogance, courage into recklessness, generosity into exploitation, perseverance into obsessive stubbornness. It was a direct assault on everything they had painstakingly refined throughout their travels.

Blunt stepped up to a spiking illusion that attempted to lure him with prideful visions of dominating the Orloj. He remembered how similar illusions once promised him power if he forsook humility. But synergy had taught him that real strength lay in uplifting others. He channeled that memory, dissolving the illusion with a calm wave of water-ward.

Checkered spotted an illusion warping curiosity into willful ignorance—a dense phantom proclaiming, "You already know enough. Stop asking." She recalled how, in an earlier trial, deception had nearly persuaded her that knowledge was a burden. That lesson forced her to merge curiosity with empathy, forging an unstoppable resolve. Summoning that balanced perspective now, she thrust her lens forward. "No illusion can stifle our quest for truth," she declared, and the boastful mirage shattered like brittle glass.

Greenie encountered an illusion turning compassion into apathy, whispering, "People will only betray you if you care." Recognizing the attempt to isolate her empathy—just as similar phantoms had tried before—she wove out verdant, empathic vines that reaffirmed caring as her true strength. Alongside her, Reddish burned away an illusion twisting bravery into heedless aggression. She had seen that tactic before and had learned to channel her embers with measured caution; the phantom fury fizzled against her controlled flame.

Firee faced a sneering illusion that tarnished perseverance into obstinate refusal to adapt. He remembered times when stubborn illusions nearly drove him to a breaking point by urging him never to change course. With clarity gleaned from their synergy, he balanced steadfastness with open-mindedness. A focused column of flame split the deceit in two. Meanwhile, Breezie swept aside an illusion turning justice into cruelty—a perverse deception once used to breed division. This time his gentle winds of fairness refused to let injustice fester.

In less than a minute, illusions across the dais crumbled, each undone by the Wizards' unified effort. Behind them, the corrupted wizard hissed in frustration, every movement sharp with spite. The gear-laden floor itself rumbled in protest, as though the Orloj recognized each small victory. Blunt exhaled, sweat beading on his brow. "We've broken illusions of twisted virtues," he murmured. Unity had held firm—but a deeper confrontation still loomed within the cosmic labyrinth.

The Circle Forms

The corrupted wizard retreated with a snarl, disappearing into a swirling vortex at the Orloj's core as if inviting them to follow. A prismatic corridor of rotating cogs opened before the Wizards, each gear etched with star symbols pulsing in time with a deep cosmic hum. The Orloj's very voice seemed to groan: a summons for them to push forward.

A faint glow from the runic crown-star guided them onward. Blunt felt the crown-star tug toward the depths where the corrupted wizard had fled. He nodded to the others. "The Orloj's hum is surging, urging us toward the heart of this fight," he said, steeling them for the final stand. Firee kept his flame at a low, ready burn—mindful that new illusions might erupt, yet trusting in their combined strength.

Greenie brushed her hand across a battered cog on the wall, compassion radiating through her touch as she sensed the Orloj's longing for completion. "We've undone illusions that twisted fear, greed, despair, and more," she said softly. "Whatever remains, we can't let division break our final bond." Reddish ignited a small ember at her fingertips, memories of near-catastrophic mistakes fueling her caution. She'd once rushed ahead alone, but synergy saved her from illusions that almost devoured her will. Now she stood among allies whose presence bolstered her resolve.

Checkered advanced beside them, lens scanning the corridor's runic script. Each phrase spoke of forging a cosmic unity that transcended illusion. She recalled times when deceptions tried to trap her in her own mind; she had overcome them by linking reason with empathy. Breezie stayed at her side, conjuring a steady, guiding breeze. He remembered how illusions once fed on his fear of being unnecessary—until unity showed him that each of them was indispensable.

At last, they reached a threshold guarded by fractal illusions. The mirages parted before them like reluctant shadows. The sense of final confrontation thickened around them—an ultimate test of synergy beckoned from beyond the archway. The runic crown-star in Blunt's hand glowed brighter, confirming they were on the right path. With a collective breath, they stepped into a new chamber, half expecting an ambush. Instead they found only an ominous stillness, as though even the lingering darkness was holding its breath for the next stage.

The Circle Holds

Entering a vast circular space lined with rotating discs, they found the corrupted wizard at its heart. His cloak undulated around him like a living tapestry woven of flaws. Threads of envy, fear, and betrayal snaked visibly through the fabric. A single overhead gear cast shifting light onto him, giving his face a twisted half-shadow that accentuated the depth of his corruption.

His lips curved into a crooked smile. His voice spilled out, rough and bitter: "Unity... your precious unity. I embraced it once—and it betrayed me. Better to stand apart, safe from the trust that will surely break you. Alone, no one can hurt you."

Blunt raised the runic crown-star high, focusing the hard-won synergy gleaned from every clock they had ever rescued. Memories of challenges overcome—humbling lessons in Philadelphia, cathedral trials in Europe, cosmic battles against greed and fear—flooded his mind. "We faced illusions in every corner of the world," he said firmly. "Unity overcame them each time. This final stand will be no different."

A whirl of illusions burst from the wizard's cloak, each tendril shaped by his personal vendetta. Breezie braced himself as a familiar lie stung at his mind—the old whisper that he had no place among his friends. He swept it aside with a crisp gust of wind. "We have no time for your divisions," he shot back, his voice uncharacteristically sharp.

Greenie's empathic senses caught the faint tremor of heartbreak fueling the wizard's corruption—perhaps once upon a time he had lost faith in unity and turned to illusions for power. Sorrow flickered in her eyes as she wove gentle vines to quell the phantoms rising around him. "No betrayal is worth forsaking unity," she murmured, resolve in her voice.

Reddish struck out with measured flames, recalling how she nearly destroyed a vital clue once by acting too rashly. Now she tempered her aggression with teamwork. "We won't let illusions prey on us ever again," she said, her emberlit gaze never leaving their foe.

Checkered noticed spectral equations swirling around the wizard's cloak—logic twisted to justify his fall. She refused to let such warped reasoning ensnare her in a maze of half-truths. "We keep an open mind and heart," she declared, her lens blazing as if to burn away the lies.

For a heartbeat, a cruel illusion stole over them. Each Wizard saw a friend wavering in doubt: Breezie imagined Greenie faltering with despair; Greenie thought Breezie had turned away in fear. Their hearts froze, uncertainty stretching between them. Then Reddish's strong voice rang out, breaking the spell. Breezie's hand closed around Greenie's, their smiles steady with trust. In an instant, unity's light banished the deception. Side by side again, they met the final wave of illusions with unbroken resolve.

Firee's flame flared and seamlessly merged with Reddish's, forging a unified wave of heat that drove the encroaching illusions back. The wizard staggered, shadows around him flickering—a sign that their combined power had begun unraveling his hold. For an instant his cloak shimmered, each dark thread writhing like a living thing. The final blow had not yet fallen, but he was clearly weakened. The Orloj's hum quickened, signifying that the ultimate test was beginning.

Unity's Seal

The six friends exchanged weary glances—they had held together, but just barely. Breezie's knees nearly buckled with exhaustion, and Checkered's hand trembled around her lens until Greenie gently steadied her. Each Wizard wore the strain of battle on their face, a stark reminder of the cost of victory.

Sensing the illusions falter, the Orloj's cosmic hum intensified, as if calling for a culminating testament of their synergy. Reddish and Firee steadied themselves for another onslaught, but the corrupted wizard merely swayed. An eerie calm fell in the cosmic swirl around them.

Blunt lifted the runic crown-star again, feeling it pulse with a wordless request—for something unifying beyond mere raw power. "We've seen fables and poems anchor each virtue," he said, voice echoing in the stillness. "Perhaps we need a final epic to seal unity's claim over illusion."

Greenie's empathic intuition resonated with the Orloj's longing. "This is how we overcame illusions in past trials," she agreed softly. "By channeling each virtue into a story that cements them all."

"The Orloj wants a definitive epic tying every virtue into a single force, or phantoms might linger," Checkered reminded them, reading the urgency in the flickering runes overhead.

Breezie glanced toward the wizard, who stood stooped and cloak-battered. "He may yet rally his illusions if we don't cement our unity now," he warned. Firee nodded, his flame burning low and steady. "Then let's speak the Orloj's final epic—something that unites all we've learned."

Reddish cupped her embers in her hands to steady them. "We overcame phantoms that tried to break generosity, justice, courage, perseverance… Now we affirm unity, for good." At her words, the gear-laden dais beneath them rumbled in agreement, as though granting a fleeting moment to deliver this final testament. Overhead, a swirl of cosmic mist coalesced, signaling the Orloj's readiness to receive the words that would finalize its cosmic order.

Greenie placed her palm atop the runic crown-star, sensing lines of cosmic text swirling through her mind. In a clear, resonant voice, she began to recite:

"The Dusk of Fracture, the Dawn of One"

Before ages were tallied and clocks first chimed,
twelve radiant virtues danced among uncounted stars.
Courage lit a bold flame,
while justice balanced each cosmic scale.
Generosity flowed to mend lonely hearts,
as perseverance refused to break beneath storms.
Compassion stirred healing, curiosity probed every dawn,
and fortitude stood steadfast against fear's gnawing night.
Innovation birthed brighter paths,
humility steered proud souls,
wisdom guided mortal wonder,
rationality brought clarity, and unity bridged them all.
Then came a fell time when each virtue spun alone,
trapped in illusions of division.
Shadows whispered,
"Stand apart," until even starlight dimmed.
Yet from that gloom arose a single star,

A hush lingered after Greenie's final line. One by one, each Wizard quietly affirmed how unity had shaped them:

Blunt recalled temptations in distant places that once promised him absolute control. "But synergy taught me humility," he murmured. "Leading means standing beside others, not above them."

Reddish thought of the time she nearly sabotaged a mission by blazing ahead recklessly. "Unity tempered my fire into a creative spark instead of a wild blaze," she admitted softly.

Greenie felt renewed empathy welling in her heart. "Whenever illusions whispered that caring was foolish, our synergy showed me it's the very thread that weaves hearts together," she said.

Checkered remembered deceptions that twisted pure logic into cold isolation. "I learned that reason thrives best when fused with empathy," she concluded. "Clarity guided by compassion can dispel any illusion."

Firee recalled how he almost abandoned the group in despair once. "Unity anchored my flame and ensured it never died out," he said firmly.

Breezie let a gentle breeze carry their words through the glowing hall. "We overcame separation by trusting each other," he finished. "Together, we extinguished every darkness."

The Harlequin Breaks

As the resonance of their epic faded into the Orloj's cosmic engine, the corrupted wizard lurched with a sudden howl, his cloak of flaws swirling anew. He unleashed one last storm of illusions, tendrils of darkness probing each Wizard's old vulnerabilities. Yet the power of the epic filled the chamber, forming an intangible barrier that the renewed illusions could not penetrate. The dais trembled as the Harlequin's final might pressed in from every side—but unified, the six Wizards held fast, repelling it.

Breezie exhaled a purposeful gust, clearing the last clinging shadows from the chamber's corners. "That epic's energy is real," he observed in a hushed tone. "We've anchored the Orloj with a cosmic story that enshrines unity as unstoppable."

Greenie's vines trailed softly around her, glowing with star-lit patterns. She sensed that illusions could find no foothold now in hearts bound by the epic. Reddish's embers fluttered calmly at her shoulders, each gentle flame-twist a reminder of how synergy had shaped her into a balanced agent of change. Checkered felt her lens lighten in her hand—no dark whisper could weigh down her logic now. Firee's flame burned steady and unwavering, reaffirming that the doubts which once threatened him had lost all purchase.

The corrupted wizard let out a final, guttural cry. His cloak of fractal illusions flickered erratically, cracks splintering across every swirling patch of flaw. Reality itself pushed back; the Orloj, buoyed by their epic, refused to yield another inch to division. Blunt lowered the crown-star, his stance unwavering. "Keep pressing," he urged his friends. "No illusion is strong enough to sever what we've merged."

The Cloak Unravels

The wizard struggled to stand, his cloak now shifting like a tattered tapestry—each frayed section representing a flaw that had once lured him away from virtue. Those lingering strands of darkness fought vainly against the epic's resonance still thrumming in the Orloj's chamber. A hiss escaped the man's lips, but no malice remained—only anguish at what he had become.

Firee studied the swirling threads of the cloak. Each thread glimmered faintly with echoes of betrayal, greed, or despair that had at one time plagued them all. "He's wearing an embodiment of every flaw illusions exploited," Firee realized, his flame steady. "No wonder that cloak held such power."

Breezie drifted a light breeze around the trembling figure, noticing that the remaining illusions in the cloak no longer lashed out but faltered. "He might once have had all the virtues," Breezie reflected, "but illusions twisted them into their opposites. If we purify that cloak, can he be free of them?"

Greenie approached carefully, her empathic senses registering the wizard's internal battle—a swirl of guilt, sorrow, and yearning for redemption. Reddish, trusting in the unity they had built, let her embers glow softly to show they came not with hostility, but to salvage what remained of his wounded spirit. Checkered kept her lens poised, ensuring no stray shadow would regain traction.

Blunt raised the runic crown-star and stepped forward. "Unity overcame illusions across continents," he said firmly. "If a single wizard fell to them, then we can still bring him back." The wizard cringed as the crown's light washed over him. One by one, the cloak's lingering illusions peeled away in shimmering fragments, revealing glimpses of the man he once was—a figure noble of bearing, his eyes etched with deep regret.

At last, the final illusions bled out in a silent cascade of sparks. The wizard sank to his knees, cloak hanging in tatters and powerless. The Orloj's cosmic hum soared, indicating that illusions no longer held sway here. A fragile hush stilled the air—unity and courage had prevailed. The freed wizard closed his eyes, tears slipping down his cheeks as he finally grasped the weight of all the illusions undone.

Restoration

With the corrupted cloak purged, the wizard knelt trembling amid drifting motes of cosmic dust. Each piece of darkness faded away like a spent ember. The Orloj's gears now hummed in smooth unison, arcs of starlight linking gear to gear in a grand cosmic design. What had moments ago been a straining mechanism was now on the cusp of full restoration.

Reddish and Greenie each offered a supportive arm, helping the wizard rise to unsteady feet. He cast a hollow gaze over the dais, seeing the space now clear of illusions for the first time in ages. In a raw, broken voice he rasped, "I… forgot the virtues we once championed." A weak flicker of sorrow crossed his face, mourning how thoroughly the glamours had twisted him for so long.

Checkered answered with a gentle, understanding nod—there was no condemnation in her eyes. "Each of us nearly fell to illusion at one time or another," she said softly. "But our bond always guided us back." Breezie sent a comforting breeze swirling around the wizard, symbolizing how shadows had once threatened to consume him as well, yet unity's light had always shone through.

Firee conjured a small, contained flame in his palm. "We overcame despair, fear, greed, division," he recounted quietly. "Now we stand for unity. Even your cloak couldn't sever that bond." The wizard bowed his head, words failing him. Yet a glint of understanding flickered in his eyes.

Blunt lifted the runic crown-star once more. The Orloj's cosmic hum thundered in response, urging them to seal this final restoration. "The illusions are gone," he declared. "Boston's Orloj can realign the city's spirit—and the world's, if needed."

The wizard stepped aside, cloak limp in his arms, allowing the group to approach the Orloj's central hub. Overhead, a faint swirl of cosmic runes still danced as though awaiting the claim of triumph. The final restoration was at hand: illusions banished and synergy unbroken. A sense of closure crept into the air as each Wizard felt that the concluding steps would cement all they had fought for.

Dawn at the Tower

A final surge of cosmic energy rippled through the chamber, sealing the wizard's redemption and the Orloj's revival. Radiant arcs of light traced each gear, aligning them in perfect harmony. Dawn broke outside the tower at that very moment, flooding the hidden gear-chamber with fresh golden light. Slowly, the oppressive shadows that had choked the city's unity dissolved into motes of harmless color.

The once-corrupted wizard stood off to the side, his ruined cloak in hand—now purged of all malice. He bent in silent gratitude, unsure if he deserved forgiveness but free at last from the dark influence that had bound him. Reddish, remembering her own near-catastrophic missteps, stepped forward to offer reassurance. "We've all battled darkness," she said gently. "You can rebuild, just as we did."

Greenie's empathic aura confirmed the genuine remorse within him, and with a warm smile she offered quiet acceptance. Checkered lowered her lens, satisfied that no trace of illusion lingered in his posture. Firee let his flame burn bright but calm—a sign that fear no longer reigned here. Breezie conjured a soft, hopeful breeze while Blunt rested a hand on the wizard's shoulder. Each gesture spoke of unity over judgment, compassion over blame.

Together they turned to gaze upon the cosmic Orloj, fully restored at last. A hush of reverence fell over them. Each recalled every trial—fear, greed, despair, division—and how together they had forged each corresponding virtue into a cohesive whole. The tangible smell of old oil and metal mingled with the crisp dawn air wafting in from the opened hatch above, reminding them of the real, physical world that their victory now brightened.

Firee paused, reflecting on how his earliest doubts had nearly driven him to abandon the group. "I see now that my flame stands for vigilance and hope," he said quietly. "When darkness threatened it, unity kept it alive." In that admission, he felt a final closure settle in his heart.

Breezie, too, had a quiet moment of introspection. "I remember the whispers that I was unnecessary," he said, letting a gentle wind stir his cloak. "But now I see how each breeze feeds a friend's flame or ward. We proved that lie wrong by standing side by side."

The wizard watched in silent awe as each of them reflected on the hard-won lessons behind their victory. Reddish's fire now burned with purpose rather than anger. Checkered had learned that logic, when guided by empathy, offered far greater clarity. Greenie's compassion had become boundless. Blunt's humility proved more potent than any solitary throne.

Seeing how each of them had been tested by darkness and emerged stronger together, the wizard finally understood the true strength of their unity.

Outside, the city's dawn beckoned. The Orloj's cosmic hum had calmed to a gentle background whisper, signifying that all shadows were truly vanquished. A subtle portal shimmered into being at the edge of the chamber. The redeemed wizard gestured for the six young heroes to step through—he would remain here, he insisted, to atone and to serve as a guardian for whatever might come next.

Blunt, Reddish, Firee, Checkered, Breezie, and Greenie stepped through the portal into the morning glow, hearts light with relief. They emerged onto solid ground like six stars linked in a single constellation, shining beyond any lingering shadow. No illusions dogged them now; no twisted reflections threatened to break their bond. From the earliest deceits encountered in old halls to the cosmic churn beneath Boston's tower, they had risen above division's final hold.

A new day greeted them—one where nothing could ever again separate their bond. The city's pulse felt gentler, the Orloj's cosmic gears fully aligned, and each Wizard's personal arc gracefully concluded. Though their grand quest now approached its epilogue, the resonance of unity would echo on, woven into the fabric of every clock they had restored and every spirit they had redeemed. And in that hopeful dawn, the great wheel turned once more, ushering in a fresh day for Boston and for all who believed that unity could triumph over even the darkest deception.

For a long moment, silence hung in the candlelit hush of the archive. Professor Erasmus Cromwell-Smith II slowly closed the leather-bound journal in front of him, its gilt pages rustling softly. He remained still, eyes unfocused in recollection, until a gentle touch on his forearm drew him back to the present. Victoria sat across the oak table from him, the golden glow of a nearly spent candle dancing in her eyes. She took a slow breath, steadying herself, and broke the silence.

"I've studied so many chronicles of magic and history," Victoria began, her voice low and almost reverent. She reached out and lightly ran her fingers over the ornately inscribed crown-star that rested between them—the very relic Blunt's team had forged beneath the Custom House Tower. A tiny flame's reflection wavered on the bronze surface of the crown as she spoke. "But hearing how you all truly united to defeat such darkness… it's different. It's powerful." Her voice caught for just an instant, but she gathered herself, eyes shining more with admiration than tears. "Those illusions you faced were like shadows on a wall—frightening shapes meant to confuse and divide. And every time, you and your friends shone a light of understanding and hope so bright that the shadows had nowhere to hide. You turned every fear, every flaw, into part of a greater strength." She smiled then, calm and resolute, the emotional quaver in her tone replaced by steady conviction. "It inspires me. It shows me that even when darkness gathers, a single spark of unity can dispel it. I promise, I'll remember that lesson."

Erasmus reached across the table and covered Victoria's hand with his own, the weight of the old journal pressing gently beneath their palms. The dim flame between them fluttered, casting soft halos of light on the vaulted archive walls. "It's why I share these stories," he said kindly, his eyes reflecting the candle's glow. He could see the resolve and wonder in her expression—the same he had felt all those years ago. Together they glanced to a tall window where the first pale rays of morning were beginning to filter in, mingling with the warm candlelight. In the stillness of that early dawn, surrounded by dusty tomes and ancient secrets, it seemed as though time itself held its breath.

Outside, somewhere beyond the archive's walls, the city bell tower began to chime the hour—a new day beginning. Erasmus gently closed his eyes, allowing the resonant echoes to wash over them. "Victoria," he said softly, "always remember what this tale has shown you." He nodded toward the crown-star and the faint reflection of their candle on its surface. "No matter how long the night, no matter how deep the shadow… the light of unity endures."

Victoria's fingers tightened slightly around his, and she returned his nod with quiet determination. The candle on the table guttered low, its flame having done its duty. Daylight was growing stronger now, inching across the wooden table in front of them.

Professor Erasmus rose from his chair, and Victoria followed. Together, they felt the gentle morning breeze slip in through a high, cracked window, carrying with it the distant sounds of a city waking to peace. Erasmus placed the runic crown-star carefully back into its silken-lined box—a treasure not just of metal and rune, but of meaning—and in doing so, he caught their two faces reflected faintly in its polished rim. The flicker of the candle's last light and the dawning glow of day met for just a moment on that mirrored surface, indistinguishable from one another.

In that quiet moment, as the first sunbeams broke into the archive, both teacher and student understood the truth carried by the Orloj's legacy. The trials had ended, but their message would resonate far beyond these pages. Erasmus rested a hand on Victoria's shoulder and guided her toward the heavy wooden door. Behind them on the table, the final wisp of smoke curled upward from the extinguished candle, disappearing into sunlit motes of dust.

Side by side, they stepped forward into the new day. And as they did, the great wheel turned once more—ushering in a dawn of hope, wisdom, and unity that would forever light their path.

Epilogue

The Garden After the Storm

Morning sunlight warmed Boston's Public Garden, its landscaping dating back to 1859—a living testament to the city's devotion to renewal. Lush willows dipped into glimmering water, while a gentle breeze carried the scent of freshly cut grass. Blunt (Erasmus Cromwell-Smith Jr.), Reddish, Firee, Checkered, Breezie, and Greenie gathered by a quaint footbridge, their Harlequin cloaks shimmering in the gentle light.

Erasmus Cromwell-Smith II, Blunt's father, and Lynn Tabernaki arrived moments later. They had guided these Wizards long ago, imparting fundamental lessons in synergy and humility. Although their roles had been mostly unseen in the final cosmic battles, their wisdom underpinned every step the Wizards took. A faint pride shone in Erasmus II's eyes as he watched the group converge in unity, recalling how the spark of this adventure ignited years earlier.

Blunt offered a welcoming nod, the runic crown—"Unitas Est Virtus"—resting quietly in his hands. This was the very crown they had forged beneath the Custom House Tower, now a symbol of their unified virtue. No glamours hovered now; the city stood at peace after the final confrontation. Light glittered on the water as ducks paddled by, seemingly unconcerned with cosmic battles. And yet, the Orloj's hum lingered in the air, an unseen chord of harmony holding everything in gentle equilibrium.

Greenie inhaled, recalling the veils that once threatened to sever her empathy from the group's synergy. She felt only calm now, remembering how each friend had overcome illusions twisted by fear, greed, or despair—each trial giving rise to newfound courage, generosity, or hope. This garden, tranquil yet brimming with historical resonance, felt like the perfect setting to finalize their vow of passing on all they'd learned.

Reddish's embers flickered softly. She remembered how her fiery impulses had risked fracturing the group in earlier trials, but synergy taught her to harness that blaze for creation, not ruin. The garden's gentle aura reminded her that even the fiercest flame could coexist with serenity.

A hush settled over them. Lynn waved from beneath a flowering magnolia, beckoning everyone closer to a circular clearing near a small fountain, runic inscriptions etched along its stone rim. Each Wizard recognized faint echoes of the Orloj's cosmic patterns. They understood this quiet nook would serve as the final stage for planting a legacy far beyond the reach of any glamour. With gentle steps, they moved toward the fountain, hearts brimming with hope for whatever next step awaited them.

Sunbeams cast dappled patterns on the fountain's runic stone as they gathered. Erasmus II stood beside Lynn, each wearing subtle tokens of the old mentors' legacy—a hand-carved clasp or a faint wizardly brooch harkening back to the earliest guidance they'd offered. Breezie took a moment to appreciate how the city had changed since they first embarked on their quest—once overshadowed by false lights, now infused with calm unity.

Checkered lingered near the fountain's edge, lens in hand. Ghostly recollections of illusions teased at her memory, half-truths that once nearly trapped her in unwavering logic that dismissed emotion. She recognized how synergy—the fusion of intellect and empathy—had shattered each cunning trap. "We overcame illusions not just by being strong individually," she mused softly, "but by weaving each virtue together, ensuring no fracture could widen."

Greenie nodded, recalling moments when glamours sought to exploit her compassion, urging her to seal off her heart. "No illusions break us when we stand as one," she said, running her fingers over the fountain's runes. The markings pulsed gently in response, a quiet echo of the Orloj's cosmic hum.

Blunt turned the runic crown in his hands. This relic embodied the final synergy they forged—the culminating piece that restored the cosmic Orloj beneath the city's tower. His humility, honed in earlier battles, had guided him to step aside from personal glory. "We've come far," he said, glancing at Reddish. She responded with a wistful smile, embers playing across her palms. The memory of illusions almost consuming her once felt distant now, overshadowed by a measured flame that served the group.

Firee caught the swirl of conversation, recalling illusions that nearly convinced him to retreat in despair. But synergy taught him that his flame was needed to keep illusions at bay. He let a soft spark dance in the mild morning breeze—a sign of the calm faith he now carried.

Erasmus II beckoned them closer. "We stand on the threshold of a new level in our quest," he said, his voice resonant. "Others may follow your path, learning these virtues. Let's see how you'll pass along the flame." The group exchanged a silent understanding. Unity thrived not just in battles won or illusions undone, but in preparing the next generation to guard the Orloj's peace. For each Wizard, a personal vow stirred—an unspoken pledge to remain watchful, ensuring illusions never gained a foothold in Boston's soul again.

They formed a loose circle around the fountain, its waters reflecting the willows overhead. Each Wizard prepared to speak a brief vow, recalling how illusions had once tested a specific virtue. Rather than delivering lengthy speeches, they distilled their promises into concise declarations.

Blunt stepped forward first, humility evident in his posture. "I pledge to guide new guardians with the same open heart once shown to me. Together, we'll keep illusions from ever taking root."

Reddish pressed a glowing ember to her chest, eyes steady. "I vow to channel my fire responsibly—lighting paths for others without scorching their hopes. No illusions will feed on hasty sparks again."

Greenie rested a palm on the fountain's stone rim, compassion shining in her eyes. "I vow to remain open-hearted, ensuring empathy links every new ally who joins us. Where illusions sow distrust, we will sow unity."

Checkered lifted her lens, a small smile tugging at her lips. "I vow to uphold curiosity tempered with empathy. I won't allow illusions to blind logic again, nor let reason drift apart from compassion."

Firee's flame danced near his fingertips. "I vow to share the spark that overcame illusions of despair. My flame will be a beacon for anyone who feels overshadowed."

Breezie let a gentle breeze swirl around them. "I vow to be the quiet wind carrying hope, ensuring illusions never isolate a single voice. Together, we remain essential."

None of them offered a lengthy soliloquy. Each vow was succinct, reflecting how illusions were undone by synergy rather than by any grandstanding. Erasmus II nodded approvingly, leaning on his staff—a keepsake from his own mentors. Lynn watched with tears glistening, recalling how she once saw sparks of possibility in each of these young Wizards. The vow circle complete, they fell silent, letting the vow's resonance sink into the fountain's ancient runes.

A hush settled in the garden, as though the entire landscape recognized the significance of these vows. Sunlight brightened, dancing on the water's surface. The runic crown in Blunt's hands flickered with a soft glow, indicating the next step in sealing their legacy. Greenie stepped forward, opening a small pouch woven with cosmic threads—inside was a runic seed etched with swirling sigils reminiscent of the Orloj's cosmic symbols.

Blunt recalled how in countless battles illusions had tried to stop them from forging synergy. He felt the star-laced energy radiating from the seed—a testament to every virtue they'd nurtured. "This is the seed that ties our final unity to a living symbol," he said quietly.

Erasmus II's eyes lit with recognition. "A seed once mentioned by the earliest watchers," he murmured, half-remembering some old lore. "It grows where synergy flourishes—a sentinel against illusions. Plant it, and the city's harmony stands watch even after you rest."

Breezie approached, letting a soft breeze carry the seed's subtle glow. "We overcame illusions that threatened to separate us," he said. "This seed can remind new guardians that synergy overcame darkness every time."

Reddish, enthralled by the seed's glowing markings, pictured how illusions once urged her toward recklessness. She realized this living token could help future watchers remember the measured flame that synergy taught her. "Let's give Boston a living testament," she said warmly.

Firee knelt to help Blunt lift a small trowel near the fountain's base. Checkered hovered her lens over the soil, ensuring no lurking illusion tainted the ground. Satisfied that all was clear, they prepared to plant the seed with great care. The garden's hush deepened as if anticipating a pivotal moment. Each friend paused, letting any lingering illusions dissolve in the warmth of synergy—a synergy they hoped to pass on through new growth.

Before plunging the seed into the soft earth, Erasmus II and Lynn shared a tender glance. They remembered how, in an older era, they had met these Wizards as wide-eyed novices, offering key insights about synergy's hidden power. Lynn gently touched the seed, her voice catching with emotion. "I remember those early days, when illusions nearly trapped you in simple anxieties," she said, eyes shining.

Greenie lowered her gaze, recalling illusions that once targeted her empathy, urging her to shut others out. "You both taught us that synergy means never letting illusions isolate a single mind or heart," she said gratefully.

Erasmus II nodded, tapping his staff lightly on the ground. "We never doubted you'd unmask illusions and rescue the Orloj's cosmic core. Still, the road was yours to travel. Now your example stands for all future watchers."

Checkered's mind flashed with images from their very first trial in Philadelphia—the first time illusions tried to confound her logic. She remembered how Erasmus II had gently teased out her curiosity back then, showing that unwavering reason alone wasn't enough; only synergy, bridged with empathy, completed the puzzle. She offered him a small, grateful smile. He returned a grave nod, perhaps recalling how even he had once been threatened by illusions.

Reddish's embers glowed softly. She felt how this moment connected the earliest instructions from these mentors to the final cosmic battles they had survived. Breezie exhaled, the hush between them bridged by a gentle wind that let everyone sense the calm of knowing illusions were forever left behind.

Lynn ran a hand over the runic crown in Blunt's grip, as if searching for her own reflection in the glistening metal. "We pass the torch to you fully now," she whispered. "May no illusions ever disrupt what you have built." With that, planting the seed became a tangible act to seal the journey's finale.

The group encircled a small patch of turned earth near the fountain. Boston's century-old landscaping provided a serene cradle for the seed, signifying the city's tradition of forging community amidst new beginnings. Blunt knelt and placed the seed into the soil, the tiny object's runic lines flickering across its surface. A collective hush fell, as though each Wizard's heartbeat synchronized with the Orloj's cosmic hum.

Reddish guided a gentle flame over the soil, warming it so illusions would have no space to hide. Firee added a faint spark of vigilance, ensuring the seed's energy remained stable. Breezie breathed out a soft breeze across the spot, symbolizing how illusions had once overshadowed him until synergy gave him the confidence to stand out.

Greenie brushed her fingers over the newly covered seed, compassion flowing into the earth. Checkered's lens confirmed no trace of illusion lingered, verifying the seed's purity. Finally, Blunt pressed the tip of the runic crown to the soft earth, sending a last wave of combined magic into the seed. "Let this be the anchor for all we've achieved," he said, his voice trembling slightly with reverence.

Erasmus II and Lynn each placed a hand over Blunt's hands, wedding their old mentorship with the Wizards' triumphant synergy. The virtues of humility, courage, curiosity, empathy, fortitude, generosity, justice, perseverance, and more pulsed into the soil. In that moment, illusions felt like nothing more than a distant nightmare—wholly undone by unity.

The fountain's runes glowed as if in recognition of the act. Nearby park-goers, if any noticed at all, simply saw a small group engaged in an unusual planting. But the Wizards felt the cosmic weight of every step they'd taken, all of it culminating in a single seed that might one day remind future watchers that illusions can never overshadow united hearts.

A faint shimmer arced from the planted seed, rising up through the soil. Moment by moment, a tender shoot emerged—slender and etched with swirling patterns resembling the Orloj's starry designs. Gasps escaped the Wizards' lips as the runic sapling unfurled emerald tendrils, starlight dancing around them. Even Erasmus II and Lynn watched with awe, tears in their eyes reflecting the hope of new eras.

Breezie's eyes glistened with wonder. "Look at it... it's absorbing each virtue we poured into the soil," he breathed. He recalled how illusions once whispered that he'd never be more than a background figure. Yet synergy had made his calm wind vital. He could see that very wind now gently ruffling the sapling's leaves, encouraging its growth.

Reddish gently shielded the tiny plant from any stray gust or ember, mindful of how illusions had once exploited her reckless flame. She marveled at how each creeping root intertwined with the magical currents beneath the garden—a living vow that their hard-won synergy would outlast any illusion. "This is the living bond we fought for," she whispered.

Checkered scanned the sapling with her lens, reading the faint runic lines spiraling up its stem. Each line spelled out aspects of humility, justice, fortitude, curiosity—virtues they had honed in the face of illusion. "The Orloj's cosmic mark is in its very fiber," she concluded softly. "No illusions can overshadow such a symbol."

Greenie pressed her palm to the tiny trunk, eyes brimming. "Compassion anchored our synergy, and this plant will anchor the next guardians," she said. The hush that followed brimmed with relief—no illusions lurked here, no whisper of division—

merely the unspoken knowledge that their quest had fulfilled an ancient promise.

For a moment, they all stood transfixed by the sapling's quiet glow. Finally, Breezie stepped closer, letting a gentle breeze swirl around its new leaves. He found words he'd never shared before. "I… I always feared illusions made me the weak link," he admitted, voice trembling. "But standing with you all, those illusions never overcame us. My wind was part of every victory—like each root, trunk, and leaf works together here."

His breath hitched, but Blunt placed a reassuring hand on Breezie's shoulder. The runic crown glinted faintly in the morning sun. "You were never overshadowed," Blunt said gently. "We needed your calm to keep illusions from fraying us. This sapling stands tall because each gust helped shape it."

Greenie nodded, recalling how illusions once threatened to single out Breezie's quieter presence. "We overcame illusions that thrived on separating strengths," she added. "Thanks to you, no illusion found a crack in our synergy." Breezie's tension ebbed, replaced by serene acceptance that illusions had no hold on him.

Checkered offered him a small smile, her lens dimmed in the tranquil morning. "Your wind balanced Reddish's flame, Firee's spark, Blunt's ward, my logic, and Greenie's empathy," she said. "That balance of elements overcame illusions every time." Breezie nodded, tears glistening at the corners of his eyes—those lingering doubts forever banished from his heart.

Checkered then lowered her lens with quiet pride, reflecting on how synergy had welded reason and empathy into an unbreakable whole. Reddish's embers flickered softly; each of them sensed that the illusions of their past were now nothing but distant memories, undone by living synergy.

Just then Erasmus II and Lynn stepped forward, each wearing subtle tokens reminiscent of their earliest lessons with these Wizards. Erasmus II placed a hand gently on the new sapling. "We never expected illusions to ripple so far, nor that your synergy would be so crucial," he admitted, his voice thick with emotion. "But from the first time you embraced humility and curiosity, we glimpsed this outcome—an unbreakable circle."

Lynn's eyes shimmered with pride. "I recall your early stumbles—illusions nearly catching Reddish's spark, Breezie's breeze, Firee's flame. Each time, synergy overcame them. This result goes beyond any illusion we once feared might devour us all."

Reddish nodded, grateful they had taught her how to channel fire responsibly. "You guided us before illusions twisted every virtue," she said. "Without that foundation, we might've fallen to despair or greed."

Checkered smiled softly, lens in hand. "Illusions threatened to isolate each of us. But your early mentorship showed us that synergy is the heart of every clock—every city's unity. We just had to prove it to ourselves."

Greenie ran a palm over the sapling's leaves, noticing how each Wizard's personal vow from moments ago seemed embedded in its runic veins. "It's a new dawn for Boston, for the Orloj—for illusions undone," she said quietly. "This plant will remain a living anchor long after we're gone." Erasmus II and Lynn exchanged a look of satisfaction, relief, and affection. Their old roles as mentors were gracefully ceding to the Wizards' new guardianship. The morning light grew brighter; illusions were nowhere in sight, synergy standing in eternal guard over the city's future.

A light breeze carried the gentle chatter of passersby in the Public Garden, most of them oblivious to the cosmic significance of the gathering under the willows. The vows had been spoken, the runic seed planted, but an unspoken cue hung in the air. The fountain's sigils flared momentarily, as if prompting them toward one final symbolic act.

Blunt sensed it first. "The fountain's runes are still alive," he observed, eyeing the glowing carvings. "Perhaps we need one more unifying gesture." He glanced at the tender sapling, newly sprouted—reminding him how illusions once tried to quench each Wizard's spark but found no purchase against their unity. "Let's give this sapling a moment of final solidarity before we depart."

Greenie took his hand; Firee reached for Reddish's; Checkered and Breezie linked arms; Erasmus II and Lynn joined in. Forming a ring around the plant, they let synergy's quiet energy flow between them. A calm hush enveloped the group, illusions a distant memory. The runic crown glowed softly from within Blunt's satchel. The bright day moved onward, future onlookers unwittingly walking past, but an ephemeral hush signaled that a final piece of closure was about to unfold.

In that ring of joined hands, a gentle warmth swirled from the newly formed sapling. None of them needed to speak— each remembered the illusions that had once tested them, and how each illusion fell when their virtues united.

Blunt detected subtle arcs of synergy passing among them, the Orloj's resonance faint but steady. Firee exhaled slowly, satisfied that illusions could never wedge into a circle so firmly bonded. Breezie smoothed a light breeze across the sapling's leaves, while Greenie stroked the small trunk with empathy. Overhead, the fountain's glimmer flickered, reflecting their unity as a dancing tapestry of sunlight.

A hush lingered, illusions utterly absent. The energy around the sapling was a tangible affirmation that all those trials were undone the moment each Wizard realized illusions could not overshadow unity. Even the corrupted wizard they once faced had found redemption. This ephemeral moment confirmed that illusions had lost their last foothold, utterly outshone by synergy's luminous coil.

Another breath of silence passed, letting each Wizard soak in the morning's serenity. For a fleeting moment, no one spoke at all. The breeze carried distant notes of city life—carriages rolling and footsteps on paths, families enjoying the garden. Nearby, a passing couple paused to smile at the tranquil scene, quietly sensing the harmony blanketing this corner of Boston. In this small clearing, the group's synergy filled the air with an almost sacred calm.

Breezie closed his eyes, the wind swirling around him like a reassuring friend. Firee stood at ease, his flame low but unwavering. Reddish felt her embers gently pulsing, with no illusion urging her to incinerate or rush ahead. Checkered's lens shimmered in the golden light, with no illusion tangling her reason. Greenie simply radiated compassionate warmth, any illusion that once threatened her empathy now fully vanquished. Blunt placed the runic crown at the sapling's base, symbolizing the final merging of cosmic guardianship with new earthly life.

This pause was a final testament that illusions had no place here. Each Wizard's personal arc had come to a soaring close. The hush lay sweet and heavy, as though time itself had paused to honor their unity. The sun climbed higher, reflecting on the pond's surface in a dazzling mosaic of radiance. A sense of awe, tinged with deepest gratitude, washed over them: illusions behind them, synergy forging a new era in Boston's public heart.

From the seedling's leaves came a gentle glow, intensifying under the brightening sun. It pulsed in time with the Orloj's cosmic beat—reminiscent of how illusions once tried to stifle that very heartbeat in cathedrals, towers, and gear-laden crypts. But synergy had proven unstoppable, weaving humility, courage, perseverance, justice, generosity, empathy—every virtue—into a single radiant bond.

Erasmus II and Lynn exchanged hopeful looks. "We sense new watchers will come," Lynn murmured, "drawn by this living sign. The illusions you dispelled might reappear in other forms, but they'll find no easy cracks."

Greenie brushed the sapling's topmost leaf, feeling a subtle tremor of possibility. She pictured young guardians following in their footsteps—novices curious about illusions and cosmic clocks. "Our virtues will pass on, weaving new fables," she said softly, imagining how illusions might someday test unprepared hearts, but trusting that synergy would rise to meet them.

Firee's flame brightened, as though anticipating a future generation that might ask him for guidance in confronting the corrosive fear of illusions. Breezie, too, felt a stirring in the air, as if the illusions of future ages might attempt to overshadow quiet souls, only to be undone by a culture of unity. Each Wizard understood that they would not stand watch forever—but thanks to this foundation, any illusions to come would find the next watchers equally prepared.

Reddish's embers flared briefly. "When illusions arise, they'll see this sapling and recall how synergy always won," she whispered. A hush framed her words; illusions were wholly absent, and synergy was fully present. The little sapling glowed with silent promise. Indeed, the orchard of future guardians would never let illusions tear them apart. Blunt sensed the dawn of new stories forming—each future caretaker destined to preserve these virtues. The seedling's gentle luminescence hinted at countless adventures yet to unfold.

A subtle hush drifted once more across the Public Garden, the soft rustle of willow branches and distant city sounds forming a gentle soundtrack to this concluding moment. Each Wizard felt a deep sense of completion in their bones. The illusions that had once plagued them—whispering fear, greed, injustice, despair—had no foothold here now, replaced by the living symbol of synergy they had planted.

Firee took a final step forward, his gaze on the sapling. He recalled how illusions had once nearly extinguished his flame. Now he crouched beside the plant, letting a mild warmth radiate from his palms. "This little seedling is a mirror of my own spark," he said quietly. "Once, illusions told me I might smother or burn aimlessly. But synergy gave my fire a home. I'll ensure others find that same guiding flame."

Breezie stood next to Firee, a reflective softness in his eyes. He had once believed the illusions that said he was unnecessary, that he could be overshadowed. Yet each breath of wind he conjured had proven those illusions wrong—tying every flame, ward, lens, and vine together. So too does this sapling stand as a living reminder that no voice is too small in the current of unity.

Checkered let her lens rest at her side. She recalled illusions from her earliest days that twisted her curiosity into doubt. "But synergy revealed that real knowledge unites, not isolates," she said, gently running a hand over the sapling's leaves. "If illusions arise in future hearts, let them see how logic, empathy, and unity overcame every false whisper."

Reddish flicked a gentle ember over the soil. Her mind touched on the illusions that once fed on her impatience. "No illusion can warp me into a reckless flame," she said firmly. "This sapling stands for how a measured spark, guided by synergy, warms but never scorches. I pray future watchers learn it well."

Greenie took in the profound quiet, recalling how illusions had tried to crush her empathy with cynicism. "So many illusions wanted me to think caring was a weakness," she murmured. "Yet synergy showed that compassion is the anchor illusions can't break. This plant pulses with that same unwavering care."

At last, Blunt raised the runic crown one final time, faint starlight of synergy pulsing in its metal. "We overcame illusions by forging a ring of virtue," he said. "Humility, curiosity, justice, fortitude, generosity, empathy, and the rest. May this seed remain a testament that illusions—no matter how cunning—fall when hearts unite."

Erasmus II and Lynn stepped forward as well. "We shall watch over this garden with you, in spirit or in counsel," Erasmus II promised. Lynn placed a hand on the sapling, a tear falling upon its leaf. "No illusion can stand where synergy blooms," she whispered.

A gentle hush sealed this final vow. Blunt lowered the runic crown at the sapling's base, humility evident in his posture; Reddish's ember glowed steadily—her once-reckless flame now a gentle warmth; Firee's flame burned strong and even, free of the despair that once dimmed it; Checkered tucked away her lens, curiosity now balanced with compassion; Breezie exhaled a contented breath, his breeze carrying quiet hope; and Greenie rested a loving hand on the new leaves, her empathy anchoring this new beginning. The sun climbed higher, warming the stone fountain, the newly sprouted sapling, and the ring of Wizards around it. In that shimmering morning light, illusions parted from every corner of memory, replaced by a living promise of hope. At the fountain's edge, the runic crown now rested beside the newborn sapling, both glistening as one in the morning sun—a final tableau of unity and renewal. The final words lingered in the air, echoing across the dawn:

No illusions overshadow synergy. No darkness endures once virtues unite.

The public garden, awakened to this triumphant hush, enfolded them in a new day's embrace, ensuring that what they built would outlive illusions in every form. Thus the saga's epilogue ended in gentle radiance—seeds of legacy planted, illusions undone, synergy eternal.

Author's Note:

A Window into the Journey

Creating The Orloj of Boston has been as much a personal voyage as it was a literary one. In my teens, I once stood in an orchard at dusk, worried that my earnest dreams might be mere mirages—fragile hopes bound to fail under life's pressures. Yet a trusted mentor offered a gentle truth: by combining fortitude and humility, no vision is too grand. That memory rooted itself in my heart, later blossoming into the saga you hold now.

Throughout the Wizards' travels—Philadelphia's early challenges and the final test beneath Boston's Custom House Tower—I channeled that orchard epiphany. Blunt's steady leadership echoes the calm conviction I found when illusions threatened to overshadow my youthful hopes, while Reddish's fiery spirit recalls how I nearly let impatience scorch my own ambitions until synergy tempered my drive into shared purpose. Greenie's empathy carries my deepest gratitude for community, for I learned—much like she did—that compassion stands firm against isolation. Firee's unwavering flame reminds me of the courage it takes to persist when doubt whispers defeat, and Breezie's gentle wind evokes the acceptance that even the quiet among us have vital roles. Checkered's logic, balanced by empathy, reflects my realization that knowledge means little if it fails to serve the greater good.

Mentors like Erasmus Cromwell-Smith II and Lynn Tabernaki stand in for the real guides who nudged me beyond my orchard's doubts. Their wisdom, woven into the cosmic threads of the Orloj's battles, exemplifies how one's own illusions can be dispelled by unity and openness.

To you, dear reader, I extend a personal invitation: carry a piece of this story into your life. Let courage, empathy, or fortitude speak when illusions loom. Like the orchard that shaped my journey—or the sapling in Boston's Public Garden (established 1859)—our collective roots deepen when we share hope. May we all nurture the virtues that bind hearts, and unmask illusions for what they truly are. And when the clock next chimes, remember: every question is a beacon of light along your path. Thank you for stepping into this cosmic dance with me.

Astronomical Clocks Index

Astronomical Clocks in the U.S.

- **Cedar Rapids' "Silent Watcher"**
Location: Cedar Rapids, Iowa
Year Built: Unknown (narrative civic clock; early-20th-century styling)
Description: A steadfast civic timekeeper that opens the saga, quietly modeling humility and unity before the journey turns toward Europe's great astronomical clocks (Ch. 1).
- **Engle Monumental Clock**
Location: Hazleton, Pennsylvania
Year Built: 1878
Description: Stephen Decatur Engle's towering showpiece with intricate figures; in the story it confronts stagnation and re-centers communal resilience (Ch. 3).
- **Old State House Clock**
Location: Boston, Massachusetts
Year Built: 1713 (mechanism updated later)
Description: The emblematic colonial clock presiding over revolutionary streets; a touchstone for innovation and civic courage (Ch. 4).
- **Thomas Jefferson's Astronomical Clock**
Location: Monticello, Virginia
Year Built: 1806
Description: Jefferson's brass astronomical timekeeper for tracking celestial cycles; anchors the "Lantern of Inquiry" and disciplined curiosity (Ch. 6).
- **Old North Church Clock**
Location: Boston, Massachusetts
Year Built: 1726 (approx.)
Description: Boston's oldest surviving church clock; its steady beat underwrites questioning, vigilance, and clear-eyed resolve (Ch. 7).

- **Wanamaker Grand Court Clock**
Location: Philadelphia, Pennsylvania
Year Built: Early 20th century
Description: The Grand Court's iconic timepiece in a vast civic hall; in the narrative, its public cadence resonates with compassion's renewal (Ch. 8).
- **Rittenhouse Astronomical Clock**
Location: Philadelphia, Pennsylvania
Year Built: Late 18th century
Description: Precision tradition in the American scientific vein; supports justice's clarity and measured impartiality (Ch. 12).
- **Simon Willard's Astronomical Shelf Clock**
Location: North Grafton, Massachusetts
Year Built: c. 1780
Description: A "home planetarium" with calendrical/astral indications; initiates the mirror-trials of reflection and honest self-seeing (Ch. 15).
- **Great Historical Clock of America**
Location: Washington, D.C. (narrative setting)
Year Built: 19th-century automaton tradition
Description: A grand narrative automaton used in the fortitude arc, tested alongside its overseas counterpart (Ch. 14).
- **Sedona's Orloj**
Location: Sedona, Arizona
Year Built: Modern (narrative)
Description: A desert-set Orloj whose dials and figures entwine with justice; paired with Franeker to balance law and empathy (Ch. 11).
- **Clock of the Long Now**
Location: Near Van Horn, West Texas
Year Built: Ongoing (initiated 1996)
Description: A 10,000-year clock reframing time as stewardship; in the generosity arc it opposes short-term greed with long-horizon care (Ch. 16).

- **Adler Planetarium Celestial Clock**

Location: Chicago, Illinois

Year Built: 1930

Description: A museum celestial display linking the scales of justice to cosmic order; paired with Münster for balance (Ch. 17).

- **Independence Hall Clock**

Location: Philadelphia, Pennsylvania

Year Built: 1753 (approx.)

Description: The founding hall's tower clock; symbolizes fortitude and civic duty en route to its European counterpart (Ch. 13).

Astronomical Clocks Around the World

- **Zytglogge Astronomical Clock**

Location: Bern, Switzerland

Year Built: 1530 (current astronomical stage)

Description: Medieval show clock with figures and celestial dials; pairs with the saga's opening chapter to frame humility and unity (Ch. 1).

- **Stará Bystrica Astronomical Clock**

Location: Stará Bystrica, Slovakia

Year Built: 2009

Description: A modern wooden Orloj with regional motifs; in-story it confronts stagnation and callousness, advancing innovation and compassion (Ch. 3).

- **Horologium Mirabile Lundense**

Location: Lund Cathedral, Lund, Sweden

Year Built: 1425

Description: Medieval wooden astronomical clock with knights and calendrical/astrological displays; centers disciplined inquiry (Ch. 6).

- **Eise Eisinga Planetarium**

Location: Franeker, Netherlands

Year Built: 1781

Description: A ceiling-mounted planetary model; its measured heavens steady justice's course beside Sedona's Orloj (Ch. 11).

- **Jens Olsen's World Clock**

Location: Copenhagen City Hall, Denmark

Year Built: 1955 (inaugurated; designed/started earlier)

Description: A civic-scientific masterpiece with thousands of parts and deep astronomical cycles; paired with Rittenhouse to complete Justice's Triumph (Ch. 12).

- **Gdańsk Astronomical Clock**

Location: St. Mary's Church, Gdańsk, Poland

Year Built: 1460

Description: Monumental medieval mechanism with zodiac and calendar; tested alongside Independence Hall in the fortitude arc (Ch. 13).

- **Ulm Minster Clock**

Location: Ulm Minster, Ulm, Germany

Year Built: 16th century (trad.)

Description: A historic astronomical ensemble within the Minster; in the narrative, its cadence steadies Fortitude's Fire with the American counterpart (Ch. 14).

- **Zimmer Tower (Jubilee Astronomical Clock)**

Location: Lier, Belgium

Year Built: 1930

Description: Multi-dial public astronomical ensemble; completes the paired mirror-trials of reflection with Willard's shelf clock (Ch. 15).

- **Wells Cathedral Clock**

Location: Wells, England

Year Built: c. 1390

Description: One of the oldest working astronomical clocks with jousting knights; entwined with Generosity's Triumph (Ch. 16).

- **Münster Astronomical Clock**

Location: St. Paulus-Dom, Münster, Germany

Year Built: 1540

Description: Planetary and calendar trains in a 16th-century masterpiece; balances justice with Adler's celestial clock (Ch. 17).

- **Salisbury Cathedral Clock**

Location: Salisbury, England

Year Built: 1386

Description: The world's oldest working mechanical clock (bell-striking, no dial); a crucible for courage (Ch. 18).

- **Strasbourg Astronomical Clock**

Location: Strasbourg Cathedral, Strasbourg, France

Year Built: 1842 (current version)

Description: A grand, complex astronomical clock; in-story it refines courage against hesitation (Ch. 18).

- **Greenwich Clock (Shepherd Gate)**

Location: Royal Observatory, Greenwich, England

Year Built: 1852

Description: The public master of GMT; frames Perseverance's Triumph before the overseas counterpart (Ch. 19).

- **Messina Cathedral Clock Tower**

Location: Messina, Sicily, Italy

Year Built: 1933 (modern tower-show and astronomical dials)

Description: Lion, rooster, and saints tableau with astronomical indications; replaces Ulm in this chapter to counter despair with steady cadence (Ch. 19).

- **Rostock Astronomical Clock (St. Mary's Church)**

Location: Rostock, Germany

Year Built: 1472

Description: Interior medieval clock with astrolabe, noon apostles' parade, and Death figure; famed for continuous operation and renewed calendar disk—central to Compassion's Triumph and its final test (Ch. 8–9).

Glossary of Characters in "The Orloj of Boston"

Orloj Wizards

The core group of magical protagonists, led by Blunt, who confront illusions and embody virtues across various clock-related trials.

- **Blunt (Erasmus Cromwell-Smith Jr.)**
  Leader of the Wizards, uses water wards for protection, champions virtues like unity, humility, courage, and reflection. Carries synergy artifacts (gears, pendants, crown) and a tome or diaries, embodying steady leadership and moral conviction.
- **Reddish (Sofia)**
  Fiery Wizard with ember-based magic, overcomes pride and haste, drives virtues like courage, compassion, and fairness. Resists impulsivity and embraces synergy, often acting as a passionate force in trials.
- **Firee (Sanjiv)**
  Precise flame Wizard, vigilant against fear and despair, supports unity with runic pendants and danger sense. Represents courage and persistence, countering isolation and doubt in clock challenges.
- **Checkered (Winnie)**
  Analytical Wizard, uses an enchanted lens to detect illusions and decipher runes, counters flaws like ignorance and prejudice with reason and empathy. Promotes trust, caution, and fairness.
- **Breezie**
  Wind Wizard, fosters synergy with breezes and Reality Sight to detect portals and illusions. Exemplifies quiet resilience, promoting unity and calm resolve against isolation and fear.

• **Greenie**

Empathic Wizard with healing vines, promotes compassion, empathy, and curiosity. Senses emotional and moral tensions, countering apathy and division with heartfelt unity.

Mentors and Mentor Spirits

Figures who guide the Wizards with wisdom, often spectral or historical, instilling virtues and countering illusions.

• **Erasmus Cromwell-Smith II**

Professor and mentor, echoes the author's real-life guide, instills humility and courage. Reflects on Boston's trials in Sedona and guides Wizards in the Epilogue's sapling planting, symbolizing nurturing wisdom.

• **Lynn Tabernaki**

Mentor figure and Erasmus II's companion, offers emotional support and early lessons. Supports Wizards with guidance, joins the sapling planting, and symbolizes nurturing wisdom against doubts.

• **Erasmus Cromwell-Smith Sr.**

Historical mentor, Blunt's father, whose wisdom guides via diaries and spectral mentor spirits like Mr. M. Instilled virtues in prior generations, referenced for synergy and moral clarity.

• **Mr. M.**

Spectral mentor with a half-cape, linked to Erasmus Sr.'s lineage, appears in Boston Common and Beacon Hill. Foreshadows trials and reinforces virtues against illusions.

• **Mrs. V.**

Maternal mentor spirit with a half-cape, offers guidance on humility, curiosity, and compassion. Appears across chapters (6, 8, 17) to affirm virtues like justice and unity.

• **The Orloj**

Silver-haired, fatherly cosmic entity of starlight and gears in Boston's Old North Church crypt. Guides Wizards post-Antiquarian trials and during puzzle challenges, embodying reflective wisdom.

Antiquarians

Mystical figures who test the Wizards with illusions tied to specific virtues, acting as both adversaries and teachers.

- **Cornelius Tetragor**

Antiquarian associated with a traveling bookstore, tests Wizards with illusions of vanity and corruption in Chapters 1 and 2. Challenges humility and unity, linked to early narrative arcs.

- **Lazarus Zeetrikus**

Antiquarian of innovation and Perseverance, tests Wizards with stagnation illusions, despair and hopelessness illusions. Provides the Synergy Gear (Innovare Est Virtus). Antiquarian of perseverance, bent-hat figure with runic scars, tests in Chapter 19.

- **Morpheus Rubicom**

Antiquarian of ignorance and courage, ragged-cloaked (Chapter 6) or trinket-cloaked (Chapter 18). Tests Wizards with half-truths and cowardice illusions, provides gears like Quaestio Iterum and Perseverantia Est Virtus.

- **Paulina Tetrikus**

Antiquarian of compassion and generosity, radiant (Chapter 8) or amber-shawled (Chapter 16). Tests Wizards with callous and greed illusions, provides gears like Caritas Iterum and Caritas Est Finis.

- **Lettizia Dillettante**

Antiquarian of justice, silver-gowned with a starlit veil, tests Wizards with injustice and bias illusions in Chapters 11, 12, and 17. Provides synergy artifacts like Aequitas Est Virtus coin and medallion.

- **Lucrecia Van Egmond**

Antiquarian of fortitude, midnight-blue cloaked, tests Wizards with fear and doubt illusions in Chapters 13 and 14. Provides synergy artifacts like Fortitudo Vincit Timorem key and Reflectio Est Virtus pendant.

Historical Figures

Real or fictionalized historical figures who appear in cameos or are referenced to teach virtues or contextualize trials.

- **Benjamin Franklin**
Historical figure in a Chapter 5 cameo, demonstrates swift synergy via a lightning rod experiment in Boston's Old North Church crypt, teaching immediate, unified action against illusions.
- **Thomas Jefferson**
Historical figure, creator of Monticello's Astronomical Clock, referenced in Chapter 6 for his curious spirit, tied to the Wizards' battle against ignorance illusions.
- **Paul Revere**
Historical figure referenced in Chapter 7 illusions and clues, tied to Boston's revolutionary spirit and the Old North Church Clock, symbolizing curiosity and resolve.
- **Stephen Decatur Engle**
Historical figure, creator of the Engle monumental Clock, referenced in Chapters 3 and 8 for his compassionate vision, tied to breaking stagnation and callous illusions.
- **Ralph Waldo Emerson**
Historical figure in a Chapter 10 cameo in his 1841 Concord study, teaches transcendental curiosity and synergy, linked to the Over-Soul concept and the Old North Church Clock.

Antagonists and Malevolent Forces

Entities or figures representing illusions and flaws, challenging the Wizards' virtues and synergy.

- **Dark Harlequin**
Rumored sinister presence, manifests as a vortex with void-eyes (Chapter 20) or through a corrupted wizard's cloak (Chapter 21). Orchestrates divisive illusions tied to flaws like betrayal, pride, and ignorance, a recurring threat across chapters.
- **Dark Goblin**

Rumored malevolent force, symbolizes illusions threatening synergy, referenced in the Prologue I, Prologue, and early chapters. Possibly distinct from the Dark Harlequin, linked to fear and mistrust.

• **Corrupted Wizard (Unnamed)**

Once-noble wizard, now the Dark Harlequin's instrument in Chapter 21, cloaked in a tapestry of flaws (envy, fear, betrayal). Redeemed through the Wizards' synergy, embodying the narrative's theme of overcoming moral failings.

Supporting Characters

Additional figures who aid or interact with the Wizards, often providing guidance, warnings, or historical context.

• **Bart Sutton-Leigh**

Blunt's uncle, provides diaries and guidance, investigates Boston's Orloj in Chapters 1, 2, and 4. Supports Wizards against illusions, tied to humility and unity.

• **Antonella Cromwell-Smith**

Blunt's aunt, supports Wizards with historical knowledge, monitors illusions in Chapters 1, 2, and 4. Aids in uncovering clues about U.S. clocks and the Harlequin's Quest.

Glossary of Latin Terms

Aequitas Est Virtus (Justice is Virtue)

A guiding principle associated with justice, featured on synergy artifacts like coins, pendants, and sigils. Emphasizes fairness and counters illusions of injustice, bias, and favoritism.

Avaritia Est Vitium; Donatio Est Virtus (Greed is Vice; Generosity is Virtue)

A clue against greed illusions, highlighting the virtue of generosity. Appears in Chapter 16, tied to the Clock of the Long Now and Wells Cathedral Clock.

Caritas Contra Calliditas (Compassion Against Callousness)

A clue emphasizing compassion as a counter to callous illusions, found in Chapter 8, linked to the Engle monumental Clock and Rostock Clock.

Caritas Est Finis (Compassion Is the End)

Etched on a bronze Synergy Gear from Paulina Tetrikus, symbolizing the triumph of empathy over callousness. Appears in Chapter 8, tied to compassion's narrative arc.

Caritas Iterum (Compassion Again)

Etched on a bronze Synergy Gear, symbolizing the persistence of empathy. Found in Chapter 8, reinforcing compassion against apathy and indifference.

Caritas Veritatem Revelat (Compassion Reveals Truth)

A clue against callous illusions, etched on a bronze Synergy Gear from Hazleton. Appears in Chapter 9, linked to the Rostock Clock and overcoming apathy.

Chronos Taceo, Hazleton Vocat? (Time is Silent, Hazleton Calls?)

A cryptic clue hinting at illusions tied to the Engle monumental Clock, suggesting a call to action. Found in Chapter 7, linked to curiosity's triumph.

Fortitudo Est Virtus; Timiditas Est Vitium (Courage is Virtue; Cowardice is Vice)

A clue against cowardice illusions, emphasizing courage. Appears in Chapter 18, tied to the Salisbury and Strasbourg Clocks.

Fortitudo Vincit Timorem (Fortitude Conquers Fear)

Etched on synergy artifacts like pendants and keys, symbolizing triumph over fear and doubt. Found in Chapters 13 and 14, linked to the Independence Hall and Gdańsk Clocks.

Fortitudo Vincit Timorem; Timor Est Vitium (Fortitude Conquers Fear; Fear is Vice)

A clue reinforcing fortitude as a counter to fear illusions, emphasizing fear as a flaw. Appears in Chapter 13, tied to fortitude's triumph.

Humanitas Sive Nexum: Rises? (Humanity or Connection Arises?)

A cryptic clue for future illusions, suggesting themes of empathy and unity. Found in Chapter 8, linked to compassion's narrative arc.

Innovare Contra Stagnatio (Innovate Against Stagnation)

A phrase symbolizing innovation as a counter to stagnation and resistance to change. Appears in Chapter 4, tied to the Old State House Clock.

Innovare Est Virtus (Innovation is Virtue)

Etched on a silver Synergy Gear from Zeetrikus, symbolizing collaborative innovation. A recurring motif across chapters (e.g., 4, 5, 8, 9, 13, 14, 15, 16, 17, 19, 20, 21), central to overcoming illusions.

Innovatio in Spiritu (Innovation in Spirit)

An inscri ption tied to the virtue of innovation, countering illusions of inertia. Found in Chapter 3, linked to the Engle monumental and Stará Bystrica Clocks.

Perseverantia Est Virtus (Perseverance is Virtue)

Etched on a starlit Synergy Gear from Morpheus Rubicom, symbolizing perseverance against despair. Appears in Chapters 18 and 19, tied to the Greenwich and Ulm Clocks.

Quaestio Iterum (Question Again)

Etched on a bronze Synergy Gear from Morpheus Rubicom, symbolizing persistent inquiry against ignorance. Found in Chapter 7, linked to the Old North Church and Granary Clocks.

Quaestio Prodevit: Mortifer Artifex? (Question Emerges: Mortal or Deadly Craftsman?)

A cryptic clue hinting at future illusions, possibly tied to the Dark Harlequin or clockmakers. Appears in Chapter 7, linked to curiosity's triumph.

Quaestio Veritatem Revelat (Inquiry Reveals Truth)

Etched on a bronze Synergy Gear from Paulina Tetrikus, symbolizing curiosity's role in overcoming illusions. Found in Chapters 9 and 10, tied to the Rostock and Old North Church Clocks.

Reflectio Est Virtus (Reflection is Virtue)

Etched on a runic Synergy Pendant from Lucrecia Van Egmond, symbolizing reflection's triumph over haste and doubt. Appears in Chapters 14 and 15, linked to Beacon Hill and Boston Orloj puzzles.

Scientia Lucem Affer; Ignorantia Tenebras Praebet (Knowledge Brings Light; Ignorance Brings Darkness)

A clue against ignorance illusions, emphasizing curiosity and thorough inquiry. Found in Chapter 6, tied to Monticello's and Lund's Clocks.

Unitas Est Virtus (Unity is Virtue)

A central narrative principle, etched on synergy artifacts like stars, crowns, and runic inscriptions. Appears in Chapters 19, 20, 21, and the Epilogue, symbolizing unity's triumph over division and betrayal.

Unitas Est Virtus; Divisio Est Vitium (Unity is Virtue; Division is Vice)
A clue reinforcing unity as a counter to divisive illusions, emphasizing division as a flaw. Found in Chapter 19, tied to the Greenwich and Messina Clocks.

Glossary of Terms

• **Antiquarians**
Mentor-like figures (e.g., Zeetrikus, Morpheus Rubicom) who test Wizards with illusions tied to virtues like compassion or justice. Guide moral lessons through clock-related challenges, often providing synergy artifacts.
• **Beacon Hill**
A Boston location, home to a runic lamppost etched with star motifs, symbolizing historical and magical significance. A focal point for fear illusions in Chapter 14 and mentor spirit appearances.
• **Boston Athenaeum**
A Boston library where Wizards confront illusions of cowardice in Chapter 18, tied to the Salisbury and Strasbourg Clocks. Represents a site of intellectual and moral challenge.
• **Boston Common**
A 2034 setting in Boston, Massachusetts, where Wizards converge in the Prologue, foreshadowing Boston Orloj trials. A public space tied to unity and the emergence of illusions.
• **Boston Orloj**
A hidden cosmic clock, depicted as the Custom House Tower Clock in Boston, central to the narrative. Symbolizes unity against illusions, not a real astronomical clock but a fictional construct.
• **Boston Public Garden**
An 1859-era garden in Boston, site of the Epilogue's runic sapling planting. Symbolizes the Wizards' legacy and the rooting of virtues like unity and compassion.

- **Boston Public Library**

A Boston site in Chapter 19 where Wizards confront despair illusions, tied to the Greenwich and Messina Clocks. Represents a cultural hub for perseverance and unity.

- **Boston's North End**

A 2034 setting in Boston, Massachusetts, where Wizards gather in a brownstone in the Introduction. A starting point for American Orloj trials, tied to humility and caution.

- **Cargo Ship's Tower Clock**

An 1850s-era clock on a Boston Harbor cargo ship, part of a puzzle pair with John Harrison's Chronometer in Chapter 15. Holds star-alignment clues for reflection's triumph.

- **Cedar Rapids' Orloj**

A newly built clock tower in Cedar Rapids, Iowa, epicenter of intensifying illusions in Chapter 1. Represents a modern American counterpart to European Orlojs, tied to humility.

- **Central Institute of Arts and Literature**

A futuristic academic setting in 2059 where Erasmus Cromwell-Smith II shares Boston's story in the Prologue I. Symbolizes intellectual reflection and legacy.

- **Charlestown Navy Yard**

A Boston site with battleships in Chapter 17, where illusions of injustice are dispelled. Represents a historical and symbolic space for justice's balance.

- **Corrupted Wizard's Cloak**

A tapestry of flaws (envy, fear, betrayal) wielded by the unnamed Corrupted Wizard in Chapter 21, serving as the Dark Harlequin's instrument. Defeated by synergy, symbolizing redemption.

- **Cosmic Gearworks**

A labyrinth beneath the Custom House Tower in Chapter 20, where the Boston Orloj's unity is tested. Represents the narrative's metaphysical climax against divisive illusions.

- **Cosmic Maelstrom**

Chaotic energy within the Boston Orloj's chamber in Chapter 21, fueled by illusions of division and betrayal. Calmed by the Wizards' unity, symbolizing cosmic restoration.

• Danger Sense

Firee's intuitive Wizard power to detect illusory traps, used across chapters (e.g., Chapter 6). Counters flaws like complacency and supports vigilance against illusions.

• Dark Goblin

A rumored malevolent force, symbolizing illusions of fear and mistrust, referenced in the Prologue I and Prologue. Possibly distinct from the Dark Harlequin, threatens synergy.

• Dark Harlequin's Vortex

A shadowy swirl with void-eyes, the Dark Harlequin's final form in Chapter 20, orchestrating divisive illusions. Defeated by the Wizards' unity, representing the climax of the narrative's conflict.

• Enchanted Lens

Checkered's tool for revealing illusion patterns, mechanical flaws, and runic inscriptions. Used across chapters (e.g., 5, 6, 7, 8, 9, 11, 12, 13, 14, 15, 17, 18, 19, 20, 21) to counter ignorance and prejudice.

• Ephemeral Shops ("The Six Statues")

Mysterious pop-up shops reminiscent of Antiquarian encounters, holding relics like the Statue of Justice. Appear in Chapters 1 and 12, tied to humility and justice.

• Erasmus Sr.'s Diaries

Historical texts carried by Blunt, containing clues about U.S. clocks and illusions. Guide Wizards in the Introduction and early chapters, symbolizing mentorship and wisdom.

• Fire and Ice Immunity

A Wizard power protecting against illusions' flames and frost, requiring ethical use to avoid misuse. Referenced in the Prologue I, tied to moral responsibility.

• Ghost Lights

Spectral illusions in Boston and Cedar Rapids, causing public fear and linked to the Dark Harlequin. Appear in the Introduction, exploiting flaws like haste and fear.

• **Glamour**

An illusion spell used to disguise or deceive, associated with flaws like vanity and corruption. Appears in Chapters 1 and 2, countered by humility and unity.

• **Harlequin Cloaks**

Wizards' magical attire with emerald, crimson, or sapphire hues, shifting to reflect emotional/magical states or warn of illusions. A recurring symbol of unity and vigilance across chapters.

• **Harlequin's Quest**

A narrative arc across cities (Prague, Venice, Paris, London, Boston), testing Wizards' unity against illusions. Referenced in the Author's Note, symbolizing the broader journey.

• **Healing Vines**

Greenie's empathic magic, organic tendrils that support unity and counter illusions. Used across chapters (e.g., 5, 6, 7, 8, 9, 11, 12, 13, 14, 15, 16, 17, 18, 19, 20, 21, Epilogue), embodying compassion.

• **Hyperloop**

A futuristic transport method used by Erasmus Cromwell-Smith II to reach the Central Institute in the Prologue I. Provides contextual detail for the 2059 setting.

• **Illusions**

Deceptive magical forces exploiting flaws (e.g., fear, pride, ignorance, division) and testing virtues (e.g., unity, compassion). Central to the narrative, countered by synergy and mentorship across all chapters.

• **Invisibility**

A Wizard power for stealth, briefly misused by Reddish in the Prologue, risking permanent translucence. Reflects ethical challenges and the need for trust.

• **John Harrison's Chronometer**

An 18th-century timekeeper in the Boston Maritime Museum, part of a puzzle pair in Chapter 15. Requires synergy to unlock, tied to reflection's triumph.

• **Lie Detection**

A Wizard power to expose truths, risking trust violations if misused. Referenced in the Prologue I, tied to ethical dilemmas in confronting illusions.

• **Magical Convergence**

A phenomenon where magical energies align, often tied to portals and clock trials. Appears in Chapter 3, linked to breaking stagnation at the Engle monumental Clock.

• **Magical Inscriptions**

Runic or symbolic writings on clocks or artifacts, guiding Wizards against illusions. Appear in Chapter 4, tied to innovation at the Old State House Clock.

• **Mentor Spirits**

Spectral guides (e.g., Mr. M., Mrs. V.) echoing Erasmus Sr.'s wisdom, reinforcing virtues against illusions. Appear in the Prologue, Chapters 6, 8, 17, and 14, tied to mentorship.

• **Mind Reading**

A Wizard power to reveal thoughts, carrying risks of mistrust if misused. Referenced in the Prologue I, tied to ethical challenges in Wizard trials.

• **North End Courtyard**

A Boston site with a lamppost etched "Donatio Est Virtus," a hub for generosity tests in Chapter 16. Symbolizes community and selflessness.

• **Old North Church Crypt**

A hidden nook in Boston where the Orloj meets Wizards in Chapters 5 and 15, a reflective hub for guidance and puzzle-solving. Free of direct illusions, tied to synergy.

• **Orchard**

A symbolic setting in the Author's Notes, representing the author's teenage reflection where doubts (illusions) were dispelled by mentorship. Tied to personal growth and humility.

• **Over-Soul**

Ralph Waldo Emerson's transcendental concept of universal connection, reflected in the Wizards' synergy in Chapter 10. Tied to transcendence and the Old North Church Clock.

• **Portals**

Magical travel methods, risking distortion by illusions, used or considered for clock journeys (e.g., Cedar Rapids in the Introduction, Chapter 3). Symbolize transitions and challenges.

• **Reality Sight**

Breezie's enhanced perception power to detect portals, illusions, and environmental shifts. Used across chapters (e.g., 5, 6, 9, 11, 12, 13, 14, 15, 17, 18, 19, 20, 21), countering deception.

• **Runic Fountain**

A Concurrent Modification Exception stone fountain in Boston's Public Garden, etched with Orloj-like runes, a focal point for vows and sapling planting in the Epilogue. Symbolizes legacy and unity.

• **Runic Lamppost**

A brass lamppost in Beacon Hill's courtyard, etched with star motifs and runes, a focal point for fear illusions in Chapter 14. Represents magical and historical significance.

• **Runic Pendant**

Firee's talisman from London (Prologue) or synergy artifacts (e.g., Aequitas Est Virtus, Reflectio Est Virtus) in later chapters. Symbolizes bravery, justice, or reflection against illusions.

• **Runic Sapling**

An emergent plant from a cosmic runic seed, planted in the Boston Public Garden in the Epilogue. Embodies virtues like unity and compassion, a living legacy against illusions.

• **Runic Seed**

A cosmic seed etched with Orloj sigils, planted to grow the runic sapling in the Epilogue. Symbolizes the enduring legacy of the Wizards' virtues.

• Runic Slip

A parchment with glowing runes, warning of Cedar Rapids' illusions and emphasizing humility. Delivered by the Courier in the Introduction, guiding early trials.

• Runic Symbols

Magical inscriptions on artifacts like scrolls or clocks, guiding Wizards against illusions. Appear in Chapter 2, tied to Tetragor's traveling bookstore and humility.

• Six Statues

The name of the "Travelling Antique Book Stores" of Harlequin's Book Antiquarian Mentors.

• Scroll

Magical literature containing runic symbols or clues, associated with Tetragor's bookstore in Chapter 2. Represents knowledge and the challenge of overcoming corruption.

• Sedona, Arizona

A tranquil setting in the Prologue I where Erasmus and Lynn reflect, and a modern clock site (Sedona Orloj) in Chapter 11. Symbolizes introspection and justice against illusions.

• Spider-Climb

A Wizard power for scaling heights, carrying ethical risks if misused. Referenced in the Prologue I, tied to moral responsibility in navigating clock trials.

• Statue of Justice

A marble statue in "The Six Statues" shop in Chapter 12, symbolizing balanced fairness. Glows when injustice illusions are defeated, tied to the Old South Meeting House Clock.

• Synergy

The collective strength of virtues (e.g., humility, courage, compassion), central to overcoming illusions. A recurring theme across all chapters, embodied in artifacts like gears and crowns.

• Synergy Coin

A bronze coin from Lettizia Dillettante, etched with "Aequitas Est Virtus," symbolizing triumph over injustice. Appears in Chapter 11, tied to the Sedona Orloj and Eise Eisinga Clock.

• **Synergy Crown**

A runic crown etched with "Unitas Est Virtus," central to defeating the Corrupted Wizard in Chapter 21 and used in the Epilogue's sapling planting. Symbolizes unity's triumph.

• **Synergy Gear**

Artifacts (e.g., Innovare Est Virtus, Caritas Iterum, Quaestio Veritatem Revelat) carried by Blunt, symbolizing virtues like innovation, compassion, and inquiry. Appear across multiple chapters (e.g., 5, 7, 8, 9, 10, 13, 14, 15, 16, 17, 19, 20, 21).

• **Synergy Key**

A silver key from Lucrecia Van Egmond, etched with "Fortitudo Vincit Timorem," symbolizing triumph over fear. Appears in Chapter 13, tied to fortitude's narrative arc.

• **Synergy Medallion**

A star-marked meddorf from Wells Cathedral in Chapter 16 or a silver medallion from Lettizia in Chapter 17, etched with "Aequitas Est Virtus." Symbolizes generosity and justice.

• **Synergy Orb**

A crystal orb from the Cargo Ship's Tower Clock in Chapter 15, etched with runic coordinates, pointing to the next clock pair. Symbolizes reflection and puzzle-solving.

• **Synergy Pendant**

Runic pendants (e.g., Aequitas Est Virtus, Reflectio Est Virtus) from Antiquarians like Lettizia or Lucrecia, symbolizing justice or reflection. Appear in Chapters 12, 14, and 15.

• **Synergy Sigil**

An artifact etched with "Aequitas Est Virtus," guiding Wizards against injustice in Chapter 17. Represents fairness and unity, tied to the Adler Planetarium and Münster Clocks.

• **Synergy Star**

A runic star etched with "Unitas Est Virtus," guiding Wizards to Boston's tower in Chapter 19 and central to defeating the Dark Harlequin in Chapter 20. Symbolizes unity.

• **Synergy Wire**

A runic wire labeled "Donatio Est Virtus," guiding Wizards against greed in Chapter 16. Symbolizes generosity, tied to the Clock of the Long Now and Wells Cathedral.

• **Tarnished Key**

A token from Morpheus Rubicom, etched with runes, symbolizing victory over ignorance illusions. Appears in Chapter 6, tied to Monticello's and Lund's Clocks.

• **Telegraph Wires**

A historical reference to 1844 Morse demonstrations in Chapter 15, symbolizing connection in puzzle-solving with John Harrison's Chronometer and Cargo Ship's Tower Clock.

• **The Long Now Clock**

A futuristic clock Near Van Horn, West Texas, designed for 10,000 years, tainted by greed illusions in Chapter 16. Symbolizes stewardship and generosity.

• **The Six Statues**

Ephemeral shops in Boston, holding relics like the Statue of Justice, reminiscent of Antiquarian encounters. Appear in the Introduction and Chapter 12, tied to humility and justice.

• **The Wanamaker Clock**

A store clock referenced in Chapter 10, symbolizing unity and hinted at for future illusions. Represents communal strength against evil illusions.

• **Tome**

An ancient book carried by Blunt in the Prologue, glowing with inscriptions guiding Wizards' trials. Symbolizes wisdom and continuity of mentorship.

• **Traveling Shops**

Mobile stores like Tetragor's bookstore in Chapter 2, containing magical scrolls and runic symbols. Represent knowledge and the challenge of overcoming corruption.

• **Water Wards**

Blunt's protective magic, creating watery barriers to stabilize environments and counter illusions. Used across chapters (e.g., 5, 6, 7, 8, 9, 11, 12, 13, 14, 15, 16, 17, 18, 19, 20, 21), embodying leadership.
• **Wizard Portal**
A magical travel method risking distortion by illusions, considered for journeys like Cedar Rapids in the Introduction. Symbolizes the Wizards' mobility and challenges.

About the Author

Erasmus Cromwell-Smith is an American Writer, Playwright, Poet, and Pedagogue. He's published 32 books in the genres of self-help, poetry, young-adults, education, and sci-fi.